Star Bird
CALYPSO'S RUN

Schultz, Robert, 1961-
Starbird II; Calypso's Run: A ScFi Novel/ by Robert Schultz –
1st edition
RJS Publishing

ISBN-13: 978-0-9960448-5-1
Titling & Cover by Anina Laird Swallow
Summary:

Deep in the clustered regions of the Spartus quadrant, the rogue planet Aster wanders, hidden from the searching fingers of the Colonian and Albion Empires. Here in exile, CJ Barker and Gunnar Conrad have established a base of operations. But Gunnar is determined to return to the planet Carolon in the Nulark system to retrieve the Asium crystals he and CJ left behind in their rush to escape the invasion forces of Queen Captain Drax Blair. With a full cluster of crystals, Gunnar's Assault Corsair, the *Constellation* can operate at full power again.

Six months has passed since Rick Niker left Aster in search of his ship, the *Athena*. All his hopes lay with the ship's AI, CORA 500, finding his first officer and wife, Jayda, before time runs out for her. The escape pod she is traveling in has only so much life support. Following a faint trail of spent pod fuel and his intuition, Rick continues his journey, a lone traveler through the uncharted regions of the Spartus.

Even as the Empires of Hadrian continue their relentless search for the renegade CJ Barker and the advanced technology of Gunnar's Starbird, all the factions of Hadrian must attend the Rite of Pintar; the christening of a newly crowned Ruler of the Hadrian. But, there is no Royal to christen. The Colonian Empire remains steadfast in their certitude that the Duchess Stephanie Benetar is the rightful heir, while the Albion Empire contends she is not a blood heir and has no right to the mantle of Galactic rule.

A Note from the Author

When I started Starbird in the late 70s, I always wanted it to be a Trilogy. Most of my favorite movies of that era were moving in that direction. I just didn't believe I had enough energy to make that happen. Certainly when life comes along and takes you away with responsibilities of family, home and work, your imagination takes a back seat. Truth be told, Starbird II was begun shortly after Starbird I was finished. But it was never completed. I got about a third of the way through it and that's when life took over. Thankfully, back when I was writing, it was all done long hand and for all these years I've been able to keep those manuscripts safe. Some days it was tough. I would bump into the boxes during a cleaning or a reorganization, sit and read for a bit, wondering why I was keeping them. Something always seemed to whisper, *patience*...

As with much of any written work, daily life and the struggles a person goes through can directly affect a storyline. At the time Starbird II was started, that was certainly true. I've tried to build on that, letting the story go where it needed to in order to bloom. As with my other works, I can see the ending in my mind and how it's all going to play out. I'm excited to get there, for the adventure is in the journey. Life took me away from finishing this many years ago, but I'm actually glad it did. Coming back to it now has allowed my imagination to mature a little and life has provided me with a variety of experiences that blend well with the character's development.

I love the characters I've created in the Starbird universe. Yes, even the bad guys; without them, there can be no good guys and no adventure to experience in one's imagination. Starbird isn't just about a spaceship, or even outer space. It's about people and their relationships one with another. I often wonder what they think of me and what they would say to me if I could ever meet them for real. I guess... I could always ask...

In a galaxy only half explored by its native populous.

In a galaxy on the brink of civil war.

In a galaxy where the knowledge to command the elements extends beyond mortality.

Two friends struggle to find each other and those they love.

"... if *normal* people can't see you for who and what you really are, then they're having issues with what's considered *normal*."
General Richard Alexander Niker, Commander, Athena SAC09

"This business is all about war and people die in war... Sometimes it hits closer to home than we would like, but it hits none the less and it's how we respond to death that's one of the things that defines who we are... At times, it takes more courage to show emotion than it does to hide it." *Doctor Fuji Yamoto, Medical Officer, Constellation, SAC10*

Starbird Assault Corsair Crew assignments

Athena SAC9

Commander/Thane- General Richard Alexander Niker
(Currently on Search & Rescue)
First Officer- Lieutenant Commander Jayda Niker (Missing)
Interceptor Pilot 1- Captain Zek Korack (Missing)
Interceptor Pilot 2- Captain Zak Korack (Missing)
Chief Engineer- Frank Cooper (Head of Starbird training on Aster)
Engineer's Mate- Cacao Walker (Colonian replacement in training)
Turret Gunner- Lance Banco (Colonian replacement in training)
Chief Medical Officer- Kelly Gibraltar (Cross replacement in training)
Medical Assistant- Mayfield Hathorne (Cross replacement in training)
Helm Pilot- Captain Lisa Dayton (In medical stasis)
Navigator- Robin Mandrel (Cross replacement in training)
Weapons Officer- Karlyn Kinoy (Colonian replacement in training)
Com Officer- First Lieutenant Laura Habba (In medical stasis)
Science Officer- Mr. Toby Mavis (In medical stasis)
Integrated Artificial Intelligence- CORA 500 (On Search & Rescue)

Constellation SAC10

Commander- Colonel Gunnar Lee Conrad
First officer- Captain Dakota Abrams
Interceptor Pilot 1- Captain Dakota Abrams
Interceptor Pilot 2- Captain Logan Dalley
Chief Engineer- William "Billy" Moon
Engineering Independent Contractor- Tiana Mantose
Engineer's Mate- Scott Brandon (Colonian replacement)
Turret Gunner- First Lieutenant Hayden Hunter
Chief Medical Officer- Fuji Yamoto MD
Medical Assistant- Alder Gantrie (Colonian replacement)
Helm Pilot- First Lieutenant Lynette Starman
Navigator- First Lieutenant Nigel Kramer
Weapons Officer- Second Lieutenant Doran Cartwright
Com Officer- First Lieutenant Lana Nevall
Science Officer- Mr. Pippin Habba
Artificial Intelligence Droid- Alex 7001

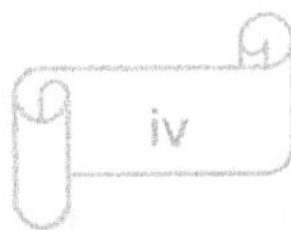

Aster Command Staff

Base Commander- Colonel Casey Janae "CJ" Barker
Command Staff Personal Aide- Lieutenant Willis Ruston
Command Com Officer- Talia "Bubbles" Reese

Albion and Colonian Command Staff

Commander of Albion Medium Fleet- Queen Captain Drax Blair
Albion Supreme Commander- King Commander Thoene Dismon
Albion Thane- Blinda Koss
Stephanie Benetar Duchess of Teleknee

Additional Characters

Administrator of Cross- Diord Vandmire
Tomplie Pirate Commander- Lou Aura
Castellian Aide- BachTL

Foreword

Starbird Assault Corsair 10: Colonel Gunnar Lee Conrad Commanding

Constellation ship's log; Flight Ministry date 3292.33-12

My first entry as Commander of this ship. Never been much of one to fill out paperwork or make vocal entries, but being assigned a command of one of these new Starbird class Assault Corsairs will require me to at least make the effort. Can't promise this will be regular, but here it goes. Colonel Gunnar Lee Conrad commanding. My wife, Audra Atlanta is the Executive officer. Our first action out of space dock nearly saw my best friend, Rick and I a floating debris field over Kalamar. Hekla sent in a bunch of bombers with heavy fighter escort to destroy all the orbiting shipyards in an attempt to keep the Flight Ministry from manufacturing any more Starbirds any time soon. The other eight ships in the squadron had already launched and weren't even in the area at the time of the attack. We barely got the _Constellation_ out before the bombers hit our yard. Rick wasn't so lucky. He got caught up in the _Athena's_ yard superstructure and I had to rescue his sorry self from pancaking on the surface of Kalamar. We got him back out by cutting him out as he fell through the atmosphere, then got him pointed in the right direction with a sling shot maneuver we had used back in our fighters days. Once we made orbit again, we tackled Crofts forces pretty handily with just our two ships. These Starbirds are amazing.

End of Entry.

Constellation ship's log; Flight Ministry date 3292.33-13

The Flight Ministry called the _Athena_ back, so Rick had to report to Midway station for battle damage inspections. The Ministry sent us on to our first assignment. A distress signal was received from four Kendalon freighters stuck in the gravity fields of the Oneida Caldron. We've been ordered to investigate and render whatever assistance we can give.

End Entry.

Commander's personal log; Flight Ministry date 3292.33-14

Have to make a slight detour to Commenor. Seems my Dialabron condition has finally caught up to me. My second heart picked a heck of a time to actually do something. It's been dormant all these years, I figured it was just going to remain asleep unless my first heart decided to check out. Doctor Yamoto and Audra insisted we declare an emergency and reroute to Commenor to get some Furlitron to treat my condition. It'll be good to see some old friends.

End of Entry.

Commander's personal log; Flight Ministry date 3292.33-17
Well, that was an adventure. Jonas tricked me into taking some orphaned rejects. He was hoping Audra and I would take them back to Kalamar for safe keeping. Seems we've gotten caught up in a domestic dispute between the children of the Mantose fortune and their stepmother. She must have wanted them pretty bad. It looked like she hired an entire army to bump off these Mantose twins, Tiana and Taron. Barely got them off the planet in one piece. They had some heavy hardware in orbit, but I let Audra deal with them. It was her first action as officer in command and she performed splendidly. She's an amazing EXO and a wonderful woman. I couldn't ask for a better First Officer. We're now on our way to the Oneida Caldron.
End of Entry.

Constellation ship's log; Flight Ministry date 3292.33-21
We saw the freighters for a moment, stuck in the accretion ring of the black hole, but then they disappeared, and thanks to some heavy action here at the Caldron, we're now stuck just outside the accretion ring. Some of Croft's ships were here waiting for us. They nearly had us buried out here, but thanks to Captains Dalley and Abrams, and my bridge crew, we were able to hold them off long enough for Rick to get here and give them a pretty good black eye. But, he got slammed pretty hard as well. We're barely hanging on by our fingernails with maneuvering thrusters only. Now we're both stuck in the ring with no way out.
End of Entry.

Commander's personal log; Flight Ministry date 3292.33-94
This black hole's gravity well is playing havoc with the ship's chronometers, among other things. Rick and I have decided to try the same sling shot maneuver we used over Kalamar to get both ships up to speed, drive as close to the Event Horizon as we can, then as we're pulling away, form a Hap void to create a worm hole which should throw us far enough away we can make repairs and get back home. Trouble is, we don't fully understand the space-time variables involved. We could end up shifting time and being sent heaven knows where.
End of Entry.

Commander's personal log; Flight Ministry date 3292.34-68
We're still in one piece, but at a terrible cost. I've lost Audra... I'm numb... I can hardly think... I can't even comprehend what's happened. There are no words...
End of Entry.

Constellation ship's log; Flight Ministry Entry 1

We have no idea where we are in space and time. I've disabled the time keeping function in these log entries as dates don't seem to mean anything where we are. There is nothing familiar out here. The wormhole operations were much tougher on the *Constellation* than anyone could have predicted. I doubt Rick or the other design engineers ever imagined these Starbirds traveling through such extreme environments.

About halfway through the wormhole, the *Constellation's* Asium crystal chamber developed a power harmonic that resulted in a crack in crystal number five. The containment chamber vents handled the resulting energy release from the antimatter burst, but it caused an overload down the back channels of the Asium power circuits. I ordered Audra to assist the engineering team trying to stabilize the containment, but it blew anyway. The explosion weakened the structural integrity of the ship at the engineering and loading vestibule. As the ship's super structure began to twist, Audra was crushed by falling debris while trying to get out of engineering. Doctor Yamoto did her best to save her, but there were too many internal injuries and she passed away shortly afterwards. I've lost the better part of myself and I feel, so alone...

End of Entry.

Commander's personal log; Flight Ministry Entry 2

I haven't even been aboard ship to make any kind of entry, so here's the short version. Rick sent the *Constellation* into the Nulark system, to a planet called Carolon, to inquire about a facility we could use to make repairs. Several malfunctions forced us to land the ship at a Colonian outpost on the planet and surrender to the base commander; a Colonel CJ Barker. Because of ongoing military action involving her forces, she released my ship and crew and gave us some raw Asium. In return, I offered assistance, but before Rick could get here to help the base was overrun by an Albion Queen Captain called Drax Blair. We were able to teleport CJ's Command staff out, but due to another malfunction, Colonel Barker, Alex 7001 and myself were left behind. We escaped through a back door in the command center, then nearly got the heck shot out of us making a mad dash to CJ's fighter. We barely got her ship into the air and away. This Drax character, chased us to a neighboring planet called Reako, but we lost her in its atmosphere. I had to set CJ's fighter down in a pond due to mechanical problems. We ended up sinking through a water layer into a biome inside the planet. While we were down there getting chased around by some ugly flop-eared looking things called Binions, we got

helped out by a young woman named Janox. I still have no idea why she was down there, alone. We brought her with us and somehow evaded Drax long enough to get CJ's fighter to light speed. We made it to a planet called Cross where a friend of CJ's was willing to help us; a Diord Vandmire. Seems like a nice sort. He fixed us up and let us rest for couple of days. He was a little short with me because CJ got hurt; I think he's got a thing for her. Our vacation was cut short because Drax had figured out where we were and sent in her henchwomen. They shot up the place, pumped me full of some kind of happy juice and succeeded in getting me to their ship. CJ and Rick managed to retrieve me, and we all made a fast get away to the planet Aster. It's in an unknown region of this galaxy. Diord has helped us get a small base of operations setup here. It makes a good place to hide, but it's about as far away from nowhere as it can get.
    End of Entry.

Commander's personal log; Flight Ministry Entry 3
    I'm attaching an amended log entry by Captain Dakota Abrams outlining what happened to the *Constellation* during my separation from the ship: Following direct orders from General Niker, I, Captain Abrams, helped escort Colonel CJ Barker's command back to the Colonian home world of Tintee. As acting ship's Captain, I ordered the ship secured and abandoned when we were surrounded by superior Colonian forces. To confuse the Colonians, we transported into a jungle area some distance away. During a skirmish with a hostile indigenous life form, MedTech Sindee Connors was mortally wounded. Then, while retaking the *Constellation* from within a Colonian facility, Taron Mantose was killed trying to board during a Colonian droid attack. A certain BachTL helped the rest of the crew get aboard by providing cover fire during the attack. As the Colonian forces were occupied out of the solar system, we took the *Constellation* and the forces loyal to Colonel Barker to the Jurass system and the planet Cross where CJ and Colonel Conrad had traveled to. End of Log Entry by Captain Dakota Abrams.
    When CJ and I got separated from my ship and crew, Rick came looking for us, but came under attack by Drax Blair's flag ship, the *Tarzana*. As we've both flown circles around it, I can say it's a sizable battlecruiser. Anyway, I guess Rick was off ship in one of the Interceptors, doing an expanded search for me and CJ when he got detoured to the planet Boris and met up with someone named Ona. I don't think Rick even knows exactly who she is. Apparently, she expanded Rick's mind to be able to manipulate matter at the molecular level. Calls himself a "Thane" now. Sounds like a bunch of hocus-

pocus nonsense to me, but he did learn how to use an impressive old school weapon called a Balkrum. Kind of like a razor sharp metal ring with some kind of ion emitters on it. If it doesn't cut you in half, it can laser slice you. The thing can pop apart into two separate rings.

While he was away the *Athena* came under attack and was nearly destroyed. Near as we can tell, the Albions thought it was going to explode and damage their ship, so they left it. Rick lost several of his crew, some of them due to an Albion Thane called Blinda Koss. She used her Thane abilities to create ILOB mind waves that can fry your brain or something like that. It appears Jayda ejected in the turret escape pod and one interceptor is missing; presumably Zek and Zak took it since they're also MIA. Rick was able to redock to the *Athena* and get all the damage under control, bury the dead and put the wounded in medical stasis. Somehow, he knew I needed help, so he programed his ship's AI, CORA 500 series to find Jayda's escape pod while he came to find me. Rick just left Aster this morning in his Interceptor to try and find the *Athena.* Hopefully Jayda will be onboard.

End of Entry . . .

Commander's personal log; Flight Ministry Entry 41

I have little concept of real time anymore. According to the *Constellation's* chronometers, Rick's been gone for six months now. I have to say I'm getting a little worried. I hope he makes contact soon. We've been on deep space probes for this long before, but it was always together so we could bail each other out if needed; he's alone. The Interceptor is an amazing fighter, but spending that much time isolated in one can be tough. We've seen only a few ships out here that don't belong, but they didn't seem too interested in us and since we haven't seen the *Tarzana* or one of the Colonian Capital ships out here, I think we're still safe for now.

End of Entry . . .

Commander's personal log; Flight Ministry Entry 48

Dakota has been working on vetting replacements for those crew members that were lost to enemy action. Doctor Yamoto will get a new medical assistant and Billy Moon will have a new engineer's mate, although it seems Tiana has become more familiar with this ship's engines than any recruit we could ever find. Billy's original Engineer's mate, Frank Cooper will remain here at Aster command to help train the replacements for Rick's crew, then assume command of the *Athena's* engineering department once it returns.

I have high hopes of Rick finding the *Athena* intact and even greater hopes Jayda will be onboard, safe. I can't even fathom my best friend having to go through what I have since losing Audra.

Audra... It's been nearly two years since she... I'm no closer to getting over life without her than I was the day we buried her in space. In fact, I feel more lost now than ever. But I feel like something else is going on inside me and I can't figure it out. I expend an enormous amount of energy to keep from exploding. The other day, I nearly took several of the ground crew apart because they had placed their work lights too close to the *Constellation*. Really? How is placing them too close going to hurt anything? This is a warship for crying out loud. I think it can handle a little bit of bright light. None of this makes any sense. I see Doctor Yamoto regularly, whether I want to or not, and she seems to be just as much in the dark.
   End of Entry . . .

Constellation ship's log; Flight Ministry Entry 54
   Talking with CJ, Dakota and Billy Moon about how to get this ship back to full power. It will require installing new Asium crystals, which means we have to go back to Carolon. It's the only place we've found it in any useable quantities. Captain Abrams and I have it all worked out, but CJ has concerns. The *Realistic* can carry us to the outskirts of the Nulark and then the *Constellation* can drive in from there. I have no doubt the Albions will be trolling around the place, but with most of our weaponry now operational, I see no reason why we can't get in and out of Carolon without any kind of lasting entanglement. Then we high tail it back to the *Realistic* and jump out of there.
   Audra used to tell me I didn't think things through and while she was usually right, this time, we've considered every reasonable contingency. It's our best chance of getting both ships back to full operational status, and perhaps... home.
   End of Entry.

Dedicated to my big brother, David Walter.
In hopes he'll give this one a better rating.

Star Bird
CALYPSO'S RUN

Starbird II: *Calypso's* Run

Aster Command

"Is that the best you can do?" Captain Dakota Abrams asked, squeezing past several technicians standing in the doorway to one of the small control rooms. Hurrying to keep up, Tiana Mantose made a half turn, breezing through the doorway after the Kalamarion officer.

"They're the best available," Tiana said, following him to a large console in the Aster control room and stopping next to the head controller.

"Talia," Dakota said tapping her on the shoulder. "Who's in charge of the personnel files?" Talia glanced up and pointed to an older gentleman at a different console on the other side of the control room. "Right." Dakota maneuvered carefully over several large cables snaking through the walkways of the control room and toward the man. Tiana wasn't so fortunate and tripped several times trying to keep up with the Captain. "I'll show you what I'm talking about," he said, touching the man on the shoulder. "Can you punch up the data files on the final replacements for the *Constellation* and *Athena*?"

"Yes, Sir," the man said turning back to his terminal and going to work. Dakota looked around at the Aster Command auxiliary control room. If there were an emergency, they'd be in big trouble. The main control room was still under construction and this auxiliary control room was only half functioning. Partly due to the lack of room and materials. There seemed to be plenty of personnel to man any station needed, but equipment logistics supplied from Cross were difficult at best. With both the Colonian and Albion Empires on the hunt for the tiny band of militia fighters, it was becoming increasingly difficult for shipments to make the perilous journey to Aster without being detected. A string of abandoned and burnt out hulks littering the different routes to Aster were evidence of the combined efforts of the Colonian and Albion Empires to find Colonel Barker and the highly sought after Kalamarion Assault Corsairs. So far, their exact position remained hidden.

"Files are up, Sir."

"Here, look at this," Dakota pointed at the screen in front of them. "This Scott Brandon character is only a third class engineer. He'll hardly be able to identify a Flux module, let alone know what one does. Then there's this Cacao Walker... I've got nothing against having females working alongside men, heck, most of them are more capable, but does she even understand you don't start working on things at her age, you retire?"

"All of the upper-class engineers are required on the *Trax* and *Realistic*. These are the only ones they could send us." Tiana pointed to the screen. "Besides, Lieutenant Brandon shows the best aptitude to learn and understand our systems faster than any of the others. And Cacao isn't that old."

Dakota took a deep breath and gave Tiana a look.

"What about this Kinoy? Tiana, she's only an ordnance bunker operator. We need someone who can run the ships guns and not have to stop, consult a manual, then point and shoot."

"Yeah, but look at her performance record. The woman never misses a target. Besides, she's the only one I could find that's even remotely familiar with our type of targeting systems."

"No one here is familiar with our targeting systems," Dakota complained. "Wonderful... I've got a couple of engineer's mates that can't tune engines, a weapons officer that can't find the trigger to shoot and look at this," he said pointing at the screen again. "Mandrel, navigator. Four ships lost in an asteroid belt."

"Well, at least you can't complain too much about the Medical doctor and the Medtecs I found," Tiana said.

"Wanna bet?"

"Come on. You're not being reasonable."

"Beautiful," Dakota threw his hands up in disgust. "The Colonel will just love this. He's already difficult enough to deal with. I can't wait to give him this report." Dakota turned and stormed from the crowded control room. His expression took on a sarcastic twist. "Nope, can't wait for this one at all. 'Oh, don't mind me, Colonel. We've found the crew replacements for you and the General. Your gunner won't be able to shoot while in motion, the navigator will get lost and run you aground and our engineer mates can't open a toolbox. But we do have some good MedTechs.'" Dakota and Tiana dodged a pack of techs working on cabling in the cramped rock tunnels. They entered the main cavern housing all the larger equipment and some of the smaller ships. The Captain homed in on his objective and started off again. "Ah yes, a couple of MedTechs. We're certainly going to need them. Better yet, how about a couple of surgeons? It's going to take a few to put us all back together when these new replacements get through with us."

"Dak," Tiana called out amid the bustle of machinery and working personnel moving all around them. "I'm doing the best I can."

Dakota stopped for a moment and collected himself. He realized he had needlessly become upset about circumstances that were well out of Tiana's control.

"I'm sorry," he finally said, turning only part way around. "I know this is tough." Dakota stepped over to a pile of containers, out of the way of any foot traffic or prying ears. "I'm just really worried about putting any of these people in front of our technology." His voice had toned down considerably as he scanned the bay. Tiana moved in close to him so she could hear and be heard.

"I know. We've vetted thirty or so people and three of them ended up being Colonian operatives. Thankfully, security has been finding these rat-bags before they ever get close to the ship. Remaining hidden here is a whole lot harder than either Colonel Conrad or Colonel Barker figured on."

"Well, if we didn't require all this constant resupply..." Dakota said looking up as a large shuttle gingerly came to rest in an open space next to several other transports. "Self-sufficiency would be our best friend right now if we could make it happen."

"There's just nothing on this rock," Tiana said, fingering the necklace under her shirt. "We're just so far away from anything, or anyone. We're pretty dependent on Cross."

"And until we can get the *Constellation* fully operational, we'll keep having these guys trying to find us. You'd think the Queen would get a little tired of looking." Dakota rubbed his forehead and looked around, focusing again on a brightly lit object in the bay some distance away. "Has Yamoto approved these new MedTechs?"

"About twelve hours ago."

"And since I haven't heard *boo* from the good doctor, things must be fine. Thank goodness for small favors. So let me ask you honestly here," he said shifting. "These new people we're bringing in from the Carolon personnel, you've vetted them. How do you feel they'll be able to perform using our tech?"

Tiana pondered a moment, thinking back to the rigorous barrage of interviews and testing she and Willis had put all the applicants through.

"Gantrie and Mayfield will figure things out the quickest. While we're all human, we have different interpretations for many of the same things. The biggest barrier is their understanding of our alphabet. I'm no linguist by any means, but I've been trying to compare theirs to ours and there are no similarities that I can find."

"Agreed. And the others?"

"Brandon will get it figured out if Billy doesn't kill him first. I know Billy would prefer having Frank Cooper back in the engine room with him, but the General is going to need Frank onboard the *Athena* when he brings it back from Boris. I think the others will acclimate just fine once they really get down to business. As with everything, there'll be a learning curve."

Tiana and Dakota turned to the center of attention in the cavernous bay and gazed silently at the Kalamarion Starbird sitting under a blaze of foot lights and lighting trees. Next to it were several

F-2 Flightstreaks and some tiny scout ships used for exploring the dark surface of Aster.

"Want to come with me to see how Billy's doing?" Dakota asked, stretching.

"I'm sure he's a little irritated with me right now," Tiana said as they made their way toward the *Constellation*. "I've been working with Willis so much on these new replacements, I haven't been able to spend as much time with him on the ship."

"Well it's not like Frank is gone."

"Yeah, but he seems to have taken a liking to me."

"He's almost old enough to be your father."

"Not like that," Tiana said, stepping cautiously over a tangle of large cables. "Him and Frank have always gotten along really well, but I think Billy loves teaching and Frank has gotten to the point he just doesn't need to be taught anymore."

"You can always learn something from someone."

"You know what I mean."

"Yeah, I know. You're going to have to decide what direction you want to go here pretty quick too. Executive officer or Engineering. But if you're pursuing Exo to get closer to the Colonel, then it's for the wrong reason and you'll find nothing but disaster."

"Guess it's been a little obvious, huh?"

"A little obvious? Do you think what Willis and I have going on is a little obvious? How well do you know the Kalamarion Flight Ministry's regulations?"

"I've been studying."

"Then you should be aware of the regs stating a husband and wife cannot serve in the same command together." Dakota and Tiana headed for one of the side loading tubes at the rear of mid-ship. "They can't even serve on the same ship together without special permission from the Ministry High Command, and only on a case by case review."

"Then how did Gunnar and Audra manage to get to the command chair?"

"The General recommended them, directly to Admiral Mandrel."

"But he did the same thing," Tiana pointed out.

"How is it you don't know anything about this?"

"Not in the service, remember?"

"Right, anyway, it wasn't just my cousin interceding and trying to push it through. The Admiral in command of the Starbird fleet was shorthanded after the Valkyrie-Kinder war. Fighter command had plenty of pilots, but there were so few qualified command personnel available to crew fleet ships, the Admiral suspended the regs."

"So why the reg in the first place?"

"Because service together as a couple can destroy the marriage. A command can't operate effectively, if at all, under those conditions."

"Makes sense." Tiana started up the boarding tube after Dakota, wondering why he was telling her all this.

"You try becoming the Colonel's Exec just for the sake of getting close to him, I can guarantee things will turn out much differently than you're hoping for."

"He and Audra seemed to make it work."

Dakota strode through the ship's main doors and to a corner, out of the way of foot traffic.

"You of all people know the kind of woman Audra was, and while Gunnar is an extraordinary pilot and commander, she was the one that completed him. She made him whole."

"After all this time, she still holds him prisoner," Tiana said using a lower tone.

"Well, that may be, but that's for him to figure out, not you."

"Ah ha!" a voice called from the open engine room doors. "Here you are," Billy Moon called, looking at Tiana. Dakota patted her on the shoulders as she rolled her eyes.

"You let me know what you decide," he said heading forward.

"Thanks, Captain." Tiana turned and walked into engineering to see a smiling Billy Moon. "Good to see you, Billy."

"Are you finished with all that administrative crap so we can get back to work?"

"That crap, as you call it, got you a new engineer's mate." Tiana's grin was infectious to the chief engineer.

"Engineer's mate…" Billy was trying to act indignant; it wasn't working. "The boy doesn't know a Flukston antimatter probe from the hole in his…"

"William Moon!" Tiana cut him off. "We'll have none of that on this ship. Now, how can I help?"

The engineer froze, knowing he was better than that. Looking at Tiana as she breezed past him to the main engineering console, he grinned broadly. He truly loved having her here. She was smart and hungry for knowledge and the wisdom he had spent his life accumulating.

"Need to figure out what's up with these sequence inductors."

"Did you have Mr. Brandon check to make sure the phase polarizers were within tolerances?"

"Oh, you think that's where the problem is, Miss Smarty pants?" Billy was testing her, plain and simple.

"Yes, I think that's where the problem is," she responded in a mocking tone. She set several controls and glanced up at the massive displays in front of them. "Where is Mr. Brandon? You didn't lock him in the Fulton access pit again did you?" Tiana started toward the engine bulkheads.

"I wouldn't put that green horn down there," Billy said, casually following her, "for very long," he added. "The boy is a walking disaster…"

*   *   *   *

Dakota stepped silently onto the bridge and moved toward the engineering consoles. He glanced over his shoulder at Lieutenant Nevall at her communications station and looking forward, Lieutenant Nigel Kramer sat working at the navigator's station. They were the only two manning the bridge. With the ship in down time for final repairs before mission departure, the other crew members were out on other assignments or extended shore leave. Leave to where could be anybody's guess. Aster was completely barren on the surface and even with the celestial heavens illuminating it through its travels, the surface was a dark place to be. The adjoining caves weren't much better. While they provided a wide range of climbing and spelunking levels, not everyone was adept or interested in such extracurricular activities.

"And why are you two in here?" Dakota finally spoke up, sitting down at the engineering console and checking several readouts. "I thought I gave everyone shore leave. Ain't nothing happening while the ship is sitting here getting a prostate exam."

"Doesn't the Colonel refer to the ship as a she?" Lana asked turning in her chair.

"Do you really want me to go the other route?" Dakota asked slowly, still focused on the readouts in front of him.

"We're just a little bored is all."

"We've been in space for how long and you got bored of shore leave?"

"What is there outside the ship, Captain?" Nigel asked leaning back in his chair. "If we could have gotten off on Cross, maybe spent a couple of days and just hung out wherever, that might be different, but this place has zero to offer anyone."

"You're just not using your imagination, Lieutenant," Dakota suggested.

"Uhm, I'm not sure you can imagine your way around nothing, Sir," Lana chuckled. "There are some of us that can use what's out there for diversion, but the rest of us are content with what our Hallavertor can produce."

"To each their own I suppose," Dakota finally said rising to his feet. "Has anyone seen Alex 7001?"

"He's overseeing the external umbilical interfacings on the port side aft and the new sensor interlays," Lana said. "Said he'd be back in to relieve us when he was finished."

"That little droid can really get around," Dakota said as the com system came alive with the quiet voice of the ship's doctor.

"Captain Abrams, are you on the bridge?"

Dakota hit the com button on the command chair.

"You've tracked me down, Doc. What's up?"

"Can you meet with me in sick bay right now?"

"Sure, anything important?"

"Just a consultation."

Dakota turned and started for the door.

"Have fun kids," he said before the door shut behind him. Heading straight past the Commander's quarters, he made his way down to sick bay and walked right in.

"I hope this isn't another physical exam. You just did one last week and bored or not…" Dakota noticed someone leaning against the wall in the far corner across from the MD's desk. Colonel CJ Barker stood with her arms folded looking at a display near Fuji's desk.

"No," Fuji replied quietly. "I don't need any more of your blood."

"Am I in some sort of trouble?" he asked nervously, watching CJ. She hadn't even acknowledged his presence.

"No, you're not in trouble," Fuji reassured him.

"Don't scare me like that, Doc," Dakota complained, relaxing a little. "How about we shift to normal voices instead of cryptic ones?"

"We need to get some information from you, Captain," CJ finally said still looking at the display.

"Certainly. What do you need to know?"

"Remember platform two-three-six on Cross when we were trying to stop Seelix and Blinda from taking Gunnar?"

"Yeah, that was a bit of a ruckus. You and I about got thrown off on that one."

"Yes, and of course you saved me from Blinda," CJ reminded him.

Dakota smiled a little abashedly.

"A base needs its commander."

"When you fired your shots from over the side, did you see Blinda or Seelix doing anything to Gunnar?"

"Doing anything? I don't understand the question. I shot Blinda and she was dragging herself away and Seelix was trying to nail me in the head with her blasters while getting Gunnar to their ship."

"You didn't see anything else?" CJ pressed him. "You didn't see either of them inject him with anything?"

"No, just what Seelix fired into him up in the Penthouse. Why? What's this all about?"

Fuji moved forward and held out several tiny darts.

"Those are what she fired into his legs," the Captain said recognizing the darts.

Fuji set them on her desk and walked over to the displays CJ was looking at. Dakota stepped up behind the two women.

"This is Colonel Conrad's blood work from when I last sampled him before the mission to Carolon." Fuji pointed to a column of information on the screen.

Looks like gibberish to me, Dakota thought, staring blankly at it.

She pointed to the other column.

"This is his blood work after CJ and the General rescued him from the *Tarzana*."

Dakota could see a difference but didn't understand the information enough to know what it was. Fuji swiped through several images and files, stopping on a scan depiction of a human form.

"This is the Colonel's internal scans," Fuji pointed out. "You'll notice some glaring differences between his body structure and ours." Dakota would have to take Fuji's word for it. The only thing he could identify was the outline of the body. "This is his circulatory system here, much like ours, just more of it on his peripherals. His actual blood is depicted here in the color blue."

"There's more than just blue there, Doc." Dakota pointed to an odd green shade mixing with the normal blue.

"Correct," Fuji agreed. "Now, look here." She pointed up at the base of the head, touching the screen and making the image larger. "Below the Cerebellum, around the Medulla and down the upper spine. This large fascia tissue buildup here; his body is trying to protect itself from something attacking it. I can't identify the substance beneath this tissue buildup."

"Attacking how?" CJ asked becoming focused. She thought she recognized something familiar.

"Whatever this material is, it's dissolving the outer layers of his Cerebellum and Medulla tissues."

"Not good," Dakota commented.

"Not good is right," Fuji maintained. "His body is amazing in the fight it's putting up to eradicate whatever this is, but it appears to be losing the battle."

"So what can be done about it?" CJ asked.

"Well, normally I'd just pump him full of Nano-Med and program it to go after whatever this is, but I've got no parameters for Dialabrons."

"Why not just use the default?" Dakota asked.

"His body would just attack and eliminate it. Nano-Med requires special programing to account for everyone's unique chemical makeup. Without it, the body's defense mechanism would perceive the Nano-Med as just another foreign invader to be destroyed. But if his body is losing this fight with whatever this *stuff* is, I can't even imagine the Nano-Med would stand a chance either."

"You could always give him some Nano-Mech," Dakota suggested.

"You want me to put mechanized Nanomites in him?" Fuji exclaimed. "No one knows what that would do."

"It's just repair mech, Doc," Dakota said. "We use it all the time on the ship. It's tough stuff."

"I'm sure it is, but does it have the correct programing protocols to navigate around the inside the human body and then make the needed repairs?"

Dakota shrugged and looked back at the display.

"So what's this going to do to him?" he asked.

"Headaches, irritability, short with everyone and everything. I think it's pretty clear to everyone that he's expending a lot of energy just trying to hold it together. As things progress, his inability to focus will increase. He'll turn somewhat bi-polar. Quick to anger, which Dialabrons are prone to anyway. But some of these 'incidents' will be sudden bursts of rage, perhaps even uncontrollable. If this is true, he'll become a danger to others and eventually, himself." There was a long pause as everyone stared at the display, contemplating. "If only Audra were still here."

"What do you mean?" Dakota asked.

"Audra and Gunnar were a matched pair."

"How so?"

Fuji touched the screen again and swiped through several files.

"I'm sure you've seen this before and we all thought it was really cool, but so what? In Audra's and Gunnar's case, it's more than just cool; it's astronomically coincidental. This was the glue that bound them together."

"Isn't that what love is for?" Dakota asked.

"Yes, of course, but in this case it comes down to their actual molecular makeup. Here, let me show you. Like I said, we've all seen this." Fuji pulled out a handheld device and pointed it at Dakota. "I already have this on file, but this will be easier." Fuji touched a couple of controls and another body depiction popped up on the display. "This is you, Captain. A snapshot of your aura; the energy you constantly emit. It's produced by your molecular makeup, your unique biosignature." Fuji paused and pointed the device at CJ and touched a control. A moment later, CJ's body depiction showed up next to Dakota's. "Here, now scan me." She handed the device to Dakota. "Press the button when you've got it pointed at me." A moment later, another depiction lined up next to the others. Fuji took the box and made several adjustments to the display. "There, you see? We all have our distinct aura. Neither is like the other. Yes, similar in some cases, but all different, just like we are all unique in our molecular makeup. CJ has red hair..."

"Auburn," CJ corrected without taking her eyes off the display.

"Auburn," Fuji repeated. "Mine is black; Dakota's is brown, and so on and so forth. You get the idea. Your aura responds to all kinds of stimulus, internal or external and even has a harmonic oscillation that makes it even more unique. As with every atomic molecule that moves to its own frequency, our auras have their own unique frequency. Most of the time, those frequencies interact at a low level when we encounter others. Usually it has little to no effect on us. But sometimes, you come across someone that just feels right, almost natural to be around, like you've known them all your life. It can go even further than that. In the case of Colonel Conrad, his energy signature is operating at multiple complex frequencies, so finding someone with an aura that complements his own or works on a favorable wavelength would be rare, even among his own race. Imagine the odds of a human having a favorable harmonic to his. Colonel Barker, your biosignature has some similarities, but there was only one that was nearly perfect. This is Audra's," Fuji said adjusting the controls to bring up the depiction. She overlaid Audra's molecular signature with Gunnar's. The oscillations moved in near perfect tandem. "This is why she could calm him with just a touch or a word. This is why he could remain ahead of his biological demons indefinitely."

"But surely he doesn't require her to maintain himself?" Dakota asked.

"Normally, I would say no," Fuji said. "But whatever this is has changed everything in the last couple of months. He was doing pretty good with coping with Audra's absence, until CJ brought him back from the *Tarzana*."

"Did they do something to him on that ship?" Dakota asked.

"We don't know for sure," CJ answered. "I highly doubt Seelix would have shot him up again once she got him onboard the Metro-star and Albion prisoner procedure would not have allowed anything to be given to him until he had gone through detox. I got to him long before that was supposed to happen."

"Well, clearly something's different," Dakota said, stating the obvious. "I can't seem to do anything right by him. I work double time running interference between him and the crew. He just seems to get upset about any and everything."

"I haven't observed any episodes of rage or outbursts," CJ remarked.

Fuji pointed at her aura display.

"Look at this. It confirms my hypothesis. He's always been a little short with me," Fuji admitted. "But not with you because your aura is similar to the harmonic of his. I haven't told him anything about what we've found here, yet." Fuji seemed relieved and worried at the same time. "He's always been able to control his inner demons, but things are progressing far beyond anything normal for a Dialabron; whatever that is." Fuji abruptly turned back to her desk, CJ looking after her.

"Are you done with me?" Dakota asked, moving toward the door.

"Yes, Captain, thank you. I'll let you know if I need anything else." Fuji sat down and started going through some of her notes on a small hand display. Once the Captain had left the room, CJ sat down in front of the doctor and waited silently. Fuji kept reading, looking as though she had forgotten something.

"Doctor Yamoto..." CJ finally started. Fuji continued to read without looking up. "How long do you think Gunnar has before whatever this is... You know...?"

"I don't know, days, maybe weeks. Dialabrons have an extraordinarily complex physiology, so it's impossible to say for sure. As the fascia tissues continue to grow, they'll constrict around his upper spine and into the base of the skull. If that doesn't kill him, this foreign matter eating at his tissues will. I wished I had a better understanding of what's going on."

CJ looked back at the display and just stared at it. The familiarity here kept repeating itself, but without some kind of concrete connection, she could only dismiss the ideas milling about in her head.

"Wished I could be more of a help," she said getting to her feet. "My knowledge of Albion procedure, barely got me to him and back out again. I'd say we were about as lucky as we could get."

"I read the Colonel's report. It was a harrowing escape," Fuji agreed. "A little more climatic than our escape from Tintee. Lost a good nurse on that one." Fuji paused a moment, then went back to reading. "And a good friend."

"How is your new MedTech working out?"

Fuji looked around the room, as if trying to find her new assistant.

"She's off ship on shore leave right now. Not that we've gone anywhere since she was assigned. But I think she'll do just fine. Hard part is getting past this alphabet barrier we all have. I think it's even harder for us medical people as we use a lot of abbreviations and you have to get them right the first time or it could be trouble."

"I hear you," CJ said.

"If you stop in on the Colonel before you head back out, could you have him come see me when he gets a moment?"

"Certainly, but you know as well as I do, you'll have to chase him down."

"I'm an eternal optimist."

CJ thanked the doctor and left, turning toward the bridge. It was oddly quiet in the hallways of the Assault Corsair. It seemed like the ship was mostly deserted. She had been onboard while in orbit around Aster and the ship had a certain life to her when in operation. Without propulsion systems functioning, the *Constellation* felt like she was asleep. Reaching the commander's quarters, she stopped at the door, hesitating. She looked back down the hallway to the engineering vestibule, then back to her left at the bridge door. She was used to capital ships like the *Tarzana* or the *Trax*. It sometimes took twenty minutes to a half hour to get from one point to another in a ship of that size. This Kalamarion vessel was quite sturdy and compact. She wasn't sure if she liked it or not. She finally pressed the door summons and waited. She was about to activate the summons again when a voice answered.

"Yes, who is it?"

"It's CJ." There was a moment of silence giving CJ cause to wonder. "May I come in?"

"Come in."

The door hissed open. CJ instantly recognized Gunnar sitting at his desk, his back to her. As the door closed behind her, she looked at the cavern outside through the overhead windows.

"What are you working on?" she asked taking a seat.

"Just admin stuff," Gunnar said without turning around. "What about you? Get the command center operational yet?" CJ found herself paying particular attention to the inflections in his voice.

"Not yet, still waiting for some modules to arrive from Cross. Aux control is a busy place right now."

"No doubt. I sure wished there was a better way for you guys to get supplied. Diord is really hanging himself out for the Empires to see, just so you get setup. On the other hand, this planet is so far from anywhere, it's a wonder anything gets here at all."

"The spy network has been ramping up as well," CJ said.

"Not sure how to help you with that one." Gunnar sounded indifferent.

"Me either," CJ said. "But I wonder if I could get your input on a similar subject."

"Ok," Gunnar said turning around and facing her. CJ noticed the memory chip usually around his neck, was conspicuously absent. She carefully shifted her eyes around the desk area, hoping to see it. If it was that important, it wouldn't be far from him.

"BachTL."

"Your Albion friend?"

"Castellian."

"Now explain all that to me again. You rescued this guy as a kid?"

"He was onboard a Pantarian hospital transport. They were transporting orphaned children from one of Altair four's moons when they struck a Ratronian mine in the Krackuss system. The ship broke apart and pieces of it impacted a slow-moving comet called *Hailstrom*."

"There's such a thing as a slow-moving comet?"

"Well, about the only explanation we have is when the ship broke up, its pieces were hurled out into space and BachTL's piece just happened to get in the path of the comet and somehow soft landed."

"We?"

"Yes, Drax and I were in command of a small corvette responding to the distress call."

"Weren't you guys the valiant ones…"

"Well, Drax was, I didn't want to be bothered with it. The emissions coming off the comet were pretty intense and what are the odds of someone surviving a collision with a comet? It was a real trick picking up the ship fragment with the carbon emissions spewing everywhere. We couldn't even get a visual sighting on it."

"Then why go down after it? Why risk your ship?"

"Our sensors were showing life readings, so Drax insisted. My view was why risk it for someone that was probably too far gone already."

"I don't get you at all," Gunnar said perplexed. "I just can't see you like that."

"Oh please," CJ responded. "You remember my story about my ship's captain on the *Meade*?"

"Yeah, I remember. In order to gain rank and command of the ship, you arranged to have your Captain ejected into space."

CJ remained quiet, thinking. She wasn't sure what it was that had finally changed her.

"We finally got it onboard and somehow got out of the comet's emissions without burning out our Isom inductors. When Drax and I went down to the hold, the techs were just getting the thing open and out pops this mess of a little kid. How in the world he survived is completely out of my realm of understanding. He had to have been out of air. He had plasma burns all over him and the poor thing just cried and cried for his parents. He wouldn't go to anyone but me or Drax. When we got him down to the infirmary, we had to take turns holding him on our lap while the MedTechs worked on him."

CJ went silent, thinking about the scene she had just created for Gunnar. There came a smile to her lips as she weaved through the years of nursing the little Castellian back to health and raising him up in their shadow.

"So how do two staunch military girls raise a young boy when you're out trying to do your thing in space?"

"Nannies and boarding school."

Gunnar raised an eyebrow.

"We took him with us whenever we were in a position to do so and the tours weren't long or in dangerous areas, but raising a boy on a military ship is no way to provide a nurturing environment."

"Why did he stay with Drax?"

"When I left, I knew I couldn't take him with me. I doubt he understands."

"So, have you been in to see him yet?"

"No."

"Has anyone told him that you're in command here?" Gunnar asked, becoming a little animated. It didn't go unnoticed.

"According to Talia, no."

Gunnar popped to his feet.

"We've been here how long...?"

"Six months."

"And you've had him locked up all this time and he doesn't even know you're here? Casey Janae, you have to go see him."

"And tell him what?" CJ gave Gunnar a lost look. "Mommy's here now, but you're under arrest for, for... I don't even know what he's under arrest for?"

"How about espionage?"

"We don't know that for sure," CJ responded.

"He's all but admitted to it," Gunnar countered. "Hasn't he?"

"So far, the only thing he's admitted to is being a Queen Captain's personal aide, and I could have told you that. He was an aide to both Drax and I. As far as stealing an entire ship or at least its secrets, even Drax isn't stupid enough to send just one person."

"Six months? Are you serious?" Gunnar popped bewildered. "I'll admit he helped save my crew and made it possible for them to get this ship out of Colonian hands. I guess that gets him on my good side. Look, you're either going to have to treat him as an Albion spy and charge him with espionage, do whatever you guys do with spies, or turn him loose. It's as simple as that."

"What would you do?"

"Told you, he's on my good side; I'd probably let him go."

CJ leaned back, letting out a big sigh. Gunnar detected a gentle tingle come to his ear and his heart rate settle.

"Ok, so if I turn him loose, how do I keep him busy? There's always going to be some kind of suspicion surrounding him. I know this guy, my staff doesn't."

"Sometimes the best way to hide something is right out in the open."

"What do you mean?"

"I mean, put him close to what you suspect him of trying to get to. You'll always be watching him and he'll always know it. He wouldn't be able to do anything nefarious if he wanted to."

"I see the logic. But if he were after your ship, then wouldn't it make sense to put him onboard with you?"

"With me? I was talking about in your operations, with you."

"We both agree he's probably after your ship or its technology, but he's more likely to figure out a way off Aster than he would your ship."

"But if you put him onboard my ship, he's already figured out a way off Aster."

"There are several shuttles that come and go from Aster every day. He has a far better chance of getting onto one and away from here, than he would confined on a high security ship like yours."

"That doesn't speak very highly of your security, does it?"

CJ paused a moment, thinking and gauging Gunnar's disposition.

"Regardless of our suspicions, he could be invaluable in getting you through your mission to Carolon. He knows all the latest Albion intel and what you're liable to find in Carolon's orbit or its surface."

Gunnar rubbed his forehead deeply, finally sitting up straight.

"Ok, you win this one. But just because he's your… whatever he is, doesn't mean I'm going to treat him any different than I would any of my crew."

"Wouldn't dream of it, and if he steps out of line, you do whatever you have to do."

CJ had no idea how much trust she was placing in Gunnar as she had no idea how she really felt about BachTL's Albion indoctrination at the hands of Drax Blair. She had hopes that he had simply chosen for himself to follow a different path.

"Now, what about you?"

"What about me?"

"I've been visiting with your Doctor Yamoto. She's a little concerned about you. There are some significant changes in what's pumping around in that machine you call a body."

Gunnar snapped to his feet and stormed across the room trying to maintain control.

"The Doctor worries far too much," he said becoming tight lipped.

"Worries too much? Gunnar, it's her job to worry. We have no idea what Seelix pumped you full of and what effect it's having on you. I've read a couple of Captain Abram's reports. You get angry over trivial things. Clearly something is going on."

"It's what we Dialabrons are known for, our tempers."

"Yes, but this seems to be going beyond that. You've always kept your cool."

Gunnar took a deep breath and held it, remaining still, looking at the opposite wall. He finally let the breath out and turned to CJ.

"Well, I see the good Doctor on a regular basis whether I want to or not," he said controlled. "I promise I'll let her know if I feel like I'm becoming psychotic."

Gunnar's response didn't satisfy CJ in the least, but she could only take him at his word.

"A couple more things," she said, getting up and stepping over to Gunnar's desk.

"You're gonna talk some more?"

CJ scanned the top of his desk, looking for the chip.

"The General has been gone how long now?"

"A little over three months, why?" Gunnar remained short with his answers.

"So, six months since we landed here… Just seems like a long time to be gone looking for a ship that may or may not exist. Shouldn't he have checked in by now; given us some kind of a progress report?"

"We all agreed when he left that he would maintain radio silence until he was on his way back or got into trouble. We both know Rick can take care of himself," Gunnar said, folding his arms. CJ took notice of the stance he had taken. His legs appeared to be locked in place, almost as if he had been ordered to stand at attention.

"Just like that? You're not worried in the least?"

"Not worried is a strong term," Gunnar admitted. "Yes, I have my concerns, but I've known that guy long enough to know he can certainly take care of himself without my help."

"So, I shouldn't be concerned when you head back to Carolon for the Asium?"

"I thought we were talking about Rick. You worry too much. I was planning on having Captain Reader scan the system for the *Athena* when we get there, and Mister Pippin will be looking for him all the way in to Carolon and back out again if necessary. If that turns up nothing, then I'll start to worry a little more."

"You just don't sound as concerned about him as you should be. You're best friends."

"Why would you worry? I'll have BachTL with me," Gunnar smirked, trying to relax again. "The hard part is getting there and that's not even that big of a deal; just takes forever because of all the different jumps your ship will have to make. We load into the *Realistic's* hold, jump to the Nulark system and unload. We drive in, scoop up some Asium from the surface and we're back out before anyone even knows we're there; provided BachTL's intel is credible. Once we get the crystals back here, we can have them properly shaped, refitted, and calibrated, then this ship has light speed again and full power to her weapons."

"Tell me again why you wouldn't just send in a couple of our F-2s or even your Interceptors, or better yet, the Orbiter?" CJ turned and folded her arms. Gunnar heard a familiar tone in her voice.

"To recap the intel from your automated drones. Drax has embedded all kinds of monitoring satellites around Carolon with several corvette class ships and even a destroyer in orbit, taking turns poking around Reako. Call me superstitious, but every time I've separated this ship, it has never gone well. If I'm going to ride into what could end up being a hotbed full of unfriendlys, I'd much rather have everything at my disposal."

"Then we should send the *Trax* in with you to run interference. She's got lots of fighters."

"For a bunch of rocks? Sorry girlfriend, but that doesn't sound like sound battle tactics from any point of view. Especially considering the butt whoopin' you took when Drax jumped into your sand box the last time."

"Still not liking your battle tactics. Nothing ever goes off the way you plan."

"The difference here is, we have to get the Asium, you don't. I won't ask you or your people to risk anything more for us. I promise we'll be careful," Gunnar reassured her. "Remember, I'll have BachTL babysitting me." He couldn't resist the sarcasm. "So," he grabbed his uniform jacket and put it on. "Would you like me to come with you to see BachTL?"

CJ thought a moment, watching him button his jacket. Before her visit with Fuji, she hadn't been looking for differences in his behavior. Now, he appeared perfectly fine.

"Sure. Nice to have the company."

Acuity

Rick Niker continued to follow the spent fuel exhaust from the *Athena.* He had been operating on calculations his Navi-computer had been providing, and intuition. While he had been traveling for a little over three months without any kind of concrete leads as to a confirmed direction, he held out great hope that he was close to catching up with the *Athena.* He glanced down at the readouts on his navigation systems. Holding this course had taken him into the unknown territories of the Spartus quadrant. He had no idea who or what he would encounter here, having only the rumors and wild stories some of the Carolon command officers had conveyed to him. At this point, he didn't care. He just wanted to find Jayda and his ship and get back to Aster. Somehow, he just knew Gunnar was twisting toward some kind of trouble and Rick would need to help protect him and whoever he was traveling with.

Rick's thoughts wandered to Jayda. He was hopeful CORA 500 had caught up to Jayda's escape pod and had her safely onboard. The notion of Jayda spending the last couple of months in the pod didn't sit well with him. The pod was designed for extended cryogenic stasis, but that provided him little comfort, especially considering the circumstances of her escape from Blinda Koss's ILOB mind waves inflicted on her and his crew. For all he knew, she had perished directly after activating the escape pod. Whenever he thought about her, he had to fight those thoughts back, clinging to the hope that she had indeed survived and was safe onboard the *Athena.*

"Hello," Rick breathed, studying his instruments as an alert sounded. He glanced out for only a moment, realizing that what was ahead of him was still too far away to see with the naked eye. He studied the readouts on the HUD display in front of him as it began to spill out information at an accelerated rate. "Computer, give me a condensed composition analysis and distance to targets." Rick continued to study the information as the computer began.

"Nearest target is a small G class planet with no detectable atmosphere. Mass composition is ten percent solid, ninety percent fluid. Ship's sensors are unable to penetrate the depth. Fluid composition, ninety-seven percent Hydrogen and Oxygen, with a two percent mixture of Sodium Chloride. One percent unidentifiable. Analysis consistent with the presence of a Berrelium core. Water is in various states of liquid and solid consistent with frozen and heated zones. Indeterminate amounts of naturally occurring material and manmade objects suspended in a neutral buoyancy. Planet measures eighty-seven Kelants in overall mass. Horizontal axis measures one hundred forty-five thousand Tanz in width by ninety-eight Tanz along its vertical axis. Circumference measures approximately two hundred and thirty-three Tanz at its equator. Distance, one hundred fifty-two thousand kilometers. Analysis of second target still in progress."

Rick studied the orbital paths of the two planets. It appeared the outer planet was moving faster than the smaller one, but on a slightly different orbital axis. Looking closer at the data, their orbits were close enough that the second planet's gravity was drawing water from the first. He ran a scan of the rest of the solar system, searching for anything that might hold clues to the enormous body of water surrounding the smaller planet. There were several larger planets in the system, but they were in distant orbits and appeared to be frozen. *Little point investigating those.* The almost nonexistent trail didn't point in those directions.

"That is one big puddle of saltwater," Rick commented, amazed to see such a body of water in space. He had encountered pockets of water in space before, even large bubbles of oxygen that would allow a human to free float in space without a breathing device, but he had never encountered a body of water of this magnitude.

"Any detail on the second target?"

"Second target is a larger D class planet, consisting of various standard ores, and an oxygen nitrogen atmosphere. Planets are running parallel orbits around a blue dwarf star."

"Can the sensors penetrate the first planet if we get closer?"

"Negative, scans are being hindered."

"What are those satellites in orbit around the second planet?"

"Detecting scattered space traffic."

"Is that another ship out there beyond it?" Rick asked looking closer at the readings.

"Sensors indicate a space station moving in an irregular orbit. Humanoid life has also been detected. Would you like to alter course?"

Rick thought a moment, considering his options. *I'm not anxious to dive down into a civilization without knowing their disposition first. Besides, the trail doesn't go in that direction.* Checking the transponder scanner for Jayda's signature, he hoped to see something show up, but the screen remained blank. He looked again at his scopes.

"Ignore all the naturally occurring material and identify all the man-made objects in the water."

"Unable to show all man-made objects. Sensor range limited to short range scan."

"So, let's go have a look at what's in there." Rick pushed his sub-light throttles forward to hasten the Interceptor's approach. As he drew closer, he scanned for any ships in the immediate area; nothing. Looking at the glassy body undulating in a shimmering matrix of waves, he could clearly see the reflection of the surrounding stars and nebula. As he drew close, he slowed the Interceptor to a crawl. The body of water took up his entire field of view. Rather than plowing right in, he turned and skimmed along the surface for some distance. After making sure he wasn't going to inadvertently collide with something afloat or just beneath the surface, he gently dipped his craft into the water, then turned straight beneath the shimmering waves. He had taken note of the water's surface temperatures, but now his instruments were registering a marked drop.

"Sensor range reduced by fifty percent," his computer announced as small chunks of ice began to buffet the fighter. "Only primary target information available."

Rick held his speed, trying not to fight the buffeting, but still hold a straight course through the dark murk.

"Overlay primary target information on the HUD." Rick looked up in time to see the display flash up onto the windshield. Most of what was displayed was identified as natural material suspended in the watery soup. Several mechanized objects appeared occasionally, but on closer inspection, turned out to be parts of probes of one kind or another.

"Larger target bearing one six, point two, mark three."

"Swing a little closer. We'll see what we can see." The Interceptor's sensors were quite limited in this soup, something he hadn't been able to figure out yet. It was, after all, just heavily salted water. But clearly there was something in here creating havoc with the Interceptor's sensors. Rick frowned as further detail began to flash in front of him. The object was a partial fragment of a ship's hull. As they drew closer, the onboard sensors diagramed the badly rusted hulk. It was clear the ship was quite old and had been derelict for some time. Heaving a sigh, Rick tried to convince himself that these kinds of findings would be the general rule and not the exception. He shook his head at his initial notion that he'd find the *Athena* right away.

"Now that we're inside this soup, can you identify only man-made objects?"

"Filtering out all naturally occurring objects and showing only man-made materials, but scanner range is still considerably limited."

"Understood, now plot a course to all other objects larger than a probe class device."

It took only a moment for the computer to compile the requested information and display it on the heads-up viewer. Nearly a third of the objects his sensors could identify were in the frozen parts of this great ocean covered planet. It was so vast it would take him a considerable amount of time to cover the course the computer had laid out. Rick let out a frustrated sigh. He couldn't even be sure the *Athena* was here. It just made the most sense. There was nowhere else close enough for it to be. Setting his controls to follow the course displayed, he tried to sit back and relax, but it was difficult as the water his ship was traveling through was rough. He looked at the readouts next to the course map the auto pilot was following and studied the time estimates it would take to complete the entire course. After examining several man-made targets, he decided to try to get some sleep as his ship traveled toward another distant target. At first, it was difficult, but after a while, the buffeting calmed as the water temperatures rose and the ice chunks disappeared. The next several objects turned out to be pieces of ship, either wreckage or unwanted salvage parts that had been discarded long ago and had ended up in this murky ocean in space. Rick would wake up long enough to have a look at the information displayed on the heads-up display; he might even catch a glimpse at what was in front of him, but then he would set the auto pilot to move to the next target and he'd be right back asleep.

This process repeated itself over and over again until Rick was so tired he fell into a sound sleep. In a dreamscape, he found himself in a dank and dreary place, deep underground. The only source of light was somewhere high above in the cavern. As he searched for a way out, he found a stream percolating through jagged rocks making up the floor of the cave. On the other side, far up the stone wall, he could make out the form of someone huddled in a depression. Making his way across the stream, he found the going difficult as the serrated rocks were uneven. Climbing carefully, he became aware of a soft weeping. The quiet sobs sounded vaguely familiar, but he couldn't bring a name or face to mind. After several more minutes of struggle, he pulled himself up into the nook and turned. A figure was curled up, clinging to the damp walls. The clothes were torn rags, almost beyond recognition, but there was something familiar about them. Rick's vision dropped to the man's feet. They were bare and filthy. He could also see they were badly cut and bruised; no doubt from climbing the rocks without footwear. The pants, or what was left of them, appeared to have once been a beige color with stripes down the outside of each leg. The shirt was nearly gone and unrecognizable. As he drew closer, he surmised that it was a man. Blood from countless cuts and lacerations covered the man's back and arms. Rick suspected the face was probably in similar condition.

"Don't come any closer, please," a voice rasped.

"I only want to help," Rick replied quietly. "What happened? How did you get here?"

"It's the safest place for me, away from everyone," the man sniffled, still hiding his face.

Rick looked around. It was about as dreary and uninviting as it could get here. The rocks and air were heavy with the smell of moisture and decomposition. While there was light enough to see, there was nothing cheery about it.

"I can't imagine anything being safe here. Come on, there's got to be a better place to be. What's the best way out of here?"

"I don't want to leave. I need to be here. I must never leave."

Rick reached out and put his hand on the man's shoulder.

"Please don't," the man cowered. "For your own sake, leave me."

Rick recognized the voice and turned the man over. The man was suddenly on his feet, swirling around to confront his best friend.

"Leave me now!"

"Gunnar, it's me! It's Rick! What's happened to you?"

Gunnar grabbed his friend by the wrists and held him. The grip was painful. Even in the shaded lighting, Rick saw Gunnar's eyes turn a flaming blue. His face contorting with a mixture of pain and anger, Gunnar pushed his friend back toward the edge of the recess.

"Gunnar, stop! You're hurting me!" Rick struggled against his friend's advance, but couldn't hold him back and did the only thing he could. Twitching his straining fingers, he took a big step backward and jumped. Startled, Gunnar released his hold on his friend as Rick levitated just out of reach. Anger surging freely through him, Gunnar backed up against the wall, pressing his hands against the rock.

"Gunnar," Rick called. "Don't do this!"

"I warned you!"

"Don't," Rick lamented, watching the unbridled rage flaring through his friend's expression. Gunnar exploded from the side of the wall, diving toward Rick with his arms flung wide. Filled with the horror for what had to happen, Rick spun sideways and pushed a blast of air at Gunnar, sending him sailing in a different direction. He watched in horror as his friend fell to the bottom of the ravine. Moving quickly, he swooped down next to Gunnar's lifeless form. In tears, Rick carefully turned his friend over and held him. Slabs of toothed rock had pierced his abdomen and arms, but somehow, Gunnar was still alive.

"They've messed me all up. I think I'm broken beyond repair."

"No, I can fix this," Rick said cradling his friend.

"You and your scientific fiddle fuddle. Rick, let me go to her." Gunnar sank in Rick's arms, his eyes fading closed.

"No, I can fix this," Rick sobbed. "I promise I can."

*   *   *   *

Rick woke with a start, sitting up to the onboard computer trying to wake him.

"Sorry, kind of tired here." Rick wiped the sleep from his eyes. "What a horrible dream," he muttered, bringing his focus to the objectives. Studying the readouts in front of him, he surmised something odd. He turned to the transponder scanner. There was a

signal directly in front of him, except… it wasn't Jayda's identifier.
Perplexed, he looked at the data again. "This makes zero sense.
Bring all the forward exterior lights up," he said, swiping the heads-up
display out of the way and leaning as far forward in his seat as he
could.

Gradually rotating, a tubular shaped object with a Kalamarion
emblem matching the one on his Interceptor appeared directly in front
of him. Rick instantly recognized Lieutenant Commander Audra
Atlanta's burial pod. It had been nearly two years since they had
buried her in space. *Her pod must have drifted into this space body
and became trapped; protected from the elements of space.* Rick
leaned back and brought the HUD system back up. Working
meticulously, he listened to his computer report on the pod's
condition. All its systems were still intact and operating.

Rick let a relieved sigh go. In early Kalamarion culture, ships
floating his planet's oceans would often bury their dead at sea. While
what would ultimately happen to the body was somewhat gruesome to
think about, it was the honorable and practical thing to do. Taking
from the past, modern space-age cultures acted in similar fashion, but
instead of leaving the body to the elements, they were placed in
cryogenic stasis, essentially preserving the body.

Watching the pod move with the gentle currents, Rick thought back
to Gunnar's grief when Rick had boarded his vessel to find him sobbing
over her cryo-tube. Doctor Yamoto had placed Audra into burial stasis
almost immediately after she had passed away. At Gunnar's
insistence, she had left Audra's transponder operational. He never
gave a reason why. Rick had struggled, watching his friend struggle
with his grief through the burial proceedings. To save Gunnar from
further pain, Rick had even tried to persuade him to leave after the
formal proceedings had concluded, but his friend persisted. As hard as
it was, Gunnar remained composed long enough to activate the
teleporter controls. Even Rick lost his composure for both Gunnar's
pain and Audra's passing as they watched the pod dematerialize.

"Computer, deploy a tracking beacon to that pod and mark its
general location in your data banks." Rick thought for a moment, until
the onboard computer acknowledged deployment of the beacon. He
watched the secured beacon flash on the hull of the burial pod and
sitting up, collected himself and refocused. "How far to the next
target?" Information flashed up in front of him again as he shut the
exterior lights off and backed the big fighter away from the pod's
location. Being as careful as he thought reasonable, he steered the
ship toward the next destination as directed by the charts on his HUD.
It would be several more hours before they reached the next target
and while he wasn't too keen on having another dream like the one he
had just awakened from, he was still very tired and could use the
sleep.

Better somewhere else

Gunnar had to admit he was getting a little tired of synthetic lighting. While light range generators were standard equipment onboard a Starbird, there was no substitute for the real thing; a sun. But on Aster, there was no hope for any sun. As he and CJ snaked their way through the Aster Command complex, he thought of the planet's calculated trajectory. If undisturbed, Aster would eventually rotate into a relatively new star system called Mercap and settle into an orbit around it's sun. There could be a problem with one of the young planets currently orbiting the Mercap sun, but the computer models were so varied with their projections, it was impossible to figure it out. Not that it would matter. These projections stretched out years in the future. He really didn't expect to live that long, even if he passed away of old age. Right now, the focus was on getting Asium for their ships and figuring out a way home. Until that happened, he and his crew were committed to helping CJ Barker and her cause. But at the moment, he wasn't entirely sure what that cause was.

As they made their way through the complex, Gunnar observed a figure crouched high up on one of the rock walls, nearly out of sight; almost a statue, watching from the dark recesses of a ledge among the lighting fixtures. He couldn't clearly see who it was, but he had a pretty good idea. A visit would have to wait, as CJ ducked through a set of guarded doors leading into a series of tubes connecting several box shaped enclosures. After winding through several hallways, they stopped and Gunnar looked around. There wasn't a whole lot of security here, but then again, there didn't have to be. Where was anyone being held in confinement going to go on a planet like this? It was virtually impossible to get off Aster and if anyone managed to do so, trying to navigate back to charted territory was difficult at best. He watched CJ take a deep breath, hesitating to enter the room.

"Maybe I should go in first, see how things are?" Gunnar offered.

CJ remained silent, keeping her back to him. He started to move past her, but a hand grasped his arm.

"I have no idea what to say to him." She looked genuinely lost.

Gunnar motioned for her to wait outside and stepped in the room, closing the door behind him. While the room lighting was a bit stark, it looked comfortable, having all the amenities one would expect to find in a comfortable home. As he looked around, he observed a figure leaning back, fully reclined in an easy chair, staring at a large display near the ceiling.

"Please have a seat and make yourself comfortable," the young Castellian said, unmoved. "I'll be glad to tell you whatever you want to know, or maybe even make up something new... again. Wanna know what I had for breakfast? Have my poo examined?"

"Deal," Gunnar said, finding a seat on one of the comfortable couches. There was a moment of silence until BachTL realized he wasn't dealing with the usual interrogators.

"New meat? Wanna know what I had for breakfast?"

"No, not at all. I just stopped in to see how you're doing?" Gunnar remarked, unmoved. The display above BachTL suddenly went dark and the Castellian turned in his chair, looking at Gunnar. The chair slowly rose back up into position as it turned around.

"No, you don't look like someone that would be interested in such things. You don't look like someone that would try to break my fingers either."

"Really?" Gunnar looked at himself. "I always felt like I was a little intimidating."

"Maybe at one time, when you were younger."

"Is that a crack about my age?"

"Well, you sort of look the part. Are you supposed to outwit me with your vast store of knowledge and wisdom? Maybe the whole father figure thing?"

"You've been in here for a long time, haven't you?"

"You'd be a little grumpy too if you were held prisoner."

"Been there, done that," Gunnar said, thinking back to his incarceration on Carolon. "Surely, they let you out for a walk, maybe some fresh air?"

"Oh, they let me out. I get a leash and everything. But you people keep me in the dark the whole time. Walk me around a cave and on the off chance I do get to go outside, it's always at night."

"You realize most prisoners are treated far worse?"

"You'll excuse me if I have a hard time showing any gratitude."

"You'd rather be back with the Queen Captain?"

BachTL remained silent, looking right at Gunnar as if trying to pick him apart.

"Come on BachTL. Lighten up. You and I have a lot in common."

"I seriously doubt that."

"I'm the superman Drax has been chasing."

"Don't flatter yourself," BachTL said emotionless.

"Well, to be fair, she's been chasing after my ship and Colonel Barker too."

"Colonel Barker is long gone. If anyone can get away from Drax, it's CJ Barker. As for your ship, the Queen Captain will find it with or without my help."

"I like the 'can-do' attitude." Gunnar smiled. "So you don't think I'm the superman your Queen Captain has been chasing? Like you said, I'm too old for such things to be real; I'd have to be young and energetic, like you?"

"I admit to the stereotype."

"Maybe if I told you something about your ship?"

"Hardly convincing. No one gets on or off the *Tarzana* without the Queen Captain's permission."

"Exactly."

BachTL continued trying to see into Gunnar. He had no abilities like Blinda Koss, the Albion Thane, but he felt like he always had the ability to read people.

"Granted, I was a little bit out of it when we escaped, but your cargo..."

"We? Whose we?"

"Gunnar and I," a soft voice interrupted from the door. CJ slid inside and leaned against the frame, folding her arms.

BachTL rose from his seat.

"Casey," he whispered, a look of disbelief springing to his face. The room fell silent for several stretching moments as BachTL processed what was happening. The young Castellian finally moved toward CJ, who stood up straight. "You're alive, and you're ok," BachTL said, still not sure he was actually seeing her. As he drew closer, his disbelief turned to relief. Gunnar instinctively came to his feet as BachTL threw his arms around her. A look of confusion mixed with relief streaked across CJ's face as she returned the embrace. Stroking BachTL's hair, she looked over at Gunnar and smiled as he quietly slipped out of the room.

"Of course I'm all right," CJ whispered softly.

BachTL pulled back, but held on to her.

"But you were hurt. Why wouldn't you let us help you?"

"Drax wasn't coming for me because I was hurt."

"There was blood all over the floor of your hangar on Carolon."

"Well, ok, I was hurt pretty bad, but I had good friends taking care of me," she said as they sat down together.

"But that's what family is for," BachTL insisted.

CJ gently caressed BachTL's cheek and smiled.

"You're such a good kid."

"Why did you leave without me? You didn't even say goodbye."

"I couldn't stay. It got too complicated."

"How?"

"I was going in a different direction than Drax and things wouldn't have ended well had I stayed. You would have ended up hating one of us. I had to do what I thought was best for you."

"Why didn't you try to take me with you?"

"Where I was going, you couldn't come. It was safer for you to stay where you were."

"I don't understand. What is this place? Why are you even here?"

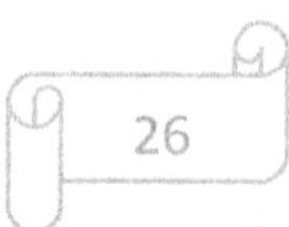

"Because this is me. This is where I belong."

"So, what about this Gunnar character? Is he really superhuman?"

CJ grinned broadly, sitting back and relaxing.

"Yes and no." Her smiled continued. "He isn't human like you and me, but he is. He can certainly do remarkable things if that's what you're asking."

"Can't imagine him being *super* anything with as old as he is."

"Hey, I'm the same age as he is."

"Not like that. You've gotta have youth to foster super anything. It's how the human machine is designed."

"Well, you know best, don't you? By the way, did he tell you he's not human? He has an alien physiology. To him, he's ordinary and we're the inferior species."

BachTL took notice of the inflection in CJ's voice and the pleasant look drifting across her face.

"You're not sweet on this guy, are you?"

CJ hesitated a moment, looking at BachTL and realizing she might be revealing something she hadn't intended.

"He's become a good friend. I wouldn't be here if it hadn't been for him. He's saved my life a couple of times and I've saved his a few times too. It's what friends do."

"So what about this ship Drax wants so bad? Have you seen it? What's so impressive about it?"

CJ fell silent, thinking of the conversation she'd had with Gunnar shortly before coming here.

"Certainly, I've been onboard. You were onboard as well."

"Yeah, your aides nearly took my head off."

"Consider who you are. Wouldn't the Albions have done the same?"

"I didn't get to see a whole lot of the ship; the medical bay and someone's quarters."

"Why were you there in the first place?"

BachTL considered for a moment, giving CJ a long look. She only looked back at him, as if she were waiting for him to reveal something.

"I was trying to help them get away."

"No... why were you on Tintee?"

BachTL sat back in his chair and folded his arms. After a moment, he turned his overhead monitor back on.

"BachTL..."

"Drax sent me to find out the disposition of the Colonian military in regard to the Kalamarion ship. I happened to be in the hanger bays when things started to get a little out of hand, so I helped them out, a little... I didn't expect your aides to try and stick their blasters down my throat. Wish I could have seen more of the ship."

"It's an impressive piece of tech. But unless you're prepared to provide Gunnar and I with some information and assurances, that description is about all you're going to get."

"You really had to say that?"

"BachTL," CJ chastised gently, but firmly. She snapped to her feet. "Come on, let's you and I go for walk."

"To where?"

"Any place but in here." CJ helped him to his feet and put her arm around his.

"Will your boyfriend be joining us?"

"I'm sure he's busy, but maybe..."

"What about guards?"

"No doubt you already know you're on a planet very far from anywhere. You can try to escape if you want. Considering your options, I don't think you do, but if you wanted to, you'd have a difficult time trying to get anywhere." They left the room arm in arm and headed out of the complex into the main cavern. "And Gunnar is not my boyfriend."

"Whatever. Why is it always dark here? Where's the sun?"

"Aster has no sun."

BachTL gave CJ a queer look as they strolled through the outer caves.

"How do you not have a sun? Shouldn't this place be an ice cube?"

CJ motioned for BachTL to follow as she boarded an open framed elevator and worked the controls. As they rose through the cave phishers, an ocean of stars suddenly appeared. Presently, the open elevator slowed and stopped at a platform constructed on a rocky outcropping overlooking a massive expanse of dark prairie for as far as the dim light would allow the eye to see.

"Where are we?" BachTL asked, moving to a safety rail for a better look.

"On the surface of Aster looking at a small piece of Thunder Prairie." CJ leaned against the rail next to him. While there was no sun or moon, the infinite field of stars more than made up for the absence of life giving light. Tall mountain ranges were easily distinguishable in the distance.

"Why the name?"

"Well, it's clear right now, but quite frequently, weather systems roll off those mountains in the distance. On the other side is a string of volcanos that super heat the atmosphere and the moisture builds up into some spectacular electrical storms. Even when they don't reach this side, they can make a lot of noise that's fairly intense; pretty to watch though."

"Trying to understand the science going on here," BachTL said, a perplexed look etched into his expression.

"You won't find Aster on any star chart," CJ offered. "It's a rogue planet that was stripped from its orbit."

"Then how come...?"

"Aster has retained a strong magnetic field, so the cosmic winds can't pull away its atmosphere. It also has seasonal cycles. We believe they're created by all the volcanic and geothermal activity planet wide. The planet is still rotating, so its atmosphere continues to move, mix and cycle. We get high and low pressure fronts similar to a planet in a normal solar orbit. Our air scrubbers keep the toxic gases in this area, cleaned out."

BachTL let his gaze lift to the heavens. Without a sun and light clutter from a crowded, civilized planet, the star field was just like being on a ship off world. During Aster's rotation, they were viewing several bright nebula and close galaxies. He found himself caught up in the grandeur of the cosmos in a way he had never experienced before.

"What are you going to do if someone comes along and finds you here?" His question was only half-hearted, as he was still caught up in the beauty of the skies.

"We have plenty of measures in place to deal with unwelcome visitors," CJ said.

"No, I mean like the attack on Carolon?"

"We've got that covered too. Similar setups all around us."

"Where? I don't see anything; not even a shield generator." BachTL scanned the area around them. He wasn't expecting CJ to give up any military secrets. But then again, who was he going to tell them to? CJ let a chuckle go.

"You're standing right next to one of the shield anodes and there's a pulsar cannon over there."

"I don't see anything."

"Exactly," CJ said, moving past BachTL and heading back to the elevator.

BachTL remained still, trying to make out the shapes of man-made machines camouflaged in the rock next to the platform. He had hoped she would elaborate, but realizing it wasn't going to happen he followed CJ onto the elevator.

*   *   *   *

Gunnar didn't care much for rock climbing. He preferred jumping. He actually enjoyed the sport of parkour, having been introduced to it in the months they had been on Aster. Since they were starting from scratch, recreational facilities were nearly nonexistent. He and his crew certainly had access to the Hallavertors onboard the *Constellation*, but there was only so far most of their programs could go without the experience feeling redundant or synthetic. The human machine required natural interaction to remain functional at peak efficiency. Many of the base personnel had organized different types of activities utilizing what the surrounding areas had to offer. Cave exploration or spelunking was a popular one, though the base command had put a limit on those expeditions because of the dangers involved. Others had taken to rock climbing, as the vast size of the cave offered just about every option imaginable, from the novice climber all the way up to the pro.

Heights weren't much of a problem for Gunnar, he was a fighter pilot after all. He had spent the better part of an hour climbing to one of the higher cliffs. It would be much easier if he could just take a couple of good jumps and be where he wanted to be. The base security in charge of safety would have had a fit had they known he was climbing without safety gear.

As Gunnar made his way toward a figure perched on a level outcropping, he looked down into the brightly lit cavern and several ships birthed below. It had been a lot of work getting up this high; now he wished he had an easier way down.

"You not sneak up on person that way," a calm voice sounded from around the rock face.

Gunnar focused on the figure ahead of him. Janox seemed perfectly at ease so high up the rock wall. He finally reached the young woman and cautiously swung his legs over the edge, sitting next to her.

"Wasn't trying to sneak up on anyone, especially you. I know better."

"Then why you here?"

"You've been spending a lot of time up here," Gunnar puffed, leaning back on his hands. "I wanted to see what was so exciting about the view."

"This not only place I like to come. Good place to think; watch things happen."

"Yeah, I know. CJ and I are always getting reports of some wild woman trekking out alone across Thunder Prairie or disappearing for days in the Bender tunnels."

"All good places for me to get away." Janox remained unmoved.

"Your speech is sounding better," Gunnar commented. "All those lesson are helping."

"Speak lessons are boring."

"You need to learn to talk right, Janox."

"Wished I was still in Reako; in my old place. Much happiness there."

"Being alone is not what makes a person happy," Gunnar said. "Believe me, I know."

"Believe me, I know too," Janox countered looking at him. "I need to go back to my place."

"Reako is not where you belong."

"I not happy here. Happy in Reako."

"Then why did you come with us?"

"You need help. CJ need help. I help. Help done. Now time I go back."

"Back to what? There's nothing down there."

"My home."

"That place is not a home to anyone; only the Binions and how in the world they ever got down there is beyond me."

"Binions are not only thing living in Reako. Many things live there. Tonnie is there."

"Yeah, you've never told us anything about your Au Pair, Tonnie, or how you even got down there to begin with."

"Tonnie and I have always been there. I not remember before. Tonnie never say anything about before. Only that she have present for me when time for me to be older."

"She was supposed to give you a present? What present?"

"Present surprise. Is why called, present."

"So you're older, how come she never gave it to you?"

"Tonnie got hurt. She sleep. She not wake up for long time."

Gunnar opened his mouth to ask another question, but stopped as a picture of Tonnie came to mind. Tonnie must have died of injuries she sustained in an accident down in Reako. Not surprising considering the hostile environment there. He looked at Janox for a long moment, still wondering how she had ever survived all alone.

"How long before CJ and I found you did Tonnie get hurt?"

"Not understand you time. Was small when Tonnie sleep." Janox shifted on her perch, facing Gunnar. "Saw you and CJ walking before."

"Yeah, I saw you too."

"How are you and her together?"

"Together?" Gunnar grinned and looked up at the dark ceiling of the cave. "There's no together."

"Why not? You not love her like your Audra?"

"CJ and I are just good friends. We help each other out."

"You love her, no?"

Gunnar hesitated, forced to think a little deeper. Audra materialized in his thoughts.

"Certainly, as a friend."

"I see you more than good friends."

"You're seeing things that aren't there."

Janox eyed Gunnar for a long moment, then got to her feet.

"Bud, hide what Bud feels. Bud, needs to look forward to what Bud has." With that, she effortlessly swung around a large rock outcropping and disappeared.

"Wished I had never told her to call me that," Gunnar grumbled.

Most would have been startled that she had climbed out into what appeared to be nothing, but Gunnar knew her capabilities well and had no concerns. He was left to think on what Janox had said. Yes, he had feelings for CJ, but he couldn't translate them into anything more than just friends. He only knew of what he was feeling now. A constant ache, occasionally spiking with more frequency into an intense pain deep within him.

*　　　*　　　*　　　*

It took Gunnar quite a while to make his way back down the cavern wall to the main floor. In his younger years, he would have made it more of a bounding jump all the way down, but now he tried to be more careful not to show off. First of all, it wasn't in his nature. Second, he noted whenever he did exert himself, his body chemistry felt like it was wrapping up tight. The stifling effects of depression would trigger certain processes in his chemical makeup, amplifying his emotional disposition. It was better to try and remain subdued and relaxed.

Making his way through the tangled weave of cabling strewn throughout the maintenance bay, he passed a myriad of fighters and transports in various states of repair. Over in one of the corners were several F-2 Flightstreak carcasses, some piled on top of the others. Stopping several times to observe what was going on, Gunnar remained far enough back as to not bother the techs working to keep the ships operational. Reaching the far end of the maintenance bay, he caught sight of the *Constellation* in the next bay, still under a blaze of lights. Stepping through the main bay doors, he observed CJ Barker and BachTL moving around the outer walls of the enormous cavern.

"Colonel Conrad," CJ called, over the noise of operating equipment.

Gunnar stopped and turned as they walked through the maze of lights and cables.

"Are you able to take on another crew member?"

"I've got a full complement already. But I might have room for the right person. Someone with intel on all the latest Albion procedures."

"Then I have the perfect candidate right here," CJ said gesturing to BachTL. CJ tightened her lips to keep from showing a smile as Gunnar gave her a glance.

"Perfect, we're loading from shore leave as we speak. By the way, Colonel Barker, thank you for the help with my crew. They all looked like a bunch of lost children. Didn't know quite what to do without metal under foot. Are you sure you're all right with your friend here coming along with us on this one?"

"Wait a second," BachTL said, realizing they were talking about him. "You want me to go with these guys? Right now? You're ok with this?" BachTL asked, turning to CJ.

"You think you're up for it?" CJ asked.

"Up for it? Anything is better than sitting staring at four walls."

"He's bright," Gunnar commented. "I'll give him that."

"I think he'll be able to supply you with any information on Albion movements and get you through whatever orbital configurations might be in place around Carolon. Having him with you on this mission sounds like good insurance."

"Laying it on a little thick, aren't you?" BachTL said, turning back to admire the Starbird.

Gunnar and CJ smirked from behind the Castellian as they looked at the *Constellation*. Alex 7001 appeared from the top side and hovered near the port side Interceptor, directing some of the final work that had to be done before their scheduled launch. Gunnar looked over at BachTL who was still staring at the Assault Corsair.

"You'll need to get familiar with at least the ship's layout before we get under way. I'll have my first officer, Captain Abrams give you a quick introductory tour, then you'll need to get your gear stowed before we leave."

"My gear consists of what I'm wearing, Colonel." BachTL remained in awe of what he was looking at.

Gunnar eyed the Albion aide as CJ took the young Castellian by the arm and motioned for Gunnar to lead the way. As they made their way into the boarding tube, Alex 7001 swung down from above and flew alongside Gunnar.

"Colonel, if I might have a word."

"What is it, Alex? Sort of busy here."

"No doubt you are aware of who Colonel Barker is escorting aboard?"

"You're bothering me with the obvious, Alex. Am I to assume you're about to quote some obscure regulation I've never heard of?"

"If you think it would help."

"There's method to my madness, Alex. We need his intel of the Albions to get close enough to Carolon to pick up the Asium and get back out in one piece. However, just to satisfy your concerns, why don't you secure engineering and the bridge."

"I can activate the new Mallory doors and dim them down, but they'll still be able to see inside."

"Try not to make it too obvious," Gunnar said looking over his shoulder as the little droid moved swiftly ahead of them. "So tell me, BachTL, what does the TL stand for? Can I just call you Bach or just TL?" Gunnar detected a quick look and head shake from CJ.

"I would not presume to call you just *Gun*, Colonel." BachTL sounded a bit indignant. "I would ask the same of you. TL is my identifier among my race. It is part of who I am."

"My apologies," Gunnar offered humbly, as they entered the midship hallway. "You'll pardon the lock down here onboard," Gunnar said motioning to the closed doors. "We're scheduled to leave on maneuvers within the hour. Standard procedure for us after every inspection is to lockdown those areas that are ready to go until we actually depart. Cuts down on unintended problems during actual operations." Gunnar stopped in front of the Mallory doors. "We just had these installed," he said looking through the darkened containment doors dividing the engineering vestibule and engine compartment. "The Mallory doors protect the rest of the ship's interior in case of a catastrophic failure in the engine room. The frame structure also doubles the strength of the ship at her midsection."

BachTL and CJ pressed their faces to the containment doors trying to make out what was inside. The room beyond was quite dark, but they could still see movement in front of a vast console and glowing displays.

"Why is it so dark in there?" BachTL asked, straining to see more detail.

"It's not. The Mallory barrier is embedded with Niobium. Excite the anodes with a tiny plasma charge and it can be manipulated to any darkness or color setting. All of our main windows are embedded with the stuff, even the bridge."

"So we can't see inside," BachTL smirked.

"Exactly," Gunnar responded turning for the main hallway. "Some crew's quarters, multipurpose rooms, storage and some other classified areas are on the lower level," Gunnar said pointing to a stairwell. "Medical bay right here."

"Yes, I'm quite familiar with it," BachTL acknowledged just as the door snapped open and Doctor Yamoto nearly collided with them.

"Oh, Colonel Barker, I was just coming to find you."

"I do have a communicator," CJ said, showing off the device strapped around her wrist.

"Yeah, but you don't seem to be answering it." Fuji looked at Gunnar, then noticed BachTL. "Nice to see you again, BachTL. Getting a proper tour of the ship this time?"

"I don't know about proper," BachTL smiled, looking over at Gunnar.

"You were coming to see me," CJ reminded the ship's doctor.

"Yes, I wondered if you could have a look at something I've found?"

"Can it wait?"

Fuji hesitated, looking back at Gunnar as Dakota came up the stairs from the lower level.

"No, not really."

"Hey, what's this all about?" Dakota asked, recognizing BachTL.

"You're about to continue a tour for our friend here," Gunnar said, motioning them up the hall toward the bridge. Dakota's expression changed.

"Oh goodie for me?"

Gunnar turned to CJ.

"See you as soon as you're done?"

"I'll wait for you in your quarters?"

"Perfect," Gunnar replied without thinking.

"Doctor," CJ motioned to the open sick bay door.

As CJ and Fuji disappeared behind the sickbay door, Gunnar and Dakota led BachTL toward the bridge.

"How's life been treating you, BachTL?" Dakota asked.

"Been locked up in solitary since Colonel Barker's aides hauled me off your ship."

"Solitary is a little strong, isn't it?" Gunnar asked, giving BachTL the eye.

"Ok, I had some company and they did let me out on a leash every so often."

"Better than I ever got when I was in the clink," Dakota replied.

"Ah," BachTL nudged Dakota. "What were you in for?"

"Let's just say some people consider betting on Killdawn racing an illegal activity."

"It's illegal on any level," Gunnar said with a grin. "You're lucky you didn't get into more trouble."

"Got a week for my indiscretion." Dakota motioned at the crew's quarters lining the hall. "I think you remember the crew's quarters."

"I'm sensing a theme here," BachTL grumbled.

"A couple of work rooms and the command ready room over here," Dakota continued.

"Do people sleep in these rooms as well?"

"Only if they're under arrest," Gunnar poked. He was starting to find BachTL's attitude annoying.

BachTL stepped into the open ready room door and looked around.

"Is the bridge secured?" Gunnar asked, leaning next to Dakota.

"Alex has it in sleep mode, but Lieutenants Navall and Kramer are at their stations with them in base mode. It'll look impressive, but that's about it."

"Pretty good droid, that 7000 series. You ever tell the General I said that and you'll be bucking engineering duty for a month."

"Don't I already?"

"Not since Billy has taken such a shining to Tiana. Are we still on track to launch on time?"

"A few of the crew are back onboard or in route."

"Everyone was informed of the schedule, weren't they?"

"Yes, Sir."

"So where do you drive this thing?" BachTL asked, reemerging from the ready room.

"Right this way," Dakota motioned, stepping to the bridge door. As it opened, Lana turned from her communications console and smiled as BachTL entered slowly. The ship's crew was getting used to the looks from individuals seeing the bridge for the first time. While it wasn't as large as most space going, military ships, its presentation of technology was impressive. At every turn, there were displays and controls that boggled the senses.

"Most of our crew is off ship right now," Dakota began, moving toward the command chair, "but we've got a couple of die-hards here doing what they do because they have no life other than this ship."

"Is that really the case?" BachTL asked, looking at Lana and moving closer to her station. Her dazzling displays appeared to flow in a visceral motion under a glossy sheet of glass.

"Contrary to conventional thinking, we do have lives other than our stations, we just happen to board a little earlier than the rest of the crew."

"Lieutenant Navall," Gunnar said stepping up next to BachTL. "Why don't you explain to our visitor here what it is you do and why you're the 'Queen of Communications' aboard our little home away from home?"

Lana gave the Colonel an odd look, hesitating to speak. She glanced at Captain Abrams then back at BachTL.

"Don't worry, Lieutenant," BachTL said smiling. "I understand you can only give me the cadet version, so I won't be offended if you skip all the top-secret stuff I'm not supposed to hear."

Everyone let out a soft chuckle except for Lana, who finally pushed back from her console to start her explanations.

*   *   *   *

CJ stepped out of sickbay and turned toward the bridge, walking slowly. Looking behind her, a few of the *Constellation's* crew were just boarding the ship. She stopped next to Gunnar's door and leaned back, thinking. Her conversation with Fuji hadn't shed anything further about the mysterious substance mixed with Gunnar's cocktail of a blood stream. This foreign material was something she thought she recognized from long ago, but she wasn't sure. She watched one of the crew walk into the bridge. She could see Gunnar talking with BachTL. As the door closed again, CJ rolled right, activating the door sensor to his quarters. Stepping to the couch, she went to sit down, but several things caught her attention. She studied the citations and souvenirs adorning the wall. Pictures of Gunnar and Rick were clustered together. There were several of Gunnar and Audra. She

made her way to his desk. His displays were on, but in sleep mode.
She felt a little guilty peeking into his personal stuff, but she had a
standing invitation from Gunnar to come in any time.

She turned to sit down on the couch but caught sight of an odd
reflection in Gunnar's window. The Lexan doors to his inner chambers
had been left open and hoping to get a better look from a different
angle, she moved back toward the desk. Glancing back at Gunnar's
window, she saw nothing. She turned to leave, but something on his
nightstand, caught her eye. Unable to quench her curiosity, she
recognized his chip inserted in his nightstand interface and stepped
into the room. Once inside, the lights dimmed and the scenery around
her transformed into a green landscape on a hill beneath a large tree.
Startled at first, CJ turned around. The door was still there, but every
other surface of the room had changed. She bent down and picked up
a large star shaped leaf. It felt real enough; cool and dry. She looked
up at a sun and shielded her eyes. It was bright and warm. Several
clouds floated lazily across a blue sky. She turned left to the large
tree and noticed someone leaning against it looking at her. The
woman was short and pretty, her dark brown hair just touching her
shoulders. She wore a shimmering blue dress coming to her knees
and a pair of black, flat shoes.

"Hello." The woman smiled and stepped away from the tree. "You
must be CJ Barker." The woman held out her hand.

"Yes," CJ finally said, taking the woman's hand and shaking it
slowly. She wasn't sure what this experience was. CJ gave the
woman a queer look. "You're..."

"Audra, Audra Atlanta. It's nice to meet you, CJ. Gunnar has told
me so much about you."

CJ looked at her dumbfounded, having no idea what to say.

"Gunnar said you two were separated and it would be a long time
before you were reunited. How are...?"

"I am a simulation of Lieutenant Commander Audra Atlanta. I was
created by General Niker and Doctor Yamoto to assist Gunnar in
dealing with his grief."

"His grief? I don't understand."

"Audra Atlanta passed away a year and ten months ago due to
injuries sustained during an accident while traveling through a
wormhole."

*　　*　　*　　*

CJ stepped from Gunnar's quarters, a stunned look etched into her
expression. The encounter with Audra had profoundly affected her.
Seeing several personnel milling about in the engineering vestibule,
she silently made her way across the hall to the command ready room
and sat down. The encounter, or whatever that was, had answered

few questions and created a myriad of others. She turned her chair and gazed out the window at the bustle of technicians hard at work. This encounter only added to the confusion of events currently unfolding. Presently, her communicator went off.

"Yes, Talia, what is it?"

"Sorry for the interruption, Colonel…"

"No interruption. I'm still onboard the *Constellation*."

"Long range sentries report a scout class vessel from Cross has just dropped out of light speed and heading straight at Aster. Its ident codes only read 'Emissary'."

"I'll be there in five."

Just the diversion she needed from the chaos building in her head. As she hurried down the hall toward the boarding tube, she heard the bridge door open. Turning the corner for the boarding tube, she saw Dakota, BachTL and Gunnar step out. Gunnar looked up in time to see CJ make the corner for the tube and quickly excused himself.

"Colonel!" Gunnar was around the corner and down the tube after her. "CJ," Gunnar called again. This finally brought Colonel Barker to a halt in the middle of the hangar bay. "Where you headed in such a hurry?"

"I'm sorry," CJ replied, looking back at the *Constellation*. "I've got an urgent call from Talia. We have a ship inbound."

"Scheduled resupply?"

"Not sure what it is. I don't remember any resupply from Cross scheduled for another couple of days."

"No idents?"

"Cross emissary."

"Should I delay our departure?"

"No, it's probably just an inspection."

"Will you be able to come see me before we depart?"

"Not if you're to leave on schedule." CJ turned without another word and hurried away, disappearing down one of the many tunnels leading into the control complex.

Gunnar kept looking after her, hoping she'd reappear, but after several seconds it was obvious she had gone. He turned back to the boarding tube as Dakota and BachTL appeared.

"Impressive ship," BachTL remarked with a brightened expression.

Gunnar folded his arms, looking behind him one more time for CJ.

"Glad you like it," Dakota said, turning to Gunnar. "You know, Colonel. BachTL here could be invaluable to us on this mission. With the insights he's got on Albion and Ratronian procedures and fleet operations, he could be a big help getting us in and out of Carolon."

"I've already cleared it with Colonel Barker," Gunnar said flatly. "Captain Abrams, help our new independent contractor get situated. Where are we with personnel returns?"

"Everyone but Starman and Mr. Pippin have made it back," Dakota replied.

"Can't go anywhere without those two. Drop by Talia's station on your way to getting BachTL's gear and see if you can locate them. I'd like to lift off within the hour."

"I'll find them," Dakota said as he and BachTL set off together.

As Gunnar turned and headed back into the ship, he was met by Alex 7001 in the engineering vestibule.

"How'd you do, Alex?" Gunnar asked heading for the control console.

"I've made the sensor array patches and have run the calibrations. It is my opinion if we were to ever build one of these in a production run, we'd just incorporate the design directly into the fabrication. But the retro-fit should work well for the *Constellation* and the *Athena*. Provided we ever see the *Athena* again."

"Have a little more faith in your creator, Alex," Gunnar mumbled.

"I am unaware of any communications between this vessel and General Niker. Have you had any personal communications with the General?" The little droid followed Gunnar around the console to the engine bulkhead and an open access pit.

"Strict radio silence unless emergency dictates otherwise," Gunnar responded looking down in the pit. Several pairs of legs moved about under a tangle of intricate tubes, wires and machinery giving him cause to wonder. "Should I be concerned with what I'm seeing?"

A head popped out next to a set of feet. Tiana looked around a descending Alex 7001 at Gunnar and smiled broadly.

"Looks a little strange, doesn't it?"

"A little? How many people does it take to accomplish… whatever it is you doing?" Gunnar felt his blood surging.

"Just showing Billy's new engineer's mate how to calibrate the antimatter control flow valves."

"I count six feet and one head."

Tiana looked from side to side realizing how this might look.

"Oh," she grunted shuffling her torso out into the open. "These are mine," she pointed to her wiggling legs and feet, "a pretty pair of Notorall women's calf boots. See the lovely heel?" She motioned to the other two sets of feet. "Billy Moon on this side showing his fashion sense, sporting his favorite Tikenese cross boots and Engineer's mate, Scott Brandon wearing your forced march, military issue combat boots."

"Does it really take all three of you to make the calibrations?" Gunnar asked, audibly irritated. Tiana wasn't sure how to respond, picking up on Gunnar's irritation.

"If I'm to teach this green horn anything," Billy called from under the machinery, "so he'll be of any use to me, it does."

Gunnar grimaced. Tiana noticed his face draw up tight. Gunnar sat back on his heels and looked away from the access pit, taking several deep breathes in the process.

"Alex! Will you get out of the way!" Billy's voice was loud and commanding. Gunnar looked back down into the pit in time to see the little white droid being pushed out from under the machinery. Alex turned his head from side to side, then his torso, scanning for an opportunity to get back into the game, but after a moment, he simply rose straight up and rejoined Gunnar.

"It would appear I'm not wanted down there, Colonel," Alex said.

"That's fine, Alex." Gunnar looked back down into the pit. "Have this thing up and running in half an hour," he hollered down at the other three. Turning, he stormed hastily out of engineering. "Alex, help Captain Abrams with getting Lieutenant Starman and Mr. Pippin back onboard right away."

"Could be problematic, Sir."

"Don't care," Gunnar gruffed in frustration. "Just get them here. We need to leave." Gunnar didn't look back, but continued briskly up the hall toward the bridge. As he disappeared behind the bridge door, Fuji emerged from the lower deck and shuffled to the sickbay door looking after Gunnar. She had witnessed the entire encounter in engineering and Gunnar's shortness with Alex in the hall, giving her cause for concern. While it wasn't uncommon for a commanding officer to be demanding, even a little curt with their orders, this was out of character for Gunnar. He and his friend Rick enjoyed a fluid dynamic with their crews that few commanding officers ever achieved. While understandably firm in their interactions, they were always friendly and good-natured, acting as "one of the guys". This mission was planned to be a quick in and out maneuver, but what if something were to go wrong? If Fuji had learned anything from her deployment aboard the *Constellation*, things seldom ever went as planned.

Gunnar tapped his fingers in a rhythmic pattern on the armrest of the command chair, listening to the bridge crew working. His eyes settled forward at the helm station where Lieutenant Nigel Kramer sat working with Lieutenant Doran Cartwright in preparation of their imminent departure. His frustration building, Gunnar glanced at the empty science station and Lana sitting between her station and Pip's empty chair working both stations at the same time. Gunnar turned anxiously when the bridge door opened, only to see Tiana walk in and move to the engineering station. He glanced at the ship's chronometers and tightened his lips.

"Lieutenant Nevall," Gunnar said without turning.

"Still nothing from Aster command on Mr. Habba or Lieutenant Starman," the com officer responded. Gunnar's armrest com suddenly came alive.

"Colonel," the voice of Alex 7001 came over the hidden speaker. "Lieutenant Starman and Mr. Habba have just boarded with Captain Abrams and BachTL. I'm closing the boarding doors."

"It's about time," Gunnar snapped.

"They must have come straight here," Lana said, wondering why Aster command hadn't alerted her.

Moments later, the bridge door whisked open and Lynette Starman and Pip Habba stormed in, followed a moment later by Dakota. Neither looked at a fuming Colonel Conrad, but assumed their duty stations. Both were loosely dressed in a mix of uniform and civilian clothes. It was apparent they had only stopped at their quarters long enough to grab a shirt and run.

"For the sake of the rest of the crew," Gunnar started angrily. "I won't go into how disappointed I am you two nearly held up this mission. But rest assured, you will be expected to make your explanations and receive a proper dressing down once we're under way. Com, signal Aster Command that we're finally ready to leave. Lieutenant Starman, as soon as you're ready, let's get this ship under way."

Captain Abrams stood at attention behind the command chair.

"BachTL is aboard and all situated down in the crew quarters, Sir."

"Probably itching to get back up here, I suspect."

"Understandably so," Dakota said.

As Lynette Starman worked the Starbird's controls, both Gunnar and Dakota looked outside as personnel cleared the support umbilicals. The ship gently rose into a hover, slowly pivoting in place, then carefully glided out of the base cavern and accelerated. Lynette made a wide graceful circle around the cavern opening, then steered out across Thunder prairie, making an upward arc towards space.

Calypso

Waking up this time went a little better for Rick. There were no dreams that he could remember; his kind of sleep. His computer was talking again over an audible alarm. He studied the information on the heads-up display and ordered the lights back up. While this was not the *Athena*, it was the hull of an intact vessel; or so it appeared.

"Ok, let's get a good look at this thing," he said more to himself than his computer. "Is it fully intact or flooded?" Information began to flash in front of him while he adjusted his instruments and listened to his onboard computer ramble off information about the ship's status.

"Partial flooding has occurred, but hull is stable. There are two energy signatures present in its forward mid-section. Sensors are registering…"

"Life forms," Rick finished. "Only two?"

"Affirmative," the computer responded. "Readings indicate one human life sign and one hybrid. Specifications…"

"Wait a minute," Rick interrupted. "A hybrid? What do you mean, hybrid?"

There was silence from the computer for several moments.

"Sensors are showing an older human life form; a male. A secondary energy signature registered human as well but containing a considerable amount of synthetic molecular matter. My programming parameters will only define it as a hybrid."

Rick considered for a moment, then finally nodded in agreement.

"Understood, continue the report."

"Specifications indicate the ship is a frigate class vessel with damage to its sub-light propulsion drives, but it has an operational Light drive. Power source is intact, but its bias regulators are inoperative. Low level ship power being drawn from the source through alternate means."

"Any way inside? Landing bay, outer hatches?"

"Landing bay doors are inoperative. The nearest available outer hatch is located on the port side bridge conning tower."

"Can we make a sealed dock?"

"Affirmative. Be advised side mounting without a positive collar lock is not advisable if outside conditions become unstable."

"Do the sensors have enough range to warn us if the water becomes turbulent?"

"A two-minute warning can be provided when turbulence is detected."

"Let's get this done," Rick said, taking the controls and maneuvering the Interceptor into position against the mammoth conning tower. Tipping his craft back, he coaxed it onto the side of the old ship and over the hatchway. After a positive lock was achieved, he grabbed his utility belt, blaster and his Thane weapon, a Balkrum. The ship's hatch acted as though it was made to fit right in with the Kalamarion design. Its external interface panel had power to it and operated with no issues.

Stepping inside, Rick found the air fresh and pleasant. Judging from the exterior, not at all what he expected. He didn't get very far before he was met by a slender, shapely figure moving toward him up one of the many hallways. Considering the walk and the silhouette, he would have guessed the person was female, but there seemed to be something odd about the walk. Perhaps she had an injury? Coming into the light, he found a pleasant face with long black hair wound up on top of her head. A little unsettling at first, her eyes were a steely black, but her smile and demeanor calmed any misgivings Rick might have developed. Her clothing was a bit odd, consisting of a white, hip hugging mini dress and matching knee-high boots.

"You took a little longer to get here than we were expecting," the woman said stopping in front of him. "We hope your journey through Acuity hasn't taken too much of a toll on you and your ship?" Her voice sounded strange; almost synthetic, mechanical.

"It was fine," Rick said, not sure what to expect. "You knew I was coming?"

"Certainly," she responded pleasantly. "We picked up your energy signature…"

"Excuse me," Rick interrupted. "We?"

The woman paused a moment, slightly cocking her head.

"Yes, we. Myself and Caidin."

Rick looked past the woman, hoping to see someone else.

"Just you and this Caidin?"

"Who else would there be?"

"Your crew?"

"There is no crew. There is only Caidin and myself."

"And you are?"

"Forgive me. We don't get many visitors. You may call me Dãsha. If you'll follow me, I will present you to Caidin."

"Don't you want to know who I am?"

"I will know when Caidin knows."

Rick raised an eyebrow, still looking around for someone else to appear. He watched her turn and start walking. *Still something odd about her demeanor. She must be the hybrid the onboard computer had mentioned.* After moving through several hallways and open hatchways, they entered the expansive bridge of the old ship. There were a myriad of windows lining every wall, all of them dark. Rick glanced around at the rows of equipment. Most of it was devoid of any life. In fact, some of it looked as though it hadn't been working for a long time. Many of the consoles had been taken apart and left. Rick took special notice of what looked like dual pilot positions. There were two control stations, side by side with differing yokes embedded into a pair of standup consoles that surrounded the pilots; all dark. Miscellaneous junk lay strewn across their dead surfaces.

"Welcome aboard *Calypso*," a voice spoke quietly. Rick turned toward one of the few consoles still working. An older man kept his eyes glued to the instruments before him. As Dãsha came to a stop next to the older gentleman, Rick noticed his bearded face. His hair was long and greyed. Trying to see what the man was doing, he observed a scar slanting across the left side of his face. Rick looked at Dãsha. She stood perfectly still, rigid, her gaze on the information flashing in front of the gentleman.

"You must be Caidin?" Rick asked. "Is that Captain?"

"No, no Captain," Caidin said turning his chair to face Rick. "Caidin Mantose. And you would be?"

"Richard Niker." Rick stretched his hand out and shook the older gentleman's hand. The name struck him odd. He had heard it somewhere before. "General Richard Niker of the Royal Kalamarion Starbird, *Athena*. Most people just call me Rick."

Caidin's look changed for a moment; someplace far off, but he promptly snapped back.

"Kalamar," he repeated. "Heard that before somewhere. As we get to know one another, I'm sure we'll feel more comfortable just calling you Rick. You've traveled quite a distance in a short amount of time."

"Depends on your definition of time and distance," Rick said folding his arms.

Caidin took notice of the weapons his visitor garnered but said nothing and rose to his feet. Rick watched him scoop up a cane and shuffle around the console toward one of the large viewing screens. Rick remained unmoved, looking back at Dãsha. She hadn't made any kind of a move but continued staring at the information moving across the screen on the console.

"Well spoken," Caidin said touching a control on the screen. "Truth is, we've been tracking you since you entered Acuity."

"Not sure how you were able to do that. My sensors could hardly penetrate this soup."

"Your ship is vastly superior to this one to be sure." Caidin looked around at the aged bridge and then faced Rick and Dãsha. "But Dãsha and I know something about these waters you don't."

"It's saltwater," Rick stated bluntly.

"You're missing that element your onboard computer was unable to recognize. I'm surprised you didn't try to discover its identity."

"Sort of on a mission here."

"Yes," Caidin agreed. "Of course, but I hope you'll take a little time to stay and relax; enjoy our hospitality for a bit before you continue. While you have a nice ship, designed for deep space flight no doubt, I'm sure you'd welcome a hot meal, some real furniture and some other company besides a computer."

Rick glanced at Dãsha, still unmoved, then past Caidin at the screen flashing information.

"I have to admit that does have its appeal."

Caidin shuffled over to Rick and putting his arm around Rick's, pulled him toward the glowing screen.

"I have something I want to show you, and a few questions I hope you can answer."

Rick felt a little uncomfortable. He knew nothing about this man and already he was to be a guest aboard his vessel? What's more, Caidin was an older gentleman and his only companion was a tall, gorgeous twenty something woman. However, he was intrigued about this hulk of a ship and how it had remained habitable in the conditions in which it was existing. But as he had indicated earlier in their conversation, he was on a mission. He was about to decline, but noticed the information on the screen ahead of him.

"*Calypso* is positioned in a specific orientation in Acuity for various reasons we'll have much conversation about I'm sure. This is Acuity's internal ice pack over here. You'll be heading there next I expect. The Rapids are here, you just passed by them as you were following your flight plan. Looking at all manmade objects? My first question is, why did you tag this?" Caidin was pointing at a blinking spot on the screen.

Rick looked closer at the myriad of displayed targets, then at the one Caidin was pointing at.

"The one before I came here?"

"Yes, this small one."

"It's a burial pod for one of my people."

"And you needed to remember where it is?"

Rick stuttered for an explanation. It was difficult to explain without a lengthy backstory.

"You knew I was looking for manmade objects only?" Rick asked, trying to skirt the pod inquiry. "How could you possibly know what I'm looking for and why would I want to go to the ice pack? It sounds cold."

Caidin grinned broadly and steered Rick to a different display.

"*Calypso* was once one of the greatest vessel in this part of the galaxy until the Drake got their hands on it. I have no idea where or how they acquired it. They certainly don't have the brains to build something like this. I think it was a gift from the Pintar Royalty of the Tau. She's a frigate class vessel, but more than that. She's fitted out as one of the greatest science platforms known to the galaxy. With her great array of scientific instruments, she can peer into the furthest reaches of space, places far outside our own galaxy borders. She was a wonder of human engineering." Caidin looked around the bridge, reverencing a once great ship. When he turned back to Rick, he realized he had lost himself and smiled. "Most of her sensor gear is still functional and as long as you know what to calibrate for in these waters, she can still see for quite a distance. Were she not here in Acuity, she would be able to see much further, in much more detail. But for now, she is here, protected. With her sensors, I can see everything within Acuity. I know where everything is. I've mapped everything and know when something comes and when something goes."

"Then you're aware the planet in close orbit with this one is pulling water from... Acuity?"

"Yes, of course. That's Skadil; a desert planet used as a Drake penal colony for deep ore mining. Eventually, these planets will collide and form a single world."

"So, if you know what everything is, why ask about a burial pod?" Rick was getting a strange vibe from the older man.

"*Calypso* can't see inside. Her tactical equipment is inoperative." Caidin put his hand to Rick's shoulder. "Will you dine with Dãsha and me? We would love to have you as our guest for as long as you can stay."

Rick looked at the display depicting the sensor arrays mounted all around the exterior of the old ship, then back over at the map. He still had questions that would no doubt lead to others, but he was hungry and anxious to eat something other than what he had stored onboard the Interceptor. He felt the air next to him move slightly and turned to find Dãsha standing next to him. He was startled at first as she hadn't made any noise. Looking at her long, curled eye lashes, he perceived that she blinked her eyes strangely. *Hybrid...?*

"It would be a welcome change of pace. I've been traveling for many months now."

"How long is a month?" Dãsha asked quietly. "We assume it is a measure of time or distance or both."

"I haven't been keeping track of distance on this mission. The objectives are the only important factor, so it's a time measurement. Here's a base line for you." Rick clapped in rhythm for several seconds. "The time between claps would be called a second. Sixty seconds makes a minute, sixty minutes makes an hour, twenty-four hours makes a day and thirty days makes a month. Twelve months makes a year, ten years a decade, ten decades makes a century and so on."

"Our time is measured in similar fashion," Dãsha announced. "We just use different terms, but I'm sure Caidin and I will be glad to use your terms, if it will please you."

"Dãsha, will show you to your quarters where you can rest for a while and freshen up if you'd like." Caidin began to shuffle off to a connecting hallway. "She will come for you when dinner is prepared."

Rick was still a little apprehensive about his situation. A feeling of foreboding lurked somewhere in the back of his mind, but it was far away and could just be his time alone in space. That was something the human soul never seemed to become fully accustomed to. He turned and took a couple of quick steps to catch up with Dãsha as she started for the hall.

"I'd like to grab some things from my ship if that's ok."

"If you'd like a change of clothes, *Calypso's* stores have plenty of crew inventory."

"Yeah, 'bout that," Rick said stepping in time with Dãsha. "Where is the crew? How come you and Caidin are the only two onboard and why is this ship here?"

Dãsha remained silent as they weaved through the halls, back the same way she had led him from his ship. Once they reached the airlock, Dãsha worked the panel and the hatchways rolled into their open position. Rick clamored into the access tube and into the Interceptor's cockpit. After a moment of rummaging around in his personal belongings, he turned to exit his ship but came face to face with Dãsha. Startled at first as she didn't seem like the type of woman to be crawling around in access tubes, not to mention she was hardly dressed for it, he sat back behind the pilot's chair and let her work her way into the seat. Once settled, she scanned the dark instruments and control surfaces, finally settling on the console in front of her. Rick watched her, wondering what was going through her mind. Certainly, she had never seen technology like this before.

"Would you like me to turn it on for you?" Rick asked, smiling.

"Unnecessary," she answered. "I understand how it all works."

"How could you, you don't even know what it is?" Rick reached for the main systems power, but Dãsha stopped him with a firm hand. Astonished, Rick relaxed and Dãsha released him. "That's some grip," he said rubbing his wrist.

"No one person should know too much about another culture. Especially one so far advanced."

"Yeah, well just because we've got a lot of really neato gadgets and gizmos doesn't make us anymore advanced as a cultural civilization than you."

"I have seen all I need to see," Dãsha said getting out of the seat and moving back through the access tube. Rick watched her as he made his way into the hatch access area and Dãsha turned to work the mechanism. Once the openings were secure, she turned to Rick. "I really like your ship. It is unlike anything I have ever seen or studied." With that, she turned and started back down the hallway.

"Advanced technology will do that," Rick mumbled, having to hurry to keep up.

*   *   *   *

Rick ate like he hadn't eaten for a week. It wasn't until he was nearly finished that he began to think about where it might have come from. He suspected there was no traffic to or from *Calypso* and the main entrée was meat. There was also plenty of food. He didn't remember seeing anything in Hadrian that came close to the food replicators onboard the *Athena*. He also became aware of an awkward silence he had probably created with his eating display. No doubt Caidin and Dãsha were watching him, wondering if he had starved himself getting this far.

"This is really good. My compliments to your chef, or whatever you call them," Rick said, still chewing.

"We've built the finest hydroponics operation in the quadrant," Caidin boasted, passing a glance over at Dãsha, who remained poised and proper. "The meat you're enjoying isn't meat at all."

Rick paused after putting the last little bite he had dished up in his mouth.

"It's a Dichlone plant, sautéed in a Gerbilaria sauce." Caidin got a chuckle out of the look on Rick's face. "It's meat. You've had that much already. Just finish it. It would be silly for Dãsha and I to try and raise meat stock here, although *Calypso* is quite capable of doing so, we just don't have the manpower to keep up with everything."

"So how did you get here to begin with?" Rick asked, finishing his Dichlone plants while trying not to think about what it really was.

"I bought *Calypso* about..." Caidin paused, trying to convert the time into something Rick would understand. "About twenty years after she was decommissioned from the Drake inventory. She spent about ten years in private service as a cargo hauler, but then was sold for scrap to a yard in the Anilox system. Somehow, she broke her moorings while waiting for the cutters to do their handiwork and drifted away in a solar storm. I bought her for the salvage rights, but she drifted into Acuity before I could get to her. My salvage tug was damaged trying to reach her; barely got onboard before the tug broke up."

"So, you're marooned here?"

"Yes, but it hasn't been all bad," Caidin said looking over at Dãsha. She smiled and continued eating quietly.

"Surely there have been search parties."

"None," Caidin responded. "Acuity is considered a no-man's area in this quadrant. Generally, ships that come in here, don't come back

48

out. This is a place that is much easier to go around or avoid altogether."

"Acuity contains several mineral and chemical compounds that make it a hostile environment for the standard space going ships to navigate," Dãsha spoke up.

"Certainly is hard to see through it. Are these compounds you're referring to the ones you mentioned earlier?" Rick asked. "Is that why my sensors have such a short range?"

"You have to recalibrate your instruments to compensate for these compounds in order to maximize the effectiveness of your sensors. Depending on the molecular makeup of your ship's hull," Dãsha nodded, "the water can have an adverse effect on it as well."

Rick hadn't observed anything adverse happening to his ship during his time here in the ocean. His computer would have alerted him to any problems. He considered himself safe, owing to the advanced technology of the Kalamarion Interceptor, both structurally and technologically.

"*Calypso* seems to be doing pretty good," Rick observed, wondering what it's hull was made of that protected them from the outside elements.

"Yes," Caidin smiled, "she's an amazing ship."

"So, a derelict ship in the middle of an ocean of murky saltwater in space. You broke up your salvage tug getting here and now you're marooned with no one bothering to try to rescue you. How did you get the power systems back online all by yourself?"

"My studies of *Calypso* reveals a design of self-containment, without the need for refueling," Dãsha continued. "You can logically conclude the cost and scale of refueling a vessel of this size to be prohibitive. Her reactors are still viable and will power our essential operating systems indefinitely. Unfortunately, they can do nothing for damaged engines and dismantled defense systems. The retro thrusters are operational, but they are only designed for docking maneuvers and won't get this ship very far."

"What about droids?" Rick asked. "Surely they left some kind of mech hardware on a ship this size."

"Nothing," Caidin shook his head as he leaned back. "All removed and sold. Many of the systems you no doubt observed on the bridge, were removed or disabled at the salvage yard before she broke her moorings."

"You'd think a ship this size wouldn't have floated away unnoticed," Rick commented taking a last drink.

"Salvage yards are kept well out of the way of space traffic and generally unmanned unless there is a need to move a vessel. By the time they figured out she was adrift, it was too late. No doubt you've encountered several wrecks getting here."

"Yes, plenty of those."

"Is there anything else you'd like to know?"

"Not right now, but I'm sure I can come up with something later."

"Then may I ask a few questions of you?"

Rick nodded and sat back.

"You're looking for something or someone. Can you tell me who or what?"

"I'm looking for both."

Caidin shifted his eyes momentarily to Dãsha. Rick observed the exchange, but remained focused.

"I'm following the trail of my ship, which is following the trail of an escape pod my first officer is in."

"How did you lose your ship?" Dãsha asked.

"Long story short, while I was out on a recon the ship was attacked. When I got back, half my crew was dead. My first officer and the Interceptor pilots somehow got away. I can only assume the pilots took the other Interceptor and the first officer jettisoned in the escape pod."

"An escape pod?"

"Yes, large sphere with mounted cannons. Grey in color."

"And you are coming from where?"

"A little difficult to indicate as I'm still a little new to this part of the galaxy." Rick noticed Caidin and Dãsha's expression shift.

"*Calypso* has a vast database," Caidin said. "I'm sure we could match something up."

"I was told this quadrant was uncharted and not a place to wander about lightly."

"Certainly, that's true," Caidin said. "The Drake and the Skillman are still a primitive, ruthless people. The Drake have wiped out nearly every rival galactic clan in this quadrant, except for the Skillman. But, at the moment, they seem more interested in other things."

"Nice to know Hadrian has plenty of hate and discontent to go around," Rick responded.

"The only way to survive an encounter with the Drake is to join them, but if they don't like the way you carry out their ambitions, you're dealt with."

"Sounds just like the Albions."

"The Albions?"

"Rival faction to the Colonians, ruling faction of Hadrian."

"I think I've heard of the Colonians," Caidin said scratching his whiskers.

"Right now, there is a big argument about the heir to the throne. If the Colonians don't produce a blood heir, the Albions have vowed to take control of the Empire."

"You're right," Caidin agreed. "Things never change from one place to another. But back to your escape pod. You have traveled a

long way and the time consumed to do so is considerable. I suspect
you weren't using light speed operations?"

"No," Rick said shaking his head while fingering his glass. "I've
had to remain at sub-light the entire time. I've stopped at every rock
from here to Boris in the Nulark system. Sometimes to scan the
planets hoping to find the pod and maybe my ship, but also to rest and
forage for food."

Caidin looked at Dãsha, who was riveted to Rick's every word.

"And this ship of yours? Just how big is it? What does it look
like?"

"Corsair class vessel. Crewed by fifteen to twenty officers and
some enlisted men and women. Bridge is the shape of a heart, long
neck in the middle and delta wing shaped aft section. Fighters like
mine attach to the wings and the escape pod is the turret, located on
top of the aft section, directly above the main engines." Rick watched
Dãsha and Caidin pass looks back and forth again, giving him hope.

"Any identifiable markings?" Caidin asked.

"Big red bird with its wings spread up in a circle, touching at the
wing tips." Rick raised his hands over his head and touched his
fingertips together, trying to illustrate the Starbird insignia. Dãsha
remained motionless while Caidin rose and shuffled to a wall screen.
After adjusting several controls to the side of the screen, an image
materialized.

"A day or so ago, Dãsha tracked a vessel moving toward the ice
pack," Caidin said.

"Because our tactical scanners are nonfunctional," Dãsha said,
taking up the explanation, "I sent one of our probes to have a closer
look. The vessel disappeared into the ice before the probe could make
an internal scan, but it was able to send back these images."

Rick turned and came to his feet, seeing a familiar shape among
giant blocks of ice. The images were a bit blurry and murky, but they
were unmistakable; a Starbird.

"Information from the probe indicates the ship was cutting into the
permanent ice pack," Dãsha continued. "The water there is so cold,
the tunnel this ship was making would have sealed back up shortly
after it was made." Dãsha stood rigid, looking at the images flashing
across the screen.

"The ice pack is an unstable and dangerous place," Caidin said
grimly. He shuffled up next to Rick, who continued to stare at the
images with Dãsha. "It is constantly moving; compressing and
releasing. Things that go in there generally don't come out looking the
same."

Rick understood what Caidin was talking about. Planet bound ice
sheets acted much the same way. Even ships designed to deal with
the hostile environment of space can be easily crushed and destroyed

if left to the icy elements. *CORA 500 must have had a good reason for going in.*

"There are countless caverns and tunnels devoid of water," Dãsha said, emotionless. "Some are filled with heavy mineral deposits, others have pressurized gases. You might find one filled with oxygen and the next one a complete vacuum. If this is your ship, your autopilot or whatever you have controlling it has effectively marooned itself."

"It's the *Athena*," Rick confirmed. *Surely the Athena's sensors could identify the danger.* "That's my ship, the one I've been following." Rick started for the door. "Thank you for your kindness, but I need go after it."

"Such an attempt is not recommended," Dãsha warned, turning to him.

"Dãsha's right," Caidin chimed, giving Rick cause to pause. "The ice pack is not a place to be taken lightly. Even the greatest of ships have met their fate, caught in the ice and crushed. I've seen some frozen so hard under such high pressure, they shattered into unrecognizable pieces."

"I think my Interceptor has plenty of firepower to cut through ice. It has externally heated skin plates to keep ice from forming on the hull." Rick hesitated a moment, then disappeared through the door. He wasn't exactly sure where he needed to go to get back to his Interceptor, but he was determined to get under way as soon as possible. He had come all this way, he wasn't about to be detoured by an ice pack. As he worked his way through the vast labyrinth of hallways looking for something familiar, the entire ship seemed to echo with alarms and flashing warning lights. A generic voice boomed out through the halls, giving Rick cause to become a bit more frantic.

"Four Drake Invader craft approaching at attack speed."

Possibly Calypso's automated early warning systems?

There came a noticeable rumble through the ship as Rick recognized a hallway and a direction to get to his fighter. Perhaps if he could get up and running fast enough, he could help defend Caidin and Dãsha from the Drake. Raising his communicator, he made his way toward the hatchway vestibule.

"Computer, activate startup sequence and charge the main guns."

"Acknowledged," came the quick reply.

"I'll give them a surprise they'll not soon forget," Rick mumbled as he hurried toward the hatch directly ahead of him. Before he could reach the access control, Dãsha appeared and stood between him and the control.

"You must not board your ship at this time."

"What are you talking about? Get out of the way!" Rick tried to push past her, but she remained in position.

"It is not safe to be out there when the Drake craft are present."

"My Interceptor is far more powerful than anything you guys have around here," Rick retorted becoming angry. "Now get out of my way." Rick tried to push Dãsha aside, but it was like pushing against a stone pillar.

"I cannot let you board your ship," Dãsha maintained, straight faced. She grabbed his wrists and held them. Astonished, Rick was unable to pull himself free of her grasp. In fact, the grip was so tight, it hurt. He observed several flashes outside accompanied by loud booming noises that shook the ship. Then there was a brilliant flash that nearly blinded him and what felt like an explosion just outside the outer hatchway. More alarms went off as the outer hatch entrance seemed to disintegrate. The concussion threw Rick off his feet, but Dãsha held him up. She remained steadfast in place, seemingly unaffected by the ensuing chaos outside. Dãsha turned her head toward a flashing panel on the inner hatch, dropped one of Rick's wrists and pulled him down the main hall, deeper into the safety of *Calypso*.

"Dãsha," Rick tried to pry her hand from his wrist. "You're hurting me!" She didn't respond but seemed determined to reach a safe point in the ship as the pounding on the outside continued. She finally released him and touched a control on the wall past a rounded archway and a sea of metal slammed to the floor, sealing the hallway from the hatchway vestibule. Dãsha shifted to the opposite wall, checked a display and touched several controls, then spoke into her communicator.

"I have him," she said quietly through the continued bombardment. "We are safe in the Zulu deck, hall nine."

"Good enough," came a response from her communicator. "Hold him there until the bombardment has finished and then bring him back up to the bridge." It was Caidin. He sounded just as calm as Dãsha did. Rick had no comprehension of how they could act so cavalier. When things start to explode around him, his first instinct is to defend with an aggressive offense.

"I am sorry about your ship," Dãsha said helping Rick to his feet. "But if I had not acted, you would be dead right now."

"How did you know that was going to happen?" Rick was spitting mad and wanted to remain angry, but it was hard to be upset with someone that had just saved his life.

"The Drake have always come," Dãsha started, leaning back against the opposite wall. "They patrol Acuity for ships that have fallen into its waters and are unable to escape. They use *Calypso* as target practice, knowing they cannot damage it."

"They just blew up my ship," Rick responded, still smoldering. "Why can't they hurt yours?"

"Have we not explained this already?" Dãsha asked, folding her arms. "This is a very large ship with a hull made of a material not easily damaged. Only another capitol ship would have enough firepower to cause concern for this ship. Even then, it would take quite a bit to cause significant damage."

"Seems silly to have mothballed it then," Rick said noticing the pounding had stopped.

"Caidin has requested we return to the bridge," she said starting down the hall. "I'm inclined to agree."

"Where else would I go now?" Rick asked, still rubbing his wrists.

A Choice

Diord Vandmire grinned broadly as he stepped from his ship and headed straight for CJ, who looked genuinely happy to see him. He looked back several times, making sure his ship was being properly cared for.

"Quit worrying about your ship," CJ said grabbing his arm. "I know you've got a whole fleet of them."

"I do, but I like this one." They held each other by the forearms.

"What makes this one so special?" CJ asked gleaming.

"It brought me to you."

CJ twisted a dismayed look.

"Really? You're going to ruin the moment with a dripping comment like that?" They held one another for a long moment and then started walking.

"It looks like you guys are doing really well with all the stuff I've been sending you," he commented, turning his gaze to their surroundings.

"That's right," CJ realized. "You haven't seen any of this."

"I need to see everything. When does the next tour come by?"

"High rolling investors think they have to be pampered," CJ snickered. "Everything should be exactly like you've envisioned it."

"And how can you be so sure?"

"Because everything fits together so well."

Diord stopped and did a slow turn, looking at everything and nodding in approval.

"It's amazing what you've accomplished in such a short of time."

"I have a great crew and a really good supplier," CJ said smiling. "Now, I know you didn't come all the way out here to look at an investment you're not going to get any return on. What's this all about?"

Diord continued to look around, but now he seemed to be searching more than looking.

"Where's Gunnar and his amazing ship?"

"You just missed him."

Diord fidgeted slightly, looking disappointed.

"You two getting along ok?" Diord took notice of CJ's shifting demeanor.

"We're fine." Her response was short, but not curt. "Please tell me you didn't hop-scotch all the way here to poke your nose into my personal affairs." The two headed toward the main hallway leading to the control complex.

"Well, partially," Diord admitted. "I do have people I have to answer to. I'm not the ruler on high you think I am." Diord studied his surroundings as they strode through the different rooms of the subterranean complex.

"Well, I'll make sure you get a look at everything."

"I wouldn't worry too much. Most of the orders I've sent you are rejected change orders from other projects that just happen to fit your parameters."

"I thought some of this design looked remarkably Albion and Ratronian."

"There's some Colonian stuff in here too. But it's all just business," Diord chuckled lightly. "Waste not, want not. I would have had to junk it all and recycle. Well, except for the Ratronian stuff. They have far lower standards than the other guys. This way, it all finds a good use and I don't have to bother with it."

"Recycled junk, huh?" CJ smiled.

"Only the best for my little red-head."

They stopped and turned to one another. A fond look cruised through CJ's expression. She moved a little closer to Diord and took his hand, squeezing it gently. He smiled slightly, feeling something rekindled.

"I don't know what we would have done without your help," she said quietly, looking away.

"You know I'm always here when you need me."

CJ smiled and squeezed his hand again then turned and started walking.

"While I know I'm at the top of your crush list and you need to answer to your board of directors, I'm still not convinced that's why you took the risk to come all the way out here for a spot inspection."

Diord fumbled with something as they walked, then stopped again. When CJ turned back to him, he was holding a small device in his fingers. She recognized it as an encoded message key.

"Casey, she came to me; alone," Diord stated cautiously as CJ took the key and they started moving through the complex again. "No battlecruiser or support armada. No personal aides or bodyguards, no weapons of any kind. She was surprisingly calm through the entire visit. Offered to pay for all the damages Blinda Koss and Seelix did to my Letoh complex."

CJ passed Diord a quick look.

"Oh, don't worry, I took her up on her offer."

"That can't possibly atone for all the security guards they killed."

"She offered full compensation to their relatives. Her only condition was that I deliver that com key to you personally and that you were the only one to view it."

"You don't think she followed you?" CJ asked, stepping up their pace toward the personnel complex.

"No, and I had my ship scanned constantly before I left and while enroute. I sent out ten other ships just like mine and had them all do multiple, complex Quadra-light jumps in different directions." The two stopped at a door. Diord noticed CJ's name on it. He had ordered the plaque special for her. "I got the distinct impression she didn't want to follow me, that she wouldn't have to."

"One can never say my sister isn't tenacious," CJ said looking at the key. "Still, I think if she had really wanted to, she would have figured out a way to find me again. Even way out here in the middle of nowhere, going to nowhere."

"Being that tenacious, Drax must be held back by forces beyond her control. Maybe the King Commander himself is restraining her. From the intel I could gather on the Carolon affair, she spent an enormous amount of assets in capturing that system and chasing after you. The repairs to my facilities alone certainly weren't cheap and you can bet I added my *pissed off* tax to it. Still, the relationship you and your big sister have isn't complex. Only the circumstances surrounding it."

"Family councilor too, huh?" CJ chided with a grin. She raised her communicator to her lips and activated it. "Talia, can you make time to give Administrator Vandmire a comprehensive tour of our facilities while I'm in conference?"

"Certainly, Colonel," came the quick response from CJ's second in command. "Is this the abbreviated version or down to the rivets and welds?"

CJ looked up at Diord.

"Somewhere in between will be more than enough," Diord responded.

CJ smiled and opened her door.

"Dinner afterwards?" Diord asked as she stepped inside.

"You're so bold in asking, Sir."

"That's me," Diord said with a laugh as CJ started to close the door behind her. He waited for the locking indicators to come on, then turned and leaned against the wall to wait for Talia. His thoughts wandered around his past with CJ. Things hadn't ended the way he had hoped. The fact that they had ended at all wasn't what he had in mind. But he held out eternal hope that time and maturity would soften them both.

*   *   *   *

Willis Ruston spun her chair around and stretched. *This job is about as mind numbing as anything I've ever had to do. I'd rather be one of those cable techs. At least they're moving all over the base. There's plenty of traffic in orbit, but directing it is about as tedious as watching mud dry. Why didn't CJ assign me to show Administrator*

Vandmire around the base? Now that would have been really nice to hang on a handsome, older, more sophisticated gentleman. What girl could resist an afternoon of being on the arm of a man like that? Sure, he was no Dakota Abrams, but still...

The bustling auxiliary control room had tight quarters, making it easy for her to see just about every station. Spinning her chair slowly, she caught a glimpse of something odd on one of the hangar bay monitors. For a split second, it looked like Colonel Barker working her way toward her personal F-2. Willis spun around a little faster and stopped to get a better look. It was CJ! She was removing the cover guards from the thruster ports and intakes, as well as all the gun barrels and sensor pods. Willis pushed away from her station, nearly giving herself whiplash when her headset cord came to the end of its length and jerked her head back. Getting herself untangled, she pulled up close to the security tech on duty.

"Did the Colonel say anything about taking her ship out?" she asked watching the monitor.

"Nothing, ma'am. Should I have a team check on her?"

Willis remained silent, watching Colonel Barker. She seemed to be in quite a hurry.

"No, I don't think so. Do you have a current location on Lieutenant Reese and Administrator Vandmire?"

"They just passed sentry check point three in hangar deck two."

Willis pulled her headset off and bolted from the control room. At the speed she was running, it took only a minute for her to catch up to Talia and Diord.

"You guys need to come with me, on the double!"

"What's this all about, Lieutenant?" Diord asked, a little bewildered.

"Not sure, but we have to hurry," Willis answered as they dashed down the hall.

"Slow down, Willis! Information please..." Talia called after the aide.

"It looks like Colonel Barker is trying to take-off without any clearances."

"Take-off?" Diord repeated. "Are you sure?" The sound of converters starting to whine began to echo down the hall as the three rushed to the open door. By the time they reached the hangar bay, the Isom engines were fully revved up and the F-2's anti-grav system was active. Talia raised her communicator to her mouth.

"Sir, what are you doing? You don't have any clearance delivery; no departure orders. Where are you going?" The three watched CJ, who seemed to ignore them as she turned her craft toward the closed doors. Diord grabbed the communicator and took a step toward the throttling fighter.

"Casey, we've got a date this evening; no welching. What's this all about?"

CJ glared at Diord. There was a completely different woman behind her expression.

"Open the doors, Talia, or I'll blow them open," CJ commanded, turning back to her controls.

"I can't open them without proper authorization, Sir," Talia yelled in a panic. "Those are your orders!"

Catching a glance from CJ, Diord suddenly turned and body slammed both women as the F-2's guns came alive. Shrapnel and debris exploded in a fiery spray as the hangar doors gave way under the powerful blast. As the dust and smoke began to clear, the three on the ground turned to see the fighter maneuvering through the blown-out doors and toward the cavern opening. They watched helplessly from the crumpled piles of broken junk as the Flightstreak receded to a pinpoint in the dark Aster sky.

"Control," Talia yelled frantically into her communicator. "Patch me through to all the fighter frequencies and make sure I've got full power on the coms." All three scampered over the wreckage of the hangar doors and ran back toward the control center.

"Did she say anything to you, Lieutenant?" Diord asked as they entered the main hangar bay.

"Not a word," Willis replied. "I just noticed her on the security monitors."

"Colonel Barker, come in." Talia kept her communicator to her lips as best she could as they hurried toward the control center. "Colonel Barker, please answer. Patrols three and nine, do you have eyes on a lone F-2 in orbit?"

"We did," a voice came back from Talia's com. "We tracked an F-2 with no clearance delivery just moments ago, but it blew into Quadra-light before we could intercept. It's long gone. Do you want us to try for any kind of directional fix from its last known jumping point?"

Talia slowed to a walk with Diord and Willis as they entered the control room.

"No, you won't be able to find anything." All three stopped at the departure controller and looked at the screens. "The Colonel didn't say anything to anyone about leaving?" The controller only turned and shook his head.

"I don't get it," Willis said. "Why would she just up and leave?"

"No idea," Talia responded trying to think of anything. "It's not like anything is going on. The *Realistic* and the *Constellation* only left a little over an hour ago. They haven't had time to encounter any trouble. She sounded fine when she asked me to give you the tour," she said looking at Diord. He stood silent, looking at the floor thinking.

"I might know what's going on," he finally said.

"What?"

"I came here to give her a message from Drax."

Talia looked all around the control room, then shuffled Willis and Diord out into the hallway.

"Did you see this message?"

"No, but considering who it was from... Which way to her quarters?"

"This way." Willis breezed past them, heading up the hall.

It took several minutes to reach the door and a few moments for Willis to work the security pad.

"Not sure we're going to be able to find anything," Diord surmised, looking around the room while Talia and Willis went directly to her desk. "It was an encrypted message on a memory key. Chances are, she took it with her."

"If that's the case, then we're sunk," Willis conceded as Talia started working the viewing controls on her desk.

"She had to have viewed it here somewhere. I just need to find the device she viewed it on."

"What good will that do? It was encrypted." Willis sounded defeated, but not quite ready to give up. Talia was busy going through all the files on her desk system, scanning everything while Diord took a seat in a corner chair. As he sat and waited while Talia continued to pour over all the data on CJ's desk, he noticed a small viewing device on the table next to him and picked it up.

"Maybe something like this?" he asked poking his fingers at the screen to turn it on.

"Stop!" Talia shrieked, holding her hand up.

"What? We're not going to know if it was this device if we don't try it." Diord had nearly jumped out of his pants.

"I just peed a little," Willis complained.

"Because, that device on startup will clear all its memory to make way for all the startup files. If I can start it up in a safe mode, it will retain the last files it used, all decrypted. If she viewed it on that device, we might be able to see it." Talia carefully took the device and sat down at CJ's desk to work with it. After a moment of fiddling, she set it on the desk and made several adjustments to her wall viewer. "Now, for all you full sound folks and large picture geeks in the audience..." She looked up at the large wall display and adjusted a control on the viewing device. Moments later, the image of Queen Captain Drax Blair materialized on the screen.

"I get chills just looking at her," Willis shivered purposely.

"You knew about this?" Talia asked turning to Diord.

"I knew about the message because the Queen Captain came to me and asked that I deliver it, but I had no idea what was in the message." Diord looked back up at the image as Drax began to speak.

"Hello, Casey Janae. I hope this transmission finds you fully healed and doing well. I feel like after everything that's happened in the last several months, I need to apologize."

"Apologize?" Willis cried, incensed.

"Ssshhh!" Talia hushed the aide.

"While the fortunes of war are usually in my favor, I feel some regret for having used my success on you."

"She feels bad? Is that even possible?"

"Willis!" Talia scolded.

"The deceptions of the Colonians put you in an impossible position and it's unfortunate you were in command of the Nulark system when the Albion Empire came to take rightful possession."

"What a crock!"

"Ssshhh!"

"As the Albion Empire stands poised to crush the illegitimate rule of the Duchess Benetar, it is my fondest hope that you will rejoin me and help orchestrate a smooth transition of power to maintain a stable government throughout Hadrian. To prove my goodwill, I'm willing to offer you several assurances. I will halt any and all attempts at locating your position. I know Administrator Vandmire is assisting you and possibly knows of your whereabouts, but I will not hold him accountable as an accessory to your exile in hiding. I will not follow or track his movements."

"Not that she could."

"Furthermore, I will dismiss any attempts at retrieving the secret weapon he has provided you in the form of the attack Corsairs. Additionally, as further incentive for your safe return to Albia, I will provide you with the antidote to what was injected into your friend, Gunnar Conrad. No doubt he is experiencing some additional side effects from his sedation therapy at the hands of Seelix Monroe."

Talia and Willis looked back at Diord, who only shrugged.

"If you do not join me within the specified time frame, using the arrival coordinates provided with this message, he is going to die. The injection happened while onboard the *Tarzana* right before you took him from the examination room. I feel certain you remember it; Kodiac Blu. Please feel free to make your verifications. If you remember, we haven't used it in a long time because its use was forbidden by treaty, and because it didn't produce the intended results for which it was originally designed. But I think in this instance, it's having the desired effects. Listen to me closely now." Drax leaned forward and held up a small cartridge filled with fluid. "Make no mistakes, my dear sister. I'm holding the only antidote and it doesn't live very long on the shelf. Since we created this variant, you'll not find it anywhere else. Kodiac Blu will gradually eat at the base of a subject's cerebral cortex, causing a complete loss of one's cognitive functions and then madness. Eventually, if they don't end up killing themselves first, they die a very painful death." Drax leaned back. "Now, it's quite simple. You will tell no one where you are going or why. You will come alone and come straight here. I'll allow you to wipe your navigation system clean after your arrival. Once you're here and have vowed your allegiance to the Albion Empire, you can deliver this antidote to wherever you like without fear of anyone tracking it. If you don't show at this location within the specified timeframe, I will destroy the antidote and the formula used to produce it. It doesn't matter if you are intercepted, your ship breaks down or whatever the reason, your fault or someone else's, I destroy the antidote. I'm sorry it has to be this way, Casey. Family should remain on the same side of everything and my little sister is no exception. Now, come join me, quickly." The screen went dark for a moment, then a star chart came up with several rows of information flashing beneath it. Talia read it carefully.

"Coordinates where she is to meet the *Tarzana* no doubt. Looks like she has only twelve hours to get there. At the bottom, it says, "Don't be late.""

"Sisters?" Willis blurted, astonished. "Are you serious? Did you know about this?" She turned to Diord.

"Yes, I knew. I've known for years, but Casey asked me not to say anything. She wanted her successes and failures to be her own and not because of some prejudice quantified by one race of people or another. She wanted to be known for the kind of person she is inside, not for who she is related to or where she comes from. Nothing has changed as far as Casey is concerned. This is blackmail of the worst kind."

"There are different kinds of blackmail?" Willis asked.

"It's one thing to put the screws to someone in business or an enemy in wartime, but to hold something over the head of a relative? That has got to be the lowest form of blackmail out there. Shouldn't you be treating those who profess to love you better than anyone?"

"So now what are we supposed to do?" Willis asked, trying to see into the future. "Can we send another ship to intercept her?"

"You heard Drax," Talia pointed out. "If CJ doesn't show up at the appointed time, the antidote and the formula are gone and Colonel Conrad is a dead man. Besides, we've got nothing that could catch her."

"What about the *Realistic*? They could stop her."

"Willis, have you not been listening?" Talia scolded. "If CJ doesn't board the *Tarzana* at the time indicated right here," she said pointing at the numbers on the display, "Drax will destroy the antidote and the formula, then Colonel Conrad is as good as dead."

"Isn't there anything we can do? I just can't believe CJ is going to go back to being Albion and fight for them." Willis sounded quite distraught.

"I think you're missing the point here, Lieutenant," Diord said with arms folded and legs crossed. "You have zero say in the matter. What you two do have a say in, is what you're going to do next to keep what CJ created alive. Are you going to go on the base sound system and tell everyone the beacon they thought was leading them has thrown it all to the wind and defected back to the other side? That everything they have fought and died for is all a big sham and they were brought out here in the middle of nowhere for no reason?"

Willis turned to Talia who was now deep in thought. Diord finally got to his feet and started for the door.

"Wait," Willis said stopping him. "Where are you going? You're not leaving?"

"Well of course I'm leaving. I've seen everything I needed to see and I have to make my reports in such a way that others don't come snooping around in my business and discover your whereabouts."

"But we need you here. Now more than ever. Who's going to lead us; take command of the base."

Diord looked over at Talia, who was still thinking.

"Oh, I think you can figure it out. Just remember, CJ hasn't changed, only her circumstances. Follow command procedures. That will put the Command Control officer in charge." Diord put his finger to Talia's chest. "Commander Reese. Just keep business as usual until you hear something different." With that, Diord slipped out the door, leaving Willis wondering and Talia still thinking.

Calliope

The nation of Castell had been forced to abandon their home worlds of Tela Nunes and Colliagose long ago. Deadly plagues from deep space meteorites striking their planets had ravaged both spheres. Unable to contain the catastrophic effects of the space borne outbreaks on the populations, this unassuming society turned to the other civilizations of Hadrian for help. After much debate, the Administrators of Cross determined that in order to isolate these interstellar pandemics from other galactic nations, what was left of the Castell inhabitants would have to be relocated. As a suitable planet wasn't possible, an asteroid was decided upon. One large enough to accommodate the entire populace, yet small enough it could be moved to an isolated area with an available sun and placed in a sustainable orbit. This setting would provide them the needed isolation and allow them to evolve independently, keeping their culture intact.

The science required to create such an environment wasn't terribly difficult to implement, but the scale on which it was undertaken was larger than anything ever attempted in Hadrian. Finding an appropriately sized asteroid for the application was a chore in and of itself. Most space bodies, such as benign comets and crushed planet debris were generally ignored. It was only after an exhaustive search, that the technicians of Cross were able to find a suitable planetoid and have it meticulously milled to fit the needs of an entire civilization. Calliope was built entirely in its interior. Much smaller than even the smallest of moons, Calliope was hardly spherical. It resembled more of a great chunk of broken rock than anything remotely round. Inside, a myriad of connecting tunnels and cavities formed what the Castellians affectionately referred to as Calliope's Maze. Large enough to take in medium class capitol ships, the interior was designed with all the facilities needed to maintain and repair just about any space going vessel.

Occupying neutral territory, Calliope was the preferred location for hosting military and governmental dignitaries for negotiations and peace talks. Only the best accommodations were afforded the dignitaries and military VIPs now assembling in the plush conference lounges. Rather than a large table to converse and negotiate over, the high command had opted for a large comfortable seating area where everyone could see everyone and not feel left out of a conversation. All were intended to be heard. Amid several men and women smoking and sipping drinks, the conversation of an Albion diplomate and a Ratronian Field Marshal rose above the quiet chatter.

"Unless we find the installation Colonia has illegally established in the regions of the Spartus, we'll end up dragging this conflict out even further," Ratronian Field Marshall Von Hoffen contended, pulling a smoldering pipe from between his teeth.

"You have deep space probes out all over this galaxy," Albion General Nassy replied gruffly, "and into the fringes of the Spartus. The Albion Empire has probes tracking your probes as well as the Colonian probes. And yet no one has detected any trace of this militia the Colonians have illegally established."

Colonian Ambassador Rigel Fixx jumped into the escalating conversation.

"You keep accusing us of having illegally established some mystery super base whose ships are poised to lay waste to the entire Ratronian and Albion fleets. The age and amount of hardware Colonel Barker has stolen from the Colonian Empire is hardly enough to worry about, unless we've grossly underestimated the strength of the mighty fleets of Albia and Krull. Colonel Barker is a traitor to the Empire and I can assure you, she has acted alone."

"Not that the Ratronians couldn't go wherever we will, but it makes zero sense to think the renegade Barker just took her command and left the galaxy never to return. She has ideals and principles and until she is located and dealt with, there can be no political solution to stabilize the government ruling Hadrian."

"There can be no stabilized government where the Colonians are concerned without a blood heir to the royal throne. Pintar Royalty has been the only mechanism that has successfully seen Hadrian through all its difficult times of turmoil."

"I couldn't agree more," Ambassador Fixx said, her voice starting to escalate. "But we have that now. Queen Benetar has proven her blood line throughout this entire dispute. This is a non-issue; it always has been."

"Hardly," General Nassy countered. "The Duchess's only claim to the throne is by marriage and subsequent disposal of the royal heirs. This clearly tries to circumvent Hadrian law, which demands a blood heir. Show us there is an actual blood line to a legitimate heir and the Albion Empire will swear its undying devotion to that heir and the fighting will stop."

"And what of Colonel Barker?" Von Hoffen interrupted. "She is still out there and has armed herself with two-heavy attack ships produced by Cross. It's clear the forces supplying and protecting her militia have chosen political sides as they have refused to provide the rest of us with the plans for these new super-weapons or working prototypes for inspection. Cross has signed long standing agreements with all of us for inspection of any new technologies. Administrator Vandmire must live up to these agreements and release the plans and a working production model."

"Yes, we do need the plans for these new super weapons," a stern voice interrupted the heating exchange. The room hushed down a bit as the cloaked figure of Queen Captain Drax Blair glided up the aisle, flanked by several officers and Blinda Koss. Drax settled into one of the plush chairs and picked up some finger food from the table next to her as Blinda melted into the dark recesses of the wall behind the Queen Captain. "And we'll have both the plans and a working prototype, very soon." Drax looked around the room. Most of the attention was now on her. Just where she liked it. "Not only will we have these new weapons Administrator Vandmire is producing, but Colonel Barker along with them. I will personally see that she is dealt with in an appropriate manner."

"How is it a Queen Captain can negotiate for either? Especially the one who has needlessly escalated tensions by attacking a sovereign Colonian outpost on Carolon and is now squatting her forces in the Nulark system?" Ambassador Fixx asked indignantly.

"What was the Duchess hiding in the Nulark system anyway?" Von Hoffen asked. "There's nothing of strategic importance there, no settlements on any of the planets, no usable commodities to be extracted. At least nothing worth all the trouble to go out that far to get."

"Colonia has purposely tried to widen its illegal expansion by setting up an outpost on Carolon," Drax said, trying to remain calm. "If there was nothing there before, then there certainly isn't anything there now. But I believed it was a steppingstone to something much larger, so the threat required equalization."

"There was nothing illegal about the outpost we set up to monitor the Spartus," Ambassador Fixx responded. "There is nothing to *step to* in the Spartus. Equalization is just another fancy term for…"

"The Duchess could have easily built her little 'outpost' on Boris if she had wanted to monitor the Spartus. What was so special about Carolon?"

Incensed, one of Ambassador Fixx's attachés sprang to her feet.

"Queen Benetar is how you will address her majesty!"

"Your 'queen', as you refer to her, is not a blood heir. Therefore, she is simply a Duchess of Teleknee." Drax remained calm, unmoved.

"This is outrageous!" The Colonian attaché jumped out into the middle of the room. "We will not sit here while our queen is openly insulted by an Albion underling. We demand you address your sovereign as Queen of Hadrian or we will have justice!"

"Your sovereign has no more authority in Hadrian than the House of Dillard," Drax said leaning forward a bit.

"We will have justice," another Colonian aide said as several sprang to their feet. Before Ambassador Fixx could stop her delegation, one of them pulled a blaster. No sooner did the weapon appear than it mysteriously started to turn toward his head. A swirl of air spun around him as he fought to keep the muzzle from his face. Struggling, he began to thrash about while slowly rising from the floor. All eyes were fixated on the Colonian as he gently spun around, the barrel of the blaster now positioned in his mouth, his eyes wide in terror. Drax took note of the fingers on the trigger and the whining sound coming from the unit's power pack.

Perhaps I've allowed this to go a little too far. "Blinda," Drax spoke up. "Please release the Colonian." There was a long pause, giving Drax cause to wonder, but then the air in the room settled and the attaché dropped to the floor in a heap. The blaster tumbled away as the other Colonian aides helped the panting man to his feet.

"We've sort of gotten ourselves off topic here," Drax said, settling back in her chair. "We were talking about Colonel Barker's attack vessel that most of us think Cross produced, weren't we?" She watched as the humbled Colonian delegation warily went back to their seats. "My aide will bring you all up to date with the latest intel." Drax motioned to Captain Morris, who snapped to attention and activated a control on a personal display. Everyone in the room picked up a device and examined the information being presented.

"Some time ago, the *Tarzana* engaged a Corsair class vessel in the Nulark system between Reako and Tanis. During the ensuing skirmish, our Hesson engineers were able to collect partial data on the vessel. Due to the advanced nature of their shielding, most of our scans were deflected so what you're seeing here is somewhat incomplete. This ship is constructed of a material we have not seen before. Additionally, it has energy shields powerful enough to repel most of the weapons we possess. Careful analysis of this shield energy supports the notion that it would be able to deflect most conventional firepower as well, at the very least, slow it down. Its weaponry is unidentifiable. Nowhere in Hadrian can these type of armaments be found. It appears to have detachable fighters that will shame anything known to Hadrian, that includes the new F-4 Flightstreak. It was impossible to get any kind of readings on its propulsion system or anything else about its interior as it's shields were scrambling most of our scans, but we have to assume it has some kind of light speed capability."

"Excuse the interruption," one of the Colonian delegation stopped the presentation. "This room is filled with Colonians, Albions, Ratronians and several others. I think it's pretty safe to say we all hate each other's guts." The Colonian turned to the Albion Queen Captain, who nodded approvingly. "So why are you sharing these military secrets with everyone when it would be to your advantage to keep it to yourself; gain the upper hand on the rest of us?"

Drax smirked slightly, looking around the room.

"Is it possible all you really see is the little picture and not the larger issue? We are dealing with a highly technological alien presence, and while they don't have four heads and suction cups on the end of fifteen tentacles, they are different from us, mentally and physically. They can run faster, jump further and are by far, stronger than anyone in this room. So, it stands to reason their intellect is far superior to ours, as is their technology. Since our disagreements can't seem to be resolved by political jibber-jabbing," she said looking around at the different delegates, "we keep knocking at each other, taking our hits, and gradually whittling away at each other, all the while this new alien threat creeps up on us and takes over before we even know what happened. We all need to know how these ships and their crews operate and what they're capable of, so we can remain on a level playing field."

The room fell silent as no one was sure how to respond. There were several looks back and forth, until Drax motioned for her officer to finish his presentation. He cleared his throat and turned back to the depiction on the large screen.

"Our Hesson engineers were able to duplicate this design from the plans you see here and reverse engineer a working weaponized prototype we've called the *Warbird*."

A murmur rolled around the room as each person studied their displays in greater detail.

"But this working prototype looks far inferior to the real thing," the Ratronian Field Marshall pointed out. "What are you trying to get at here, Blair?"

Captain Morris gave the Queen Captain a glance and seeing she was not going to respond, continued.

"Our hope is to draw the second ship out. No doubt they're in search of their sister ship. They seem to be particularly interested in Carolon. Our intelligence indicates they might try to make a landing, though we're not entirely sure why. Since the first ship was lost in the Nulark system, it stands to reason they would come back to that area to search for it. If we can get close enough to the other ship with the *Warbird*, maybe even disable and capture it, we should be able to discover its secrets."

Another quiet roll of whispers and chattering meandered through the room.

"You're talking about setting a trap for this ship, and from what you've described, it's capable of wiping out several larger ships. Who's going to volunteer for that kind of mission and how will you ever get them close enough?" Von Hoffen folded his arms and waited for an answer with a look of supreme confidence that it wouldn't come.

"The first ship appeared to be damaged before the engagement began. But even then, *Tarzana* took on some heavy damage to its gun emplacements. The fatal blow was struck to the alien vessel's aft section. From this encounter, we've concluded that it would be unwise to engage this ship one on one. It's also reasonable to deduce that such a vessel wouldn't fall for just any trap. Just the hint of larger ships and it would avoid the area. Our plan is to lure it close using its own identifiers and general physical footprint."

"You're hoping it doesn't bring its shields up before the *Warbird* can disable it," Von Hoffen said. "Then what?"

"We call in the tugs to bring it here, to Calliope."

One of the Colonian delegates raised a hand.

"You realize, we had this very vessel in our marshalling ports on Tintee and it made short work of our matrix hangar system and blew through our outer security defenses?"

"No, we weren't aware of that," the Albion Captain said, one eyebrow raised.

The Colonian aide shrank back into his seat, realizing he might have just given up sensitive information. He gave the ambassador an embarrassed glance.

"If this is truly the case," the Captain began again. "We'll have to exercise even more caution."

"Thank you, Captain Morris," Drax said getting to her feet. "Because the Albions were first to engage this ship, we have an idea of what to expect and will therefore bear the cost of the second ship's capture. Of course, we'll be happy to except any financial assistance. Manpower and equipment are also welcome."

"I'll be happy to provide you with several tugs for the operation," Von Hoffen volunteered. "They're slow, but powerful and have the strongest tractor beams of any ship, even your beloved *Tarzana*."

"The Colonian Empire will provide perimeter security, to make sure nothing gets in or out of the system during the operation."

Drax eyed the group suspiciously. She was a little surprised that an unsteady accord had just been brokered without anyone even realizing it. No doubt the technology before them had their full attention and all were willing to do whatever they could to lay their hands on it. She reached for her wristband and motioned for her officers to follow as she started from the room, but before she could make her exit, a voice called to her from the far corner.

"Queen Captain Blair, I'd like a word."

Drax stopped short, recognizing the voice. A hush fell across the room as the Albion Supreme King Commander, Thoene Dismon came to his feet. Blinda Koss materialized from the shadows, standing several steps behind the King Commander. Sporting a plain, light blue uniform, Thoene Dismon gestured toward a private cubical. Drax drew in a deep breath, preceding the supreme leader to a tiny table and sitting down.

"Staff meetings like this one make the military fun again. Clearly, I need to join them more often." Thoene sat down, facing the Queen Captain. "The only thing missing was dinner."

"Wars would go much smoother if it weren't for diplomates and politicians," she grumbled.

"A smooth war isn't a war, but a diplomatic discussion," the King Commander countered. He seemed delighted at the consternation gripping the Queen Captain. Drax checked her wristband impatiently.

"Is there something I can do for you, KC Dismon?" she finally asked.

Thoene instantly picked up on the Queen Captain's irritation and leaned closer.

"There is, QC," he hissed quietly. "That ship could finish this conflict once and for all. It's just the weapon to tip the balance in our favor and I want it, not excuses."

"I thought that's what I was trying to do?" Drax replied cautiously.

"Mind where your focus is," he said drawing closer. "Imagine my concern when I get reports back that one of my top Queen Captains is off chasing after some rumored superman for cloning purposes or destroying a civilian Letoh complex and pissing off our only military grade contractor, all to try and hunt down her baby sister. Keep your mind on your job or I'll have someone else do it for you." Thoene was nearly on the table, glaring at Drax. "By the way, nice job expending a crap load of my assets in taking a system that has zero worth to the Empire."

"Carolon holds a strategic purpose to the Colonians, otherwise they wouldn't have put an outpost on it. They're hiding something."

"Well, whatever you think it might be, if I catch you anywhere near it again, I won't be as forgiving as I am now. You get one warning, and this is it."

"So, what would you like me to do with the outpost we've setup on Carolon?"

"Leave it where it sits. The people you have manning it are idiots anyway and it will keep them out of the way of where the real issues are."

"And where are the real issues?"

"With Cross and Administrator Vandmire. I want that ship and the technical plans for it. I'm certain he has them."

"You know as well as I do," Drax snarled right back, "Cross's security force is large enough to cause some serious damage to any one of our fleets. No one dares attack him for fear the others will gang up on the weakened one. If you're so concerned about your assets getting in harm's way, then going after Diord isn't the smartest move. It would take all three of our fleets combined to do it."

"Back off, Koss," Thoene growled, feeling the air begin to compress around them. Several of the King Commander's bodyguards instantly produced powered up weapons, pointed at Drax and Blinda. Blinda glanced across at Drax, who hastily shook her head. The air pressure promptly relaxed, but the guards held their weapons at the ready.

Thoene grimaced. His vision shifted to the room full of politicians and high ranking military officers. He passed a heavy sigh and looked back at Drax, eyeing her carefully. "Bring me this ship and these so-called aliens that come with it. You will report directly to me of any activity in the Nulark system and if there is so much as an asteroid passing out of place, I better hear about it." He pointed a threatening finger in Drax's face. "But let me make myself perfectly clear. You are not to enter Nulark, Colonian or Jurass space for any reason. Nor am I to get any reports of you chasing after your sister. Is that clear?" Thoene got up and waited for the Queen Captain to exit.

Drax held her breath for a moment, biting her tongue. Most coups were well planned. Very seldom could one just happen off the cuff, but were the King Commander's guards not here, she would certainly have killed him where he stood or let Blinda finish what she had attempted. Clearly those conditions weren't present, so she clenched her teeth harder.

"Perfectly clear," she grumbled barely audible.

"I'm sorry," Thoene spoke up reentering the main room. "We couldn't make out what you said. Can you repeat that?"

Drax stepped out and looked at everyone waiting for her to respond. No one could have heard the bulk of their conversation, but the fact the King Commander had drawn her out in the open, meant public humiliation.

"I understand you clearly, King Commander Dismon." Making sure everyone witnessed her contrite posturing, she bowed her head and took a step back.

"Very good. You're dismissed and good hunting." Thoene motioned his guards to stand down. As they melted back into the room, the King Commander turned as Blinda breezed past him. "Blinda, I'll have a word privately before you go."

Drax and Blinda turned, surprised there would be more reprimand forthcoming. Thoene motioned her into a private room at the far end of the conference room.   Both women headed for the door, but Thoene stopped them.

"I said Blinda. Drax, you may go. Don't worry, I'll have her onboard before you leave. "You're not in that big of a hurry."

"Actually, Sir, I am," Drax responded, impatiently checking her wristband.

"It can wait."

Drax hesitated a moment, then turned and left without the Albion Thane.

The King Commander gestured to the private room and followed Blinda in, closing the door. Twiddling his thumbs behind his back, Thoene moved to a large screen at the other end of the room and activated the control. After making some adjustments, the partial image of the alien ship flashed up. He studied it for a moment then turned to the Thane.

"Love the new outfit and what you've done with your hair."

Blinda remained motionless as the King Commander circled her admiring her new attire. Her emerald body suit appeared to have been sprayed on and there seemed to be no conceivable way she could have gotten her spiked knee-high boots on. Her long hair was now a silky raven color. She had also darkened her eye makeup. Her Balkrum and blaster were in their usual places on each hip.

"I read Commander SoKnack's report on the *Tarzana's* encounter with the alien ship, but didn't see yours," the King Commander complained.

"I didn't submit one," Blinda declared quietly.

"Seems like you would be anxious to make sure your actions were well documented. Keeps people from formulating inaccurate speculation."

"I'm not in the military, KC," Blinda answered coldly.

"No, but you serve the military." Thoene turned to Blinda. "Perhaps you'll convey your version to me?"

"I've read Dalton's report as well. It's accurate."

"But your version," Thoene persisted.

"There is nothing to add," Blinda held firm.

"Then make something up," Thoene growled.

Blinda stared at the ship on the screen, considering. Thoene went to move for the door, but the silence was finally broken by her response.

"I could sense the crew were human just like us; their minds just as fragile."

"Could you see into the ship's structure?"

"No, it was not my priority at the time."

Thoene turned back to the screen, frustrated.

"Drax ordered us to take the ship intact, not its crew. I will say the crew had a much stronger will than most other human minds I've encountered."

"Stronger willed?"

"They were well disciplined; the focus on their jobs was strong. It's difficult to cut through such intensity. They were highly intelligent, well trained; a tight knit group. It was a shame they had to be destroyed."

"Why did you order Commander SoKnack to fire on them a second time?"

"I'm fairly sure his account has all that detail," Blinda said.

"I will hear your account," Thoene insisted, coolly.

"I could not penetrate the ship's shield energy well enough to reach into their minds in order to get the job done. But the fatal blow that stopped the ship was also the blow that destroyed it."

"How big was the blast?"

"Dalton withdrew the *Tarzana* far enough away, we never saw the blast. Drax gets angry when her ship is damaged."

"She likes to think it's her ship," Thoene smirked.

"Is there anything else, KC?"

"Yes, your recent adventures have given me cause to wonder about Drax and her loyalty to the Albion Empire."

"You've never questioned her before," Blinda replied. "Why start now?"

"This whole Carolon affair has me concerned. Something isn't right. Even if the Colonians produce a legitimate blood heir to the throne, I'm not inclined to capitulate. We've come too far and gained too much to simply roll back and fall in line."

"But Hadrian law..."

"I'm not concerned with Hadrian law."

"What would you like me to do, KC?"

"I'm relying on you to keep the Queen Captain on task, and me informed of her activities."

"Drax does as she wills and I cannot interfere in what she has in mind. She can have me killed just as easily as you can. I've seen it done before."

"As have I, and have done so myself. For the good of the Empire, you will do this."

"Since I seem to have little choice in the matter," Blinda said looking straight ahead. "Reports will be provided as they become available and it's prudent to do so. Is that all, KC?" She bowed respectfully.

"Who are you loyal to?" Thoene asked, looking down at her.

"I am loyal to the Empire, Sir," she answered remaining bowed.

"As a Thane, who are you assigned to?"

"I have no official charge," Blinda said, hesitating.

"You mean after all this time, you still haven't received a new assignment?"

"It's of little consequence as I failed to adequately protect my original charge."

"Oh," Thoene raised a finger sarcastically to his temple. "Weren't you originally assigned to protect a Pintar Princess? What happened to her?"

Blinda remained silent, her lips drawn tight. Shifting her eyes up through her bangs, she let her vision burrow into the back of the King Commander's head.

"She died in a drowning accident."

"Drowning," Thoene tisked. "Such a tragedy, and you weren't there to protect her?"

"I was occupied elsewhere," she hissed.

"Yes, those things do happen, don't they? Well, see that you remain focused on your current assignment. Do I make myself clear?"

Blinda slowly stood erect, her fists tight and feet spread. The King Commander put his hand to his ear and leaned a little closer to her, ignoring her aggressive body language.

"What was that? I didn't quite make out what you said."

"Crystal clear, KC." She clinched her fists a little tighter, trying to maintain control. She could feel her fingernails trying to swell. She kept her eyes looking at the floor as she knew they were dilated.

"Ah, good. We have an understanding. See that Drax stays out of trouble and remains focused. Now, go." Thoene turned back to the viewing screen, clasping his hands behind his back. Blinda spun on her spiked heels and started for the door, but before she could exit, the King Commander called to her without turning.

"And Blinda? The contents of this meeting are to remain private."

Blinda paused a moment, then exited the room, breezing past the King Commander's guards and down the hall.

*   *   *   *

The *Tarzana's* support flotilla consisted of several different classes of war ships. Several Corvettes, a couple of Frigates, a number of Destroyers, along with armed freight carriers for resupply of the larger ships without having to pull them from front line battle operations. It wasn't difficult to identify the *Tarzana*, even from a distance as it was the largest of all the vessels. Surrounded by her flotilla, she ran at Quadra Light toward an unremarkable point at the edge of the Spartus boundary, ordered by Queen Captain Drax Blair. On the bridge, Commander Dalton SoKnack stood conversing with several of his support staff when a com officer delivered a hand display unit to him. After studying it for a moment, Dalton nodded and looked up through the overhead windows at the command lounge high above. The Queen Captain hadn't spoken a word since arriving back from her meeting on Calliope Station several hours ago. She had walked right past him without a word and ascended to the lounge. Usually when she acted in similar fashion, she was in a foul mood, yelling insults at anyone in her way. This time, she seemed deep in thought. Dalton almost preferred the yelling and condescending attitude. At least he knew exactly what to expect under those conditions. This felt like a powder keg that was about to blow. He was also aware Blinda Koss had boarded the ship, but had not followed the Queen Captain to the lounge, opting instead to head straight to her quarters. This troubled him even more. He understood well that the relationship between Drax and Blinda was a tenuous one at best, and to have the two board separately and not speaking to anyone, let alone each other, meant something ominous was on the horizon.

Taking a deep breath, he stepped into the command elevator and a moment later was entering the command lounge where he found Drax sitting with her face in her hands. He approached timidly, then stood at attention while holding out the device.

"Yes, Commander. What is it?" Drax asked quietly.

"Navigational analysis of the coordinates you've ordered the *Tarzana* to have been sent back for review. There's nothing out there at this location. I'm checking to make sure we got the information correct."

Drax didn't move for several moments while Dalton waited patiently. She finally pulled her hair back and examined the information on the device. A wearied look was etched across her face.

"Yes, this is correct. And yes, I understand there's nothing out there. Can you be sure we can reach this location by the time indicated?"

"Yes, QC. We can be there right on the mark."

"Can you make it there a couple of minutes before the mark?"

"Yes, certainly. Is there anything specific we'll be looking for when we arrive?"

"Follow the instructions as indicated. No fighter launches and minimal patrols."

Drax handed the device back to Dalton and leaned back in her chair, closing her eyes. Dalton watched her for a moment; wondering, but finally bowed slightly and headed for the elevator.

"Commander," Drax called quietly.

Dalton stopped at the door and turned.

"Where will I find Blinda Koss?"

"She has not reported in, but I was notified earlier that she did board and headed straight for her quarters." Dalton waited for a response, but Drax remained unmoved. "Should I summon her to the Command lounge?"

Drax finally opened her eyes, looking out through the overhead window.

"No, I'll find her myself."

"Would you like me to summon your aide to accompany you?"

"No, I'll go alone."

"As you wish. Is there anything else?"

"No. Be sure to let me know before we reach those coordinates."

"Certainly." Dalton turned back to the door, but hesitated, turning back to his commander. "QC, is everything all right? You don't look well. Should I have your chef prepare you something?"

Drax sat forward rubbing her eyes and finally looked at Dalton.

"I haven't eaten or slept in a while. Perhaps I'll have something in an hour or so."

"Very good, QC." Dalton turned and disappeared into the elevator.

Once the commander was gone, Drax got to her feet and moved to the window, looking out at the vastness of space, contemplating. Wondering if she was on the right path; if she had ever been on the right path. Was power really the ultimate goal of her life's pursuits? Had Casey found there was more to existence than just power? Drax stood for a few more moments watching the surrounding flotilla traveling alongside the *Tarzana* at Quadra-light. Her thoughts wandered to earlier times with her sister; when things seemed easier to navigate. She found herself wandering in and out of those memories with her then, best friend and little sister, Casey Jenae. The times they would discuss, even argue about how BachTL should be raised. Turned out to be an even split as to who would win those arguments. She thought of BachTL and where he was and what he might be doing. Was he all right? The Colonian delegation hadn't said anything about him being on Tintee, so he must be still at large, trying to accomplish the task Drax had given him to procure the second Alien assault ship. She hoped he would either come back, admitting to failure or somehow bring the alien craft in. At least make contact with her. Nothing would give her more pleasure than parading the alien ship in front of the King Commander. The other Queen Captains would have something to aspire to. Yes, she did still love the spotlight and yes, there was still that element of thrill in wielding power, but now there seemed to be something tempering it. Perhaps it was something coming in the future; she didn't know for sure. Taking one last look at the stars, she turned and headed for the elevator.

Hurry up and wait

The spearheaded shape of the *Realistic*, sported long opposing tail fins around a square main thruster port. Its nose was cone shaped with a large conning tower mounted just behind it. Large gun emplacements adorned the structure in the most strategic locations. This craft, being an older galaxy class research ship, had been retrofitted for military use. Within its upper hangar decks, many of its craft had been left behind on Aster to make room for the Kalamarion Assault Corsair, *Constellation.* Still unable to perform light speed operations, their mission to Carolon was to rectify that condition. Even without FTL engines, the Starbird was considered a deadly opponent to ships much larger than itself, though that had yet to be proven to the factions of Hadrian.

The crew of the *Constellation* waited patiently for word to come that the *Realistic* had successfully navigated through all their Quadra-light jumps into the Nulark system. With operations shut down, Colonel Conrad had taken Captain Dalley with him to observe the jump procedures of the *Realistic*. Dakota was left as the officer in charge and had taken BachTL down to engineering to make some operational explanations.

"This place is incredible," BachTL said, standing just inside the engineering Mallory doors. "The *Tarzana* is an amazing ship as well, but there's no way to ever get to know it completely. It's just too big. But this ship has everything, and it doesn't take you all day to get from one end to the other."

"I've been on a couple of those," Dakota smirked. "Thankfully, our Capitol ship designers understood the need to sleep next to your gun or fighter."

"Are there restrictions here?" BachTL asked not daring to move from the door.

"As long as either myself or one of the engineers are with you all the time, you are free to look at anything and ask any questions."

"Any questions?"

"Oh, don't worry. If you ask about something top secret, I'll make sure you get a bunch of BS and make you feel good about it."

BachTL looked all around the engine room, not wanting to miss anything. He focused on the engineering consoles at the center of the room, right in front of the main engines and power converters assemblies. He turned to the closest wall and worked his way around the perimeter of the room, looking at everything.

"Where does this go?" he asked, looking at the body cradle in the Interceptor tube.

"Fighter access," Dakota replied. "One on both sides of the engine room."

"Is this the only access?" BachTL peered up the tube lit with tiny clearance lights.

"You can access from the outside, but where's the fun in that?"

"I mean, what happens if the engine room has a problem and has to be sealed off? How do you get to your ships?"

"Both fighters are manned during alert operations. Were something catastrophic to happen in engineering, standard procedure is to launch both fighters."

"And this elevator here?" BachTL stepped to a shaft door beside the engine bulkhead.

"Turret," Dakota said from the middle of the room.

BachTL continued around to the front side of the engine bulkhead, finally stopping in front of the massive glass touch console.

"Utterly amazing," BachTL gasped. "I've never seen this kind of tech before. Can you tell me what I'm looking at?"

"Sure," Billy said, stepping forward. "We have command and configuration of all the ship's systems at our fingertips here. We can't use weapons or navigate, although we do have limited control should the need arise."

"If for some reason the bridge becomes incapacitated," Dakota interrupted, "the ship can continue to function by using an auxiliary control console in another room."

BachTL let his eyes wander about the vast console, trying to figure out what the information being displayed was. It was difficult not to get lost in the myriad of pictorials and readouts swirling in a fluid dance before him. He looked up at several overhead displays, trying to decipher the information before him.

"How do you keep track of everything?"

"It's not hard when you work with it constantly," Dakota said.

"Doesn't hurt we've been using this since it was invented," Billy added.

BachTL observed something beyond the displays, mounted directly in front of them on the engine bulkhead. It was a curious structure, housing several glowing stones held in place with spider like fingers behind a glass plate.

"So, you monitor everything that's happening on the ship from here?"

"Everything that has to do with power and propulsion. We have a station up on the bridge that is used for real-time monitoring, command, and control. It's not as big and comprehensive as these controls are, but it gets the job done."

"What if you wanted to look at that box with the glowing stones in it?" BachTL asked, pointing at the Asium crystal assembly.

Billy Moon, tapped the bottom left section of the glowing display, and a pictorial of the Asium Crystal assembly expanded forward on the glass.

"You're looking at the Asium crystal assembly," Billy said swiping a finger around the corner of the picture, causing it to spin slowly. "We can look at it from any angle. Look at any areas that might be developing a problem and adjust its configuration."

"It looks like there should be six stones in your assembly here," BachTL said pointing at an empty set of claws. "There's only five."

"The reason for this mission," Dakota said tapping the screen, causing the image to zoom in on the empty claws. "We lost a crystal on our journey here sometime back. Carolon has the raw materials we need to manufacture a replacement."

BachTL looked closer at the display, then up at the actual assembly.

"I imagine there's a lot of energy running through that little box."

"You imagine correctly," Dakota responded.

BachTL reached up and tapped the glass next to the display of the Asium assembly, but nothing happened. Billy touched the glass and the image shrank back to its original size, then swiping it to the left, the image shrank further and moved back to its original location on the left lower corner of the console.

"I don't understand," BachTL said perplexed. He touched all over the glass, but nothing responded. "How come I can't make anything work?"

"Because the ship doesn't recognize you as a crew member," Dakota said.

"Nice security protocol. How do I get on the list?"

Dakota smiled and stepped back, allowing BachTL to move around the console to the engine bulkhead. After walking the length of the engine and examining the interior plumbing of the rear thrusters, he bent down and followed the contour of the engine cradles and mounts all the way forward.

"This looks like it would slide right out if you wanted it to," he said, still bent over.

"It's a modular design," Billy said. "If we have a major problem with an engine for whatever reason, we can remove the unit and replace it with another. Saves on valuable downtime in space dock. We can make a change out and be operational again within days instead of months."

"Now what?" BachTL asked, stepping back to the engineering console.

"We wait for the *Realistic* to finish its light speed operations."

"Can we go back to the bridge to wait?"

"Sure, we'll stop off at sick bay first and see Doctor Yamoto. She said she wanted to visit with you since she didn't get a chance when you first boarded."

"Lead the way," BachTL said as they started for the Mallory doors.

*   *   *   *

The bridge crew sat causally in front of their stations talking.

"You mean to tell me you spent your entire shore leave here on the ship?" Mr. Pippin was flabbergasted at both Nigel and Lana.

"Not the entire time," Lana answered. "We left the ship to have a look around."

"But since there was basically nothing out there, we came back," Nigel jumped in.

"You're serious," Lynette chuckled. "You guys didn't try to do anything outside the ship? Just got off and got back on?"

"No, it wasn't that bad." Nigel looked around the bridge at all the disbelieving faces. "We just didn't outfit ourselves and go river rafting or plain dragging."

"There just wasn't anything of interest for us. So, we would just make short trips out for fresh air and a good walk as far as the base personal were allowed, then we came back." Lana was feeling like she and Nigel were being mocked a little too much. "I mean you guys have to admit there isn't a whole lot to do on Aster."

"While I can agree with you to a certain extent," Mr. Pippin finally conceded, "popping outside for a quick smoke just doesn't seem like an effective use of a shore leave."

"Nobody smokes anymore," Nigel quickly added.

"Well, in our galaxy that might be true, but there are lots of cultures spread across the universe that partake of a variety of inhalants in an equally diverse manner. One shouldn't be surprised to encounter humanoid and nonhumanoid life forms engaging in such activities."

"Geez, Pip," Lynette Starman chuckled. "You're starting to sound like Alex 7001."

"Thank you," Pip responded. "I'll take that as a compliment."

"It's not," Lynette muttered behind a grin.

"So, what about you two?" Doran Cartwright asked from his weapons console. "What was so exciting that you two nearly made us late and got left behind?"

Lynette looked across at Pip, but remained silent. All eyes turned, wondering who would make the explanation. Mr. Pippin finally took a deep breath and let it out.

"We were playing Shogi."

"Shogi..." Lana repeated, looking across at Lynette.

"Yes, Shogi," Pip reaffirmed. "It's a game utilizing many multi-level game pieces that are moved strategically around a board in an attempt to out-maneuver the other player."

"Yes, Mr. Pippin," Doran spoke up. "I think we all know what the game is and how to play it. What we don't get is how you two..."

"Mr. Pippin we get," Lana pipped up. "But Lynette, I would have never figured on you liking a game as boring as Shogi."

"It's not boring; I love it." Lynette didn't seem insulted or terribly defensive about the revelation. "It requires you to think ahead to out-maneuver your opponent. Stimulates the brain. Besides, that wasn't the only thing we were doing."

"Ah," Doran jumped in. "Now we're getting to the juicy parts."

"We hiked and camped Thunder ridge."

"You did not," Lana and Doran erupted in unison.

Nigel chuckled, closing his eyes and putting his hand to his forehead.

"Of all the stupid things," he muttered, bringing Lynette's attention to him.

"We were within sight of the base the entire time," she defended.

"You two are lucky you're even onboard right now," Lana burst, spinning around in her chair. "How in the world did you avoid detection from perimeter security?"

"Despite the planet's current status, there are a multitude of indigenous life forms still living on Aster. Aster Command doesn't scan the surface of the planet for life forms, only energy signatures. We took nothing with us that could create such a signature. The idea was to go off grid and be on our own. Roughing it as you will."

"You're definitely going to be roughing it when the Colonel gets through with you."

"We'll be lucky if he doesn't impose something on all of us because of you and your *roughing it*."

"Not likely. Were we aboard ship and creating a ruckus so as to affect the entire crew and this ship's performance, it could come back on you. But once explained under controlled conditions, we're only likely to receive a reprimand." Mr. Pippin sounded quite confident in his assessment of the situation, but the looks from the other three told a different story.

"Guess we're going to find out pretty quick," Lana announced looking at the displays on her console. There were several feeds showing the exterior of the ship. One of them was trained on two figures moving toward the open boarding door. The expression on Colonel Conrad's face wasn't too reassuring. She brought up the exterior mics and adjusted the gain. The Colonel sounded infuriated and all Captain Dalley could do was listen.

"I hope your theory holds up, Mr. Pippin," Lana said cautiously, listening closely to the Colonel's rantings as they continued to approach from outside. "He doesn't sound like he's in a very good mood."

"Seems like he's never in a good mood anymore," Lynette complained. Everyone turned back to their stations to make it look like they were busy. It felt like an eternity before Captain Abrams entered the bridge with a ruffled look. He glanced at the empty engineering station and turned to the command chair, touching one of the comlink controls.

"Tiana, to the bridge." The message echoed ship wide as Dakota sat down with a heavy sigh.

"Orders, Captain?" Pip asked turning in his chair.

Dakota stared blankly at Pip for a long moment, then sat up.

"We're still holding for another six hours."

"Six hours?" the bridge crew erupted.

"Are we in the Nulark system or not?" Doran asked.

"We're here," Dakota confirmed. "But Captain Reeder wants to drive the entire perimeter first, before he starts pushing past Boris to Carolon. They aren't detecting anything different than what the drones have reported, but we're too far away from Carolon to know what's in orbit."

"Anything on the *Athena*?" Pip asked.

Dakota shook his head slightly, thinking.

"Let's just blow the doors and go straight in," Doran suggested.

"That's just what the Colonel is suggesting," Dakota said smiling slightly. "But I can see the Captain's reasoning. The *Realistic* is out here alone with only the fighter groups you see here in her hangar bays. It could get ugly if they encountered an Albion or Ratronian flotilla dropping out of Quadra-light somewhere close."

"Bring it," Doran continued defiantly. "We've been out here all by ourselves for almost two years and we're not worried about someone sneaking up on us."

"Well, to be fair, we were hiding out in the middle of nowhere for part of that," Nigel interjected.

"For now, we hold stations. It'll give Billy's crew more time to make sure everything that can work, works like it's supposed to." Dakota fell silent, watching everyone turn back to their duty stations. He let a sigh go and turned to Pip. "Mr. Pippin, the Colonel wants to see you and Lieutenant Starman. You are to report to the conference room immediately."

Everyone on the bridge froze, until Mr. Pippin got to his feet, followed by Lynette Starman. The two straightened up and made their way silently toward the bridge door. As they reached it, Tiana entered, moving to the side to let them out.

"Maybe I should come with you," Dakota offered as they stepped through the threshold. Pip shook his head, following Lynette out into the hallway and disappeared as the door closed behind them.

"Come with them where?" Tiana asked looking after them as the door closed.

"Where are you and Billy with the induction sequencers?"

"We're tuned up as well as we can be with five crystals. Come with them where?" she persisted.

"The Colonel is giving them a formal reprimand," Dakota finally said in a low tone. He turned to Tiana, who had done an about face to follow the two officers. "And you weren't invited."

Tiana stopped and turned to Dakota to object, but the Captain had turned back forward. She looked around the bridge at the crew. They all remained silent, facing their stations. Glancing at the engineering consoles, she turned back to the door.

"Tiana," Dakota said.

"I need to see Dr. Yamoto." With that, she stormed out, heading directly to the medical bay.

Lana turned and leaned back in her chair.

"Captain, what's the Colonel likely to do?"

"They'll certainly get a butt chewing," Dakota said after a short pause. "But it's hard to say for sure. He's already fuming at Captain Reader. He's been on edge as of late and it's not getting any better. There was a time when this kind of thing would require only a stern word and that would be the end of it, but ever since we lost Commander Atlanta, he's not been the same." Dakota fell silent for a moment, then cracked a smile. "Don't worry too much about it. He'll do the right thing."

*   *   *   *

Dr. Fuji Yamoto strolled casually up the main corridor of the ship. Halfway up the hall she took notice of two officers moving toward the bridge, disappearing behind the closing doors. A moment later, Gunnar stormed straight across the hallway and into his quarters. She couldn't see his expression, but his demeanor and walk told her enough. Continuing slowly, Fuji entered the bridge and let the door shut just behind her. She stood looking around at the personnel manning their stations. The bridge was quiet and with the exception of the occasional com burst it felt like you could hear a pin drop. The mood was tight and somber. She finally moved up between the command chair and the com station, still looking around.

"Hi, Doc," Dakota finally said quietly. "What brings you up here?"

"Just checking on the welfare of the crew." She glanced back at Lana Nevall, then at Mr. Pippin. He looked sharp and focused, his attention enveloped by what he was doing at his station. Fuji gradually made her way forward, making a gentle sweep behind the pilot and the navigator's station. Passing Lynette Starman, she paused a moment, taking note of her demeanor. The pilot's face was

reddish in color and her expression was rattled, upset. Fuji then
continued around the bridge, stopping at the command chair again.

"Is the Colonel in his quarters?"

"There or the conference room, ma'am, but I suspect he doesn't
want to be disturbed," Captain Abrams replied.

"I suspect you're correct." Fuji turned for the door, passing Tiana
as she entered and headed directly to the engineering consoles. Once
back out in the hall, Fuji turned to Gunnar's door and tried to listen for
activity inside. When she couldn't hear anything, she pressed the
summons control. Still nothing happened. Starting to leave, she
turned and inadvertently activated the door sensor. Startled at first,
the doctor peered inside, scanning the room. Gunnar never left his
door unsecured and while Fuji hadn't meant to open it, she was still
concerned for the welfare of the ship's commander. The main living
room lights had been dimmed, even his desk systems were off, though
there was a shaft of light beaming from a port window. Light filtered
through the dark Lexan doors that separated the living space from the
sleeping quarters. *Gunnar must be across the hall in the command
conference room.* Fuji turned around and looked through the open
door, into the conference room directly across the hall. She glanced
behind her at the Lexan doors then crossed to the conference room.
Empty. She turned again, facing Gunnar's door then looked up and
down the main hall. Billy was moving around beyond the open Mallory
doors, still no Gunnar. Stepping back over to his door, she reactivated
the sensor. The scene remained unchanged. This time she walked in
and headed straight to the Lexan doors. Fuji tried to look through, but
could only see the distorted view of the opposing wall and part of the
ceiling. There were quiet voices inside. This struck her as odd.
Activating the doors, she stepped inside and froze, seeing a couple
embracing in the corner.

Gunnar instantly pulled away from Audra, a look of mixed
astonishment and anger coalescing across his face. His eyes swirled
different shades of color. Stunned, Fuji tried to back out, but Gunnar
was already coming at her.

"Gunnar, stop!" Audra demanded.

Dr. Yamoto backed into the Lexan door, even after Gunnar had
stopped his advance.

"What are you doing in here?" Gunnar roared incensed. "You have
no right to be in my quarters! It's against regulations for any officer to
enter a commanding officer's quarters without their expressed
permission."

"As medical officer, it's my responsibility to see to the welfare of
the entire crew," Fuji fumbled sheepishly. "That includes you,
Colonel." Fuji looked past Gunnar at the form of Audra. "What's going
on here?"

Gunnar's angry look melted, shifting to embarrassment. He reached for his shaded glasses and put them on. After the initial shock of what she had walked in on, Fuji now wondered if the Hallavertor program had been such a good idea.

"I'm…" Gunnar stuttered, not exactly sure how he wanted to explain himself. "I mean, we were…" Audra stepped forward.

"You of all people know what's going on here, Doctor. I am fulfilling the program parameters you and General Niker created for this purpose."

"Are you sure?" Fuji asked, perplexed. She watched Gunnar suspiciously. Even through his glasses were on, she detected his eyes doing weird things. Even the color of his skin seemed to continually modulate. "Colonel, I'd like a word with you privately. Please turn your program off."

Gunnar looked at Audra, but hesitated.

"Pardon me, Doctor," Audra objected. "But if this has anything to do with Gunnar's disposition, then don't you think it would be better if I remain active and part of the conversation? I can provide you with valuable feedback and insight into how Gunnar is progressing that he would otherwise be hesitant to mention. If I am to remain an integral part of his therapy, then you need me to be part of this conversation."

Dumb struck, Fuji stared at Audra's determined look.

What have we done? Fuji thought.

She had approved the program parameters Rick had originally proposed and hadn't foreseen any problems. There were some concerns about how real the experience might be for Gunnar and the possibility of him becoming attached, but the realism had been deemed necessary to get Gunnar to open up and express his feelings. What neither had counted on was how closely the program could emulate Audra's feelings for Gunnar. Indeed, it appeared the program had actually assumed Audra's role.

"You may well be correct," Fuji finally said. "But, I'd still like to speak privately with the Colonel before I discuss any psychological diagnosis with a program. Now, Colonel, please."

Gunnar looked at Audra for a moment, then back at Fuji, who waited patiently.

"Freeze program."

Audra's image instantly froze, but remained visible. Gunnar waited for Fuji to say something, but clearly she was expecting him to begin first.

"I have a mission to command, Doctor? What do you want me to say?"

"Well, for starters, don't give me any of that command mission crap. Captain Abrams has already told me we won't be leaving this hangar bay for several hours. The mission is planned and executed. There is nothing to do here but wait for clearance to launch."

Gunnar sat down on the end of the bed, glancing over at the image of Audra.

"More to the point, what are you doing? This isn't Audra. It's a program. It's a replica, designed to help you find closure and move on."

"Yeah, well it's not working," Gunnar snapped, his anger ratcheting back up.

"Then I'll ask the question again. What are you doing? Rick and I created this program to help you get through your grief and the pain associated with it. It was never designed for you to fall in love with it."

"I keep hoping it'll help," Gunnar finally said, working to calm himself. He turned his gaze back to the image of Audra. "You and Rick did a magnificent job of recreating her."

"Apparently too good of a job," Fuji admitted. "Why didn't you tell me you were having this much difficulty?"

"I kept hoping it would get better, and when I'm with her, I feel a little better, but as soon as I leave, I'm right back where I was before, maybe a little worse each time."

"May I see your hands?" Fuji asked.

Gunnar slowly raised them up, still looking over at Audra's motionless image. The tops of his hands were unremarkable. Fuji grimaced a little when she examined his palms. The centers had deep dig marks burrowed into them. Clearly from clinching his fists too tight. She looked at the image of Audra.

"It's getting harder for you to maintain control, isn't it?"

"Yes," he admitted, shifting and burying his face in his hands.

"I didn't hear the reprimand Lieutenant Starman and Mr. Pippin received. Did the punishment fit the crime?"

"Yes, but I'm afraid I may have come across a little too strong. Starman was in tears when I dismissed them."

"Is that how you want your relationship with your crew to be?"

"No, of course not. But it's like I step out of my body and I'm watching me lose control and I do nothing to stop it. It's almost surreal. How do I fight something that's coming from inside me? What's happening to me, Doc?"

"I'm not sure, Colonel," Fuji replied. "But once this mission is complete, if we haven't figured out a way around this, you need to remove yourself from command until we can get a handle on it."

Gunnar looked up at Fuji, then over at Audra.

"So, what about her... the program?"

Fuji glanced over at the image of Audra, then looked back at Gunnar's expression.

"The fact that you're still calling it a program means you haven't completely lost your mind." Fuji smiled. "But only you can decide what to do. Allow me to remind you of something you already know so well. The longer you continue on your present course, the harder it will be for you to let go. You know better than anyone that Audra would not have wanted you to be caught in a never-ending cycle of virtual reality. This is a program and that's all it'll ever be." Fuji turned to leave, but Gunnar stopped her.

"Doctor, does CJ know about Audra?"

Fuji looked back at Gunnar.

"Only what you've told her," Fuji said continuing out.

Gunnar heard the outer door close, but remained unmoved, thinking for a long moment. He finally turned and looked up at Audra. He gazed at her longingly. The likeness was perfect in every detail. He reached up to touch her hand, but in freeze mode, his hand only passed right through hers. He finally dropped his hand back to the bed, looking at the wounds in his palms.

"Unfreeze program."

"Ok, so what was that all about? What did Doctor Yamoto have to say?"

Gunnar let out a sigh and stood up.

"Nothing but praise for you."

"Then what's wrong? You look as though you've lost your best friend."

"I have... I did... A long time ago."

"But I'm here now." Audra took his hand and squeezed it. "I'm here for you whenever you need me. Did the Doctor have any special instructions on how I can be of more help to you? Tell me what you want me to do."

Gunnar could only look at her with a lost expression.

*   *   *   *

Six hours of waiting took an eternity, but Lana finally turned to Captain Abrams.

"Signal from the *Realistic*, Sir. We are go for launch in ten minutes."

"Finally," Dakota grumbled, hitting a button on the command chair. "Colonel to the bridge. Lieutenant Starman, let's get this thing revved up. Engineering, we good?" He asked looking over at Tiana.

"As good as we could make it, Captain."

"Lieutenant Kramer, download our flightpath coordinates from the *Realistic's* Departure control just as soon as we leave the doors. This ought to be fun people. Last time we came through here, we were chasing our tails for Tintee in a bucket that could barely move."

"This ship has a lot more get up and go now, Sir," came a confident reply from Tiana.

"Thanks to you and Billy."

"We ready?" Gunnar asked, stepping hurriedly through the bridge door, tucking Audra's memory chip under his shirt.

"Our independent contractor here seems to think we're good to go," Dakota replied, getting out of the chair. Gunnar motioned the Captain back down.

"You got this one, Dak. Just remember, I wanna be bragging to Colonel Barker and the others about how we got in and out of there without a hitch." Gunnar looked up through the overheads and watched the enormous hangar doors scroll open, revealing a sea of stars surrounding a distant nebula.

"*Realistic* signals all clear, Sir," Lana announced.

Gunnar glanced down at Dakota and gave the Captain a thumbs up.

"Ok helm," Dakota said, taking command. "Let's go. Lieutenant Nevall, please have BachTL report to the bridge."

After touching several points on her displays, Lynette took hold of her controls and guided the ship up and out of the hangar deck into open space. Feeling like it was only a moment ago, she handled the Assault Corsair like the day they launched from the orbiting shipyards over Kalamar. As they powered away from the *Realistic*, BachTL entered the bridge.

"You all know the drill; we've gone over it enough," Dakota spoke up calmly as he came to his feet.

"It sounds like you guys already have a plan in mind for this mission," BachTL remarked, looking all around the bridge.

"Yes, there's a plan, and you're here to make sure that plan goes off the way it's supposed to."

"Can you let me in on your plan?"

"We approach from Reako's far side. Since the planet lays at an angle to Carolon, we'll skim along the underside of its asteroid ring toward Carolon to shield our approach. Then as we emerge, Lieutenant Starman will make this bird go as fast as she'll go straight at Carolon. Mr. Pippin will locate the largest concentration of Asium and we'll go in after it. Captain Logan Dalley will launch his Interceptor right before we reach the atmosphere to provide top cover. We'll select the easiest deposits we can find and send in a team. We then get back out the same way we came in, rendezvousing with the *Realistic* on the far side of Boris. Questions; concerns?"

"Unless you stay out in the open, you should be able to remain hidden from Albion detection until you reach Reako." BachTL stepped to one of the displays of the Nulark system. "There are probably detection buoys on the outer rim, just inside the Boris orbit, and several more in random spots between Tanis and Hinge. Because Nulark is so far out, there won't be any capital ships here."

"Aster command reported at least one destroyer and several corvettes."

"Yeah, smaller stuff. Certainly bigger than this ship, but definitely not capitols. There will be the possibility of fighter sweeps too, but they usually have the less experienced pilots out here on long boring duties like this, so you should be able to dodge them, jam their transmissions or do away with them completely. If you can make it to Reako undetected, they won't see you coming at Carolon until you come out from under its belt."

"We'll be sure to drive hard and fast," Dakota said.

"Have you made your extraction team assignments?" Gunnar asked.

"Yes, Sir. Mr. Pippin will lead a team of four. Himself, Lieutenant Kramer, MedTech Gantrie and our independent contractor, Tiana Mantose."

"Why not Doctor Yamoto?" Gunnar asked quietly as Dakota came back to the command chair.

"Regulations, Sir. Senior staff should remain onboard. Besides, Lieutenant Gantrie has heavy field medic experience and was part of Colonel Barker's personnel staff on Carolon. She'll be familiar with the base layout and its environment. I'm afraid Doctor Yamoto would be clueless."

"Not sure what I'm doing here," Gunnar remarked, keeping his voice low. He was impressed with the progress Dakota had made as an executive officer. His abilities to assume command of any special operations made him a great candidate to lead as the crew had full confidence in him; Gunnar being no exception.

"You're here to save my bacon should I screw up, Sir. Yellow alert," Dakota ordered looking at Lana.

"Good enough," Gunnar smirked. "How fast can we get this bird to go?" He asked turning to Tiana.

"All sub-light speeds available."

"Weapons?" Gunnar turned forward to Doran Cartwright.

"All ordnance weapons fully operational; light pulse at half capacity. Full complement of Pin missiles and Mark V torpedoes."

"Just need some Asium and we'll have light speed," Gunnar said.

"Not quite, Colonel," Tiana said without turning. "Light speed engines aren't quite functional yet. Billy still has some bugs to work out."

"I'm assuming it's technical."

"Would you like me to spell it out for you?"

"No need," Gunnar replied. "I trust you." Gunnar took note that in the entire exchange, Tiana never once turned to face him, but kept her back to him. Thinking on it, her voice sounded short, almost curt. Lynette Starman gave the ship throttle and turned toward the coordinates the navigator had provided her.

"Colonel Conrad, this is sick bay."

Gunnar rolled his eyes and looked down at the com panel. *How is it, Fuji always seems to pop up at the worse possible moments? She must have a gift or something.*

"Yes Doctor, what is it?"

"Lieutenant Gantrie, Sir."

"You're Doctor Yamoto's nurse," Gunnar confirmed.

"MedTech, Sir."

"MedTech," Gunnar repeated looking at Dakota. "I stand corrected. How can I help you?"

"Doctor Yamoto and I were just running the confirmation scans of all personnel onboard and the numbers aren't matching up."

"How so?"

"We've got fourteen registered personnel onboard and two non-registered; Tiana Mantose and BachTL. We're tracking all fourteen transponders and the two unregistered life signatures, but we're picking up a seventeenth signature."

"You mean transponder. Whose is it?"

"No, Sir. No transponder, just an extra life signature."

"Can you locate it?'

"Not with our equipment down here. We were wondering if you could have Mr. Pippin track the location?"

Gunnar made a quick glance at the science officer who was already on the job.

"Confirmed," Pip said, focused on his instruments. "I'm picking up fourteen transponders, two unregistered and an extra life signature in the aft section of the ship. Individual is stationary; located in Interceptor one."

"Someone stowed away in my bird," Dakota said flatly. "I'll go back and have a look."

"You're in command of this mission." Gunnar stopped him. "I'll do it. BachTL, you stay here."

"There's a pistol in the holster pocket on the back side of the seat," Dakota said. "Hopefully it's still there."

"Lieutenant Gantrie, have Doctor Yamoto meet me in engineering at Interceptor one's entry hatch."

"Yes, Sir."

"Whatever happens back there, Captain, complete the mission. I'll be back to watch and give you a grade directly afterwards."

"Thanks. Just what I need. Criticism from a perfectionist."

"It's how we learn."

"Permission to accompany the Colonel?" Tiana bolted from her chair as Gunnar headed for the door.

"Denied," Gunnar snapped. He was in no mood to be lectured by Miss Mantose. He knew full well she was looking for a reason to chew his ear off about whatever was bothering her. She should have just come out and said something earlier. "There's only so much room in a cradle tube and Captain Abrams needs you right where you are."

Bristling, Tiana melted back in her seat and turned to her consoles, but all she could see was red.

*   *   *   *

Entering engineering, Gunnar found Fuji and Billy waiting for him in front of Interceptor one's access tube.

"Whoever's up there, isn't coming out," Fuji announced trying to get a reading from her small medical scanner.

"I can vacate the atmosphere in the cockpit and the cradle tube," Billy suggested half serious.

"Not very funny, Mister Moon," Fuji responded still looking at her scanner. Gunnar hid a snicker with a hand over his mouth.

"They'll come out about the time their eyes start to bug out."

"Mr. Moon!" Fuji looked up from her equipment.

"Has anyone seen Alex?" Gunnar asked, turning away to keep from showing his amusement.

"Just making suggestions, Doctor."

"You're doing nothing to improve my sense of humor."

Gunnar made a quick scan of the engine room, straightening his expression and stepping to the cradle.

"Well, I guess someone better go up and have a look see at who it is."

"Be careful, Colonel," Fuji cautioned.

"You know me. I'm always thinking ahead." Before Fuji could get another word out, Gunnar activated the cradle mechanism and was whisked out through the main wing and into the seat of the Interceptor. From this vantage point, he could just make out the dark sphere of Reako looming ahead of the *Constellation*; it's asteroid ring clearly visible.

"We're making pretty good time," Gunnar said aloud. "We're just getting ready to pass under Reako's outer rings. We'll be out the other side in about ten minutes." He listened closely for movement, but heard only a gentle whisper. More of a feeling of movement than something audible. He waited for a response, feeling a presence next to his shoulder. He carefully reached back behind the seat, feeling for Dakota's gun in its holster. It was empty. He slowly turned his head to one side, catching sight of the muzzle of said pistol pointed at his temple.

"You good teacher. Know how to use this."

"You really going to shoot me?"

"No want shoot friends, but Janox must go home."

"Janox, I thought you and I had already discussed this? Reako is not a home. You and Tonnie were marooned there by the Duchess

91

Benetar. You are the only living heir to the throne of Colonia. Hadrian needs you and it's up to CJ and me to see that you take your rightful place on the throne." Gunnar could already feel himself starting to rev up and did everything he could to maintain control.

"No believe I royalty. Tonnie is only mother I know. Reako is only home I know. You take me home and I prove to you. You and Alex heal Tonnie and she tell you."

"I can't heal Tonnie and I have no idea where Alex is right now."

"He right here behind you."

Gunnar twisted around to see the form of the small droid sitting deactivated on the back floor of the Interceptor.

"Well, that would explain why I didn't see him in engineering. What did you do to him?" Gunnar spread his fingers out to keep from crushing something important on the instrument panel.

"He sleeps." Janox pointed at the charging arm attached to a power socket on one of the back walls.

"I need him down in engineering!"

"He fine," Janox reassured Gunnar. "You must be calm or I shoot."

"Where will that get you?" Gunnar snipped, gritting his teeth. "You can't fly this thing."

"No, but you can."

"Not if I'm dead!"

"Janox no kill one best friend. Stun maybe, but never kill."

"You wouldn't dare," Gunnar said glaring at the setting on the pistol. Before he could react, there came a blinding light and a horrible jolt accompanied by what amounted to a board being broken over his head. A myriad of sparks sprayed through his vision and his brain felt like it was vibrating at a frequency impossible for the human body to handle in a conscious state. He tried looking around at the interior of the fighter but saw only a sea of sparkling dots of light. He wasn't even sure he was moving his head. For a moment, he felt sick. Blinking brought some relief as his vision started to clear. Something still wasn't right. His vision was partially blocked by something and as he was finally able to focus, he found his shaded glasses were sitting askew of where they ought to be.

"Holy…! What the heck?" he groaned, finally able to sit up and straighten his glasses. "Did you just stun me?"

"Work better than thought, now we go or stun again."

"Stunning me isn't going to get you to Reako!"

"It will if I stun a couple times."

"Look," Gunnar growled, rubbing his aching shoulder. Every joint in his body ached now, but the blast point where she had stunned him hurt the worst. "Tonnie is dead. She died a long time ago. You said so yourself; she fell. Not even Dr. Yamoto can heal Tonnie. We're on a mission to Carolon, to get some crystals that will make this ship fly faster and be even more powerful than any ship in Hadrian. Once we have that, we can come back to Reako and bring Tonnie home so you can bury her properly."

"No wait, go now or stun again. This ship fast. Much better than CJ's ship. Not all broken. This is good ship. Make trip quick."

"Janox, be reasonable. I promise, if we don't have any trouble with the Albions, I'll take you back down to Reako and we'll find Tonnie and you'll see."

Gunnar noticed her finger twitch and the generators on the blaster started to whine up again. Not wanting to experience the stun again, he finally reached for the headset and hit the master switches on the control console in front of him.

"Ok, but I'm not launching until you put that thing away." He meticulously worked the instruments in the cockpit as he brought the fighter to life and prepared to depart. Touching a control on the yoke, he adjusted his mic pickup.

"Lieutenant Nevall, put me through to Captain Abrams please." He waited a moment as the engines started to turn up. "Dak, it looks like I need to make an unscheduled stop down to Reako. Complete the mission and pick me up on your way back to the *Realistic*. Please inform Billy and Doctor Yamoto I have Janox and Alex 7001 with me."

"I think I know better than to ask why. Just don't get lost like you did the last time."

"I promise I'll find a whole new way to get lost." Gunnar glanced back at Janox who had holstered the pistol and was gripping the back of the pilot's seat.

"Why like to fly this ship, better I think, than CJ ship?"

"Yes," Gunnar said, looking back at a still motionless Alex as he finished his preparations for launch. "It's got a little more get up and go. If you wouldn't mind too much, could you please reactivate Alex? And be ready for one pissed off droid. He hates being shut off."

"You feel ok? Much anger inside you I know."

"Ya think? How would you feel if you just got stunned?"

"Don't know. Not been stunned before."

"Here, I'll give you your first lesson."

"Yes, you very angry, but not with me. See, feel and hear anger in you. You need sunggo."

"I'm not even going to ask what that is."

"For you, very difficult to find. CJ have some, but not enough for you. I feel it here in ship. You love to fly ship I think."

"I love to fly anything, especially fighters like this or CJ's." Gunnar fell silent, listening to the soft hum of the Interceptor's engines. Lieutenant Nevall's voice over his headset brought his attention back to his controls.

"Mission guidance parameters have been downloaded into your Navi-computer, Colonel. Transferring all launch controls to Interceptor one. Good luck; launch when ready."

Gunnar touched several controls on the panel next to him and pushed the thruster button on the control yoke. As the Interceptor jumped from the wing tip of the Assault Corsair, the star field rolled until the *Constellation* spun into view. Guiding the big fighter around the Starbird several times, he throttled away toward Reako's dark form.

Prison

As Dãsha and Rick entered the bridge, he slowed, noticing something a little odd about many of the dead consoles in the vast cathedraled control room. Some had a light coat of dust on them, others were taken apart and set neatly around their supporting structures, but most were only opened. There was no sign of damage or missing parts.

Must have been internal, down to the component level?

"Thank goodness you're all right," Caidin said, relieved to see Rick come up behind Dãsha. "I am so sorry about your ship. The Drake ships raked the entire side of the coning tower this time. Usually they aim for harder targets. My only thought is they saw your ship docked to the side and zeroed in on it. I wish we would have had more of a warning."

"I thought this thing could see anything coming from outside the Ocean boundaries?" Rick asked, finding more to remain angry about.

"*Calypso's* sensors are quite directional. I don't know if you noticed when you approached earlier, but she rotates angularly."

"I did notice it's rotation. You're saying you have her programed to rotate along all axes?"

"We're constantly scanning Acuity," Dãsha cut in. "When we find something, we're able to use our retro thrusters to alter the ship's rotation to track it. But if we move too quickly, or in an abnormal fashion, the Drake are quick to remind us of our place."

"I had *Calypso's* antennas pointed at the ice when the Drake came." Caidin stood up and moved to another console. "We were trying to get a better fix on your ship. Trouble is, there's more than just your ship stuck in the ice."

"Yeah, you said earlier there were other ship's marooned in there," Rick agreed, starting to relax a little.

"What we're saying is," Dãsha said stepping over to a display and pointing at several images. "Aside from the normal wrecks that have drifted into the ice and become caught and crushed, there is a cluster of four other ships that became entombed in the ice quite some time ago. It appeared to me at the time, they were trying to evade the Drake. Considering their size, we believe they are freighters or something similar. Your ship appears to be moving in their direction."

Rick stared at the images. They were distant, greyish, and fuzzy, but their shape seemed familiar to him. He looked closer. Dãsha pointed to a couple of other images on the other side of the display.

"Infrared scans show a heat signature at the aft section and a smaller one at the bow. Here is the tracking information on her movements."

Rick studied the information for a moment, then realized what it all meant.

"She's definitely cutting through the ice, but why?" Rick puzzled for a moment, looking back at the images. "CORA will follow her orders unless she is somehow incapacitated. She was ordered to find the turret. She wouldn't go into the ice unless she reasoned it necessary to fulfill her orders." Rick came to his feet and turned to Dãsha, realizing there could be only one answer. *CORA has found the escape pod!* A surge of hope filled him and momentarily losing himself, he threw his arms around the tall brunet. Grinning from ear to ear, he grabbed Dãsha's face and planted a big kiss squarely on her lips. When he pulled back again, he looked into her black eyes and realized how foolish he was acting. Dãsha smiled, her cheeks flushing a subtle color. Rick released her and composed himself. He had never kissed anyone else since he had married Jayda and now he felt quite awkward.

"Sorry," Rick said, stepping back and turning to Caidin who was smiling.

"You have this CORA onboard your ship with orders to find your escape pod?"

"Yes," Rick was still smiling. "Well, not exactly. I have injured crew onboard in critical stasis. My onboard AI, CORA 500 is running the ship."

"Well, she must be close to her objective."

"That's my hope," Rick said.

"Caidin," Dãsha said motioning to the sensor images. Both Caidin and Rick examined what she was pointing at. "These are the Drake craft that just attacked us. It would appear they have detected movement in the ice. No doubt they have figured out there is value here."

"What are they doing?" Rick asked, trying to understand what the images were showing.

"Difficult to know for sure," Caidin said slowly, assessing what was happening. "But I'd say trying to blast through the ice to get to your ship."

"Try all they want," Rick said defiantly. "Even if they reach her, there's no way they could get past her shields."

"They don't have to," Caidin responded. "They only have to reach it. They'll call in some heavy-duty equipment to pull it out of there if they decide it's worth the time and the risk."

"Is there any way to calculate how long it would take them to reach the *Athena*?"

"The Drake Escey assault craft is a tough ship, but it is built for combat," Dãsha informed them. "It was not designed for deep space travel or utility work. It has no cutting lasers or concussion charges for ice breaking. They will have to call in a bludgeon vessel or specially outfitted tugs with cutting lasers. It will take them a considerable amount of time to figure out how to get to it and then get the right equipment here."

"Hours? Days? What?"

"At least a day."

Frustrated, Rick went from elation to worried and took in a deep breath as he paced around the bridge, looking at everything. Dãsha and Caidin watched him as he stopped in front of the large bay windows and looked out into the dark water surrounding them. He threw his arms behind him and grabbed a forearm. His wrists still hurt from Dãsha's vise grip on him. He paced a moment, then abruptly turned.

"You don't have any other craft onboard? No small tugs, shuttle craft or haulers?"

"No," Caidin said. "They were all removed long ago when she was sent to the scrap yard. I'm sorry, but your fighter was the only means of getting off *Calypso*."

Rick continued his slow march around the bridge, looking at everything. At several areas, he stopped and examined a console and the insides of opened gear.

"Would you mind showing me your power induction coils?"

"Why?" Dãsha asked folding her arms.

"I think I may be able to do something with them."

"We have tried to make repairs and leave Acuity many times but have been unsuccessful. There is little point to trying where we have failed." Dãsha sounded indignant, but Caidin held a hand up to quiet her.

"My dear, just because we have failed, doesn't mean someone with a different perspective and skill set can't succeed. Our knowledge of the inner workings of a ship's systems are admittingly limited. I suspect the General might have a better ability to understand such things. What else do you require?"

"I recall your cargo and landing bays are full of water. Can you provide me with a structural synopsis of the extent of the flooding and hull integrity in those areas? Also, do you have any weaponry onboard?"

"Nothing, not even cutting lasers," Dãsha answered.

"You said this ship was built for exploration as well as war. Can you provide me with structural specifications of the bow's hull?"

"Yes, but what good will that do you?" Dãsha was scrambling to figure out what Rick was thinking.

"Caidin, with yours and Dãsha's permission, I would like to use *Calypso* to reach the *Athena* before these Drake guys do."

"Completely out of the question," Dãsha replied sternly.

"*Calypso* is of no use," Caidin pointed out. "She has no weapons, she can barely move, and when she does, the Drake see that we are reminded of our status here."

"All things I'm fully aware of and that's why *Calypso* is perfect for what I have in mind." Rick continued to examine the consoles around him. "I want to use her to break through the ice to the *Athena* before the Drake have a chance to get to her. Once free, *Calypso* will have the engine power to take you to wherever you want to go, away from the Drake."

Dãsha didn't move, but the concerned expression etched across her face spoke volumes. Caidin ran his fingers through his beard, looking at the display.

"I suppose it's possible the concussions on the ice pack would carry to the Drake position and hinder their ability to blast through the ice or try to come back to our position."

"If we could get the sub-light engines up," Dãsha offered, "it would be possible to outrun most of the Drake craft."

"That's if they even notice you leaving," Rick pointed out.

Caidin looked at Dãsha, who remained motionless.

"Well, my dear? What do you think?"

"Here, we only exist. Perhaps it is again worth the effort and risk trying to leave."

"We would both be glad to help if you think we can." Caidin smiled and shuffled next to Rick. "Dãsha, please provide the General... I mean, Rick with the requested information." The tall woman turned without objection and exited the bridge to carry out the request.

Rick grinned broadly and turned back to the dusty old consoles.

"Can you give me a hand with these?" Rick asked, gesturing to the dark navigation consoles. "I'm assuming you just have power turned off to most of this stuff," Rick stated.

"There seemed little point to having any of these systems up if what they controlled didn't work. Besides, we felt that saving the power was most important."

"Do you remember how it all goes back together?"

"Yes, I think I can manage."

"I'll start over here and you start over there. We'll meet in the middle." Rick turned and went to work. While the technology was old and foreign to him, it all still made sense. Where it didn't, he used his Thane powers to focus in at a closer level to see better detail and gain greater understanding. Hours rolled by as they worked, gradually bringing the bridge back to life. Coming closer to where Caidin was working on the navigation station, Rick passed a glance at the displays coming online. There was little if any information being displayed, only empty suffix fields.

"I'm assuming you have some type of central processing room driving all this gear?" Rick asked, standing back and taking in the entire view of the vast bridge.

"Yes," Caidin puffed, finishing what he was doing. "It's many decks below us, beyond one of the main landing bays. Are you ok? What happened to your wrists?"

"Dãsha pulled me back at the airlock during the attack. She has quite the grip." Rick rubbed his aching wrists gently.

Caidin noticed the bruising around Rick's wrists and chuckled softly.

"Yes, Dãsha forgets her own strength sometimes."

"Forgets?" Rick repeated, letting Caidin look at the bruising. "I'd hate to be around when she remembers."

"If you'll allow me, I think I can correct this."

"What do you have in mind?" Rick asked a little hesitant.

"I've learned a thing or two about healing the organic. It won't hurt. It'll just take a minute."

Rick had thought about trying to repair the damage to his wrists himself. There had been several times he had attempted injury repair, but he knew next to nothing about how the body worked. Ona had warned him about going into places he knew nothing about and causing unintended consequences. Best to have someone who knew what they were doing look at it.

"So, what did you do before you came here?" Rick asked as Caidin gently examined his wrists.

"I was a physician."

Ok, now Rick felt a little stupid for being skeptical of Caidin's abilities. He watched the doctor turn his wrist this way and that, being careful not to extend beyond what his damaged tissues would allow. Caidin then closed his eyes and using a series of gentle touching motions with his fingertips, lightly caressing the skin all around the damaged portions of the wrist. He repeated the process with the other one. When he had finished, Rick twisted them in every direction. There was no pain and he had full range of motion.

"Impressive technique," Rick said smiling. "I won't ask where you learned to do that. I've known similar doctors where I'm from that can do that, but they are few and far between. Most of them are generally shunned by the majority of medical people."

"They'd like to think medicine is best handled by computers and droids these days?"

"Exactly," Rick agreed still twisting his wrists as Dãsha approached. *Is it possible this guy is a Thane?*

"I have retrieved all the data you have asked for and have uploaded them to our sensor station," Dãsha reported stopping in front of them. She looked at Rick's wrist motions with a cocked head, as if trying to figure out what he was doing. "Caidin has repaired the damage to your wrists. I knew he could do it. He is quite skilled with all things medical as they pertain to the organic."

Rick looked at Dãsha, looking at him. Her black eyes were emotionless and seemed to be trying to look through him. There was still something not quite right about her; *synthetic* was all that came to mind. Rick turned to the sensor station and looked at the information.

"What's your hope?" Caidin inquired, looking at the information in front of them.

"Well, thankfully your alphabet is the same as mine. Hadrian's isn't anything like mine and so written communication is a little difficult."

"I think you'll find our language fairly common and other languages the exception," Caidin said. "A Millennia ago, there was a great purge of those who were deemed to have spoken the lower form of languages. Anything that didn't conform to the language you and I are using right now. If you couldn't speak it, you were either banished and taught it or you were eliminated. Of course, people aren't nearly as civilized about making such differentiations now. They just blast you if they don't like the way you look or talk."

"Life goes on as it always has," Rick agreed, still focused on what was in front of him. "So, we need to have a good look at those power induction coils, and," Rick said turning to Dãsha, "we need to get to *Calypso's* central processing control room."

"If you'll follow me," Dãsha said turning to escort them out of the bridge. "The ignition coils will be simple; the processing room will be more difficult."

"Dãsha, my dear," Caidin called after her as he shuffled to keep up. "What's wrong with the processing room?"

"There is nothing wrong with the processing room. I have rerouted power to it and it's ready to bring back online."

"Ok, so why the gloom and doom?" Rick asked.

"The access hallways have all flooded. I have tried to figure out a way to circumvent the access, but there is no way to gain access except through the halls."

"What about the ventilation infrastructure or the ship's internal super structure?" Rick asked.

"No," Caidin said looking at the back of Dãsha's head as they followed her into an elevator and started down into the bowls of the ship. "When she says, you can't get through, even by unconventional means, she means it. There really is no way to do so."

"Well, perhaps a solution will present itself," Rick said refusing to give up. For some time the elevator remained in motion, but finally came to a halt and opened up. They walked down several halls and came to an open lift platform. After it had dropped for some length, it stopped on a brightly lit deck with a labyrinth of piping and machinery. There was plenty of room to walk as the space was a cavernous echo chamber of smooth floors and vaulted ceilings that disappeared behind bright punch hole lighting.

"Whoa," Rick gasped, taken aback by the sheer size of the mid-section engine compartment. He had seen capitol ship engine rooms before, but not with nearly as much supporting machinery within its confines. He had to keep telling himself this was old technology.

"Power couplings are over here," Dãsha directed as they continued through the maze of machinery. Presently, they came to a halt in front of a relatively small mound of pipes, conduits and mechanized bulk.

"Is the power up in here?" Rick asked, examining the inducer.

"Yes, you should be able to navigate through all its menus," Dãsha said. Punching in several commands into a built-in keyboard terminal, she studied the information on the overhead monitor. "I can bring up the schematics on the coupling subassembly and pinpoint exactly where the malfunction has occurred."

"Do you remember what was happening when the unit malfunctioned?" Rick was already focused on understanding the theory of operation behind this old equipment. While it was alien in nature and archaic in terms of his own tech, there was a familiar basicness to everything.

"It was the last time we tried to restart these engines," Dãsha said in a hypnotic fashion. "We were trying to drive her out of Acuity."

"Never forget that day," Caidin said looking over at Dãsha. "We had just gotten hammered by the Drake for moving too fast, about four times that day."

Rick looked up at Caidin.

"I can't really understand why they even bother."

"They just want to make sure we stay right where we are. So they can keep an eye on us."

"After all this time, you'd think they'd quit messing with you."

"What is your assessment, Richard?" Dãsha inquired, watching him go back to studying the induction power coupling. Rick meticulously looked at everything, then examined the schematics Dãsha had pulled up on the display.

"Yes," Rick whispered with his eyes starting to brighten. "Yes, I can see this. This makes all the sense in the world. Normally you'd have to replace this. They weren't made to be repaired, but I think I can do something with it. We're going to need the central processing engines up and running first."

"Well, there is no point in going any further then," Dãsha said coldly. "There is no way to get through the flooded halls and compartments to access that room."

"Let's go have a look," Rick said, remaining upbeat and focused. Dãsha shook her head and started off with Rick right with her and Caidin struggling to keep up. After some foot travel, an elevator and a set of stairs, Rick sensed a sharp rise in the humidity and the smell of stale saltwater filling the corridor. Rounding a corner, they stopped at the edge of the water filled hallway.

"There are stairs at the end of the hall," Dãsha said folding her arms, "and a paravator that moves across the upper decks of the hangar bay and then down again to another corridor before the water levels drop enough to get through to the processing decks."

"And *Calypso* doesn't have another route to get there?" Rick asked, wondering why it was so complicated to get to a main operations room.

"There are three other access ways. One is from an elevator that services the main hangar bay. Two more from the other side are completely under water with damaged or inoperative doors."

"Just seems like the designers would have put the brains of this place a little closer to the control center," Rick complained. "You said there was another one?"

"Yes," Dãsha said accessing a map from a wall display. "From beneath. There is a maintenance corridor leading straight from the central processing room to an exterior loading door at the rear of the ship, beneath the main thruster ports."

Rick frowned. He was certain he could get the old-style power couplings up and if the engines were in even partial running condition, he was sure he could get this hulk moving fast enough to accomplish what he had in mind. But without control, they would just sit with idling engines. Rick knelt next to the water and dipped his fingers into it. It was cold and slimy; probably due to how long it had been standing.

"No bilge pumps I'm guessing," Rick said putting his fingers to his nose.

"Normally if a ship took on water, you'd just vent it to the outside and let the ship's pressure blow it out," Dãsha said.

"Good for you," Rick complimented her, standing back up. "You didn't say sucked out. No G-suits, I'm sure."

Caidin slowly shook his head.

"Didn't you say your tug broke up? How did you get onboard?"

"We were docked and off-loading our gear when the tug broke up on seal," Caidin said looking over at Dãsha. "Dãsha pulled me from the wreckage and into the ship."

"You were in the tug when you lost seal? Didn't that flood the tug?"

"Not only did it flood, but it broke up and pinned me inside one of the pieces as it floated away from the hatch."

Rick looked Dãsha over trying to picture the events. Her strength would explain how she could save the older gentleman. What didn't make sense was, Dãsha was tall, slender, and shapely; her bone and muscle structure didn't lend itself to her exhibited strength. Unless she wasn't human. His onboard computer had indicated there was a *hybrid* onboard. He took in a deep breath and held it, thinking.

"Are there any doors or hatches a person would have to go through to get to the other side?" Rick asked.

"Several," Dãsha replied. "And they've been under water for a considerable amount of time, which means..."

"Even if there is power to them, they aren't likely to want to open too easily."

"And even less likely if the manual releases have to be used."

"Ok," Caidin said. "How do we get this done?"

"With your permission," Rick said looking back at the water. "Dãsha and I will make our way to the central processing room while you get the power transducers opened up so I can repair them when we get back."

Dãsha looked at Rick, an expression of disbelief piercing from widening eyes. Caidin gave Dãsha a quick double take and turned to Rick.

"There is no hope of success here," Dãsha blurted, irritated. "This mission will fail,"

"Relax my dear," Caidin said trying to calm Dãsha's fears. "I suspect that not only can the General explain it to us, but he has an uncommon ability to make it happen."

"Yes," Rick said with a smile. He turned to the display on the wall and studied it for a moment longer. "We're going to move the water that's in the flooded hangar bay here, to the other landing bay, here."

"What?" Dãsha cried. The color drained from Caidin's face.

Rick chuckled, as it seemed quite elementary to him.

"We close these hatches, here, here and here," Rick said pointing to sections of the display. "Open these over here and make sure everything is watertight in this area. We'll then use your retro thrusters, we call them maneuvering thrusters, to turn the ship along its axis to this point, then tilt the bow up and lean her over on her side. We'll have to leave your anti-grav in its current configuration in order to keep the water from going places it's not supposed to."

Caidin took in a deep breath, shaking his head slightly.

"That's too much movement. The Drake will pick up on it and be all over us."

"We'll have to work quickly then," Rick said.

Dãsha studied the display, following the Kalamarion General's logic.

"You're talking about maneuvering a lot of water through this ship by tilting and twisting it," Dãsha said. "Tilt too far too fast and you could over run the water's path and flood the wrong compartments, mainly the engine room."

"Part of the water's main pathway will put it against the far walls of the engine room," Rick said. "There is nothing there the water will bother, but if the maneuvers aren't just right, it could turn it into the main engine compartment and flood the whole thing."

"Won't the water want to wash back?" Caidin asked. "Anyone still in those passages could get halfway to the processing room and get blind-sided with a wall of water?"

"I admit the possibility exists, but if we leave *Calypso* in the final maneuver position until the processing room is accessed, we should be fine." Rick glanced over at Dãsha who abruptly turned.

"The General's logic is sound, but without processing systems running, the maneuver will all have to be done manually. Too much for one person to handle *Calypso's* controls alone."

"Ok, so new plan," Rick said, "Caidin, you and I will handle *Calypso's* controls manually and Dãsha, you go bring the central processing room online."

"I'm not so sure either one of us is qualified to be performing such a maneuver," Caidin said letting out a chuckle and shaking his head. "Dãsha is far better able to handle this type of maneuver."

"Do you have the strength and agility it will take to get to the processing room if something out of the ordinary should happen?" Rick asked. "Do you know how to bring all the central processing engines back online? While I could figure it out," Rick continued, "I don't know how to drive your ship, but it looks like *Calypso* was intended to have two pilots anyway. You and I are the best candidates for performing the maneuver. Dãsha knows how to get through and turn on the processors."

"Richard is correct." Dãsha turned to Caidin, reading the worry sliding across his face. "I trust you both completely. Don't worry about me, I can take care of myself. I will change into something better suited for this type of operation," she said, turning and making her way back up the corridor. Rick helped steady Caidin as they turned to follow the tall dark haired woman. The floor was a bit slick and Caidin struggled a little to keep his footing. Grateful for the help, Caidin held onto Rick as they worked their way back toward the engine room.

"She's an amazing woman," Rick commented as they walked together.

"Yes," Caidin puffed as they walked a bit further in silence. "Please ask your question, Richard. I sense you have many."

"Yes, there are several," Rick said looking at their darkened surroundings as they approached an elevator. "What in the world is Dãsha doing with you? You have to be at least twice her age."

"A little more than twice," Caidin smiled, stepping inside behind Rick. "She has made life here in isolation bearable."

"I have no doubt," Rick replied as the elevator began to move. "I think just about any man could live like this with a woman like her on his arm. But, what's she doing with you?"

"You don't think a man such as me, could have a woman such as her?" Caidin's inflection was one of amusement. "I rescued her from execution at the hands of the Drake on Himtar."

"Sounds like an adventure."

"Long story short, I was provisioning my tug for the salvage of this ship when I got caught up in the middle of a medical squabble. Dãsha was being sold as a test subject for medical purposes I won't bore you with. She asked for my help and we made a break for it. Now I ask you, wouldn't you have done the same thing?"

"Possibly," Rick answered. "But for entirely different reasons."

"Your benevolence is above reproach. We were pursued by a Drake security force into Acuity's ocean. We were able to evade them once inside these waters, but not without incurring damage. We were just able to reach *Calypso* and dock before the tug finally gave up the ghost. The rest you already know."

Rick gave Caidin a long look, studying the years streaked through his gray beard.

"You love her," he stated flatly as they stepped from the elevator.

"She's my wife."

Operation Carolon

Captain Abrams tapped his fingers on the armrest of the command chair. He was a little disturbed by Colonel Conrad's sudden exit from the ship. A better explanation would have gone a long way at alleviating his concerns, both for the mission and the Colonel's eventual retrieval from whatever wild adventure he was sure to get mixed up with. The last time they were separated, it felt like an eternity getting everyone back together and not without peril and loss of life. Still, this was an excellent opportunity for him to show he could get the job done. Perhaps, if he did well, he would have a command of his own.

"Mr. Pippin, make sure you track Interceptor one at all times. I want to make sure we don't leave the Colonel hanging out here in the middle of Nowhere-Ville while we're hiking around on Carolon."

"Keeping him on scope three, Sir," Pip said, motioning toward one of the overhead displays.

"Any sign of that Albion destroyer that's supposed to be puttsing around Reako?"

"Nothing so far."

Dakota turned back to BachTL, but found him leaning over Tiana's shoulder, looking at readouts and asking questions.

"BachTL," Dakota spoke up. "Where's your destroyer?"

BachTL looked forward and stepped up next to Dakota.

"What do you mean where is it? How am I supposed to know?"

"Not seeing anything on the short-range scans. Mr. Pippin, anything on the long-range scans?"

"Seeing several returns around Carolon and something just outside scanner range on the outer rim of the Nulark, but nothing here around Reako."

"I'm a little nervous here," Dakota admitted, folding his arms. He looked up at the asteroid belt just above them, then over at Reako as they passed by. Shrouded in heavy dark clouds, constant lightning flashes lit up its dark atmosphere.

"Can't say as I blame you," BachTL agreed, looking back at Mr. Pippin's scanning displays. "Always nice to know where all your game pieces are."

"Lieutenant Starman, hold her here at the edge of the ring until we find our missing destroyer. Mr. Pippin, do you still have the Colonel?"

"Just lost him, Sir. You duck down under those clouds and nothing gets through."

Dakota turned to BachTL.

"Any way an Albion destroyer can get down under that soup?"

"I wouldn't think so," BachTL answered, thinking. "Fleet operations expressly forbids such maneuvers. Besides, most fleet commanders are afraid to bring a capitol, large or small, down into any atmosphere without some kind of automation assistance, either ground based or tug assisted."

Dakota looked out at the underside of the ring again, considering.

"Lieutenant Starman, let's go for a little joy ride, shall we? Steer us back to about halfway the width of Reako's ring and do a couple of orbits; stay under the ring. Mr. Pippin, look that planet over with a fine-toothed comb." Dakota returned to the command chair and sat down with BachTL standing next to him, looking at the scanning displays.

"Picking up some low powered marker buoys," Pip said. "Not sure what they're doing here. They're Colonian, not Albion though. May have just been left over from Carolon Command."

An eternity elapsed as everyone waited for several orbits to be completed and Lynette brought the Starbird to a halt at the edge of Reako's asteroid ring.

"Three orbits completed, Sir." Lynette turned around and faced Captain Abrams. "Holding position on the underside edge of the ring, facing Carolon."

Dakota and BachTL turned to Pip.

"There's nothing here, Sir," the science officer finally said. "Just the Corvettes over Carolon."

"Maybe those primary targets outside the system are the destroyers?" BachTL offered. "Could be something out there that has drawn their attention."

"Ok," Dakota finally said. "Let's get this done. Lieutenant Starman, let's make a break for it. As soon as we make the atmosphere, the away team needs to report to the teleporter."

Lynette Starman spun back around to her controls and executed her assigned maneuvers as everyone else seemed to tense up a little, focusing on their jobs. The defined ring of asteroids around Reako disappeared behind them as the Starbird bolted away toward Carolon. Still a little nervous, Dakota came back out of his seat and gave the scanning displays a quick glance, then stepped forward next to helm control.

The Starbird controls were immense and complex. While there were analog controls used to steer the ship, it could be controlled synthetically using just your fingers on the glassy touch surface. Dakota much preferred something a little simpler, like the controls in a Tempest or even a Viper. Able to find his way around the instruments of the *Constellation*, he much preferred the simplicity of the T6. Even the Interceptor was less complex than the Starbird, and it was about the largest fighter class ship he had ever flown. Still, it was a hand full at times.

Watching Lynette work her instruments and controls, he was impressed with the Starbird pilot. The situational awareness required was almost superhuman. Still, she seemed quite at ease, surrounded by her consoles and controls.

"ETA to Carolon, Lieutenant?" Dakota asked, folding his arms, and looking out ahead of them as an orange brown orb grew in size.

"We should be able to cruise into orbit in about ten minutes, Sir," Lynette answered glancing at a readout to her right. "Things sure go a lot faster when everything is working like it's supposed to."

"Yes, they do," Dakota agreed, turning to the rest of the bridge personnel. "Here's how this is going to go down. We'll do two cross pattern orbits of the poles. This will give Mr. Pippin time to find the best Asium deposits. It will also draw off those Corvettes. Doing a cross pole orbit will confuse them even further as I'm sure they're not use to such maneuvers. Any concerns should be brought up right now, otherwise, good luck people." Dakota turned back to the command chair and sat down.

"You're right about a cross pole orbit," BachTL said leaning a little closer. "I doubt any Albion commander would know what to do if they weren't over the equator."

For several stretching minutes, the bridge remained quiet as the orange brown orb of Carolon loomed larger.

"Two corvettes have seen us," Mr. Pippin announced.

"Make 'em chase you, helm," Dakota responded.

Lynette Starman steered the *Constellation* toward the upper pole of Carolon, keeping an eye on her short-range scanners.

"When they finally get it figured out, they'll call the ships on the other side of the planet to intercept," BachTL said.

"I'm counting on it," Dakota replied, his voice steely.

As Lynette steered the ship down the back side of Carolon, she observed something else appear in several locations on her displays, but before she could announce her concerns, Mr. Pippin spoke up.

"Found your destroyers, Sir. They're just coming out from under Reako's asteroid rings." Dakota came to his feet, studying the displays in front of Pip.

"Three of them," he rasped. He looked back at BachTL who stood wide eyed.

"They must have been hiding in Reako's atmosphere," he gulped.

"Getting Asium returns," Pip said touching several points on his glass. "Two more corvettes and a squadron of fighters moving to intercept us from the back side of Carolon. There are four other corvettes in orbit, but they don't seem to be changing course."

"Red alert," Dakota ordered. "How long will it take those destroyers to reach us?"

"They're not very fast," BachTL assured him. "Maybe fifteen minutes."

"Confirmed," Pip agreed. "They'll reach Carolon orbit in fifteen minutes, forty seconds."

"That's not going to give us enough time if we wait for two pole revolutions." Dakota looked out the front windows. Lynette was holding her course as ordered, just starting past the equator on back side of Carolon. "Have you got enough Asium returns to pinpoint a suitable pickup location?"

"I have two, Sir," Pip answered. "Not sure you're going to like either one of them." Pip pointed to one spot on his displays.

"That's only one spot. Where's the other one?"

Pip touched the glass again and enlarged the spot he was pointing at. Dakota rolled his eyes and stood up straight.

"You have got to be kidding me?"

"It was one of the first returns we picked up."

"Isn't there anything else down there?"

"Probably, but we're not going to be able to scan for them and still get out of here before those destroyers reach orbit."

"What's the issue?" BachTL asked looking at the displays. Dakota pointed at the two spots on the screens. "So what, they look like good deposits of whatever you're after."

"These two points are at the original location of Colonel Barker's Carolon base. Can you tell if its occupied?"

"Pretty sure that's where Drax planned to setup a new Albion outpost," BachTL said.

"Pretty sure this is a stupid coincidence. Anywhere else, Mr. Pippin?"

The science officer slowly shook his head as he continued to scan.

"There are lots of other locations, but the deposits are scattered and most of them are underground."

Nervous, but still confident, Dakota took a deep breath and looked up at the tracking screens. He finally turned to helm control.

"Lieutenant Starman, we're going in. It'll be just like old times."

"Like that would be something I'd want to commit to memory," the Starbird pilot mumbled as she made the course adjustments and dipped the ship down into the atmosphere.

Dakota turned back to Mr. Pippin, who was already on his feet.

"Bravo team to the teleporter room for immediate transport. Good luck, Pip."

Tiana and Nigel Kramer popped out of their seats and followed Mr. Pippin from the bridge. Dakota sat down in Mr. Pippin's chair and studied the readouts in front of him.

"Sir, may I?" Lana Nevall said rolling her chair over. "Bridge protocol, Sir. When Mr. Pippin is out, the communications officer shall perform both science and com duties."

"There's no such protocol," Dakota said, moving out of the way. "Does it really say that?" Lana gave him a flashing glance and went to work between both stations. "Can you get a good look at the transport site?"

"Yes, it's right here," the com officer said, pointing to several pictures on the console.

"It looks deserted," BachTL commented from behind.

"We didn't see any destroyers either," Dakota replied pointing at the scanner display.

"Still, what choice do you have?"

"Lieutenant Starman, you decide when they can teleport."

"Aye, Sir."

Dakota and BachTL watched as the ground rose up to meet them, the wrecked Carolon base coming quickly into view.

"I thought Colonel Barker said she set the base destructors before she and Colonel Conrad left?" Dakota observed most of the ground structures of the base were still intact. "It should be just a great big hole in the ground."

"Drax's defuser teams are second to none," BachTL said.

"Big concentration of Asium in the far structure," Lana Nevall announced pointing at a bright return on the screen.

"Where's the other location?"

"Out here, but it appears to be scattered, much of it is buried."

"There's no cover out there either. Be better for them if they went into the buildings. At least they can evade if someone comes along. Where's the new outpost located?"

"On the back side of the old one, in the forest."

"Get them just as far into those structures as you can," Dakota ordered. "They can pinpoint the Asium with their rifle trackers."

"Coordinates sent to the teleporter, sending them down now, Sir," Lynette announced as she buzzed the ship directly over the old outpost.

"Corvettes and a squadron of the Starhoppers directly overhead. The Starhoppers are peeling off and coming down," Lana announced.

"Launch Interceptor two. Have Captain Dalley try to draw off as many of them as he can. Weapons, pick up the first target that gets too close. Hold your pin missiles for my command."

"And torpedoes, Sir?" Doran Cartwright asked.

Dakota hesitated, glancing at the tracking returns.

"Have one armed, but I'll give specific orders if we have to use it." Dakota looked back at BachTL.

"You've sure stirred up a real hornet's nest," BachTL said.

"Ok, helm, get us out of here."

"Any particular heading, Sir?"

"Anywhere they aren't. Draw those corvettes off to the far side of Carolon along it's equator. We need to be as far away from that outpost as we can, but still be able to get back at the appointed time."

"What if they finish early?" BachTL asked.

"Hopefully they won't. We need to try and draw those destroyers away from this side as well. They can't drive as fast as we can, so I want to be able to lead them away and then come back and pick up our people without harassment."

"You hope," BachTL responded.

"You've got more intel?"

"The Starhopper is slightly faster than the Black Tiger, but not quite as maneuverable as the Flightstreak. The corvette commanders tend to think of themselves as capitol ships, so they try to perform their maneuvers in the same way. Their weak spots are the aft quarters, around the thrust clusters and under its nose."

"How do they deal with a fighter assault?"

"They're armed with only snuff canons and a heavy gun on top of its bridge pod. I think their hope is that they can maneuver enough to deal with such an assault."

"Corvettes closing on our position," Lana reported. "Starhoppers are almost on top of us."

"Has Captain Dalley launched yet?"

"Just now."

"Here's where you guys earn your pay today."

"Wait a second," Lynette said taking hold of her analog controls. "We're supposed to get paid for this?"

"Just today," Doran said. His scanners and scopes were target rich and he was anxious to make a mess of anything that came in close as the Starbird pilot maneuvered the ship into the upper stratosphere of Carolon.

"Paid or not," Lynette grunted. "It's about time we got into some action. I'm sick and tired of doing nothing but pushing buttons and sliding my fingers around these controls.

"Let's not get caught up in any toe to toe entanglements," Dakota cautioned. "Remember, we need to lead these guys as far away from this location as we can. Do our fighting on the other side of Carolon, then make a run for it back here when the time comes."

Lynette pushed her throttles forward and put the *Constellation* into a gentle turn, staying just inside Carolon's upper atmosphere. There came a blur of another ship as she flashed past one of the corvettes firing on them. Within the envelope of Carolon's upper atmosphere, they could hear the muffled shots fired at them, and feel the concussion of explosions all around them. Lynette glanced at her displays, taking particular note of the aft turret depicted in operation. Several fighters buzzed angrily after them as they throttled along, just inside the atmosphere. The Starhoppers were able to keep up with the Starbird but couldn't organize any coordinated attacks due to their inability to get out in front of the Kalamarion ship. All they could do was fire as opportunity presented itself. Behind them, the Albion corvettes followed, sending a volley of shots after the fleeing Starbird.

It wasn't long before the four corvettes were joined by two more. But catching the Kalamarion ship was proving to be problematic.

"Is there going to be some point in all of this? When do we start doing a little damage to these guys, Sir?" Doran asked, aiming his aft guns at a Starhopper that wasn't taking fire from the turret.

"Be patient, Lieutenant. When we get on the other side, we'll do some maneuvers that will bring us into close quarters with these guys and I'm sure you'll have plenty of opportunities to show them what a Starbird can really do." Dakota smiled. Things hadn't gone exactly how he and Colonel Conrad had planned, but being able to change and make things work with the situation he was confronted with, made him feel like they had a pretty good chance of success. He hoped everything went as well for the landing party.

Unhappy reunions

The room was dark. Blinda had purposely set it that way to
heighten her senses. She stood motionless in the middle of the
practice hall with only dim foot lights melting along the floor around
the perimeter. She had pulled her raven hair up in two braided ropes
on top of her head. Wearing only a thin mid-drift, she sported
spandex shorts and a pair of friction moccasins. She held perfectly
still, her eyes closed with her Balkrums in her hands, waiting. In her
mind, she reached out to everything scattered around her. Planters
full of various plant life and several inanimate objects. Small training
droids used to help combat cadets hone their skills with hand
weapons, zipped all around the room. Several larger, more lethal
drones, used to assist ground troops with real combat operations,
waited along the borders of the room.

"Begin," she said softly, striking a defensive stance. Focusing on
the plant life, she remained aware of the drones maneuvering directly
above her. In her mind, she discerned all the plant life begin to grow
at an accelerated rate, reaching out to her with long twisting vines and
roots. Some even picked themselves up out of their potting anchors
and skulked about the room, spreading their branches and roots like
tentacles all about the floor and walls. The drones overhead revved up
and dispersed making loud buzzing noises from every direction. Blinda
flung her Balkrums in opposing directions and swirled her hands above
her head, creating a rising vortex that gently lifted her from the floor.
Pulling her blaster, she fired into the darkness, a brilliant ball of
expanding, molten metal appearing a short distance from each shot
she took. Swirling madly, she continued to shoot, hearing her
Balkrums whizzing past her position and striking the rising plants as
they flung their branches and roots at her, trying to knock her from
her position. Holstering her pistol, she reached out and grabbed both
Balkrums as they spun past her and with a twitch of the finger, the
swirling air settled, dropping her to the floor. The moment she
touched down, she activated the radium anodes. The blades now
snapped and crackled as she swung them at her attackers.

Blinda abruptly sprang forward, jumping and tucking as several
blasts from the assault drones echoed in her ears. Rolling along the
ground, she held her glowing blades out on both sides, effortlessly
slicing through reaching vines. Coming up out of her roll, she landed
on her feet and threw one of her Balkrums, its red glow streaking out
into the darkness. She turned on one heel and sliced through a
branch with the other Balkrum, then pivoted again to slap away
several blasts from an unseen assault drone. A number of shots

peppered her position from above and both sides. Hearing her first Balkrum whizzing about the room and only catching a blur of red color, she took several running steps and jumped, swinging her other weapon into the darkness. Contacting metal, her blade seared through the body of an assault drone at the same time her other spinning weapon passed through a second on her other side. Shrapnel scattered in all directions, raining down around her as she softly landed on her feet. Catching her Balkrums, she fused them and swung directly behind her, stopping the advance of more vines, then all was quiet.

Remaining still, she held her eyes closed. Her weapon remained poised behind her as she probed the air immediately around her. She perceived everything was either dead or destroyed. Several moments passed before she relaxed and opened her eyes. The darkness hung heavy with only the light from her activated Balkrums to illuminate the area immediately around her. A light from an elevated observation deck suddenly lit up the entire hall. The floor was littered with drone fragments and plant carcasses. Blinda brought a hand up to shield her eyes.

"End exercise," Blinda said, deactivating her weapon and clipping it in place. As her eyes adjusted to the change, she began removing her gloves, taking notice of a lone individual sitting in the observation room. "Clean up," she called out. Immediately, several ground droids appeared and started scooping up the mess left by the training encounter.

"Impressive," a voice said calmly over the hall sound system.

Blinda looked up at Drax and then around at the mess being cleared away as the lights came up to full. Checking that everything was in place on her person, she exited the training hall and entered the observation deck.

"You didn't report onboard," Drax said coolly.

"I don't have to," Blinda replied. She leaned against the entry wall, back into the shadows. "I assume you're here in hopes I'll tell you what the King Commander had to say after you left."

"I am understandably curious."

"I was commanded not to speak of it. But you needn't worry about your position as top Queen Captain. KC Dismon has every confidence in your ability to carry out his designs."

"So why the secrecy?"

"Apparently he felt like I should have detailed my encounter with the alien ship better."

"But you didn't detail it at all."

"Exactly. I will say it would be unwise for you to go chasing after Casey any longer."

"Yes, I got that message loud and clear." Drax fell silent looking back down into the training hall and watching the last of the debris being cleared. "So, am I to understand you'll be reporting on all of my activities now?"

"Do you really expect an answer to that?" Blinda sneered. "Are you going to disobey a direct order and go chasing off after Casey?"

"Why would I tell you?" Now Drax sounded irritated. "I will say it's not likely as I'll be occupied with other matters."

"Meaning?"

"Other matters."

"Just see that you don't fly off and do something stupid," Blinda counseled, smirking from the shadows. "Now, if you'll excuse me, I have *other matters* to attend." Blinda turned without another word and left the observation platform. Moments later, Drax observed her reenter the training hall, taking a position in the middle of the room.

"Begin exercise delta four," Blinda called out. She pulled her Balkrum and separated the discs, activating the anodes and striking a defensive pose. Moments later a Vivitar droid appeared from each corner of the room with their guns blazing. Drax watched for a few more moments, listening to the clatter of machine gun and laser fire bounce all around the practice hall. She checked her wristband and got up, walking from the observation platform without looking back.

*   *   *   *

Dalton SoKnack studied the ship's scanners thoroughly, but was getting only black coming back from every station. While the cosmos was brilliant with an infinite cluster of stars and galaxies in all directions, they were still out in the middle of nowhere and it was about as black as it could get at this location. An aide handed him a hand device and saluted, turning smartly and marching away. Dalton looked at it for a few moments and turned to the command deck.

"There's nothing out here, QC," he informed Drax as he took the last step at the top of the stairs. Drax remained motionless, her arms folded neatly beneath her green cloak.

"Nothing?"

Dalton held out the device.

"Nothing within a couple of parsecs. I'm not very comfortable out here, QC."

"We have the flotilla with us, why are you worried?"

"It's just we're out here in the middle of nowhere on the edge of the Spartus. The Colonian Second fleet was reported in this area not three hours ago. We took a terrible pounding running from their Fifth fleet just outside the Jurass system. I would hate to be caught out here alone. If one of the other factions should find us..."

"I'm sure you understand they are more afraid of this sector than we should be. Stop worrying, we won't be here long." Drax turned and took the hand device from the Battlecruiser commander and

glanced at it. After scrolling through some of the information, she stepped to the edge of the command platform and looked down at the ship's positioning monitors. She checked her wristband again and considered for a moment. "Have your pilots turn the ship one hundred and thirty-three degrees on your Y axis and thirty-four degrees on the X axis."

Dalton developed a puzzled look. Drax looked back out at two of the flotilla's destroyers milling about in front of the Battlecruiser.

"Have the *Terrence* and *Mikal* hold their positions at thirty degrees off the port and starboard bow."

Dalton turned and gave the orders, then silently returned to watch the maneuver as the great ships began to move into their ordered positions. Once the maneuver was completed, he recognized the V-shaped opening directly in front of the battlecruiser.

"Open the landing bay doors and make sure we have no fighters or assault craft outside," Drax ordered, still watching.

"Scout vessels?"

"Nothing outside. No charged guns and no energy shields of any kind."

"But regulations..." Dalton started to object until he received a steely look from a surprisingly calm Drax. "Yes, QC." Dalton turned and gave the orders as Drax checked her band again. She looked up in time to see an orb of light flash directly in front of the bow of the battlecruiser and a small white ship appear, dropping out of Quadra-light.

"Right on time," Drax mumbled with a crooked smile.

"Colonian F-2 approaching the bow," a voice from the pit below called out. The command personnel nervously waited for Commander SoKnack to give the order to open fire or at least grab the fighter with the ship's tractor beams, but no such order was given.

"Transmit standard landing instructions and have the pilot taken to the executive quarters until called for." Drax watched closely as the Flightstreak made a wide turn and disappeared beneath the belly of the great ship. "Commander SoKnack, bring the flotilla back together and set your course for the Jurass system, then meet me in the command lounge in fifteen minutes."

The battlecruiser commander acknowledged and disappeared to carry out his assigned task, leaving Drax alone on the command deck. After several minutes, she disappeared into an elevator.

*   *   *   *

As Drax sat thinking in her quarters, she reached for a viewing device and activated it. Thumbing through several files, she opened one she had been studying previous to her meetings on Calliope. The first sets of images were taken from gun camera footage of both airborne fighters that made it through Carolon's planetary defenses and other ground machines that had participated in the Albion advance. She watched closely, the work of death and destruction her troops inflicted on the Colonian foot soldiers and the mechanized armaments going head to head. Drax found it interesting the Duchess Benetar hadn't supplied the Colonian outpost with nearly enough military hardware to hold it against a prolonged assault. Scrubbing through the moving images in fast forward, she reached a point she had gone over and over again, trying to see something she hadn't seen before. She stopped at the image of Gunnar Conrad working to disable an attacking ROACH. She gazed at the images moving through its timeline frame by frame. It still amazed her a human could perform such feats of strength and agility. As the video ticked through the frames, the ROACH exploded and Gunnar walked casually back to where he had left CJ and his small droid.

"He just sweeps her off her feet," Drax chuckled, watching Gunnar scoop CJ up and make a run for it. The next scenes were taken from the other ROACH's head cameras as it approached CJ's personal hangar. Then it switched to the body cams of several of her infantry soldiers that had reached the building before anyone else. The scenes tightened up a bit as they made their way into the building and toward the hangar. There were images of CJ and Gunnar climbing into her fighter with the little white droid, but no one else. She then proceeded to her encounter with Gunnar and CJ inside the planet Reako. The body cams of her pilots and the camera files from their parked fighters, showed Gunnar and another woman running together in the caves and then running with CJ down the hillside to the riverbed. She froze the frame several times, studying the image of an unfamiliar young woman, trying to get a clear picture of who she might be. A couple of times, Drax stopped and looked up, thinking, trying to piece the puzzle together. Presently, there came a summons at her door and turning the unit off, she reached for a control on the table next to her.

"Come in."

She heard the sound of the door pulling back, then slow footsteps walking toward her. Drax looked up to see Casey Janae Barker dressed in a jet-black uniform with white seamed accents, black pants and shiny black knee boots, standing across the room.

"Casey," Drax beamed, springing to her feet and throwing her arms around CJ. "You're here! You have no idea how good it is to finally have you back, safe! How are you feeling? Fully recovered?" Drax was a little dismayed at CJ's lack of enthusiasm, but remained upbeat. She slid her arm around CJ's and walked her into the room.

"I'm here as ordered, Drax," CJ finally scowled. "Now where's the antidote?"

"You never were much for small talk."

Drax motioned for CJ to sit down while she reached for a small box on the table next to her viewing device. Turning back to CJ, she produced a small vile and handed it to her.

"Just like that?" CJ asked, still not happy.

"As promised," Drax replied.

"And how will I know this is the real thing?"

"You're welcome to send it down to the lab for analysis and confirmation. We can put Doctor San Sann on it."

"Where did you get it?"

"As you are aware, we were injecting all prisoners with Kodiac Blu, but due to the 'side effects', the Sanchian treaty required that we cease the practice and destroy our inventory. Your boyfriend was given an injection from a variant version I acquired from a private source. It was meant to keep him calm until we could find suitable accommodations for him. Seelix was gracious enough to provide me with the antidote formula. I had Doctor Sann synthesize a single dose; you have it in your hand. Took him quite a while as it is somewhat fragile and has a very short shelf life."

"And how am I supposed to get it to where it needs to go?"

"Name the place and we'll get it there."

"The only one I trust is Diord."

"Why am I not surprised? As it happens, we're passing close to the Jurass system. The *Tarzana's* flotilla isn't allowed to enter the system, but we can stop on the borders long enough to make a transfer. Then, I expect you to take your place here."

"When I have confirmation this is the real thing and has been delivered, you'll have my undying loyalty."

"As promised," Drax agreed, smiling. She pulled the tie on her cloak and leaned forward. "Now, tell me all about your adventures."

"You want me to divulge Colonian military secrets?"

"I want you to do your duty to the Albion Empire. Come on, a little information isn't unreasonable here. Most of it I already know anyway. Why did Benetar put you on that worthless chunk of nothing, out in the middle of nothing?"

CJ looked at Drax for a long moment.

"You're a real piece of work, ya know that?"

"What? It's not like you didn't give the Colonians information on us. You pretty much hung me out to dry to get them to let you keep your rank and offer you a command."

CJ fell silent, knowing Drax was right. As she had no intention of ever coming back to anything with Albia stamped on it, it seemed pointless to withhold information.

"I really have no idea," CJ finally said. "It was a start. I was just grateful I wasn't spending time on a penal ship or stuck in some mine doing security duty."

"So, you didn't receive special orders?"

"No, in fact every directive I received was pre-screened and low priority. I guess that's understandable considering, but I was only ordered to build the defenses of the outpost and report on any comings and goings in the system."

"How were they about keeping you supplied?"

"They were pretty good about sending in supplies and troop build ups on a regular basis, but as you know all too well, it wasn't enough. I would have had you kicked if Benetar had sent me any of the new stuff in any kind of useable quantities."

"In your dreams," Drax retorted good-naturedly. "We both know you were too far out to withstand a prolonged campaign. Did you ever see anything in that system while you were there?"

"Did I ever see anything?" CJ repeated, not sure what Drax was asking. "No, not really. Carolon itself is fairly unremarkable. What you saw when you landed, was what there was."

"What about Reako?"

"What about it?"

"You don't need a scanner to look at it," Drax commented. "It's pretty close to Carolon. You can see the asteroid rings plain as day from the base."

"It's just a swamp," CJ responded. "I expect in a few million years the two planets will collide and form one really nice place."

"Did you ever go there?"

"You know I did. Why are you asking?" CJ asked.

"I mean did you ever have it explored. Surely you knew all about the subterranean world inside."

"We suspected there was something inside, but never could get any probe telemetry back. It was too deep."

"Who was the girl you and Gunnar brought out with you?" Drax probed.

CJ hesitated for a moment, then nodded.

"Her name is Kara Americ. Her ship crashed there years ago and sank into the underground caverns. She and another woman were the only two survivors. She was alone when we found her. Her friend was killed by Binions. We left her on Cross with Diord."

"Interesting," Drax responded quietly. "What do you think the odds are that you and Gunnar ended up down in the same spot you found her?"

"Pretty astronomical," CJ said. She took notice of Drax's inflection, but didn't acknowledge it. Drax was fishing for something.

"So, Gunnar..." Drax said in a mixed tone. She picked up the viewer again and started cruising through it.

"What about him?"

"You two are pretty tight."

"We're good friends."

"Yes, good friends," Drax gave CJ a glance. CJ tipped her head at Drax.

"It's not what you're thinking."

"And what do you think I'm thinking? I chase you two halfway across the galaxy. He saves your life how many times? You spend how long in close quarters together? You risk everything to pull the dumbest maneuver ever, to get him back off this ship, which by the way, was brilliant, and you've no doubt worked closely together, one must wonder how long you've been married. And now, you've abandoned everything you believe in and worked so hard for, all so you can save his life, again. Just what do you think I'm thinking?"

"You think I'm in love with the guy?" CJ finally said.

"The evidence is pretty overwhelming," Drax smiled.

"I admit, I love him," CJ said.

"Ah, see!"

"I love him, but I'm not in love with him."

"Semantics!"

"I don't see you hanging off anyone's arm," CJ snapped indignantly.

"I don't hang off any man. Anyway, the man who can handle me, doesn't exist in this dimension."

"Are we gonna sit here and bandy words about our love lives, or is this going somewhere?"

"Just wanting to know more about him."

"What's to know? Sounds like you've already made up your mind." CJ was growing weary of the interrogation. "He's a nice guy from a different galaxy and he's just trying to get home; that's it."

"What about his strength?"

"He's the only one that has his makeup, if that's what you're asking."

"I won't deny having troops like him would be a nice addition to the Albion arsenal..."

"You mean your arsenal."

"Just wondering what he's like that you find him so likeable."

"Drax, Gunnar is just like you and me," CJ maintained. "Two arms, two legs, two eyes and two ears. He's got gifts and talents just like you and me, except he tries to use them to help people."

Drax fell silent for a moment, a pleasant smile drifting across her face.

"Yes, well, we all have talents," she finally said, sitting forward. "And you have yours. It's time to put them to good use. Let's go."

"Go?" CJ asked watching her sister get to her feet. "Where are we going?"

"You didn't think I was just going to lock you in a room and hold you indefinitely, did you? Here, you're gonna need these," Drax said tossing CJ a small box. "I've got several projects I need completed

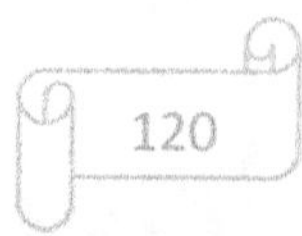

and as I have restrictions placed on me from the King Commander, you're just the person for the job."

"And just what are these projects?" CJ asked opening the box while following Drax into the outer hall. She stopped and pulled a set of Albion Colonel clusters from the box.

"Here, let me help you with those," Drax said taking one and pinning it in place. CJ just looked at the other one as Drax straightened her collar and turned for an elevator. "Follow me please."

As they moved between decks, CJ finished pinning the other cluster on and straightened her cuffs.

"Where's BachTL?" CJ asked quietly.

"Oh, you're just now getting around to asking about him?" Drax asked snidely. "Wasn't sure if you had missed him at all?"

"I left him for you," CJ defended. "It was the best thing I could do for him."

"Best thing for him, or best thing for you? I'm not sure that statement counts as having a conscience."

"I didn't want to put him through what I was going to have to endure."

"You're so full of compassion," Drax growled.

"Look who's talking!"

"Don't you even begin to judge me. We needed you and you left!"

"You're a big girl and he is a grown man. You've never needed anyone, and he's old enough to decide for himself what path to follow."

"Oh... my noble sister being parental."

"He should be free to decide..."

"You are the one that left," Drax bellowed, becoming incensed. "Don't lay your benevolence at my feet. He never voiced it, but I could see it written all over his face, utter contempt for what you did to him."

"Are you sure that's how he feels and not you?"

Silence echoed in the elevator as they traveled through the bowls of the ship, until CJ turned back to her sister.

"Tell me where he is, Drax."

Drax returned her sister's determined gaze, but finally flinched.

"He's on an extended assignment."

"What assignment?"

"That's classified."

"What assignment, Drax?" CJ persisted.

Drax stood firm as the elevator opened to the bridge.

CJ had to move quickly to remain on Drax's flank as she strode onto the upper platform of the *Tarzana*. Dalton SoKnack turned and smiled at CJ as the two women approached.

"Is everything ready, Commander?" Drax asked, coming to a stop in front of Dalton.

"As per your instructions, QC." Dalton turned to CJ. "It's really good to see you again, Casey."

"Hi, Dalton," CJ greeted. "It's good to see you too. *Tarzana* is a big ship; you've handled it pretty well since we last served together. It'll be good to serve with you again."

"Yeah, well, as nice as that might be," Drax said cutting in. "I've reassigned the commander here to another project. As of this moment, you, Colonel Barker will assume command of the *Tarzana*."

CJ suddenly felt very uncomfortable. She hedged a look in Dalton's direction, but he didn't seem to share her apprehension. In fact, he seemed pleased.

"Very confused here," CJ said folding her arms.

"Come on, Casey," Drax firmed up. "It's not that complicated. Be the *take control of everything* sister I know so well. Use to be you'd be shoving the commander here to one side to take the helm."

"That was then, this is now. What's this all about?"

"You've got plenty of other things to concern yourself with right now, just as the commander here does." Drax turned to Dalton. "How long before we reach the Nulark system?"

"About an hour."

"Then you'd better get going. Good luck, Commander."

"Thank you, QC." Without another word, Dalton saluted and turned for the elevator.

CJ carefully eyed Drax as she stepped to the forward bridge windows.

"Nulark?" CJ asked.

"Just dropping something off on our way to the Jurass system. I do have other commitments you know."

"As commander of this vessel, is this something I need to know about?"

"Come on!" Drax elevated a bit. "Where's the Casey everyone respects? You are commander of this vessel..."

"And you are the Queen Captain of this fleet," CJ retorted.

"You know your responsibilities."

"Show me what you have in mind."

"That's a little better," Drax said toning down a little. "This, goodie two shoes act you've got going on doesn't suit you in the least. Follow me," Drax insisted, a stern look etching her expression. The two disappeared into another elevator that took them deeper into the bowels of the great ship. After making several elevator changes and hall transport rides, they arrived at a small hangar bay overlook.

"Special Operations," CJ recognized the area. "Ok, what are you up to, sis?"

"I won't insult your intelligence by threading through an entire back story of what I've gone through since you left me high and dry some time ago." Drax walked to the window and looked down into the small hangar bay, at a single craft sitting on the shiny black floor. A look of shock crossed CJ's face as she stared down at the white hull of a Starbird sitting in the bay. There was an army of maintenance personnel surrounding the vessel working to clear away support gear in preparations for departure.

Fighting her impulses, CJ folded her arms and studied the craft realizing there were some noticeable differences. The aft Interceptor locations were not separate crafts, but just structured parts of the rear wing section. The aft turret had no gunner position on it, but looked to be converted to some kind of observation dome. The entire structure of the ship seemed to be the same as the *Constellation* with some differences where the forward guns were located and the thruster pods. Clearly a clever look alike.

"Very impressive," CJ whispered, still awestruck at the Albion copy. "And you plan to do what with this?"

Drax hedged a glance at her sister and looked back down at the ship, watching Dalton SoKnack make his way toward the boarding door at the rear of the mid-section.

"Do I really have to explain it all to you?"

"You've got a working copy…"

"Only part of a working copy," Drax corrected. "Basically, the guts of a Torag TL235 pulsar assault ship, but the outside looks pretty convincing, don't you think?"

"A Torag? That's a big gun, where did you put it?"

"Muzzle out the front," Drax pointed at the nose. "Control breach in the back. The turret dome is just for looks; the pressure piston just behind."

"Where are the engines?"

"Here," Drax said touching a control on a screen next to the window and pointing at the image of the fake Starbird in cutaway form. "The outer hull is just a shell. We couldn't get a good look at what's inside the real thing, so the Hessons improvised. They stripped a Torag to fit the outer dimensions and remounted the engines on either side of the control breach in the back. It won't go for very long, but it doesn't have to. All they have to do is fool the other ship into thinking it's the sister ship, so they can get close enough to disable it, then we can come in and tow it or carry it back to Calliope." Drax turned back to CJ. "Of course, any information you'd like to lend would go a long way to helping this project along."

CJ shook her head, keeping her arms folded.

"I'm afraid I won't be able to help with what you have in mind here."

"You were onboard their ship. You know what it's like inside. What their technology is and how to work it."

"I was onboard, yes, but I never got to see anything or learn how anything worked. It's a beautiful ship inside and there's a lot of fancy tech in there. They can do some considerable damage if they chose to, but both ships were damaged when they came here. You blew up one of them and it's not likely they'll make that same mistake twice."

"So, you don't think sending the *Warbird* out to fool them is going to work?"

"I didn't say that. You're just asking someone who is a bit biased here. These people are my friends. Gunnar is my friend."

"And you like him a lot."

"Yes, I like him a lot. Why would I want to compromise my friendship with Gunnar or risk killing his crew for the sake of letting you get your hands on his ship?"

"For the good of Albia. For the good of Hadrian."

"How about, for the good of Drax Blair?"

"Sure, who wouldn't love to have the credit for bringing in a prize like this? Just think of how far a person could go in their career with this highlighted on their resume'."

CJ considered for a moment.

"Is this the line of logic you used on BachTL when you sent him out on special assignment?"

Drax flared her nostrils, taking in a deep breath to hold her anger in.

"Suit yourself," CJ said, speaking up before her sister had a chance to explode. "But you'll get no help from me." She looked back out at the *Warbird* as Dalton disappeared into the ship and the last of the equipment was cleared from around the vessel. "I'll provide escort and cover for your little operation, but that's where I draw the line. You want me to command this ship and its flotilla, fine, I'll command and see that nothing happens to her, and that includes putting her into a compromising situation. Let me know when you need to stop and drop that thing off." CJ gave the *Warbird* one final look and briskly exited the overlook room. Drax looked after her, wondering, then looked back out at the *Warbird*. She could see figures moving around inside the tight bridge section as they prepared for departure.

"Well, that could have gone a little better," a voice spoke up calmly from the shadows. "But at least you know where you stand with her."

"Not really," Drax said turning to Blinda as she materialized from a far corner. "Not sure I can fully bring her back from where she went."

"Then why put her in command of this ship? She's going to go off the deep end when she finds out where you sent BachTL."

"No doubt," Drax said starting for the door. "But if you think it through, you'll see I've put her exactly where she'll do me the most good."

Blinda pulled her hair back and looked down at the *Warbird*, then after Drax.

"There's a lot of gambling going on here and the odds are certainly not in your favor."

Landing Party

Standing next to a wrecked anti-fighter emplacement, the *Constellation* landing party gazed out at an eerily quiet Carolon base. There wasn't a lot of time to waste examining the devastated area. Pip had his scanner up and zeroing in on the Asium signature before everyone else had their weapons out, making sure they weren't caught unaware. Nigel Kramer stepped forward, followed by Tiana, then Pippin and finally Alder Gantrie. The four piled up against a crumbled hangar bay wall and looked up into the dusk sky.

"Give me a direction," Nigel whispered. He looked at his proximity scanner, turning in several directions. Pip studied the display and pointed toward a dark recess across the collapsed hangar bays. "Looks dark and nasty."

"Nothing on the prox scanners," Tiana said nudging him forward. "And it's very quiet."

"A little too quiet," Nigel said moving forward. "I don't suppose you've got a layout of the base complex?"

"I remember some of it from when we were here the first time, but I don't think the Colonel figured we'd be going into the complex to find what we're looking for."

"I was stationed here with Colonel Barker, remember?" Alder whispered forward.

"Get us into that hallway and Alder can help get me situated with the complex layout," Pip said, putting his hand on Tiana's shoulder and following them across the rubble in the wrecked hangar bay. The four remained silent as they worked their way toward the gloom of the main hallway, relieved to be in the relative safety of the outer corridor. Standing in the darkness with only the displays of their devices to illuminate their faces, they detected a strong odor that quickly turned their stomachs. As Pip worked his equipment, Alder Gantrie gazed back out at the wreckage in the hangars. The ceilings were completely caved in and shuttle, fighter parts and burnt out Albion ROACH machines lay everywhere. The Lieutenant turned her rifle light to the floor of the hallway and put her hand to her mouth. She had seen plenty of field action before, so she was used to just about anything. Gathering her wits, she pulled up her filter piece and put it over her mouth and nose.

"What is that awful smell?" Tiana asked switching on her light.

"Smell? You're calling that a smell?" Nigel complained. "That's a stench, what the…?"

He followed Tiana's light as he reached for his. Before he could sight his light on the floor, they all witnessed several large lumps.

"Holy..." he choked, fumbling with his filter. Directly at their feet were the badly decomposed bodies of Colonian and Albion ground troopers.

"No time for this," Pip said in a hushed voice as he pulled his filter up. "Alder, can you confirm this layout?"

Alder looked at the display for a moment.

"It's quite a bit out of date, but I think I can fill in for the inaccuracies. About thirty feet ahead, turn right, then left, then right again. About halfway down the hall should be a narrow hall."

"Ok, you take the lead and Nigel brings up the rear. Go," Pip ordered. "We're running the clock."

Moving cautiously, they made their way around a constant heap of rotting corpses and down the hall, following Alder's lead and Pip's directions.

"How effective are these proximity scanners in an enclosed place like this?" Tiana asked.

"A little range reduction, but they should still give us a good indication if something shows up," Nigel said. "Who knows what the heck in lurking around in here."

"Nothing hungry for meat," Pip commented, looking down at a corpse.

"Can we talk about something else?" Tiana complained as they turned a corner.

"This placed was rigged to blow when the Colonels got away," Alder stated. "Clearly they disabled the charges. Which means the Albions were going to come in and clean the place up; rebuild it. So why is it still just sitting here? It's like they ran everyone off and left it. Makes zero sense."

"Maybe they haven't gotten to it yet?" Pip offered from behind.

"These are the Albions we're talking about here."

"Gotta say," Tiana grumbled. "I'm a little scared here."

"Well, if you weren't, we'd all think you had some kind of death wish," Nigel said turning another corner with his rifle up.

"Ok, I'm a lot scared."

"How many ground deployments have you been on?" Alder inquired.

"Including this one? One."

Everyone looked at Tiana, Alder being the only one surprised. Tiana shrugged and nudged Alder forward.

"Yeah, ya gotta start sometime."

"Just wished it wasn't on an extraction like this," the MedTech mumbled as she probed further into the darkness.

"Does anyone know if this is the way Colonel Conrad and Alex 7001 used to extract Colonel Barker and her ground staff?" Nigel asked.

"I'm using Alex's overlay," Pip informed them as they proceeded cautiously through the black passages. "Right here is where it starts."

Everyone stopped. To their right was a narrow hallway that had been partially destroyed by weapon's fire.

"This is a maintenance access," Alder informed them as she started through the broken interior. "It leads to the back side of the command center."

"There's an intersection just ahead. Looks like a main corridor," Pip said from behind.

"It will take you around to the main doors of the command center."

"Will that be faster?" Pip asked noticing the timer on his display.

"Depends on where your target is," Alder replied.

Pip stopped everyone at the main hallway and dialed in his scanner.

"Shorter through the maintenance hall," he said pointing his rifle light at the narrow opening. "But I get the feeling it'll take us longer." There appeared to be something in the hall. Alder poked her head into the darkness with her light up.

"You would be correct," she announced, turning left and starting down the curved hallway. Tiana glanced her light into the darkness of the side hall. She could only see a static cascade of rubble and cables. Nigel nudged her forward to keep up with the other two as they made their way around debris and body mounds strewn all over the large hallway. Nearing another intersection, they took note of the walls and floors. They were nearly completely destroyed, leaving bare rock showing through piles of bodies. Even with their filters on, the smell was becoming overpowering. In some instances, they had to crawl over moldering carcass piles, their hands and knees sinking into the rancid flesh.

Picking himself up, Pip checked his scanner and turned to a large opening in the wall. Not waiting for the others, he entered the wrecked command center. As he moved toward a set of metal stairs, Tiana and Nigel entered, looking around the main floor. It was difficult to tell there had been technology installed as the ceiling had fallen in, burying any remnants of command and control equipment. Tiana heard Pip's boots clamoring up a set of metal stairs leading to a partially collapsed overview deck, as Alder shuffled through what was left of the main blast doors.

"Times up!" she called out.

Tiana checked her proximity display for the timer, but noticed returns forming on the edges of her display. Her heart skipped several beats, watching the objects moving toward the center of her display.

"We need to get back to the extraction zone now," Alder called again, a little more frantic. Nigel moved back toward the main blast door with Tiana who turned to make sure Pip was with them. *No Pip!*

"Mister Pippin!" Alder yelled, looking up at the metal overview deck. "We've got company!"

Pip turned left then right, trying to get a fix on the return. Even with the small scanner, he hadn't gotten as good a return on the Asium signature as he had with the ship's onboard sensors. He should be standing almost on top of it. He fumbled around in the dark, shining his light back and forth, listening to the scanner squawk and chirp, trying to announce where the Asium was located. There should be whitish stones laying under the soles of his boots with as much noise as the scanner was making. He heard an odd noise against a far rock wall and turned his light toward a dark hole in the stone. Scampering toward it on his hands and knees, the sound seemed like it was coming from the hole, but he couldn't be sure. There was a commotion rising in pitch down on the main floor at the blast doors. Pip glanced back to see Nigel and Alder swinging their weapons around, their rifle lights stabbing into the darkness of the hallway. He continued forward, noticing something square off to his left as he perched himself next to the hole in the flat rock wall. He could hear a sick hissing sound coming from the hole next to him, and ignoring the screaming scanner, peered into the hole.

A barrage of weapons fire erupted from the blast doors and he caught the flash of a rifle's light beam streak across a metal box only feet away. Looking down the hole, he could feel air moving past him. He pulled his light up, listening to Nigel and Alder yelling something about retreating from the command center. There was a slither of tentacles and long black fingers reaching toward him. A bubbled head materialized with a set of red eyes flaring back at him. Shocked, he froze, disbelieving such a creature could exist and that it was here, coming up an air shaft at him. He could hear more yelling and more weapons fire, then the clatter of metal against metal. There was an unholy screech issuing from the hole and the creature launched at him. A sudden flash accompanied a deafening blast in his ears, catching him completely off guard. Pip rolled away as Tiana continued to fire her weapon, even after falling back against a twisted railing.

"Where is it?" she screamed.

"Where's what?"

"The Asium? Where is it?" Tiana kept her rifle and light pointed down the hole and squeezed off several more shots. A horrible shrieking noise continued to wail from the hole.

"I think it's in that box right next to you," Pip pointed at her right side. Tiana looked down and almost knocked the box off the tilted platform. Something reached out at her from the hole and she let out a scream. Pip pulled his gun up and fired. Muzzle flashes illuminated the hole as a creature tried to pull itself through the threshold.

"Shoot it!" Tiana screamed as she fumbled with the box and tried to fire her rifle at the same time.

"I'm trying to," Pip yelled back, pulling the trigger again and again. "Get the box and get out of there!"

"I'm trying, but it's got my leg!"

"Shoot it!"

"I'm trying! You shoot it!"

Pip's rifle popped out of his hands as one of the tentacles swatted his arm. His rifle light flashed across the head of the disgusting looking beast. Riddled with ordnance holes, he recognized the glint of light reflecting off fluids running from its head. Fumbling for anything to fight the creature back with, he finally pulled a lunar grenade.

"Tiana!" he yelled over the noise while showing her the flashing object in his hand. Horrified, she continued to fire at the mass holding onto her.

"Do it," she screamed, frantically kicking at the head of the creature. She caught the flash of white razor-sharp teeth at the same moment she heard the grenade hit the side of the hole and start tumbling down the air shaft. Instinctively, she grabbed the metal box, turned over and curled up into the fetal position. She felt something pulling her closer to the hole, then there was a blinding flash accompanied by a loud boom. The roar of flame and intense heat rushed over her. The creature screamed, blowing apart as it was forced through the metal railing above Tiana. A rain of entrails and creature fluids rained all over her, and then everything was silent, but only for a moment. Pip grabbed the balled-up Tiana and pulled her away from the hole and around the backside of a smashed console.

"Are you ok?" Pip asked grabbing his rifle and taking the box from her.

"Yeah, I think so." She looked back at the smoking hole. "What was that?"

"We'll ask Alder when we get back downstairs." Pip opened the box and pointed his light and scanner inside. Tiana peered in at a load of whitish stones. "Jackpot," Pip snapped with glee, looking at the off-scale readings on the display. "Let's move." He helped Tiana to her feet, grabbed his rifle and tucked the box into Tiana's pack. They scrambled down the twisted remnants of the stairs and to the blast doors where they met Nigel and Alder retreating back into the room.

"Those things have never tried to come in here before," Alder complained checking her weapon.

"Leave the place unlocked and anything comes in," Pip commented, breathing hard.

"It takes nearly an entire clip to slow these things down," Nigel said.

"Why don't they just eat the bodies?" Tiana asked.

"With a smell like that, would you?"

Pip pulled another grenade and activated it, then stuck it in Alder's face.

"Have another one ready," he said tossing it down the hall.

Alder pulled one of her grenades and activated it at the same time the first explosion erupted. Creature bodies and parts expanded out in every direction. Several live creatures snarled viciously, reaching out as they lunged past the four crouching combatants. Nigel abruptly found himself struggling with one of the creatures on his back. Using one hand to pry the shell hardened tentacles from off his shoulders, he tried to use the butt of his rifle to strike at it from behind. He was having little success until Alder brought out her blaster pistol and pulled the trigger several times at point blank range. Before she checked to see that the animal was dead, she tossed her activated grenade back up the hallway and turned in time to see Pip struggling with another creature. As she scrambled to get to him, another blast rocked the hallway and the ceiling in front of the command center blast doors crumbled and gave way. Picking herself back up, she pulled her service knife and with a quick thrust and a twist, dispatched the creature Pip was struggling with.

"I could have gotten it," Pip said puffing. Alder smiled and wiped the mess off her knife. They pointed their lights at a commotion at the nearby wall. Tiana was kneeling over something striking it repeatedly with the butt of her rifle. The creature was certainly dead, but she kept smashing it where she thought the head ought to be. It was only after Alder grabbed the barrel of the gun, did Tiana finally stop and slumped back, out of breath.

"Whatever those things are, it isn't going to take them long to figure out another way to get at us," Nigel said. Everyone pointed their lights back at the wall of concrete rubble and rock blocking the passage in front of the command center blast doors.

"They're called the Quid," Alder said. "Indigenous life form of Carolon, among others. With tentacles like that, you would think they would rather be on Reako. Everyone good enough to move?" Alder asked, checking the others. There were cuts and abrasions in many places, but it appeared there were no serious injuries so far. Pip pulled his scanner and looked at the countdown timer.

"We've only got a little over a minute to reach the pickup zone," he said moving down the hall toward the service corridor. Everyone understood the urgency of their situation and even though they were shaken and a bit battered, they hurried through the narrow hallway, following Alder back out the way they had come in. As they worked their way back through the maze of hallways, Alder stopped, looking at her prox scanner, but motioned everyone to continue. It was only after there was an explosion from behind, did they realized they were being pursued.

Stopping near the main hallway leading to the demolished hangar bays, Tiana felt something pulling at her waist and turned to find Alder pulling her four grenades from her utility belt. Tiana noticed returns appearing on her scanner and glanced back at Alder's.

"Are they gonna catch us?" she asked anxiously.

"I don't think so. Nigel, you hang back here with me. We'll cover Mister Pippin and Tiana while they get to the extraction point and call for pickup. How many grenades do you have left?" Alder looked at Tiana's rifle. She had somehow damaged the barrel; probably when she was bashing her attacker with it.

"Looks like three, two ordnance magazines and a couple of power packs."

"Here," Alder said pulling Tiana's magazines from her belts. "We're going to need these, you're not. Take my service pistol and use yours to get you to the pickup point."

Mister Pippin looked back at Alder as she activated a grenade and tossed it up the pitch-black corridor. As soon as they heard the metal explosive clanking along the floor and walls, they all took off running toward the broken opening to what was left of the hangar bays. A moment before they reached it, they heard the blast from behind and the subsequent squealing of creatures dying, then the concussion reached them. Alder motioned Pip and Tiana forward as she tossed another grenade back into the darkness and raised her rifle. She glanced over at Nigel as he brought his rifle up in one hand and grasped a grenade in the other. Both waited; listening and watching their proximity scanners as Pip and Tiana sprinted through the hangar bay toward open sky. Pip gave his scanner a glance as it started making noise and changing color.

"Does that mean the ship is back?" Tiana asked from behind.

Pip looked up as the sky appeared through the massive crushed opening.

"It means we're supposed to be at the pickup point." He didn't tell her he couldn't detect the *Constellation's* presence, but his scanner was picking something else up. "We need to be right up there," he said pointing at a large mound of dirt next to a smashed cement bunker. Tiana recognized the destroyed remains of an anti-fighter gun next to the dirt mound. It was where they had been deposited only a short time ago. Now it seemed like hours since they had been there. Tiana pushed ahead of Pip, anxious to achieve the relative safety of the pickup zone. She no longer paid attention to her proximity scanner, nor did she have her pistols up. The only thing in her vision now was that mound of dirt. Moving to keep up with her, Pip put his wrist to his mouth and activated his communicator.

"Alpha one, this is Bravo leader. Mission successful, we're ready for pickup."

"Understood Bravo leader," came the cool reply from Lana Nevall. Pip seemed to relax a little. She sounded like she was standing right next to him. "We're inbound now. ETA to your location, five minutes."

"Five minutes?" Pip answered back. "What's the hold up?"

"A little more than anticipated sky traffic up here."

"This is going to be a hot pickup, isn't it?"

"Very hot. What's your situation?"

Pip looked back into the hangar at several muzzle bursts and a blast flash. Just as he was turning forward he caught sight of Nigel and Alder sprinting from the hangar corridor.

"Hot down here too, but we have the package secured. Don't take too long, our butts are kind of hanging out here."

"Understood. Hang tight, we'll have you in a few."

Pip watched as Tiana reached the base of the mound and started clawing her way up the loose dirt. Having no idea what the other returns on his scope were, he wasn't too excited about being so exposed. Reaching the base of the mound, he glanced up, seeing Tiana sitting near the top of the pickup zone, looking at something in her hand. He looked back at Alder and Nigel making their way out of the hangar and toward them. Occasionally, Alder would turn and fire her weapon, but he couldn't see anything following them. Pip looked down at his scanner, then in the direction of the returns. He turned to Tiana to yell a warning, but it was too late. She was already surrounded by troopers with their weapons pointed at her head. He turned to warn Alder and Nigel, but was cold-cocked with the butt of a gun.

*   *   *   *

"Here," Dakota directed BachTL to the command chair. "You sit here in the advisor seat. Whatever we can't figure out right away, you fill in the gaps."

"Sure," BachTL said sitting down. He realized this was probably more to keep him out of the way as Captain Abrams was moving back and forth from the navigation consoles and the sensor control station.

"Do these corvettes have any surprises loaded in their firing tubes?"

"Corvettes aren't large enough to carry anything really upscale when it comes to firepower. They're designed mainly to take on fighter groups. They've got lots of small guns and missiles, several cutting beams and a single blaster cannon. As I indicated before, weakest spots are the thrust clusters and under the nose."

"Any particular moves they like to use when they're all together?"

"Ship commanders don't normally work in groups. That would require someone to be in charge of everyone else and since the military is based on egos and who can get the most power, unless you have a cell, which I very much doubt is what you're dealing with here, it'll be just whoever can get the closest to fire off a shot."

"Good to know. Lieutenant Starman, you have free reign to get us to the other side of the planet however you see fit," Dakota said, sitting down next to Lana.

Lynette grinned broadly, passing Doran a quick glance. Still holding onto her controls, she pushed her throttles forward and rolled the Starbird inverted. BachTL looked through the overhead windows, down at the surface of Carolon. A gaggle of fighters were swarming below them, keeping pace with the throttling Starbird. One of the fighters looked larger than the others. Watching it curiously, he suddenly realized it was the *Constellation's* Interceptor number two. Stunned at first, he watched in awe as the Interceptor appeared to be leading the Albion Starhoppers along, parallel with its mother ship. He also detected a trail of disabled fighters, most probably doomed to burn up in reentry.

"Is your Captain Dalley talking to you?" he asked Lana.

"Unless he's working directly with someone or in distress, he doesn't say much," she answered. Lana pointed to something on the far displays in front of Dakota.

"Yeah, I'm looking at them," he responded.

"What's the matter?" BachTL asked.

"Looks like your friends have called in reinforcements. Can't tell exactly what they are yet as they've just appeared on the outside of this system, but they're there, who or whatever they are."

"Are they going to be a problem?"

"No, we'll be long gone before they can reach us."

BachTL looked ahead as the binary suns breached the curved horizon of Carolon's terminator. The glass auto-dimmed and ahead he could make out two distant objects directly in their path; a pair of corvettes coming right at them. They had already opened up on them even as Lynette adjusted her speed.

"Switching to pin missiles, Sir," Doran announced.

"Make your aim count," Dakota ordered.

"Aye, Sir."

Lynette rolled the ship ninety degrees, matching their orientation with the two corvettes. She pulled back on the throttles, slowing even more.

"Lieutenant Hunter, feel free to join in if you have a moment," Doran called back to the turret gunner.

"Oh, I imagine I can miss a couple of shots and accidently on purpose hit something else." The turret gunner sounded calm and collected, as if he were sitting at a desk doing paperwork.

"Light 'em up," the Captain called as they passed between the two Albion ships.

Doran jammed all ten fingers at the launch points on the glass in front of him, sending pin missiles bursting from both sides of the bridge pod. The *Constellation* took a heavy hammering as they passed between the corvettes. But the incoming fire abruptly stopped as the missiles found their marks, exploding on the gun positions and launchers of the Albion ships. Doran let several more pin missiles go from the *Constellation's* aft launchers as they passed. The fast-moving ordnance swiftly found their mark, exploding on the thruster ports of the corvettes. Two more of the Albion attack crafts tried the same maneuver, only to experience similar results. Even though there were four disabled ships, there were plenty more to elude.

Reaching the far side of the planet, Lieutenant Starman turned the *Constellation* in a long wide turn and circled. Lynette studied her scanning displays, taking note of what was following them and what was trying to maneuver into position for some kind of a stopping tactic. She wasn't so worried about the corvettes anymore, no one was. They had proved that even without full ship's power, they could stand alone against them without sustaining any damage of consequence. She took particular notice of Captain Dalley's Interceptor, in a lower orbit, making a smaller circuit, but remaining in sync with the Starbird. The Starhoppers numbers were significantly smaller. Watching his maneuvers, it appeared he was just toying with them. Just keeping them busy. As she held her course, she considered the Captain's tactics. The conditions here would change dramatically when the destroyers arrived. There would be more fighters and firepower that could prove far more dangerous than what they had experienced so far. But everyone held their confidence that the Starbird was well enough protected and equipped to handle anything the Albions could bring against them.

Lana touched Dakota's shoulder and pointed to an alarm at the top of his displays. He nodded and touched several points on the glass, his main displays instantly changing.

"They really mean business, don't they?" he commented, watching the Albion destroyers breaching Carolon's horizon and coming at them from both sides. "Four of them."

"Each ship has a small squadron of fighters onboard," BachTL spoke up. "But they likely won't launch any of them unless things get ugly."

"I don't want to make things bad for them," Dakota said. "I just want to keep them busy and then leave them in my dust."

"Sir," Lana summoned, putting a finger to her earpiece. "Bravo team reports success. They're moving back to the pickup zone."

"Understood," Dakota answered, studying the destroyers converging on them. "Lieutenant Cartwright, send a couple of volleys of pin missiles into two of the nearest corvettes. Put them out of commission."

"What's your play?" BachTL asked.

"I want to really piss them off. Make them want us bad."

"I thought that was a foregone conclusion?"

"I want to get them angry enough they won't be thinking straight."

"As a general rule, that's not too hard."

"Missiles away, Sir," Doran announced.

All eyes turned outside to watch as a volley of missiles launched
from both sides of the bridge pod, each cluster streaking toward two of
the Albion corvettes trying to gain an inside turn on the Starbird.
Hayden Hunter slung his turret around and held the triggers down,
both barrels blasting out powerful blasts of destruction on the Albion
ships as they tried to advance on the circling *Constellation*.

The first volley of missiles struck the lead corvette along it's port
side and upper decks back to the main thruster ports. The impacts
sent the ship off course, veering into the path of its sister ship. Before
a collision could be avoided, the second ship was struck by several
more missiles. The corvette's command tower and bow section
erupted into a flash of explosions. A collision was now unavoidable,
the jagged bow raked into the starboard side, tearing a long gash
along its main bulkheads. Hopelessly tangled, both ships dropped
back, spinning downward toward the upper atmosphere of Carolon.

"Lieutenant Starman," Dakota said. "Standby to alter your
course."

"That's how it's done," Doran whispered gleefully, passing Lynette
a glance. She held a fist up and Doran immediately gave it a
triumphant bump, then focused on his next target.

"Two of those destroyers just sent a couple of torpedoes at us,"
Lana announced, pointing at several objects in red on the tracking
displays. Dakota passed a look at BachTL.

"Are they tracking us?"

"Affirmative."

"Two-dimensional thinking," Dakota smirked confidently.

"Helm, I'm tired of this turn."

"Aye, Sir." Lynette acknowledged.

"Get us back to the other side of Carolon as fast as you can get her
to go."

"Mind if I take a little short cut, Sir?"

"I'm counting on it. I'd say right between those two destroyers."

Lynette checked her tracking returns and pushed her throttles
forward, bringing the *Constellation* out of its long turn and headed
straight at two of the Albion destroyers.

"Boy, you guys aren't scared of anything, are you?" BachTL asked,
taking a bit of a gulp. Dakota gave BachTL another glance.

"You better get those safety locks down into position. This could
get a little rough." Dakota reached over and tapped a button on the
command chair and the safety locks slapped down over BachTL's
thighs. The Castellian looked around the bridge, taking note that
everyone else already had their locks in place. *Wonder when I missed
that order.*

"Lieutenant Cartwright," Dakota said looking at the readouts on the
fast approaching Albion Destroyers. "Arm forward torpedo pod A-1
and aft torpedo pod G-1."

Everything on the bridge seemed to go quiet. The Mark Vs had never been fired from a Starbird before. General Niker was the only officer in their ranks that had ever seen a demonstration of the Mark Vs destructive power and he was hesitant to ever use it, advising Colonel Conrad to do the same. It was to be used only in extreme circumstances.

"I need a target, Sir," Doran stuttered.

"Program the forward torpedo with a deck penetrating delayed trigger. Give it their energy source as its target. Launch only one at a time on my order."

"Aye, Sir." The weapons officer glanced at Lynette, his expression surging with uncertainty. He went to work, arming the torpedoes and making sure they were properly programed. After finishing, he sat for a moment, contemplating. He finally turned and faced Captain Abrams.

"Torpedoes armed and ready for launch, Sir."

"Good enough, Lieutenant, stand by."

"Sir, permission to speak freely?"

Dakota turned, faced the weapons officer and nodded.

"I'm concerned about setting one of these off with us still in such close proximity. No one on this ship has ever witnessed a demonstration of the Mark V. We have no idea what its really capable of."

"I assume you've read the specs of all the weapons at your command?" Dakota asked.

"Recreational reading, Sir," Doran snapped, sounding a little indignant.

"Then you know what it will do and I'm trusting on your expertise as weapons officer to put that ordnance exactly where I tell you to put it."

"Yes, Sir. I'm just concerned about the damage path these things are going to cause."

"They're going to cause a big mess and make the Albions think thrice about coming after us. It's either us, or them."

"Aye, Sir." Doran turned back to his consoles and made himself ready.

"Untested weapons?" BachTL echoed, now wishing he were still in his cell on Aster.

Dakota considered for a moment, but only that. These would require testing sooner or later. With four Albion Destroyers bearing down on them, he couldn't think of a better time.

"Destroyers in ten seconds," Lynette announced. She gave her tracking screens another glance. So far, the Albion torpedoes were faster than they were, but that condition was by design.

As the ship began taking fire, the hull jolted violently. Dakota gave the shield readouts a hard look, then turned his gaze out toward the two destroyers looming ahead of them. He looked at the upper decks of the Albion ships, taking note of the command towers of each destroyer. He glanced back at the tracking displays and the two torpedoes coming up from behind.

"Lieutenant Starman, what do you say we have a closer look at those command towers? Any chance you could do a circle around them?"

"Aye, Sir," the Starbird pilot agreed without hesitation. Griping the controls, Lynette gently pulled back on the yoke amid a constant barrage of gun fire hailing against the *Constellation's* energy shields. Keeping an eye on their tracking returns, everyone watched as the upper decks of the giant destroyers became visible. As the Starbird passed between the two ships, even BachTL was taken aback at the size difference and the fact they were on the offensive here. Lynette pulled back harder on the control yoke and leaned the ship to the left, toward the command towers. It seemed the destroyer had ordered its entire compliment of gun emplacements to fire on the relatively small Assault Corsair. Several shots landed against the *Constellation's* energy shield, nearly knocking the ship off its flightpath. As Lynette brought the ship into a steep turn around the back side of the first destroyer, Dakota couldn't help but wonder if this wasn't what it had been like for the *Athena* blasting through the Ratronian fleet on his way back to find Colonels Conrad and Barker. He passed a glance at the tracking returns, then looked up watching the two Albion torpedoes splitting their trajectories, trying to follow the tight maneuvers of the *Constellation*.

Holding her course, Lynette leveled out, heading directly at the command towers of the second destroyer. Still nervous, Dakota waited as the ship streaked from the first structure toward the second. He looked back at the returns, seeing the torpedoes making a tight arc, trying to reacquire their assigned target. Lynette pulled back on the throttles, giving the torpedoes a chance to catch up. Turning the ship into another steep turn around the back side of the second set of command towers, she checked her timing. The torpedoes wobbled in their flightpath, dodging the super structures of the first destroyer and streaking towards them as the *Constellation* came out from behind the command towers and started to level out, moving past the big Albion ships toward their rear. Watching the inbound torpedoes converge on them, at the last moment, she shoved the throttles all the way forward and pulled up. Unable to follow, both torpedoes slammed into the command towers. One torpedo exploded instantly, while the second was thrown clear of the blast, but in trying to reacquire its target, its momentum carried it down into the lower decks of the super structure where it bounced along the side surface of the hull and finally exploded.

Lynette focused on vacating the area as hastily as possible. Taking notice of several fighters still keeping up with them at a lower altitude, she pushed the throttles to the stops, heading into a higher orbit. She looked at the tracking screen. Several more torpedoes had been launched, but they were rapidly falling back.

"That was impressive," BachTL said from the command seat. He was trying to figure out how to unlock the safety locks holding him down.

"Well, not exactly what I had in mind," Dakota said standing up. "But I think we got our point across. Well done, Lieutenant Starman. Lieutenant Nevall, please remind Captain Dalley to keep up the good work with those fighters and be ready to redock when we're outbound."

"Aye, Sir."

Dakota reached down and touched the control for the safety lock release on the command chair. BachTL stood up, looking back down at the control and wondering why he hadn't tried that.

"ETA to Bravo team pickup point?" he asked, moving forward next to helm control.

"Five minutes," Lynette answered, still vigilant.

"What's behind us?" Dakota asked.

"A couple of torpedoes. What's left of those destroyers and corvettes are falling back now," Lana informed them. "But I'm getting a reading on another ship, Sir."

Dakota and BachTL turned back to the tracking displays as the image of another Albion destroyer was displayed on the dimensional readouts.

"Where did they come from?" Dakota bolted back to sensor control, BachTL right next to him.

"Judging by the direction its coming from, I'd say the southern pole," Lana surmised.

"Why didn't we detect it when we approached?" Dakota studied the readouts carefully.

"They must have come in after the first four, just as a contingency," BachTL offered.

"Any other surprises up their sleeves?" Dakota looked back at BachTL, who only shrugged. "This is starting to get a little too complicated for my comfort level. Lieutenant Starman, we gonna make it?"

"Skin of our teeth, Sir," the helmsman answered after a quick look at her displays.

"I've got com with Bravo team," Lana announced. "They report mission successful, but their location is hot. They need immediate pickup."

"Have the teleporter room standing by to grab them on Lieutenant Starman's signal." Dakota looked forward. "We're only going to get one chance at this, Helm."

"One is all we're going to need," the Starbird pilot responded quietly.

"More fighters coming from that destroyer," Lana announced, bringing Dakota's attention back to the tracking screens.

"This is getting more exciting by the second," Dakota mumbled, bringing up the dimensional on the new craft.

"Black Tigers," BachTL affirmed grimly.

Dakota frowned. Captain Dalley had his hands full of Starhoppers, holding a parallel course in a lower orbit. It would be impossible, even for him to intercept and hold both Albion fighters at bay. Dakota had the urge to leave the bridge and launch Interceptor one, but then remembered the Colonel already had it. Together, he and Captain Dalley could have made short work of those fighters.

"Torpedoes," Lana said, pointing at the tracking displays.

"Lieutenant Cartwright, pin missiles. Take out any torpedoes that come at us."

"Our Mark Vs are still armed and ready for launch," the weapons officer reminded Captain Abrams.

"Not ready for those yet." Dakota sounded a bit flustered. He closed his eyes and took a deep breath. An image of him at the controls of his Tempest flashed to mind. He was about to wing over into a large squadron of Valkyrie fighters with only Captain Dalley on his wing. He recalled they were hopelessly outnumbered, but they dove in on them anyway. The thought of being beaten or destroyed hadn't even occurred to either of them when they did it and they succeeded in breaking up the entire squadron before they were forced to make a run for it as they were out of ammunition and running low on power reserves. He smiled confidently and stood up straight. *Action is what I'm all about.*

"Those fighters are going to make it to us head on," Lana announced.

"Lieutenants Cartwright and Hunter, make 'em pay for it."

"Starting our descent to the pickup point," Lynette said pushing her controls forward.

"How come you have to go down into the atmosphere to teleport your people back up?" BachTL asked. He watched the Albion destroyer shift its flight path to try and intercept the smaller Kalamarion vessel.

"This engagement has become a bit more complicated than I'm comfortable with, so I'm not leaving anything to chance. I want to make sure we get a proper lock on them. Better to come in right over the top of them and pick them up. Less chance of a mistake..." Dakota's voice dropped off, his eyes fixating on the scanning equipment.

"Mistake?" BachTL repeated. "You've had mistakes with this equipment?"

"Sometimes, it's all technical..." Dakota tapped the glass in front of him. "Lieutenant, can you identify what this is?" He pointed at a return moving towards Carolon from the system edge.

BachTL stepped next to Dakota and looked at the small return moving away from a cluster of ships that had gathered on the edge of the Nulark system.

"It's about the same size as us, Sir. Take just a second or two to get a better look."

The ride became rough as they descended through the atmosphere of Carolon with several Black Tigers and Starhoppers tailing them. Lynette deepened her dive but held her throttles in place as the *Constellation* screamed through the cloud layers toward the surface.

"Dimensional coming in now, Sir," Lana announced, shifting her attention to the display Captain Abrams and BachTL were looking at.

"Lieutenant Nevall..." Dakota trailed off, not believing what was being displayed.

"Working on trying to raise her now, Sir," the com officer said, sliding back to her controls.

"Hey," BachTL said looking at the picture. "Is that...?"

"The *Athena*," Dakota whispered.

"Isn't that your other ship? I thought it was destroyed by the *Tarzana*?"

"Almost destroyed. I was starting to wonder if the General was ever going to find her. Let's get our people picked up while we check in with the general. Then we can really *whoop some smack* on these guys." Dakota looked over at the com officer. She was shaking her head and sliding back between the two stations.

"More fighters," Lana spoke up. Dakota and BachTL turned forward as a squadron of Albion fighters swung up to meet them.

The ship buffeted as it was set upon by a swarm of Black Tigers. The first attack was over in an instant, but the destruction to the fighters took longer. The moment they passed, several were obliterated and several more were damaged. Even as they turned to catch the Assault Corsair, the powerful turret cannons blew them apart; one after another. Even with the accuracy of the turret canon, there were too many of the dark wing shaped fighters for one turret to handle effectively and as they began to swarm the ship, the rear shields started taking heavy hits. Doran took his shots with the rear guns at every opportunity, but as soon as one fighter disintegrated, another was right there to take its place. Even as they plunged into Carolon's atmosphere, the Starbird was being overwhelmed until a brilliant barrage of powerful gunfire tore into the Tiger's ranks, nearly obliterating half of what was left of the squadron. Interceptor two blitzed across the brow of the Albion squadron with a line of

Starhoppers hot in its wake. Several of the remaining Starhoppers burst into crumbled junk as the *Constellation's* turret swung in a wide arc across the aft section, its twin canons blazing. The Tigers scattered, fearing they were being set upon by superior numbers as the Starbird dropped away, down into the dusty sky of Carolon. A few followed, but had fallen so far back they were no longer a factor. The others, milled about in the upper atmosphere, trying to engage superior numbers they couldn't locate.

*   *   *   *

Pip heard the roar of engines overhead and opened his eyes. His face hurt where he had been struck, but his wits came back to him quickly. He felt a hard kick to his backside and jerked up into a sitting position next to Tiana. A rifle barrel appeared in his face and looking at the other three with him, surmised that he needed to put his hands on his head.

"Are you all right?" Tiana asked quietly.

"I'm fine," Pip groaned. "Everyone else ok?"

Nigel and Alder nodded as they looked around at the growing numbers of Albion troopers milling around the immediate area. There were various military vehicles, but nothing large. Several small scout craft buzzed overhead, some circling, while others maneuvered over the ruins of the Carolon base.

"Ok, boys and girls," a small trooper gruffed, approaching the group. "My name is Major Tickan. Ask my squad here and they'll gladly inform you that I'm the orneriest SOB in this military." The Major paused and looked at all four of them, waiting. "Well?"

"Well what?" Pip asked. His response was met with the Major's backhand.

"Who told you to open your smart mouth?"

Pip sat back up wiping the blood from the corner of his mouth. He looked up at the Major.

"I've been on this rock for over six months without any kind of leave to my version of paradise, so you'll have to excuse me if I seem a little… 'tense'." The Major gritted his teeth as he looked Alder over, then caught a good look at the other female. "Well, well, well. What have we here?" He stopped at Tiana. "Now, you're my version of paradise. Let's have a good look at ya," he said, motioning to a couple of his troops. Tiana was brought to her feet, with the Major stepping around her, letting his gaze settle on her figure. "Take the pack off," he ordered.

Tiana hesitated, looking back at Alder, then peeled the straps from her shoulders and let the bundle drop. Everyone heard a heavy rattling coming from the pack as it rolled several times. Major Tickan raised an eyebrow and knelt next to the pack, looking back up at his four prisoners. He cautiously opened the pack, pulled out a beat-up metal box and shook it.

"What are you guys up to? Collecting junk?" He opened the clasp and looked inside. "Rocks? You're collecting rocks?" He pointed to their equipment. "You do know this is a restricted area and you seem to be carrying a lot of hardware that a science team looking for rocks wouldn't have? I've got a bunch of enemy ships sneaking around this worthless planet and now a group of wet behind the ears, egg farmers are down here trying to stir up trouble down here with the Quid. How many more of you are there?"

"Wouldn't you like to know," Nigel smirked quietly, looking over at Alder.

"You've got some explaining to do. So, who's telling the first lie?" Major Tickan asked spilling the Asium and tossing the box. He picked up one of their rifles and turned on the proximity scanner, then turned to Alder.

"I doubt you'd believe the truth," she said looking up at him.

"That's why I'm giving you the opportunity to tell the first lie, then we can get to the truth."

Pip's wrist com came alive with a sudden burst of chatter, bringing Major Tickan back.

"I knew there were more of you guys here. This is a treat. Why don't you check in with your buddies and we'll all get to know everyone?"

Pip's eyes widened. He slowly raised his wrist to his mouth, but the major warned him.

"Careful, guns with safeties turned off will get to you before your friends can."

Pip nodded deliberately and looked at the others, then raised the com back up.

"Bravo team confirms, ready. Come on down."

Major Tickan smiled confidently and looked around at his men and machines. Having the whole bunch of whoever these people were that weren't supposed to be here, would certainly get him transferred off this lonely rock.

"So, what's so interesting about these rocks?" he asked, pushing them around in the dirt in front of Tiana.

Tiana carefully bent down and picked several of the white opaque stones from the loose dirt.

"Well, if you hold them all just right, they make a really funny sound and things start to disappear." Tiana heard a sonic boom overhead and the sound of a missile approaching. Major Tickan and his men looked up, trying to find the source of the boom.

"Why don't you give us all a demonstration, little lady," he suggested with a lustful grin.

Tiana smiled and handed the rocks she had scooped up to Nigel, then picked up the rest.

"It's quite simple. I have an arm full and my friend here has an arm full. If we stand in just the right spot," she said moving a little closer to the Starbird navigator, "and wait for just the right moment…" Alder and Pip glanced up as the *Constellation* streaked into view from across the southern plateau.

*   *   *   *

"Bravo team is in position," Lana said, working the scanning equipment. She looked harder at the displays, not sure what she was seeing. "Sir, you're going to want to have a look at this."

"What?" Dakota asked, leaning down and giving the display a double take. "Are they having a party down there?"

BachTL leaned in closer, his eyes widening.

"It's an Albion garrison patrol. I'm sorry, but it looks like they got to them before we did."

Dakota shook his head, noticing the pattern of the transponder signals coming from three of his crew. A fourth was in the correct place.

"Lieutenant Cartwright, you have control of the teleporter."

"Aye, Sir."

"Wait," BachTL started, perplexed. "You're going to try to bring them back up anyway?"

"Sure, why not?"

"Don't you have to stop or something?"

"We didn't stop when we teleported them down, why would we now?"

"What about that garrison?"

"What about it? Let them find their own ride out." Dakota turned back to helm control to watch the operation unfold as they leveled out, soaring across the dusty surface of Carolon toward the wrecked base.

*   *   *   *

"You guys weren't kidding," Lana burst from Pip's com. There came a funny sound surrounding the four and a shaft of color. Major Tickan looked back at Tiana, who smiled teasingly, and waved a hand at him.

"Bye, podbrain," she said as all four of them disappeared at the same instant the Kalamarion Corsair blitzed directly overhead and arched skyward. Moments later, several fighters and two Albion Corvettes appeared, trying to match the alien craft's ascent. Before anyone could sight in on the alien ship, it was already above the thin Carolon cloud layer and out of range.

Major Tickan looked around for anything else that might be out of the ordinary, but found nothing but the bent-up metal box the Asium stones had been in. In his frustration, he could only give the box a hard kick and motion for his men to head back to their base on the other side of the wrecked Carolon outpost.

*   *   *   *

"We have them," Doran announced, giving Captain Abrams a thumbs up.

Momentarily relieved, Dakota backed up and sat down in the command chair, a smile forming on his lips until he gave the tracking displays a look.

"Helm, let's see if we can do one more fancy dance and meet up with the *Athena*."

"Already on our way up and out," the Starbird pilot said as the nose of the ship tilted hard skyward. They were buffeted several times as a few Black Tigers passed by them firing, but they were left far behind as the *Constellation* climbed higher into the outer atmosphere of Carolon. As the dusty skies began to fade into the blackness of space, the bridge door snapped open and Mr. Pippin, Lieutenant Nigel Kramer, and Tiana hurried in.

"I look forward to hearing all about your adventures," Dakota said smiling. "Just as soon as we're back onboard the *Realistic* and running at Quadra-light for Aster."

"You guys are a mess," BachTL observed, looking at the soiled attire and smudged faces. "I take it, an Albion garrison had some questions..."

"And we gave them answers," Tiana responded, exhausted.

"Mister Moon has the Asium, Sir," Pippin reported taking his place at his station.

"Well done, people," Dakota said. "I'll see that you're all given commendations. Now let's see if we can get out of here as easily as we got in."

Au Pair

Gunnar chose a reentry point a little more hospitable than the first time he had come to the dark, dismal planet of Reako. Unlike the blind landing of their previous encounter, Gunnar was quickly able to locate the entrance to the water tube. Once down and traveling through the correct tube, he set his auto controls and turned in his seat while Janox was just turning Alex 7001 back on. Gunnar was correct; angry droid.

"I will know the person responsible for shutting me down unexpectantly!" Alex could only raise his voice volume and color his panel lights red to express his displeasure. Right now, he was quite colorful and loud.

"Chillax, Droid," Gunnar sniped, instantly ramping up.

"Colonel, there is a right way and a wrong way to perform certain tasks. Doing things the wrong way can cause damage where none was intended. You, of all people, understand that."

"You seem to be operating just fine."

"Only because of the nature of my circuit design."

"Then why are you complaining?"

"Because it's wrong and I don't like it. You've been asked many times not to do it."

"I did it," Janox cut in.

Alex turned his head. His panel lights instantly dimmed.

"Why would you shut me down without my permission?" His volume had dropped as well.

"I need your help."

"I don't understand. Why not just ask?"

"Because..."

"It's a kidnapping, Alex," Gunnar announced sounding annoyed.

"Kidnapping?" Alex became airborne, scanning the view outside and looking at the readouts on the instruments. He spun around and faced Gunnar. "Colonel, this is a joke."

Gunnar just shook his head. Alex turned to Janox, then back at Gunnar, then looked back out the cockpit window.

"Did we learn nothing from our last encounter here?"

"Janox insisted we return to learn something new. She wants us to find Tonnie."

"No offence, but aren't you the one in command? Don't you decide where we go and when?"

"She stunned me, Alex."

"You probably deserved it," Alex shot back.

"Hey, it hurt," Gunnar growled, rubbing his shoulder.

"I fail to understand why you need me to come along on this kidnapping?" Alex asked turning back to Janox. "If Tonnie is hurt or lost, then the ship's new MedTech or the good Doctor herself and one of the Interceptor pilots would be better suited to accompany you."

"You and Gunnar will help," Janox insisted.

"And if I refuse?" Alex retorted.

"She'll stun you too," Gunnar scowled. "Trust me, it hurts bad."

Alex looked at Janox who was clutching the holstered pistol, then looked back at Gunnar.

"Doesn't your Dialabron physiology make it so you can take more punishment than a droid?" Alex asked.

"It still hurts," Gunnar flared. "You're stuck, Droid. Might as well make the most of it. The sooner we find Tonnie, the sooner we can get back to the ship. It appears we have better conditions this time around. We know where we're going and we're in a ship that isn't about to fall apart, and it's not going to take us forever to get back down into the caverns," Gunnar said checking the readouts. "Can you tell me which direction we need to go once we arrive?"

"Home not far from Binion caves. Much higher than cave. We land on top. You see when get there. There tunnels to home from top."

"A split level, sounds nice," Gunnar said. "How hard will it be to get to Tonnie?"

"Tonnie very near. She fall getting water. Hole deep, very full of water. It very dark."

"Still not sure what we can do," Alex complained.

"And you're sure the Binions can't get to your house and this water well?" Gunnar asked, noticing the exterior start to brighten. He turned and touched a couple of controls in front of him.

"No, Binions move fast, but no climb rocks good."

"Oh, yes," Gunnar said, taking hold of the yoke control. "Eight minutes beats eight hours any day." He grabbed the throttle controls and slowed his craft while pulling briskly back on the yoke. The big fighter nosed up at the same moment it burst through the surface tension of the water and glided gracefully over the enormous canyon far below.

"Alex, were you ever able to figure out how this water stays up on the ceiling and in the tubes? This is the strangest thing I've ever seen."

"No, Colonel. When last we were here, I did not have the time to examine the hydraulic pressure dynamics at work. Someone had me working on a Colonian fighter craft that could only speak in a confused mass of binary gibberish."

"Tell us how you really feel, Alex."

"Isn't fixing ships what Alex for?" Janox asked, pointing at a cliff out cropping up the canyon a ways.

"Certainly I am not," Alex retorted indignant, his voice elevating.

"Now you've done it," Gunnar scoffed, steering toward a large level area above the outcropping. "That's the second time you've ticked him off in the same hour."

"Not understand," Janox responded, looking curiously at the little white droid.

"I designed the Starbird Assault Corsair," the little droid announced indignantly.

"Careful there, Spanky," Gunnar cautioned, making a wide circle over the flat area below them. "Don't take more credit than you're responsible for."

"I designed many of the systems found onboard the *Constellation* and the other Corsairs in the Starbird fleet."

"But you didn't design them all and many of the ones you did design were the brainchild of General Niker."

"My apologies," Alex toned down. "My twin, Felix 7000 and the General assisted in the designs and construction management of the Starbird project."

"I like how you use the term, 'assisted'," Gunnar said, activating the landing gear and bringing the Interceptor into a hover over a suitable spot.

"Alex, very smart for helping design Starbird. Janox proud to be friends with such smart Alex."

"Careful not to spread that goo on too thick," Gunnar jeered.

"At least someone appreciates what I do," the little droid commented. "Her vocabulary really has improved."

"Now see why Alex friend must come with Janox to find Tonnie? He smart to help Tonnie."

"Wow..." Gunnar muttered sarcastically.

The little droid fell silent, staring at Janox until the fighter settled to the ground and Gunnar shut everything down.

"Ok, you've got the gun. Where to now?"

Janox handed the pistol and holster to Gunnar and crawled down to the hatch.

"You work gun better than me, you go out first."

"Now, you're sounding like a little droid I know," Gunnar said working the mechanism.

"No, I not know how to work door."

"That makes a good excuse." Gunnar dropped down the hatch opening and looked around. Moments later, Janox and Alex were beside him scanning their surroundings. "You're sure the Binions can't get up here?"

"No Binions, but always good to make sure nothing else up here."

"Alex, you getting anything?" Gunnar asked.

"There are a myriad of indigenous life forms all around us. Most of them are quadrupeds, but my sensors are picking up some subterranean life forms of various sizes. Hard to pinpoint anything down here; something in the rock strata is making it difficult to see any detail."

"Anything else?"

"There are what appears to be some flying life forms roosting in the cliffs on the other side of the canyon. But they don't look like they are want to leave their perch."

"Tonnie call them, air-claws," Janox announced wearily. She walked cautiously to the edge of the cliffs and looked out across the wide expanse.

"Air-claws?" Gunnar asked. "Not sure I want to know why."

"If we make not much noise, we be fine."

"You know this from firsthand experience?"

"Yes, have been taken several times when much younger. I see them take Binions, fly high and drop them to kill. Then take to cliffs and eat."

"Good thing they don't eat metal," Alex said floating next to Janox.

"They try take Tonnie several times too," Janox said looking at Alex. "You very small. No problem for them to take you. Alex be much careful."

The little droid spun his head, looking all around to make sure nothing could catch him unaware.

"Perhaps I should remain onboard the Interceptor," Alex hedged.

"You did that on purpose," Gunnar accused Janox. He turned back to Alex. "Stay put tenderfoot. We'll take care of this. Janox, lead the way."

"We go," she said pointing to a lump of rock toward the upper canyon wall. She worked a makeshift mechanism to a wooden door and stepped through. Gunnar didn't even get turned back to the Interceptor before Alex came flying past him into the dwelling. Once everyone was inside, Janox secured the door behind them and reached for a torch. Alex already had his headlamps on and moving forward. A short distance into the rock, the passage opened into a spacious living area that was well maintained. While the basic surroundings were still rock formations, it had been dressed up with various things to make it look homey and quite comfortable. Gunnar noticed two private living spaces, not much larger than a person could fit, located on opposites sides of the dwelling. The ceiling was at a standard living height with several crude light fixtures hanging in different areas. Janox moved to each one, lighting their sources until the room was well lit.

"This is my home," Janox presented, turning to Gunnar and Alex. "Not on other planet, or in space on ship. This is home."

Gunnar continued to gaze all around the room, taking notice of a couple of small manmade items in a corner next to a large metallic box with cords hanging from it. Stepping closer, he glanced at Alex, who was drawn to the box as well.

"Those belong to Tonnie."

"It's a power generator," Gunnar recognized.

"Still operational," Alex said, scanning it. "It has a power core similar to our Seezeum cores. Indefinite power source."

"But why would Tonnie need something like this?" Gunnar asked. "Unless it's to provide power for lights and appliances. But shouldn't it be hooked to something?"

Alex had no answers.

"This way," Janox said, motioning for them to follow her down a darkened passage. "Water well not far."

"Did you guys build this place all on your own?" Gunnar asked looking at the walls a little closer. Most of the living space appeared to be formed naturally, but some looked as though it had been hewn with drilling lasers.

"It is my home. It is as I have always known. I know no other place."

Gunnar held back at the summons of Alex 7001.

"Colonel, the cables on this generator haven't been used in a long time."

"How can you tell?"

"There is a considerable amount of oxidation built up on the contacts and the internal circuitry."

"Can you tell what it would have been used for?"

"I do not recognize the socket attachment. It is possible it could have been for a droid, but I have seen so few examples since we have been here, I have nothing to compare it to."

"You saw those Vivitars blow the doors out at Diord's place on Cross."

"I didn't see a whole lot of anything after I was struck. What I am trying to say is, I have no basis from which to draw any kind of conclusion."

"Are you two coming?" Janox called up the passage.

"Right with you," Gunnar called back as he turned and ducked down the passage with Alex right behind him. Presently, they caught up with Janox standing next to a circular hole in the wall. At its base, a glassy stream of water poured out and followed the contours of the passage down into the blackness of the rock tunnel. After mounting her torch inside the hole, Janox pulled her head out and pointed inside.

"Tonnie fall here."

Gunnar poked his head into the large hole and looked down. The water was glassy smooth and so clear you almost couldn't tell it was there. Even as clear as it was, he couldn't see the bottom of the shaft. Examining the ceiling, he pulled himself back out.

"Alex, come in here and have a look see with your lights."

Alex hesitated; looked at Janox, then back at Gunnar. Finally, he proceeded to the hole, floated through and hovering just above the surface of the water. Pointing his lights down, he turned them up to full intensity.

"What do you think?" Gunnar asked, poking his head back inside and looking into the abyss.

"It is a very deep hole, Colonel."

"Your brilliance is astonishing," Gunnar mumbled.

"I cannot read the depth of this shaft. It runs far too deep and the water has something in it that's interfering with my sensors."

"Janox, is this the same kind of water that was in the cave you found me in?"

"Yes, same water, but much colder. Very cold, very clean, very clear, very good for you. Very bad for Alex. Make sure he do not get wet."

"And Tonnie fell in here?"

"Yes."

"Are you sure she fell?"

"Yes, saw her fall."

"Are you sure she didn't fall in and then climb back out when you weren't looking?"

"That question not make sense to me," Janox answered, puzzled. "Why Tonnie climb back out and disappear?"

"True enough," Gunnar said nodding.

"Colonel," Alex called. "If I may. I am detecting something at the extreme range of my sensors in this shaft. Something abnormal appears to be attached to the wall down there. It does not show any of the same characteristics of the surrounding rock formations."

"Human remains maybe?" Gunnar suggested quietly.

"Impossible to say. We would need to extend my sensor range or somehow get down there to look at it firsthand."

"I try to swim down to find Tonnie," Janox said. "But it too deep; too cold. I sleep for whole day afterwards."

"If it's too deep down there, then we're looking at a body; Tonnie drowned. If that truly is her down there, then we're likely detecting her bones. I'm sorry, Janox, but I think we've proved pretty conclusively that Tonnie died a long time ago. There is nothing more we can do here."

Gunnar shifted how he was standing to allow Alex to come back out of the hole, but in doing so, slipped on the wet rock beneath his feet and fell sideways into the well, inadvertently taking Alex down with him. The frigid water bit at him as he struggled to right himself. Opening his eyes, he saw Alex sinking below him. The little droid had trac motovacs and articulating arms with artificial gravity cathodes located in various places around his case. He had no thrusters of any kind as his design parameters didn't call for such things. Now there was nothing to keep him from sinking, except his anti-grav system, but clearly something wasn't working as it should.

Gunnar dove hard, reaching for the still illuminated lights turning up as the droid's decent increased in velocity. Kicking hard, he reached again and caught hold of one of Alex's antenna. He tried to turn back up, but even with his strength, unless he had something to exert energy against, he was just as helpless as any human. Gunnar found himself struggling harder to find something on the wall to grab hold of while still holding his breath. Running out of air, he looked up and reached for something stabbing down at him. A small but strong hand grabbed him and pulled him to the surface. Breaching into the air, Gunnar gasped violently and pulled Alex from the water. Janox promptly reached over Gunnar and pulled the little droid out and over the edge of the hole, letting him tumble to the floor while she pulled Gunnar out as well.

"Alex," Gunnar gasped, trying to get his breathe. Shivering violently, Gunnar flopped out onto the slippery tunnel floor and rolled over, looking at Alex as the little white droid worked to right himself using his motovacs and arms. "Alex, are you all right?"

"Unknown at this time, Colonel."

"How can water be that cold and not be frozen?" Gunnar continued to gasp uncontrollably as he rolled over onto his hands and knees. "Janox, that water wasn't this cold in the Binion cave."

"Of course not," she responded. "Remember? It not come from same place."

"And it's the same kind you had me bathing in?"

"Yes, very good for you, especially if hurt."

"Yeah, but very bad for anything metal or electronic."

"Yes, very bad."

"Alex, your internal sensors?"

"Still running a full diagnostic now, Colonel. However, I am not detecting any moisture intrusion on my internal structure."

"How long will a full diagnostics take?"

"Almost finished now, Sir."

"Gunnar, need get you dried off and warm," Janox said helping him to his feet.

"Incredible," Gunnar shivered uncontrollably. "I've done suitless deep space drills many times in my career, but I've never lost body heat like this before."

"What in water, make lose heat fast," Janox said as they made their way back up into her living place.

After Gunnar had stripped down, Janox threw several coats of fur over him as he plopped down on a fur covered bed. Turning to a dark fireplace, the young woman began working to get a fire going. Gunnar rolled over in time to see Alex rolling back into the room and coming to a halt next to the bed.

"I am unharmed internally, Colonel," he announced.

"That's good news," Gunnar shivered.

"However, my exterior has sustained substantial damage."

"How so?" Gunnar asked trying to sit up. He was promptly pushed back down by Janox, who went right back to making the fire.

"All of my external sensor probes and anti-grav cathodes are completely burnt out. My transmission antennas are still functional. I can reroute my sensor logics to the antennas, but my range will be greatly diminished. Nothing I can do about my anti-grav. The cathodes are a special corrilium alloy. There are replacement parts on the ship, but we're down here and..."

"It's on its way to Carolon. I get it, Alex. You're on your tracs until we get back. I'll try to remember that."

"You two stay here," Janox said backing away from the fire she had built. She turned and grabbed a homemade bow and quiver of arrows. "I get some food. Be back quick." Janox was gone before either of them could object. Gunnar was grateful for the fire and the warmth it provided. As it was producing more heat than his body was, he opened the furs a bit to let in the heat. Alex moved a little closer.

"Colonel, may I ask you some personal questions?"

"Personal questions, Alex? Why would you possibly need to ask for personal information at a time like this?"

"I've been trying to ascertain your disposition ever since we came to this galaxy."

"My disposition?"

"Yes. I'm trying to understand human emotion more fully."

"Is that possible?"

"General Niker designed my artificial intelligence parameters to learn all there is to learn so Felix 7000 and I could more fully integrate and have empathy for humans and their struggles."

"But you understand you can never achieve that state, right? You'll never know what it's like to feel emotion."

"While that may be true, my programing requires I continue to try."

Gunnar looked at Alex for a long moment. He turned and looked at the fire, enjoying its heat as he gradually gained control of his faculties and the shivers began to fade.

"Ask your questions, Alex."

"With the permission of Doctor Yamoto, I have accessed your medical history and current files."

"Not sure how I feel about that. I might have to have a little talk with the good doctor when we get back."

"I am under strict orders not to divulge any information to anyone other than the doctor and you."

"I feel so much better. Go on..."

"Are you able to describe what you were feeling when Lieutenant Commander Atlanta passed away?"

Gunnar sucked in a deep breath.

"Wow, that certainly is personal."

"If you are uncomfortable, I can retract the question."

"Alex, you can't just retract a question like that!"

"Why not?"

Gunnar rolled back on his back, watching the light from the flames flicker on the ceiling making for uneven shadows dancing all around.

"You become physically sick. In my case, both my hearts began to beat irregular, to the point of it being painful."

"Physically pumping against the other."

"Yes, then comes the feeling of someone pulling parts of your organs from you while you're conscious."

"Have you ever experienced such an operation?"

"Certainly not!"

"Then how...?"

"It's a metaphor, Alex! A way to describe what's happening inside. I imagine what it would be like in order to describe what the pain would be like."

"I understand."

"Then there is the mental anguish of knowing I will not see her again, not be with her again in this life."

"It seems illogical to me that humans would voluntarily engage in lifelong relationships knowing they face a painful separation at an arbitrary point in their life span."

"I suppose there is some truth to that and if you believe that humans just fade away into nothing when they die, it would certainly support such a notion."

"But you don't believe that," Alex said after a moment of processing. "You believe in a Deity."

"Yes I do," Gunnar replied. "Otherwise, what's the point of any of this that's happening to us now? Whether it be here in this galaxy, solar system or here inside this planet; what's the point to it all? I just can't believe that everything Audra was to me, everything we shared together is meaningless now; that we'll never be together again. To me, there is no logic to existence if there isn't something that comes afterwards. If we don't live on or move to another plane of existence, then why exist at all?"

"Then you feel you will be with Commander Atlanta again?"

"Audra, Alex. You can call her Audra."

"I would not feel comfortable calling a commanding officer by their first name," Alex responded.

"Well, she's not your commanding officer anymore."

Alex fell silent for a minute, not moving.

"Do you understand what is happening inside you, chemically, when you become angry?"

"Sure, happens to every human. Dialabrons aren't any different."

"But you are experiencing something above and beyond what humans have to deal with. I understand from the files I have been able to access, that while Dialabrons already have aggressive tendencies, what you're experiencing isn't even documented."

"No, it wouldn't be. We don't live long enough to ever get this far. It's a wonder my species can even survive with such a high mortality rate."

"Then why would Commander Atlanta... Audra, ever consider forming a lasting relationship with you if she knew you could die at any time?"

"Love, Alex. Because we were in love."

Alex fell silent again for several passing moments, processing.

"What is going on with you now?"

"Just starting to feel warm again," Gunnar said pulling the furs around him.

"No, ever since Colonel Barker and General Niker rescued you from the Albion ship, you haven't been the same. You were fine on Cross, but not after the rescue. Do you know what has happened?"

"That's the frustrating part. I have no idea. The doctor believes the Albions did something, but she can't pin-point it. Frankly, I don't think she's telling me everything." Gunnar thought for a moment, occasionally looking down at a motionless Alex. "Here's some input for you. I'm laying here, and you and I have been having this conversation, and right now, I feel like I want to pick you up and throw you across the room. Or better yet, throw you back down that well. How's that for anger?"

"Why? I have done nothing to offend or annoy."

"That's just it! As a Dialabron, I have to practice self-restraint to keep from becoming angry anyway. Too lose it over nothing, is ridiculous! The amount of energy I expend just to keep from smacking someone for doing something minor is exhausting, and it's only been getting worse. I'm just not this way. I conquered this Dialabron demon a long time ago, even before I met and married Audra, but my ability to control anger, went with Audra when she died."

"It sounds like we need to stop talking about this," Alex suggested.

"Did you have any more questions?" Gunnar asked. There was a certain measure of relief talking about what was happening inside him. If he could just think it out and bring it forward, instead of it always lurking somewhere inside him, trying to lash out at the worst possible moment, he could keep it in check.

"Only one more," Alex said, his volume and inflection lowering. "What is it like when you lose control?"

"It doesn't feel pretty," Gunnar said quietly. "I try to remove myself from anyone before I lose control. I would hate to injure someone. It's like standing beside myself and watching me do things I would never think of doing, but I've got zero control over. Does that make any sense?"

"I think I understand what you're trying to convey, but it will take me some time to properly process this. Thank you for your indulgence on my behalf."

"I'm sure I don't have to tell you to keep this conversation to yourself. I suspect the crew already talks about it when I'm not around."

"They are understandably concerned. Losing Commander... Audra was difficult for everyone. Imagine if they were to lose you."

"Captain Abrams is a very capable officer."

"But he's not Colonel Conrad."

Gunnar stared into the flames, letting the random movement sooth him. As his body temperature gradually returned to normal, he became drowsy and let his eyelids droop closed. As he drifted off, he felt about as comfortable as he had felt in a long time. He wasn't sure it didn't have something to do with the water. It quickly didn't matter.

Regrets

Rick walked in time with Caidin's hurried shuffle as they finally reentered the cavernous engine room and made their way toward the power couplings and the disassembled inducer. His mind was on something completely different. Dãsha's age and their timeline together weren't matching up. He had zero doubts as to Caidin's affections toward the young woman. It was quite obvious. He didn't have any reservations about Dãsha's feelings for Caidin either. There was just something off here, besides the timeline. Rick couldn't put his finger on it, nor did he really have the time to try to figure it out. Besides, was it really any of his business what the feelings were between another man and woman? He had Jayda and his ship to think about and the operation they faced was a means to find her.

Rick stopped at the inducer and watched as Caidin continued to another door. A moment later Dãsha reentered the room wearing a thermal wetsuit. Rick pretended to immerse himself in the inducer's schematics, but watched the two exchange an embrace at the door. A moment later, Dãsha stepped quietly up to Rick.

"Caidin fears greatly for my welfare," she said quietly. "I've tried to reassure him that you know exactly what you're doing and that I will be all right."

"I think it's good he's so worried. Shows how much he really cares about you."

"Do you think there will be any problems you didn't think about earlier?"

"I have little doubt that you can make it to the processing room. I wished I had had your strength when I was your age."

"Do you think you and Caidin can steer *Calypso* as you have indicated?"

"We'll be fine."

"Do you think he will be fine if something were to happen to me?"

"Has anything ever happened to you before?"

"Yes, I have been damaged before. But he has always been able to repair me."

"Damaged? Tell me, Dãsha, why doesn't he fix his leg and scars?"

"He says it reminds him of his mortality. He maintains that it keeps him grounded."

"Why did you agree to go with him?"

"I asked him to take me with him."

"But why have you stayed with him?"

"Where else would I go? There is no means of escape from *Calypso*."

"Do you love him?"

"Deeply. Why do you ask these questions?"

"I don't know," Rick finally said. His suspicions remained unsatisfied. "Couples of your makeup are unusual where I come from."

"You're not used to seeing a young woman with an older man."

"That's one way of putting it."

Dãsha handed Rick a small communicator and headset as she started for the hallway leading to the elevator.

"Make sure you and Caidin are belted in securely. Your proposed maneuvers will tilt the ship in several different directions." She slipped her headset into place and then she was gone.

Rick looked around. He hadn't even thought about having to deal with a fixed antigrav configuration being tilted and turned in differing directions. Thankfully these wouldn't be aggressive maneuvers. Making sure everything was secure in the engine room, he turned and headed for the bridge.

"Dãsha," Caidin's tentative voice came across the communicator as Rick approached the pilot's station.

"I'm in position in a sealed room, just off the main corridor next to the hangar bay access," Dãsha announced.

"General Niker, are you ready for this?" Caidin asked as Rick belted himself into the second pilot's station.

"Just need a crash course on how to work this thing," he said scanning the console in front of him and to his left.

"Basic operation is deceptively simplistic. My controls are for the X axis, yours are for the Y axis. We adjust the Z axis together. Of course, there is a lot more complication available on these controls if you feel the need to tax your thinking. Because *Calypso* is so large, she has retro thrusters or maneuvering thrusters, all over to help her move with precision. Normally a tug would do all the positioning work, but in the absence of a tug, these controls aide the pilots in making the movements as accurate as possible. Just concentrate on this small panel and control stick here. The rest is for propulsion operations. Make sense?"

"Clear as mud," Risk answered studying the controls.

"These little displays here give you a real time pictorial representation of *Calypso's* orientation along a preset plane. We're going to leave her in her rotational axis and use that as our baseline. Ready?"

Rick studied the panel for a moment, making sure he understood how it worked and then nodded.

"Then let's get this done," Caidin said trying to sound positive. "Beginning roll maneuver now."

Rick worked in unison with Caidin as they began the delicate maneuver of the giant ship, positioning it to move the water in the

flooded bays, into other areas of the ship. Items not locked down, started to slide across the floor as the ship rolled on its side.

"Ok, bring the vertical axis over," Caidin instructed, tense.

They listened anxiously as *Calypso* groaned, made several booming sounds deep within the structure accompanied by several episodes of intense vibrations.

"How are you doing down there?" Caidin asked anxiously.

"The noise is incredible," Dãsha yelled. "It feels like it's going to come right through the blast door."

"Halfway through the tilt," Caidin announced.

"We're gonna be hanging upside down before this is over," Rick said, trying to remain aloof of the noises he was hearing from the surrounding bulkheads.

"It's good for blood circulation," Caidin replied.

"Are we sure all the doors to the landing bay were opened up?" Rick asked, becoming a little worried.

"According to the door controls I'm looking at, they are," Caidin said, glancing up at several displays. "Landing and launching bay cameras on your right, above you."

"I guess I should have asked how full the hangar bay was," Rick grunted, looking up and seeing water blasting through the open inner doors into the bays.

"Just a little bit further," Caidin called out.

Rick felt more heavy vibrations from somewhere deep within the ship and detected muffled booming noises. With the water rising in the hangar bays, his concerns that maybe something was obstructing its path to the landing bay grew. Perhaps one of the automatic doors had malfunctioned and hadn't opened properly. Closing his eyes, he cleared his mind and concentrated, his thoughts moving through the turbulent water in the lower parts of the ship and through the flooded hallways toward the landing bay. He passed through, one, two, three doors in the halls, all of them opened all the way. Then he came to several large double doors that opened into the landing bay. The first set was open all the way, as was the second set, but the third was still mostly closed as was the fourth. There were no other doors, at least not on this side of the bay. Zooming in on the controls, he sensed the electronic circuits were working, but the sensors that made the indications for the doors, were not. This would indeed send false readings to Caidin. He focused in closer on the circuits, locating the problem and made a quick tweak to their molecular structures to affect a repair. But fixing the indicators would only send Caidin a message that the doors weren't fully open. He needed to get these doors all the way open or risk flooding the entire engine room. He zoomed into their mechanisms, locating the jammed areas, and started working to reverse the problems until the doors began to operate. Once finished, he moved onto the last door, finding it in the same condition and working to affect the same repair. As he pulled back in his mind, he perceived something in the landing bay. A larger object was pushed up against the far wall of the flooding landing bay. Because of the turbulence of the water, he was unable to get a clear view in his mind, but for a moment, it looked like a scout sized vessel. He finally let it go and blinked, looking at the position readouts in front of him.

"Proceeding to dip the bow," Caidin announced.

"Transient door confirmed closed?" Rick called out, as the ship started to tip forward.

"Transient doors?" Caidin repeated.

"They are the large doors at the top and bottom of the landing bay that connect the hangar bay to the landing bay," Dãsha called out.

"Yes, my dear. Of course I closed those. That would be foolish not to do that."

Rick noticed the groaning of the ship go silent. He glanced up at the overhead displays.   Half of the views were obscured by murky water, while others showed water, once again moving. Indeed, the ship started moaning again as the bow tipped forward. A moment later, Caidin fired the correction thrusters and the groaning abruptly went silent as the ship came to a stop in its new position.

"Dãsha, I think you're clear to go," Rick called into his mic pickup.

"The General is correct, my dear," Caidin confirmed. "The bow maneuver is complete. Please proceed as fast as you can and be careful."

"I will," Dãsha replied. "Are the lights on in the corridors and hangar bay?"

"If any of them are working, they're powered up," Caidin reassured her.

"I'm in the hallway," Dãsha reported. "It's a real mess down here. Really slimy. Amazing what can grow down here without any light. It's gonna be rough trying to get through all this mess with everything tilted all wrong."

"I have no doubt that you will be just fine," Caidin lied unconvincingly. "It goes without saying that you need to be extra careful, but more than that, remain vigilant, my dear. We don't have a clear picture as to what created the flooding in that section of the ship. There are living organisms in these waters that could have found a home down there and may not be very happy about it being drained of water."

"Yes, we've discussed this in great length many times before," Dãsha grunted, working her way along the halls toward the hangar bay.

"I didn't detect any aqua life during my travels to get here," Rick interjected.

"Remember the conversation about recalibrated scanning equipment?" Caidin asked.

"Oh, yeah. So, what are we talking about here? Slimy little worms or swimming bugs? What?"

"Certainly all those things will be present in Acuity's waters," Caidin said. "But you should consider what you might find in an ocean on your own planet. There's no reason to believe Acuity doesn't have everything your world would find in that ocean, probably a little more."

"Gentlemen," Dãsha interrupted. "I am concentrating on getting to the processing room through all this muck. I don't need to hear these things."

"Do you have any lights down there?"

"Yes, for all the good they're doing. Some of these are so covered in gunk, it's a wonder you can see them. I'm in the stairwell to the hangar causeway."

"There she is," Rick burst, pointing at one of the display windows. "She can sure move fast," Rick marveled, watching the tall woman streaking across the causeway and down the dripping stairs.

"Yes, she can," Caidin said tight lipped. He knew every surface down there had to be slippery and one slip could be catastrophic. His heart nearly leapt from his chest when several warning indicators started to blink and make noise.

"Uht-oh, what's that all about?" Rick asked looking toward the source of the noise.

"Drake attack craft inbound," came the automated early warning. Caidin twisted in his position to look at one of the scopes behind him.

"The sensor equipment here at the pilot's station doesn't work very well. There are several primary objects inbound. They should just be Raider ships. I fear they have detected *Calypso's* movement and when they see her sitting in a different configuration, they will call in for something larger and attack with greater ferocity. Dãsha, you must hurry."

"I'm going as fast as I can in these conditions."

"Are you sure they're only Raiders?" Rick asked. "Didn't you say the two that attacked earlier were looking in the ice pack where the *Athena* is? You said they would have to call in for something bigger to get to her."

"I'm trying to get a better reading on what they really are, but the scanners here at the pilot's station are not working well. Perhaps if the processors were up and running I could get a better reading. Dãsha, you must hurry!" Caidin's inflection had changed from worried to alarmed. As Rick watched Caidin work, he felt a faint vibration developing throughout the ship's inner frame, followed by a distant thumping noise that grew more violent.

"I can't see outside," Caidin called, "but those strikes feel like something a lot bigger than a Drake Raider craft. Dãsha, hurry!"

Rick changed several of the camera windows until he found the one to the processing room. As he waited for Dãsha to arrive, a thought came to mind that had been dawging him since he had arrived. Caidin had said the Drake used *Calypso* as target practice; a rite of passage for the younger pilots. *How many younger pilots could there possibly be? And why bother with a shipwreck anyway? It made zero sense.*

"I'm in the processing room," Dãsha announced over the comm. "Sorry, I'm making a mess all over the floor in here."

"I'm sure the equipment doesn't mind," Caidin responded.

"It's been so long since I've been in here, it may take a moment to remember how to get everything back up and running."

"Work as quickly as you can, my dear."

Calypso was unexpectedly rocked by several violent strikes, shaking the entire ship to its core. Rick glanced down at his controls, sensing something wasn't right. The little displays showing *Calypso's* tilt were starting to move off the prescribed numbers. As the entire ship shook viciously, he carefully brought *Calypso* back into the prescribed positioning.

"Target practice my eye," Rick mumbled, trying to refocus on the instruments in front of him. Catastrophic thoughts began to form as he considered what could go wrong. Perhaps the hangar bays were flooded because the doors were broken or there was a hole blown in one or worse; one or more were completely missing. Maneuvering *Calypso* to remove the water may have only been temporary. If that scenario were even half true, they'd have to get the engines up and running quick or risk more flooding that may not be able to be contained.

Scanning the images in front of him had him disconcerted. There was water flowing everywhere and trying to keep track of where it should be and shouldn't be proved impossible. Rick noticed several displays and consoles starting to light up as *Calypso's* systems started coming back online with a myriad of noises and blinking lights.

"Pilot's station exterior sensors are coming back online," Caidin called out. "These are Drake craft all right, but much larger than what we've seen in this part of Acuity."

"But you've seen them before," Rick reiterated.

"Yes, but only when they're after something. These are utility craft. Not very fast, but lots of heavy firepower and tough to damage."

"It's a good bet they're here for the General's ship," Dãsha called out over her headsets, "and whatever else they can find in the ice."

"That was fast," Rick said still working to keep *Calypso* under control. "Thought it would take them a while to figure it out and get something big enough here to do the job."

"Must have been in the area."

"So why the heck are they shooting at us?" Rick asked as the great ship shook again.

"This is a big move for *Calypso*," Caidin said. "With her in a different configuration they get really testy."

"What?" Rick asked completely perplexed. "I'm not buying that load of crap. We're in an XYZ plane of existence. Whether we're in water or just free floating in space. They've been able to get at any part of this ship in any configuration since it wandered in here; if it wandered in here at all."

"What's that supposed to mean?" Dãsha asked in an angry tone. The great ship shook repeatedly.

"Not now, Dãsha!" Caidin sounded almost panicked. "Please get out of there!"

"Just finishing the last one," she responded. "I'm about to head back out the door."

"Make sure you seal that door when you leave," Rick instructed.

"I know what I'm doing," Dãsha snapped.

The ship suddenly pitched abruptly, straining both Caidin and Rick in their harnesses. Horrified, Rick watched the monitors as the water rushing through the different camera angles became even more violent.

"Caidin," he called frantic. "Hold her steady." Even Rick was having difficulty holding the great ship within the parameters specified.

"I can't," Caidin came back. "They're using concussion ordnance on us. The retro thrusters can't compensate for that kind of disruption."

"They're trying to breach the hull this time," Dãsha called.

"Dãsha, get out of there now!" Caidin sounded terrified this time.

The ship rocked again. Rick watched their readings begin to fall out of parameters. The whole ship acted as though it were going to topple over as it began to tip back on its keel and over to its side.

"I'm out," Dãsha called.

Rick watched as water started to gush from the landing bay halls and race back down toward the hangar bay corridors.

"If you know another way out of there, better take it," Rick called.

"Dãsha?" Caidin called frantic. "Dãsha?"

"Caidin," she called back. "Hold *Calypso* where she is. I'm trying to get back over the causeway."

"I can't," Caidin yelled. "Dãsha, find another way back!"

"No, I can make it..."

Rick and Caidin both recognized her com going dead. After giving each other a horrified glance, they worked to bring the great ship back into its original configuration. After several long, painful minutes, the readings settled back to their original numbers and the moaning stopped. Rick was out of his harness and dashing to the door in an instant.

"What are you doing?" Caidin asked.

"I've got to try to help her," he said, sprinting down the halls and stairs leading to the engine room and the other passages that would take him deeper into the ship. But even though *Calypso* had returned to her level configuration, the water that had filled her bays wasn't finished moving. After several tormented rides down different elevators, Rick arrived at a partially flooded engine room. Zeroing in on the far doors leading to the hangar bay causeways, he soon found himself being forced along with the current.

The hydraulic surge Rick found himself in nearly swept him out of control as the water continued to flow back toward the hangar bays. The water was so cold, his lungs involuntarily exhaled, blasting his air supply in a split second. As the current carried him into the adjoining hallway and toward several open hatches and cross grid railings, he realized he was going to drown or get torn apart in the ship's structure if he didn't figure something out fast. As he rushed through the sweeping torrent, he slapped his hands together and then pulled them apart as if he were moving through a curtain. A pocket of air instantly developed around him and with a flick of a finger, the pocket he had created warmed, bringing heat to his chilled, wet skin. Rick dove over the side of a railing, following the fast-moving current, deep in the bowels of the ship. Moments later, he was weaving through the lower halls and beyond where they had stopped at the original flood line. As he made his way up the stairs, he burst from the water and landed on his feet.

"Dãsha," he called, looking around the causeway over the flooding hangar decks. "Dãsha," he repeated trying to project his voice over the noise of the rising water. *She could be anywhere!* He took off running across the steel grating of the causeway to the other side, looking on both sides in the water as he went. Stopping on the other side, he turned and checked the flooding hangar again. "Dãsha!" Nothing. He looked down into the swirling water in front of him. He had no idea where he would go from here. Only the scant description the tall woman was giving as she had made her way to the central processing room.

Slapping his hands together again, he dove into the water, creating another warm pocket of air, and propelling himself down into the flooded halls. Turning this way and that, he searched for the familiar form of Dãsha. He was hoping he'd find her trying to swim to a safe air pocket or still be safe in the upper halls above the processing room. As he swam about the submerged hallways, he passed a door clearly marked as the central processing room. The water had already engulfed where it had been safe before. Swimming a bit further, he surfaced in a brightly lit portion of a hallway, near a closed hatch.

"Dãsha," he called as he emerged from the water. Moving up and down the halls, he noticed most of the water was no longer moving. *Certainly, these halls would soon flood behind him. They would soon flood! The door was closed; surely Dãsha would have closed the door behind her to keep the water from flooding the halls.* Rick carefully worked the door control until it suddenly pulled to one side. Making his way through several other closed doors, he went to open another and as the door pulled open, he was met with a pressurized wall of water. Not ready for it, he was blasted back along the halls and through the open hatches. He was pushed back into the flooded central processing hallway before he could gather his wits enough to create his air pocket. Warming it, he dried himself, then fought the current to get back to where he had been. As he passed through the open door, he noticed an object floating past him and reached out and grabbed it, pulling it back into his air pocket. *Dãsha's headset!* Rounding a corner, he became entangled in a pair of arms and legs floating at his level. Grabbing an arm, he pulled Dãsha close, bringing her head and shoulders into his envelope. Her face and head were badly damaged; he could detect no breathing. The force of the water coming back in at her when she opened one of the doors must have rammed her into one of the bulkheads.

Rick remained motionless, holding her close for several moments. *Caidin will be devastated.* He wasn't even sure it was a good idea to bring her body back up to him. It might be better to take her to the flooded hangar deck and release her body to the elements of the water. There she would possibly float outside and Caidin would be spared the indignity of seeing her in such horrible condition. With that in mind, Rick worked his way back down the passages, following the receding currents back to the causeway. Once he arrived, he stood with Dãsha in his arms, ready to drop her into a frigid grave. He paused, looking down at Dãsha's limp body, his thoughts turning to Jayda and where she might be. He had expended a considerable amount of time and energy searching for her. His travels had led him here to Acuity and *Calypso*. Meeting and befriending Caidin and Dãsha, couldn't have just been happenstance. There had to be a purpose in all this. Jayda's chances of survival were slim now; yet he continued to search for her. He had to know. Even if it was as painful as what Gunnar had had to endure when he lost Audra almost two years ago. Would he rob Caidin of closure? Either way it would be painful to bear. Ultimately, he reset his hold on Dãsha's limp form and made his way to the other end of the causeway, entered the water, and made his way back up to the engine room.

When Rick entered, he caught a glimpse of Caidin sitting next to one of the power coupling units. The older gentleman came to his feet, leaving his cane where he sat. Even with his limp, he was to Rick in an instant. There were no words to be spoken as Caidin took Dãsha's broken body and held her close. Rick could only watch as Caidin turned with tear filled eyes and carried her slowly from the engine room.

Rick stood silent for several minutes, wondering if he should follow him; be with him for support and consolation. But he got the distinct impression that for now, it was better for Caidin to be alone. After leaning against an engine bulkhead for an extended period of time, his thoughts turned back to the ship. With the processing room back online, he could work on the inducer and *Calypso* would be operational. He could get to the *Athena* before the Drake and he could take Caidin off this old shipwreck. Working his way back over to the power coupling, he removed the covers and focused on the task to be done.

The finish work was a little more difficult than he had calculated, but after some time, everything was in perfect order on the inducer circuits. Once he had finished, he turned to the display and ran as many tests as he was able with his limited understanding of the symbols used to indicate information. Putting the covers back in place, he started for the bridge. Upon entering, he found just about everything alive with lights and sounds. Displays, gauges and readouts flashed information at a dizzying rate. Rick stepped to the windows and examined them closely. Caidin had indicated that he kept them dark on purpose, but Rick couldn't see how it was accomplished.

"The controls for the windows are over here," a voice said quietly from behind. Caidin shuffled to the sensor control station and pointed to a small panel covered by a clear plastic lid. "But it isn't wise to open them."

"Because if the Drake see you trying to pilot the ship, they'll fire?" Rick asked. Caidin just stared blankly past Rick for a long moment, finally turning and leaning back in the navigator's seat.

"Caidin," Rick said quietly. "Did your tug really break up getting here?" Caidin remained silent for quite some time, leading Rick to think he didn't need to answer the question.

"No, it didn't," Caidin finally said. "But what I told you about a tug breaking up and Dãsha saving me was true."

"I saw a ship in one of the landing bays. It's the one you and Dãsha came here in, isn't it?"

"Yes, it's a small scout vessel I stole when Dãsha and I left Gillard. We found the tug in one of the upper hangar bays sometime after we got here. It took some time for Dãsha and I to repair it. I should say Dãsha did most of the repair work. She was always good with that kind of thing as my talents were stronger in other areas. We were trying to use it to make repairs to the exterior hangar bay doors. They are the reason those decks are flooded. Something is obstructing them. We tried to use the tug to remove the obstruction, but the Drake caught us and fired on us. The story of Dãsha saving me as indicated earlier, is accurate."

"Why the ruse?" Rick asked, leaning against the blacked out bridge windows. He had run every possibility over in his mind and couldn't figure any of it out.

"We are exiles here," Caidin began. "We can never leave and this ship cannot be moved from its current location. The Drake make sure of it. There are orientation buoys attached to her hull and constant patrols monitoring *Calypso's* position."

Rick folded his arms, feeling comfortable about the revelations coming from Caidin.

"The Drake Grand Council deemed us as unnatural; an abomination to all that is scientific."

"Both of you?"

"Yes, both of us. You see, I am one of you; a Thane. Called and trained by Ona Tusk."

"Ah, she does have more to her name than just plain Ona. How'd you know I'm a Thane?"

"Ona paid me a visit not too long ago, telling me you'd be coming. She instructed me to help you in any way I can. That there was a higher purpose than what Dãsha and I were about here in exile."

"She didn't happen to let on what that higher purpose was, did she?"

"She mentioned your ship and your Jayda were of vital importance, but more importantly, the freighters caught in the ice. They must be rescued at all costs. She said that you will have need of them."

"I don't suppose she let on what I would possibly do with a bunch of shipwrecked freighters frozen in ice?" Rick asked.

Caidin shook his head.

"Figures," Rick complained. "She isn't one to provide a whole lot of detail."

"No, she isn't."

"So why is a Thane considered an abomination to your Grand Council and sent into exile?"

"A Thane is not, only myself. I was a doctor of many things before I was chosen by Ona to become a Thane."

"She certainly can get around, can't she?"

"There are many Thanes in this quadrant you call the Spartus. While all are charged with protection in some form or another, they all have differing talents, natural abilities. Judging from the weapons you carry and the fact you hold the rank of General and command a warship, I suspect yours is as a warrior."

"Forgive me if I seem a little befuddled here. Ona left me with the impression all Thanes were taught how to fight using the weapons of a Thane." Rick held up his Balkrum so Caidin could see it.

"May I?"

"Certainly," Rick said handing it to him. Caidin carefully examined it.

"I was shown one of these. Even used it once or twice, but it was never in my DNA to fight with one. That's not where my talents lay. Much like you, I am a man of science, but in a different field than you."

"Yes," Rick agreed. "You're Caidin Mantose, inventor of many of the medical devices we use now. Your investment Empire grew vastly larger after your departure from Kalamar."

"I thought I recognized where you said you came from. If memory serves, Kalamar is in the Delta Beta quadrant. The Caney system, which is adjacent to my home system of Yunkin."

"Yes, it is. Your inventions paved the way for so many wonderful advancements in medicine and biological research. What happened to you? How did you get here?"

"I could ask you the same question," Caidin countered, turning and looking at the information flashing on the displays in front of him. "I was traveling on business from Tarlow to Kerson when I got caught in a solar storm that nearly broke the ship apart. Certainly, it was disabled. A couple of weeks drifting into the path of a comet that swept my ship past the Oneida Caldron and flung me across space and time to here. I lost everything to that part of the universe, my wife... my family."

Rick had to smile a little. The irony of fate woven so closely together, even across the expanse of the universe, sometimes mystified him.

"Seems we came by similar roads," Rick said, still smiling. "The *Athena* and her sister ship, *Constellation*, got caught in the Oneida while on a rescue mission. We used a sling shot maneuver to break free and then wormhole travel to get a safe distance away. A tiny glitch in our calculations put us here."

"Where's your other ship, the *Constellation*?"

"I have zero doubt its off somewhere in Hadrian getting into trouble."

"I don't understand."

"My friend, Gunnar Conrad, commands the *Constellation*. He has a propensity for getting into trouble."

"I think I've heard of you two," Caidin chuckled. "Just curious and you don't have to answer if you don't want to, but how does the burial pod of one of your crew fit in here?"

"Gunnar's wife was killed during the worm hole operations. We buried her in space and somehow her pod was caught in Acuity's ocean."

"I'm sorry to hear that."

Rick considered a moment, wondering whether to reveal more to Caidin.

"You should also know that your daughter, Tiana is onboard the *Constellation*," Rick said, not sure how the older gentleman would take the news.

Caidin nodded blankly, giving Rick cause to wonder if he had even heard what Rick had just said. He waited for a response, but nothing came.

"Caidin, did you hear me? I said your daughter, Tiana is serving onboard the *Constellation*. She's here, in this galaxy. She still believes you're alive."

"Yes, I heard you," Caidin finally responded. "I'm glad she's still alive, though I admit I'm a bit surprised."

"How so?"

"I became aware that my second wife was making plans to try to cut my children out of my will. I suspected she was going to try to have me killed in some mysterious manner." Caidin paused a moment, considering. "During my time here, I've come to realize that I didn't need any of that anyway. She can have everything and all the headaches that go along with it."

"Well, she tried to bump off your children too. Colonel Conrad had a battle on his hands to get them to safety."

"Well, I'm glad for that. They're better off without all the mess I left behind; probably safer with you guys anyway."

"Not exactly."

"What do you mean?"

"We lost Taron some time ago in a fire fight."

Caidin pulled his hand over his face and down into his beard, letting out a heavy sigh.

"Seems like there's no escaping one's fate." Caidin dropped his head into his hands.

"If you're a Thane, may I ask who you're protecting?" Rick asked.

"Were you not instructed by Ona to keep such information confidential?"

"Ona wasn't very clear about anything," Rick said.

"I'm sorry, but Ona forbad me from saying anything further," Caidin finally said.

"I'm so sorry for your loss," Rick said bowing his head. He couldn't help but feel responsible for Dãsha's death. Perhaps if he had tried for the central processing room instead of Dãsha, he would have survived the flood. "It looked like she tried to..."

"Please don't," Caidin said, his voice shaking. "It's not important and she would not want either of us to dwell on it. She did what she thought was best to ensure success."

"I'll be glad to help you bury her if you'd like," Rick offered, wondering how Caidin could be this composed with the prospect of facing the rest of his mortality alone.

"No," Caidin responded politely. "Thank you, but I'll take care of it on my own. Of course, my scout ship is yours to use as needed. I probably should have told you about it before we tried to make repairs to *Calypso.*"

"Does your scout ship have any way to cut through the ice?"

"Only a set of low power beamers," Caidin said shaking his head. "They were designed for geological core sampling of comets and asteroids, but you might be able to adapt them to cut through the ice."

Rick thought for a moment, then stepped out into the middle of the enormous bridge, looking all around.

"Do you know exactly where all of the positioning devices are?"

"Yes, Dãsha mapped all of them. They're in the sensor data banks."

"Did she identify how they were attached?"

"Simple magnetic gas sealed couplers."

Rick walked over to the sensor control consoles and started looking at the displays.

"Did you ever do a seismic mapping of the ice pack?"

"Yes, of course. When you're stuck out here with nothing to do, you find the most mundane of things to keep yourself occupied. I can tell you anything about the ice, the water, any of the shipwrecks here in Acuity's ocean, all the objects."

"Yes, because of *Calypso's* calibrated sensors. Are you able to reorient *Calypso* toward the ice without pissing off the Drake?"

"No," Caidin admitted. "We generally get fired on every time we move any faster than what a normal eddy or current would produce. A ship of this size generally wouldn't move very much on its own anyway."

"Yeah," Rick said becoming focused. "We'll have to chance it and hope they aren't scanning too closely to discover this old girl can move now."

"Chance what?"

"I'm continuing my mission," Rick said stepping to the engineering consoles. Caidin watched the Kalamarion General studying the engine monitoring readouts. "Gonna need a little help here," Rick said looking toward Caidin. He slowly got to his feet and shuffled over to where Rick stood searching. "I'm assuming you know where the engagement drivers are on this old tub?"

"They're here," Caidin said, pointing to a panel close to the end of the long row of consoles. "The Star drive is over here, but it looks like it's still offline. The sub-light drive is here. I'm reading full power from the Furelium core. She'll give you as much speed as she's got to give."

"Perfect," Rick said moving back to the sensor station. "Can you bring up the information on the ice pack? We're specifically looking for any major weaknesses in its lined structures near the *Athena* and the freighters."

Caidin sat down at a set of terminals while Rick hurried back over to the pilot's station.

"Does *Calypso* have enough automation working for you to pilot her alone?"

"Yes, but what good will that do?" Caidin looked across at Rick. "Information on the ice is up. *Calypso* is pinpointing several locations where the ice is the most unstable."

Rick shifted back over to look at what was being displayed. Caidin pointed to several locations and looked at the readouts connected with those locations.

"Which one of these is the closest to the *Athena* and which one has the hardest ice?"

"The ice is most dense here, but this one over here is the closest and has lots of water pockets honeycombed through it."

"This is perfect," Rick mumbled, studying the information in front of him. He turned back to the navigation consoles.

"What's perfect?" Caidin asked. He had an idea of what Rick had in mind, based on previous conversations, but was having trouble following the logic.

"Yes, this will do nicely," Rick grinned. "And it will make it easier for you." Rick straightened up. "Are the Drake still pounding at the ice?"

Caidin glanced at the sensor information.

"Yes, they're starting to drill and from the looks of it, the heavier equipment they just brought in will make quick work of it. What's your plan?"

"I'm going to take your scout ship, knock off all the marker beacons and then drive it as fast as it will go in this direction. That will draw off the sentry ships," Rick said pointing at the sensor screen returns. "When I'm far enough away, you need to wake this ol' girl up and steer a wide turn in this direction and run her as hard as she'll go in the opposite direction. Don't look back; don't stop for anything, just run her hard. You should be able to breach Acuity's surface before the Drake ever figure out you're gone."

"Where am I going?"

"That way," Rick pointed off into nothing. "Out of there. You'll know where you're going when you get there. Maybe when you do, you could point these antennas toward home, see if you can find it. For now, I can't ask you to sacrifice anymore on my behalf. You've sacrificed enough."

"But what about you?"

"What about me? I can take care of myself."

"I mean what are you going to do, dodge those guys out there forever? They have guns, you don't."

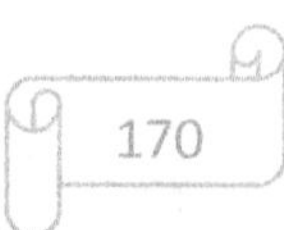

"I don't have to out gun them, just outrun them. I'll lead them all over this ice sheet, maybe give them a little what for, then maneuver back to this point in the ice and start drilling," Rick said pointing at the images on the screen. "If there are any sentries left after I lead them on the ride of their lives, they'll try to follow me in, giving you even more time to disappear."

"Well, I'm not so sure about that," Caidin commented sounding more worried. "That little scout ship is fast to be sure, but you won't have anything to defend yourself with."

"Not going to need anything," Rick said confidently, heading for the door. "We best get to it."

"Rick," Caidin stopped him. "Thank you. You've shown me a brighter side of humanity. I wish Dãsha could be here to help." Rick turned back to the older Thane.

"I can't express how badly I feel about Dãsha. But if you can get *Calypso* out of here and run her as far away from here as you can, maybe her death won't be in vain. I'll find you when I have the *Athena* back." Rick turned and was gone before Caidin could get another word out.

Not for the faint of heart

"Destroyer," Lana announced excitedly. This time, instead of looking at the scanning displays, she pointed straight ahead of them. Everyone looked up except for Mr. Pippin, who remained focused, tapping the glass in front of him as if he had never left the bridge.

"Two more converging from opposite sides, Captain. Along with four corvettes," Pip reported. "The two destroyers on either side just launched torpedoes. Impact in thirty seconds."

"Lieutenant Starman, can you get around the destroyers and those corvettes?"

"That's a pretty tight bottle neck, Sir."

"Can you do it?"

"Not without taking some heavy hits."

Dakota glanced at the tracking displays, then turned forward again.

"Lieutenant Cartwright, stand by to send five Pin missiles each at those incoming torpedoes on my command. First, I want you to target the command decks of the lead destroyer and send a Mark V into it. Tell me when you're ready."

The weapons officer turned back to his controls and made a series of adjustments but hesitated a moment. He glanced at Lynette, then leaned back in his seat with his finger hovering over his glass controls.

"Mark V ready, Sir."

Dakota paused as they drew closer. After giving the tracking displays another glance, he turned forward again.

"Let it go."

Doran touched the firing pad on the glass.

"Torpedo away."

There was a flash from the nose of the *Constellation* and a blue flare rocketed away, heading straight at the Albion destroyer.

"Helm, drive right past them. The explosion will mask our course."

"Ten seconds to Albion torpedo impact," Pip announced.

"Fire Pin missiles," Dakota ordered, "and dim the glass, this could get bright."

Lynette touched a control on her console and the windows dimmed just as a brilliant burst enveloped them. Everyone shielded their eyes as the Mark V found its mark, passed into the lower command decks of the destroyer and erupted. The flash intensified as internal ordnance began its grim work of consuming any fuel it could find. As the fiery blast continued to find oxygen, internal explosions and subsequent concussions broke the ship apart. The entire series of command decks instantly shattered, followed by a massive secondary detonation that broke the ship in half.

Lynette tried to steer the *Constellation* away from the eruption, but they were already in the thick of it. Surrounded by fire and debris, the ship rocked violently.

"This is not good," Dakota hollered. He grabbed BachTL by the shirt as the Castellian was sent tumbling. "Starman, get us out of here!"

There seemed to be no space outside the ship; only fire. Every workstation blinked, fuzzed momentarily, then all the displays smeared into a flash of colors, making it impossible to discern their orientation to the horizontal axis of Carolon. Several warning alarms squawked for attention in front of Tiana as she worked frantically to identify the problems. The bridge lights winked out, leaving everyone with only failing instrument lights to see with.

"I need information!" Dakota bellowed. He felt himself sliding out of his seat, and trying to hold himself down did little to stop it. Recognizing weightlessness, he slapped down the safety lock control. As the thigh covers pulled him back into his seat, he turned and grabbed a hold of BachTL again, keeping him from floating into something. "Do we have any emergency lights?"

"Working on it, Sir," Tiana grunted from her station.

A flash from helm control revealed a partial picture from Lynette's displays. They were on for only a moment, but it was enough to see everyone was still at their stations and safety locked in place. Looking outside, the space around them was still aflame with glowing gases and molten debris. The ship's hull shuttered, being struck by broken and torn pieces of vessel. Several large jolts reverberated through the ship's frame, then an enormous crash slammed the hull, nearly jarring the seats from their mounts. Dakota looked over at Mr. Pippin, but found it difficult to even turn his head. He was also having a hard time holding on to BachTL. In fact, everyone appeared to be having difficulty holding themselves upright. Outside, the glow of exploding gases finally dissipated, and all was dark except for large pieces of hull fragments spinning past the windows. Carolon suddenly spun past their view, revealing a wild, out of control spin. The emergency lights abruptly popped on.

"Mr. Pippin," Dakota grunted loudly. "Anything working over there?"

"Negative, Sir. Everything is offline."

"Tiana, can you tell us anything?"

"I don't even have coms, Sir. There's no way to ascertain any damage to the ship."

Dakota observed the helmsman holding her fists to one of her eyes, looking out at the spinning stars and Carolon. He recognized the simple trick all space pilots were taught when their instruments were compromised, and they found themselves in an uncontrolled spin. It was an easy way to sight in on their speed and direction from a heavenly body, using time and size references.

"Helm, please tell me we're moving away from Carolon." Dakota waited several anxious seconds noticing several displays flash and go dark. He was still holding onto BachTL, who was trying to regain his feet, but the ship's spin kept him completely off balance. All he could do was wrap himself around the base of the command chair and hang on.

"Affirmative, Sir," came the response from Lynette. She grabbed the control yoke to hold herself upright against the inertia of the spinning ship. "We're still moving away from Carolon at an accelerated rate."

"I've got Billy on my personal com, Sir," Tiana announced.

"Good thinking," Dakota said, struggling to turn his head toward the engineering station. He finally let go of BachTL; he wasn't going anywhere.

"He says he'll have power restored in about a minute."

"We don't have a minute!"

"They're in the dark back there too, Sir."

"Captain Abrams?" Dakota's personal com came alive. "Lieutenant Hunter, Sir."

"Are you dark back there too?" Dakota asked.

"I was, but I'm on my own backup power now, Sir."

"Our backups are offline. Can you see anything from your vantage point?"

"Standby, I'm having my tracking control computers match the turret's spin with the ship's spin. This is a pretty significant cartwheel we've gotten ourselves into here. The ship was hit by a big piece of enemy destroyer when it broke up. Those Mark Vs really pack a wallop."

"Don't they though?"

"There, now at least I don't feel like I'm going to puke," Hayden Hunter commented over the com. "We're moving away from Carolon at a pretty fast clip and I don't see anything following us. There are still several ships back there in orbit, but they look disabled. I can't get a read for how bad, but there's nothing trying to follow us yet."

The main lights flashed twice and came on along with several engineering, com and helm displays. Tiana waited a moment, then information began blitzing across her workstation.

"If I'm to believe this information," Tiana said, trying to interpret what she was reading, "Our main power core is completely offline. That means our sub-light engines are offline as well as our environmental systems. We should still have maneuvering thrusters and some lateral control now."

"Helm?" Dakota asked.

"Confirmed," Lynette said working her controls. "I have limited thruster control now. Attempting to correct our spin, but this could take a while."

"You've got nothing better to do," Dakota said. "See if you can keep as much of our forward motion going. Tiana, can you get the environmental systems back online from here?"

"I'm sure Billy could use my help in engineering," Tiana said, "but without the anti-grav systems working, there's no way I can even get out of this seat, let alone make it down to engineering." Tiana had to hold herself back from being pressed against her consoles. If Lynette could manage to stop the spinning, at least they could move around in a weightless environment.

Several anxious moments creped by as everyone held on, waiting for the spinning to stop. Gradually, the pressure exerted on everyone from the spin's inertia, began to relax. The com channels suddenly came alive and Lana had to act fast to quiet down the noise. Dakota looked over at the sensor control station. Pip's displays were on, but only a jumble of gibberish and blank readouts were visible. Then the main lights came back on.

"Does this mean we have power back?" Dakota asked, looking around.

"It means Billy has the core back online," Tiana stated. "All other systems are still down."

"As soon as you can manage it, make your way back to engineering and see what you can do to help." Dakota anxiously tapped his knuckle on the armrest of the command chair.

It took a few minutes longer before Lynette managed to stop the ship's cartwheel. Continuing to work on correcting the other axis issues, she found the ship was now in a constant turn and everything she tried did nothing to correct that condition. It was a broad turn, one that would eventually have them turned right back into the Nulark system.

Tiana unlocked from her seat and worked her way out the bridge door. Carefully navigating the hallway using the handrail, she finally reached the closed Mallory doors. Inside, she could make out the form of Billy Moon working his way around one side of the immense monitor control console. Making her way to the door controls, she keyed in a sequence of numbers and symbols, then turned back as the large doors separated. Billy peered out from the opening in the floor as his apprentice shoved off from the door frame and stopped herself at the engineering console.

"It's about time you got down here." Billy sounded irritated.

"Hey, we've been pinned to the walls up there until we could stop the spin."

"What did Starman hit?"

"She didn't hit anything. We got hit by pieces of a destroyer."

"Lucky it didn't break us in two. I think our shields saved our bacon on that one."

"Helm has only limited directional control now and we're stuck in a wide turn. What have you got going on down there?"

"A big mess," Billy said working with something in the pit. "That blast has scrambled everything with an Atheon driver. I'm having to reset every one of them manually."

"What's wrong with the Helix control modules?" Tiana pulled herself down to the floor and looked around in the pit.

"I don't know," Billy admitted exasperated. "Burnt out, froze up, inactive for whatever reason."

"Ok, calm down," Tiana said watching him work. "Where's Brandon?"

"Infirmary."

"Ok, no problem. Your favorite independent contractor is here to help. Let's have a look at this logically. Right now, we need environmental and the antigrav systems."

At the moment, Billy's thoughts were elsewhere.

"He got slammed against the engine bulkhead when we were struck. I don't know what kind of shape he's in." Billy seemed to freeze, thinking about what happened to his engineer's mate. "I should have had him buckled in instead of wandering around looking at numbers on a display."

"Billy," Tiana said grabbing him by the head and turning him to face her. "You need to focus. No one had any idea that Mark V was going to do what it did. You can't blame yourself for people doing their jobs. Now, antigrav; what do you know?"

The chief engineer looked into her eyes for a moment. What he saw brought him back to his normal gruff exterior.

"I know it's not working," he said resetting another module. "But we need to get those engines back up or I expect we're going to be in a lot of trouble."

Tiana grabbed the engineer by the shoulders and pulled him up and out of the pit.

"What the...?"

"I'll take care of these engines, you take care of the antigrav."

Billy smiled, catching himself before he struck the ceiling in their weightless environment.

"Geez, you teach someone a little something about modern Massey and Fulton light drives and they think they own the place."

"I've got a feeling the problem with the environmental systems are somehow tied to the antigrav problem," Tiana said diving into the pit headfirst. Billy looked back, but saw only the bottom of her boots.

Gliding back to the floor, Billy maneuvered around to the engineering console and started to work on the systems still operating. After several minutes of searching through subsystems, he moved to a small panel next to the Mallory doors and activated a key sequence. Moments later, a door sung open and a large mass slid out. The antigrav Klystron had the appearance of a small glass castle with anode spires. The entire unit was designed to glow when in normal operation, but only half the glass structure seemed to be operating. After examining several of the readouts located around the delicate looking apparatus, he began to work with several parts located on either side of the antigrav device. Fiddling with it for several minutes, most of the antigrav systems began to operate again, but they were still free floating in a weightless environment. Moving back over to the engineering console, he smiled, delighted with his success. Most of the glass panel was displaying coherent information now. Either they were returning to normal on their own, or what he and Tiana were doing was making a difference. Feeling the urgency of their situation, he touched the glass on the com panel section of the console.

"Bridge, this is engineering."

"Nice to hear from you, Billy," Captain Abrams responded. "How are things progressing back there?"

"Still a lot of systems offline, Captain, but we're getting there." Billy was momentarily distracted by several readings in front of him, but then came back. "Make sure everyone is sitting down and locked in place. I'm going to try and bring the antigrav back online."

"Standing by."

"Tiana," Billy called out. "Get on your feet, I'm bringing the antigrav back online."

"Let her rip," Tiana called from the engine pit.

Billy tapped a myriad of points on the glass, then waited. He looked over at the antigrav system, noticing it was all lit up now, but they were still free floating. Shaking his head, a frustrated look twitched across his face. He maneuvered his fingers all around the glass display, trying to figure out what was wrong. His frustration levels were building.

"Did you reset the gravity flux sequencers?" came a voice from the pit.

Billy paused, thinking. There were a lot of systems that relied on each other for either power or critical data feedback in order to remain in harmony with the other systems. As he thought back to everything he had done, he realized in his haste that he had forgotten several key procedures. Tapping his fingers across the glass at a blur again, he made sure not to miss anything, finally tapping the last control. A soft whine issued from the antigrav unit and its countenance sharply brightened as it came to life. Moments later, his feet settled to the floor as the weightless environment was corrected. All around the engineering compartment, he could hear the sounds of objects settling as the gravity returned to normal. He always loved seeing results, especially when under pressure. With renewed confidence, he turned for the engine pit.

"The air is getting stale in here, what's taking so long down there?" He dropped to his knees and bent down to the hole at the same instant Tiana popped her head up.

"I don't suppose it ever occurred to you to get down here and help me?" Tiana dropped back down the hole, crawling around in the maze of piping and cable trays. "It might have been better to not have the gravity working while I'm trying to crawl around down here."

Billy watched her struggle, working with several mechanisms and a jumble of piping. Several valves seemed to be non-functional while others acted as if they were going to rupture. He finally dropped into the pit to help with her struggle.

"I'm not sure what you're trying to do, but you're sure expending a lot of energy doing it."

"The oxygen flow sensors from the scrubbers are jammed up. They're not allowing the air through. Without it, nothing works in the environmental systems."

"Did you try resetting the flow control sensor circuits?" Billy asked.

Tiana abruptly stopped working and slowly turned her gaze at the chief engineer. If her eyes had daggers, he would have been cut to ribbons. Billy smiled playfully, leaning over to a small panel, and touching several colored buttons. He then held three of them for several seconds. The panel changed color, flashed several times, and then went solid. Tiana looked at the sensors readouts as they stabilized then turned back to the engineer, who was making a quick exit from the pit. Once out of the pit, she slid up next to him as they examined the readouts on engineering control console. Just about everything seemed to be displaying as it should.

"Bridge, you should have all your systems back online, or at least be able to access them for a reboot." Tiana turned to Billy. "Ok, let's figure out what you did to these engines."

"Medical bay," Billy said touching his com panel. "How's that greenhorn I brought in?"

"He's doing ok," Fuji answered. "He doesn't have a clue as to where he is, but at least he's conscious now. By the way, thanks for the gravity. Weightlessness has its advantages in medicine, but I think Lieutenant Gantrie was getting tired of me kicking her in the head every time I flew past her."

"Thanks, Doc. I'll be in to see him as soon as we get back to the *Realistic*."

"If we get back," Tiana mumbled, tapping the glass in front of her and looking up at the displays over the engine bulkheads.

"Come on, homegirl," Billy smirked. "We know these engines forward and backwards. If we can't fix them, no one can."

"Yeah," Tiana said becoming focused. "That's what I'm afraid of. You're gonna have to help me with the details here."

Billy leaned closer to the glass and tapped several points, bringing up several windows of information.

"Here's all the failsafe's that have activated. I suspect some of these are because of that Mark V detonation and subsequent collision with those pieces of ship. Look, the venting induction channels are completely plugged. Some of that junk has made it into the plasma cooling filters. We'll never get a restart unless we can get that crap cleared out of there."

"Have you got any good ideas of how to reach those?"

"Well, the filters we can do something with," Billy said thinking. "The induction channels are a bit more problematic." Billy expanded the image on the glass in front of them. "The induction channels are only accessible from outside of the ship and if you haven't noticed, we don't have Alex 7001 here with us."

"Then I guess one of us gets to suit up and go for a little space walk." Tiana looked closer at the induction channels. "Why in the world wouldn't you make an access from the inside?"

Billy brought up the short-range scanning equipment tied directly to the ship's sensor arrays.

"Because there's supposed to be grills in place to protect the channels, but I think they must have been assigned to future models."

"It's a military vehicle." Tiana said. "It's going to blow things up and drive around in the muck. Something is bound to get in there, whether it's the first model or the last."

"Another design flaw on the A model we'll have to put on Alex's think list. Walking around outside is going to be a bit rough."

"How so?"

"The ship is moving pretty fast right now," Billy said pointing at the scanning displays. "Thankfully Lieutenant Starman has been able to stabilize our flightpath and we're no longer cartwheeling. I suspect Captain Abrams is having her hold a steady course, trying to put as much distance between us and our Albion friends back there, so until we can get engine power back, we'll hold our course for now. Trying to do a walk during an unstable flightpath is only for the advanced walking technician. The biggest problem whoever faces right now is all the bits of debris flying around out there. Our suits are tough, but some of that stuff is going to be razor sharp and flying faster than some of our ordnance. You could be full of holes in a split second without even knowing it."

"You don't really need to sell me on this," Tiana mumbled.

"I'm glad, because you're not going to be the one that has to do it; I am."

"No, it would be better for you to be in here. You know everything there is to know about this ship. Clearing those channels is grunt work."

"...and how many space walks have you accomplished since you've boarded this vessel, young lady?"

Tiana fell silent, thinking. She shifted her eyes from the glass to Billy and back again.

"Including this one?"

"Yeah, I'll go for that. Including this one?"

"None."

"This conversation is over."

"What about someone else?" Tiana objected. "Captain Abrams is a fighter pilot. Surely he's seen his share of walks."

"I'm certain he has, but he's also the Officer in Command. During military action, unless deemed necessary for rescue of life or limb, the commanding officer in charge will remain at his post until such time as action ceases or he can be relieved of command by an equal or superior officer."

"Hang the regulations, Billy. You are needed right here. I'm not."

The Chief Engineer turned for one of the suit lockers and opened it up.

"Don't make me turn you over my knee kid."

"You wouldn't dare!"

Billy stared at her for a moment.

"Fine, maybe we can figure out something different. I need those Asium rocks you guys brought back up with you. Where are they?"

"What do you want those for?" Tiana asked, turning for the engineering vestibule. The moment she stepped outside the door frame, she hesitated, hearing the hiss of the Mallory doors sliding shut behind her. Turning back, she tried to slip back inside before they could close, but the halves were slanted and slotted, making it completely impossible to simply slip through.

"Billy! No!" Pounding on the doors, she pressed her face against the glass and watched helplessly as Billy moved toward the suit lockers. Continuing to pound on the doors, she tried to work the door controls several times. Livid, she jammed her finger at the wall com.

"Bridge, emergency alert in engineering! I need assistance down here right now!"

Moments later, Fuji Yamoto materialized from sick bay with Dakota only a few steps behind her.

"What happened?" Captain Abrams asked puffing. "What's wrong?"

"Engineer Moon has sealed the Mallory doors and won't let me in."

"Now what did you do?" Dakota asked a little irritated, pressing his face against the glass. Billy was donning a space suit, preparing to exit the ship.

"I haven't done anything," Tiana retorted. "He's getting ready to leave the ship."

"Leave the ship?" Dakota repeated, stepping to the Mallory controls. "What for?"

"We've picked up some debris from the explosion the Mark V caused. Some of it has gotten caught in the venting induction channels. The only way to get it cleared is to go outside and do it by hand."

"So?" Dakota stopped short of overriding the Mallory lockout control. "That's his job and we're right in the middle of one tough engagement. We need those engines back up and running or we're going to be in a world of hurt."

"But it should be me going out there, not him."

"Why is that? Do you have more experience than he does? You've had how many space walks? You out rank him by how much? Oh, wait. You don't have a rank, Miss Mantose. You're an independent contractor."

"But with all the junk flying around out there, even with a suit on he's likely to get killed." Tiana tried to beat on the doors again, but Dakota stopped her.

"Listen to me," he said holding her wrists. "Billy knows what has to be done and who best to have doing it. Sometimes we have to take chances or make sacrifices in order to save the lives of others. Billy knows the risks to you and to himself. Give him the chance to do what he does best, engineer."

Tiana looked into Dakota's eyes for a moment, then relaxed. Dakota released her, and they looked into engineering in time to see Billy open an exterior airlock door and move inside. Once the door closed and the environmental panel next to the door signaled the airlock had sealed, Dakota reached over and punched in the commands to override the lockout. As the Mallory doors hissed back open, Tiana rushed to the engineering console and tapped the com panel.

"You've got a fat lip coming when this is all said and done," she hissed tight lipped.

"I look forward to your attempt, little lady," Billy answered back as he exited the airlock. "You need to get to work cleaning those interior purifiers. I don't want to be waiting for your sorry little behind when I'm finished here."

"I'm on it," she responded angrily.

Swiping through a myriad of diagrams and schematics, Tiana finally stopped and expanded several. Tapping the glass, she heard a panel door pop open on the far side of the engine bulkhead and hurried to find the access. After examining the apparatus for several seconds, she touched a control and a thin tray slid open, revealing a large square membrane. It was coated with all sorts of material.

Plucking several pieces off, she realized that using her fingers wasn't going to get the job done. After a lengthy search, she pulled a small hand vac from one of the tool shelves and used it to clear the debris. It worked perfectly. She could hear all the little metal bits filling the vac container as she ran the wand back and forth over the membrane. Once she had finished with the first one, she moved on to the next, until she had finished and reinstalled everything. Back at the engineering console, she was delighted to see most of the failsafe's had cleared.

"How's it going out there?" she asked touching the com and looking down at Billy's displays.

"I've finished two and have two to go, but this third one is in tough shape. It's not ruptured or blocked, but I've got something jammed up in here really good. It's gonna take some time to get it out."

"Just be careful out there. I have no idea how fast we're going and I don't want to lose you."

"Don't worry; I'm tethered and I have a transponder. If I come free, you guys can always come back after me. Funny thing here is, you can't even tell we're moving at all, unless you look back at Carolon. Outer space is kind of funny that way."

"You just concentrate on what you're doing."

"Yes, Ma'am."

Captain Abrams leaned over Mr. Pippin, watching multiple targets moving toward them again.

"Still no contact with the *Athena*?" the Captain asked, passing a glance at Lana who shook her head.

"The General's coms must be completely down and still too far away for our personal coms to work. I'm getting a whole lot of nothing," the com officer informed him.

"Maybe he's in worse shape than we are," Mr. Pippin offered. "We're too far away to scan for transponder signatures. In our present condition, we're going to have to be practically right next to him."

"Still rebooting?" Dakota asked.

"That and it'll take some time to recalibrate all our sensors. I imagine we lost a few to that Mark V engagement," Mr. Pippin replied.

"I thought Alex 7001's new design was supposed to keep that from happening?"

"This will be its first practical test."

"Do we have weapons and shields back up yet?"

"Negative, subsystems are still rebooting." Mr. Pippin worked with his limited instruments, but ultimately had to get up and step to the back wall of the bridge, looking at the readouts of the equipment mounted there.

"Why is it taking so long for your systems to come back online?" BachTL asked, watching Mr. Pippin work.

"That Mark V explosion caused more damage to us than I anticipated," Dakota explained. "There's a lot of stuff here that has to be synchronized in order for it to work properly. If it doesn't come on in a specific sequence, it can throw everything else off."

"You didn't know this would happen?"

"It was an untested weapon."

"I guess it's tested now."

"There'll certainly be a lot of logging data to go over when we get back to Aster." Dakota examined the tracking information of the primary targets coming at them, then fumbled for the com in front of him.

"Lieutenant Hunter, this is Captain Abrams."

"Yes, Captain. How can I assist you?"

"Do you still have a visual on our pursuers?"

"Most of them."

"Do you have a visual on Interceptor two?"

"Give me a moment."

"Tiana, this is Captain Abrams."

"I'm a little busy, Captain."

"I have no doubt. We're still a little blind up here. Any chance you have an update on Sub-light power?"

"Just a sec. I'm up to my elbows in Fulton injection catalyzers."

"As soon as you can, please."

Dakota turned to the bridge crew.

"I am considering options from anyone, at this point."

"Can we call Captain Dalley back and have him redock?" Doran suggested. "Use his engines?"

"We could," Dakota agreed sitting back. "And when he came, he'd bring all those Albion fighters back here with him."

"How about having the *Athena* grab us with their tractor beam and haul us out of here?" Nigel offered.

"An option that's right up there, provided we can make contact with them and they're in a position to do so." Dakota nodded at the ship's navigator.

"Captain Abrams, this is engineering," Tiana's voice blared from the com panel. "Afraid it's still going to be a while before we can have Sub-light power back up."

"Thanks, engineering. Carry on."

"The *Athena* is close enough we ought to be able to see her," Lana announced.

"That's a big affirmative on seeing the *Athena,* Sir," Hayden announced from his turret. "By the way, no sign of Captain Dalley."

"Sir," Lana turned in her chair. "Regulations clearly state we should be in full defensive posture when any vessel that has not established communications with us comes into close quarter maneuvers."

"What would you like me to do, spit on them?" Dakota blurted. "We've got nothing to defend with. We don't even have shield power or launch capabilities."

"I've got my Quads trained on them, Sir," Hayden called forward. Pippin returned to his seat as the conversation continued, but he didn't seem too interested in what was being said. Working with his equipment, he hardly paused long enough to point at something for Lana to activate.

"Bridge, this engineering."

"Go."

"I've got partial power back. Enough to maybe restart the Fulton. If it will come alive, I can't guarantee how long it will go. I've been able to temporarily increase the maneuvering thruster output, but if you put the screws to it too hard, it's liable to blow the nozzles right off the directional ports."

"I'll take it," Dakota exclaimed, turning forward. "Helm, standby."

"Billy is still outside working on the induction ports," Tiana came back.

"Tell him he's got one minute to haul himself back inside or tuck in tight."

Tiana fought the urge to argue. She understood their situation and the need to try anything, but she could also feel a nervous ball form in her gut when she realized what it would take to get the engineer back inside the ship in that amount of time.

"Billy, you've got to quit what you're doing and get back inside, right now."

There was no answer from the engineer. Tiana checked his cameras. He was still there, and she could hear him breathing.

"Billy?"

"I heard you."

"Come on, you don't have much time."

"I don't have any time."

"What do you mean, you don't have any time?"

"It means I can't possibly move that fast, even with my boosters. I'm going to keep working to get these guys cleared out and you keep working to make sure they have as much power to the Fulton as you can give them."

"Billy…"

"It's simple math, young lady."

Tiana watched on the cameras as the engineer continued to pull large pieces of debris from the conduits.

"What math are you using?"

"We're locked in a low probability scenario here. That Mark V basically knocked us out of commission. I can stop doing what I'm doing and try to make it back inside before they try to restart the engines. One way or the other, it's going to work or it's not. If it doesn't work, I've lost time trying to fix these other conduits and we'll get picked up or destroyed by the Albions. If the Fulton fires up, my tether will pop as designed or I'll tuck myself up close to this 'ol girl to stay inside her inertial dampening field. Either one of those options isn't a lot of fun. Regardless, you guys will do some fancy fighting and kick some Albion ass. Then I can climb back inside or, this suit is good for two days before the air scrubbers burn out. Plenty of time for you to find my transponder and pick me up."

"No we won't, and you know it! Captain Abrams will run like hell. There won't be time to come back and get you."

"At least I'll have a front row seat to all the action for a change. Seems like I never get to see what goes on up front."

"That's not simple math," Tiana choked. "That's stupid math!"

"How are you coming with those catalyzers?"

"Don't try to change the subject on me, Mister!"

"Tiana, this is a military vessel that deals in destroying things and killing people, both on the giving and the receiving ends. Now, like you pointed out to me earlier, you need to focus on what you need to

do or we're going to be on the receiving end of that equation.
Everyone onboard is counting on you to get that Fulton up."

"I hate your math," Tiana sniffled, wiping big tears from her eyes.

"Get to it girly girl," Billy encouraged her.

Tiana blinked and focused in on the readouts in front of her. She
brought up the Fulton engine monitoring controls and activated her
bridge coms in time to hear Captain Abrams order the engine start.
Touching several points on the glass, she felt a gentle vibration
emanate from the engine bulkhead and glanced down at the readouts,
trying to smile. Instead, she burst into tears as the engine came alive
and helm control applied forward power.

Looking down at Billy's cameras, she wiped away the moisture and
watched him tuck himself up tight against the conduits and hold on
with one hand while he worked the last of the debris out with the
other. Nearly out of her mind with the *what ifs* of his situation, Tiana
knew if he were to move outside the ship's inertial dampening
envelope, even a little, he could be torn apart by even the slightest
change in speed or direction.

Several alarms took Tiana's attention from the engineer's struggle
as she focused on adjusting the Fulton catalyzers. Overanxious for his
safety, Tiana was back at his cameras before she had even finished
the last adjustment. For now, Billy was safe, or at least secure.

"Billy, don't you move."

"I think I've got a pretty good handle on what I'm doing."

"Just see that you're careful."

*   *   *   *

"Lieutenant Starman, how are we doing now?" Captain Abrams
asked, stepping anxiously up next to helm control.

The Starbird pilot cautiously tapped several controls on the glass in
front of her and after examining the readouts, ran her fingers up the
thruster slides. Everyone held their breath as the injured vessel began
to accelerate. Not wanting to push the engines too hard, she throttled
back to a slower sub-light cruise setting, then turned her chair to the
Captain.

"She's a little sluggish, but it beats waddling around with just
maneuvering thrusters turning in a big circle."

"Primary target, ahead of us, Sir," Mr. Pippin called out, bringing
Dakota back to sensor control.

"Sensors back online?" Dakota asked.

"Still waiting for the arrays to calibrate."

"Target approaching off the port bow," Lynette announced
watching her tracking information.

"Weapons or shields?" Dakota asked.

Doran only turned and shook his head solemnly.

"Lieutenant Hunter, you're up. We need defensive fire ready to track on my command."

"Sir? We gonna fire on our own ship?"

"Only if we have to."

In the turret, Hayden checked his battery power and charged his cannons. Following the regulation of defensive posturing until communications were established, he turned his turret around and tilted the four stout barrels at the approaching craft. As he got comfortable, he noticed more of his short-range scanning systems coming online. A bit surprised, he touched several points on his scanner and tried to focus his equipment in on the *Athena*. Thinking of their own design, he studied the bridge pod carefully. It certainly looked like a Starbird. Working with his scanning equipment, he punched in several commands into his dimensional computer. Immediately it began working to scan and assemble its findings on one of the displays to his left. He looked back out at the approaching ship, taking notice of how close it was now. He could clearly make out the outline of the bridge pod and the aft Interceptor fins. But there was something else; something he didn't recognize. It looked like something had struck the nose of the craft. Perhaps this was some of the damage she had received during her engagement over Tanis with the *Tarzana*. He looked over at the dimensional readout as the outline of a Starbird appeared, then down at the technical information the scanners were gathering. Now, it looked as though the *Athena* had indeed had a run it with something large. There was a large round maul protruding from the nose of the bridge. *What has General Niker concocted now?*

"Bridge, this is Hunter in the turret. Are you getting this?"

"Our scanning equipment is just starting to draw her out now. That's quite the snout."

"Something is happening here," Hayden said, looking out at the approaching ship. Surrounding the snout were several bright colored lights and the snout itself was beginning to glow. "I don't like the look of this," Hayden mumbled, looking back at the technical data pouring across the scanner display. "That looks like an energy..."

There came a brilliant flash as the snout suddenly discharged, sending a brilliant payload at the *Constellation*. Hayden's ball turret abruptly went dark and he blacked out for a moment. When he came too, he could hear static blasting in his coms and his emergency lights had come on, but all his instruments and his weapons were completely blank. He looked outside, but saw only rolling stars.

"Bridge," Hayden yelled into his wrist com. "They've fired on us! The General fired on us! Bridge?"

"Bridge here," Dakota yelled back. "What's your status?"

"All my systems are down. I've got nothing up here. He fired on us!"

"Standby, Lieutenant. Are you intact? Are your environmental system operational?"

"Yes, I'm good for now. Just sitting here in the dark, but I've got nothing right now."

"I haven't heard from engineering yet. See what you can do on your own. Report when you have something."

"Aye, Sir," Hayden said, unbuckling himself and opening up the nearest access panel he could find.

*   *   *   *

It took Tiana a couple of moments to realize she had come too and was aware of her surroundings. She was lying in a far corner of the engine room, half buried in containers and equipment. She didn't hurt, which was a bit of a mystery considering she remembered being thrown across the room and into the wall she was lying against. The emergency lights were on and there were several warning alarms blaring in her ears, but she could detect no other imminent danger. Pulling herself from the corner mess, she looked around. The Mallory doors had automatically closed, but there appeared to be no damage. As the initial shock of the attack began to wear off, she became aware that her wrist com was making a horrific noise. Switching it off, she made her way back over to the engineering console. The glass was still glowing, but there were only a few systems being displayed. Still not quite sure what had happened, she started going through her checklist of things to make sure everything was still operational. After bringing several sub-systems back online, she remembered Billy and brought his camera systems back up. To her relief, she could still see him tucked in the number three vent well. Studying the cameras, she realized the ship was rolling and she expanded a com panel.

"Billy? Are you ok?"

"What was that?"

"I have no idea. I think we just got attacked."

"Yeah, and by our own ship. It was a good thing I had my arms wrapped around these conduits or I'd be sailing off to parts unknown right now. What's your status in there?"

"They knocked most of our system back offline, but I think I can bring them back up fairly quick. It'll just take some time."

"Bring up the MT monitors. I can't see any of the ports from here. Is Starman trying to do something about this?"

"Yes, she's on top of it."

"You get that engine power back to them as fast as you can and then get them some weapons. Nobody kicks my ship and gets away with it, even if it is the General."

Tiana felt great comfort hearing the angered resolve in the engineer's voice. With that kind of determination, she was sure they could get themselves out of this mess.

*   *   *   *

"Lieutenant Starman, how are we doing?" Captain Abrams asked.

"Maneuvering thrusters are dark. We'll spin until I can get some control back."

Dakota turned to Mr. Pippin, who was busy trying to bring his systems back online.

"What happened?" Dakota asked.

"As Lieutenant Hunter indicated, we were fired on by the *Athena*," Pippin replied.

"Fired on? I don't get it. What's the General doing?" Dakota asked perplexed.

"That's some friend you've got," BachTL grumbled from the engineering seat he had found refuge in.

"Captain," Pippin spoke up. "That isn't the General, nor is that the *Athena*."

"Are you sure?" Dakota asked, looking at the sensor control screens, hoping to see something.

"I'm certain. We got a full log of information on that ship before they fired. I don't know what it was, but it wasn't the *Athena*, and they're not shooting Mark Vs at us either. Whatever their weapon is, causes major disruptions to our central energy systems, and unless we can get power back up in the next two to five minutes, they'll have time to come back around and fire on us again."

Dakota turned to BachTL.

"Any idea what we're dealing with here? Did you know about this?"

"I knew Queen Captain Blair was working on plans to get her hands on your ship, but I didn't know anything about any decoy ships."

"Are there any other desires the Queen Captain has we should know about?" Dakota asked.

"None that you haven't already surmised long before this mission," BachTL said. "I've seen this type of weapon before though. My guess is they've taken an Albion Torag and built a shell around it to make it look like your Starbird; they're similar in size."

"So what did they hit us with?"

"A pulsar energy disruptor. The Torag is built with ship compartments assembled around the weapon and several low power thrusters to maneuver with. It's meant to be a field piece, dropped onsite to disable other ships or installations without doing permanent damage to the target."

Dakota thought a moment. BachTL appeared to be genuine with his information, but there were still some lingering doubts about whether he was wholly with them or looking for an opportunity to facilitate their capture at the hands of the Albions. At the moment, that didn't seem likely.

"Systems coming back up," Pippin announced.

"We've got systems back up here, but there's no telemetry," Lynette informed them, looking across at the navigation and weapons consoles. Indeed, the displays were on, but there was an acute lack of control information.

"Engineering," Dakota called, pressing a button on the armrest.

"Yes, Captain," Tiana responded. "I imagine you have a lot of questions."

"Only one that counts right now."

"Whatever you have going on out there is making it next to impossible to keep our systems up long enough to make a fast get away."

"You would be correct."

"Give me two minutes, provided everything else is still working."

"I'll take it."

"Captain, they do that again and there's a very real possibility main power won't be an option."

"Understood. Is Mr. Moon still outside?"

"Yes," Tiana said giving the engineer's cameras displays a glance. "He's trying to make for the last vent now."

"Lieutenant Starman," Dakota said tapping the com button and looking up. "Put as much distance between us and the Torag as you can."

"Aye, Sir," the Starbird pilot responded.

"How maneuverable is the Torag?" Dakota asked turning to BachTL.

"Like I said, it's mainly designed to be dropped off and picked up. As I'm not familiar with this particular modification, there's no way of knowing for sure, but if it's going to take a couple of minutes for it to get into position to fire again, then it's not likely it has any enhanced maneuvering capabilities."

The noisy com system abruptly went quiet, bringing Lana's attention to her displays.

"Something's happening," she exclaimed, touching the glass in front of her. "I've got com control again."

Dakota leaned closer to Mr. Pippin as information started to fill in the empty spaces on his displays.

"I've got Maneuvering thrusters," Lynette Starman called out as her console came alive.

"Thank you, Miss Mantose," Dakota muttered as more systems came back to life. "We need to know exactly where that Torag and the other ships are, just as soon as you can make it happen." Dakota turned to the command chair and touched the com panel. "Turret, what's your status?"

"Still down, Sir. I'm getting some power from the ship now, but not enough to charge my guns."

Dakota frowned and looked up at the weapons officer. Doran only shook his head after looking at his displays.

"Primary target, Sir," Mr. Pippin announced. "Trying to come around for another pass."

"Helm, can you outrun them?"

"No, Sir. Our thruster output is only about thirty-five percent."

"Can we at least stay away from the rest of those ships?"

"They're still quite a distance away," Mr. Pippin said. "Right now, it's just us and that Torag. They'll be in firing range in about thirty seconds."

"Engineering, any weapons power you can give us would be a big help right about now."

"Wished I had it to give," Tiana responded. "If you can give me another minute, I might be able to figure something out."

Dakota hardened his gaze out the forward windows, watching the Starbird shaped Torag maneuvering towards them again. Without main power, it was impossible for them to launch or shoot anything at their pursuers.

That's Too Much Water

Gunnar smelled outdoor cooking. He remembered it as a youth, camping with his family, his friends or by himself. There was nothing like it. He missed it. He and Rick had gotten themselves into situations where they had had to camp out before, but they always had their fighters with them or some sort of space transport close by. Only occasionally did he and Audra ever go camping. She was never much of an outdoorsy kind of girl, but as long as Gunnar made sure she had all the comforts of home, she didn't have any aversions to stepping out for a hike.

He so wanted to remain asleep, but the sounds and the smells were too much to ignore and he finally cracked an eyelid and rolled over onto his side. The fire was still going; not as big as when he had fallen asleep, but now there was a spit erected with some kind of animal flesh roasting on it. *That smells amazing!* Most of the foods Gunnar was used to were synthetically processed and didn't have the flavor raw food had. He admitted that even the food CJ had provided them during their stay on Carolon was better than what the processors on the *Constellation* had to offer.

He popped the other eye open, scanning for Janox or Alex. He found the little droid by Tonnie's power generator, somehow drawing energy from the old unit. He finally caught sight of Janox when she materialized from the shadows to test how well the meat was cooking.

"You sleep long time. You got very cold I think."

"Is it just me or is your English getting better?" Gunnar yawned and sat up.

"I like think I learn better talk from friends. Tonnie taught me before she fell."

"How long was I asleep?"

"Couple of hours. Good for you to sleep long. Water great for drinking. Very bad for swimming."

"Now ya tell me."

"Alex charging when I got back and hasn't said anything. Is he going to be ok?"

"He said none of that water got inside him, but it made short work of his sensor probes and anti-grav cathodes."

"Don't know cathodes."

"They're what make it so he can fly."

"You can fix him when you get back to your ship?"

"Yeah, sure," Gunnar said looking over at the spit. "Been a long time since I had base food."

"Not understand."

"Base food hasn't been processed and compacted for long term storage. Our version of meat, like you have there, would be a cube the size of a small pebble. Our food generators will rehydrogenate it for consumption. Not terrifically appetizing, but it's still classified as edible. This looks and smells great!"

"I make this all the time. Tonnie taught me how to hunt and prepare..."

"Wait, I don't want to know what it is. Last time someone told me what something was, I about brought it back up. Just pass me a big piece."

Janox produced her knife and sliced off a large piece of dripping, well-cooked flesh. Gunnar tossed it back and forth to keep from burning his hands. It tasted amazing. He wished there was a way to have food onboard the *Constellation* taste this good. At this point in their technological evolution, they hadn't figured it out yet.

Janox cut off a couple of pieces and sat back on the other side of the fire to eat.

"So now what happens?" Gunnar asked.

"Not understand question," Janox said with a mouth full.

"We've found Tonnie. We know where she is and what happened to her. Can we all climb back in the ship and get out of here?"

Janox didn't look up from her food.

"I know you could have left any time you and Alex wanted. I know you well enough to know what you can do. You just as curious to know about Tonnie as me. I think Tonnie just hurt. I think we can still save her, maybe."

"How do you save someone whose been dead for such a long time?"

"Alex survive in water, Tonnie might survive too."

"Janox, I wouldn't have lasted more than a minute in that water. Look what ten seconds did to me... And I'm not even human!"

"Maybe Tonnie not human either."

"What are you saying?"

"No remember for sure. Something different about Tonnie. I was young when she fall; I not remember for sure."

"What do you remember?"

"Tonnie fall in, but never come back out."

"Do you think Tonnie was alien?"

"What alien?"

"You know, like me. I'm alien."

"Bud very strong, but even you hurt by water."

"I know, but..." Gunnar pulled his britches on under the blankets, then grabbed his shirt and stood up, bumping his head on the low rock ceiling. "Ouch!"

"Careful, head not harder than rock."

"Funny little girl." Gunnar felt his anger spike as he rubbed his head. He stepped over to Alex and checked a readout on his chest plate.

"Alex ok?" Janox asked.

"Yeah, he's asleep. He'll probably come back on when his batteries are all the way charged." Gunnar stared at Alex for a moment, then glanced back at Janox. He looked back down at Alex, thinking. He shuffled around the room, deep in thought, coming full circle in front of Alex. He squatted down in front of the sleeping droid and looked through some of Tonnie's possessions.

"Those Tonnie's things," Janox said again, becoming a little anxious.

"Yes, you said that before," Gunnar said picking up a pair of electro-binoculars. "These are Tonnie's?"

"Yes, she not use them much. She always see good, but she let me use them till she fell."

Gunnar examined them closely, continuing to puzzle with something in his head. He finally reached down and tapped Alex on the head.

"Alex, wake up."

The droid's lights instantly came on, turning its head.

"Janox, do you have any rope? A really long rope?"

"Have many long rope. Use for climbing big places. Why need long rope?"

"Colonel, I wasn't quite finished charging," Alex complained.

"I know, but I need you to look at something." Gunnar held the binoculars out in front of the droid.

"They're binoculars. Really? You needed me to tell you what they are? This power generator is old and it takes a while to charge. Can I finish please?"

"No, ya dope! Can you scan them? Tell me if they're waterproof?"

"Well of course they're waterproof." Alex was still quite bothered. "It says so right on the label. Oh look! Vandmire Industries made them. Must be good stuff if Diord had anything to do with it."

"Will you please scan them and tell me if they're still waterproof?"

"I cannot comply with your request as the well water has rendered my external sensor probes nonfunctional. I can however perform a visual scan that will accomplish the same thing."

"What do with binoculars?" Janox asked.

"Yes, Colonel, they are still waterproof." Alex said, after a quick look.

Gunnar held them up to his eyes and turned them on.

"Do you think you could readjust the optical pickups in these for close up work? While you're in there, see if you can adapt the astro transmitter so you can receive their telemetry."

"Simple alterations, but why would I need to see through binoculars remotely? I have far better sight capabilities than an old pair of Electro-binoculars."

"Get to work." Gunnar turned to Janox. "Your long rope, let's have it."

"What size you want?"

"You have more than one?"

"Much time on hands. Make many sizes and lengths." Janox motioned Gunnar to a small room off the main room. Inside were rows of stacked rope, neatly coiled. Gunnar examined the expertly woven twine braid, a little surprised by the numbers that lay before him.

"What in the world would you ever use something this big for?" Gunnar held up the end of a large coil. It was the size of his wrist.

"Tonnie made that one. She big and need big rope."

"That's some woman," Gunnar muttered. He looked around and chose a thin coil. "Alex, you finished yet?" He asked, reentering the main room.

"Yes, Colonel. The resolution of these binoculars isn't the greatest, but I've got some pretty good range. Now can you tell me what this is all about?"

Scooping the little droid up, Gunnar headed for the well hallway with Janox right behind. Alex turned his headlights on as they neared the well opening.

"I have to wonder if you need to be stunned again, Colonel. I do not wish to be thrown down into that water again, even if you can pull me back up."

"No, I'm not going to throw you in. I need you up here to be our eyes down there." Gunnar set the droid down and took the binoculars. Making sure they were turned on and the tiny kernel lights were working properly, he tied the rope to them and lowered it into the water. "Let's have a look," Gunnar said holding the rope and squatting down in front of Alex. The little droid's front panel lite up, the screen showing what he was receiving from the binoculars. With the lights turned on they could clearly see the rock face of the well shaft.

"Not sure how far my range will be in these conditions," Alex announced.

"The alternative is to tie the rope around you," Gunnar said letting out more rope.

"Careful, you don't let it hit the sides," Alex said, anxious for Gunnar's plan to work.

Gunnar and Janox watched the display on Alex as the binoculars dropped deeper into the darkness. Several minutes elapsed as they watched the rock wall pass, meter by meter. As they neared the end of the rope, Janox quickly tied another onto it. As they neared the end of the second rope, Alex stopped him.

"Can you turn the rope? There is something here."

"Alex, we're all looking at the same image. We didn't see anything, just rock." Gunnar looked at the display a little closer. "I think if we get to the end of another rope, all we were seeing was just a rock sticking out."

"Turn the rope," Janox urged.

Gunnar turned his lips down, then reached over and started twisting the rope. It took a couple of moments for the image to start to turn, but it continued to send back images of rock. Gunnar detected a dark blur move across the screen as the image continued to turn.

"Sorry," he said trying to be careful. "There must be a current down there."

"No, not a current, Colonel," Alex said. "Hold it right there and see if you can pull away from the wall anymore."

"Not likely. That's a long piece of rope and a narrow shaft." Gunnar stretched his arm out across the pool of water and held it there.

"Far enough away, Colonel, look," Alex said.

Gunnar did his best to hold the rope still as he looked down at the display. There, on the screen was a gloved hand. Gunnar looked harder at the image as Janox pointed at the hand.

"Tonnie!"

Gunnar glanced at Janox who knelt reverently next to Alex, looking at the hand of her Au Pair. He tried to twist the rope ever so slightly to follow the wrist to the arm and perhaps see the rest of the body.

"Well, I guess this confirms things," Gunnar said looking at the sleeved arm. He let a little more rope out and twisted again. "Not too excited about seeing the bones of a dead person. Not that you'll be able to tell for sure, but I don't know how many other people would be inside this planet and drowned in a well."

The image slowly spun around until it came to rest on the head and face. Startled by the image, Gunnar nearly lost his grip on the rope.

"Colonel?" Alex said, letting go of a few chirps.

"This is not even possible," Gunnar exclaimed looking at the perfectly preserved face of a middle-aged woman with long white hair. The woman's eyes were closed, looking as though she were sleeping. "That's got to be some really cold water to preserve a body for that long."

"Perhaps the temperature and whatever the compounds are in the water prevent microbes from feeding on the body tissues or hinder decomposition somehow," Alex offered.

"There it is," Janox pointed excited.

"What?" Gunnar looked harder.

"My present. Tonnie promised to give it to me when I old enough. She keep around her neck. Now time for me to have present."

"I'm not going down there to get that," Gunnar exclaimed. "And as much as I give Alex a hard time, I'm not going to send him down there either."

"Thank you," the little droid commented.

"Then bring Tonnie up here." Janox spoke like it was as easy as walking into the next room.

Gunnar gave the young woman's determined expression a long look.

"Alex, any ideas?"

"I'm not understanding why we've come this far. Now you want me to figure out how to pull the dead weight of a body out of a shaft full of ice water?"

"Alex and Gunnar heal Tonnie," Janox insisted.

"You don't heal someone whose been dead for who knows how long," Gunnar yelled, losing his temper. "You don't heal anyone who's dead, period!" Gunnar held onto his faculties long enough to hand the rope to Janox and storm out. Janox quickly tied the rope off, making sure Alex was ok where he was and took off after Gunnar.

"Don't worry about me in this dark, wet tunnel, I'll be fine," Alex called out.

"Bud, wait!" Janox called. She sped through her dwelling space and out the entrance to find the Kalamarion Colonel pacing back and forth at the edge of the bluff. "Gunnar, please wait. I sorry."

"Sorry for what!?" Gunnar brooded.

"Sorry for forcing you to come here," Janox said.

"You didn't force me to do anything."

"Then why you angry?"

"Because I am who I am and I can't change it! Because I'm more torn up inside now than I ever was. I don't want to see anymore dead people; I've seen enough death!"

"Death is part of life."

"Whoever told you that is a naïve idiot."

"I not know what, how you say, naïve idiot is, but you were the one that told me that."

"Well, in any other circumstance, it's idiotic! I won't participate in death anymore! I can't!"

"Bud, know it not a choice."

"Stop calling me that," Gunnar sputtered. "You know my name!"

"You told me to call you Bud!"

"I was joking," he seethed. "I hate that name! My name is, Gunnar..." he picked up a nearby boulder that would tax even a hydro-lift. "Lee..." He exerted as hard as he could, tossing it against the canyon wall. "Conrad!" The large rock shattered into pieces on impact as did part of the canyon wall. Gunnar turned back to Janox with a fiery look of rage contorting his face. Breathing hard he wasn't so far gone he didn't recognize the puzzled look on Janox's face.

Calming slightly, he realized she wasn't looking at him at all, but beyond him. Whirling around, the dust was just settling in front of a large section of rock that had simply vanished, exposing a mechanism of circuits and piping. Several lights blinked sporadically next to a couple of displays behind multiple layers of technology.

"What the...?" Gunnar exclaimed. He looked over at Janox as she stepped up next to him. "What is this?" he asked.

Janox returned his look with an equally puzzled expression.

"I not know. Have never seen this before? What is it?"

Gunnar stepped forward for a closer look, but motioned back to Janox.

"Go bring Alex back out here."

Without being prompted a second time, Janox disappeared and returned a short time later with the little droid. As she set him down, Gunnar peered inside the broken barrier.

"Alex, what do you make of this?" Gunnar asked.

The droid rolled quickly forward, stopping just short of the opening.

"This is Albion and Colonian technology, Colonel."

"Both?"

"Yes, I recognize the alphabets and symbols being used."

"It looks like it's operating. What's it supposed to do?" Gunnar asked.

"I am without my external sensors, Colonel. It is impossible to know what its purpose is." Alex turned and sped back down into Janox's dwelling.

"This is nuts," Gunnar muttered angrily. Examining the mechanism carefully, he tried to follow where everything snaked off to. "What were you and Tonnie even doing down here?" He turned back to Janox, his anger boiling back to the surface.

"I not know," Janox answered quietly. "It our home..."

"No! It's not a home! It's a prison! You were sent here to die! Tonnie is dead and you just happened to survive! Can't you get that through your thick head? You're supposed to be dead, for whatever reason!"

"Tonnie not dead. She fall. She is hurt."

"Janox, Tonnie is dead, and not you, Alex or me can bring her back!"

"Tonnie like Gunnar and me," Janox said after a long pause. "But, I think Tonnie like Alex too."

"Tonnie... is... dead!" Gunnar yelled the words at the top of his lungs, then finally dropped to his knees, his fists slamming against the ground several times. "She's dead and she's never coming back, never..." He let his head sink to the ground, puffing hard, trying to regain his composure. Janox tried to comfort him, but he pushed her away. "You need to give me a moment."

After several minutes of stillness, Gunnar looked out across the expanse of the canyon before them, noticing the fowl on the other side becoming restless. Occasionally a couple of them would take flight and soar up and down the canyon. He took several deep breathes and closed his eyes. Trying to relax his hands from digging further into his palms, he imagined himself somewhere else. Under his tree amidst a great pile of leaves. Here, there was no internal pain or scrambling of thoughts. Only quiet and comfort. He felt relaxed as he enjoyed the feel of leaves all around him and their odors. In his mind, he cracked an eyelid and peaked up at the sun, then over to the great tree trunk. Leaning against it was Audra. She smiled and spoke his name.

"Gunnar," Janox repeated.

"Wait!" Gunnar's eyes popped open. "You said, Tonnie is like you and me?"

"Yes, I think she is, but different somehow. Not remember well. Very young when she fall. Strong like you, but she need to plug in, like Alex."

"Alex?" Gunnar developed an odd expression. "Tonnie's a droid?" Gunnar asked.

"Not like Alex. Need power, but not like Alex. More like you and me."

"An Android."

"Not understand what android means."

"Like Alex, but like you and me, human. In my culture, they were built to integrate into human society better; an Alex made to look human. But we had problems with it and decided something less humanoid worked better." Gunnar thought a moment. "The droids I've seen in this galaxy are far less sophisticated than ours, so it's a little hard to believe you guys would have androids."

"Colonel," Alex called from the dwelling door. "You need to come look at this immediately."

Refocused, Gunnar and Janox bolted to the door and were headed back down the dank hallway toward the well. Gunnar scooped Alex up and carried him the rest of the way, gently setting him down next to the opening. The display on the front torso of Alex came back on as Gunnar and Janox knelt closer.

"What are we looking at?" Gunnar asked as Tonnie's face reappeared.

"Just wait a moment," Alex said.

"Alex, do you have the history of android development in Kalamarion society in your data banks?" Gunnar asked.

"I do, but why the interest now?"

"I think we're dealing with an android here, but I know at least Kalamar used to have them."

"Androids became widely used for a myriad of things in Kalamarion society a century ago, but because the human populations were trying to give them the same rights the humans had, it became too complicated for any government entity to regulate what was real and what was synthetic. Some humans tried to bond with them. It was all unraveling into the unnatural and so they were abolished. Androids are still present, but only in illegal pockets of black-market sales and trading on outer rim systems where enforcement is difficult."

Janox suddenly gasped, putting her hand to her lips. Gunnar passed her a glance.

"Colonel!" Alex said.

Gunnar looked down at the display, seeing Tonnie's white hair floating in front of her face. As her hair drifted away, one of her eyes opened, a green glow emanating from the retina.

"Tonnie alive!" Janox exclaimed.

"Not possible," Gunnar refuted. "Maybe it's just residual battery power discharging from her core?"

"Are you willing to chance your knowledge of the internal workings of a Hadrian android on this?" Alex asked.

Gunnar stared at Tonnie, watching the eye close again.

"Janox, come help me," he said springing to his feet and heading back up the hallway to where the ropes were. "These are all the same length?" Gunnar was pulling on the coil of large rope.

"Yes, but how you pull her up?" Janox asked.

Gunnar dropped the coils just outside the well hallway and looked around.

"You get these down there and I'll be right back." Gunnar hurried back out to the plateau and headed straight for the Interceptor. Climbing back inside, he fumbled around for the tool bin. Grabbing the largest tool he could find, he made his way back to the well shaft. Janox already had the two ends of the thick rope tied together when Gunnar returned. Passing the large tool to her, he pulled the lengths of rope out straight while Janox worked to tie the hook shaped tool to the end of the rope.

"What are you hoping to do with this?" Alex asked as Gunnar dropped the tool and rope into the well.

"The clamp hooks on those spanners should be strong enough to hold Tonnie while we lift her up," he said playing the rope out.

"Strong enough, yes, but how are you going to attach it to her?"

"She's an android, Alex. She should have something on her we can hook to. Janox, move the image around and see if you can find something." Gunnar pushed the rope in faster, slowing only when the tied ends slid over the side of the well.

"This would be a whole lot easier if we had a gear-maged winch set in here. We could have this done in half the time." Gunnar continued to play out the rope until he started coming close to the end. Stopping the rope from running through his hands was a little harder than he had anticipated, but he was sure the real work was yet to come.

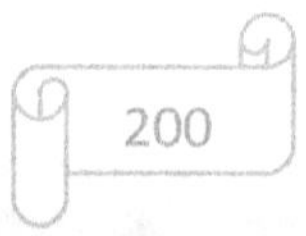

"Colonel, stop," Alex called out. The spanner appeared in the image, bumping into Tonnie's head. Her eyelid cracked open again and the green glow reappeared.

"Find anywhere to hook this thing too yet?" Gunnar asked, watching the android slowly blink its eyelid.

"Nothing," Janox said, still trying to spin the image in new areas.

"Wait," Alex said. "Go back to her face."

Janox gently twisted the image back around until the face came into view again. Between the eyelids, the green eye was moving.

"She's looking at her hand," Janox said, maneuvering the image up.

"That's it!" Gunnar exclaimed. He pulled back on the rope and waited. Holding his breath, he watched the spanner gradually drifted towards the hand. Bumping the fingers at first, he applied a little up and down motion and the hook shaped tool slipped into the android's palm. After several anxious moments, the hand closed around it.

"Here..." Janox shoved a pair of gloves at Gunnar. "You need these. Water make rope very cold; these help."

"As I pull, you move this rope out of the way," Gunnar said, pulling up the slack, reaching toward the water and pulling as hard as he could.

With his feet firmly planted against the rock, he heaved, pulling the rope up meter by meter. Starting to breath hard, Gunnar tried to get himself into a rhythm to maximize his energy use. Halfway through the rope, the large knot appeared and he stopped to rest. Leaning against the tunnel wall, he looked at Janox. She had her head against the rock, listening to something. He turned around and looked down into the darkness.

"Where does this passage come out?" He could feel an ominous presence starting to build in the mountain. The rock itself felt like it was beginning to vibrate.

"It opens to the canyon below," Janox replied. "I have many ladders placed on cliff wall to valley floor."

"Colonel," Alex hedged. He spun his head. "Are you detecting anything odd?"

"You're the one with all the sensors, Alex. Why would I be able to detect anything? What's wrong with you?"

"Is he talking about ears hurting?" Janox grunted hard as she moved a large pile of rope out of the way.

"I think so," Gunnar said securing the rope around a stone pillar. "How long will it take to get to the end of this tunnel?"

"Faster to go out top to look," Janox said. She turned in front of Gunnar and they trotted out to the rock bluff beside the Interceptor.

"So, this doesn't look right at all," Gunnar said turning in a circle. Great plums of water were gushing from the canyon walls. Looking up, he could see the great pools in the ceiling starting to bulge, as if being pushed up by some unseen force. Looking over the canyon rim, the water had flooded the entire bottom and while it was moving down in the direction of the Redle caves, he could just make out an equal amount of water coming from that direction.

"Not right," Janox exclaimed. "Even in rainy season here there no be waterfalls that high up. Too much water coming down." They looked around. There seemed to be water coming from everywhere. Even on their side, water was starting to seep from every crack in the canyon wall. Gunnar turned to the blinking mechanism embedded in the rock wall. The readouts were flashing a myriad of information and the warning lights were blinking erratically.

"Wonder if I broke something? I'd say we better get out of here as soon as we can."

Heading back inside, Gunnar could feel his ears pop several times as they went.

"Can you tell me what's happening outside?" Alex inquired.

"Waterfalls are popping out of nowhere all over the place. If it keeps up, we could be getting wet," Gunnar said grabbing the rope.

"Not to alarm anyone, but I have detected a change in the atmospheric pressure from the last time we were here. Even down here, I am detecting a constant change."

"My ears have popped a couple of times in just the last couple of minutes," Gunnar said, glancing at the display.

"What mean, ears pop?" Janox asked.

"Differential pressure between the outside air and the inside of the inner ear…"

"Alex, she's not going to know what you're talking about." Gunnar snapped.

"Ear hurts, but if I swallow, they clunk and feel better?" Janox offered.

Gunnar looked over at Janox, then down at Alex.

"Not going to know?" Alex teased.

"Just means those speech lessons we've been giving her aren't as boring as she's been letting on. Remind me to have the General dial back your humor setting a little," Gunnar said starting to pull on the rope again.

"No, lessons still boring," Janox said.

"Colonel, can you hear something?" Alex asked, turning his head toward the darkness of the hallway past the well opening.

"I can hear me puffing to pull this dead weight up."

"It sounds like rushing water," Janox said.

"Colonel," Alex had raised the volume of his voice. "I am detecting large amounts of water filling into the lower portions of this tunnel. My range is far too limited to ascertain what's happening on the outside to cause this."

"There's water all around us, Alex," Gunnar said heaving. Getting into a rhythm, Gunnar pulled, then held it while he grabbed for more rope.

"How we doing?"

Janox looked at the display and nodded.

"She hangs on."

"Usually droids don't need any power to hold onto something."

"Must pull harder," Janox encouraged, looking back down the shaft behind her. She could hear the ominous rumble of water against rock and the wash of waves moving up the hallway toward them.

Gunnar leaned into it, trying to increase his rhythm.

"You need to pull harder," Alex beckoned.

"Feel free to get up here and help anytime," Gunnar puffed. Even with his strength, he was starting to tire and the sound of water working its way up the hallway towards them did nothing for his comfort level.

"Tonnie!" Janox yelled as the android's hand appeared coming over the edge of the well.

"Alex, get back to the ship, now!"

The tone in Gunnar voice was anything but calm as he pulled the heavy bulk of the lifeless android from the hole. Water was just beginning to work its way around their feet. While the little droid couldn't fly anymore, it's tank tracks still worked well and propelled him back up the hall and into the dwelling toward the outer door. Janox and Gunnar pulled the android up the hallway, out and away from the knee-deep water. Dragging the rope with them, it caught several times as they moved toward the door.

"Tonnie," Janox called. "Let go of rope!"

Now everything was wet and weighing them all down as the water swelled out of the hallway and into the dwelling after them. Struggling to get out the front door and up onto the plateau, Gunnar turned and picked up the android as it let go of the rope. There was only a moment for him to look around as he followed Janox toward the awaiting Interceptor. The canyon was gone; submerged under a cascade of roaring water pouring from the walls and the pools in the ceiling. The air lashed at them while they ran to the ship as the engines started turning up.

"We need her power generator," Janox insisted as they climbed into the ship.

"And where would you like me to put it?" Gunnar asked, setting Tonnie on the hatch threshold and climbing over her. He looked back at the dwelling door as water began to boil out.

"But you not be able to fix her without it," Janox insisted.

"We'll figure it out." Gunnar pulled Tonnie up inside and hit the hatch mechanism. "I'm sure between me and Alex, we can think of something. Alex, get us airborne!"

"Not much air left in here to get into, Sir."

Gunnar climbed up into the cockpit and dropped into the seat as the fighter lifted from the plateau.

"It's gotta be going somewhere."

"Wonder what caused all this?" Janox asked, looking back at the mechanism being engulfed. She took her place behind the pilot's seat and steadied herself.

"Much of the water is coming from those," Alex said, activating a screen over Gunnar's head. Banks of manmade valves appeared on the display. Enormous amounts of water gushed unchecked into the cavern from the open valves. "My best analysis shows this subterranean world was created by valving the water entryways and pumping the cavern full of air. The differential pressure was meticulously balanced to make sure the water didn't come in and the air didn't get out."

"Either we broke something or someone's discovered we're down here," Gunnar said maneuvering the fighter away from any cascades of water that would surely pound the craft out of what air was left.

"Or the mechanism was set off automatically. Perhaps something we did?"

"We need to get up one of those shafts, but I'm not liking how much water's coming out of them," Gunnar said. Janox strained to see out the overhead windows, trying to find a hole they could exit from. Gunnar steered his ship out into the middle of the enormous cavern and set the craft down on the turbulent surface.

"Not seeing your logic, Colonel," Alex hedged, uneasy.

Gunnar checked his instruments as the fighter was tossed by giant waves. Reaching for the throttles, he pushed the yoke forward and nosed the ship beneath the waves.

"Best place to be in a storm is as far away from it as possible." Gunnar turned on the infrared sights on the forward glass and guided his ship to the bottom of the submerged canyon bringing it to a gentle landing on what used to be the sandy river bottom. They were now fathoms below the rising surface water. Shutting the engines back down, he turned off most of the ship's systems and settled back in the pilot's seat. "Whadaya think of that?"

"In all this excitement, the bottom had not occurred to me," Alex admitted.

Gunnar looked back to find Janox absent. Turning all the way around, he spotted her down the access shaft, huddled next to the lifeless form of Tonnie.

"I guess we might as well haul her up here so we can have a look while we wait for the turbulence to settle."

"I calculate about half an hour, Sir," Alex informed him, turning his head toward the shaft.

Gunnar settled on a perch just above Tonnie and watched as Janox carefully pulled something from around the android's neck. Holding it up, she gazed at a large locket on a stout chain.

"My present," Janox announced.

"Ok, so what is it?" Gunnar asked.

Janox continued to stare at it, but finally looked at Gunnar.

"Not know. Only know it for me when I old enough."

"You have no idea what it is or what to do with it?"

Janox shook her head and climbed up the shaft past Gunnar as he helped Alex down, setting him next to the lifeless android.

"What do you think?" Gunnar asked, watching Alex scan the surface of Tonnie's torso and head.

"There's an energy signature here, quite minimal. Not enough to power up her systems. I can only postulate she had just enough to manipulate her eye and hand for a short while."

"Can you rig something to get her charging. Maybe get enough in her to activate her systems?" Gunnar asked.

"I think I can adapt the Interceptor's charging systems to provide enough power to bring her back online. But if she's as old as we think she is, and being submerged for as long as she has, her batteries may be compromised and will have to be refitted or regenerated. That can only be done onboard the *Constellation*. We don't even know if the water has compromised any of her internal circuits or mechanisms. It's a sure bet if she has anything external, they are long gone."

"Well, see what you can do," Gunnar said.

After climbing back into the pilot's seat, Gunnar checked a couple of readouts, then turned to Janox who sat with her back against the pilot's seat.

"So, what do you think?" he asked.

"I wait long time to have this, now I holding it, I not know what to think." Janox gazed at its shiny metallic surface. Gunnar recognized the Colonian symbols etched into its surface. There were symbols on the other side as well, but at the moment he couldn't see them well enough to know what they were.

"Did Tonnie ever say what it does or how to open it?"

"No, only that it special and guide me when I older."

"That's cryptic," Gunnar mumbled sarcastically.

Janox looked up at the back window of the fighter. It was dark and foreboding and there were strange noises swirling all around the parked fighter.

"I have nothing now. Home gone and only thing have is this."

"We have Tonnie," Gunnar gestured toward the lower hatchway.

Janox looked at the locket and then up at Gunnar.

"I not sure I want to talk to her."

"But she holds the key to what that locket does or where it leads."

"I angry with her now."

"Angry? Why would you be angry with an android? She took care of you. She was your protection while you were here."

"She leave me alone. I just little girl when leave me alone."

"Janox, it was an accident. You said it yourself, she fell into the well and couldn't get back out. It was too deep. Geez, I fell in and nearly died!"

"She android. She made to take care of me. Androids not slip and fall."

"Hate to break it to you kid, but they certainly do. Alex is always bumping into things…"

"I heard that," came a call from below.

"You know it's true," Gunnar called back. "I guess my point here is, you need to first be grateful we were able to bring her out of there and second, wait to see if she can explain what happened before you pass judgement."

"She the only mother I ever know."

"All the more reason to be patient."

Janox thought a long moment, rolling the locket in her hand.

"I be as patient as you."

"Not fair," Gunnar said trying to smile. "I'm expending far more energy than you are."

"Colonel," Alex called.

Gunnar crawled past Janox and down to where Alex was examining with the internal workings of the android.

"Very sophisticated designs for the type of tech we've encountered in this galaxy," Alex observed. "I'm actually sort of in awe at what I'm seeing here."

"Now, Alex, no falling in love. It would be illogical." Gunnar grinned broadly.

"Really, Colonel?" Alex sounded less than amused.

"Can you get power hooked up to her?"

"Yes, I have and her batteries seem to be responding to the charge. It'll be a couple of minutes before we can attempt a startup. The better news is, even as long as she was submerged, she has remained watertight." Alex chirped several times as he continued to scan the internal workings of the android.

Several dull thumps against the hull of the resting fighter brought Gunnar back up to the pilot's station. Unmoved, Janox continued to examine the locket as Gunnar checked several readouts on the scanning panel. Several more thumps vibrated the hull.

"Alex, any objections to lifting off a little sooner than later?"

"Can you provide more information?"

"There's some kind of undertow forming down here. It's picking up all kinds of crap and tossing it around. I'd hate to have another run in like we almost had last time we were here."

"Not likely, but prudent thinking all the same," Alex said.

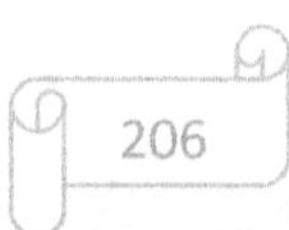

Gunnar settled into his seat and restarted all the systems, bringing the engines back online. As he carefully brought the fighter off the bottom, there were several more bumps, followed by a substantial strike. Janox was up in an instant with her hands clamped around the back of the seat.

"Well, that was different," Gunnar said checking his readouts.

"Is a rock like last time?" Janox asked looking outside into the black.

Gunnar watched something slip past the front of the ship, just touching the glass as it slunk around out of sight. He reached over and brought up all the exterior lights. Startled, he counted four pairs of red glaring eyes staring back at him. Holding the fighter steady, he waited to see if there were more; there were. Another long, single finned form slid past the window again, this time knocking it several times as it went.

"And what would you call these?" he asked, strapping himself in.

"Not know," Janox breathed, terrified at the size and number of razor teeth.

"Should I blast them?" Gunnar suggested.

"You should get us out of here," Janox said, bracing herself as two of the long-finned creatures charged the ship, slapping it abruptly right on the nose.

"Rubbish," Gunnar gritted angrily. "Sometimes I wonder if the speech lessons were a good idea. Now you talk too much." He pulled back on the controls and adjusted the reverse thrusters.

"Colonel, could you please hold the ship still," Alex called from below. "I'm trying to work."

"Leave her where she is for now," Gunnar called back. "I've got my hands full here and it's gonna get bumpy for the next couple of minutes."

The creatures slapped the ship again, this time from multiple angles. Two of them wrapped themselves around each wing and started to squeeze. Another one attached itself to the front end, blocking the forward windshield. Gunnar looked up as an eye pressed against the overhead glass. There came a loud scraping sound against the hull from several locations and a moment later, several rows of long teeth were leveraging against the upper glass.

"Ok, nobody scrapes the paint," Gunnar said turning the shields up to full power. This seemed to stop the teeth, but did nothing to free them from their grasp. "Ah, nuts!" Gunnar finally activated the weapons systems and pulled the triggers. A pulsing flash lit up the exterior followed by dark clouds of something mixed with pieces of drifting material. There came a horrible wail from outside and the fighter bucked violently from side to side. Gunnar fired again. Again, more flashing light, dark inky clouds and fleshy material accompanied by high pitched wailing noises. Finally, the creature that had pasted itself to the nose of the craft, slipped away, revealing large gaps where flesh had once been. All of the creatures finally abandoned the attack except for one. Sporting several wounds that flowed dark fluid as it hovered just in front of the ship, it stared back at Gunnar.

"We go," Janox insisted.

"Unless we can lose it… that… whatever it is, will probably dawg us all the way to the surface."

"You best pilot ever. Fly faster and better than it swim."

"You know this how?" Gunnar edged backward again. He could easily kill the creature, but surmised it was just a scared animal that got caught up in the flush of water from the surface.

"I fly with you and CJ last time. It charge again," Janox warned, watching the creature posturing.

"Counting on it," Gunnar said, shoving the throttle all the way forward as the creature lunged. Instead of hitting it head on, Gunnar dipped the nose, ducking the craft just beneath the charging beast, then he pulled back hard on the yoke, giving the scanners a glance and steering toward the surface.

"Is still following us?" Janox asked, barely hanging on to the back of the seat by her fingernails.

"Probably," Gunnar said, holding the yoke back and letting the fighter invert onto it's back. Leveling out, he rolled it over and turned sharply to the right.   A quick look at the tracking screen showed the creature tailing them. "Nimble little minx."

"How know where going?" Janox asked. She couldn't see a thing outside but the dark mirk of the unsettled water.

"I just do," Gunnar reassured her. Giving his scanner a glance, he touched several controls on the navigation panel and eyed the readouts over his head. "Just wanna make sure our friend back there doesn't catch up to us. Ah, here we go." Gunnar rolled the ship again and turned it sharply up, firing his weapons. Several explosions flashed ahead of them, rocking the fighter with concussions as it sped through a cloud of bubbles and falling rock. As the debris cleared and the ride smoothed out, Gunnar checked his tracking instruments, then turned to the navigation panel and activated several controls. Letting go of the yoke, he turned to Janox.

"To the surface," he said climbing out of the seat and peering down the hatchway shaft at Alex. "Still in one piece down there?"

"Yes, Colonel," Alex said as he closed the access panel he had been working in. "I think we're ready to see if she'll power up."

"Ok, let's give it a try."

Alex touched a spot under Tonnie's hairline on the back of her neck and rolled himself back. Nothing happened. Gunnar watched the lifeless android for a long moment, then looked at Alex. At least he had lights to let people know he was operating.

"Is she still plugged in?" Gunnar asked.

"Yes." Alex turned his head back to the android. "Perhaps there is damage I cannot detect?"

"Well, maybe we can have a better look at her when we get back to the ship. Let's face it, a lower hatchway isn't an ideal spot to make repairs on an android."

"Agreed," Alex said, pulling himself back up in the cockpit.

Gunnar climbed back into the pilot's seat and checked his instruments.

"What is your plan once we reach the surface?" Alex asked.

"What do you mean, what's my plan? We follow standard procedure; run a couple of orbits around Reako until we find out where the ship is, then meet back up and *whoosh*, we're outa here."

"Haven't I heard similar plans like this before?"

"Come on, Alex. Have a little faith."

"As you are so fond of pointing out, I am incapable of such human platitudes. I can only operate on facts and logic."

"Alex, Alex, Alex. Weren't you the one who indicated the General programed your AI engines with the ability to leap beyond logic? You wanted to seek after what makes us humans, human."

"While that may be true, there are some humans who are both unpredictable and predictable at the same time."

"Sounds like you have a real quandary trying to figure that out." Gunnar turned and checked his readouts. "Ha! Let's see that fish follow us to the surface that quick." He took a hold of the controls and slowed the fighter as they broke the surface. Letting the ship float on the water for several minutes, he ran a scan of the area.

"Nuts," Gunnar frowned. "Forgot about not being able to see much of anything on this planet. We'll need to get into orbit before we can locate the ship."

"If it's still here," Alex said. "We've been down in this planet much longer than Captain Abrams would have been prepared for."

"His orders were to get to Carolon, get the Asium and then get out. If there were any problems, he was to abandon the mission and high tail it back to Aster. But like you said, the *Constellation* and *Realistic* are probably already gone."

"What we do now?" Janox asked.

Gunnar craned to see all around them. Nothing had changed with the atmosphere of this dark planet. It was still a mixture of dark clouds, lightning storms and rain.

"Ace in the hole for this swamp you used to call a home is it has a nice big ring of asteroids we can hide in while we have a good look around."

"We could always just make a lightspeed jump to Cross and then back to Aster," Alex offered.

"Let's make that plan B," Gunnar said throttling the Interceptor into the air. "We'll get up to the ring first, find out where the ship is

and then decide what to do from there." Gunnar did a number of sweeps across the dark surface of the area, then steered for a hole in the clouds. But it was a hole to multiple layers of other clouds. There would be no escaping the lightning reaching out at them as they climbed higher through the mirk, finally blowing out the tops and into the darkness of space. Reako's asteroid rings quickly came into view, providing cover from seeking eyes.

Rubbish

"This is complete and utter rubbish," Blinda fumed. "I will be reporting this to the KC immediately. You're going to have a lot of explaining to do."

"You must do what you feel is best," Drax replied. She stood relaxed with a firmly implanted smile as she let her gaze wander all around the top of the *Tarzana*. Encircled by its flotilla, the massive battlecruiser held its position at a precise location in space, just outside the Jurass system. In the distance, a cluster of ships held their position as a few envoy ships made their way to the open landing bays of the Albion flag ship.

"Are you at least going to go down to meet him?" Blinda blurted in frustration. The Thane paced anxiously to another window to get a better look at the shuttles maneuvering through the flotilla.

"Why? That's what the ship's commander is for." Drax remained calm. Her supreme confidence was getting the better of Blinda, who couldn't hold still.

"This is madness," Blinda sputtered, taking her cloak and starting for the door of the Command lounge. "I'll go down and then I'll make a live report to the King Commander. I expect you to be present as he's going to want to have a talk with you anyway."

"Shall I provide you with the fast link to his personal communicator, or shall we use the council frequencies to make sure there are more witnesses to your transmission?"

Blinda stopped before she reached the elevator door. Completely bewildered as to the Queen Captain's behavior. *Why isn't she bothered by my threats?*

"What are you doing?" the Thane asked, turning.

Drax remained silent until the envoy had disappeared under the great cruiser.

"I'm relaxing," Drax finally mused. "I have a plan and everything is working out exactly how I have envisioned it."

"You launch a wild idea to strike Diord's alien ship in a system you've been forbidden to enter, lure your sister back onboard and give her command of Albia's greatest battlecruiser and accompanying fleet, then let her drive it to Cross…"

"Outside Jurass," Drax corrected.

"Now you're letting her cavort with Diord Vandmire, her known accomplice?" Blinda countered.

"For the life of me, I can't understand what you're so upset about. Can you see anywhere in any of what you just said that runs counter to what KC Dismon has ordered of me?"

Blinda opened her mouth to speak, but stopped, thinking.

"Tell me," Drax said. She sat stretching her arms and clasping her hands behind her head. "What could Administrator Vandmire and my sister possibly say or do together that's going to alter the outcome of the Pintar rite of Hadrian?"

"Of all the people that could possibly interrupt your grand plans, those two would be the first two I'd finger," Blinda retorted. She stomped back into the lounge and dropped her cloak over one of the chairs. Drax smiled at the Thane and waved a hand in her direction.

"Then by all means, if you really think they're going to cause such a ruckus onboard this ship or in any other place, then you need to be down there to monitor everything they say and do."

Blinda grabbed her cloak again and threw it around her shoulders as she headed back to the door. Before she boarded the elevator, Drax called to her.

"But if you do, be prepared to get even less information out of Commander Barker while she is in command of this ship."

Blinda paused at the threshold for a moment, twisting her head to the side, then entered and disappeared behind the closing door. Drax sat for a moment, smiling confidently. She leaned back further and brought her communicator up from under her cloak.

"Captain Jarvis. Get me an update on the *Warbird* mission as soon as it becomes available."

"Right away, QC," came the quick reply from the com.

Drax swung her legs up onto the couch and crossed her arms over her chest. After staring through the glass roof of the command lounge at the cosmos for several minutes, she drifted off to sleep.

*　　*　　*　　*

Remaining just inside the open doorway of his shuttle craft, Diord looked anxiously outside at the crowd of officers and emissaries for a familiar shade of auburn curls. Looking in both directions, he finally spotted CJ walking toward the group, surrounded by several deck officers, aides and bay guards. Dressed in uniform black with her hair stuffed under a service cap, Colonel Barker tried to keep her stride as mechanical as possible, holding with the Albion military's regulations when receiving visitors aboard ship. As her group faced the lead envoy from Cross, she remained long enough to greet the highest ranking politician, then faded back to let her aides greet the rest.

Diord could hardly hold himself back. The transmission sent directly to him on his cruiser, the *Hampton*, had been coded with her Albion credentials. His heart pounded as he worked up the courage to step out. As he continued to wrestle with himself to move, one of the shuttle pilots called to him from the cockpit.

"Administrator, landing instructions require we be empty, and all doors closed before we shut down. I need you to exit the craft."

Diord acknowledged the pilot and stepped down the short walkway, purposely looking away from the crowd of people. He pretended to check the shuttle behind him to see if the pilots were still seated and their doors were closed. Having no other excuses not to look, he finished his descent to the bay floor and turned toward the crowd. He hadn't noticed them when they landed, but there was a large contingent of troopers and military hardware on display; nearly filling the landing bay. Most of what he was looking at was all equipment that had come from his factories; just painted in Albion colors.

As he made it to the bottom of the steps and stood between two armed soldiers standing at attention, he realized they had created a walkway for him. The only thing missing now was the red carpet. He moved away from the shuttle and turned down the row of troops toward a small cluster of aides and military officers. His heart suddenly jumped into his throat as he recognized CJ Barker turn and face him. He felt himself broadening his step to reach her and everything in the landing bay became muted as she smiled pleasantly and started toward him. Diord fought the feelings he knew all too well, trying to keep his relief and admiration for her bridled. Finally, he stopped in front of her and smiled broadly. Fighting the overpowering feeling to throw his arms around her, he bowed and took her hand, gently kissing it. He felt her pull back a little when he didn't release her immediately. When he looked back up at her, he saw a broad smile and flushing checks.

"I suppose you think I owe you a date?" CJ said in a quiet voice.

"A date?" Diord repeated. "I don't remember the promise being for a date. Now, dinner, yes, but not a full-blown date." He looked around at the interior of the landing bay and at all the troops assembled. "Besides, I can think of far better places to take you on a date."

"Oh," CJ mussed, teasingly. "So you wouldn't want to date me here aboard ship? And I wore my best uniform."

Diord grinned broadly, wishing he could just take her by the hand, load her back in his shuttle and take off.

"Do you think we can wrap up our business early enough to at least get dinner in?"

"I'm so counting on it," CJ replied, turning and walking leisurely with Diord by her side. The rest of their entourage fell in line behind them, a few paces back.

"If I had known you were going to show me spit and polish, I might have worn my dress cloak," Diord said looking around at the sea of troopers holding at attention in the bay.

"The one you're wearing is doing a pretty good job, not that you need any help," CJ commented, keeping her gaze straight ahead.

Diord turned a circle as they walked. It was nice to look up and see many of his machines hanging above them or hangered in multi layered shelves all around the landing bay. Most of what he was seeing looked as though they had never seen action. In fact, they were so well polished, he wondered if they hadn't just accepted delivery.

"Where's the stuff you actually use?" he asked looking at several ROACH transports sitting in a row next to a long row of Black Tigers.

"What are you talking about? We use these all the time."

"Oh course I believe you," the Cross administrator chided good-naturedly. "I bet we pass the storage rooms holding all the cans of polish and a bunch of dirty rags."

"I bet we don't," CJ responded confidently. "Those rooms are on the other side of the bay. We're going this way," she said pointing to a set of doors at the end of a long line of troops and officers.

"You need to loosen up a little," Diord said nudging her enough to make her waiver from her straight line.

CJ didn't flinch, but corrected her path. A few steps later, she nudged Diord, causing him to veer off; almost into the line of officers just feet away from them. He had to spin around to keep from crashing into the line. When he was facing forward again, he was right back in step with CJ. A few more steps and Diord gently bumped her shoulder with his. A few more steps and CJ repeated the maneuver. They held a straight face as they bumped into the other the rest of the way to the double exit doors of the landing bay. Neither of them noticed a solitary figure sitting next to a stowed Starhopper in an open fighter shelf, high above the landing bay. Blinda watched the two disappear below her, but remained on the open shelf, thinking.

*   *   *   *

An inspection of all the fighter decks, all the assault craft decks and an example of the armory took way longer than Diord was hoping. He was anxious to know what was going on in CJ's head. He understood why she was here; the ultimatum Drax had given her made that quite plain, but he was sure there was more to it than just Gunnar's life. And there was something else worrying him; where was Drax? Shouldn't the Albion Queen Captain be greeting the highest ranking official of the manufacturing juggernaut producing nearly all their fighting hardware? He was grateful to be walking next to CJ and listening to her voice, but the absence of the Queen Captain bothered him.

"As you can see by this list," CJ continued, handing Diord a small display. "There are several improvements we're needing on the indicated fighters and some trouble areas requiring an immediate field modification."

Diord studied the list carefully.

"Geez, you weren't nearly this picky with what I was sending you on Aster." He passed the display back to one of his aides.

"I wasn't paying for what you were sending me on Aster," CJ replied, still focused on the business at hand.

"Most of that list will require some major reworks. It will take quite a while to come up with a good refit," Diord said, keeping pace with her.

"It's my job to see that this ship and all its associated components, including auxiliary craft, are operating as specified. If it isn't right or still under your manufacturer's warranty, then wouldn't you want to know about it?"

"I suppose so," Diord agreed.

CJ stopped and turned to the rest of the group.

"I appreciate any input your team can provide on these issues. I know you're all anxious to get back to Cross and get to work on these field repairs and modifications. If you'll step into the ship's cafeteria, you can pick anything you'd like from the menu."

Diord moved to enter the crowded lunchroom, but CJ stood in his path.

"Where do you think you're going, Mister?"

"Getting a bite to eat."

"I think not," CJ said, taking his arm. "You owe me a dinner and not with the rest of the crowd. So, if you'll come this way, I've had something special prepared." CJ walked him down a long hall and into an elevator. After exiting, they made several turns before entering a small, quiet room with a view of the stern of the *Tarzana*. The room had been darkened with small light stems illuminating the table and its sparkling dinnerware. An attendant took Diord's cloak, then CJ's uniform jacket and service cap as they took their seats. Before they had a chance to even look at each other, they were being served. Once they started eating, Diord looked up. Music started to play from the room's hidden sound system. He looked back at CJ with a tipped head and a raised eyebrow.

"Really?"

"Too much?" she smiled.

"A little," he agreed leaning in closer.

CJ snickered softly and touched a control on the corner of the table; the music becoming quiet.

"So just how alone are we?" Diord asked as they went back to eating.

"About as alone as we could possibly get without being in suits outside or down in the maintenance bay. Why?"

"I don't normally do field inspections on production equipment, only beta gear. And then only the, *really blow your mind* kind of stuff." They ate the rest of the meal in silence, then made their way to the window with their drinks to look out across the broad stern of the great ship. The gunners were performing maintenance on the enormous turrets, swinging them back and forth and raising them up, then back down. It had the appearance of a complex dance. As they stood close, sipping their drinks, CJ set her glass on the sill and turned to Diord.

"I imagine you have some questions," CJ finally said.

"A few."

"You know the last thing I wanted to do is to pull you into a political skirmish. I know how you and Cross feel about your sovereignty, but I couldn't think of anyone else to turn to."

"Well, it looks like you turned to your sister and Albia."

"I'm sure it does. I assume you and Talia were able to view Drax's message."

"And Willis... and her commentary."

CJ chuckled softly thinking of her aide.

"I sort of knew they'd figure out how to access it."

"That was a pretty rotten thing you did to Talia and all those people you left on Aster."

"What else was I supposed to do?"

Diord drew in a deep breath and slowly shook his head.

"I don't know. But I assume that's not the reason I'm here."

"You're right," CJ said, pulling something from her pocket.

"The antidote for the Kodiak Blu," Diord said looking at a small vile of fluid.

"A variant of it. You already know most humans die within a week without the antidote."

"I don't know much about your friend, but I assume he's not like most humans."

"No, Gunner isn't human at all; at least not like you and me. Which is why he's lasted as long as he has. You've got to get this to him as soon as he returns from Carolon; sooner if possible."

Diord set his drink down and took the small container from CJ.

"Silly stuff," he mumbled, examining the vile.

"How so?" CJ asked.

"Our chemical research department created Kodiac Blu and several of its variants. We determined it was too unstable for safe use and buried it in *the never use* bin."

"I can only surmise Seelix Monroe stole the formula and sold it to us," CJ offered. "Our Doctor San Sann can synthesize an antidote in small quantities."

"Fortunate for Gunnar." Diord put the vile in his pocket.

"Promise me you'll get it to him as soon as you can," CJ pleaded quietly.

"Does he really mean that much to you?"

Reading the inflection in Diord's voice, CJ melted back a little.

"You know he's a good friend to me and our cause."

"So, there is still a cause?"

"I'm doing what I have to do; what I'm forced to do."

"But at what cost?" Diord asked. "Do you really think sacrificing yourself to your sister will save Gunnar and somehow magically heal Hadrian?"

CJ stared at the glass on the sill and ran her finger around the rim, lost in her thoughts.

"I have to think there is a place for all of us in bringing Hadrian back together and the parts we'll end up playing can have some meaning; for good or bad."

"How cryptic," Diord grumbled watching her stare. "So, where do those parts leave you and me? What about us?"

CJ looked up into Diord's eyes and gently took his hand. Diord turned his eyes to their hands as they touched. This was what he had come for. He felt mildly guilty wanting to be close to CJ; to rekindle what once was. As their fingers intertwined, he looked into her lovely green eyes. They were an unmistakable reminder of the day he had first met her. A silly red headed Albion Lieutenant with a big wad of curly hair stuffed beneath a service cap sitting next to her big sister, Drax. The years had not dimmed or changed their beautiful color.

"I once thought a career was my best destiny," CJ spoke quietly. "To be with my sister to ensure the Albion way of life was the greatest goal I could aspire to. I left that way of life because I had started to see what it was doing to me. I guess I was being selfish."

"You don't have to recount this to me," Diord replied. "We've been through this already; a long time ago. I can repeat it to you verbatim. The outcome wasn't at all pleasant the last time."

"No, it wasn't, for either of us. I'm so sorry for what I've put you through. I've been totally unfair to the both of us. But these last months on Aster have taught me something I'm not sure I can put into words. I guess in my old age, I'm feeling more of a sense of loneliness and it's caused me to look back at my life and rethink some of the decisions I've made. Most of them, I can't do anything about..." She squeezed his hand a little tighter. "But some I hope I can correct." She drew close to him, feeling his hand slide around her waist. A warm shiver blasted through her, one she recalled from a long time ago when he had first held her in his arms. It was exciting then and the years hadn't diminished that excitement. They brought their lips together with a purpose and control only the years of maturity could produce. But even under control, the electricity of a younger era transposed itself on them as they enjoyed the embrace. Finally pulling back a little, CJ rested her forehead on Diord's lips, her eyes remaining closed as she let the years and the loneliness melt away.

"I wish we could just take off without having to worry about anything else. Maybe get away to that place on Terran Pahe you were going to take me to years ago."

"Wouldn't that be nice?" Diord agreed. "I'm afraid your sister wouldn't be too keen on the idea. At least not right now."

CJ turned around and let Diord wrap his arms around her as they looked out the window, watching the gun turrets move back and forth. Several fighters swept around the stern and flew directly over the top of the great ship towards the bow.

"There has to be a way out of all this," CJ said, enjoying his warmth.

"Things certainly seem quite a bit more complicated, that's for sure," Diord agreed.

"To add to the complication," CJ said turning in his arms. "I think Drax suspects something about Janox."

"What do you mean?"

"She quizzed me pretty good about who Gunnar and I were running with inside of Reako. I threw her off with a phony name and story about finding her there from a shipwreck. Still, I got the impression she knows something about Janox, but isn't letting on what. I know Drax. She not only likes to make an entrance in front of everyone, but she likes to be holding all the cards when she does it."

"You think she suspects Janox is the Princess?"

"I don't know, but why else would she bring it up? To the casual observer, Janox is just another kid who got the short end of the staff in life. I know before I left Aster, she wasn't very happy, but she would never sit still long enough for me to try to talk to her about it."

"The Princess belongs on the throne. Somehow, someone has to convince her of that."

"But how, and even if you did convince her, how would you ever prove to Hadrian that she really is the rightful blood heir to the throne? And on top of all of that, how would you get her in front of all the factions at the same time? The throne is surrounded by those who don't want a blood heir on the throne."

The two fell silent for several long moments, watching several flotilla ships maneuvering around the stern of the ship.

"The Pintar rite of Hadrian," CJ whispered.

"This is no time for joking," Diord responded quietly.

"The Pintar rite of Hadrian," CJ repeated out loud. "Why didn't I see it before?"

"See what before, the joke?"

"It's the Hadrian ceremony confirming a royal to the throne."

"I know what it is. I just don't see why you're bringing it up." Diord suddenly pulled away from her and turned her around. "Hold on a minute. Are you serious? You're not actually thinking of trying to crash that kind of party?"

"No one would be expecting it, and it is the only place all the faction representatives are together in one place."

"CJ, there's no way you could possibly make that happen. No one, and I mean no one is going to let you waltz into the great Hall of Pintar trying to present a girl you think is a blood heir. Even if you had proof, they're still not going to let you in. You'd have to have a fleet big enough to push its way through neutral space to reach Calliope and even then, once the rite starts, there's no opening of the chamber until the ceremony has been completed."

"You're telling me that if we wish for change that we need to wait until all the conditions are perfect and we can present Janox in a calm and controlled manner where no one will object and everyone will welcome her with open arms? Is that what I'm hearing?"

Diord thought a moment, seeing the anxious look on CJ's face.

"I guess it does kind of sound that way. What would you have me do?"

CJ drifted to the other side of the room, thinking, then turned to the window. She watched as the turret gunners finished their maintenance maneuvers and moved their weapons into their stowed positions. Several fighters swung around the back side of the conning tower, swooping low over the settling turrets. The scene reminded her of when she and Gunnar had orchestrated their escape from the *Tarzana* in her F-2 with his friend Rick flying their wing. She smiled slightly thinking of how effortless Gunnar made it look. It had been as if he was unaffected by the fighters chasing them.

"Recall the Aster force," CJ said, folding her arms. "Bring Janox to Calliope and force the factions of Hadrian to deal with her."

"How am I supposed to get the Aster force past the other faction fleets, and if I do, how will I get Janox into chambers?"

"You get her to Calliope, and I'll get her into chambers."

Diord stepped over to CJ and took her in his arms. Letting a sigh go, he looked into her beautiful green eyes.

"You know I can't refuse a girl with freckles and red hair."

"I'm counting on it."

"How will I know you're ready for me to bring her in?"

"I'll give you a signal."

"How? You and I both know you're being watched, if not by your sister then surely Blinda has her eye on you."

"I'll figure something out. Just be ready. As a faction of Hadrian, Cross is obligated to be there with at least a part of your fleet."

"How come they won't let me into the ceremony then?"

"Because Cross has declared itself neutral, your emissary is the only one allowed to attend."

"Clearly, I'm taking a side now."

"Yes, but not one recognized by Hadrian."

"I wouldn't be doing this for anyone else," Diord smiled and drew closer.

"Yes you would," CJ protested gently. "You knew Janox was the Princess the moment Gunnar and I landed on Cross. You want to see her repatriated just as much as we do."

"Hate it when you're right."

"Get used to it," CJ whispered coming closer. "Maybe this will simplify life a little and we'll have time for what's important."

"Something to look forward to," Diord breathed, so close their lips weren't quite touching.

CJ rose up to meet his lips as they came together in another embrace. After holding each other for several lasting moments, they finally gathered their belongings.

"Thanks for dinner," Diord said, pulling his cloak over one of his shoulders and attaching the clasp.

"You get to host the next one," CJ said pulling her jacket on and working the buttons.

"It's a date," Diord agreed as they headed out the door. "I'll get a message about the antidote off to the *Constellation* as soon as I can." Retracing their steps, they came to a waiting room where they were met by their aides. As they all made their way back toward the launch bays, a short slender figure in dark garb, silently shadowed them from far off. Never in view, but always within contact.

The display troops were absent and the launch bay was oddly quiet. It kind of had Diord spooked as he walked next to CJ toward the cluster of waiting shuttle craft. Diord was used to normal battle maneuvers on a ship this large. Fighters and other craft would be constantly coming and going, but right now, it seemed every ship present had been put to bed for the evening. Diord felt like he was departing under the cover of a late night or the wee hours of morning on Cross.

"Kind of quiet, isn't it?" CJ remarked as they stopped in front of the boarding stairs to his shuttle.

"Yeah, what gives?" Diord asked looking around.

"I have a schedule to keep. This ship is due somewhere else; as soon as you're clear, we'll be off. Everything needs to be buttoned up for that to happen."

"Sorta leaves yourself open to attack from the Colonians doesn't it?"

"Not this close to Cross." CJ held out her hand and smiled. "Thank you for coming personally. I hope we can have another one of these meetings again soon."

Diord took her hand and squeezed it gently, but firmly.

"It's always good to meet directly with the client. I'll be in touch, Colonel." With that, he turned and ascended the stairs and the shuttle door closed up behind him.

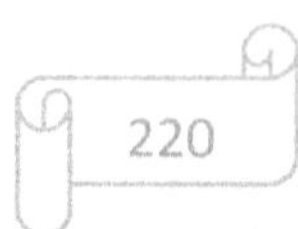

Outside

Tiana glanced at Billy's cameras, noticing he was just pulling the last of the debris out of the fourth venting conduits. A feeling of relief came to her as she watched him turn in the venting port and prepare to make his way back to the hatch.

"How we doing in there?" the engineer asked working his way to the next port.

"Looks like Lieutenant Starman is trying to make a run for it, but all she has are the maneuvering thrusters. Whatever that thing out there is will be on us in about fifteen seconds."

"Why don't they just put a couple of missiles into it and call it a day?"

"We've got no launch power. Barely anything available for thrusters and instruments. Sounds like the turret is down as well."

"Can't launch, huh?" Billy repeated, turning and looking ahead of the ship. "Where's the other ship?"

"Directly ahead of us. They'll be in firing range in about ten seconds. Have any good ideas?"

"Not what you would consider a good one."

"Then let's not try it. We've tried enough stupid ideas for one day."

"What stupid idea?"

"The one you're currently thinking of."

"Can you access the weapons power matrix?"

"Sounds harmless," Tiana said nervously as she worked to bring up the requested information. "Not sure what good this will do. All the power matrix's are offline. It looks like every energizer relay is either burnt out or non-functional."

"Hence no power to the weapons, and getting to them will take time neither one of us has."

"Hang onto something," Tiana interrupted. "They're in firing range." Tiana watched as the engineer tucked himself firmly inside the second vent port and waited. It wasn't long before the ship was racked again by the high-powered energy pulse. Tiana could clearly see the rolling star field from Billy's vantage point as he looked out from his perch in the venting port.

"Get them maneuvering thruster power back as quick as you can and then let's get to work," Billy ordered.

"Get to work doing what?"

"Well, I can't do anything until Starman can get this ship stabilized. Get that power back on."

Tiana went to work as fast her fingers would allow, going through much the same procedures she had the first time they had been hit. Several times she had to step away from the console and reach down into one of the open engine pits to make an adjustment or just plain hit something in order to get it to work. This time, it took her only a couple of minutes to bring their limited power back up.

"I think you've got it," Billy announced, able to see one of the thruster ports firing. "Do you still have the weapons power matrix up?"

"Yeah, but not sure it's going to do any good," Tiana complained. "This shows the laser crystals are disintegrated or the focusing mirrors so far out of alignment that if I could get anything to them, they'd likely melt down. The torpedo bay doors are nonfunctional and the thrust ignitors are offline. Like I said, nothing works right now because we just don't have enough power in the right places."

"You need to go forward and access the weapons maintenance shaft."

"I'm not liking the sounds of this," Tiana grumbled.

"You're gonna hate what I have you do after that."

"Then let's not do it."

"If we don't stop that ship out there from blasting us again, we're gonna be left with nothing. Now get to it and let me know when you're in the access shaft."

"Fine," Tiana gritted, grabbing a couple of tools and dashing from the engine room.

Flying down the stairs to the lower level, she barely touched any of the metal grated stairs. Tearing up the hallway in an all-out sprint, she almost couldn't stop before hitting the closed hatchway. Working the code pad as fast as her fingers would go, she pulled on the handles of the heavy metal door as soon as she heard the mechanism release. Inside, a dimly lit access tunnel curved forward, beneath the heart shaped bridge. As she climbed in, she bumped her head on one of the many weapons tubes stacked in long rows above and below the crawlway.

"Ok, I'm in the access tube," Tiana announced activating her wrist com. "By the way, thanks for the heads up on the low clearance."

"Ahead of you, you should see large tubes below the access and smaller ones above. As you move down the access, you'll see a lot of the smaller tubes squeezed in between the larger tubes on the bottom."

"Yes, I see them."

"The smaller tubes are the pin missile launchers. The larger ones are the Mark V torpedo launchers. You need to count to the number five overhead pin missile tube and you should see a small panel on it. They all have the panel, but this one is the quickest to get to."

"Ok, I've found it. It's glowing red and says *fired*."

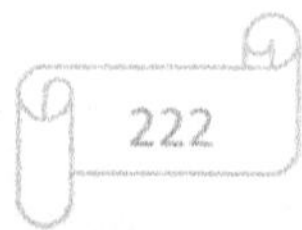

"Ok, you now know what you're looking for. Just work your way around the upper row until you find a panel that's glowing green. And make it quick. You're short on time."

"Yeah, yeah, yeah. I'm moving as fast as I can," Tiana grunted, scurrying through the forward magazine access.

"Keep count of which tube you find that's green. It should tell you on the display. Ah, that's much better," Billy commented. "Our Lieutenant Starman is on the job. She's got us stabilized again."

"Number thirteen is green," Tiana announced. "Great, lucky thirteen. Now what?"

"The tubes are designed to release their ordnance manually. That's how we load them, one at a time, by hand. We can unload them by hand as well; which is exactly what we're going to do with number thirteen. Just push the little black lever forward. You'll hear a click and that's it."

"Then what happens?"

"I just pull it right out."

Tiana heard the click and then heard the sound of something sliding through the tube.

"Wait, you just pulled it out? How?"

"I reached in with my hand and pulled."

"I thought you were coming back inside? What are you doing up here?"

"Launching a missile."

Tiana froze, her thoughts running wild, trying to picture what Billy was trying to do.

"Billy, no!" she yelled, clamoring to get turned around and scrambling back around the access tube to the hatch. "Billy Moon! Don't you dare! Dancing around outside the ship while it's getting kicked all over the place is one thing. Lighting off a missile while you're standing next to it is something completely different!"

"Oh, don't worry about that. I'm not going to be anywhere near this thing when it goes off. Now haul your butt back to engineering and get that power back up."

Gritting her teeth, Tiana tumbled out of the crawlway and accelerated back down the lower hall to the stairs and back into engineering. Skidding to a stop at the engineering console, she widened Billy's helmet camera display. By now, he had made his way around to the front side of the bridge pod and lodged himself in the various weaponry mounted in the nose of the ship.

"Boy, that thing is ugly looking," Billy puffed from his perch on one of the main cannon barrels. He adjusted his comlink on the forearm of his suit. "Captain Abrams, this is Billy Moon."

"Captain," Lana said turning in her chair. "I'm receiving a signal from a cruiser called the *Hampton*, Administrator Vandmire."

"Stand by," Dakota said, holding a finger up. "Mr. Moon, how are the repairs on the conduit vents?"

"Completed a few minutes ago, Sir. We can't take another punch from those guys, so I'm gonna give 'em one of our Pin missiles."

"That would be all well and fine, except how are you going to deliver it? We've got no weapons and no way to launch."

"I'm going to hand deliver it."

"You're gonna do what? Where are you?"

Billy stood up on the barrel of the Starbird's forward cannon and waved at the bridge crew looking out at him with shocked expressions. Lynette and Nigel waved tentatively back at the engineer as he held up the Pin Missile.

"What the...?" Dakota muttered. "Where did you get that?"

"Does it matter?" Billy replied. "All that matters is that you steer right at that ship. I'll do the rest."

"And just what is, *the rest*? You've got no way to light that thing off; no way to deliver it."

"You get this ship up to speed, hit the brakes and I'll see that it gets to where it needs to go."

"Don't let him do it!" Tiana yelled, dashing into the bridge and skidding to a halt next to Captain Abrams.

"Why aren't you back in engineering?" Dakota exclaimed. "We need that power back or nothing we do up here is going to do any good."

"Trying to keep your most valuable person from killing himself."

"Tiana, we've been through this already. Now please, I'll handle this. You can do the most good back in engineering."

"But..."

"Go! We need that power!"

Tiana opened her mouth to protest again, then looking back out at Billy, turned and stormed from the bridge.

Dakota watched her leave, then turned back to the engineer. He gave Mr. Pippin a glance, then looked over at Lynette Starman.

"Helm, steer right at them."

"Aye, Sir."

"Standby to hit the brakes and execute emergency evasive maneuvers," Dakota ordered.

"Standing by," Lynette said, setting her controls and waiting for the order.

Dakota looked back at the sensor control displays, then back forward.

"They're in range," Mr. Pippin announced, turning forward for the maneuver. The muzzle of the Torag weapon was starting to glow.

"Ready for this, Billy?" Dakota asked moving next to helm control.

"Hurry up, before I change my mind," Billy responded.

"Good luck. Now, Lieutenant," Dakota ordered firmly.

The Starbird pilot touched the glass in front of her and twisted on the yoke while working several slide controls on the glass. Everyone watched breathless as Billy launched from the front of the ship. The Torag and the surrounding stars tilted hard as the *Constellation* gently twisted right while Lynette held the maneuvering thrusters at full power.

Billy's heart raced as he stretched his arms out in front of him with the missile held firmly in both hands. He touched the booster controls of the tiny retro directors built into his suit. Every second, he made small corrections to his flight path, heading directly at the cannon on the front of the Albion ship. Watching the ring of the muzzle glowing brighter, he realized the Torag was about to fire its weapon and for a moment he wondered what his demise was going to be like passing through the weapon's beam. Those thoughts were soon replaced as the Albion ship turned, trying to keep the Starbird in its gun sights. He tried to make the needed adjustments to his trajectory, but the maneuver was too great. As the Starbird rolled by the Torag, the Albion ship fired its weapon, appearing to score a direct hit to the bottom aft section of the *Constellation*.

Billy only caught a glimpse of the Starbird as it tumbled away; a moment later he struck the nose of the Torag. The force of the impact knocked the missile from his hands and sent him sliding back along the hull of the Albion ship. His head spinning, he tried to roll and grab at anything. The thoughts of spinning out into open space never to be seen again had him petrified. His helmet banged against the hull several times and his interior lights, HUD and com systems went completely dead. As he continued to bump and roll along the hull, his hand caught hold of something, spinning him violently. He tried to hold onto whatever his hand had caught, but he was still moving too fast and it ripped through his fingers.

Sliding halfway across the back side of the vessel, he dropped his feet and hands to the hull, trying to slow himself down. Tumbling back along the mid-section, he struck enough surface protrusions to correct his spin. Approaching the aft section, he pushed his hands out in front of him and worked his suit thruster controls with no success; they were dead. Still moving faster than he was comfortable with, he pulled the tether hook from his suit and clawed at anything he could find. Finally passing the aft dome structure, he hooked a stout pipe and grabbed the tether, letting it slide through his gloved hands. Straining to slow himself before he got to the end of the tether, he was abruptly yanked to a stop. The whiplash nearly cut him in half, but somehow, the tether held and he was pulled back to the pipe where he hauled himself in close to the dome of the Albion ship. Working to calm himself, he carefully felt around his helmet and shoulders, as far as his arms would reach. There seemed to be nothing broken or loose, but the only system working was the air supply. His suit would get cold as time went on, but for now, breathing was of paramount importance.

He looked back at the rear edge of the ship. It was dark here and only the reflection of the distant sun and dim glow from Carolon striking the hull in other places allowed enough light for him to see. Two large bell-shaped cones protruded out the back of the ship and nestled neatly between them was a massive recoil cannon breach. It looked like it was calibrated to rest in the middle of the recoil. If he were to be anywhere close to this weapon when it was fired, he would likely be injured or killed. He looked around for anything he could use to possibly jam the mechanism, but anything he considered strong enough could not be easily removed.

Turning forward, he peered around the base of the dome toward the front. In the distance, he saw the *Constellation*, still tumbling helplessly. He grabbed hold of a handle and pulled himself up and began making his way to the top of the ship, pulling himself along with a set of handles running up the spine of the entire craft. As he worked his way forward, he noticed most of the seams in the hull were poorly assembled. Some had cracked welds and there appeared to be airsoft material pressed into the wider gaps in the hull seams.

Either this ship was put together so poorly it wasn't space worthy, or its weapon's discharge is so violent it shakes the hull to pieces.

He passed several port windows, making sure he wasn't observed, and continued forward down the middle until he reached the bridge pod. From here, he had to find another way to the front as there were no hand holds and no way to remain unseen if he remained on top. Cautiously nudging up to the top of the bridge windows, he peered inside. It was brightly lit, but crudely designed. There were two seats in the middle behind a large console and a third seat directly behind the first set. Two other seats, one on each side of the middle chair, were mounted in front of a couple of bulky consoles. An officer manned each station with several others surrounding the center seat of the bridge. A short man sat rigid in the middle seat; obviously the ship's commander.

Billy pushed back away from the window and made his way down the side and to the underside of the ship. Still following the handles, he turned forward until he pulled himself into a cavity on the nose, next to him was the cannon barrel. An enormous maul, he had to wonder how it ever fit through the interior of the ship. Working methodically, he hovered all around the nose, looking for something he could use to disrupt the weapon's ability to fire. Inspecting the barrel, he detected something wedged in the weapon's aiming nozzle. Without his helmet lights, it was impossible to make out what it was, but after tugging on it, he pulled a long, slender white tube with fins, out into the light. The Pin missile!

As he was checking its condition, he felt the cannon barrel start to vibrate and turned his attention to the muzzle. It was starting to glow. He looked out at the *Constellation*, but he couldn't tell if they were under power or not.

I don't want to be anywhere near this thing when it goes off, he thought, turning back to the bottom of the ship to move to the rear. *But I've got to disrupt this thing before they have a chance to fire it again.* He looked at the barrel of the ship's gun, then at the missile. *I'm dealing with a pulse weapon here,* he thought looking back at the snout. *There's no ignition source. If I try to shove this missile down it's throat it will just spit it right back out. This missile is concussion activated. I bet if I hammer on it hard enough, it'll go off. But the whole idea is not to be anywhere near this thing when that happens.*

He glanced back at the disrupter barrel as it continued to glow brighter. Turning around, he pulled himself up on the top side of the nose and pushed off toward the back of the bridge pod to the rear of the ship.

"Hello boys," he smiled as he passed up across the bridge windows waving at the occupants.

Commander Dalton SoKnack dipped his unibrow, dumbfounded as he watched the lone astronaut streak up past the windows and disappear. He looked side to side to see if either of the bridge officers had been witness to the odd occurrence. It wasn't often you saw an astronaut sliding along your ship out in open space. Neither officer was willing to look at Commander SoKnack. He thought about the possibilities for a moment, then shrugged and turned his attention back on his work.

Skimming along the hull, Billy grabbed hold of the top handles and pushed off again, gliding back to the aft portion of the ship. Arriving at the cannon breach and exposed engine thrusters, he observed the breach slowly sliding back into firing position. Once in position, the recoil would be released and the enormous piston would spring forward. Billy didn't quite understand the operating dynamics of it; it seemed rather mechanical for an energy disrupter. He pushed off again and grabbed a hold of the cannon assembly, then scrambled further back to where the breach was sliding back into position. Moving quickly, he jammed the missile head into the slide path of the breach, then took hold of the thruster bell and pushed off as hard as he could. Instinctively, he jammed his thumbs down on his booster controls. They instantly came to life, thrusting him into the black of open space. He glanced back as the Torag receded. Moments later, there was a brilliant flash with an accompanying jolt that visibly shook the Albion ship. There were no flames, but he could clearly see one of the thruster bells tumbling away in a shower of debris while the other one hung uselessly twisted, swaying in the Torag's wake. The blast had sent the Torag barreling in a different direction from the

Constellation. As the Albion ship tumbled further away, he watched the *Constellation* holding a stable course in the opposite direction.

It worked! The pin missile went off before they could fire their weapon. Now there's no way for them to fire it again. He could only imagine what the back end of the ship looked like up close. *That gun has to be a mess.* In any case, he was making it up as he went along. He turned and looked at where his trajectory would now take him; in the opposite direction of both ships. Carolon was still close by and Reako was only a tiny orb in a vast ocean of tiny specks of light. He took great comfort in his boosters mysteriously working again. Billy checked his environmental systems. His com and most of his electrical systems were still off-line, but the environmental systems seemed to still be functioning properly. These new suits were designed to keep a person alive for days if necessary, although he couldn't think of a reason anyone would want to remain in one for that long. He had done what needed doing and that meant having to make a sacrifice. Now he had to face the consequences of the decisions that had brought him to this point, and come to terms with it.

Ice Hockey

The hallways to the landing bays were still wet and slick as Rick made his way carefully along the main passage. As he had seen in his mind's eye when he had to open the large access doors, he could now peer inside the cavernous bay area while making his way further down the hall. Finally, he caught sight of a machine sitting on its side, its landing gear facing out. Once inside the bay he made his way toward the scout ship, glancing at the enormous outer bay doors. There was some kind of creature thrashing about in the idle water at the far end near the bay doors. Thoughts of Dãsha still weighed heavy on his mind and it wasn't until he was climbing through the side hatch of the scout ship, that he realized just how lucky he was. He could have become fish food when he dove in to find her.

Easily finding the cockpit of the craft, Rick wasted no time powering the systems up. Getting into the seat was a little tricky, but he was used to having to wrangle a bit to get into a fighter. Once he had gotten himself situated, he righted the small craft and started to search for the communications panel.

"Ok, Caidin," Rick said, pushing a small earpiece into place. "Let's close all the interior landing bay doors and get ready to open the main doors. Once you get clear of Acuity, make sure you open all the outer doors to both the landing and the hangar bays. You got all kinds of goodies swimming around down here. I'm sure there are other places they'd rather be."

"I'd just as soon they not be onboard with me," Caidin responded.

A moment later, Rick caught a glimpse of the line of interior doors slamming shut on both sides of the landing bay and the lights went dark. Rick maneuvered the scout ship toward the top back of the landing bay and waited. He felt a vibration, followed by a loud groaning piercing through the hull of the tiny vessel. Switching on his exterior lights, he was confronted by a massive gush of water rushing through the two enormous door halves sliding open. As the wall of water reached for his ship, he gunned the throttles, sending the vessel catapulting straight into it. He fought for only a few seconds before he was through the turbulence and outside.

"Caidin, can you hear me?" Rick asked touching the transmission control to his left.

"Barely," came a static filled reply. "Not sure whose radio is having the problems."

"Can you send me the locations of the marker beacons?"

"No, there is too much noise in our transmissions. The information will corrupt by the time it gets to you. Turn left and I'll guide you to all of them. You should know when you're close. They all have marker lights on them, bright red ones."

"Let's get to it," Rick said, maneuvering left around the giant hull of *Calypso*. "Won't the scanners in this thing locate them?"

"No, too small for those scanners. Straight ahead, you should see one just out there in the open. The Drake weren't too clever with where they put them. Just where it was easiest I think. There should be three more following a straight line all the way back to the thruster ports."

Rick bumped the thruster controls a little, just skimming along the bottom side of the great ship, looking for any signs of flashing lights. He pulled back on the throttles and shut off most of his exterior lights. Through the dark gloom, he spotted a beacon, it's light slowly blinking under a coat of ugly brown film. Taking careful aim with the small beamer, he touched the control and the little beacon abruptly popped in a flash of bubbles and floated away from the hull.

"Now if you can do that fast enough, you'll have them cleaned off before they have time to send up any Raider ships to find out what's going on."

"Just exactly where do these Raider ships come from?"

"There are bases in several locations. Gillard is the closest. It's the Drake home world in the system next to this one. Directly ahead of you again."

"Got it," Rick acknowledged. "How many of these did you say there were?"

"Two hundred and thirty-six."

Rick let out a slight sigh. At least this would give him a chance to get to know Caidin's scout ship before he tried to take on the Drake. For more than an hour, Rick worked his way all over the hull of the great ship, popping the beacons as he went. Most of the time, he could see the blinking lights in the darkness and destroy them without even having to slow down to take aim. Several times he had to stop long enough to scrape the mucky slim covering the beacons. Then he'd make quick work of them and move on.

"I've counted two hundred and thirty-five," Rick announced, driving up the front of the massive bow, moving toward the last beacon anchored to the tip of the old vessel.

"Last one is at the very tip of the bow," Caidin said nervously. "I sure hope this plan of yours works."

"Don't worry," Rick tried to reassure the older Thane. "Just make sure you have this old tub full throttle when you're heading the other direction and don't stop for anything." Rick tapped the firing trigger on the control grip and swung the scout ship around, putting it into a hover above the bow of *Calypso*. "Ready for this?"

"Best to go now before I have any more time to think it through. Good luck, Richard."

"Good luck, Caidin." Rick hit the throttles and the little ship blasted away from *Calypso*, back toward the ice. As he put the great ship behind him, he perceived the water brightening all around him and looking back, saw the thruster ports of the mammoth vessel blasting thrust gases behind it. If Caidin followed his directions, it wouldn't take much time for the great ship to breach the outer surface of Acuity's ocean and be moving away from its watery prison. Rick now had to focus on his next objective materializing directly in front of him; a wall of ice.

*   *   *   *

Rick methodically worked to reconfigure the beam laser on the nose of the scout ship. This wasn't terribly difficult for him as he had already become familiar with the Drake technology working with *Calypso*. Nothing had to be done to the laser itself, only the power supplies and the control Diacs regulating the laser engine's output. He had just about finished when a sickly sounding buzzer began to make noise on the front control panel. He gave the readout a glance as he continued to work, taking note of several moving dots on the small monochrome screen.

"'Bout time you guys showed up," he said out loud. "Question is, are you coming for me or are you looking for something bigger?" He popped the panels back into place at the same moment he felt several concussions and a flash of splintering ice to the left of his ship. "I guess that answers that question."

Rick pushed the reverse thrusters to full, pulling away from the ice shelf and the splintering shards pelting the hull of the small craft. Turning away, he shoved the forward throttles to full and started out, skimming just along the shelf. Being this close to the shelf might not be the best idea as the scout ship was constantly pummeled by near misses, showering his vessel with ice and concussion waves. He turned away from the shelf and weaved his way back toward his pursuers. There were several flashes to his right and then nothing. Flying through water, in the dark, had its advantages, though having the Interceptor with all its instruments would have been even better.

Rick kept checking the numbers on the navigation display. He had to buy himself enough time to use the beamer mounted to the nose of the scout ship. It didn't take long for the pursuit ships to catch up and they were again throwing a barrage of fire at him that seemed more like it was aimed at anything but his ship. Either he was incredibly good at flying this old ship or they were incredibly poor at shooting at him. Certainly, he liked to think the first was true. It appeared there were at least four ships in pursuit with several stationary targets further down the ice shelf. Maneuvering his ship in an erratic fashion, he steered for the ice wall, coming upon four larger ships using their blaster cannons on the ice shelf in the same spot. The tunnel they had started cutting was already quite sizable. All four ships were tucked neatly inside the tunnel they had opened, each taking turns blasting away at the ice, then using their cutting lasers to smooth out the edges.

It seemed to Rick they working overly hard for what little results they were netting. As he passed by the large cavern, an idea popped into his head. If they were as good at making holes in the ice as they were at shooting at him, he might be able to make this work to his advantage. Hauling back on the controls, he headed straight away from the ice shelf for some distance and waited. It wasn't long before his pursuers discovered his location and pressed an attack. Maneuvering to keep from getting hit by a lucky shot, he headed straight back at the ice, directly toward the cave opening. As he neared the ice shelf, he slowed his ship to half power and activated its laser. As the beam disappeared into the gloom, he held the activators down until he heard the overload alarms come on. When he shut off the beams, he brought his ship to a halt right next to the ice wall inside the cave. Ice chunks rained down on his little ship as his pursuers followed him into the cave, firing. Before they got close enough to actually land any hits, he gunned the throttles again and took off, weaving around the four larger vessels, still cutting, and blasting at the ice. Rick repeated this procedure several times, each time the ice wall was pushed back a considerably further. Continuing with his success, he started to feel a little sorry for how hard his assailants were trying without any results.

Pulling in again close to the crumbling ice wall, he waited for the Drake ships to begin to fire at him. Watching the tracking returns on his tiny screens, he heard a loud thump. Certainly, more ice blocks hitting his ship as they floated away from the shattering wall. There were several more thumps and then a loud thud, setting off a couple of alarms on the console in front of him. The Drake ships were using their exterior lights to aide in their work and from what he could see, a large chunk had just separated from the wall and was now pushing him back between the four larger ships, making him an easier target for the near-sighted pursuit vessels. He tried using his throttles, but he was stuck fast. Several explosions rocked his ship as they struck all around him, peppering his hull and setting off more alarms.

"Not good!" he yelled, realizing his situation. His ship began to rotate as the berg he was stuck on was tumbling with each hit. He watched as one of the utility ships still blasting at the ice came into view. A thought sprang to mind. He touched the laser control and a beam of light streaked through the murk and across one of the fins of the ship. Only when a few pieces fell away, did the Drake ship turn its guns on Rick's helpless scout ship. There were several blasts from the large Drake ship and several smaller ones pounding the berg from behind. All at once, the entire ice block shattered, throwing Rick's ship back. Trying to right his craft and get some directional control, he saw the wall coming at him at an accelerated rate. The strike would surely breach the hull and fill his ship with ice cold water. He wasn't sure what would kill him first, the temperature of the outside water or the drowning. To his astonishment, he never felt his ship hit the wall. The lights from the Drake ships faded and then came back into view as his craft tumbled through an open fissure and into an ice canyon beyond. Gaining control, he steered his ship deeper into the fissure, away from his assailants.

Bringing the exterior lights back up, he carefully navigated through the open canyon of ice. Making sure he wasn't being followed, he slowed to a crawl while he assessed the damage to his craft. Glancing all around the cabin, he detected no water leaks; always a plus. Flooding generally wouldn't be a problem as everything inside was usually trying to get out, not in, but any cracks in the hull could spell disaster for other factors. After careful inspection, he found one of the directional thruster ports were damaged. It still functioned, but would not give him full range of steering. He was certain there were several dents and scrapes on the outer skin of the space craft. As he ran a diagnostic scan of all the ship's systems, to his dismay, he found the coms systems were no longer functional. The exterior antennas must have been torn off in the melee, but more importantly, now the laser was damaged. Looking out the front window, the tube protruding from the nose of the ship, was gone.

"Nuts," Rick grumbled, sitting back to think. He needed that laser to cut through the ice. He glanced down at his relative position in relation to the *Athena*. He wasn't too far from her now, but without the laser, there was no way for him to reach her. CORA 500 might see him coming, but would reason he was an enemy ship and just ignore him. Even as close as he was, he was sure the ship's AI wouldn't be able to hear him. He glanced ahead, watching the ice walls widen and vault until he couldn't see top, bottom or sides. He wasn't even sure he was still in the ice anymore.

The water had cleared considerably, but the instruments indicated it was starting to move a little faster. He pulled his throttles back to idle, but still the ship kept moving. *Certainly, there could be forces acting on the water to cause it to move so rapidly, even in a cavernous space such as this fissure was, but what? Gravitational forces from nearby Skadil drawing Acuity into a wide oval shape? Only gravity could cause veracious currents to sweep this little ship through small tunnels or worse, crush it against the ice.* Unable to see what was ahead of him, he could only allow the current to sweep him along. The good news here was he was moving toward the *Athena*. It wasn't until the walls started to converge ahead of him that he realized just how fast he was being carried along. Engaging the reverse thrusters slowed his craft to something a little more manageable, but he wasn't feeling terribly confident in holding them in reverse for long. Even more worrisome, he discerned the top and bottom of the fissure starting to close in on his ship.

He pulled back on the reverse thruster controls as far as they would go, but still the little ship continued forward. There came a flash of reflected light in front of him and then, nothing. He could feel no movement for several moments, then a rumbling from the rear of the ship followed immediately by a shudder and then the nose pitched up violently. The ship seemed to settle for a moment, but then repeated the process, each time the windows of the ship would blur. Trying to figure out what was happening, he shut off the reverse thrusters and the bucking action ceased. Taking the controls, he carefully turned the ship one hundred and eighty degrees only to find an enormous waterfall directly behind him. He was now hovering just above a torrent of high pressure water spouting out of an opening in the ice shelf. The stream dropped away into another chute leading in the direction of gravity's pull. Not anxious to follow the water's path just yet, he steered his ship to a wall and started moving up and across in a diagonal path.

What the what? Rick focused on the information in front of him. Oxygen was present outside, and not just air, but warm air. He steered away from the ice wall and pointed his ship vertical, hoping to see the ceiling or perhaps the source of the heat. The higher he got, the warmer it became until it would be easy for him to open the hatch and step outside without worry of getting a chill or gasping for breath.

Continuing to rise, the ceiling remained dark and out of sight, or so he thought. As he rose, it appeared there was something there. Looking at the walls, there was a definite line. He finally slowed his ship on approach to the ceiling, but it wasn't made of ice. He glanced at his navigation readouts. He still had a little way to go to reach the *Athena* and whatever this was, was the wrong color anyway. Pulling back a little farther to get a better look, he turned and skimmed along the bottom of a ship's hull until he came to an external hatch. It looked strangely familiar; Kalamarion. Positioning his little ship beneath the hatch, he activated the magnetic clamps and locked his ship in place.

Rick cautiously opened his own hatch and took a breath. The air was clean and refreshing. Looking up at the hatch, he recognized the access panel to the side and popped the lid. Inside was a small glowing keypad. There was power, something that made him both nervous and hopeful. He wasn't sure what to expect as he worked the combination using number codes he knew. After a couple of attempts, the panel turned green and the hatch door snapped open. The adjoining tunnel was dark, and a little dank, but it wasn't full of water and to be honest, he was kind of tired of water. He thought it might be nice to be on Skadil.

Once inside the access tube, he found the door control, closed the hatch, and turned on the access lights. The access ladder stretched nearly out of sight, up into the belly of whatever ship this was. After climbing for several minutes, he emerged into a hallway. So as to not surprise anyone or anything, he moved silently about the labyrinth of halls until he found an information terminal. Access was simple and a moment later, he was staring in disbelief at the information scrolling up the screen. This was a Kendalon freighter, the *Stark*, commanded by Captain Constance Fowler. The ship was carrying military grade hardware.

"The *Stark*?" he gasped audibly. It was one of the freighters he and Gunnar had tried to rescue at the Oneida Caldron. "Constance and Manx were always too smart to be just freighter Captains," he said aloud, shaking his head.

"What do you know of Captain Fowler and Captain Quayle?"

Rick whirled around and came face to face with several crewman guards flanking a woman and several officers. He looked at the blaster pistols pointed at him and raised his hands, smiling.

"If you'll just check my transponder, it'll save you some embarrassment," Rick said, as he was promptly disarmed. One of the officers stepped forward and waved a hand scanner in front of him and then glanced down at the readout. There were several double takes and eventually, everyone came to attention.

"General Niker," the lead officer bellowed. "We had no idea. We're tracking the *Athena* inbound. How did you get here before your ship?"

"By a very different route," Rick said, retrieving his weapons. "Where's Captain Fowler?"

"I'm sorry, Sir. She isn't here. Captain Fowler, Quayle, Puche' and Darton were taken by marauders over a year ago."

"You mean to tell me you've been in this frozen block all this time?"

"We've been wandering this quadrant for a year, Sir. We've been stuck in this ice for about ten months."

Rick thought about the chain of events that had lead everyone to this point. Some of the ramifications seemed astonishing to him.

"What are the odds?" he said shaking his head.

"Sir?"

"Nothing. There'll be plenty of time for explanations soon enough." Rick motioned to the senior officer to take the lead. "Please, Lieutenant, I'm sure your ship has some comfortable surroundings we could all relax in."

"Certainly, Sir. Right this way."

After a brief tour of the freighter, the group stopped at the landing bay. It was small to be sure, this was after all, just a freighter and not intended to be outfitted for combat.

"These look familiar," Rick said folding his arms and looking down at several Drake Marauder craft parked in the landing bay.

"Drake H-90 fighters and a couple of Escey Assault ships," Chief Petty officer Greg Tanetto announced from behind.

"We were boarded by five Drake ships." Lieutenant Terry Gillespie glanced back at the Petty officer. "These fighters and an assault craft. Those things look like they should have been crawling around on a planet, not spinning around in space. But they had all the guns and we had next to nothing to defend ourselves with. They took our Captains away in one of the assault ships and left the others to drive our ships to their planet for looting."

"They didn't tell you what they wanted?"

"They didn't have to. It was clear they were after anything they could lay their hands on. They were really unhappy they couldn't get into our holds. I'm pretty sure their intent was to get us to where they could get them open or come back with something bigger to get the job done."

"Sounds like a bunch of pirates," Rick commented.

"They didn't seem to like that label," Terry Gillespie said. "After the assault ship took our command personnel, we set course for a planet called Tantil. Some kind of military base I guess. As we passed Acuity, we got brave and overpowered their pilots, then ducked into Acuity's ocean. Evading was a little difficult as they patrol these waters all the time, but we managed to drive up inside one of the ice pack's big canyons to hide. We didn't count on the canyons freezing up and trapping us in here."

"Well, they've found you now. They're trying to blast their way through the ice to get to you. I got ahead of them in a little scout ship I borrowed."

"Yeah, about that, Sir," Greg Tanetto piped up again. "We thought you'd be onboard the *Athena*. How did you end up in that squeaky little thing? And how did you ever get it through the ice to the *Stark* before the Drake?"

"It's a very long story, Chief Tanetto," Rick said with a far-off smile. "I promise you'll hear the whole tale soon enough. Have you got room for the *Athena* when she gets here?"

"Certainly," the Petty officer perked up. "We can move those three fighters out of the way and you can park it right here. It'll be a real treat to see an actual Starbird in our landing bay."

"Lieutenant Gillespie, do you have an ETA on the *Athena's* arrival?" Rick asked.

"She's very close, Sir," Terry said looking at a device she pulled from her belt. She was about to say something when the ship wide com system came alive.

"Lieutenant Gillespie and Chief Tanetto to the bridge. The *Athena* is requesting landing instructions."

Rick turned to Terry with arms folded.

"Mind if I meet her down there in the bay?"

"Usually against regulations, Sir. But I think in this case we can make an exception."

"Mind if I tag along?" Greg Tanetto asked anxiously. Rick gave Terry a glance and shrugged.

"I'm not in command of this ship."

Greg looked anxiously toward Terry.

"General, if he gets in your way, just push him out when your ship comes in. I'll be on the bridge." With that, Terry headed down the hall followed by the other officers.

"Lead the way, Chief," Rick said, motioning he was ready.

They were quick to make it into the landing bay and while they waited for the doors to open, Rick walked over to one of the Drake fighter craft as it was being maneuvered out of the way. He walked around it, looking carefully at its armament and mechanical workings.

"You said you overpowered the pilots?"

"Yes, Sir. Two of them are dead, but we still have one here on the *Stark*."

"Seriously?" Rick asked looking at the Chief. "You've had him locked up all this time?"

"Oh no, Sir. Not at all. After we got stuck in the ice, it seemed pointless to keep him locked up. We weren't going anywhere and neither was he. He's a decent guy. I'll introduce you as soon as we get you and your ship settled. Tell me, Sir, is the Starbird as amazing as we've heard?"

"I don't know. What have you heard?"

"I've read all the specs on them. At full power, they can take down a capital ship and still have power to beat up on its support ships if it wanted to."

"Well, it's designed to do that, but it's never been tested. They certainly can pack a pretty good punch when needed." An alarm sounded in the landing bay and several warning lights started blinking.

"Warning, stand clear of the yellow markers," an automated voice boomed. "Corsair class vessel entering the landing bay." Both officers turned as the enormous doors pulled back to reveal the darkness outside. Rick strode to the middle of the bay as the white, battle scored nose of the *Athena* entered the freighter's bay. He felt his eyes tearing a little as his ship silently slipped through the doors towards him. Once inside, the big doors began to close and Rick stepped up to the hull, letting his fingers streak across its surface. He felt a tingle of excitement fire through his hand and up his arm as he started toward the aft boarding doors. He could hardly contain himself as he popped open the door access panel. Working the panel locking code as quickly as he could, the door finally slipped away and he climbed inside.

"CORA," he called anxiously. The lights instantly came on and the welcome voice of the ship's AI echoed through the entire ship.

"Rick! You're here! Wait, how did you get here? Never mind, you're here!"

"CORA, you have no idea how good it is to hear your voice." Rick's mindset shifted. "Were you successful? Did you find Jayda?" There was a long pause giving Rick cause to wonder.

"No, Rick. I found the escape pod. It's redocked on the turret tower. But Jayda wasn't in it."

"Not in it? I don't understand. Where is she?"

"I don't know, Rick. I found the pod on the surface of this water body. But it was empty. There were no returns from a scan for her transponder."

"Permission to come aboard?" a voice asked from below.

Rick looked back at Chief Tanetto who stood anxiously just outside the doors. Rick looked back at the interior of the ship. All the doors were closed and he would be going into engineering anyway. The tech there wasn't any different than what he was used to dealing with already.

"Come aboard, Chief, but please stay with me. I haven't been aboard ship for some time and I want to make sure everything is ok before we let personnel lose."

Greg was standing next to the General before he finished his instructions.

"CORA, open all the aft compartments," Rick ordered.

"They'll be a little cool as I just started turning the environmental systems back up," CORA responded.

"Amazing AI," Greg said. "Is it integrated through the entire ship or is it a droid?"

"Integrated. CORA is the *Athena*," Rick said, moving through the engineering doors and starting for the elevator shaft leading to the turret.

"I thought there was a 7000 series assigned to each Starbird? Holy smokes, Sir!" The Chief interrupted his own question. "You guys have seen some serious action." Greg walked over to the large hole in the floor of engineering. Examining the damage, he looked up through the matching hole in the ceiling. "How did you guys survive this one?" The Chief looked all around noticing something odd. "Better question, who survived? Where's your crew?"

Rick stopped next to the engineering consoles and looked back at the Greg.

"The survivors should still be in stasis in the sick bay. Chief, please keep up." Rick was focused solely on what he would find in the turret. There would plenty of time for explanations and further discovery later. He hurried past the glimmering engineering consoles. Greg couldn't help but pause for a look. This was his realm and it was nearly impossible for him to keep walking as the General activated the elevator door to the turret. "Chief?" Rick coaxed the *Stark* engineer. Rick activated the door, reached inside and deactivated the hoisting mechanism then started up the access ladder. Greg gave the engineering room one last look, then followed the General.

"CORA, any analysis on the pod's external condition?" Rick asked examining it closely.

"I could find nothing out of the ordinary. Any marks of note are consistent with prolonged exposure to the elements of space. All cosmic shielding has remained viable."

Reaching for the access panel, Rick punched in the key sequence and opened it. The pod door immediately swung up out of the way, exposing the interior of the gun turret. Sitting in the cushioned chair, he activated the turret's systems and studied the readouts.

"What's so important about this turret, Sir?" Greg asked.

"My second in command was in it when the attack on the ship occurred. She jettisoned when the ship's systems went critical. The life support systems are nearly exhausted."

"Meaning?"

"Meaning she activated the stasis system. It'll keep a person alive for an extended period of time if necessary. But clearly the pod was intercepted."

"Intercepted? How can you tell?"

"Well, these systems show an exterior interruption, like the pod was forced open by someone. She can't de-activate the systems while in stasis, and now she isn't here…"

"And this would be why," Greg said, bending down and picking something up from the floor of the pod. Rick looked at the object, then thoroughly searched the rest of the pod for anything else. He found another object, or piece of one and held it up to what Greg was holding.

"I know where these came from," Greg said, recognizing the pieces. "This is what's left of a Drake service dagger."

Rick studied the pieces carefully, then turned to the stasis couplings.

"Are you sure?"

"When we overpowered the Drake pilots, they all had these. I'm sure Dacey would be glad to confirm it. He's the pilot that survived."

Rick held one of the pieces up to the coupling. Sure enough, there were marks matching what the dagger could produce.

"If I had to make a guess, I'd say the Drake got to this pod before your ship did."

Rick let the possible chain of events stream through his thoughts several times, finally handing the dagger pieces back to Greg.

"Could you have your Lieutenant Gillespie and your medical personnel come aboard. I have some seriously wounded crew that require attention."

"Will you require an engineering team to help you get everything back together here?" Chief Tanetto was hoping to get his hands on the ultimate technology of his career. Rick smiled.

"There will plenty of time for that a little later. You have your orders, Chief."

"Yes, Sir," Greg said and disappeared back down the ladder. Rick sat back in the seat for several more minutes. It seemed these Drake were going to be a prominent part of his immediate future.

*   *   *   *

Rick gazed through the stasis pod glass at what was left of his crew while the *Stark's* medical officer analyzed the readouts on the side of each pod. After several minutes of study, the medical officer turned to the General.

"This is beyond my expertise," the doctor admitted grimly. "These people need several different types of surgical specialists, the least of which would be a Neurologist. There is some serious damage to their central nervous systems that I can't even begin to explore. I'm a general ship's doctor; basically, I can treat the common cold if they had such a thing anymore."

"I understand what you're getting at doctor," Rick said, quietly looking through the glass at Captain Dayton.

"The best thing you can do is leave them right where they are until you can get them to someone more qualified than me."

Rick nodded slowly, then turned as the sick bay doors popped open. Terry and Greg walked in flanked by four other officers.

"Reporting as requested, General Niker." They all saluted sharply and remained at attention. Rick looked them over after a double take. This was going to take some getting used to. He and Gunnar had been out of military circles long enough now, he felt a bit out of place. They ran their commands a bit more casual.

"Good, you're here." He decided to let them remain at attention. It was what they were used to. "Meet what's left of my crew," he said motioning to the stasis pods neatly lined up. "My pilot, Captain Lisa Dayton, Com officer, Lieutenant Laura Habba and my science officer, Toby Mavis."

"I take it their condition is serious," Terry affirmed.

"Serious enough I can't do anything for them," the doctor admitted.

"At least not right now," Rick said. "And we don't have the time for it. Please, if you'll all follow me, we'll adjourn to the *Athena's* conference room and discuss our options." Rick motioned everyone out the door and led them up the hall to the conference room just before the bridge.

"First of all, I need a general condition of each of your ships," Rick said as everyone sat down.

"I think I speak for the other commanders," Terry spoke up. "Generally, each vessel is in fair condition considering what we've been through since leaving the Oneida. We lost our light speed engines during our ensuing wormhole operations and were left tugging around in space for months trying to make repairs."

"I feel your pain, Lieutenant," Rick agreed thinking back to when he and Gunnar had arrived in Hadrian. "Please continue."

"We were approached by several alien ships offering help, but scans of their vessels showed inferior technology, so to keep our tech from getting into their hands, we opted to politely refuse and continued on our way."

"So tell me again, how you guys ended up in here?"

"The Drake didn't want to take our *polite no* for an answer. They kept coming and we kept refusing. Freighters aren't armed like a Starbird. They had us surrounded in Acuity's orbit, but we managed to slip past them and dove for the ocean. They chased us in and cornered us again against the ice flows. At that point, we had no choice but to surrender. They boarded us and took all the commanding officers with them, leaving a few of their own officers behind to guide us back out. We overpowered them before we breached Acuity's ocean and then made a run for the ice flows. No doubt you've figured out some of these canyons are deep and seem endless. We made our way back inside as far as we could to make sure we were out of sight. We ended up staying too long back in here and our way out closed up on us. The water's mass is constantly moving though, always shifting due to Skadil's heavy gravity pulling on Acuity's water mass. I think it has kept us hidden, until now. If they reach us again, it's likely we won't be able to stop them from boarding us again."

"Shortest route out of the ice?" Rick asked.

"Our scanning equipment doesn't work very well in this ice for some reason. We never could figure it out."

"Something in the water," Rick smiled, thinking of Caidin. "You have to calibrate for it."

"It's saltwater," Terry replied. "How difficult can it be? The short answer is no, Sir. We really have no idea. Our hope was the shifting ice pack would eventually open the canyons back up and we would drive back out the same way we came in."

"Seems like they would have left more than just a couple of pilots to enforce a take-over," Rick said shaking his head.

"Dacey can provide you with any further information as to their battle tactics."

"So, do you have a projected time of arrival of the Drake ships?" Rick asked.

"Like I said, our scanners range is limited, but it appears they have broken through to several large cavities. With what detail we're able to gather, it looks like they're making sure there is plenty of room to pull us back out when they reach us."

"If they're following the same path I took, which would make sense, you don't have much time at all."

"Excuse me, General," one of the Lieutenants spoke up. "But why don't we just man the *Athena* and launch. Those Drake ships should be less than a bump in the road for a Starbird."

"Any of you ever serve on a Starbird before?" Rick looked around the room at the sullen, quiet faces. "No doubt you put in for transfer onboard one; who wouldn't? They are an amazing piece of hardware, but they are also very sophisticated, requiring a crew that knows exactly what they're doing to handle one. I haven't even been on the bridge yet or looked at the engineering logs of her trip here. When I left her, this ship's condition was pretty weak. I have no idea if she could even launch a torpedo right now."

"She cut her way to this point," one of the officers pointed out.

"Yes, and I am grateful CORA 500 was able to pull it off, but did you see the bow and the aft section of this bird? She's a little more beat up now than when I left her. In fact," Rick said getting to his feet and stepping to the door. "Let's go have a look."

He was certain at least a few of them had seen some of the technical specifications of the Starbird, but apart from Greg Tanetto, that was about as far as it went. It took his crew months of training to even qualify to drive the *Athena* out of space dock. Except for himself and Gunnar, you couldn't just walk in and make this ship move. Everyone was quick to their feet as Rick was out the door and walking into the bridge.

"CORA, activate all ship's systems," he ordered. Display panels lit up all around the bridge and the main lights brightened. "Have you had time to run a ship wide diagnostics yet?"

"Have I had time? Do you know how long I've been in operation alone?"

"Yeah, yeah," Rick chuckled. "Didn't think that question through very well."

"Yes, General Niker. I've had plenty of time to create a full report."

Rick was glad CORA knew him well enough to read the situation and adjust her address protocols to match the conditions. Being informal in front of officers other than his own could cause a problem.

"Let's have it then."

"All sub-light speeds at your command. Light speed drive is currently off-line. Asium count is at five viable crystals. Defensive armament is currently off-line. Missile and torpedo launchers are currently off-line. Gun systems are at twenty percent. Shield energy at twenty percent. Maneuvering thrusters and navigational systems are fully operational. Sensor systems are at forty percent. Environmental systems operating at seventy-five percent."

"You'll also notice both Interceptors are missing," Rick pointed out. He stopped next to the pilot's station and faced the others. "I had one of them, but it was destroyed a short time ago by a Drake attack while I was docked to a shipwreck just outside the ice sheet. It's believed one or both Interceptor pilots escaped in the other, but their whereabouts is unknown. So, while the Starbird is an amazing ship, this one has seen a fair amount of action and in need of repair before it goes out again."

"So where does that leave us, General?" One of the other Chiefs asked. Rick thought for a long moment, then looked up.

"Lieutenant Gillespie, I'd like to speak to Mr. Dacey as soon as possible." Terry saluted and exited the bridge. "Chief Tanetto, are all four ships stuck in place or can you move?"

"We move them around every so often to keep the ice from compressing the hulls. We're able to keep the water and air around us warm enough that we're never frozen solid, although that's been getting a little harder as of late. We think we're in a compression cycle right now. If you look here," Greg pointed at a display. "There's an air cavity directly below us, where you came in. The *Stark* is currently sitting on top of a small crack in our chamber. We're kind of acting like a plug right now."

"So, if you're moving your ships around every so often, what's stopping this upper chamber's currents from becoming active?" Rick asked.

"You would think it would be tough to hold any kind of a stable position when we move, but surprisingly, it's not. Natural currents pull us down a little when we move, but as soon as we move another back onto the crack, everything calms right down."

"That's not likely to last much longer." Rick stepped over to the sensor control station and started working with the glass controls. The others followed for a look.

"Can you orient your ships in this configuration?"

Greg studied the readouts for a moment, then looked over his shoulder at his fellow Chiefs.

"It'll take some doing, but I think we can manage it. As long as we can keep one of the ships sitting right where the *Stark* is, we should be fine."

"With the permission of your commanding officers," Rick said looking at the other officers in the room. They all collectively nodded, somewhat relieved someone was here that actually knew what they were doing. "Make sure you bring my scout ship inside before you go. Report when you're ready."

"General," one of the other officers spoke up. "If we're to go into actual combat, regulations require you to assume command of the operation."

"So noted, Lieutenant. CORA, please record that as of this moment, I General Richard Alexander Niker, due hereby assume command of the *Stark*, *Huntly*, *Merc*, and *Tommy-Lee* for this operation. Suitable officers in command will be appointed here-after. CORA, prep for launch."

"Are you driving, or am I?" the AI asked.

"You've come this far all by yourself," Rick said as everyone left the bridge for their duty stations. "Be a shame to change a winning combination."

"And you will be where?"

"In constant contact with everyone. I'll clue you in once I've spoken with this Dacey fellow."

"How long will I be on my own this time?"

"Just until we can get these Drake guys taken care of."

Tonnie

"Hey, Alex," Gunnar said grinning while turning the ship. "Recognize this?" Ahead of them lay Reako's asteroid ring. More to the detail, Gunnar steered toward several spots in the ring where the material had been blown out the top and bottom, forming great plums.

"Colonel," Alex responded in a low tone. "Need I remind you what I am?"

"Come on, Alex. Engage your interaction protocols. You're dealing with a human, remember?"

The droid was silent for a moment, then raised its arms and flashed its lights in bright colors.

"Oh yes! This is amazing! It's like we were just here! Can we drive through one of them, please?"

"Ok, now you're just being ridiculous," Gunnar said.

"Something else I can never get use to; you can never please a human." Alex lowered his arms and shut his lights off.

"Not understand what you talk about," Janox puzzled, watching the inner line of the ring draw closer.

"We had quite a ride getting here the last time," Gunnar said, concentrating on piloting the fighter through the thin boundary of the ring. "Those plumes are where an Albion battlecruiser tried to flush us out of the ring layers."

"You never boring," Janox said, watching the asteroids grow in size as the Interceptor winged through the ring.

"What are you talking about?" Gunnar asked, focusing on flying.

"Your plans never go the way you say."

"Now you're getting it," Alex jumped in.

"Things go as planned all the time," Gunnar defended. "Remember that time... Wait... Ok, bad example and you weren't there anyway." Gunnar fumbled for something, but ultimately had nothing. "Things just go as planned, all right?"

"Certainly," Alex voiced barely audible.

Gunnar stopped the Interceptor and checked his instruments.

"This is as good a place as any." They looked out at the asteroids completely surrounding them now. There was only an occasional glimpse of the black of space.

"We should be able to see what we need to see from here without being spotted by anyone." Gunnar started working the scanning equipment. "I'm not nearly as good with this stuff as Mister Pippin is, but at least this gear works."

"Colonian scanning equipment works, Colonel," Alex said. "Just not well in these conditions."

Gunnar's expression hardened as he continued to work the equipment, checking and rechecking the readouts.

"Alex, can you think of any reason why we wouldn't be able to see the *Constellation*?"

"If it lost power you would not see it's ident transponders. Otherwise, it should be the first ship to come up."

"Well, that's what I thought, but I've got nothing."

"Have you scanned for the *Athena*?" Alex inquired.

"Just did," Gunnar puzzled.

"Maybe they on Carolon," Janox suggested.

"Maybe, but even if they were, we ought to be able to pick up the *Constellation's* transponder signals," Gunnar mumbled. "We've been inside Reako long enough, they should be sitting here washing the ship down waiting for us. Alex, is it possible the asteroid rings are interfering with our scanners?"

"Anything is possible. If you remember the first time we came in here," Alex said, "Colonel Barker's equipment had some difficulty seeing through the belt. Certainly the Albion scanning equipment wasn't any better."

"Would I be able to see any personnel transponder returns?" Gunnar checked the smaller scope off to the side, but saw only a blank screen.

"Not at this distance. They are short range only."

Gunnar pondered a moment, then took hold of the fighter's controls.

"I'm gonna take us up and out so we can have a better look around. Maybe we'll head toward Carolon and see if we're just missing them on the surface."

"I suggest caution, Colonel," Alex warned. "Remember the Albions have overrun that planet and destroyed the outpost under Colonel Barker's command. There would be every reason to believe they would have setup an installation of their own in place of it."

"We can always bug out if something comes up at us." Gunnar delicately maneuvered the Interceptor up through the asteroids, leveling out to skim along the top layer toward Carolon. Cautiously piloting his ship, he glanced at his scanning equipment, focusing on the readouts next to him.

"Oh goodie… Look at all this," Gunnar frowned.

"What matter?" Janox asked, looking over his shoulder.

"This party is spread all over the place."

Alex moved closer.

"We all understood the operation was bound to attract some attention," the little droid emphasized.

"There are several Corvette class ships in orbit, and… Geez, what a mess! That's a lot of wreckage out there."

"Out where?" Janox asked, glancing back.

"Colonel, these returns are all Albion ships," Alex pointed out.

A look of glee developed on Gunnar's face as he studied the scanning displays.

"Or, what's left of them," he said pointing at separate clusters of returns.

"It would appear there was a recent battle here."

"And from the looks of the aftermath, I'd say the Albions lost their pants on this one." Gunnar put a finger to his temple. "Wonder what caused all this?"

"Is the *Realistic* still on the outer rim?"

"Not seeing it," Gunnar said, shaking his head, still focused on the readouts. "Not seeing the *Constellation* either. Just what's left around Carolon and this cluster out here," Gunnar said pointing at the screen. "Since neither the *Constellation* or the *Realistic* are here, I'd say Captain Abrams gave them what for and bugged out."

"So, it would be only logical to assume we need to, *bug out too*, as you put it," Alex reasoned.

"Yes," Gunnar mumbled, ignoring a shuffling behind him. He looked up to see the outer edge of the asteroid ring approaching. They would need to decide what to do pretty fast or be fully exposed against the stark backdrop of space. "Alex, what's the best way to get a reading of the other side of Carolon?" Gunnar continued to work his gear, but got no response from the little droid. "Alex?"

"Colonel," Alex finally said. "You better have a look at this."

Irritated, Gunnar turned around. Looking past Janox, a set of green orbs glowed from the top of the lower access shaft, looking right at them. Startled at first, he fumbled to bring the interior lights up to full, exposing the top torso of the android, holding itself up. He glanced back down at the scanner, then back at the android. This was neither the time, nor the place to deal with this. There was no telling what this machine might do. It was programed to take care of a royal child and if in protection mode, things could unravel fast. He finally turned back to his controls and steered the ship back down into the thickest part of the belt, then secured the fighter next to one of the bigger rocks. Once certain they weren't going to hit anything, he turned back to find the android still frozen in position. Its eyes glowing a solid, bright green. The skin was a shriveled white and the hair a tangled, white gray color.

"Alex, are you getting anything?"

"It has no external receptors or transmitters, so I can't even try communicating with it unless directly connected. I can see no facial manipulations, so I'm not sure if it was designed to show expression."

"Well those creepy eyes are sure expressing something to me," Gunnar replied reaching for the pistol still holstered on the back of his seat. He gave Janox a glance as the young woman tried to back up over the seat and into the pilot's chair. "Give direct communication a go."

"Me?" Alex elevated his voice a little and his panel lights flittered.

"Yes you."

The little droid slowly rolled toward the still android, stopping just in front of its hand. The android did not move, but remained fixed, gazing forward.

"Tonnie, can you hear me?" Alex voiced plainly.

"Oh good grief," Gunnar said getting on his hands and knees. "I could have done that."

"You said communicate directly," Alex retorted.

"Whatever." Gunnar crawled up next to the little droid, looking directly into the android's eyes. "I wonder if she would let you interface directly?"

"I'm not sure I want to try," Alex said, hesitant.

"Hey, I'm this close. I'll save you if something happens."

"And who will be saving you?"

"Steady, Alex."

The little droid inched closer and extended his arm down toward the android's access door, but before Alex could get it open, the android gently took his arm and pushed it back. Alex and Gunnar looked at each other. If Alex could have managed it, he would have looked just as surprised as Gunnar. The android held its hand out to Gunnar. Even more surprised, he got up on his knees, took its hand and pulled. The android sluggishly raised itself out of the access shaft, kneeling on the floor directly in front of him. After some curious study of his facial features, the android bent over and gave Alex a good look. Once it had finished its examinations, it looked around Gunnar at the figure peering out from behind the pilot's seat.

"Tonnie, my name is Gunnar Conrad. I'm your friend. Are you all right?"

Tonnie looked at Gunnar again, then back at the pilot's chair.

"I seek… the Princess, Jana Oxlind." Her voice was shrill, garbled and her mouth movements didn't match her speech. "Is that her… behind you?"

Gunnar wasn't sure how to respond; *Jana Oxlind*?

"I can answer that," he said carefully. "But we need to find out how you're doing first. What is your condition?"

Tonnie tried to move around Gunnar, but a strong hand stopped her. She looked down at Gunnar's hand, then up at him. She relaxed and leaned back on her knees.

"Where is, the child?"

"The child is safe. Tonnie, your condition?" Gunnar demanded.

"I am… operational. Repairing degraded, operating systems. Memory… banks are intact. Cybernetics operational. Optics operational. Attempting repair, of speech center functions. All cognitive... functions are online. Is this, the child?"

"Does this woman look like a child?"

"Where is, the child?"

"The child is safe," Gunnar maintained. "Do you require assistance to repair damaged functions?"

"My diagnostics engines... are overwhelmed. If you, can render assistance, it would be... helpful."

"Alex will assist you in repairing your damaged systems."

Tonnie looked down at Alex, then back at Gunnar.

"Alex is, a friend too?"

"Yes," Gunnar reassured her.

"Then he, should assist... me in repairing, my damaged systems."

Tonnie lowered herself to the floor, allowing Alex to open her access doors and begin the work of figuring her systems out. In the meantime, Gunnar leaned against the back of the pilot's seat.

"You stun me and then threaten to do it again, all so we can get her off Reako and now you won't even go near her?"

"I still angry at Tonnie," Janox said in a hush. "She left me when I just little. Now she not even remember me."

"You're being about as ridiculous as a person can be right now, you know that?" Gunnar whispered back. "You're angry with an android? First of all, that's about the stupidest thing I've ever heard of. Second, weren't you the one that was just lecturing me about being angry?"

"Different type of anger in you. Besides, you get angry with Alex all the time."

"That's different, he deserves it. I suspect you're more scared than angry."

"I angry. How she leave me and not remember?"

"How is she supposed to know it's you? You've grown up, changed from a little girl to a woman. The last thing she is likely to remember is some snot-nosed little girl who was totally dependent on her."

"I never snot-nosed," Janox retorted.

"I think you understand my point," Gunnar said. "Where's the fearless woman I found here the first time around?"

"Sitting here in angry mood."

"Well, if we're to have any hope of getting to the bottom of what that thing is around your neck, you need to get over it."

"Colonel," Alex summoned. "This is a remarkable piece of hardware."

"Hardware? You're calling me, a piece of... hardware?" Tonnie's voice had cleared considerably, the pitch dropping several octaves and her lip sync improving. Gunnar knelt back down next to Alex.

"I will refer to this mechanism as a *she* for the sake of keeping the peace," Alex said.

"I think you are wise, Alex. What is it?" Gunnar asked, lowering himself to have a look.

"Look at this. They're using macro magnetic servos to emulate human internal functions like breathing, and appendage movement. Her respiration acts as a cooling system, and there are chemical cell extraction systems in here that actually produce power to augment the main source…"

"Alex, I'm a fighter pilot and a ship commander. If you want to impress someone, please wait till we get back with General Niker. Are you able to help her or not, and remember, that was a simple yes or no question?"

"Yes, but…"

"Uht, uht, uht!" Gunnar leaned back against the seatback. "Yes or no?"

"Yes."

"Best droid ever. Can I talk to her while you work?"

"Yes, but…"

Gunnar held a finger up to quiet the little droid. Alex went back to work while Gunnar got comfortable.

"Tonnie, are you functional enough yet to answer some questions?" Gunnar asked.

"There are a number of high priority questions in my que requiring immediate attention," Tonnie answered.

"I'll ask one and then you can ask one."

"Proceed."

"How did you get down into that well?" Gunnar felt a pair of hands grasp the seat cushion.

"I jumped in."

Janox immediately popped up to speak, but Gunnar held up a hand.

"Ssshhh… You jumped?" Gunnar continued.

"Yes," Tonnie, said.

"Because?"

"Where is the child?"

"I thought I answered that already?"

"You haven't told me where the child is."

Gunnar glanced up at Janox, her eyes riveted on the android.

"This is Janox, she is the child you speak of."

Tonnie looked up at Janox.

"This is a woman, not a child. I seek the child, Princess Jana Oxlind."

"The condition of your memory banks, Tonnie?"

"Accessing information. Corruption present. Implementing raid data protection. Rebuilding corrupted memory. Accessing time frame adjustments. Tonnie shut down… after secured at the bottom… of the well. Adjusting time reference parameters." Tonnie froze.

"Colonel," Alex spoke up. "I've achieved a direct connection into her cybernetic network. I'll see if I can help her with her time references. She genuinely doesn't know how long she's been down there."

"Good work, Alex," Gunnar said. "Stay in there. Tonnie, Alex is helping you remember. Do you understand?"

"Yes." Tonnie looked back up at Janox. "You are the child?"

Janox nodded silently.

"How can you be the child, Jana Oxlind?"

"She doesn't remember you because her memory banks are corrupted," Gunnar said looking back up at Janox. "Not because she forgot about you. I'm sure the memory is in there, she just has to figure out how to access it."

Janox remained silent.

"I left you." There was inflection in Tonnie's voice now, regret. "Alone..."

"Tonnie, why did you jump into the well?" Gunnar asked.

"To save the Princess," Tonnie answered.

"To save the Princess?"

"Yes."

"Alex, are you sure she isn't still scrambled?" Gunnar asked.

"Her network is amazingly resilient. This can't be Colonian hardw..."

"May I touch the Princess?" Tonnie asked.

"Why?" Gunnar inquired.

"I must confirm her identity."

"Colonel, she hasn't been able to access all of her diagnostic functions yet," Alex announced. "I have scanned her exterior. There are no functional sensors or probes. She likely doesn't know that yet."

"Tonnie, the water has rendered your external sensors inoperative. You'll have to take my word for it. This is the Princess. How did jumping down the well save her?"

"Are we out of the biosphere?" Tonnie asked.

"Yes, we had to leave," Gunnar confirmed. "It began to flood."

"My prime program function is to protect the Princess at all costs. I was sent an external directive, Terminal Twenty-One. The Princess was to be drowned by flooding the biosphere. I jumped into the well so I could not execute that directive. I knew the water would render all my external systems nonfunctional. While I was isolated in the depths of the well, the biosphere could not flood."

"Either we broke the mechanism holding the biosphere in equilibrium or when we brought her up, her presence triggered the external sensors and initiated the directive, flooding the biosphere." Gunnar looked back up at Janox again. A glint in her eyes indicated tears.

"Young Princess Jana. Do you remember your name?"

"No. I am Janox. It only name I know," Janox choked.

"You are Jana Oxlind," Tonnie said. "Fifth daughter to Tiev and Mila Oxlind. King and Queen of Colonia."

"If she is the fifth daughter, where are her siblings? Her parents?" Gunnar thought back to the conversation he and Rick had with Diord as to what happened to the royal family.

"Jana is the youngest of seven," Tonnie began. "Four sisters and two brothers. Her mother, Queen Mila, died, giving birth to Jana. King Tiev remarried sometime later to the Duchess of Teleknee, Stephanie Benetar, but without any royal claim, unless something were to happen to the royal line. It was rumored one of the servants of the House of Oxlind murdered the king, but no one was ever identified. Two of Jana's sisters were lost in a transport accident on Tintee. One died of a sudden illness and the fourth went missing on a trip to the Jurass system. Both sons were killed flying TL-42 fighters in the Trepid incident."

"That's how Queen Benetar came to power," Gunnar stated.

"Technically, she is not royalty. She holds the title of Duchess only. As long as there is still a legitimate blood heir to the royal throne, she cannot legally assume the throne."

"I hate to break it to you, but I'm afraid she already has. How is it she missed Janox, I mean, Princess Jana?"

"As the royal care giver of the Princess, I suspected it was only a matter of time before the Duchess created a convenient accident for Princess Jana, so I did the only thing I could. I took the child from Tintee under the cover of another accident to a safe place. But the Duchess found out about our departure and sent her secret service agents after us. I was able to evade them for some time, but eventually they caught up to us on the planet Colbix. We were about to be taken when agents of the Albion King Commander, Thoene Dismon, interceded and took us to Zepplin, on Albia. We were held there for a long time, all the while, I was allowed to continue to care for the child. We were finally taken to the biosphere inside the planet Reako where we have been since. No one has ever checked on our welfare or come to provide any kind of supplies or aide. We were just brought down and left. I have cared for the Princess, taught her everything she needed to survive in the environment we were placed in, until I received the transmission to my cybernetic network to invoke Terminal Twenty-One."

"Have you ever received any other transmissions while you were there?"

"Only monitoring telemetry," Tonnie responded. "Just something to know we were still there. The termination command protocol setup a direct conflict with my prime directives, so I did the only thing that would satisfy the command parameters of both. In the well water, I knew my external sensors would be rendered inoperative as long as I was at the bottom. If someone did discover the Princess in the biosphere, she would remain safe."

"Like I said, either we broke the regulating mechanism or when we pulled you up, it allowed Terminal Twenty-One to activate, but since we had a ship that could handle the conditions, we got you out."

"I am grateful you have made sure the Princess is safe."

"So what's so special about the necklace you kept for Jana?"

"It is the key to records containing her royal lineage. Proof of who she is, her rights as a Princess of Colonia and rightful blood heir to the throne of Hadrian."

"Is the file inside the necklace?"

"No, it is only a key used to access the records containing the information."

"Where are these records located?"

"The Zepplin special collections repository on the Albia moon, Dither."

"Zepplin?" Gunnar repeated. "Didn't you say that was an Albion city?"

"Yes, the capital city of the Albion home world, Albia."

"Nothing's ever easy," Gunnar grumbled. He drew in a deep breath and looked up at Janox, who remained silent, holding the necklace and looking at Tonnie.

"How can I be sure you still won't try to carry out this Terminal Twenty-One command?" Gunnar asked.

"The command protocol contained transfer commands that would open the biosphere balancing values. Once that was accomplished, the protocols were satisfied. It would be assumed the Princess would be drowned. There are no further instructions in my cue that would conflict with my primary directives; protect the Princess at all costs."

Gunnar rubbed his eyes, trying to think things through. He understood Janox needed to be cared for and as the blood heir to the throne, she would have to take her placed on the throne, but he had figured when the time was right, he'd hand her over to Diord and he would present her as the blood heir and Benetar would be forced to step down to allow Janox to assume the throne. Then all this fighting and bickering would cease and he could go back to trying to figure out how to get home. Clearly it wasn't going to be that simple. He glanced over at Alex. The droid's arm was still extended inside the access panel of the android.

"How's it going, Alex?"

"I have been able to help clear most of her systems. Of course, all her external sensors will remain nonfunctional until suitable replacements can be fitted, but she should have access to all her memory data. If it is corrupted, she'll have to access the backups in her raid tiers. However, it is quite likely there is some that will not be retrievable. Her physical functions are at about sixty percent. She might have a little trouble balancing as her internal gyro-gimbles are slow to recover from being down for so long. Her outside features; hair, skin, eyes and overall muscle tone will take time to recover."

"So no more ghoulish green eyes staring us down, zombie colored skin and white scraggily hair?"

"Eventually... She is truly a remarkable feat of engineering, and that presents an important question that may not have an answer. Where did she come from? The cultures in this part of the galaxy have no such technology. Who created her? Whoever did, didn't leave any kind of identification marks in her. Even her bit streams are clean."

Janox crawled past Gunnar, crouching timidly across from Tonnie. Gunnar crawled back up into the pilot's seat and started working with the instruments. A moment later, Alex tried to join him, but struggled to position himself where he could see the instruments.

"The safe bet here is to pull up out of these rocks and bust a light speed maneuver back to Aster," Gunnar said mulling the options before them.

"Wouldn't Captain Abrams have deployed some kind of a marker beacon indicating what he did if he couldn't hang around to pick us up?" Alex inquired.

"Standard operating procedure," Gunnar confirmed. "I've been trying to scan for that, but haven't really had any luck yet because of the interference from Reako and these asteroids. Amended option would be make an orbit of Carolon while scanning for the beacon or the ship on the surface. If nothing's here, we hightail it back to Aster."

"I feel certain you are considering other options."

"Alex, you know me so well."

"I often wonder if my twin, Felix is having similar experiences."

"You love me, you know you do. The other option is to orbit Carolon, if no ship or beacon, we plot a course to Albia and try to find this repository."

"We are in an alien military ship, Colonel."

"Nobody needs to know that."

"It is a little obvious, isn't it?"

"Can you think of a better ship to get in and out of a place like that?"

"Yes, I can provide you with a number of examples." Alex went silent for a moment. "But as they are all Kalamarion craft and not readily available, there is little point to mentioning them. Are you sure taking the Princess into such dangerous territory is a wise option? Were she to be discovered, she could be terminated or used to gain power over the throne."

"Do you think anyone has a clue as to what the Princess looks like, or that she even exists? The last time anyone saw her was when she was a young child."

"Ok, but what about this repository? Surely it is a high security facility. You're talking about a moon in orbit around the Albion home world."

"I have to think it's just like any other place. Unless it's a high security installation, as you are suggesting, people have to have access to it or what's the point of having it? If we find it heavily guarded, we can just keep on driving and head home."

"I suspect you've already made up your mind, Colonel."

"I have, it would just be nice if I had everyone onboard with the same idea, starting with you."

"Colonel, I would think after all the time we have spent together, you would know that I will follow your orders, no matter how idiotic they might be."

"Nice to know you've got my back, buddy." Gunnar turned in his seat to ask a question of Janox and Tonnie, but remained silent, watching the scene behind them. Janox was kneeling behind an upright Tonnie, combing out the android's long white tangles and humming softly. The android's eyes had softened, her eyelids half closed, giving the appearance of enjoyment for the simple attention.

"Tonnie, can you direct us to Dither and the repository?"

"Certainly. It is not a difficult facility to access. It is more of a galactic library, containing records and knowledge spanning this quadrant of Hadrian."

"Then you think we can gain access to Jana's records?"

"With the key the Princess now possesses, we can."

"Is there anything you can think of that could be a problem?"

"As you and Alex discussed, no one will recognize the Princess. But if an agent of the Albion secret service recognizes me, it could create a problem as we are supposed to still be in the biosphere."

"Would there still be agents that would recognize you?"

"Not likely, but it is possible."

Gunnar glanced at Janox, who smiled softly as she worked the comb through Tonnie's hair.

"Let's go explore new places," Gunnar said turning forward and activating the Interceptor's engines. Carefully guiding the big fighter back out of the asteroids, he checked the scanners. There was no movement in their direction, so he steered toward Carolon, hopeful that Captain Abrams had left a beacon detailing the outcome of the mission. His scans revealed nothing but wreckage around Carolon and not wanting to tempt fate with the Albion Corvettes that had surely detected them, he plotted a course to Albia and moments later, shifted to light speed.

Resurrection

Rick stepped slowly around the Drake raider craft, methodically examining every part of it. It seemed simple enough; built to handle the rigors of space combat. Checking the turrets on the corners, he observed a couple of shadows.

"Chief Tanetto and Crewman Dacey reporting as ordered, Sir." Rick turned as they saluted. He gave a half salute back and shook Dacey's hand.

"Interesting you being so friendly when you come from a people who seem bent on destroying everything."

Dacey hesitated a moment, then straightened up.

"You must understand the mentality of the Drake culture, General."

"Can you enlighten me in twenty-five words or less?"

"My people have never come together as a centralized culture. It has been tried many times over the course of a millennia, but something always happens to steer the meeting of the minds apart. The Drake rely on primitive warfare instead of building constructive relations and fair trade with adjoining systems. When the Kendalons took me captive, I came to understand that there really are people who are good and not out to cheat or kill you just because you're different. I found friends here, General. Good friends."

"That was more than twenty-four words," Rick replied. "Do you still remember how to fly these things?"

Dacey glanced at the Chief, then strolled over to one of the fighters, touching the canopy release. The entire top of the cockpit, including all the windows, opened up, swinging forward.

"This is about the simplest fighter there is to fly."

"How many different types of fighters and ships do the Drake have?" Rick asked, peering inside to look at the instrumentation.

"There are only four different types of fighters. There are many different types of military ships, ranging from fighter, to assault class and leading up to capital class. But there aren't very many capitol class ships. No one has the know how to design and build one the right way, in my view. The ones we have in our fleets are stolen or salvaged."

"Interesting," Rick mumbled still looking at the cockpit. His thoughts turned to Caidin and *Calypso*. *That ship could certainly be classed as a Capitol, and a very capable one if it still had armament.* He hoisted himself up into the cockpit and settled in. Dacey wasn't overselling the simplicity of the fighter's controls. Everything was at your fingertips and there was little else. "How do you navigate?"

"Here," Dacey pointed to a tiny panel.

"This?" Rick asked astonished.

"There's a network of navigation buoys maintained by my people directing us to all the places we need to go. We don't venture beyond where the buoys can direct us. We just follow the readouts in whatever direction we want to travel."

"Talk about connect the dots," Chief Tanetto said, looking into the cockpit from the other side.

"Any limitations on these guns?"

"Well, if you're good at pointing your ship at what you want to hit, there are no limitations; they'll keep firing as long as there is something to fire."

"That explains why you guys have a hard time hitting anything," Rick said working the controls. "Light pulse or ordnance?"

"Ordnance only; loaded from wingtip to wingtip. Only assault and tug craft have light pulse tech."

"You willing to go head to head against your own people? Fire on your own ships?"

"They are no longer my people, General. These are my friends now. These are my ships."

Rick looked up at Dacey. The expression on his face told him everything he needed to know. He glanced over at Greg Tanetto.

"Are you up for this, Chief?"

"I'd rather be onboard the *Athena*, Sir. But as that doesn't seem to be what you have in mind, I'm up for a little fighter work."

"You ever do any combat flying?"

"Did some gunnery practice in a Thumper back in my cadet days."

"Didn't we all," Rick said smiling. "Get yourself ready." Both Dacey and Greg turned to get to the other two craft, but Rick stopped Dacey. "Dacey, one more question if you don't mind."

"Yes, Sir."

"If a Drake craft were to happen upon an escape pod or small ship with someone still alive onboard, would they destroy it or pick them up?"

"Depending on the craft they have available at the time, they'd be picked up and sold on the slave trade unless they thought they could use them in combat. But it's doubtful they could be picked up if they were found by a fighter like this one."

Rick nodded.

"Where would they take someone to be sold on this slave trade?"

"First they would have to be taken through space detox. It's kind of a long process. Slave traders won't take anyone from space unless they're certified clean. The only Detox station close by here would be Conti Nine space station. It's mostly automated, very minimal staff."

"In orbit around a planet?"

"No, Sir. It runs a guided course on the far side of Skadil."

"Marker buoys out there?"

"Sure. You got someone taken there?"

"Could be. What about Captains Fowler, Quayle, Puche' and Darton? Where would your guys have taken them?"

"There's a mining colony on Skadil. Unless you join the ranks of the Drake and perform as desired, that's usually where you get sent. It's a pretty tough place to be."

"The other officers?"

"If they were female, they were probably taken to Conti Nine. The men would have been put into service or sent to the mines."

Rick started to strap himself in and work the controls to get the craft up and running.

"Thank you, crewman. Stick around, I may need you later." Rick brought his communicator up as the canopy dropped down over the cockpit. "CORA, ya with me?"

"Certainly, General. You have instructions for me?"

"Yea, you could say that. Ready for another adventure?" Rick worked with the gravity compensation controls, finally bringing the Drake fighter off the bay floor.

"I didn't care much for the last one, but if this is a means to an end, I'm as ready as I can be."

"You got the positioning information for this little maneuver I sent you earlier?"

"Affirmative. I just don't understand what good this ship is going to be in actual combat. I have no operational weapons; I can't even fire any of these torpedoes."

"All part of the master plan, my dear. I wouldn't want you to fire those torpedoes in such close quarters anyway. Those things will probably blow us all up. You just need to sit right where you're supposed to with your shields up and look menacing."

"I can do that."

"Lieutenant Gillespie," Rick spoke into the headsets he slipped over his head. "We're ready to go. The *Athena* will back out first, followed by Crewman Dacey, Chief Tanetto and then myself. Please have all exterior lights on, including running lights. Remember not to start firing until I give the order."

"What if we start taking damage, Sir?"

"Did you really believe you were going to get through this without taking some damage?"

"Well, I was hoping..."

"Just keep your shields forward and you should be fine." Rick steered his ship into position in front of the *Athena* as the bay doors began to part, revealing the dark void outside. He waited patiently as the *Athena* rose from the bay floor and backed out. Dacey followed, then Greg. Finally, he gently nudged his fighter out after them just as the surrounding freighters turned on all their exterior lights. It was enough to illuminate the surrounding ice walls. Most of the light was

reflected back, giving everyone a good view of what their prison looked like. Rick pulled his fighter alongside the other two, directly behind the *Athena* as she took her position between all four freighters, two on top and two on the bottom, spaced as far apart as was practical.

"CORA, what's their position?"

"Just breaking through now, General. Left wall directly ahead at our level."

Rick let the fighter sink a bit so he could see under the *Athena's* belly. Seeing ice chunks flying away from the wall at the other end of the cavern, he pulled back up out of sight and waited.

"They're making that hole plenty big," CORA observed.

"They have to if they think they're going to get these freighters back out. Give them a little help with your cutter beam. They'll think they're really something. Lieutenant Gillespie, just as soon as they poke their nose through, you open up."

"Yes, Sir."

Everyone watched the hole grow while more ice chunks spewed from the gaping hole. For several minutes, it appeared the side blowing volcano of ice would never stop. Just as it began to subside, a beam of light filtered through the clouds of pulverized ice. All eyes were on the cloud of ice as it was abruptly sucked back through the wide hole. Several more anxious minutes passed and finally the beam pushed forward, leading a bulky looking vessel as it entered the cave. No sooner did it reveal itself, than the *Stark* and the *Huntly* opened fire. As soon as the Drake assault vessel started to take fire, another Drake vessel appeared directly behind it and opened up on the source of their punishment. Moments later, several smaller fighters appeared, banking hard into the cavern and opening up on the freighters. As the fighters weaved closer to one of the freighters, one unexpectedly spun out of control, it's wing severed as it crossed directly in front of the *Athena*.

"Nice work with the cutter, CORA," Rick exclaimed. "Let's see what you've got, Crewman Dacey." Rick dipped his fighter directly under the *Athena* and gave chase to one of the fighters. Tracer ordnance spewed in crisscross directions as two more Drake assault ships appeared at the cave opening. Rick felt a thumping in the frame of his ship as he maneuvered around to get a shot at one of the fighters. He looked out at his wings, seeing pock marks appearing, several working their way toward the fuselage. He checked the mirror above his head. A fighter had locked onto him from behind. Spikes of light pulsed from the nose and wings of his pursuer. He rolled his ship and maneuvered away, nearly slamming into one of the ice walls. Rick was almost as good as his friend Gunnar. But while he was a truly gifted pilot, he didn't have the talent of being able to jump behind the controls of any machine and know immediately how it all worked like Gunnar did. He could pick it up quickly, but his learning curve was still quite steep at this point.

"Need a little help over here if someone has a minute," Rick grunted, maneuvering in close quarters.

"Which one are you, Sir?" Dacey called out.

"I'm the one with the wings and fuselage. The one getting the heck shot out of it."

"Need to be a little more specific, Sir," Chief Tanetto called. "I'm getting hammered too."

"Here!" Rick wagged his wings violently while dipping and spinning.

"Oh, yeah," Dacey spoke up. "You're the one with the wingtip shot off."

"That would be the one," Rick answered. He looked to his left in time to see a fighter crash into the ice wall and break apart. The pilot struggled with his face mask as he floated free of the debris. Rick glanced back up at his mirror, noticing another fighter coming in behind the one still dawging him. Tracers flashed past his cockpit as he swerved again and pulled up. The fighter behind him didn't pull up and impacted the wall. Rick rolled over and looked down at the *Athena.* She was pivoting slightly toward the cave opening, bringing her cutting beam to bear against the two assault ships still poised in the opening. Both were heavily damaged, having taken the brunt of the fire fight from all four of the freighter's guns. No sooner did the cutting beams cut the two ships in half, than two more appeared and took their place. One of the fighters started directly at the *Athena,* firing straight at her nose.

"CORA, shift back to the right," Rick bellowed, watching the high-powered ordnance striking the gun assemblies on the nose of the Starbird. Rick dove on the muscled craft and pulled his triggers. Seeing his tracers track behind the fighter, he shifted, leading the ship as it closed in on the *Athena*. His tracers disappeared into the back of the fuselage and the wing roots. He adjusted some more, closing in to nearly point blank range. His tracers walked across the wing and right into the cockpit. The fighter shuddered midflight and swerved, glancing off the side of the *Athena's* bridge pod and disintegrating. Rick turned and a moment later felt several strikes on his own craft. Warning lights began to flash on his thruster controls, feeling the fighter sputter and slow. He glanced back behind him, seeing gases spewing from the rear of his ship. He tried to steer, but there was little control left and he only managed to duck behind the *Athena* before he skidded into the ice wall and ground to a halt in a large crack.

"I'm out guys," he called out. Looking back at the cave opening, he saw one of the assault ships starting to break up, but the other one moving out into the open and turning for the five ships clustered together.

"Me too," Chief Tanetto called out as he steered his disabled fighter up to one of the freighters for protection. One of his wings had been blasted off. Dacey continued to dogfight with the remaining fighters, taking intense pot shots at the assault craft moving closer to the cluster of larger ships.

"We're down to about two guns between four ships," Lieutenant Gillespie called. "And we didn't have very many to start with."

Rick watched as two more assault craft entered the cavern and started moving toward them. There came a noticeable vibration through the frame of his fighter. He glanced at the walls of ice all around him. The entire cavern appeared to shiver.

"What was that?" Dacey called out. There came an audible booming noise and the entire cavern shook again, this time with more conviction.

"CORA," Rick called. "Talk to me."

"Sensors are detecting a massive release of energy in the ice sheet. The energy signature is extending from the outside ice sheet wall to this point. Sensors will not give anything further in this environment."

It seemed that everyone in the cavern froze, listening to the sounds being transferred through the ice. Even the Drake craft abandoned the chase for a moment, trying to ascertain what was happening. Finally, as the sounds died off and the cave stood still, the opponents picked up the fight once again. Dacey made quick work of the last fighter in the cave and started in on the assault ships working their way to the closest freighter. He swung in with a voracious attack on the lead assault ship, raking the entire top of the ship and then fading quickly in front and below the ship to escape it's firing line. He glanced back as he dove, hearing the tell-tale sounds of ordnance striking his fighter. He tried to swerve and roll; a maneuver to confuse the assault craft's gunners, but it seemed there was an invisible thread connecting his ship to their ordnance. Trying to pull back up, his right wing assembly shuddered, folded back and tore away. Pulling back on the throttle, he shut the engine down to keep the stricken craft from breaking up. As he had been traveling down, his craft continued to dive to the bottom, out of the fray. Now all he could do was look up and watch.

"I'm done. I'm settling to the bottom. I'm not losing any air, so I should be fine. Now what?"

"We pray for a miracle," Rick said grimly, watching the last of the freighter's guns being blasted away. As the guns went silent, there came a terrible tremor shake through the entire cavern again. This time it was far more violent and the accompanying noise was enough to pierce through even the thickest hull.

"CORA, can you give us anything this time? Sounds closer." Rick looked all around the cavern. The Drake craft had stopped, no doubt trying to ascertain what was happening as well.

"The left wall, something large is approaching through the ice."

"Through the ice?"

Rick shifted his gaze at the same moment there was a sudden explosion in the ice wall, ice debris spraying against the opposite wall. The entire wall fractured wide open, ice fragments floating away from a large object pushing through. Rick's eyes widen as the bow of the great ship *Calypso* appeared and came to a stop against the opposing wall. The cavern had been cut nearly in half by the massive bulk of the blunted bow of the old warship. Rick checked all their ships. He could still see Dacey floating somewhere below everyone and Chief Tanetto was still tucked between the *Stark* and the ice wall. He searched for both Drake assault craft. One was still hovering right in front of the *Stark*, but the other was nowhere to be seen until it suddenly materialized from behind the first one. Both craft were moving into position to board the *Stark.*

"Am I too late?" came the welcome voice of Caidin Mantose over Rick's coms.

"Right on time," Rick said, shaking his head and still awestruck by the size of the bow of the great ship; and this was just the tip. "Now if you could get rid of those two Drake Assault ships."

"Two? I'm counting four. Two on your side and two on my side... Wait, check that, they're on your side now."

"I've got them. Seems we're in a bit of a pickle here." There was the sudden flash of gun fire coming from the third assault ship. "What in the... Wait a second!" Rick watched curiously as the third ship opened fire on one of the assault ships while another familiar looking craft appeared from behind and started firing on the second ship. The first assault craft broke apart right away, its insides curling out. The last Drake ship turned and started firing at the smaller craft shooting a hailstorm of canon fire at them and for a few moments, they played a game of hunt the Wampus until the assault ship exploded, it's fragments piercing into the ice wall and its insides free floating where the destruction had taken place. The rouge Assault craft maneuvered into position right in front of the *Athena* as the familiar design of a Kalamarion Interceptor pulled up next to it, both waiting.

"General Niker," CORA called. "You need to hear this."

"I'm certain I do," he said, nearly in tears. "Can you patch it through? This thing's coms are a nightmare to work, not to mention they seem to have just three frequencies." A moment later, a familiar voice blasted over his headsets.

"General Niker, this is Captain Zek..."

"And Zak..." another voice added.

"Captains Zek and Zak Korack reporting in. Are you ok?"

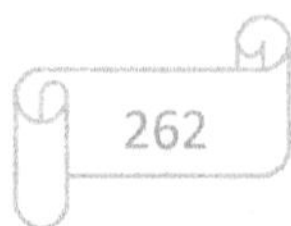

Overcome with relief for finding more of his crew, or rather they finding him, Rick was unable to speak for a moment.

"General Niker, do you read?"

"Yes, I read you," Rick finally choked. "What in the... How did you... Where have guys been?"

"A very long story, Sir. Request permission to dock or come aboard one of these freighters. We're both in a bad way."

"If you wouldn't mind, do you have enough ship left to do a little rescue. We've got a fighter below us and one tucked up next to the *Stark*. I'm slammed against the wall behind the *Athena*. We're in need of a tow back to the *Stark*."

"If the *Stark* still has any kind of mooring tractor hawsers, I think we can manage it."

"You get them close enough, Captain," Terry Gillespie called out. "We'll get them back in."

"We're on it," Zek responded.

"CORA, you're coming back in as soon as we have the other ships back in the *Stark's* landing bay."

"Gladly, General."

"Caidin, I'd like to have a word with you at your earliest convenience."

"My place or yours?"

"I wouldn't dream of making you walk that far. I'll meet you with my new staff as soon as we can get everyone back on board and any injuries attended to."

"I look forward to meeting everyone."

*   *   *   *

Once back onboard the *Stark*, Rick couldn't help but embrace both his missing Interceptor pilots. Normally he wouldn't be showing such emotion in front of other crew members, but his relief for their safe return was so great he didn't care about how a General was supposed to act in front of subordinates.

"It sure is good to see you two," Rick said, wiping his eyes. "I had no idea what or where."

"It's great to see you and this wonderful Starbird again," Zek said turning to the *Athena* as she settled in the *Stark's* landing bay. "The amount of time we spent in that Interceptor together was a little more than either of us could stand."

"I don't even want to get into that thing until it has a thorough cleaning." Rick couldn't help but smile. He knew what it was like to fly an extended deep space probe, alone. He could only imagine what it was like with two of them.

"We took turns with the stasis harness," Zak said. Chief Tanetto only shook his head thinking of what the smell might be like.

"So, what's our next move, General?" Zek asked, stepping over to the *Athena* and running his hand along it's white hull.

"We need to find Commander Jayda. If Mister Dacey's information is correct, she was taken to a space station a short distance from here. Lieutenant Gillespie, what was your cargo?"

"I don't know," the Lieutenant stepped up. "I'm not even sure the Captains knew and even if they did, they were under strict orders of secrecy."

"Didn't Colonel Conrad say something about Starbird spare parts?" Zek asked.

"Wouldn't that be something?" Rick chuckled. "If there's something we could sure use right now, it's spare parts. Do you have the required security codes needed to access your cargo holds, Lieutenant?"

"No, Sir," Terry said. "The Captain kept that confidential. If they were in her private documents locker, they aren't there anymore. We've looked everywhere for them and tried everything to gain access to the holds. You're not getting into those without some kind of high level clearance."

"Wonder if maybe I could have a crack at it." Rick felt confident in his security clearances. Maybe there would be something useful in those holds. "Do the security protocols have retinal scans, print mapping or both?"

"No, Sir. Just command codes. But they do have Trident characters in them and our computers haven't been able to run them for possible cyphers."

"Command certainly didn't want anyone getting into them," Zak said excitedly. "Trident character protocols are nearly impossible to decipher."

"We don't have a lot of time here," Rick said getting down to business. "Zek, you take the *Huntly's* command officers and open the holds; see what's in there. Find something we can use. CORA," Rick said raising his communicator.

"Sitting right here, Sir."

Rick detected a little inflection in CORA's voice. He glanced back at the ship. She must be tired of the wait and the formality.

"Give access to my personal code locker to Captain Zek Korack."

"Captain Zek Korack does not have the proper security clearance to receive access."

"Yes, I know, but we're going to give it to him anyway."

"This is against regulations, Sir."

"Report me to Admiral Mandell." There was silence for a moment and then CORA finally answered.

"Access granted to Captain Korack."

"Good girl," Rick said, turning back to everyone with a bit of an eye roll. "Zak, Chief, Gillespie and Dacey, you're with me. We need to pay the *Calypso* a visit."

*   *   *   *

"Wouldn't it have been faster to just beam aboard? How big is this thing?" Captain Zak complained as the group of officers made their way down a corridor in the bow of *Calypso*. The silence within the great hull of the empty ship was deafening.

"Transporters are down. It's a capital," Rick said scanning the hallway for any sign of the floor transport Caidin had told them about.

"I think we saw this thing when we came to the ice cap," Greg Tanetto said.

"Looked derelict to us so we just left it," Terry said. "Besides, we had bigger problems to worry about."

"Tell me about Jayda's pod again," Rick said to Zak. "And please don't leave out a single detail. The smallest thing could be important."

"It's simple enough, Sir. When we launched from the *Athena*, there was no thought to try and defend the ship as we were all about to explode."

"Yes, completely understandable, Captain. You both did the right thing."

"Never been hit with anything that powerful before. I mean it felt like my head was going to explode."

"Your report matches CORA's exactly," Rick said still looking for the floor transport. He finally found a wall communications panel and started working with it. "I've experienced it firsthand as well. It's not an easy thing to combat."

"We didn't regain consciousness for hours and by then we were so far off the beaten path from anyone or anywhere, we had almost no idea where we were. It took a couple of days just to get back to our original launching point. By then, the *Athena* was long gone. We had no idea what happened to her. I guess we do now," Zak said with a grin.

"I'd say we all had a very long trip to get to this point," Rick said, agreeing with the assessment of their adventures.

"We found the trail of the escape pod and decided it was the most likely place to find you and the *Athena*. That ball can really travel."

"That's its function when in escape mode." Rick continued to struggle with the com panel. Dacey finally stepped forward to help.

"Well, it works really well," Zak said.

"Thank you, Dacey," Rick said as the panel appeared to start working. "Caidin, we're up front in the bow, but I'm not seeing the ground transport you were talking about."

"What hall are you in?"

"I don't know," Rick answered, looking around. "One of them?"

"Hallway Zulu four," Dacey said, pointing to an identifier plate on the opposite wall.

"You're almost there," Caidin said from the speaker on the com panel. "Two more hall blocks and it'll be on your right. Just climb in, belt yourself in and touch the location you want to go to on the front panel. The transport will do the rest." The group continued forward.

"We almost lost the trail a couple of times," Zak continued. "We finally caught up to the pod on the surface of Acuity, but those Drake guys were already pulling Jayda out."

"They were going to take the pod with them, but we sort of interrupted their operation," Zak said.

"How many of them were there?"

"Four fighters and three assault ships."

Rick glanced back at crewman Dacey, who was quick to speak up.

"Standard scouting and retrieval compliment, Sir."

"And what happened?" Rick asked, noticing the transport entryway just ahead.

"The fighters were almost a non-issue. It was like a bunch of kids were flying them. They couldn't hit the broadside of a black hole."

"Yeah," Rick agreed turning to Dacey again. "What's up with that? The pilots that came in the cave were pretty good, but the ones I was dealing with on the outside were a little less than useless." Everyone entered the transport loading area and climbed into a shuttle car situated on a rail mechanism.

"Experienced combat pilots are hard to come by," Dacey began, "so the Drake have a high mortality rate among its fighter pilots. Command gives the younger trainees patrol duty and they're supposed to call in for the more experienced pilots when they find something. Sometimes, those pilots don't arrive before an engagement begins."

"Makes sense," Zak said, watching the General work the control panel in front of him. "We had our hands full with the assault ships. We destroyed one and disabled a second, but the third got away with Commander Niker."

"The assault ship crews didn't mind you taking over their ships?" Greg asked.

"They didn't have too much to say about it," Zak said. "One was dead when we boarded and the other three couldn't shoot to save themselves. They're still on the assault ship, in one of the lockers."

"It was a good decision," Rick reassured them.

"Zek took command of the assault ship while I stayed with the Interceptor. I scanned several ships entering the water on the far side, so we pursued, thinking they might have taken Commander Jayda to some kind of underwater base in all this soup. You can't hardly scan any further than you can see through that muck," Zak said. "We had to tuck and duck into this soup several times while we skimmed a surface orbit. There's a lot of water here. There's a lot of junk here too."

"When we get back to the *Stark*, we'll mount a rescue op for Commander Jayda right away," Rick said.

"Do you even know where to look?" the Captain asked.

"The Conti Nine station," Dacey announced. "That's where every person found in space is taken for detox and processing. If you're female, chances are almost certain you'll be sold into the slave trades."

Rick looked at Dacey for a moment, hoping there were other options for prisoners, but when Dacey only shrugged, Rick's expression hardened.

"As soon as you can get things organized, Captain." Rick said, touching a button on the panel in front of him. A moment later the transport accelerated into a glowing tube.

"Is this thing pneumatic?" Zak asked, looking at the smooth walls flying by at a blur.

"Most of the older capital ships used pneumatic systems in their transport drives, but this one was state of the art for its time," Dacey said, admiring not just the moving walls around them but the enclosure itself. "This one is magnetic. It rides on a huge field coil. Zero moving parts making it about as smooth as coasting in space."

"Very nice," Rick said. "Anything else, Captain?"

"Not really," Zak said. "We followed a cluster of ships into the water some time ago and have been wandering around in here when we finally detected you guys in the ice. Apparently, the Drake saw you too, so we decided to let them do all the work and follow them in. Didn't count on this big momma of a ship crashing the party. Who is this Caidin person anyway?"

"Caidin Mantose?" Rick said. "Ring any bells?" Zak stared blankly at Rick.

"Uncle or grandpa to Colonel Conrad's Mantose twins?" Zak finally blurted out.

"Close, but no; Father."

"Small universe."

"Indeed," Rick said.

"I don't suppose he knows where we are and how we can get back home?" Zak asked.

"He's an odd fellow," Rick said, thinking. "I've found him to be full of surprises."

"What about what's left of the crew, Sir?"

"They stay right where they are until we can get back to the *Constellation* and Doctor Yamoto can have a look at them."

Everyone was jostled a bit as the transport turned in several directions and then started curving up at an angle. They slowed and leveled out, finally coming to a stop at another terminal loading station. Rick spotted a com panel on the wall and activated it.

"Made it this far, Caidin. I'm not recognizing anything on these levels."

"There's a set of elevators right in front of you. Step in and press the button labeled 'conning'. If you still don't recognize where you are when the door opens, call me again and we'll go from there."

"Hard to believe this ship was moth balled," Terry commented, getting into the elevator.

"I bet their updated version is pretty impressive," Greg said.

"If there is one," Dacey said. "I don't know anything about it. I haven't seen any capital ships in the Drake arsenal that could hold a candle to this ol' girl."

"Makes you wonder why they let her go," Terry said. Presently, the elevator slowed and stopped. Rick looked down as the door started to open to see where he would be walking, but stopped short. He was looking at a set of white high heeled boots. He slowly looked up at a tall, slender young woman and stepped back. Dãsha smiled pleasantly at him, pulling back her long flowing hair.

"It's good to see you again, General Niker."

Shuffling back further, Rick lost his balance and toppled the others in the elevator.

"You know this girl, General?" Zak asked with a stupid grin. "And you didn't tell us about her?" The Captain was enthralled with the beauty of the woman standing before them.

"Dãsha," Rick whispered, not believing his eyes. "But you're…"

"I can assure you, General, I am quite alive and well. Here…" She offered her hand to him. "Please… Feel it."

Rick looked at Dãsha carefully, trying to see where her injuries had been, but couldn't see any disfigurement. Nothing to indicate she had half her head crushed. He finally took her hand and stepped out of the elevator. Circling around behind her, he looked her over thoroughly. The short dress she was wearing was the same cut as before, just a different color. He stopped on one side of her and examined her face closely. There wasn't a blemish, no scares, nothing. She turned her head to him and let her black eyes gaze into his own.

"I'd like to take your hand," Zak said, stepping out of the elevator towards them.

Rick finally broke from his disbelief, realizing Caidin had a lot of explaining to do; *a lot of explaining.*

"Captain Zak Korack, I'd like to introduce you to Dãsha Mantose, Caidin Mantose's wife."

"Wait, what?" Zak asked, realizing what the title meant. "You're kidding. She's a daughter, right?"

"Nope," Rick said stepping back.

"Married…" Zak said, dejected.

"You'll have to excuse the Captain's manners, Dãsha. He's been in space a long time."

"You said you have women on your ships, did you not?" Dãsha asked. Tilting her head curiously back at Rick, then at the other officers coming out of the elevator.

"Yes, we do, but they've heard the same tired, worn out lines from Zak and his twin brother. Dãsha, I assume Caidin sent you down here to escort us to the bridge?"

"Yes, of course, please follow me."

"To the ends of the galaxy and beyond," Zak said in a stupid tone. Everyone started walking, but Rick remained in stride with the tall young woman.

"Would you like to explain this to me now or do I have to wait?"

"What is there to explain?" Dãsha asked, leading the group through several hallways. Presently, Rick recognized where they were. "I am here and so are you. There is no more. By the way, did you like the way we brought *Calypso* through the ice to help your people? The ice breaking was my idea. Clever, huh?"

"Dãsha, I pulled you out myself."

"And for that, you have mine and Caidin's thanks."

"You were dead; as in, not living; as in, without life, as in dead."

"Yes."

Rick waited for an explanation, but much to his dismay, it wasn't going to come. He slowed a bit, letting Dãsha pull several steps ahead. He wasn't sure what to think and could come up with only a couple of scenarios that all seemed equally fantastic. For now, there were more pressing issues at hand. As they entered the bridge of the giant war ship, Caidin turned in his chair at the sensor station and smiled.

"Welcome aboard *Calypso*, ladies and gentlemen." Rick and Caidin's eyes met, but Caidin was quick to avert contact, focusing on the other officers. Dãsha made her way around everyone and stood next to Caidin. "I'm Caidin Mantose and you've met my wife, Dãsha."

"Yes we have," Zak said under his breath.

Normally, Terry would have rolled her eyes at the foolish behavior of the fighter pilot, but she understood the mentality. In this instance, her focus was on trying to figure out the attraction between the older gentleman in the chair and the young, shapely woman behind him.

"Thanks for coming back," Rick said. "But as I recall, you were told to go in one direction and stay going in that direction. Now you're right back where you started."

"Begging your pardon, General," Terry interrupted. "But if Mister Mantose hadn't rammed into our cavern with his ship..."

"*Calypso*," Caidin corrected. "She's called, *Calypso*."

"*Calypso*," Terry repeated. "We probably wouldn't be standing here thanking him."

"No doubt, Lieutenant," Rick said smiling. "What I'm getting at, is why did you come back? You were free and clear. The Drake had no idea you were gone."

Everyone but Dãsha looked to Caidin for the explanation of his logic. Caidin glanced up at Dãsha, then looked around at everyone in the room, finally settling on Rick.

"You helped me. Shouldn't I act in similar manner?" he finally asked, hoping the question would suffice. "For so long, this ship has been my prison with Dãsha as my universe." Caidin rose from his chair, leaning on his cane. "General Niker, you helped release us from our prison."

"Acuity was your prison," Rick quietly pointed out. "*Calypso* is your home."

"You saved my only reason for living." Caidin looked back at Dãsha who returned his gaze with an adoring smile.

Rick watched the exchange between the two and realized their affections for one another weren't some lop-sided relationship. Dãsha wasn't brainwashed or held here against her will. They truly loved one another, just as Rick and Jayda loved each other and maybe even as much as Gunnar and Audra had loved one another.

"For all you have done for me and Dãsha in your short time with us, we owe you an eternal debt of gratitude and I would be honored if you would allow us to help get you and your ships out of the ice and on your way, home."

"Home is a very long way from here," Captain Zak said. "We don't even know where we are to know where home is."

"Truly you are correct, Captain." Caidin smiled, stepping past Dãsha and over to the immense navigational consoles. "There is no way you or anyone else could hope your sensor equipment could reach far enough into the cosmos to find anything recognizable."

Rick's eyes widened as Caidin began to work the instruments before him.

"But this is *Calypso*, a wonder of all man-made space going wonders. Her sensors can peer into the darkest regions of space, far beyond anything that has ever been or, I dare say, ever will, and see things that could never be imagined."

The images on the displays above the console seem to blur as they raced through a myriad of mathematical equations, star charts and infinite lines of code. A star chart depicting a cluster of galaxies suddenly appeared, several locations highlighted. Caidin stepped out of the way, while Zak studied the chart carefully. Everyone pushed a little closer for a better look. Rick realized his lower jaw had dropped as he recognized the depiction of a black hole known as the Oneida Caldron. Stepping closer, he could see Commenor and finally, Kalamar. Caidin had found the Caney system!

"I'm no navigator, Sir," Terry Gillespie said, turning to Rick as he stopped behind the rest of the officers looking at the displays. "So, I'm not sure exactly what this is telling us, but is that…?"

"Home," Rick breathed, not daring to believe it. This had to be just a map pulled from a Kalamarion data bank. Or more likely, one Caidin had brought with him when he was thrown here, so long ago. Zak looked back at Rick, not sure if he should believe it either. Rick glanced at Caidin, who only smiled and nodded.

"You mean Mister Mantose has found a way home?" Greg asked, looking closer.

"He's found home, not the way home," Rick said. He knew what *Calypso* was capable of and after several more moments of thought, was finally willing to believe what he was seeing. "Incredible," he whispered.

"It's a gift for all your kindness," Caidin said, shuffling close to Rick. "Please be patient and Dãsha will make the explanations from here to there." Caidin motioned to his wife, then grabbed Rick by the arm and lead him back over to the pilot's station. "I suspect I have some explaining to do."

Rick looked back again as Dãsha began to make the presentation, the shock of the past hour weighing heavy on him. One surprise after another, but he knew he would have to endure more. He and Caidin sat down at the pilot's station and looked up at the vaulted windows and the ice surrounding *Calypso's* conning tower.

"I suspect you're correct. Caidin, she was dead," Rick finally said. "Dead."

"Yes… Well, not technically," Caidin popped back in a whisper. "And she would still be dead if you hadn't brought her back to me. If you had left her down there, I wouldn't have been able to get to her in time."

"In time? What do you mean, in time?" Rick kept his voice low. "Caidin, I'm stuck on the dead part of this. She was dead. Her face was caved in; her brain was crushed. You don't come back from that. You can't just glue a person back together and expect them to magically get back up. With all we have; with all we know, we can't bring someone back from the dead. It isn't possible!"

Caidin raised a hand, waving him to silence, then got to his feet and motioned for Rick to follow. They made their way off the bridge and back to Caidin's personal quarters. Caidin carefully opened a locked box beneath his work area and pulled out a tiny chip device, plugging it into a small holographic hand projector. He held it up to Rick and activated the control. A figure about a foot tall materialized above the projector unit. Rick recognized the slender form of Dãsha and looked through the projection at Caidin. His eyes were riveted on the image before them.

"This is Dãsha when I first married her on Tilus Three."

"Yes," Rick agreed. "So, what…"

"She died giving birth to our maternal twins, a boy and a girl. Taron and Tiana."

"Wait, she's a clone?"

"No," Caidin shook his head and turned off the projection. "I created a replica."

Rick couldn't follow. This exceeded everything he knew and understood. He clung to the only thing he understood.

"That's what cloning is, isn't it?"

"No, cloning in its basic form requires, at the very least, a complete DNA string of the individual you're trying to reproduce. By my time reckoning, Dãsha passed away over forty years ago and I have nothing of her except this hologram. One cannot extract DNA strings from a hologram. So I figured out a way to recreate her."

"How?"

"Nano-Mech and Molecular manipulation."

"I don't understand. How does that bring Dãsha…?"

"When I came here those many years ago, I was forced to put my life in the Tilus system away. But the one thing I could not forget; the one thing I never wanted to forget, was Dãsha. Somehow, I had to keep her with me. I'm sure you have at least a small sense of what I'm talking about."

Rick nodded.

"But with no way home and no prospects of ever finding that life again, I had to move on. Eventually, I ended up finding the Drake, or rather they found me. I had little choice but to join them. Either you do and perform to their expectations or you're blasted or worse, sent to their mining colonies. They're nice enough to let you choose which one you want. All of them are the same. After finding out my field of expertise, I was assigned to work in their medical field. With my background, it wasn't long before they reassigned me to their biological research division. Part of my work there was to figure out a way to stop the aging process in humans. Of course, we were given test subjects for our research. Most of these individuals were criminals or used up slaves. The amount of flesh pedaling that goes on in Drake culture is like nothing I had ever witnessed before." Caidin fell silent for a moment thinking. "The stories I could tell would astound anyone with even a spark of humanity."

"That bad?" Rick pondered. Caidin nodded grimly.

"I was assigned several test subjects, one of which was a woman my age. Her name was Danis Knox. Long story short, we fell in love during testing. She had been a slave nearly her entire life. I won't go into a female's life as a slave as I'm sure you can figure it out. Whatever depravity you can image, she experienced it. She was so damaged, physically, emotionally, and physiologically, there were several times she begged me to end her life. Her scars were so deep,

I could see no hope for this poor creature, but I loved her as I had once loved my Dãsha. In her times of quiet and calm, they were few and far between, she would listen to me tell her stories about Dãsha and I. She wished with all her being that she could be like Dãsha. I tried to keep all my research on Danis as benign as I could, but the other researchers were becoming suspicious. It was at this point, I was visited by Ona Tusk and my mind was opened to the world of the Thane. She commissioned me to be Dãsha's protector. I pointed out that Dãsha had died a long time ago, but Ona reminded me of my expertise in the field of medicine and my new ability to manipulate matter. She told me there was a higher purpose in all this and in time, I would discover what it was. That wasn't much to go on. I'm sure you know what I'm talking about."

"Like we had discussed before, she's not very chatty."

"Shortly after I considered myself the master of my abilities, I discovered that Danis had only a short time to live as her internal organs had begun to break down. A product of years of severe abuse no doubt. In one of her moments of calm, we decided that, using my new powers, I would try to heal her; make her a new woman. Danis begged me to remake her in Dãsha's image. The process took me a couple of weeks and while I was repairing and rearranging her structures, I placed Nano-Mech in her newly repaired body to help guide her physiology in a preprogramed direction."

"You gave the Drake Nano-Mech technology?" Rick rebuked.

"Heavens no," Caidin responded with a chuckle. "I gave Dãsha Nano-Mech, not the Drake. They have no knowledge of Nano-Mech. It has created many benefits to her as you have no doubt experienced. She looks the same as when I married her; she doesn't age. The tech has made her immensely strong. There are no artificial parts in her, unless you consider the Nano-Mech artificial. In this case, I don't, because it has become a part of her and she it and together they make her what she is. She is mostly Dãsha, but occasionally I catch glimpses of Danis and something else; something mechanical."

"Now it makes sense," Rick nodded.

"I hid her for as long as I could, trying to figure out how to get away, but the other researchers finally figured things out and we were brought before the Drake grand council. I tried to plead our case indicating what Ona had provided me. They were actually very receptive to having a Thane with my skill set among them, but they had no understanding of Dãsha and were frightened by her existence, by what they thought she might be capable of. They wanted her destroyed and they wanted whatever it was that made her what she was. I kept the Nano-Mech secret from them but was unable to convince them that Dãsha was harmless. They deemed the whole thing as unnatural and an abomination, even for their culture. It was just fear," Caidin said, appearing to conclude his explanation.

"But what about the mind, Caidin?" Rick asked quietly. "That's still Danis standing there?"

"True, Danis is the body template, but in making her into what she has become, she wanted every part of her mind, especially her memories, altered. I gave her one of the greatest gifts I could think of; a gift to the both of us. I gave her Dãsha. Everything I could remember about Dãsha and our life together. Certainly, all of that was in basic form, but the Nano-Mech and her mind did the rest; filled in any blanks. So, while yes, Danis was the canvas, out of love for her, she became the masterpiece that is the Dãsha you see now."

"So, explain the accident," Rick said with a sigh. "She was dead. Her skull was crushed. I can see how you can fix the physical, which by the way, you're certainly a master of reconstruction. It's like it never happened. But how do you get around the natural decay of damaged brain cells and the death of the soul?"

"The brain is like any other organ in the body. It's made of the same stuff, just arranged in a specific manner. With my knowledge of neuro mechanics and brain neuropathy, the brain can be easily repaired; it isn't difficult at all. It was before becoming a Thane, but not now. If only more of the human race could access more of their brain..."

"We'd all be in a better place and chances are, there would be no need for militaries and cultural exchanges would be the prevalent business of life." Rick and Caidin both smiled.

"There's a catch here," Caidin warned. "You asked about the mind. Danis already had a soul housed within as we all do. Once the soul leaves the body, there is no going back. You're correct, once you're dead, you're dead. That's why I couldn't just take any dead person and create another person. The energy has to be there. Yes, you can create a living body, well, one that is functioning, but without the energy of the soul, that's all it is. Providing a soul is far above what a Thane could ever do. You brought Dãsha back to me before her soul energy had left her body. Without a functioning body, the soul energy will eventually dissipate, or leave. Repair the body and the soul continues inside."

"You're saying even though she was clinically, dead, she wasn't really dead because her soul energy was still present?"

"Exactly," Caidin agreed. "There are many factors affecting how quickly the soul energy leaves the physical body, so some will leave sooner than others. There is no way to know for sure what that time limit is, but generally it's between five to as much as twenty minutes. There are a few instances where soul energy is still detectable in individuals for as long as two to three hours after physical death. It just depends on the circumstance."

"So why haven't you repaired your leg and kept yourself looking young? Doesn't Dãsha have any feelings on this?"

"She does, but she'd tell you that she loves me as I am. I keep my injury to remind me of my humanity and that I should never think of myself as superior over other human beings. As you see me now, is a product of what I have become and without it, I'm just something more artificial than human."

"Then, have I got a job for you," Rick said as his communicator went off.

"General, this is Captain Zek."

"Yes, Captain. Report."

"Uhm, yeah, 'bout that report, Sir." Zek stumbled. "I think you better come back over here and have a look in these cargo holds."

"You can't tell me over the com?"

"Yeah, I could, Sir, but I doubt you'd believe me. You're gonna wanna come see this for yourself."

Rick looked back at Caidin.

"I'd love to have a look at your great experiment," Caidin said smiling.

"Understood, Captain. We'll all be back over as soon as we can get there." Rick dropped his communicator back to his belt. "Are you up for this?"

"I may be old and crippled, but I can still walk. Don't your ships have teleporters?"

"It's not working, otherwise I wouldn't waste time whizzing through *Calypso*."

Rick and Caidin made their way back over to the bridge where they found all the male officers huddled around Dãsha, still making her explanations on how things worked on the bridge of *Calypso*. Terry and the other female officer were left on the outside of the circle trying to see over the men's shoulders.

"Ladies and gentlemen, we're needed back on the *Stark*. Are we ok to leave *Calypso* by herself?"

The group dispersed as Dãsha emerged from around the console.

"I should stay with *Calypso*," she said flatly.

"It's fine if you come along," Rick beckoned her. Dãsha only looked at Caidin, standing firm.

"You go, I will stay with *Calypso*."

"Really," Rick beckoned. "It's fine, I want you to see the *Athena*." Dãsha stood erect with her hands clasped behind her back, her black eyes looking straight ahead at the bridge windows.

"Dãsha, *Calypso* will be fine where she is. The ice is not due to shift for some time," Caidin said stepping over to the slender young woman and taking her by the hand. "We can back her out before Acuity's compression cycle begins again." Together, they turned and headed past Rick to the elevator.

Complicated

Dakota dropped back into the command chair and turned to Pippin and Lana. "Anything on Billy?"

"Systems are still down, Sir," the science officer reported without looking up. Lana shook her head grimly as Dakota turned forward.

"Helm, can you see that Torag out there anywhere?"

"Facing the wrong direction, Sir," Lynette answered.

"It's not likely your man was successful," BachTL suggested from behind. "We wouldn't have gotten that last hit if he had been able to place his weapon before they fired. What you're going to have to worry about now are the tugs."

Dakota frowned, came to his feet and paced nervously behind the helm and navigation positions. *No mobility and blind!*

"Do we even have external communications?"

"Ship internal coms are barely working," Lana said shaking her head. "We can't talk to anything external."

"We're lucky the lights are still on," Pippin added.

Dakota gave the com panel a double take and poked his finger at a control. "Hayden, are you still back there?"

"Not sure where you think I would have gone," came the instant reply. "I've still got nothing back here, Captain."

"But can you move?"

"Barely, battery power is next to nothing. Whatever that ship was throwing at us really sucked the life out of everything."

"See if you can track what's coming at us and report back as soon as you see anything."

"Be a little easier if you could get helm to straighten us out."

"Yes, wouldn't it though," Dakota agreed.

"There's something out there," Lynette announced pointing out the windows. Everyone turned and strained to focus on a couple of specs moving across an ocean of stars. As the *Constellation* had no directional control, the ship was starting to list in the direction of the moving objects.

"One of them is probably the Torag," BachTL observed, pointing at one of the specs. "Coming back around to make sure we're harmless before the tugs come in close. Not sure, but the others look more like corsairs or destroyers."

"Great," Dakota mumbled, turning back to the command chair and sticking a finger at the comlink. "Tiana, progress report."

Silence. Dakota opened his mouth to repeat his request, but the engineer's mate finally responded.

"Scott Brandon, Sir. She's not back here. I thought she went forward to the bridge."

Dakota touched a control on his wrist communicator.

"Tiana, where are you?"

Silence. Dakota glanced all around the bridge and seeing the engineering station vacant, sat down and shifted to a different button on his armrest.

"Doctor Yamoto, do you have Tiana with you in sickbay?"

"No, Captain, though I was starting to wonder why not."

"Sorry for the bumpy ride. Have you seen her?"

"Thought she was in engineering."

"She's come up missing at a bad time."

"Would you like us to have a look around?"

"Do you have anything you can use to find her?"

"I think we've got a couple of hand gadgets we could try."

"Let me know what you find." Dakota shifted the com back to engineering. "Mister Brandon?"

"Aye, Sir?"

"Are you able to give me a report on your condition back there? How soon can you have main power back?"

"Uhm," the engineer's mate fumbled. "I've got no way to even give you an educated guess... Half an hour?"

Dakota looked up at BachTL who was looking out at the growing specs of light.

"Not sure how educated that was," Dakota mumbled tight lipped. "Do the best you can."

"They'll have us before that happens," BachTL commented, trying to judge the distances between them and their quarry.

Dakota turned to Pippin and Lana, but didn't wait for them to respond, seeing their consoles were still dark.

"Battery power is the only thing running the lights," Pippin commented. He was playing with a small hand scanner he had picked up. "Environmental systems are off-line. It's going to get cold and stuffy in here pretty quick if we don't get them back up. Interesting the inferior Albion tech has been this effective against us," Pippin grumbled, passing a glance at BachTL.

"That's how the energy disruptor works," BachTL indicated. "The design is not to destroy, but disable."

"Very effective," Dakota muttered.

"Well not in your case. They should have had you on the first strike."

"Still..." Dakota clinched his fist under his chin, thinking back to when he and Gunnar had first come to Carolon. Presented with a no win scenario, the Colonel had to surrender the Orbiter because of a malfunction and no way to get away. His thoughts shifted to what they had gone through when they landed on Tintee. *Blacking out the*

windows and beaming away from the ship had worked pretty good. Wonder if maybe something similar could work in this instance.

"Somehow, we've got to buy ourselves a little time. Pip, how long did it take for our systems to recover before the last hit?"

"Recover, Sir? We still haven't recovered from that Mark V blast."

"How long before you had your instruments back online?" He looked over at Lana as well.

"Five, maybe ten minutes; if they come back at all."

"Is there any way to force some of our basic systems to function?"

"I don't follow the question, Sir," Pippin responded. "We can't do anything without power."

"But if you had the power, could it be done?"

The science officer thought a moment, trying to follow the Captain's train of thought.

"Yes, we have some manual controls designed to interface with some systems besides what we have here on the bridge."

"Lieutenant Starman, since we have no power to black out the windows, I want you to shut down the bridge. Go completely dark; I mean nothing is to be producing any light. You and Nigel will remain here on the bridge. The rest of you will locate and test those manual controls." Dakota came to his feet. "I'll be back in engineering. BachTL, you're with me."

"What have you got in mind?" the Castellian asked trying to keep up with the Captain. Dakota didn't answer, but headed straight back, seeing movement through the open Mallory doors.

"If you've got next to no power, how come your antigrav systems are still operating?"

"Good question," Dakota replied.

The pair stopped at the top of the stairs to the lower deck and looked down, trying to see if Tiana might have gone below to work on something, but the staircase was dark and empty. Dakota poked his head into the teleporter room, but seeing no one, turned to the Mallory doors just as Fuji Yamoto appeared. Holding a small hand scanner, she held the small unit out in front of her, keeping her eyes glued to the tiny display.

"Got anything?" Dakota asked joining her as she slowly made her way through the Mallory doors.

"Not sure. This thing is kind of old. I've only kept it because it was my first instrument. It can only read life signs, not transponders. I have to get a reading on anyone that's back here so I can blank out their biosignatures. That should allow me to at least get a general idea of who's where."

"Can't even imagine one of your crew disappearing on a ship as small as this one," BachTL said.

"You'd be surprised," Dakota responded, thinking of Janox.

Fuji worked her way around the engineering console and stopped in front of the engine bulkhead. She fumbled with the instrument for a moment, then looked around.

"I can't get a reading. Too much interference from something in here."

"Could be Engineer Moon's little contraption over there," Scott Brandon offered, pointing at the cavity the Antigrav unit was housed in. There was a light blue glow shrouding the entire device and a high pitched humming sound emanating from it. Everyone stepped towards the unit for a closer look.

"Be nice if we could use what he's got here to shield the ship from that Torag," Dakota commented examining it closer.

"Be nice if I had even a hint as to what he did to produce it on such short notice," the engineer's mate commented.

"Captain," a voice called from the other side of the engine bulkhead. "I think I've found who you're looking for."

Everyone turned to see Lieutenant Hunter's head poking around the corner of the turret elevator door. Making a quick trot to the shaft, Captain Abrams peered inside.

"I was in the service crawlway when I heard her..."

Dakota dropped to his knees and peered into the lower shaft. In the shadows of the corner, behind the access ladder, sat Tiana Mantose, balled up with her arms holding her knees under her chin, softly crying.

"Tiana," Dakota spoke gently. "What's going on?"

No response.

"Tiana," he said with a little more emphasis.

"Captain," Fuji interrupted. "Command your ship. I'll take care of this."

Dakota hesitated a moment, but then pulled back.

"Thank you, Doctor," he said sounding relieved. As Fuji knelt down, Dakota turned back to Scott Brandon. "When did you last see her?"

"She went tearing out of here forward about twenty minutes ago when I came out of sickbay," Scott said rubbing a big knob on his forehead. "I assumed she went to the bridge."

"She did," BachTL confirmed.

"Let's let the doctor work. Lieutenant Brandon, for now, you're the chief engineer."

"Where's Mr. Moon?" Scott asked turning white.

"On assignment," Dakota said. "And with Tiana indisposed, that means you're in command back here. Can you give me any more detail on what it's going to take to get our power back online?"

"Not much more than I told you earlier, Sir. Only that it will take some time for our systems to recover. Some might come back on by themselves, others will need help, but I've got to tell you, Sir, I'm so

new at all this, I hardly know where to look to find anything and if I do find it, I don't even remotely understand how to make it work. That's where Tiana was such a big help back here. Her and Mister Moon understood all these systems."

"Understood," Dakota sighed. "I can help a little back here. What do you need?"

"If you'll step over here to the console, I could really use some assistance trying to get this panel to work."

"I'll do whatever I can," Dakota responded anxiously. He looked back at Fuji as she disappeared into the elevator shaft.

*   *   *   *

"Tiana?" Fuji slid around the ladder towards the figure in the darkness. "Tiana, what's wrong? Talk to me." There was no response, only continued sniffling. "Tiana, I can't help you if you don't talk to me." Fuji slid up next to her and put her arm around her. Tiana abruptly turned into Fuji's shoulder, bursting into a fit of tears. Fuji wrapped her other arm around her and held her close. "Tiana, what is it?"

"He's... gone," she sobbed, her face buried in Fuji's shoulder.

"Gone? Who's gone?"

"Billy..."

"Engineer Moon? Gone? Where'd he go?"

Tiana pulled back, trying to gain control of her emotions. It took her several tries, opening her mouth to speak, but she couldn't get the words to form. Through running tears, she finally pushed them out.

"Billy... went outside... during... the attack. He... had to... clean out... the ducting vents... from when... we torpedoed... the destroyer. He was... supposed to come back... in when he was finished, but... they kept attacking... and we couldn't... fire anything back... at them. He had me... release a pin missile... and he carried it... to the other ship... to disable it. He didn't... make it back."

"I am so sorry," Fuji said, shocked. "Maybe his coms are just damaged?"

"He launched himself... at the other ship holding the Pin missile..." Tiana struggled to regain her composure, dabbing the tears from her face.

Fuji slowly shook her head trying to picture what the scene must have been like. She tried not to think on it too much. She recalled her own feelings of peril when she and Audra had rescued Tiana from her crew quarters after their encounter at the Oneida Caldron.

"It was a brave thing he did," Fuji said softly. "I'm very sorry. He was a good man."

Tiana looked out beyond the shadows of the elevator shaft. A stillness came over her as she stared out at the entrance to the Interceptor elevator shaft on the wall.

"Seems like I lose all those I love." She wiped her nose again and planted her chin in her hand while gazing out at nothing. "My parents, my brother, and now Billy." She fell silent for several moments. "I feel so alone..."

"Oh, I like that," Fuji said trying to nudge Tiana. "What about the rest of us?"

Tiana forced a smile to her lips, giving the ship's doctor a quick glance.

"Tiana, people come and go in our lives. It happens to everyone. My limited experience in the military leads me to understand it happens more often than anyone hopes or plans for, but that's the nature of it. This business is all about war and people die in war." Fuji developed a distant look. "Sometimes it hits closer to home than we would like, but it hits none the less and it's how we respond to death that's one of the things that defines who we are." Fuji looked back at Tiana. "If Billy were sitting here instead of me, what would he be telling you?"

Tiana considered for a moment, wiped her nose again, then hedged a look over at Fuji, smiling through renewed tears.

"First of all, he wouldn't have crawled in here to get me. He'd be yelling at me to quit being a bawl-baby and get off my sorry butt and get back to work."

"And how would you respond?"

"I'd be telling him off." Tiana chuckled, thinking of her relationship with the chief engineer. "Then I'd push him aside and get back to work."

Fuji watched her for a moment as she rebuilt her courage.

"This ship needs you now more than ever."

"I know, I'm sorry I'm such a big baby," Tiana said nodding her head and moving around the ladder to the shaft door.

"It takes more courage to show emotion than it does to hide it," Fuji said crawling after her.

"What great philosopher said that?"

"That would be me," Fuji admitted getting to her feet.

Tiana grinned and wiping her eyes once more, did her best to straighten up as she turned to Lieutenant Brandon and Captain Abrams working at the engineering console.

"If you'll allow me, Captain," Tiana said scanning the jumbled glass surface of the console. "I think I can do something with this."

Dakota hesitated, then moved aside, watching the independent contractor start to work with the scrambled console.

"You're not going to get anywhere with this until you can get this control console to work. The pentode transducers on this display are scrambled with Xenon plasma energy; sort of like static electricity," she explained, letting her fingers streak across the smooth surface. "Until you can get it to discharge, you're just fighting with the display."

"How did it get in there in the first place?" Scott asked.

"All the display filters are probably overloaded by whatever charge that ship threw at us. The only way to get it out now is to physically press on the glass. The pressure bleeds the energy away from the florascan display emitters."

"I get it," Scott said, watching her closely.

Dakota faded back next to Fuji.

"Thanks, Doc," he whispered.

"I was sitting on my hands with nothing to do but get thrown around sickbay." Fuji stood with her arms folded, watching Tiana work. "How does it look out there?"

"Not good I'm afraid," Dakota sighed, stepping back to where BachTL was standing looking at the shielded antigrav unit. "A lot depends on what Tiana can do here and now."

"What? Are we talking getting blown to bits or captured?" Fuji asked.

"Oh, they definitely don't want to blow us up," BachTL stated coldly, still looking at the antigrav unit.

"Well, that's a relief," Fuji said, watching Hayden Hunter step next to Tiana and Scott.

"They want this ship and all its secrets." BachTL finally turned back to Dakota and Fuji. "...and speaking from firsthand experience, the person at the other end of the rope you're almost tied to, isn't going to waste time with who she considers expendable."

"What does that even mean?" Fuji asked not believing the ramifications.

"It means we need to figure out a way to get our shields operating." Dakota looked over his shoulder at Tiana and Scott. "Even if we can't move or shoot."

*   *   *   *

Tiana swept her fingers across the glass engineering console as if she were finger painting. Amazed Tiana understood what was happening, Scott joined in with both hands, pressing his fingers on the glass and sliding them around as if he were pushing liquid from the surface.

"Got to learn how to show it some love," Tiana said smiling.

"Miss Mantose?" Dakota interrupted from behind.

"I don't know at this point, Captain. Until we can get this console display cleared up, I can't even start on any kind of diagnostics."

"I was wondering if you had any idea how Billy got this shield generator working for the anti-grav unit?" Dakota stepped to one side as Tiana leaned back from the console and looked over at the glowing unit.

"Yeah, it was fairly simple."

"How?" Dakota asked. "We have next to no power right now. I'm surprised the lights are still on."

"Well, they won't be for very long if I can't get to the ship's systems. It's already starting to get cold in here." Tiana gave Scott a double take and grabbing his hands, slid them across the glass. "Here, do it like this; it works better. As the display clears, just press on it a little harder. That'll keep the display drivers clear while you get another spot working." Tiana walked over to the anti-grav unit with Dakota and BachTL. "He placed a couple of the ship's spare shield emitter antennas on either side of the unit. One acts as the emitter cathode and the other the anode. The unit itself is powering the shield energy."

"Where is the unit getting its power?" BachTL asked.

"From the dielectric discharge the antigrav generators are producing. It won't run forever, but it sure works great for staving off the effects of that beam weapon, or whatever they were hitting us with."

"Any way to adapt this idea to the ship's shield emitters?" Dakota asked, thinking.

"No," Tiana answered. "We've got to have engine power for that. At the very least battery power. Right now there is next to nothing here."

"Engine power or any power?"

Tiana looked at Dakota oddly, trying to figure out what he had in mind.

"The engines will be offline indefinitely until I can figure out what's got to be done. Until we can get these subsystems back online, there's no power."

"Understood," Dakota agreed. "But I'm looking to the future. We've got tugs and destroyers coming in to pick us up and I really don't want anyone to get aboard this ship. I'm thinking the only way to stop them is if we have shields."

"I can't give you any shields," Tiana announced.

"I realize that, but let's say just for the sake of argument, you get the subsystems back online. What would you need in order to get the shields back on?"

"I already told you," Tiana said becoming a bit indignant. "Engine power or at least battery power. Right now we have neither. Without subsystems, I can't access what's left, if anything, in the batteries and without the batteries, I can't make the engines go so they can recharge the batteries. Sort of a catch twenty-two scenario."

"What about the Mark Vs?"

"What about them? They are where they are. No way to launch them."

"I'm not talking about launching them," Dakota rebutted. "I'm talking about using a Mark V to power the shield generators."

Tiana looked at the Captain as if he had lost his mind. She glanced at BachTL and Fuji, who had equally bewildered expressions. Hayden moved a little closer, overhearing part of the conversation.

"I haven't got a clue as to how those things work," Tiana cried. "And I dare say neither do you!"

"They have an engine on them, don't they?"

"Well, yeah…"

"And every engine uses an energy core to produce some kind of propulsion, doesn't it?"

"Yes, but you're talking about bringing the same weapon that created our current situation, into the engine room. This is the same weapon that blew an entire Albion destroyer to pieces, and you want to bring it in here, stick a straw in it and suck all the power out of it? You're off your noddle!"

"Can you provide me with a better alternative?" Dakota asked.

Tiana stammered indecisive, looking to those around her for some kind of backup or a reason not to do what the Captain was suggesting.

"I don't know…" Tiana stuttered for a quick response. "No, I can't think of anything right now. I only know that trying to do what you're suggesting is suicide."

"You may well be right, Miss Mantose, but right now, it's all we've got."

"Well, you're going to have to find someone else to do it then," she rebutted stubbornly.

"That's fine," Dakota relented confidently. "I can't order you to do anything as you're not a part of the crew." Dakota turned to the engineer's mate. "Mister Brandon, you and Lieutenant Hunter will see to tapping into the most convenient Mark V available and replicate what Mister Moon has done here on the anti-grav unit. You'll need to work double time as we're about to have company. The rest of us need to stay out of their way unless they specifically require help."

Dakota motioned for Fuji and BachTL to follow as he headed for the Mallory doors. Tiana remained in place, her arms folded defiantly. Dakota looked back as they exited engineering and seeing Tiana still standing in place, turned around.

"You're either part of the problem or part of the solution, Miss Mantose. Your choice, but make it and either help, or get out of the engine room." Dakota turned back to the main hall and headed forward.

Tiana looked after him for a moment, trying to reconcile her anger with her intense desire to be useful. She turned as Scott was pulling out several large coils of cabling.

"What are you doing with that?"

"We've got to find something long enough to make it forward to the torpedo bays under the bridge."

"That's not going to work," she responded sharply. "That run is way too long, besides, you have four Mark Vs right over your head."

"What?" Scott asked looking around the ceiling of the engine room.

"She's right," Hayden agreed, looking up at several long tubes running along the ceiling on either side of the main engine bulkhead.

"The rear magazines..." Tiana said pointing at the overhead torpedo tubes.

"Those have been up there this whole time?" Scott asked, his eyes widening.

"Hayden?" Tiana motioned the turret gunner toward one of the tube hatches.

"I'm on it," he answered, heading for several small Lev-lifts stored against the wall.

"Mister Brandon, on the far side of the turret elevator, at the top you'll find a manual release for the internal torpedo clamps. Climb up there and give it a tug when I tell you to." Tiana grabbed Scott by the arm and coaxed him toward the other side of the turret elevator.

"Yes, ma'am."

Tiana completely forgot about her anger and focused on the job ahead. Dakota, BachTL and Fuji reappeared just outside the Mallory doors watching Tiana and Hayden work to set the lev-lifts into place under one of the overhead magazines.

"You called that one," Fuji said congratulating Dakota with a fist bump.

"She's got the stuff," Dakota said. "Now, let's see if we can help the others with what they're doing."

"Anything Alder and I can do to help?" Fuji asked. "Like I said, we're just sitting on our hands in sickbay."

Dakota looked back through the Mallory doors at the engineering console.

"Did you see Tiana and Lieutenant Brandon working with that console back there?"

Fuji looked over her shoulder.

"Yeah, why?"

"It didn't look terribly complicated," Dakota suggested.

"You think we can do something with it?"

"How hard can it be?" Dakota suggested. "Press the glass in the affected areas until they clear."

"Not sure if I'm supposed to feel insulted or useful," Fuji said.

"BachTL, you take the lower deck; go through all the rooms and make sure everything is turned off. I want this ship to be as dark as we can make it."

"We need to look dead?"

"I want your friends out there to feel like they can take their own sweet time picking us up and getting us to a safe place before they try to gain access. That should give us more time to get our shields working."

"You have a lot of faith in your crew."

"Yes, I do. Meet you back up here in a couple of minutes."

As BachTL started down the stairs, Dakota turned to the nearest door and forced it open. Moving from room to room, he noticed the temperature had cooled considerably and worried about how much time they had before it became intolerable. Once he had finished with the commander's quarters, the command ready room, and the main hallways, he met BachTL coming back up the stairs. As they reentered engineering, they stopped to watch Hayden Hunter and Tiana standing on individual levi-lifts, rising into place.

"Any luck back here?" Dakota asked stepping up next to Fuji and Alder. The console images were looking a little more recognizable.

"We're getting it there, slowly but surely," Fuji answered.

"Fingers are starting to get a little cold," Alder complained.

"It's going to get a lot colder before it gets warmer," Dakota said.

"It's a big console," BachTL commented, stepping up to the glass. "Perhaps I can help?"

"Have at it," Dakota said, turning back for the Mallory door. "I'll be forward checking on the others."

Fuji pointed to an open section of the console as BachTL stepped forward and started working his fingers around the glass like the others.

Making his way forward through the darkness, Dakota saw Lana and Pippin working their hand scanners in separate access doors on either side of the bridge doors.

"Report," he said peering into a labyrinth of cables, conduits and circuits.

"It'll take some doing," Pippin said, "but I think we can make this work."

"Cumbersome," Lana spoke up from the other access door. "But, we should have enough to get the job done."

"Sir, what have you got in mind?" Pippin inquired.

"We're working on a plan to tap power from one of our Mark V torpedoes to get the shields operating."

Lana and Pippin immediately stopped what they were doing and looked at the Captain.

"I know what you're thinking! I'm open to any ideas, but so far, no one has provided me with anything better." Dakota paused a moment, then looked at Lana. "Lieutenant Nevall, you said you received a transmission from a ship before communications went down."

"Yes, from a ship called the *Hampton*. A cruiser class vessel from Cross."

"Administrator Vandmire?"

"Yes, Sir, but I only had a chance to read part of the message before we lost coms."

"Do you remember any of it?"

"Yeah, it said: 'Kodiac Blu antidote obtained from Colonel Barker on the *Tarzana*. Provide current location for immediate delivery. Response required'."

"Kodiac Blu?" Dakota repeated, perplexed. "Anything else?"

"Coms went down, so I never got a chance to respond," Lana said.

"What's Kodiac Blu," Pippin asked.

"You're guess is as good as mine. Maybe when com is back online we can find out if there's more to it." Dakota pulled the bridge doors open and squeezed through observing the dark silhouettes of the ships helmsman and navigator sitting on the front bridge windowsill above their stations. Both were looking out at the bright canvas of the universe open to their view. The entire crew had worked in space long enough they should have been accustomed to seeing the stars, but as Dakota stopped behind them, he too was taken in awe at the scene open before them. Quietly folding his arms, he let his eyes wander about at the infinite expanse encompassing them. He found himself caught up in the beauty and grandeur until he detected a dark shadow crossing his vision and focused on the aberration. He moved closer to the window as Lynette Starman pointed to another one on the other side of the window. Nigel Kramer pointed to another one, the flash of marker beacons becoming apparent. Dakota slowly brought his wrist com up.

"Tiana, company has arrived. Please tell me you've got everything figured out."

"I haven't even figured out how to open the back access plate on the launch tube, Captain."

"It might have been helpful if Kalamar Command had given us a *how to manual* on these fish," Hayden chimed in, grunting. "Turn the wrong knob or switch and things could get really hot, really fast."

"Yeah, that would make for a very bad day. I'll be back down in a minute." Dakota turned to leave.

"Captain," Lynette stopped him. "What should we do?"

"Stay put. You two are the first to go operational when and if we get power back and I want this ship moving as fast as it can, when it can."

"Sir, without power, we can't dim the glass," Lynette pointed out. "What if the Albions start poking around outside?"

"Stay out of sight. I want to keep them guessing for as long as we can. I want this ship to look like it's automated or dead."

"What if they look in and see us, do we pretend we're dead?" Nigel asked.

"Don't let them see you," Captain Abrams said turning for the door.

"Aye, Sir."

As Dakota made his way back down the hallway toward engineering, Lynette and Nigel watched for some time as the three curious shadows grew closer. There came a sudden ominous presence overhead and as they looked up, the entire starfield above them disappeared. Lynette started to move as she recognized the enormous bow of an Albion destroyer gliding overhead.

"Nigel, get down!" Lynette yelled as she tumbled from the sill. No sooner had the navigator rolled to the floor than a flood of light filled the bridge.

"Do you think they saw me?" he whispered, looking wide eyed from under his console.

"No, I don't think so," Lynette whispered back. "We need to get out of here."

"But the Captain just said we were supposed to stay on the bridge."

"I know, but he also said we're not supposed to be seen and without any power, we can't black out the glass."

"Should we call him?"

"Let's get out of here first, then let him know." Lynette started after Nigel as he turned, crawling under his own console and back along the dark recess behind the engineering console toward the bridge door.

"I have a question," Lynette whispered from behind.

"What's that?" Nigel whispered back.

Lynette let out several grunts from behind as she worked her way around the engineering station to the bridge door next to Nigel.

"Why are we whispering?"

"I don't know, it just seems like the thing to do," Nigel whispered, looking back at the Starbird pilot. He looked out the bridge windows at the tugs as their work lights came on. Drawing closer, their bright beams tilted into the dark recesses of the bridge. Lynette pushed the navigator to the door and helped him pull it open. After squeezing through, they pushed the doors closed as the tug beams filled the entire bridge. Turning around and leaning against the doors, they noticed Lana and Pippin giving them wary looks.

"You two all right?" Pip asked.

"Yeah, I think so," Nigel whispered.

"I think we're over the whispering part now, Nigel," Lynette said.

"Why are you guys whispering in the first place?" Lana asked.

"The Albions are right... over the top of us," Nigel said, starting to whisper, but changed to his normal speaking voice midsentence.

"The tugs are moving into place to take hold of us," Lynette finished.

"So why aren't you two still on the bridge?" Pip asked.

"Because they've turned their flood lights on," Lynette said. "They would have seen us. We figured Captain Abrams would rather have them see an empty, dead bridge."

"Good call," Pip agreed. "You better get back to engineering and report to the Captain. We're right behind you."

Lynette and Nigel quickly got to their feet and headed back toward the open Mallory doors as Lana and Pippin finished what they were doing.

"Doran, tie a bow on it and let's go," Lana called as she put her instruments away.

"It's about as basic as it can get," replied the weapons officer from the shadows of the conference room. "I wonder what the Captain has in mind for this one?"

"I doubt any of us want to know," Lana commented, following Pippin and Doran. Arriving in engineering, they found everyone standing around the main console while Tiana and Hayden worked from floating Lev-lifters next to an open torpedo tube.

"Well, this is fun," Hayden grunted.

"Problem?" Dakota asked, looking up from the engineering console. Hayden and Tiana were running a tiny extraction hoist, slowly pulling the tail end of the Mark V torpedo from the back of its launching tube.

"You have to manually turn this thing in several directions to get it to slide backwards so we can get to its engine systems," Tiana said adjusting the controller in her hand. "It only has to come out a little further so I can reach the access panel."

"I'm afraid we're all charting new territory here," Dakota commented, watching Tiana examine the smooth black surface of the weapon. "I've never seen one of these up close and personal before."

"I think Billy and Frank said they had some experience with them," Tiana commented looking at the propulsion end.

"They were required to at least examine them before they were loaded," Dakota announced.

As the torpedo inched its way out the back of its launch tube, Tiana popped an access door and examined the inside of the propulsion unit.

"This is some sophisticated stuff," Tiana uttered, barely audible. Hayden looked a little closer.

"You're telling me," he mumbled next to her.

"You've seen this kind of interface before?"

"Yeah, but not on the thruster end of a torpedo."

"Do you know how to access the induction coil relays?" Tiana asked.

"If I'm right, they don't have any."

"There's got to be something or we're finished here," she whispered back.

"What do you think up there?" Dakota asked. "How long do you think it going to take?"

Tiana and Hayden looked at each, then back at the cluster of tiny displays inside the open panel.

"Think you can find a place to tap power out of this thing?" Tiana asked in a hush.

"The alternative is?" Hayden asked quietly, glancing over his shoulder at a waiting Captain Abrams. "You get to go down and figure out how to duplicate what Billy created with the antigrav unit."

Tiana looked back at the glowing unit on the other side of the engine room. Hayden let a chuckle go as Tiana started to drop her lift.

"I'll let the chief engineer handle those details," Hayden said turning back to the torpedo.

Dakota met Tiana as she touched down and she headed to the engineering console.

"Tiana?" Dakota waited impatiently.

"Hey, you guys have made some real progress here," she said ignoring the Captain, focusing instead on the glass surface. Alder moved to one side as Tiana started sliding her fingers across the display. A look of dismay developed across her face as she examined the information in front of her.

"Tiana," Dakota repeated impatiently.

"I was hoping for more than this, but it is what it is," she said, finally turning around and facing the Captain. "Dakota," she said folding her arms. "I can't tell you what I don't know. If Lieutenant Hunter can figure out how to tap into that Mark V's propulsion unit, and I can figure out how to replicate Billy's design on a larger scale, then yes, we can do it."

"How much time?"

"I just don't know. You're asking questions that don't have all the numbers available for the equation."

Dakota gently pulled Tiana toward the glowing antigrav unit. His expression was as serious as she had ever seen from him.

"I'm guessing here as well, probably using the same unfinished equations I'm forcing you to use. I'm guessing, we'll be in tow in a manner of minutes, if not sooner. I'm guessing, because we look dead in space, they're not going to bother with trying to get onboard immediately. I'm guessing, what BachTL tells me of Drax Blair, they won't try to gain access until she's present. That should give us some time. But, what if I'm wrong? We've got a matter of minutes before they've got us secured in one of their landing bays and start trying to pry this thing open. I'd sure love to give them something to think twice about and at the same time, give us time to get this ship operational again. So I'm faced with a decision to make that I need information for in order to make the best decision I can. What's your best guess?"

Tiana looked at Dakota long and hard, then at the antigrav unit, then up at Hayden with his hands still in the access of the torpedo. She looked back at the engineering console and the overhead displays, then back at Dakota.

"If it's going to work, we should know in about twenty minutes."

Dakota thought a moment as Tiana turned, but Dakota stopped her.

"Tiana, you make this work and I'll put those Lieutenant bars on your collar myself."

Tiana smiled as she turned for the tools and parts storage room.

"If this works, who says I'll want them?"

Terrorists

Interceptor One had been in light speed operations for several hours. Gunnar had fallen into an uneasy sleep shortly after making the jump to lightspeed. Janox and Tonnie remained at the rear of the cockpit taking turns combing each other's long waves of hair and talking. Tonnie's hair was still white, but Janox was noticing shades of light brown starting to manifest themselves close to her roots. While her skin was still pale, it was beginning to show some tone. Her eyes still glowed green, but Janox didn't seem to be affected by their ghoulish appearance. They talked about a wide range of emotional issues Janox had dealt with on her own as a young girl in the biosphere. As they conversed, their conversations wound around to what it was like for an android to sleep for so long and the minimal processes her cybernetic network had used to remain viable. Janox had no comprehension of what the android was talking about, other than the dreaming, if an android could do so.

"I'm not going to ask you what the tactical advantage is here," Alex said quietly, noticing Gunnar blinking his eyes.

"Is that because you can see it, or because you can't?"

"You told me once that sometimes doing something isn't always the smartest things to do, but it is the right thing to do."

"I remember that." Gunnar stretched broadly. "Is that the lesson you took from that day?"

"No, the lesson I took was, never follow you into any adventure without a clear-cut plan."

"We've served how long together and you're just coming to this realization?"

"I hold out eternal hope that you'll follow the council of Commander Atlanta and think things through before you act."

"Audra, Alex. You can call her Audra. We made a plan before we left Reako and Carolon."

"Yes, Colonel, but sometimes it is better to pause before action is taken, just to make sure it is the right thing to do."

"You don't think this is the right thing to do?"

"I probably should have phrased my opening statement differently. Of course it is the right thing to do, but is this the right time to do it?"

"Is there anything we missed in our planning? Do you know something I don't?"

"No," Alex paused a moment. "But my experience has shown that every time you embark on a mission or project of any kind, something out of the ordinary usually happens."

"Perfect," Gunnar smiled. "Never have a dull moment when you're with me."

"I hate to be bearer of bad news, Colonel. But most droids work best when it's dull."

"I have no doubt." Gunnar sat up and looked behind him. "How are our two charges doing?"

"Like they were never separated," Alex said turning his head backward. "Tonnie is truly remarkable. I am detecting a slight change in her eye color."

"They still look creepy to me."

"Her skin is looking a little better, but as it and her hair were exposed the longest, it will no doubt take longer to regenerate. Janox has combed out her hair well enough, but I suspect it will take some time before it starts to look normal again. I have also observed that she has taken up helping Janox with her speech lessons."

"She still hooked up to the ship's chargers?"

"No, I took her off an hour ago. Her batteries are at full capacity now."

"How often do you think we'll have to recharge her?"

"Depends on how much she exerts herself and how much she eats."

"How much she eats?" Gunnar repeated.

"Yes, as I had indicated before, she employs chemical cell extraction systems. She can eat the same foods you do, digest them and her extraction system draws the converted energy from the food and sends it to her power cells for storage. Just like the human digestive system, and the waste is expelled in the same manner."

"Nice to hear; android doodie," Gunnar said, sounding a bit nauseated. "Tonnie," Gunnar spoke up while turning around. "We're getting close to Albia. I'm going to need you up here to help me navigate into Dither. Are you able to move freely?"

"I will help her," Janox volunteered helping the android crawl forward.

"I do not have knowledge of planetary defenses," Tonnie began. "Only the repository itself."

"What's Dither like?"

"It is a tropical planetoid. It is not inhabited by human life; only animal and plant life."

"Why put a repository on a moon where nobody lives?"

"The climate there is too aggressive for humans. There are several repositories located all around the surface in places where the tropics are at their weakest. Even then they must employ measures to hold the animal and plant life back."

"Are we able to land there or do we have to be shuttled from Albia?"

"There are landing facilities available if there is room. The number of people using the facility we're going to will depend on the landing space available."

"What if there's no room?"

"Then we would have to land at another facility and shuttle to where we need to go."

"Can't we just land outside the facility?"

"Yes, if you could clear the jungle and then access the wall tight barriers."

"You said hold the animal and plant life back? It's really that bad?"

"It's that bad."

"Well," Gunnar said, turning back to his controls at the summons of an alarm. "Here's hoping we can find a parking spot close to the front door." He touched several controls and took hold of the yoke as the stars streaked in front of them. A blue and green planet whisked into view, zooming up close. Gunnar wasn't sure what he had expected, but this wasn't it. He sort of got the impression there would be warships milling about in orbit and patrolling the space around the planet. While there was a lot of traffic, most of it appeared to be civilian in nature. Slowing his craft down to match the cruise of other vessels approaching the planet, he was a little relieved no one was trying to contact him for identification or directions.

"Remember, this is not military space," Tonnie cautioned him. "This is civilian travel space. The military only maintains a few isolated corridors directly down to Albia and they're pretty strict about staying within those corridors, so as long as you avoid those, we should have only the civilian travel authority to deal with."

"Do you have any clearance codes?"

"None required here. Just tell them your craft number and where you're heading; they will give you directions."

"Do we have a craft number?" Gunnar asked, turning to Alex.

"GR 9526 Uniform."

"Really, I had no idea."

"The *Constellation* has one as well. GR 2838 Lima."

"When would we have ever used those idents?" Gunnar asked, steering toward a line of ships moving toward the planet. He was starting to get annoyed with a headache that had been ever present at the base of his skull.

"Whenever we travel through civilian airspace on nonmilitary missions," Alex replied.

"I've never used such an ident, ever." Gunnar slipped his headsets down over his head and started working the com equipment.

"This sounds promising," he mumbled, listening closely.

"Would you like me to assist?" Alex asked.

"I think I've got it. Approach, this is GR 9526 Uniform requesting Dither approach vectors." Gunnar listened for a moment, then leaned

back, an odd look of embarrassment streaking across his face. "Alex, you wanna have a crack at this?"

"You got the wrong frequency, didn't you?" Tonnie asked teasingly.

"Sounds like a transport frequency of some kind," Alex said, listening to the chatter. "Here we are. This sounds better. I'll make the call," Alex volunteered.

Gunnar hedged a look at Janox and Tonnie, finally shrugging and looking back out at the myriad of ships now moving about in front of them.

"I talk on military frequencies. There's no rhyme or reason to this civilian stuff. How do they keep from killing themselves?"

"Colonel," Alex spoke up. "Take a heading of ninety-three point two eight. You should see the Dither approach corridor momentarily."

Gunnar turned the ship in the direction indicated, maneuvering between several lines of ships moving in different directions over and under them. His thoughts slid back to his fighter pilot days, coming back from a mission. After seeing heavy action, he and his squadron would be tired and stressed. The voice of the approach controller was always so soothing, comforting. He would hear Audra in his ears and know his squadron mates would be flying a little more relaxed, especially the ones that had taken damage. The only thing he looked forward to more than hearing Audra's voice coming over his helmet headset, was holding her in his arms.

"Colonel, did you hear the controller? You need to drop down into the approach path."

Gunnar snapped back to reality, trying to focus on the information in front of him. The headache he was dealing with was making it next to impossible to concentrate on the instructions blaring through his earpiece. He had hoped the nap he had taken would have helped, but the throbbing continued to dog him. He blinked several times as his vision seem blurred. *Probably just the sleep.*

"The approach path, Colonel," Alex reminded him. "Are you ok? Did you hear the controller?"

"No, I got a blast of static and missed it."

"Follow approach path Alpha Tango, right below us."

Gunnar made the adjustment and set the controls on auto for the moment. Alex turned to Gunnar.

"Are you all right, Colonel? I am sensing elevated blood pressure, but a slowing in the function of your hearts. Your biotics are fluctuating as well."

"I don't know what that means. I've just got a really good headache going on here. It's messing with my concentration."

"Would you like me to pilot the ship down?"

"No, I'll be fine," Gunnar said rubbing his forehead. He stretched and arched his back hard, then twisted his neck from side to side as if loosening up for a fight. Still having no effect on the headache, he tried to relax as the Interceptor's autopilot made the descent into the atmosphere of the deep green shaded moon. As they drew closer to the surface he took command and followed Tonnie's directions to the described repository.

"Dither Repos Four, this is GR 9526 Uniform on short approach to land, instructions please."

"Negative GR 9526 Uniform. Our landing platforms are closed for maintenance. Please divert to Repos one and take the tube shuttle. Be advised the landing platform at Repos one is full and you will have to find temporary parking beyond the wall tight barriers. I'll let them know you're enroute. They will make a clearing for you. What's your business here?"

Gunnar pulled his headset and handed it to Tonnie.

"Ancestry research for the Billings line."

"That's a tough line, good luck. Please see the station docking master at the wall tight and they'll give you directions to the next tube shuttle."

"Thank you," Gunnar said taking the headset back. "Wonder how they're going to clear a spot?"

"They used to place a cutter ball out in the spot they want cleared," Tonnie said from behind. "It is a limited range disc laser. Depending how big of a swath they need, they set its range and clear whatever size is needed."

"Is that it?" Janox asked, pointing at a large facility rising from the dense treetops.

"I don't see any other building around here," Gunnar noted. Suddenly, a section of the jungle disappeared in a flash of red light. As the debris settled, a large round clearing materialized and a figure appeared from the edges, waving a set of lights in both hands.

"GR 9526 Uniform, you are cleared to put your gear down. Please follow my visual signals for landing."

"Interesting they don't have docking assist," Gunnar mumbled, bringing the Interceptor into a hover and gently setting the ship down as indicated by the signalman. "Ok, Tonnie. We're in your hands."

"There is nothing to be afraid of here, however, I suggest Alex remain onboard as he could be an oddity and draw unwanted attention."

"Hear that tenderfoot? You're an oddity."

"And what would they consider a Dialabron?"

"I can mix, you can't."

"Understood," Alex relented. He was in hopes of examining some of the records. Something to broaden his data base of Hadrian.

"You could access the repository's data portal," Tonnie suggested. "If we didn't need to physically be onsite to gain access to the information we're looking for, we would have just remained in orbit and accessed the data portal."

Gunnar climbed out of the seat and made his way to the lower hatchway. He reached for the handle, but stopped and looked up at Tonnie.

"Speaking of mixing and attracting attention," he said pulling his shaded glasses off and handing them to the android. "If those eyes don't yell, look at me, I don't know what will."

"Colonel, perhaps you should take this," Alex said holding out Captain Abram's holster and pistol.

Gunnar gave the pistol a glance as he assisted Janox in getting Tonnie back down the access shaft to the hatchway.

"I think I'm going to pass. Like Tonnie said, it could draw attention." Gunnar squeezed his eyes shut again, put his fingers to his temples and applied pressure.

"Are you sure you're even up for this, Sir?"

"No, I'm not sure I'm up for this at all," Gunnar reacted angrily. He took several deep breathes and buried his face in his palms. "I'm good." He turned and exited the craft after Janox, helping Tonnie walk.

"That's a really nice ship," the signalman remarked as he looked the three guests over. "Where you folks from?"

"Dorrington, on Tellarus Three," Tonnie piped up with a smile and stepping tentatively. "Sorry, I'm a little wobbly on my feet after such a long trip."

"Understandable. You folks are heading to Repos four?"

"Yes, when does the next tube shuttle leave?"

"In about ten minutes. If you'll just step inside, the tube gate will be on your right and the shuttle conductor will get you all situated. I really like that ship." The signalman motioned them toward the building while he turned to the Interceptor for a closer look.

Gunnar kept an eye on him as they went. Something didn't feel right, but the headache pounding him and the painful glare seem to redirect his focus, so he followed Janox and Tonnie into the building and to the tube gate. As they got under way, Gunnar got a good view of the Interceptor before the tube pitched underground. The signalman was still milling around the ship talking on a device, but then the forest swallowed the shuttle and plunged into the darkness of the underground. It took only a minute for the tube shuttle to reach full speed and while the clear pod was well lit, there was nothing to see but a blur of rock flashing by. It was easier for him to just shut off his overhead reading light and try to nap. The course readout in front of them indicated it would take several hours to reach Repos Four. Might as well make the most of it.

Finding escape in sleep, Gunnar began to dream in an uneasy, repeating cycle. The colors of bright red and purple painted his mind as he was carried through a dreamscape of the past and places he had never seen before. All the scenes seemed pointless until he reached the last one where he was driving himself through a myriad of opposing forces, from battle seasoned ground troops, to mechanized war machines. With each encounter, he became more out of control with the ferocity of the destruction he would exact on each element. At the end of each cycle, there was a cool blue colored pause and the feeling of calm, but only for a moment and then the cycle started over again, turning to a blur of killing and destruction. As the scenes flew by, the feelings of anger and rage intensified and the destruction continued at a pace he could barely comprehend. Then the blue colors flooded him and he abruptly stopped. With red colors all around him and a swath of destruction on every side, he stood in the midst of a calm blue glow, facing Audra. Dressed in her shimmering blue dress, she took his hands and smiled.

"Gunnar," she said softly. "Let me go."

"I can't."

"Yes you can… Let me go," she repeated.

Gunnar tried to look into her soft brown eyes, searching for her calming influence, but the colors surrounding them were glaring out her image. Rage filled him as the colors enveloped him. He pushed her hands back and jumped into the killing and destruction again. He caught only a glimpse of the blue color fading away and the vision of Audra along with it, then there was only the blinding anger within him.

Gunnar opened his eyes, feeling cold sweat creeping down his temples and the pounding in his head, ever present. The base of his skull felt like it was tied up in knots, but nothing he did to try and loosen the muscles had any affect.

"May I?" Tonnie asked putting her hands to the back of his neck.

Gunnar recoiled, but relaxed when he realized she meant him no harm. Her hands didn't feel mechanical at all, but were soft and warm. She seemed to know exactly where to rub to gain the maximum effect on his knotted, sore muscles.

"You've got something going on right here that's pretty intense," Tonnie said. "With your permission, I can add some ultrasonic waves and mild heat to this location."

Gunnar was already starting to relax somewhat from the soothing massage.

"Sure," he said. An instant later, a gentle vibration issued from Tonnie's fingertips. "Oh my word," Gunnar groaned. "Where have you been all my life?"

"That hits the spot, huh?"

"Oh yes." Gunnar's eyes rolled back, letting his head swing from one side to the other.

"If I had my externals available, I could really get this knot to melt fast."

"I don't think I could stay conscious if you did." Gunnar let his head drop to his chest as Tonnie continued to work her magic.

"More wrong than just stiff muscles," Janox commented leaning over the seat back and watching. "His sunggo out of balance. His mind not right."

"My mind?" Gunnar grumbled, almost euphoric. "Are you calling me crazy?"

"I not mean your mind," Janox recanted. "What is the word I look for?"

"If you were Doctor Yamoto, you would be asking about my emotional state of mind. You're not going to have Tonnie try to psychoanalyze me, are you?"

"No," Tonnie said. "I would need my externals in order to make any kind of analysis."

"Good, cause what you're doing right now is about as good as it gets. I may just have to keep you around. I could use a good nanny."

"I am for the protection of the Princess."

"Yeah, yeah, yeah. Geez, is there nothing you can't do?" Gunnar was nearly drunk with the relaxation taking over his body.

"I cannot reproduce."

"Well, I wouldn't think you'd be capable of that anyway. You are an android after all."

"I am fully functional as a female with the exception of reproduction."

Gunnar sat up and turned to Tonnie.

"Wait, you mean to tell me you can…?"

Tonnie nodded, smiling lightly.

"Of all the crazy things," Gunnar mumbled. "Why in the world…?"

"I have no information in my data banks on the matter."

Gunnar sat back, letting Tonnie continue to work on his neck and even his shoulders.

"I can only imagine the look on some duncecap's face when he makes a pass at you."

"I have received several of what you would call, 'funny looks', from uninformed human males that have mistaken me for a human female."

"How did we get on subject?" Janox complained.

"Sunggo?" Gunnar asked. "What were you talking about, Sunggo?"

"It is color of your glow."

"My glow?"

"Yes, everyone has glow."

"Are you talking about an aura?"

"What is aura?"

"It's the body's biosignature," Gunnar explained. "Like any sun emitting energy, the human body does the same. You can actually see the glow with special equipment, although it appears some can see it without special equipment; Alex being one of them."

"I can see your aura," Tonnie announced, still working the last of the kinks out of his neck.

"You're an android," Gunnar moaned as he continued to melt. "I would have been surprised if you couldn't."

"I see aura too," Janox admitted. "It light blue color right now, very good for you."

"Yeah, a massage like this will do that to you," Gunnar replied.

"Not only I see yours, but I see it change color, see it is off."

"My aura is off? What do you mean, off?"

"I am not, how do you say, scientific, yes. I not have knowledge about such things. I can only say what I see."

"I think what she means is..."

"Wait," Gunnar stopped Tonnie. "You're not going to go all techno gibberish on me are you? That's what my pal Rick is for."

"I'll dumb it down," she chuckled.

Gunnar looked at Janox, who grinned broadly. It was the first time they had heard the android manifest emotion. Tonnie pulled her hair back. It was still a sickly white color, but thanks to the good combing it had received at the hands of Janox, it wasn't sticking straight out. Her skin remained unchanged.

"As we are all formed of atoms and molecules, we naturally have a lot of energy in our individual chemical makeup. The atoms that make up your unique self are constantly modulating or moving. The electrons rotating around their nuclei are moving at a certain frequency. It's that frequency that produces your individual aura, or sunggo as the Princess put it."

"Had to call it something," Janox admitted.

"Every living thing has it in one form or another," Tonnie said.

"I see yours," Janox said looking at Tonnie.

"Even a machine has one?" Gunnar asked.

"While nonbiologics aren't considered by humans as living, we are all still made up of the same atoms that are doing the same things as the atoms comprising a human. It's just a different type of aura; usually not as colorful. What color do you see around me, Princess?"

Janox looked at her for a moment.

"It light-yellow color."

"Yours is pink," Tonnie said, "and Gunnar's is blue, right now, but I think you're right. There is something off."

"Much pain inside him," Janox offered. "He mourns for sealed mate. Have seen it in him; I see it still."

"I cannot see into you the way the Princess can and I have no idea why she can. She did not exhibit this ability when she was a tot."

"I have a woman currently serving on my ship that seems to have the ability to see into other people's emotional state." Gunnar was nearly entranced in relaxation. "Are females the only ones that can do this?"

"A sixth sense appears to be prevalent in human females. They are generally more attuned on an emotional level than males. That

certainly doesn't mean males cannot feel a wide range of emotions at a similar intensity; they just experience them differently and it's that difference that leans the sixth sense in the direction of the female. There," Tonnie finished both her lecture and the rub down. "Now you know more than you ever wanted to about female intuition. How's the neck feel?"

"I think you've paralyzed me," Gunnar said. He slumped further into the chair.

"If I may be so bold, may I ask what has been the cause of your aura being off and the pain inside you the Princess has spoken of? You mourn for an absent mate?"

Gunnar fingered the memory chip under his shirt for a moment, then looked at Tonnie for a long moment. Now that he was relaxed and calm, he could collect his thoughts and ponder.

"I'm not sure I can explain it so you could understand."

"Try me," Tonnie encouraged.

Gunnar looked up at Janox, who was resting her chin on her hands on the seatback in front of him.

"I am not human as you would define one. I'm a Dialabron. Yes, I look human, but my physiology is a bit different. My species produces an anomaly where some of us are born with extra organs. In my case, two hearts. Couple that with a dense bone structure and tough skin and I have abilities above the average human. This anomaly generally creates a weakness though; we're prone to episodes of anger that are difficult to control. Somehow, I've beaten the odds and not only survived my metamorphosis into adulthood, but mastered my temper. I married a human woman, Audra Atlanta. Not exactly sure how she could do it, but she was always able to calm my anger with a word or a touch. I couldn't help but love her. We did just about everything together. My friend, Rick Niker and I came to this galaxy almost two years ago by way of a worm hole we created to escape the gravity of a black hole. Audra was killed during the maneuver from damage sustained to our ship during the wormhole operations. I've never felt so out of balance since she's been gone. There were months when I could barely function. Now, I've been getting these horrible headaches and my neck has been balling up like a Gundarion juice sphere."

Janox and Tonnie remained silent for several passing moments, watching Gunnar stare off into nothing while fingering the memory chip around his neck.

"May I?" Tonnie asked holding her hand out toward Gunnar.

Gunnar looked at her, then at the chip, finally pulling it from around his neck and handing it to her. The android studied it carefully, turning it over several times.

"It's a Hallavertor program. I use it onboard my ship to help me grieve." Gunnar stretched his hand out to take it, but Tonnie turned, holding it up. Pulling open a small access panel on her inner wrist, she inserted it into an internal slot. The android froze for a moment, then slowly looked back at Gunnar, a deep expression rippling across her face. Tears pooled in her eyes as she gently tipped her head to one side. Her expression shifted from pain to sadness. She opened her mouth trying to speak, but nothing came. Finally, she carefully pulled the chip from her wrist and put it back into Gunnar's hand, gently closing his fingers around it.

"I understand now." Tonnie wiped the tears from her eyes. "She was an amazing woman. You are fortunate for having been bonded to her."

"What did you just do?" Janox asked.

"Yeah," Gunnar echoed, giving the android a stunned look. "What was that all about?"

Tonnie sat back and wiped the residual moisture from around her eyes.

"Well?" Janox pressed.

"I cannot have empathy for what Gunnar is going through unless I can experience it for myself." Tonnie looked at Gunnar. "You provided your side of the equation, but I needed the other piece to understand the other side."

"But you had no idea what was on this chip. Anyway, how were you even able to interface with it let alone decode the encryption?"

"It just fit into my interface and the encryption didn't seem foreign to me at all."

Janox settled back into her seat while Tonnie and Gunnar sat quietly.

"So what kind of hoops are we going to have to jump through when we reach the end of the line?" Gunnar asked looking at the display in the seatback in front of him. They were approaching Repos four.

"A Repos is basically a library. There is a main desk that will direct you to a specific wing of the facility. From there, you step on a conveyer to that wing and then access an automated kiosk that will pinpoint the exact location of the material you're looking for. They should have either automation to help you examine what you're looking for or maybe some kind of droid."

"Why isn't it all on just one big data base in a giant core commanded by some super artificial intelligence?"

"Technically, it is, but without the AI. They've created large partitions or virtual raids in their data cores so if something were to happen to one facility, it would be backed up somewhere else. At least that's the way I remember it being done."

"Interesting you know so much about Albion tech?"

"I was an android held here. It stands to reason I would become aware of the technology around me."

An alert signal began to flash on the screen in front of them and the tube shuttle started to slow as a voice came over the sound system announcing their arrival at the Repos station. Tonnie moved ahead, followed by Gunnar and a slightly apprehensive Janox. Gunnar picked up on her nervousness and pulled the young woman forward.

"Stay close, Princess. You've got the key to what we're looking for. I'd hate to find whatever it is only to lose you."

"I not believe this all happening. I not feel royal." Janox looked at the ball shaped locket as they exited the shuttle.

"I don't feel very strong either, but apparently I can bend steel." Gunnar winked at her and motioned her a little closer to Tonnie. After being directed to a specific wing of the Repos, they boarded a set of chair shuttles and were whisked away, down long endless hallways. The facility appeared to be mostly deserted, with only an occasional sighting of other humans doing research or a records droid performing maintenance on a kiosk. It was hard for Gunnar to comprehend there weren't a lot of people here, or at least a lot of security personnel.

Are the Albions really that confident in their own strength not to have a level of protection everywhere? What had him more worried than his suspicions, was how Janox was acting. Yes, she was nervous about finding out the truth about her heritage and blood line, but he could tell she was sensing something else. She had a way about her; that sixth sense telling her something wasn't right. And while there seemed to be only a few people here, even he had a feeling of foreboding.

After some initial searching, Tonnie led them down a long row of file interfaces, finally stopping at a stack of rolling compact storage containers.

"Shouldn't we just be trying to access the information at one of the input terminals?" Gunnar asked, watching the android activate the correct section. As the containers robotically separated, Tonnie turned to the other two.

"Because we're not looking for a file, we're looking for a book."

"A book?" Gunnar repeated. "They have those here?"

"Sure, it's a repository, why wouldn't they?"

"In my galaxy, books are something to be viewed from behind a glass case. An antiquated form of file storage."

"Well, to be fair, the same conditions exist here, but this book is special."

"So why isn't it behind glass somewhere?"

"Because I hid it here before we were taken to Reako." Tonnie walked down the aisle looking at all the compartment doors. "I couldn't let it be discovered by the Albions or the Colonians. They would have used it and the Princess. And, here it is." Tonnie touched a sequence of numbers and characters on a keypad mounted to the door of a small compartment. Looking up and down the aisle, she popped the door open and pulled a small box from the container, then a large book. "Keep that locket hidden," Tonnie instructed as she shut the door and motioned everyone back out the same way they came in.

"Aren't we going to have a look see at what we came here for?" Gunnar asked.

"Yes, but not here."

"Why not? There's no one here. Be nice to know we have the right item."

"We have it," Tonnie said, quickening her pace as they exited the containers. "Now, the trick is keeping it."

"You're not making me feel warm and fuzzy," Gunnar complained trying to keep up.

"No doubt you have a funny feeling about being here?"

"Yes, how did you know?"

"I can see it written all over the Princess's face. She knows something is wrong and like the Terminal Twenty-one command sent me, I wouldn't put it past whoever sent the command, to have this Repos watched. I can't receive any telemetry because I have no externals, so you two are safe with me for now. They can't track me, but someone might recognize me. We just need to get out of here as quickly and as unassuming as possible."

Gunnar and Janox didn't need any convincing. Now, they moved ahead of Tonnie, back the way they came, occasionally looking behind them as they went. Feeling a small sense of relief once they made it back to the tube shuttle station, they waited impatiently for the next tube car to dock. As they waited, the station conductor eyed them closely, leaving his station repeatedly and disappearing into another room, only to return a short time later. Finally, the shuttle arrived and they boarded. As they waited, several other people boarded and took their seats in various places in the tube pod. Gunnar watched silently as the conductor began talking to someone on his communicator, while looking in their direction. Even as the shuttle began to move, the conductor held his gaze on the three, still speaking to someone. As they pulled away from the station, he observed a cluster of men and women arrive at the entry desk, surrounding the conductor, then the shuttle accelerated and they were descending through the jungle and into the ground. As they traveled underground, Gunnar studied the display in the seatback in front of him.

"I take it you're not feeling very good about our departure," Tonnie suggested softly as she leaned her seat back.

"You're feeling it too?"

"No, I can't feel much of anything, but between you, the Princess and the activity at the station, I don't need to feel anything to know something isn't right."

"Afraid I've become a bit spoilt having Alex around. But he's not here and you can't scan." Gunnar slowly looked around the tube pod at the other passengers sitting quietly, getting comfortable for the long ride back to Repos three. There appeared to be no cause for alarm at the moment as no one looked out of place. He hadn't even seen weaponry on anyone at either station.

"What do you know about this shuttle system?" Gunnar asked.

"It's a magnesphere pulse drive pod," the android replied.

"Basically a big glass jar inside a tube with a magnet on the bottom?" Gunnar suggested.

"Basically," Tonnie nodded. "There are no intersecting tubes and only one pod can be in a tube at a time. At least that's the way I remember it."

"Any way to stop this thing in case of an emergency?" Gunnar looked all around at the interior. There were the main doors on the side, but there were also compartment doors at either end.

"I don't know. I have no detailed information on the shuttle's construction."

"What you thinking?" Janox asked.

"Just looking for options. Tonnie, what's your status?"

"Core is at ninety-seven percent. Diagnostics have resolved eighty percent of my internal issues, which should be about all it can until my externals are replaced. Do you have specific instructions for me?"

"Not yet, but stand by, my mind is always coming up with something." Gunnar paused a moment, then looked at Janox. "So, should we figure out what your locket is hiding?"

Tonnie set the small box to one side and held the book up to Janox.

"It must be the Princess that opens the book. It is not for me. I am the appointed Au Pair. It can only be opened by an Oxlind."

"Why didn't the Albions or the Colonians just destroy that thing if they were intent on taking over?" Gunnar asked.

"As I indicated previously; they didn't know I had it or that I had hidden it in the Repos. Anyway, it is made of a material that is difficult to destroy. The first and second pages are a little wrinkled from someone trying to tear them out."

"Amazing you know all this," Gunnar remarked.

"I was there when it happened," Tonnie replied. "Your Highness?"

Janox pulled back a little, still holding the locket in her hand.

"Here, give it to me and I'll do it," Gunnar said taking the locket from her and the book from Tonnie.

"You are not..." Tonnie started.

"Someone has to get this done. I've been listening to little missy pants here moan and complain about how she's not a royal blood and all she wants to do is go home for the past six months and now when she has the chance to prove me wrong, all of a sudden she's lost her nerve. Well, let's put this to rest right now." Gunnar inserted the locket into the indentation on the book cover and waited. He touched it several times and waited. He carefully turned it both ways and waited. Looking befuddled, he examined the locket for any damage and proper fitment.

"You're not a royal blood," Tonnie smiled. "The locket is encoded to a specific biosignature."

"Ok," Gunnar passed the locket and the book back to the nanny. "You're the royal nanny, you try it."

Tonnie opened her mouth to object, but a quick nod from Gunnar sent a message.

"Very well," she said inserting the locket and trying it several times. She finally set it in her lap and put her hands up. "I can't work it either."

"Ok, you made point," Janox said taking the book. As she set the locket into the indentation, the small orb began to glow, tiny words spinning around its surface with various colors.

"Do you ever wonder why lock designers build such things with all these cute little gizmos and pretty lights?" Gunnar asked.

Tonnie and Janox looked up at Gunnar. He passed looks back at them and shrugged.

"Just wondering..."

"It is coded to her DNA. She's the only one that can open it," Tonnie reiterated.

Janox looked closely at the words spinning around the little glowing orb.

"I hope you can read that, cause I certainly can't," Gunnar observed, watching Janox examine the words. Tonnie remained silent, watching the Princess struggle to make it out.

"I see these before," Janox whispered impatiently. She passed a glance at Tonnie. Janox turned the orb in one direction for a moment, then paused, trying to understand the words on the orb. After a brief struggle, she turned it a different direction, then turned it again and stopped. Staring at the glowing words, she then pushed on the small ball and pulled her hand away as the mechanism securing the book lit up and beeped several times. Then the orb went dark and a moment later the mechanism began to expand on all sides and several fingers extracted themselves from the main body, releasing the front binding of the book. Tonnie and Gunnar watched with guarded smiles as Janox opened the cover and looked inside. Several sheets of parchment lay smooth across a flat screen. Beneath the screen, lay sheet after sheet of parchment until the other side of the binding. Janox picked up the facing page and examined it. It was handwritten in ink and lavishly signed at the bottom with a curious seal next to a signature. She looked hard at the other pages, trying to make out what the words were, but became so overcome, she handed it to Tonnie.

"Will you tell what says, please?"

The android smiled and took the pages, holding up the first one.

"This one is a signed proclamation from your father, outlining his state of mind when making out the following legal documents and stating the source of his royal ancestry. It validates all the remaining documents, plus the data contained on the display."

"You know everything that's here?" Gunnar asked, realizing she was familiar with the contents. It didn't even occur to him that she was technically a machine. Her cybernetic network was capable of recalling a vast quantities of information instantly.

"Certainly," Tonnie replied. "I was ordered by his majesty, Tiev Oxlind, to compile all these documents in one place and safeguard them from the Duchess Benetar and her secret service as well as the Albion King Commander and his agents. I hid them here while we were exiled on Albia."

"How did you manage to get up here to put it in place without anyone seeing you?" Gunnar asked looking at the pages. He couldn't read the language, but there were some pictures and illustrations; all quite interesting.

"It wasn't hard. I insisted the Princess be allowed access to intellectual materials not found on Albia. Since they didn't want to draw attention to us and it wasn't likely we could escape, our security was minimal when they accompanied us here on Dither. I told them the book was her study materials."

"A lying android," Gunnar chuckled. Alex was not capable of telling falsehoods and would be insulted were anyone to ask him to.

"Providing misinformation does not go against my programing, provided it helps to achieve my primary directives to protect the Princess first and these documents. Everything else is secondary."

"So what's on the display?"

"It contains a video-graphic record of the royal family from marriage to the birth of all the children, including all their DNA sequences and vital statistics. There is also a personal entry from the king, indicating who murdered him."

"He knew who killed him?"

"He was gradually poisoned to make it look like he had fallen ill. He found out about it too late. He lays out the proof in his entry."

"No second guessing who that would be. What I don't get is what the Albions have to do with all of this?"

"The connection is unknown to me." Tonnie turned back to Janox and pointed to a name on the parchment. All the writing was in fancy royal script. Having not seen much writing, let alone script, Janox had a hard time making out the name. "This is your name, Princess. Jana Tilee Oxlind, Hadrian Princess of Colonia. Fifth daughter and seventh child of their royal majesties, King Tiev and Queen Mila Oxlind of Colonia." Tonnie took Janox by the hand and pressed her finger to a glowing box on the display. "This is your recorded DNA signature, unique only to you, and here is the DNA signature of the Princess Jana Oxlind." Tonnie pressed a series of buttons next to the display and turned it so the others could see. "It is an exact match, your Highness; you are the Princess."

Janox looked at the display while Tonnie opened the small box she had taken from the compartment with the book. She looked at a large ring Tonnie was holding up.

"This is your father's royal seal. Anything stamped with this becomes royal law." Janox took the ring and tried it on all her fingers. It was so big, she could almost put two fingers in it. Tonnie held out a smaller ring. "This was your mother's ring. I think it will fit you better. It carries the same sealing power as your father's, but you must be in possession of both rings in order to make claim to the throne of Hadrian, your Highness. May you rule in the light of truth and knowledge as your parents always tried to."

Janox took the smaller ring and studied it, finally putting it on her finger and admiring it. She looked back at the documents, then the display, then at the documents. Sensing her indecision, Gunnar leaned a little closer.

"Janox, you do not have to accept any of this. I'm sure we can get you back to Cross or maybe even Aster and you can live your life as you want. I might suggest Cross over Aster. A lot more variety in the landscape and wildlife."

"He's right," Tonnie agreed. "You are under no obligation to pursue any of this. There will always be rulers of Hadrian; legitimate or otherwise. There was long ago and there will be long after we've all advanced to other plains of existence.

"You will move onto another life?" Janox asked.

"Well, I don't know. I'm sure there will come a time when I will no longer function. But if one is to adhere to the teachings of the Thane, everything is living, so it makes sense I would have a life after this one."

Janox sat back with the book and her parent's rings, looking at everything, trying to process all of it. As the trip in the tube shuttle stretched on, she studied the documents, forcing herself to read every word. She didn't comprehend all of it, but she was determined to figure out the words and at least have a basic understanding of what the documents were. Scanning through the display device, she listened to her father chronicle the steps of his demise and the evidence he had collected before he passed away. She studied his face carefully, watching the video several times. Scanning through the family pictures, she started to feel robbed of a happiness she had never had the chance to enjoy. There were only ghostly shadows of something that felt vaguely familiar to her left in her mind. Now it was clear who her family and parents were. Her lineage was laid out plain before her. *I haven't been raised to be a monarch, a ruler of a galaxy.*

I have no idea what I'm supposed to do or how to do it. What do you do with something so large and spread out? How do you help a people who have divided themselves and are constantly warring with each other? I have no idea what cultures are even involved in the conflict ravaging Hadrian. How could one person get everyone's attention and bring them all together in agreement, living in peace again?

*   *   *   *

During the hours traveling back to Repos One, Gunnar continued to wrestle with an uneasy feeling that something wasn't right, and taking the time to move about the pod, studied everything about it. The pod had three sets of doors. The main doors on the side of the compartment and one on each end. On closer examination, he found the doors on the ends didn't just open straight to the outside of the pod, but there was some kind of small compartment on the other side. Straining to see through the little window in the door, he caught sight of a control panel with a display and several controls with lights winking randomly. Eyeing the other end, he surmised it was a duplicate. The compartment looked a bit cramped for an operator.

Casually making his way back to his seat, he glanced at the display on the seat back and sat down. Janox was still engrossed in her documents, while Tonnie sat fixed. Her hair now had long streaks of light brown running randomly through it, but her skin was still wrinkled and pale. Gunnar waited a moment for the android to notice him, finally passing a hand in front of her face. After a moment, she blinked and looked at Gunnar.

"You ok over there?" he asked.

"Yes, I am sorry for my inattentiveness," the android answered. "I was running some complex computations while finishing up my diagnostic logs."

"You're starting to look a little better," Gunnar said flipping her hair with a finger. "Your skin tone is coming back, a little. There's still a glow in those eyes, but only if you look right into them."

Tonnie pulled his shaded glasses from her face and handed them back to him.

"You probably need these far more than I do now." She ran her fingers through her hair, then held some up.

"My hair still has a way to go, but at least it doesn't feel like a bundle of bare wire. Have we arrived at the station yet?"

"We're just coming up on it now. I've got a good headache coming on; must be something bad about to happen."

"You think you're developing a female's intuition?"

"Oh gosh, I hope not." Gunnar scanned the people around them getting ready to disembark. "I just have a bad feeling. Have had since we left the other station. Didn't like the look on that conductor's face. If things go sideways, just follow my lead."

"Not much we can do about anything in here until we're stopped," Tonnie pointed out.

"Janox," Gunnar tapped the young woman on the shoulder. "Let's get ready to go." The jungle suddenly reappeared all around the pod as the tube rose to the surface. "Alex," Gunnar said in a low voice into his communicator. "Fire up the ship and activate the shields. We'll be out in a couple of minutes."

"Were you successful, Colonel?"

"Yes, I believe so."

As the pod slowed, everyone got up and gathered their things. Helping Janox out of her seat, Gunnar felt something blunt poking him in the back, but before he could turn to find out what it was, there were several pistols pointing at them from the front. Looking all around them, it appeared everyone was armed.

"We'll need to have your weapons," a gruff voice from behind him ordered.

Gunnar and Tonnie put their hands up as the pod pulled into the station. He passed a glance at Janox, who was moving out of her seat with the book clasp locking into place. A swell of anger abruptly filled him, feeling like he should have been more observant of the occupants in the pod. Surely he should have noticed their weapons.

"If you can find any weapons on me, you can have them," Gunnar fumed, his hands beginning to shake.

"Check the woman," the man behind him ordered, motioning to Tonnie as Gunnar was patted down. After a thorough check, they turned to Janox as the doors opened. There was no time to search the younger woman as Tonnie and Gunnar were herded out the pod gates. Looking out the main building doors, Gunnar saw a dust cloud rising from the jungle and heard the familiar sound of the Interceptor engines turning up. They were taken to the station desk where a couple of military officers stood waiting. Gunnar noticed another form appear from around a corner.

Blinda Koss eyed Tonnie carefully, turning toward her. Something seemed familiar… but then her attention was pulled to Gunnar.

"No weapons and no identifications," the plain clothes man informed Blinda as she came to a stop next to the lead officer.

"Oh, Drax is going to just love this," Blinda mused. "I admit, I almost didn't bother coming down, but I'm so glad I did." She adjusted her ponytail, making sure it was tight.

"We've committed an entire garrison from the *Tarzana's* Special Forces group to picking up these three," the officer next to Blinda complained. "Not sure what we were so concerned about. Just a couple of women and this old guy."

"Old guy?" Gunnar repeated.

Gunnar suddenly found himself on his back, holding his jaw where the officer had decked him. His rage boiled, but he somehow managed to maintain control. He detected a couple of pistols pointed at his head and glancing outside again, saw something familiar moving through the trees toward the entrance.

"You will speak only when spoken to," the officer hissed arrogantly. "Now, on your feet, old man."

"Careful, Captain," Blinda warned, leaning in a little closer and still grinning from ear to ear. "You're messing with someone you should be careful of, or so I've heard." Gunnar noticed her weapons beneath her black cloak as she brought her hands to her hips. "Hold the others here. I will speak with this one alone."

As Blinda backed Gunnar away from everyone else, she leaned triumphantly against the wall next to him and let her head rest against the corner.

"You've caused me a great deal of embarrassment."

"You're Blinda Koss," Gunnar said, finally surmising who she was based on the description he had been given. "Nice to put a face with the name."

"Oh, that's right, you were under the influence of Miss Monroe's prescription medications when we took you from Alvadore. I have to admit; Miss Barker is one tenacious woman. To come back and single handedly retrieve you from the Albion flagship…"

Gunnar's blood was still boiling, but he somehow kept everything in check.

"Well, I have that effect on people. Everyone just loves to be with me."

"I see," Blinda said. She rolled a little closer to him and motioned in Tonnie and Jana's direction. "And why are these two with you?" She eyed Tonnie again.

Gunnar glanced outside as the engine noise continued to ramp up.

"Because I'll be the one who sees they make it off this moon."

"I seriously doubt that," Blinda stated, turning cold.

"Patience," Gunnar breathed, stoic.

Blinda looked through his shaded glasses at his eyes. His pupils appeared to be rotating with changing colors. She pulled back, a little astonished, then glanced at the others as the Albion Captain turned to Tonnie and Janox. "Hold this older one here for just a moment while I have a word with the girl." He grabbed Janox by the arm and lead her away to a more secluded spot. Once away, his smile turned wicked as he let his hand slide down her arm.

"You are quite the fetching little creature," he slathered. "I think I'll be the one to interview you." He ran his hands back up to her check and then her chin, looking her over lustfully. "And what is this book all about?"

"It is mine," Janox replied. Uncomfortable, she didn't understand what was happening.

"You'll show me a little later," the man seethed, "along with everything else." He let his hand drop to her backside, giving her buttock a firm squeeze. There came a sudden, sharp pain to the left side of his abdomen, while noticing the young woman jerk slightly. He looked down at the blood-stained blade of a knife drawing back from his uniform.

"This is what I will show you," Janox whispered, sliding the dagger back into its sheath.

Astonished at the trauma streaking through his nervous system, the officer stood immobile as Janox side stepped him and started back towards her friends. Trying to call out, he could only manage a sick gasping sound while staggering backward.

As Janox casually walked toward her companions, Gunnar suddenly exploded. Slamming Blinda's head against the wall, he tossed her across the floor, sending her crashing through the tube pod turnstile. Knocking the other armed officers to the ground, he grabbed one by the head, giving it a sharp twist, then tossed his limp body into his dying commander. The others tried to bring their guns to bear, but a flurry of boots and hands knocked them lose. Gunnar turned to Tonnie and Janox, feeling one of the officer's wrist translators in his hand.

"Get to the ship!" Nearly blinded by his own fury, Gunnar could see the Interceptor hovering on the other side of the compound, the lower hatch popping open. Tonnie and Janox tried to hop past two troopers getting back to their feet, but got caught up in a scuffle. Spinning to get past them, Janox felt something fly free from her fingers as she broke for the door with Tonnie right behind her. Looking back, Janox caught the glint of her father's ring bouncing along the floor as the android pushed her forward toward the outer doors. As the two troopers brought their rifles up, they were clothes-lined by Gunnar as he bolted for the doors after Tonnie.

"Go, go, go!" Gunnar called from behind over the rising noise outside.

"My father's ring...!" Janox tried to turn for it, but Tonnie had already pushed her out the doors.

Gunnar looked back, spotting the big ring bouncing toward a far wall. Seeing Blinda staggering to her feet and not wanting to deal with an understandably angered Thane, he burst through the doors behind Tonnie and Janox.

Focusing solely on the hovering fighter, both women rushed into the humid air filled with the low throttle of the waiting ship. Janox continued to resist as they ran, seeing Gunnar sprinting toward a ground transport wheeling to a halt to their right. As its doors swung open, troopers piled out with rifles up. The android shifted to Janox's right side, running beside her. Several rounds of fire riddled the jungle to their left and in front of them as they continued toward the open hatch. As the troopers opened up on the two women, a body slammed across the entire line, knocking them all down. Springing up on one knee, Gunnar grabbed a lose rifle and started popping shots off at point blank range. Troopers scattered in disarray, some diving back inside the transport, as Gunnar laid down a circle of suppressing fire. He glanced in the direction of the Interceptor, seeing Tonnie pushing Janox toward the lower hatch. He got to his feet and bolted toward the ship, firing the rifle at anything that moved. As he approached the ship, a blast from a grenade exploded near him, knocking him to the ground. His ears ringing and his head spinning, he tried to look around. The Interceptor's engines were only a muffled sound in his ringing ears. Trying to focus, he spotted a figure coming toward him. Tonnie pulled on his arm to help him up, but his equilibrium was still swirling. As he rolled painfully over, he glanced back at the Repos station, seeing Blinda Koss staggering into the open doors. As Tonnie reached down to help Gunnar to his feet, he grabbed her, pulling her on top of him. He heard a Balkrum ring whistle just over them as he forced Tonnie into a roll. As they stopped, he looked back at Blinda who was moving toward them with her pistol drawn.

"On your feet," Gunnar said pushing Tonnie vertical. Gaining her balance, the android pulled Gunnar up and throwing his arm over her shoulder, they struggled toward the open hatch, Janox screaming encouragement. As the android pushed Gunnar toward the safety of the ship, a flurry of rounds pummeled the side of the ship. Janox heard several strikes thumping through the open hatchway, not against metal, but something soft. She turned to help Gunnar inside, but recoiled as a spray of hot metal peppered her. Monitoring the foray at the hatch and the gunfire outside, Alex turned the hovering ship around to provide cover from their assailants. Tonnie pushed Gunnar at the hatch, but the Kalamarion Colonel insisted the android climb in first. Another volley of rounds ricocheted across the bottom fin of the Interceptor, hitting Gunnar in several places. As Tonnie hoisted herself inside, she turned and grabbed Gunnar as he began to melt away from the hatchway.

"Alex, take off!" Gunnar called, grabbing a hold of the hatchway threshold.

The Interceptor rose as the troopers continued to fire at them. Several more rounds struck around the hatch, hitting Tonnie and Gunnar as the big fighter skimmed over the jungle. Gunnar looked back at Blinda standing in the middle of the Repos compound. At this point, he didn't care what her disposition was as he struggled to hold on while Tonnie attempted to get a better grip on him. He looked down at the dense foliage passing beneath them and then strained to look back up at the android.

"Tell Alex, I'm ordering him to get the Princess to Cross," he yelled over the noise of the throttling engines.

Tonnie looked into Gunnar's eyes at the same moment he let go of the threshold. Janox watched horrified as he fell into the thick of the jungle and disappeared.

"Gunnar!" she screamed, trying to crawl over Tonnie to get to the hatch. The android held tightly to her, keeping her safe as rounds continued to hammer the ship. "Alex! Don't leave him!" Janox was almost in tears as she turned to the cockpit. "Circle around and we'll pick him up."

"I have been ordered to leave immediately," the droid responded.

"No, I order you back!"

"I cannot comply," Alex reiterated. "I was given a direct order from my commanding officer. There are four Albion military ships closing on our position. I have to comply with my orders." The ground abruptly dropped out of sight as the fighter rocketed skyward.

"No," Janox sobbed. "Don't leave him. He is our friend, Alex. Don't leave him!" Janox felt a set of hands touch her shoulders. Instantly turning, she buried her face in Tonnie's chest, sobbing.

"I'm sorry, your Highness," Tonnie said trying to comfort the Princess. "He understood what had to be done. He sacrificed himself for the greater good."

"No, not for greater good! He not want to see more death. He saw enough. He said himself. No greater good, good enough for Gunnar to die."

"His purpose was the same as mine, to protect you at all costs," Tonnie reiterated.

"No, his purpose was to get home. Is all he wanted. Must go back for him. This ship strong. Alex, use guns to destroy other ships and troops. We go back!"

"My apologies," Alex said after a moment. "I cannot pilot a ship the way the Colonel could. It is not in my ability to do so. Were I to try, there is a ninety-seven percent possibility of failure. I have been ordered to take you to Cross. You will be safe there."

"No," Janox cried. "Not way this supposed to be. I made him to cheat death, to find Tonnie. Must do same for him."

Tonnie held the young Princess as she cried, processing the events and their ramifications. In doing so, a tear dropped from her eye while rocking the sobbing Princess. Nearly numb, Janox held tightly to the android, letting her hands slide down her back. As she did so, she felt the holes that riddled the back of her shirt. She pulled from Tonnie's arms and wiping her nose, turned the android sideways.

"Tonnie, you hurt!" There was orange colored fluid seeping from several entry wounds.

"Yes, it would seem I have sustained some damage."

"Some?"

"I appear to still be functioning normally, I think."

"What mean, think?"

"Attempting to run an emergency diagnostic now." Tonnie sank back against a bulkhead.

"Lay down; I look." Janox found focus away from her grief, helping the android to the floor and examining the holes in her back. "What is this wet?"

"My blood; it is not like yours. It is a silicon based hydraulic mixture."

"Not know what that is, but you leak all over your back and leg."

"Try not to be too concerned," Tonnie said. "My flesh layer is built with self-sealing compounds. Except for anything larger than your index finger, they should seal back up in a moment."

"You make mess."

"Do you require assistance?" Alex inquired from the cockpit.

"Maybe in a minute. Get us out of here first," Tonnie said.

Janox did the best she could to dress Tonnie's larger wounds as most of the smaller injuries had sealed up by the time she got to them. Tonnie finally sat up, looking over the pilot's seat as Alex guided the ship out of the traffic patterns surrounding Dither. Outside she could still see a myriad of craft, most notably several larger ships surrounding one mammoth sized capital ship.

"That is the Battlecruiser, *Tarzana*," Alex announced.

"It wasn't here when we came in, was it?"

"No, it would appear we have somehow attracted some attention."

"Can go around?" Janox asked, getting a feeling of Deja Vu.

"I am trying to work with departure control, but the military is interfering with all transmissions."

"Can you jump to light speed from here?" Tonnie asked.

"Certainly, but there is a little risk as I do not have all our star chart jump parameters entered yet."

Janox took note of several specs moving in their direction and gave the tracking screen a glance.

"Maybe make a short jump with what you have and then jump again?" Tonnie suggested.

"Like did with Colonel Barker's ship," Janox said.

"Standby," Alex said, making a short series of chirps. A moment later, the stars streaked past the windshield as the little droid shifted into light speed. Moments later, the stars streaked again as they dropped back out. "Ok," the little droid assured them. "I have all the information we need. It will take approximately two point seven hours to reach the Jurass system."

"I believe the sooner we are there, the better off we will be," Tonnie said. "Do you know this Diord Vandmire well?"

"Yes, good friend to Colonel Barker," Janox said as Alex shifted the fighter into light speed. "He know what do."

Stunningly Functional

"So, this is what our intellect has produced in my absence," Caidin said, admiring the *Athena* as she sat in the bright light of the *Stark's* landing bay.

"I have to think they've already made some improvements on the design," Rick said standing next to Caidin.

"What requires improvement?" Dãsha asked curiously. She examined the ship closely, but didn't seem to want to touch it.

"Well, to start with, there is a flaw in the design of the powering crystal assemblies. Asium crystal number five becomes unstable under heavy loads and fractures. In the one case I'm aware of, it was nearly catastrophic." Rick's thoughts chased away to his friend's loss, but he promptly came back. "There are a number of other things, but that one seems to be the biggest deficiency so far."

"Your design engineer should have thought of those deficiencies beforehand," Dãsha said curtly. "He or they should be notified immediately."

"Pretty sure he found out the hard way," Rick responded quietly. "Let's go onboard and have a look." Rick motioned them toward the loading doors as Zek appeared and handed Rick a viewing device.

"The manifest of all four freighters, Sir."

Rick studied it for a long moment, scrolling through several pages of data and looking up at Zek periodically.

"Have you actually opened the doors and visually inspected this cargo?"

"No, Sir," Zek answered. "After looking at this, I thought it might be more appropriate if you opened it."

"Lieutenant Gillespie," Rick called, looking around.

"She's standing by the main hold doors, Sir," Greg Tanetto answered from nearby.

"Captain Zak, you'll carry on with showing our guests through the *Athena*."

"Yes, Sir," came a quick call from the other side of the Starbird as Rick motioned for Zek and the chief to follow to the nearest hatchway.

After a couple of minutes of fast paced walking and directions from behind, Rick arrived at a large access door where Terry Gillespie stood waiting. She saluted smartly and stood to one side. Rick looked at the door control. The indicators were showing green; unlocked. Taking a deep breath, he activated the opening control. As the door slid to one side, the interior lights came on. Rick stepped inside, a look of shock forming across his face. Directly in front of him was the nose of a Starbird. Flabbergasted, he couldn't even begin to imagine what a Starbird was doing in the hold of a freighter. He walked slowly around the bridge section and looked back to make sure he could see all the way to the rear of the entire hold. The ship appeared to be complete and after looking at it for a moment, he noticed a couple of Interceptors stored on raised lifters on either side along with several complete main engines and secondary thruster pods. There were boxes and crates stored neatly on either side of the ship and as Rick made his way toward the aft section of the ship he saw two more Interceptors already docked in their positions on the aft wing-tips. Directly above the engine compartment, sat a turret in its place. He spotted several turrets stored on lugging mounts on the floor behind the Starbird. Stopping at mid-ship he turned to the door control and worked the key sequence. A moment later, the activators began to blink green and the doors on both sides slid open revealing a dark interior.

"Captain Zek!"

"Right here, Sir."

"Oh," Rick turned with a toned-down voice. "Why don't you and the Chief see what kind of condition this bird is in and then get over to the other freighters and get into those holds. Report back to me." He shook his head, chuckling.

"Sir?" Zek stopped.

"Nothing, Captain. I was just thinking. This is just the kind of stunt Admiral Mandell would pull on me. Please, continue with your assignment." Rick watched Zek and Greg climb inside, dawning hand lights. Once out of sight, he turned to Terry.

"I don't understand, Sir. I thought there were only ten of these produced? If the other holds have the same contents, there would have been almost enough for half a fleet."

"Enough for a good squadron anyway. Where were you guys bound when you were chased into the Oneida?"

"We were supposed to rendezvous with a capital ship called, the *Zebra Phar*, over a planet called Genis Two, somewhere near the Androlus Quasar complex. That's all Captain Fowler would tell us. What does this all mean, General?"

"I wish I knew," Rick answered, thinking hard. A moment later, the interior lights came on and Zek reappeared from the engineering doors.

"She appears to all be here, Sir, except for a complete Asium Crystal Assembly. The assembly housing is here, plugged into its spot, but no crystals."

Rick's expression turned deeper trying to work the puzzle. *Had Croft Heckla been more of a problem than Kalamar Command had led everyone to believe? Something must have been happening at the highest levels that even he and Gunnar had been kept in the dark about. If that were the case, what was it that scared Command so*

*much they felt the need to build another fleet of Starbirds? Maybe I'm
reading too much into this? Not that it matters right now anyway.
We're a very long way from home with still no way to return.* That
made Rick the Officer in Command of this small fleet of Starbirds. It
was up to him to figure out what to do with them.

"Have Chief Tanetto help you bring all her basic systems online and
give me a report on her condition. Find out if she's loaded with
anything."

"Loaded, Sir?"

"Armed, Captain. What's she packing? Once you're done here, get
over to the other freighters and do the same. I'll be on the *Athena*."

"Mind if I assist the Captain, General?" Terry inquired, hoping for a
glimpse inside.

"Don't worry, Lieutenant," Rick said, smiling as he turned for the
hold door. "You'll get your chance. Right now, you're with me."

*   *   *   *

After some searching, Rick found Captain Zak, Dãsha and Caidin in
the *Athena's* sickbay.

"Well, I was going to make sure you got a tour of the ship first, but
ok, this is where we were going to end up anyway. What do you
think?" Rick asked, stopping next to Caidin as he studied the medical
readouts on the stasis pods of the three surviving crew of the *Athena*.

"This is pretty bad," Caidin said without looking up. "What was the
cause of this?"

"A Thane named, Blinda Koss," Rick said taking a deep breath. His
encounter with her was still fresh in his mind. "I lost half my crew to
her. These are the only ones that survived."

"Ilob waves..." Caidin finally looked up and peered inside the pod.

"Caidin, can you help these crewman?" Dãsha asked, examining
the other pods.

"I'll do what I can," Caidin said. "But there are no guarantees
when it comes to this kind of damage."

"You can't do the same thing you did for Dãsha?" Rick asked,
pushing close to Caidin.

"Certainly," Caidin said, looking into Rick's hopeful expression.
"But I can't repair a damaged mind. Ilobs are the most dangerous
wavelengths you can manipulate through the mind. I can repair the
brain, but personality and memory are created and nurtured at a
rudimentary subatomic level. Ilobs destroy those particles and it's
tricky to replicate them."

Rick looked down at Toby Mavis as Captain Zak walked in.

"General, everything is ready for the rescue op. You probably
should leave immediately."

Rick remained motionless for several seconds, then turned back to Caidin.

"Do what you can. I'll be back as soon as soon as we've found Jayda."

"Richard?" Caidin stopped him as the General turned to leave. "I look forward to meeting your Jayda. Good luck."

"Thanks," Rick said, stepping out. He stopped in the door and looked back at the three pods and Caidin. "Caidin, they're my family."

Caidin nodded and turned back to the readouts as the General and Captain left for the boarding doors.

Disembarking from the *Athena*, Rick turned to the Drake Escey assault ship. Dacey and one of the Chief Petty Officers were making hasty adjustments to the huskie craft.

"Wish we had Mister Moon here to help," Rick commented, watching them work.

"Well, the good news is," Dacey said, not looking up from what he was doing, "Drake hardware isn't terribly complicated and even easier to fix. The gun turrets on this thing belong on a capital cruiser."

"They are big," Rick agreed. "Can you have this thing ready to go in five minutes?"

"We're just putting these thruster injection pipes back on the directional ports. You should be good to go in five," Dacey said.

"How many to man this thing?"

"One can drive it, but you should have at least two others to act as gunners. Works best with six gunners and the pilot."

Rick looked around. There weren't that many crew to spare, yet if they ran into trouble with the operation, it might be nice to have extra fingers on the triggers. Captain Zak stepped up behind Rick with a small arsenal of weapons.

"Not just Starbirds and associated spare parts in those holds, Sir," the Captain said, handing him a rifle and pistol. "Some of that inventory, I've never seen before. What's really disturbing is nothing has an insignia on it."

"Well, most preproduction equipment comes plain. They put the insignias on after deployment," Rick said.

"Agreed, but the Interceptors are a little different than ours. It looks like they have different guns and more of them. It'll take time to get the detail. It's weird the Starbirds don't have the new Mark V torpedoes."

Rick passed Zak an odd look, then shrugged.

"Do the best you can." Rick passed a pistol to Greg, who looked up just in time to catch it.

"Chief, you and Dacey are coming with me."

"I thought I was coming with you?" Zak asked a little surprised and dejected.

"Got a better idea, and I need my best pilots and engineers right here to pull it off," Rick said, taking the weapons from the Interceptor pilot.

"Sounds very administrative and dull," Zak replied, his disappointment deepening.

"I need you and your brother to see what it's going to take to get those four Starbirds operational. Then you're to take the *Athena* and lead everyone out of the pack ice and head back to the Nulark system as fast as you can go. I'll get your full report when I catch up."

"What about you?"

"Don't wait on me," Rick said, stepping to the threshold of the Drake craft. "Chances are, I'm going to be half a step ahead of whoever we end up pissing off. I'll know where to find you and you should know when I'm coming."

"You expect to stir up a hornet's nest?"

"Seems like that's where I usually end up."

"What makes you think the other Captains are even still alive?" Zak asked.

Rick thought a moment.

"I have to think at least some of them are and I'd like to believe we're just like our infantry counterparts; unwilling to leave a man behind. You have your orders, Captain."

"I will go with you," Dãsha said, materializing from behind the assault ship.

"You most certainly will not," Rick objected, trying to stop her from entering. Dãsha hesitated, noticing Rick was a little tentative about blocking her path. "We're going to a place no woman, especially the wife of Caidin Mantose, should ever go."

"All the more reason for me to be with you," Dãsha said moving to pass, but Rick held firm his ground.

"Dãsha, I'm trying to save my wife from getting into the hands of the slave trade..."

"And I have been through the slave trades. I know the Conti Nine Detox station. I know how to get to your Jayda before she is sold. I will be coming with you."

Rick looked into Dãsha's black eyes. Somewhere behind them were the tortured memories of Danis. Perhaps there was some payback for her here.

"Wished you were wearing something else," Rick said moving out of her way.

"A mini dress and high heels are the perfect guise to blend in. I should be showing more cleavage," she said trying to adjust her bosoms up a little. "This top was not designed to show any more than this." She looked at everyone else standing there watching her. "All of you would do well to get out of those foreign uniforms and into something the Drake will understand and feel comfortable around." Dãsha boarded the ship and climbed into one of the gunner's chairs.

Rick looked down at his own uniform.

"She makes a good point. Dacey, do you still have those uniforms from the crew of this thing?" Rick asked turning and closing the door behind him. A moment later, the engines came to life and the assault craft left the landing bay, maneuvered around the bow of *Calypso* and back into the ice tunnel.

*   *   *   *

As they left Acuity, they made a broad orbit around the spherical body of water in space.

"What are we to expect at this detox station?" Rick asked.

"If you're looking for a fight, you won't find it there," Dacey said, adjusting the controls on the assault craft. He turned to the navigation receivers and homed in on the correct navigational beacons. "At least not at the drop off point. It's easy to get into that place. Not that you can do anything about it once you're there. All detox subjects are sealed in a detox chamber when they come in and monitored through the entire process. If a subject doesn't live through the detox, they're vaporized."

"Nice," Rick said giving Dãsha a glance.

"Those that do make it through are prepped for whatever they might be good for."

"I'm not very impressed with this culture of yours."

"Me either." Dacey turned and faced the General.

"Who determines what they're good for?"

"Conti Nine's central computer has a scanning program that makes all the determinations. Takes all the guess work and corruption out of the process."

"Corruption? What possible corruption could there be?" Rick asked, sarcastic.

"Think about it. Yes, the whole system is corrupt, and I know that's what you're getting at. It's sort of like gambling. Everything about gambling is corrupt except for the actual gaming part of it. Everything is closely monitored and regulated. Cheating is not tolerated in any form and is dealt with quite harshly. My point is, the system is designed to keep individuals from skimming off the top or pulling specimens in through the process for themselves. The outbound specimens are thoroughly inspected and monitored as they are presented to potential buyers."

"Can anyone be a potential buyer?"

"As long as you're Drake, and you've got the credits, you can buy whatever you want," Dãsha snapped casually.

"No special permits, not background checks?"

"They don't care. As long as your credit clears and you take the merchandise immediately, no one asks any questions. And they don't want to know what you're going to do with your purchase. That's strictly the buyer's business."

"Do we have any credits?"

"I checked the crew of this thing before we left," Dacey said. "I think there's enough to make a purchase, provided there aren't any high rollers."

"What if there are high rollers?" Greg asked, listening in.

"There are always what you call, *high rollers*," Dãsha commented.

"Then we'll have to take an alternative approach," Rick said fingering his weapons.

Dacey gave Rick's Balkrum a wary look and turned back to the controls. It took only a couple of hours before they were able to identify the Conti Nine Station beacons ahead of them on a marker buoy's path. From this distance, they could see the planet Skadil in its orbit around the Drake sun. It's gravity affecting Acuity's mass; pulling a great funnel of water into space, freezing it and sending it hurtling into Skadil's atmosphere. As they drew closer to the station, they began to mingle with other ships coming and going from the station.

"Should we be worried?" Rick asked, watching several larger ships make a departure from the station. "I thought you said this place was mostly automated?"

"The drop off is," Dacey said, concentrating on his controls. "Unless they've changed their schedule, something they've never done since I've been coming here, you're just seeing merchant ships moving freight in and out. The larger platforms are used as drop off points for incoming and outgoing."

"Is there a way to tell if Jayda is in there?"

"She will be identified on a list of subjects published several days before bidding begins."

"What about the female officers taken from the freighters?" Rick inquired. "Will there be anything in the station's data banks about their whereabouts?"

"Not likely," Dacey replied grimly. "Conti Nine doesn't want to be held responsible for any 'merchandise' that comes through the station, if you get my meaning. Once a subject passes to their new owners, what records they have, go with them. There's really no reason for the station to keep anything on them. I'm sorry."

Rick nodded, disappointed.

"Mister Dacey," Dãsha instructed the pilot. "Pull up the facing pages to Conti Nine's data advertisements. If she is here, she will be on display there."

Dacey handed the controls over to Rick as he worked with the instruments to find the required information.

"Here we go," he finally said as the Conti Nine station information flashed up on an overhead monitor. "Here's the advertisement file." It took only a moment to get it open and start scrolling through the information.

"Don't expect to find her by name," Dãsha said. "Given names mean nothing in the slave trades and it's not likely anyone brought here for processing gave it out anyway. Mister Dacey, please go back to the front of the page and open the symbol that looks like a crescent moon."

"You can just call me Dacey, it's ok."

"I don't know you well enough for that," Dãsha replied.

Dacey did as instructed and a moment later had a multi-screen of pictures coming up on the display. All the subjects were full body depictions, dressed in various outfits. Most of the females pictured were scantily dressed in alluring clothing designed to please the eye for what a potential slave might be used for.

"Look closely, Richard," Dãsha instructed. "Your Jayda may not look familiar to you in this setting."

Rick smiled slightly. He was certain he would know Jayda when he saw her. Like Gunnar and Audra, he would know. Watching the images flash by, he couldn't help wonder what Dãsha might be thinking as she watched with him. *This has got to be difficult for her. She was once a prisoner of this life and now to be going back to…* He became worried as Dacey neared the end of the list. Once or twice the list was stopped and backed up to make sure a picture wasn't missed or a resemblance wasn't mistaken.

"Maybe we better abort this," Greg said as they came to the end of the list for the second time. Rick closed his eyes and rubbed his forehead.

"It may be better to get our people out of Acuity and back to find your friend," Dacey suggested.

"I really thought she'd be here." Rick let out a heavy sigh. "You're correct, of course," he agreed with a heavy heart. "Let's get back to the *Stark* before we draw any attention here."

"Mister Dacey," Dãsha spoke up. "Please go back to the front page and open the starred symbol on the bottom corner of the page."

"What is this, Dãsha?" Rick asked, rubbing his eyes and looking back at the display.

"Late arrivals submitted after the main page was created."

Everyone watched as the images flashed one by one in front of them.

As Dacey neared the end of the page, Rick's heart sank further. Still no recognition of Jayda.

"Now at the bottom of that screen there is another symbol resembling nothing you will recognize. Open that one," Dãsha instructed.

Rick came out of his chair.

"That's her!"

"She is prepped for a closed auction to a special clientele," Dãsha informed him. "Those who are rich and powerful, will be the only ones allowed to bid on her. She will likely be sold into royalty."

"How fitting," Rick said, thinking of her Kalamarion heritage.

"She will be used as a concubine; sexual gratification for her new master."

"Yeah, that's not going to happen."

Rick understood how it worked. She would be used for the pleasure of the buyer and once she had outlived her usefulness, she would be disposed of.

"What's your plan, Sir?" Dacey asked, still holding his inbound course to the station. "It's a good bet we won't be able to gain access to the bidding chamber where she'll be held."

"Even if we could, we don't have enough credits to ante up for an opening bid," Greg pointed out.

Rick looked around outside. They were now among many inbound ships. It would be better if they could intercept Jayda before she reached the bidding chamber. Unfortunately, because they had little idea of where that was or how to reach it, that seemed out of the question. Then there was the problem of how to intercept her from being loaded onto the buyer's transport vessel and if she did make it onboard, how would they stop and board such a vessel? Surely if a buyer could afford such a high price as anticipated, they could afford lots of security and heavy ship defenses. This Drake assault ship couldn't possibly be any kind of a match for what that kind of credit could buy.

"I know of a way," Dãsha announced. "I told you, you would need me." Dãsha unstrapped herself and turned in her chair adjusting her knee-high boots. "Dock the ship in the number four pickup hangar on the far side."

"We can't remain there," Dacey pointed out. "That's for hot pickup and deliveries only. The platform is reserved for sky hook and space claw equipped vessels only."

"You will not be docking there. Just touch down on the platform long enough for me to get out." She stood up and straightened her mini dress, worked her hands through her long black hair, then looked at Rick for approval. "How do I look?"

Rick stared at her for a moment, trying to fathom what she had in mind, but more importantly wondering how he would ever be able to stop her. As the ship neared the platform, Dãsha suddenly remembered something important.

"Oh, almost forgot," she said, fumbling with something on her finger. "I want this back." Dãsha handed Rick her wedding ring.

"And just how am I supposed to get this back to you if you're in there?" Rick asked.

"If you don't see me and Jayda before we get on whatever ship we end up on, which will be one of those four over there," she said pointing to several fancy looking ships docked down the platform. "I'll make it obvious how to pick us up."

Rick was dumbfounded at the tenacious attitude standing before him. She didn't appear to be frightened at all.

"We're just supposed to drive aboard a Royal vessel and pick you up?" Greg inquired, not believing what he was hearing. They were running out of time as Dacey guided the assault ship down toward the platform for the drop.

"Royal vessels leaving this station are all subject to ground security searches as well as sentry searches once they leave. It's standard procedure for them to leave their landing holds open until they are out of Conti Nine flight space. You can drive right in and pick us up. Rick, how do I look?"

Rick was still hung up on what she was purposing. He was having a little or a lot of difficulty getting over the whole chivalry concept. Shouldn't it be him that was going in? He was a Thane; he had the weapons; he could weld a mean Balkrum. Why was this young, shapely woman going in to rescue his wife instead of him?

Exasperated, Dãsha turned to the door and touched the activator as the ship slipped inside the protected shield barrier and set down on the platform. The droning of the assault ship's engines growled through the open door as Dãsha moved to the threshold.

"Dãsha!" Rick jumped to the door. She turned her head to him, her hands grasping the door opening. He gave her an *OK* gesture and winked. "You look stunning, as you always do." Dãsha smiled and blew Rick a kiss, then stepped from the ship, disappearing through a service door moments later.

"Wished she'd blow me a kiss," Greg complained wishfully. "Sir, do you think it is a good idea, letting her go in alone?"

Dacey brought the ship up off the deck and throttled back out just as another larger craft was making its run for the platform.

"Chief," Rick finally said with a developing smile. "I don't think any of us have any say in the matter."

"So, what do we do now?" Dacey asked, piloting the ship away from the congested side of the Conti Nine station.

"We wait and watch those four ships. I think now would be a good time to try on those Drake uniforms these guys left us," Rick suggested.

"We can't just hang out here," Dacey said.

"Just fly around so you don't attract any attention from anyone."

"How do you do that?"

"I don't know, fly casual."

The Kalamarion General's instructions seemed quite vague to Dacey. What he didn't realize was the General was every bit as much in the dark as the others were.

*   *   *   *

No sooner had Dãsha entered the station, than she stumbled into a platform worker. Once they had recovered from the collision, they just stared at one another. Dãsha was waiting to see what the worker was going to do and the worker was checking out the curves on the beauty standing before him.

"Where did you get loose from?" The dock worker asked still looking her up and down.

"I don't remember for sure," Dãsha said, acting disoriented. "I was being dressed for the royals, got pushed through a door and the next thing I know, I'm wandering the halls. It's a good thing I ran into you when I did. Can you lead me back to the prepping chambers?"

"Not sure how you could have possibly gotten out of there without someone noticing," the worker said. He seemed to be trying to calculate something. Perhaps keeping the subject for himself. If no one had noticed her missing, she could be long gone before anyone was the wiser. Several guards materialized from the other end of the hallway, helping the worker make up his mind.

"Security," he called, getting their attention. "I've got a wayward subject here. She needs to be taken back to the high end chambers for final prep."

"Which one are you from?" One of the guards asked as they stopped in front of her.

"I don't remember for sure," Dãsha said, trying to think.

"Still disoriented from detox," one of the guards suggested.

"Do you remember which chamber you came from?"

"No."

"It can only be one of four," another guard said. "How hard can it be?"

"Have you ever gone through detox?" another guard snapped.

"This happens far too often," another one complained. "Especially in this section. We get this kind of crap happening all the time in the general sections, but that's to be expected. Not sure how this keeps happening in this one. Come on," a guard grabbed her arm and positioned her between himself and another guard. "Let's get her back before she's missed."

Dãsha had to exercise a bit of restraint to keep from tearing the guard's fingers off one by one as they escorted her down the hall.

"Do you remember anything about the room you were in?" One guard quizzed her.

326

"That's a stupid question for a chamber female," another guard complained. "All the rooms are the same."

"Do you remember anything or anyone in the room?" the first guard rephrased his question.

Dãsha shook her head in an uncertain fashion as they turned several corners and passed through a few security check points. Presently, they entered a hallway lined with many doors and smaller adjoining halls.

"There was another woman being prepped with me. She was blonde, not quite as tall as me."

"That narrows it down a little."

"Is this her?" a guard asked opening a door.

Dãsha looked in at a woman still being dressed. The woman turned and looked at her, her eyes filled with fear. For a moment, Dãsha froze, flashing back to her first time being sold as Danis. The fear she saw in the woman's eyes was the same. Painful as it was, Dãsha shook her head and turned, knowing she was helpless to prevent what this poor creature was about to be subjected to.

"If it's not this last one, you're in a lot of trouble, woman." The lead guard reached for the other door and deactivated the locking mechanism.

Dãsha looked in, afraid to see another face riddled with fear and uncertainty. The woman inside turned and looked at her. Dãsha nodded carefully.

"Try a little harder to keep a leash on your females," one of the guards ordered, shoving Dãsha into the room and closing the door before anyone could object.

The two female attendees stopped what they were doing and one approached the tall slender woman standing in front of the door.

"Where did you come from? You weren't in here before." The attendee circled Dãsha, checking her for presentation purposes.

"Doesn't matter," the other attendee said as she finished dressing their subject. "Better make her as ready as you can with what she has or Gatheos will be angry. It doesn't matter if she was in here before or not. Let them be sold and they can fight out the financial tangle later. That's not something we should have to deal with." The attendee refocused on her subject.

"Well, you're not the best I've seen, but I think we can make what you have on work. It's your hair that needs the help," she said pulling on Dãsha's flowing mane.

"I thought her hair looked just fine," the other attendee commented. She didn't even look up when there came a sharp thump and a gentle rustling sound. "Just hurry, we only have a minute or so left before they open our wall for display and bidding. Maybe you could just cut it off at the neckline really quick. You're good with hair cutters."

"There will be no hair cutting," a commanding voice said from behind. "My hair is perfect the way it is."

"Don't worry, Finney is very good with…" the attendee couldn't finish her sentence as a firm hand slapped over her mouth and she was pulled away from the short pedestal. Dãsha put a finger to her lips to quiet the attendee as she pulled her over next to her companion lying motionless against a wall. Dãsha set her down next to her companion, but held her hand firmly over her mouth.

"Now, it is important for you to know that my head is far stronger than yours and if you make a sound, I'll head butt you like I did your friend. Don't worry, you won't be in trouble. I will be sold right alongside this woman." Dãsha gestured for an understanding and the attendee nodded, her eyes wide. After reiterating her silence, the attendant was released and Dãsha maneuvered next to the woman on the pedestal just as the opening indicators on the facing wall began to glow.

"Do exactly what I tell you and we'll both have a chance of getting out of this together," Dãsha whispered as the door gave way. "Smile and look sexy."

"Who are you?" the bewildered woman asked.

"You are Jayda Niker."

"Yes, but…"

"Explanations are best kept for later. Right now, we must stay together. Now sell it, Jayda Niker!"

Both women looked out at the private audience numbering fifteen to twenty individuals. Soft techno music began to play as Dãsha started to gently swing her hips and move forward. Jayda watched her wide-eyed, wondering if she had ever been able to move in such a manner at that age. But as it seemed their lives might depend on how well she *sold it*; whatever *it* was, she started to gently sway back and forth as well. Feeling extremely self-conscious about stepping down off the little pedestal, she nearly lost her balance trying to make sure she didn't expose herself. The mini skirt she was wearing was shorter than the one her younger counterpart had on. Having her bosoms half exposed did nothing for her comfort level either and bending over was out of the question as she was sure she would spill out. After several uncomfortable minutes of twisting and swaying around the display area, Jayda observed several men and women get up and approach. Frightened, Jayda looked over at Dãsha as they were examined closer. She noticed a few were reaching out to touch the tall beauty, but got their hands slapped away. Jayda graciously spun away from the small group trying to surround her and over next to Dãsha.

"How long do I need to keep this up?"

"You'll know," Dãsha whispered while gyrating her hips.

"I'm not one who enjoys other's putting their hands on me."

"Nor do I, but when your life is on the line, you do what is required."

"My life? Who are you? What are you doing here?"

"Preserving our dignity."

"This is hardly dignified!"

"Just keep moving. We're almost finished." Dãsha slapped another hand away and Jayda followed her lead until a loud tone rang out. Everyone around the two women dispersed and sat back down, while Dãsha and Jayda were instructed to sit in a set of chairs off to the side of the display area.

"Now what's happening?"

"Do not speak," Dãsha warned with a raised hand. She scanned the room carefully, looking at the dark faces before them. There seemed to be movement towards the back of the room and several people got up and hurried out. Moments later, a couple of guards escorted the two out of the viewing area and into another room where several men and women were waiting.

"You, the light haired woman," one of them ordered looking at Jayda. "You will come with us." Two men reached out and grabbed her, while a third installed wrist binders and a mouth guard. Even more frightened, Jayda did her best to look back at Dãsha as the same was done for her. A neck collar was installed on both women and they were escorted to the door. Before leaving, a woman came forward and installed some kind of an electronic device on the collars and encoded something on a hand-held device she was working with.

"You both have privileged new homes. Serve your new masters well and you'll live a long life in their service." The attendant motioned for the two women to be separated and taken to waiting ships a short walk to the landing platform.

Jayda looked back at Dãsha horrified. Things were happening too fast. She had a pretty good idea what having a new master meant, but she had been holding out hope that maybe this nightmare was just a mistake and she would be offered an apology, set on a transport and sent back to her ship and husband. Now she was being led away like an animal toward a grand looking ship for a life of unspeakable things. She looked over as Dãsha was led away, toward the ship docked next to the one she was being loaded onto. She caught one last glimpse of Dãsha as she started up the ramp and into the ship. Once inside, Jayda was taken to her own birth and her mouth guard removed. Still wearing her wrist shackles and neck collar, she was left, locked inside. Now, she could only wonder. She knew what was to come and decided it would be better for her if she had perished in the escape pod or even back on the *Athena* when the alien battlecruiser had attacked. Her circumstance was no different now. If she was to survive, she would have to fight to do so.

Shortly after she felt the ship depart, she looked out the port window, noticing several blinking warning lights on the platform and several guards scrambling toward the ship. She expected the ship to stop and return to the platform, but the Conti Nine station continued to recede. Moments later, a man in flowing robes entered the room. He secured the door and turned to the woman huddled on the long-padded bench beneath the porthole.

"There is no need to be frightened, my dear," he said removing his outer garments. "I treat my women very well as long as they reciprocate." He sat next to her and let his hand slide up her knee toward her thigh.

"Reciprocate this," she growled. Adrenalin burst throughout her being as she swung a leg over his head and locked her ankles around his neck, then rolled over, taking him right to the floor. She felt his fingers gouging into her thighs as he pulled to free himself from the head lock. Feeling him winning his freedom, she wrapped her shackled wrists under his chin and pulled as hard as she could. As he shifted his attention to the new threat, Jayda flexed her thighs even harder. Gritting her teeth, something inside her seemed to snap as all she could think of was cutting this man's air supply off until he quit moving; quit breathing. As she continued to fight for her life, she felt the ship jolting slightly and glancing up at the porthole, saw the stars shift direction. There came a pounding at the door, that turned into a booming as someone tried to gain entry. A moment later, there was a blast from the outside, sparks flying from the door mechanism and the door was forced open. Even the commotion didn't avert Jayda from continuing her death hold on the man. His rescuer would have to shoot her and then it would be over anyway.

"Well, I see you have things well in hand," a familiar voice said. "Maybe I should wait outside until you've finished him off?" Dãsha chuckled and bent down to free Jayda's assailant, but found that even she had to use extra strength to loosen Jayda's death grip on the unconscious man. "Come on," Dãsha said trying to coax Jayda back from defensive mode. "I think you've made your point. Let him go." Jayda finally released him and rolled away, crouching on the floor against the bench like a frightened animal. "You're all right," Dãsha tried to calm the wild-eyed woman. She finally sat down on the bench, pulled her up next to her and held her. "Don't worry, we need to just sit tight for a few minutes. Our ride should be here shortly."

Jayda was shaking. The adrenaline high was crashing and it was all she could do to keep from bursting into tears. She looked up into the black eyes of her new-found friend, wondering how she had ever made it through the door, let alone onboard the ship.

"Who are you?" Jayda realized she was almost hyperventilating and did her best to slow her breathing.

"You may call me Dãsha, Dãsha Mantose."

Jayda felt like she should know the name, but nothing came to mind, nor did it seem important. The first thoughts of logic coming back to her was to get out of this room and to an escape pod; get off the ship. She tried to get up, but Dãsha held her firm.

"Hey, there is no hurry for now. You go outside this room and the crew will know something is up. Right now, we're just being sampled by our new master." Dãsha gave the unconscious man on the floor a nudge with her boot.

"What about you? Did they see you come in?"

"If they had, they would have already been in here."

"How are we going to get out of here and if we do, where are we going?"

Dãsha strained to look out the porthole.

"If things go the way they're supposed to, we should be boarded shortly by a Drake assault vessel and we'll catch a ride out with them."

"Why are they coming? Didn't we just get away from them?" Jayda was missing something here and in truth, Dãsha meant to keep as much from her as she could, for now.

"Different guys," Dãsha said, stretching her leg out and giving the man starting to rouse a swift kick to the side of the head. The man dropped back to the floor motionless.

"How did you get out of your binders?" Jayda asked looking for some kind of marks on her. It couldn't have been easy.

"Oh, yes. I'm sorry," Dãsha said. She grabbed Jayda's binders and holding them just right, gave them a quick twist at an odd angle and the binders fell away from Jayda's reddened wrists. "You would think after all this time, they would fix that problem." Dãsha carefully pulled Jayda's hair to one side and worked the mechanism to release the collar, then dropped the articles on the floor and stomped on them. Both women detected something flash past the porthole and got up.

"Ah, here they are, as I knew they would."

"So, what are we supposed to do?"

"Give them a minute to land and start their search. Once I'm caught, I'll see that they take you with me."

"I'm not getting this at all," Jayda responded.

"Just be patient and all will make sense in good time." Dãsha moved to the door and peered outside, listening quietly. A wall com came alive in the room they were holed up in. Dãsha looked at the com unit and frowned.

"I was hoping they would try to take care of this by themselves," she complained as she activated the com. "You dare to disturb my Master during love making. Whatever it is, can wait."

"We've been boarded by a Drake sentry party. They require a full search of the ship." The voice sounded insistent.

"Then let them search the ship, but leave us to our privacy."

"It is the new slave acquisition. They're insisting on making match verifications. One of the other slaves escaped her master and they claim she boarded our ship."

"Let them search until they are satisfied. We will be out to make the verifications when we are finished." The com went silent and Dãsha turned to Jayda, who looked at her bewildered. "Come on, time to go."

"Go? Where are we going? You've just announced where we are to the entire ship. We might as well stand out in the hall and call for them to come and get us."

"Nonsense," Dãsha said helping Jayda to her feet. "We need to get to the landing bay and get on that sentry ship as soon as we can."

"You're insane!" Jayda cried. "I'm not moving from this spot until you tell me exactly what's going on."

Dãsha looked back at Jayda. Exasperated, she turned back to the door, then turned back to Jayda, who stood defiant with her arms folded. Dãsha had a good mind to just belt her unconscious and carry her to the landing bay. It would have been more efficient, but decided against it as she had already formed a bit of an attachment to her.

"The General has come for you. He's waiting in the landing bay!"

Jayda dropped her hands, her expression shifting to disbelief.

"What General? General who?"

"Niker! Richard Niker! Your husband! We have to go now!" Hearing a fire fight developing down the hall, Dãsha's tone was near to panic.

"Rick is here?" Jayda rushed to the door right behind Dãsha. "How did he find me?"

"Is that really important?"

"No, we need to get to the landing bay as quick as we can. Stop wasting time! Go, go, go!" Jayda held a hand to Dãsha's back as they bolted from the room and down the hall. Both women slammed against a wall next to the tiny landing bay and peered across at the assault ship sitting only feet away. Trouble was, there was a wall of laser fire and ordnance tracers in their way. Dãsha looked at both ends of the bay and then back at the assault ship. The door was right there. A couple of steps and they could be inside.

"You stay here," Dãsha said taking a couple of steps back.

"Wait, what…?"

Dãsha breezed past Jayda, diving through the fire fight and into the open hatch.

"Not very lady like," Jayda muttered, watching Dãsha get up and pull her dress down over her exposed bottom. Dãsha motioned for Jayda to remain where she was and disappeared deeper inside the ship. A few moments later, Jayda observed one of the side gun turrets moving, its barrels swinging forward at the line of combatants firing at the other end of the landing bay. Jayda studied the situation carefully.

There was something not right about the cargo the ship's security guards were taking cover behind. Some of it was starting to burn quite robustly. There was a riddle of tracer rounds that shattered one of the crates, spilling its contents across the landing bay floor. Jayda's eyes widen, recognizing explosives. Out of her peripherals, she saw someone rushing up the hall behind her. She took a couple of steps back and then sprang forward, leaping as Dãsha had. She came to an un-lady like landing on the floor of the assault ship just inside the open hatch. Not worrying about whether she was still covered, she ran forward into the cockpit just as Dãsha started firing rounds into the line of guards.

"That looks like some kind of ammunition you're shooting at!"

Dãsha looked out her window at the shattered boxes that were now burning briskly.

"Oops!" she exclaimed, changing her aim to the bay wall. Jayda looked at the pilot's station and scrambled into the seat. The instruments were laid out in a simplistic manner. *How did these people ever colonize space in a craft such as this?* She touched the start buttons and the engines immediately fired. *Anti-grav over here and maneuvering thrusters over there*. It was almost too easy. Feeling the ship come off the bay floor, she eased the thrusters backward and started to pull out as one of the crates in front of them abruptly exploded. *Why was a royal transport carrying a bay full of explosives?* As the ship found the threshold of the bay, there came a clamor from the side hatch behind the two women.

"What in the heck do you two think you're doing?" Chief Tanetto hollered as he picked himself up off the floor. Crewman Dacey stood in the hatchway spraying a stream of tracer fire from his rifle and then stepped back as another form jumped through the door and fell to the floor.

"It's called a rescue," Dãsha yelled indignant. "Floor it!" she barked, taking aim at the line of crates in front of the retreating assault craft. There was a loud clang from the hatchway as the door slammed shut and moments later, brilliant fire balls erupted from the bay as the crates began to explode. Jayda pulled the reverse throttles all the way back to full power as a wall of fire enveloped the front end of the ship. There was a sudden flash and then the blackness of space surrounded them.

"Go, go, go!" Dãsha called from her turret. Jayda shut down the reverse thrusters and shoved the other set of throttles all the way forward. Moments later, there was an enormous jolt as the shock wave from the exploding transport rolled past them. Dacey was quick to make it forward, Jayda gladly vacating the pilot's chair. When she turned around, she came face to face with the man she had only a slim hope of ever seeing again. Rick smiled broadly, hefting a rifle over his shoulder.

"I see you two girls have gotten to know each other rather well."

For a split second, Jayda was a little upset Rick wasn't more emotional about their reunion. But she couldn't hold herself back and her arms and legs went into overdrive as she flung herself onto him. Heavy kissing and mauling were the order of the moment, until Greg Tanetto called out sentry fighters approaching from the rear.

"Thought you'd never find me," Jayda gasped, out of breath. She looked into Rick's eyes, still wondering if she were dreaming.

"You sure know how to get away from it all," Rick answered, still wanting to embrace, but the urgency of their situation called for other measures.

"Crewman Dacey, let's get on to phase two of this operation."

"What about those sentry ships coming up behind us, Sir?" Greg inquired heading to the port aft gun turret.

"Are we headed in the right direction yet, Mister Dacey?"

"No, Sir," the pilot answered. "I'm still a little disoriented due to our little escape maneuver from the red flames of death."

"Saved your sorry behinds," Dãsha shot back. "What kind of a rescue do you call that anyway?"

"Sorry," Rick said, setting Jayda down. "Their guards thought something was up when there were two assault ships trying to board at the same time. That ordnance stockpile was a little unexpected, but got us out of a sticky fix. Here," Rick said holding something out to Dãsha. "You said you wanted this back."

Dãsha smiled, taking her wedding band and slipping it back on.
"Thank you, Richard."

"Mister Dacey?" Rick dropped his rifle on the floor and pulled his jacket off. "How much punishment can this bucket absorb from those fighters?"

"You've seen them at work in the ice, General. We can take a few hits."

"Bring 'em in closer," Greg said defiantly as he slipped behind the controls of his gun turret. "Sir."

Rick looked up at the elevated control chair of the top turret and then down at the bottom turret's chair sunk in the floor.

"You up for this?" he asked turning to Jayda.

Jayda didn't even hesitate. While she had no desire to ever get back in one, she knew these weren't escape pods and if they were mortally wounded, there would be no way out this time. She grabbed both Ricks hands and swung herself down into the bottom turret chair and started working the controls.

"No course corrections until after we've gotten rid of these guys," Rick ordered as he climbed up into the top turret. "I don't want them communicating to anyone where we might be headed."

"Aye, Sir," Dacey responded.

"Hold your fire until I give the order." Rick was just getting into place when a stream of tracers swung out to their starboard side and touched one of the fighters maneuvering ahead of their position. There was an instant burst of flame as the ship broke apart and then nothing.

"I said hold your fire until I give the order." It was a somewhat hollow reprimand as the shot had been pinpoint accurate. Rick looked down at Dãsha taking aim at the next fighter trying to maneuver into position. "You're not going to wait, are you?"

Dãsha only gave him a glance and pulled the triggers, giving Rick cause to grumble.

"Glad you're not on the *Athena*," he mumbled swinging his turret around and squirting off a short burst at an incoming fighter. "Let's light 'em up," he ordered pushing his headset into place.

The little assault ship was promptly filled with a nearly unbearable amount of noise as the ordnance guns banged with every squeeze of the trigger. Even the old Thumpers he and Gunnar used to fly didn't make this much noise. He found himself thinking about how much nicer it was on board a Starbird. There was almost no noise except what the crew was chattering about during a battle. As a fighter made a sharp swing across the top of the assault ship, Rick watched its tracers pound into the assault craft's armor plating, small pieces popping and twirling off in their wake.

"Little help down here," Jayda called into the com system. "Two of them coming up from below!"

Rick spun his turret around looking into his scope visor, anticipating where the attacking craft would pop up. He waited with his fingers on the triggers, but nothing happened. He looked away from his scope in time to detect two flashes from below off the starboard side. When he looked around, there was nothing. Both attacking fighters had disintegrated. He looked down at Dãsha. She was moving her turret back into a defensive position.

"The last one is trying to make a frontal," Dacey called out.

Rick and Jayda spun their turrets forward, sighting in the last fighter as it turned to rake them with its powerful guns. Rick heard a clamor from below as the fighter made its turn and came right at them. Tracers streaked past his turret as he pulled his triggers and sprayed a quick burst at the incoming craft. Jayda's tracers also reached out toward the fighter as it weaved toward them. There came a sudden burst from the forward port gun turret and the fighter blew apart, scattering in pieces. Rick saw the pilot's limp figure narrowly miss his turret as they blew through the debris. When he looked down into the main compartment, Dãsha was just getting out of the forward port gun turret.

"These guns are poorly calibrated," Dãsha said, sitting down in one of the crew chairs behind the turret stairs. Jayda took Rick's hand as he helped her out of the lower turret and into his arms.

"That's about as far away from you as I ever want to get," she said, hugging him tight.

"Ditto," he said looking forward. "Mister Dacey?"

"Plotting a roundabout course over to Skadil right now. Estimated arrival time at full speed; about six hours."

"Good, I suggest we all get some rest. We still have a long day ahead of us." Rick and Jayda sat down across from Dãsha, who sat upright in what looked like an uncomfortable position. "I suspect you've got a couple of questions you'd like to ask."   Rick smiled as he relaxed a bit, taking the opportunity to look over every part of Jayda's face. He had been so focused on her rescue and their subsequent escape, he hadn't been able to really look at her. Now he could take the time to get reacquainted with every feature he had come to love over the years.

"I'm not sure six hours is enough time to answer all the questions I have," Jayda finally said softly. She leaned into his shoulder and closed her eyes, feeling his arm come around her. She snuggled in as close as she could and tried to absorb the moment. She could take command when needed, but right now, she was content to be a woman with her man as her protector. She pulled on the hem on her mini dress, trying to cover herself, but it felt like there wasn't enough material to do so.

"I'd be a lot more comfortable if I were in a suit or something besides this thing that hardly covers my butt. Don't know how she can stand it," Jayda said looking over at Dãsha.

"I might be able to do something about that," Rick said, sizing up Dacey and Greg.

"She can have my pants; we're about the same size," Dacey said without looking back. "They're behind the seat back there."

"Thank you," Jayda grinned, reaching back and grabbing the clothes, she pulled them on under the mini dress. "I'm way too old to be wearing something like this."

"Hey, remember I'm your age," Rick pointed out, giving Dãsha a glance. She appeared unphased by the comments, keeping her eyes closed.

"You wouldn't look very good in a mini skirt anyway," Jayda teased. "So, what can you tell me about where in the universe we are? I activated the stasis system shortly after I ejected and have no idea how long I was in that turret pod."

Rick gave a heavy sigh, wondering how he would ever explain everything without causing a great deal of confusion.

"I reached the *Athena* shortly after you jettisoned, but didn't dare pursue for fear that Albion ship would come back and attack again."

"The last hit we took nearly blew the ship apart. What happened to her?"

"After I got back onboard, I was able to stabilize it and make some repairs. I would have just left her, but there were wounded onboard."

"Understandable."

"We lost nearly half the crew."

"I watched the engineers die," Jayda said, staring off at nothing.

"It's what happens in war. You have to put it out of your mind."

"Those were our friends; our family."

"Yes, and so are you. Sometimes bad things happen to good people."

"I know," Jayda said putting her face in her hands and rubbing her eyes. "That doesn't make it any easier to take. Who survived the attack?"

"Lisa Dayton, Toby Mavis, Laura Habba and the Korack twins."

"They launched in Interceptor Two."

"And followed your trail."

"Any sign of them?"

"Yes, they found me during a little skirmish we had earlier. Came along just in time."

"How long was I in the pod?"

"Nearly six months. I was only about a day behind when I finally caught up to you."

"I don't understand," Jayda said, a perplexed look on her face. "How come it took you so long to catch up to me?"

Rick drew in a deep breath, wondering how to explain his encounters in becoming a Thane and charged with protecting Gunnar, CJ and Janox.

"Trying to figure out how to track where the pod took you was a bit on the technical side. That and Gunnar got himself into a bit of a fix. Took a little time to unravel."

Bewildered, Jayda looked at Rick for a long moment. His deep expression told her there was a long story as to the whys and she would come to understand them in time. She trusted him enough to know there was a good reason he had put Gunnar ahead of her wellbeing.

"Ok," she said, accepting the explanation gap for now. "So, you know Dãsha and I had an eventful introduction. Tell me about how you met her."

"The universe is a small place," Rick said chuckling softly. "You're looking at the wife of Caidin Mantose." He looked to Jayda to see the recognition. It took her a moment to put the puzzle together. She looked at the younger woman, then back at Rick.

"*Thee* Caidin Mantose? Mantose surgical instruments, Inc.?"

"And Toberrian synthetic growth systems."

"Don't forget about the Thulport holographic analyzer." Dãsha said without opening her eyes.

Both Rick and Jayda looked across at Dãsha.

"Any relation to Tiana and Taron?"

"He's their father."

"What about…?" Jayda nodded toward Dãsha.

"It is complicated," Dãsha said remaining unmoved and eyes closed. "Richard will explain it to you at a later, more appropriate time and place."

Jayda stared at Dãsha for a moment, then looked at Rick.

"I found her and Caidin marooned on a disabled ship called *Calypso*, in a planet called Acuity."

"Acuity?" Jayda repeated.

"The water planet on the other side of Skadil."

"Ah," Jayda nodded. "Now I know as much as I did before."

"I'll show you a sectional when we're finished with this next operation."

"What is this next operation anyway?"

"While I was a guest of Caidin and Dãsha, he showed us where the *Athena* was and…"

"Wait, the *Athena* is here?"

"Sorry, there are a lot of gaps here. When I left to go find Gunnar, I sent the *Athena* to find you. CORA had specific orders not to deviate from her task to find the escape pod. When she caught up to it, you were already gone. She reasoned that you had been picked up by four freighters stuck in the ice pack deep in Acuity's ocean. She was cutting through the ice to reach those trapped ships when Caidin and Dãsha detected the *Athena* and the other ships. Unfortunately, the Drake had found them too and we had a bit of a fight over ownership. This assault ship is one of the spoils of war from that encounter. The *Athena* is parked in the *Stark's* hold while our two Korack twins unpack all the goodies they found on the freighters."

"Where did the freighters come from?"

"From the same place we did," Rick burst quietly. "They are the four Kendalon freighters we went to rescue from the Oneida. How astronomically improbable is it that we ended up, not only here, but in the same time they did?"

"Wherever here is," Jayda grinned.

"Anyway," Rick paused, thinking. "Where was I?"

"This operation?"

"Oh, yes, operation. The freighters have been in this area for some time, dodging would be takers of their cargo. They were finally boarded by the Drake and the Captains and First officers taken prisoner. Some were sent to the Oslerian mining colony on Skadil."

"And we're going in to try and bring them back out."

"No man left behind."

"How long have they been there?"

"Too long," Greg said, only half awake.

Rick hesitated, but Dacey leaned back.

"The Skadil mines are no place for anyone who wishes to live very long. It's dark and hot. You're not allowed to get sick or hurt. If you do, you're either vaporized or turned loose on the surface. Humans don't last long on the surface, at least not yet."

"If they're still alive, we're going to try to save them," Rick said.

"Save them?" Jayda repeated. "How are we going to save people from a place like that? You're not even going to be able to fight your way in and if you did, you certainly aren't going to be able to fight your way back out. We barely got off that royal transport and those fighters back there."

"Mister Dacey tells me you can request people be brought back out for a price or to answer to other charges. Our hope is to go in as Drake officers and pull them out without anyone making any noise about it."

"And what if they do make noise?"

"We'll have to get out fast."

Jayda was hardly convinced, but understood the need to try something.

"I think we need to rest a little for now," Rick said getting comfortable next to Jayda, who snuggled in closer. She couldn't wait to get back to the *Athena* and enjoy some semblance of home, but for now, this was heaven.

Good people

Gunnar's head struck a huge tree limb, sending his mind reeling into a mass of chaos. Cartwheeling out of control, he thought he heard something make a cracking noise.

Was that a tree branch making that sound? Why is my arm hurting so bad? What is that falling next to me? Blink the eyes, Gunnar! That'll clear the vision right up. He hit a larger branch. *Grab it! Ouch! Moving too fast... That's not working. Ouch, I think my hands are on fire! Gotta get stopped before I hit the ground! Vines! Ouch, that hurts! Gotta get stopped! Gotta get stopped! Come on, Gunnar! Get yourself tangled up in these. That's the only thing that's going to save your life.*

Forming a natural netting, the tangle of vines and falling branches caused him to come to an ignominious stop. Wildlife scattered at the sudden ruckus, their noisy calls and chatter continuing for several moments after he had come to a halt. Somehow, he had kept his arms up in front of his face and his forearms had prevented the vines from wrapping around his neck. With his head still spinning out of control, his body throbbed from his outer skin to his inner organs. Battered and bruised, he wasn't sure what his condition was. He tried to turn his head up, but now the trauma was starting to register and he felt quite sick. He opened his eyes, but saw only billows of blackness and sparkles drifting through his vision. Trying to breathe normal, he realized everything was starting to go quiet. Then he saw nothing, heard nothing, and felt nothing.

Well, that was a lot of fun. Maybe when I find out where my brain fell out, I can climb back up and do it again? Something is poking at my arm and it hurts. I can't move; actually, I don't want to move. Is anything else hurting? Nope, guess I got lucky; at least for now. Let's see, what was I doing that got me into this ridiculous situation? Gunfire... Running... I can't remember what I was doing. Come on, Gunnar, think... He opened his eyes and looked around. *What the devil is poking at me?* Gunnar struggled in the tangle to see his arm. Finally able to get his head turned far enough, he found a strange looking fowl poking its beak at one of his many open wounds. Wiggling and contorting had no effect on the creature. Tipping himself in one direction, he then rolled back the other way. The bird squawked loudly, flapping its wings, but Gunnar continued and rolled over on top of it.

"How does that feel?" he gritted angrily. "You like it? That's right!"

The bird stopped moving and fell silent. Gunnar figured it was just pinned in place and waiting for release. He wanted to stay right where he was, just to torment the animal for pecking at him, but he was uncomfortable enough. He had no idea how long he had been unconscious. Grabbing the vines above him, he hoisted himself up into a sitting position and almost fell out of the vines. Looking down toward the ground, he watched the bird's limp body fall. It hit a large tree trunk and disappeared under the ground foliage.

I've killed it. Serves it right! My arm still hurts.

Surveying his surroundings, he paid special attention to the ground, or at least where it should be. The growth was so thick, he couldn't see dirt. Perhaps more importantly, he couldn't see any movement. All he could hear were noises of the jungle. He had no idea how he had gotten here or what direction to go. The upper canopy looked the same no matter what direction he looked. Feeling wet from perspiration and blood loss, he was about as uncomfortable as he could remember. His arms and hands were tiring, not to mention the pain returning to his extremities. In fact, he was starting to feel all the places he had received an injury, especially his head. He carefully started swaying in the vines, gradually freeing himself and working his way onto a large tree branch. Standing against the huge trunk, he felt a little safer now. He made his way around the trunk and found a larger branch intersecting with the branch he was on. He found the higher up he was able to go the easier the branches were to climb and the more they intersected. He had only to find another one and step up.

He finally broke through the canopy layer and looked around. He had to nearly close his eyes as the bright light stung, causing streams of tears to form. All he could see were treetops and there was just as much animal noise up here as below. A light breeze carried some of the heat and humidity away, but it wasn't enough to ease much of his discomfort. An ominous wall of dark clouds was forming, moving rapidly in his direction. Sharp flashes of lightning spiked from the cloud bases as they approached, and the roll of thunder became more prominent.

He looked at his arms and legs, seeing large tears in his clothes and bloody wounds still weeping. Several spots on his legs and side hurt more than the others and upon closer examination he found large holes in his flesh. *What has happened to me?* A couple of the holes had something hard in them and with a little careful digging, he pulled a metal object from his muscle. *It's a bullet! How did that happen?* The other wounds were far too painful to attempt to extract the metal projectiles. He would require help getting them out and the wounds properly tended.

Before the sun disappeared behind the towering clouds, he turned his gaze up, catching sight of a large ship in orbit. It's distinctive shape looked familiar to him.

"I should know what that is," he thought. A moment later he turned around, hearing the roar of engines behind him. A small craft rose from the jungle canopy some distance away and arced skyward. *I should be able to find help over there… I think.* He needed to get out of this jungle to someplace more hospitable and find some help.

The rain came in warm torrents. Gunnar ducked under the canopy of broad leaves, trying to use them as a shield to avoid being pelted. Negotiating the thick tangle of jungle vegetation was slow going as the tree surfaces had become slippery with the rain. Traversing back and forth on the huge tree limbs was somewhat frustrating. To get to one path leading him forward, he had to navigate through several others that took him in a different direction. Each time he ventured down to move in a straighter line, he would get slowed down in the tangle of branches and vines. Doing his best to stay as high up in the canopy as he could, he found the foliage thinner and walking a little easier. The rain finally stopped, but the clouds remained overhead, keeping him from knowing for sure if he were moving in the right direction. He couldn't tell if it was still daylight or not.

Several times he stopped to rest, only to notice the jungle actually moving. At one point he paused in a high clearing on an enormous tree branch and sat watching the jungle move. Plants were in a constant state of growth and decay. Some were reaching up to find light, while others were being choked out. Their remnants were quickly consumed by the other life forms; even the animal life moved in a similar fashion. Some creatures appeared ominous and ferocious, but were easily subdued by others or by the jungle itself. As he watched, he could see the vines growing, in constant motion. Even the trees moved, their growth clearly visible.

Continuing to struggle along the branches, he unexpectedly found himself standing out in the open on a tree branch. Jumping back behind the thick leaves, he peered out into a clearing. There was an elevated landing platform in front of him. Scanning the area, he observed various types of craft sitting parked in several rows. Moving back into the trees, he worked his way to the edge of the platform and stepped down onto its hard surface.

Access to the platform was through the building below. Taking notice of the security cameras mounted on the four quarters of the platform, he moved from ship to ship, but found all of them well secured. Hanging around until someone decided to leave wasn't much of an option. Making his way to the other side of the platform, he looked over the side at an entrance. It was a long way to the ground and with open wounds and constant pain plaguing him, he was in no condition to jump. He carefully climbed back into the trees and went about working his way down to the jungle floor, keeping close to the building wall. The further down he descended, the more he had to fight the plant life and an occasional animal. By the time he reached the ground, he was exhausted. There was almost no room next to the wall for him to move and the jungle seemed more determined than ever to keep him from making it to open ground. Finally reaching the corner of the building, he was forced to lay on the ground in order to see all the comings and goings of whatever this installation was. Still feeling sickly and tired, now he could barely stay awake. Remaining pressed against the building, sleep finally took him until the roar of engines woke him with a start.

The sun was gone now and looking out from his hiding place, he observed a small military transport hovering close by. It hung in the air for quite some time before finally dropping its landing gear and settling to the ground on a small maintenance pad next to the building. Moments later, its engines shut down and all was quiet again. A blaze of lights illuminated the ground directly around the transport as the doors opened on both sides and several crewmen disembarked carrying equipment. With the doors down, Gunnar looked up inside the transport. It appeared to be full of equipment, with a minimal crew.

"I still don't understand why we have to be the delivery boys for this stuff," one of the crew said to the other. "A civilian courier service could have done this easier than us."

"For the tenth time," the other replied, irritated, "we already had this stuff onboard and it was just a short detour from our normal route. Unless you're in a huge hurry to get down to Albia, this isn't a big deal. Come on, be part of the team instead of the problem."

"I'd just like to get back before the next hour."

"You've got someone waiting?"

"As a matter a fact, I do."

"Well, it's about time and I feel sorry for the poor girl that has bad eyesight." The crewman stopped and turned, hearing something behind him. "Did you see anything?"

"No, I didn't see anything, nor did I hear anything. Now come on, let's get this stuff delivered and get out of here."

The two men walked into the foyer of the Repos station and to the shuttle pod gate.

"You boys missed all the excitement," the station conductor said, clearing a spot on the counter for the delivery items.

"Sorry, I've seen excitement before, it's highly overrated," one of them said.

"Did you have another Gronck get in the building?" the other asked.

"Colonian terrorists stealing Albion artifacts."

"What's that again?"

"Your Special Forces received a tip that a radical faction of Colonians were here stealing artifacts that had to do with the Thane, Blinda Koss. She nearly got her head taken off by one of the terrorists. She was sporting a shiner and a fat lip when she left here. One of the terrorists killed several of your guys. They all got away, but I'm sure your boys caught them when they tried to leave orbit."

"So what did they get away with?"

"Not sure they got away with anything. One of the MedTech's found a big ugly ring under one of your officers that was killed."

"What kind of ring?

"Told you, a big ugly one. I'm sure they gave it to their Incident Commander."

The two crewmen looked at each other, then shook their heads.

"Well, we just fly transport duty. We generally don't get to hear much about Special Forces or fleet operations. There wasn't anything in orbit when we came down."

"But like you said, if those fanatics did get to orbit, I'm certain ASF caught them quick enough."

The conductor left his imprint on the documents they had presented and the crewman headed back out to their ship and up the boarding ramp.

"You ever wished you had joined the fighter branch, or at least fleet service?"

"Me? Are you kidding? I'm the biggest coward in the armed forces. I like to fly and I like to get paid for it. But I don't like to get paid to die. Come on lover boy. Let's get you down to Albia so you can meet up with whoever this poor girl is. Maybe I should interview her; find out what's wrong with her?"

"What's wrong with her? There's nothing wrong with her."

"Must be, she's interested in you."

"Ha, ha. Very funny."

Both crewmen laughed as they closed the doors and climbed back up into the cockpit. It didn't take long for them to become airborne again, and skimming the jungle tops for only a moment, they piloted their craft skyward. Once obtaining delivery clearance from Dither, they switched over to the Albia Approach frequencies and started down to the capital city, Zepplin. As they reentered the planet's atmosphere, the ride became rough and several alarms came on, giving them cause for worry.

"Never had the intermix coolers shut down before," one of them said.

"There's nothing to them," remarked the other. "The mechs set it and that's it. We can't even access it from here."

"Ok, so we're both at a loss here. We're just coming out of reentry and our engines are dying. How do we get this thing on the ground in one piece?"

"I don't think we can. Contact Zepplin approach control. Tell them our engines are out. We'll steer the ship towards Pantera flats on the dry lakebed and bail out in about two minutes."

"Bail out... I hate free falling and canopy landings. I like it when we're in the Vanguard shuttles. They have escape pods. Let's make it four minutes, just in case something bad happens."

Both crewmen strapped on their exit packs and went to work getting ready to bail out. One started talking on the com system with approach while the other worked to get the ship steered in the right direction.

"Estimated time to impact, five minutes. I'm just gonna shut everything off and let her freefall. No sense taking a chance on this thing wandering off where there might be people."

"Sounds good. Approach says they'll send rescue right out."

"She's been a good ship. If only this had happened before we reentered. Ready?"

"Let's go."

They got out of their seats and worked their way to the aft compartment, activating the controls to open the bay doors. Once the doors were open, they waved to each other and jumped. Making sure they were well clear of the ship, they dove as far and as fast as they could to give the falling hulk plenty of room. There was no need to follow the stricken transport's progress down, as the doomed ship would crash in a dry lakebed. The military would come and clean up the mess after the dust settled.

Gunnar popped his head out of the engine compartment and looked around. Cold air whipped through the cargo compartment and as he moved forward, he realized the cargo doors were wide open on both sides of the ship.

"What the...?" His eyes widened realizing the ship was starting to yaw and he had no safety harness attached to anything. The ship didn't seem to have an operational antigrav either; or it had been turned off. With his hands and feet tingling with the notion he could be swept out of the ship at any moment, Gunnar grabbed hold of the cargo tie downs and pulled himself up on top of the load and toward the front of the hold. Once safely on the front side, he pulled himself into the cockpit. *All the instruments are dark. Where did everybody go?* Looking at the ground below, he surmised there wasn't much time to figure out some course of action. Scanning the cockpit for emergency departure packs, it was obvious the pilots had taken the only two with them. Climbing into one of the seats, he strapped himself in and looked curiously at the controls.

"How hard can it be?" he grumbled angrily. Nothing looked familiar at all, but punching several buttons brought the power back online. Studying the instruments in front of him and to his right, he gave them a sneer and worked the engine throttles to bring the ship out of its plunge. *I can do this... I think.*

Something's wrong; the engines don't feel right. He had corrected the ship's flight attitude, but the ground was still coming up faster than what he was comfortable with. A grin popped across his lips as he touched the retro boosters and wrestled with the controls. Several warning lights began to flash erratically, and alarms blared when he tested the maneuvering thrusters again.

All of a sudden, the ship rolled left and bellied over, diving straight for the ground. Gunnar touched the boosters again and pulled briskly back on the control yoke, bringing the ship out of its dive. With the ground coming up fast, there wasn't a whole lot of time left to make any more attitude corrections. He tapped the boosters again bringing the nose up and leveling out. There seemed to be nothing on the throttle anymore and a quick glance behind him in a turn revealed smoke issuing from the thruster ports. Turning back to the controls, he kept his right hand on the booster controls and the other hand on the yoke. Blowing through a bank of low clouds, a small settlement surrounded by thick forest on the shore of a dry lakebed came into view.

Holding the ailing ship level became nearly impossible as the controls became less effective and the stricken craft veered toward the trees. Flying over a small cluster of buildings, he tried to slow the transport down; maybe put it into a hover for a moment and then drop it in the trees. Several more warning alarms began to sound as he pulled back a little more, but now, pulling back didn't seem to do any good. Gunnar tapped the boosters again, but found only a small change in speed. He looked up in time to see a windshield full of treetops and then everything was obscured. A noisy ruckus ensued as the small transport crashed through the trees and careened to an unceremonious halt on its back.

Still strapped in his seat, Gunnar blinked and looked around. Somewhat stunned, he perceived his vision was inverted. His head pounding, now every part of him felt like someone had beaten him with a big stick. Hanging upside down, he felt something wet coming down his back and chest and brought his hands up to his chin and neck. There was blood running everywhere.

Alarms continued to blare in his ears as smoke filled the cockpit. He looked down at the cockpit ceiling and then up at the buckles on his seat harness. *Well, there's no getting around it; I gotta drop.* Exasperated, he finally pulled the handles on the seat buckles and fell. Crashing to the ceiling, Gunnar let out an agonizing groan and tried not to move, waiting for the pain to pass or see if passing out was what came next. After a long moment, he rolled over and forced himself to his hands and knees. Crawling from the cockpit, he slowly made his way over several wrecked cargo containers. *I'm lucky this stuff didn't blow up.* Squinting, he moved toward a bright stab of light and rolled out one of the open bay doors. Adding insult to injury, he landed on a rock and tumbled against a broken tree stump. This proved too much as his vision rapidly clouded. Turning onto his side he heard footsteps approaching, but it all felt like part of the wild dream filling his mind as everything went dark.

*   *   *   *

Gunnar could hear nothing, which was a real problem. There should be some noise coming from somewhere, anywhere. Birds chirping or wild animals circling his broken body for an afternoon meal, but the only sound was a ringing noise piercing through his head. He hurt from head to toe and felt utterly sick. Hoping to mitigate the pain and nausea, he rolled up onto his side.

Nope, just as painful as before. Best stay on the back. The light stung his eyes when he tried to open them. Squinting seemed to help… *Wait, I'm not outside! Where am I and how did I get here?* As the fog began to clear from his mind, he realized his neck and back were throbbing.

The room was cluttered with various personal belongings. It all looked antique, even the room itself. Much of the furniture was handmade, including the door frame and door. There were windows on two of the walls, but only trees were visible outside. *Maybe I did something to my hearing in the crash?* Checking under the sheets, Gunnar discovered he was no longer in his clothes… or underwear… He settled into the bed a little more, looking around for his clothes.

Uhm, I seem to be without apparel…

Realizing he wasn't covered in blood anymore, he checked his arms and neck, then looked under the bed sheet at his wounds. Still throbbing painfully, they had been cleaned and bandaged.

Bewildered, Gunnar scanned the room again, finally noticing several items on a dresser on the other side of the room. He strained a look at the door, then gingerly swung his legs out from under the covers. As he sat up, the pain increased exponentially. He looked for his clothes again, but they were not to be found. *Perhaps this was a first line of defense for his captors in keeping a prisoner from trying to escape; take all their clothes.*

"Oh, buddy," he grimaced trying to stand. His feet felt like they were going to crumple beneath him. Using a small nightstand to steady himself, he took a tentative step forward. Just the act of trying to walk was painful. Looking down at his legs and feet, he saw bandages all over them. Letting go of the table, he shuffled over to the dresser and looked curiously at the items placed neatly on the top. There were two wrist communicators and a memory chip. He had to think hard, but finally recognized his wrist band. The other one was even more difficult for him. Recalling the chaotic escape from the Repos station, he remembered pulling the band from one of his assailants. Turning back to further the search for his clothes, he stopped long enough to look out the window. Trying to see what was outside, he was caught off guard when the door to his room swung opened. Gunnar put his hand up to shield his already smarting eyes from the glare now streaming into the room from the open door. The silhouette of a human filled the doorway, but the light hurt his eyes so much, he had to close them. Once his eyes stopped throbbing, he realized he was fully exposed and forgetting the pain in his extremities, shuffled back to the bed and covered up.

"Tomah dun teak Malian vomay naliot," an older sounding male voice rasped from the doorway.

"Say what?" Gunnar replied, embarrassed.

"Deenah, mayoy. Tomah balovan fomay dun teak vollie moe." The man sounded a little irritated. He held up his hand, pointing to a wrist band.

"I literally have no idea what you're saying."

"Tomah," the man repeated, pointing to the items on the dresser.

"Uhm, until I can get some britches on, I ain't moving from this bed again."

The older gentleman turned to the dresser and picked up one of the wrist bands, then handed it to Gunnar.

"Tomah dun teak naliot palov vomay whoteedee… you look like you need something to eat."

Gunnar paused as he positioned the communicator on his wrist. He looked at the man bewildered.

"That sounds more like it."

"Me and the misses took your translators and ID chip off so we could clean you up." The older gentleman turned and closed the door. "Not sure why you've got two of them. Is one broken? We couldn't get it to interface with anything. We weren't sure if you were using the language functions or not; I guess you are." The older man pointed at his own wrist translator. "We don't wear them much around here; no need to. Yours is different than ours. You sound like you're from somewhere in the Jurass system." Turning to the wall, the man adjusted the lights up a little until he noticed Gunnar squinting and ran them back down to a more comfortable level. "Sorry about your ship. Looks like you couldn't hold it in a hover long enough to get it to the ground?"

"Well, to be honest, that ship lost its engines sometime after reentry. I was just trying to get it down without digging my grave."

"Well that makes for some fancy flying then. Apparently, your friends thought you had bailed out?"

"My friends?"

"Yeah, your boys came and picked up the wreck already. Didn't even stop to look for you. Should I try to make contact with them? Have them come pick you up?"

"No, that won't be necessary." Gunnar tried to think. There was something he should be remembering. "I think I could use a couple of days of R & R."

"Won't your unit get worried?"

"No, I don't think so."

"You're not one of those obnoxious commanding officers everyone would just as soon was dead?" The gentleman tossed a bundle on the bed next to Gunnar and turned back for the door. "Some of my old clothes. They should fit all right. If you're feeling up to it, why don't you join the misses and me for dinner? I think we've about got it ready, if you think you can manage it."

Gunnar realized he was starving and considering his condition, a meal was probably the best thing for him.

"Thanks, I think that would do me some good."

The man closed the door, leaving Gunnar to work out how he was going to get the clothes put on without it being a painful process. After an extensive amount of grimacing, he made his way out into the hall and followed his sense of smell into an open kitchen area.

"We're out here," came a call from an open patio door. Gunnar felt like he must have stepped back in time; way back in time. The knotty pine wooden cabinets and furniture looked quite rustic. A finished wood slate bar separated the kitchen and indoor dining area. Moving toward the open patio door, he was met with a wide view of the entire lakebed. Sitting at a brightly set table, the older gentleman sat next to a woman of the same age, holding hands. The food placed around the table looked inviting and the smiles on the couple's faces were contagious.

"I'm sorry, I couldn't save your uniform. You look so much better than when my husband brought you in. How do you feel?" The woman's voice was cheery and fast paced. Gunnar smiled politely and cautiously stepped out onto the open patio, looking all around the skies, squinting.

"Well, I'm standing. I guess that's a good sign."

"That's what I like to hear; the glass is half full. Here, have a seat and try these out, see if they help." The man handed him a pair of mirrored sunglasses. "I suspect your eyes got some flash plasma burns. These will help until they heal. Dish up."

"Thank you," Gunnar said putting the shaded glasses on. "I am hungry." Shuffling to the chair, he sat down, but continued to scan the skies and the immediate area around the house. "This is quite the view."

"We like it," the gentleman said. "Have at it," he gestured to Gunnar. "If you go away hungry from this table, it's your own fault."

Gunnar chuckled and dug in, feeling like he hadn't eaten for some time. As he ate, the slightest noise would grab his attention. Most of the time the foreign sounds were created by a tiny animal creeping up onto the deck.

"Certainly are jumpy," the woman observed.

"I'm sorry," Gunnar said between bites. "Just never been in an environment like this before. I'm a little out of sorts."

"What environment are you used to?" she asked.

"I'm just really turned around," he said hesitating. "I can't seem to remember much of anything right now."

"Ah, post traumatic Mio-Campus."

"Post traumatic, what did you do to yourself?"

"Mio-Campus," the man repeated. "You've jumbled your short-term memory. It's normal for crash victims. It'll come back to you."

"Yeah, that's what it is. Just couldn't think of the right term."

"Why are you carrying two translators? Is one of them broken?" the woman asked. "We couldn't access any of the information on one of your ID bands or the chip on your neck chain."

"You accessed my personal information?"

"Only to get your name, rank and identification number."

"I sort of don't remember any of that. Can you at least tell me what my name is?"

"Captain Mace Bridger: Chief pilot; Albion Special Forces Regiment Twenty-Six. You're stationed aboard the *Tarzana*. Do you want your id number? It's kind of long."

"No, that won't be necessary."

The older gentleman eyed Gunnar carefully.

"You look too old to be in the Special Forces, even for a commanding officer."

Gunnar shrugged.

"Maybe the other two devices were damaged in the crash?" the woman offered.

"Maybe."

"I really think we ought to try to contact your unit. Let them know you're here. From the looks of most of those wounds, you were in some kind of a fire fight and someone is probably missing you or reporting you dead. We got all the bullets out of you, but you need better medical care than what we can provide."

"No," Gunnar held his hands up. "Really, it's ok. I just need some rest."

"Guess you're stuck with us for as long as you're here. My name is Eldon Grant. This is my lovely wife, Rayna."

"Pleased to meet you," Gunnar said, taking a swallow of drink.

"Captain Bridger, you're welcome to stay here for as long as you'd like," Rayna said pleasantly.

Gunnar smiled, feeling a little more relaxed. The back of his neck and head were still throbbing, but having food in his stomach seemed to help with his other aches and pains. After having his fill, he leaned back in his chair and tried to stretch. Every place he had been wounded still hurt, but at least his entire body didn't feel like it was on fire.

"Can I get you anything else?" Rayna asked, starting to clear the table with Eldon's help.

"A refill on whatever this drink is, would be great," Gunnar said, downing what was left in his glass. Rayna quickly refilled his glass and disappeared into the house.

"Come take a load off," Eldon motioned, getting up and sitting back down in a reclined patio chair.

Gunnar slowly got up and worked his way around the table to the other chair. After some careful maneuvering, he settled back and tried to relax. Under normal circumstances, he would probably have been able to just fall asleep in this position, but his wounds were in all the right places to keep him from getting comfortable. From this vantage point, other dwellings similar to this one, were visible. Every house was facing the dry lakebed.

"What happened to your lake?" Gunnar asked.

"Government drained it a long time ago. Said they needed the water elsewhere. It's a big lake, or was. Now they use the other side for military maneuvers and testing. If they have problems with a ship coming down in the wrong place, or like yours, it gets in trouble and they don't want to take a chance of it coming down in a highly populated area, they'll divert it to the other side of the lakebed."

"How long have you lived here?"

"What, in an actual house instead of a cube? Most people live in a sterile box now a day. No one appreciates living organically anymore, the way we were intended to live. This little community was started right after I retired from Albion service. A couple of us got together and decided we didn't want any part of the mechanized urban existence you'll find in the big cities like Zepplin or Haumpton, so we came out here, built a couple of cabins and we've loved being here ever since. Even after the lake dried up."

"Who thought up this kind of design?" Gunnar asked, looking around at what could be seen of the house.

"We all did. It's what naturally comes to mind when living off the land. Doesn't matter where you are, it's about what the land can provide."

"So nothing synthetic?"

"Are you kidding?" Eldon tapped several points on his wrist band. "We like being close to nature, not living in the stone age. Every house here has proximity sensors to repel wildlife and that includes any insects. We have a telecommunications unit in the house, but we rarely use it. There's a Talladega Five Hundred sitting in the garage under the house, but it's been a while since we've run it. I can't seem to get it to start. I guess maybe I'm losing my ability to operate it. Too bad, it's really a hot rig. Anymore, we usually just catch a ride with one of the other couples when they make a run into Pantos for supplies."

"Sounds like a great way of life."

"We think so."

Eldon and Gunnar fell silent, watching the last rays of the sun tilt away from the horizon. The air was starting to chill a little, but Gunnar didn't mind. He had become engrossed in the display of stars and the three moons of Albia. He had an unfettered view of the skies from horizon to horizon.

"You can't get this in the city," Eldon finally said quietly. "Too much light-clutter."

"It sure is amazing," Gunnar agreed.

"Yeah, it's pretty neat."

Gunnar let his gaze drop to the horizon directly across the dry lakebed. He thought he could see light moving far off in the distance and beyond. A dim, wide glow lined the horizon.

"Looks like there are maneuvers tonight," Eldon observed, seeing Gunnar watching the lights. "The glow is Zepplin city."

"How far away is it?"

"A good six hours by ground transport. That thing you were flying could do it in fifteen to twenty minutes."

"You seem to know something about flying," Gunnar commented.

"I was a pilot when I was in the service." Eldon let out a deep sigh.

"You sound like you miss it." Gunnar glanced over at Eldon. He could tell he was far off in his past, reliving an adventure.

"Sometimes."

"What did you fly?"

"Bombers; they were my favorite."

"Really? A bomber?" Gunnar felt something familiar about the way Eldon talked.

"A fighter will go just about anywhere you want it to. In the hands of a skilled pilot, they can be a lethal weapon. But I always felt like getting a bomber or transport to do things it wasn't designed to do, more of a challenge."

"Can you pull a pin-view roll and stop a bomber on a dime?"

"Well, maybe not a bomber, but certain transports you can."

"I can't imagine any amount of head knocking that can make anyone forget how to fly." Gunnar chuckled and thought a moment. "I guess there's something to be said about being able to put something right where you want it."

"Shouldn't matter how big it is."

"Very true."

Both fell silent, enjoying the view of the cosmos, and contemplating just how small they were in relation to the expanse of the universe. After several minutes, Rayna joined them, squeezing into the seat with Eldon.

"What makes you think there's room for you here?" Eldon asked, trying to sound put out.

"There's room here because you love me and you want to be close to me," Rayna answered, putting her arms around Eldon's neck and snuggling in tight.

"You couldn't just sit in the chair next to me and hold hands?" Eldon was trying really hard to sound irritated.

Gunnar cracked a smile, but kept his gaze up.

"Well, no. I can't snuggle with you if I'm sitting in the other chair. Now give me some suga."

"Not in front of company."

"Do I need to let you two have the deck?"

"Mr. Bridger isn't going to mind. I'm sure he misses getting a good scrug from his wife."

"Ray!" Eldon croaked.

Gunnar laughed. While what Rayna had just described sounded funny, it sounded familiar too. He fingered his ring, then put his hand to his chest. There came a gnawing emptiness, bringing with it a flood of memories of his life with Audra. The smile quickly melted, leaving him with intense feelings of loneliness and depression.

"Hey, Mace. You ok?" Rayna asked wondering if he was close to losing his composure. "Did we say something wrong?"

"No, I'm not sure what's the matter."

"Did you remember something?" Eldon asked.

"I don't know. Just feeling something from a long time ago…" Gunnar turned his head away and wiped the moisture from his eyes.

"Are you sure we shouldn't call someone?" Eldon asked again.

Gunnar took several deep breathes trying to clear his mind.

"Maybe I just need a good night sleep," he suggested, working his way out of the chair and standing up on stiff, painful legs.

"Can we help you back to your room?" Rayna asked, getting up. Gunnar started to motion no, but the aching in his chest and the pounding in his head dictated otherwise and he nodded. Eldon sprang from the chair and took hold of Gunnar on one side while Rayna supported him on the other.

Gunnar had nearly lost all of his energy by the time he reached the safety of his bed. He couldn't even pull his legs up into the sheets, but was happy to let Eldon lift them up and pull the covers up. Rayna was busy fussing with his pillows as he lay back, completely exhausted.

"I sure don't like this," Rayna complained, feeling his forehead. "There's no fever, so an infection probably isn't the culprit here."

"I think I just over did it a little," Gunnar whispered, feeling sleepy now. It felt good to have Rayna fussing over him.

"I'll see if I can do some more searching on the military data base," Eldon offered, turning from the bed.

"Don't call anyone just yet," Gunnar requested. "If I don't feel any better in the morning, we can pull more information from my wrist band and find a direct contact." Rayna got up to leave, but Gunnar held her hand. "Thank you for your kindness. You and Eldon are so nice to help a complete stranger."

"You would do the same, wouldn't you?"

"I'd like to think so. But you really don't know that much about me. You could be harboring an escaped prisoner or a convicted murderer or something."

Rayna smiled and squeezed his hand.

"I think we'd be dead by now if you were a murderer. As for an escaped prisoner, there is no such thing on Albia."

"How so?"

"Because if you're even suspected of being a criminal, you're carted off to the penal colony on Panora. If you're convicted, you don't come back, ever."

"I promise I'm not a murderer," Gunnar replied, drowsily. "Just someone in the wrong place at the wrong time."

"Goodnight," Rayna said, leaving him.

*   *   *   *

Once Gunnar's aches and pains subsided, sleep overtook him swiftly. In his dreams, he wandered in and out of scenes of people he didn't recognize. Some made no sense at all while others felt familiar. One in particular was that of a large tree overlooking a rolling meadow; similar to his favorite Hallavertor program. As he stood beneath the tree, he could look through the large green leaves and see the sun filtering through. It was a pleasant experience, full of comfort and good feelings.

"Do you always come here?" a voice from behind the tree spoke softly.

"It's a source of comfort," Gunnar said, not looking at who was there.

"What are you looking at?"

"Nothing really. Just enjoying the sun and watching the leaves move in front of it. I'd love to climb this tree."

"So why don't you?"

"I'm a little old for climbing trees."

"When did you get too old to be climbing trees?"

"We all have to grow up sometime."

"And grown-ups can't climb trees?"

"Not generally."

"You know you aren't a general type person."

"What do you mean? I'm like anyone else."

"No you're not. You're unique."

"Aww… Don't say that! No one likes to be called that."

"You are what you are."

Gunnar looked toward the voice.

"And you think I should be climbing this tree?"

"If it's what you want to do."

"Ok." Gunnar looked around and then reached for the lowest branch. To his dismay, he couldn't quite touch it, but with a slight hop, he found himself standing on the branch. "Wow, that was fun." He jumped to another branch with little effort. He found it quite exhilarating and the more he jumped, the further he could go until he had reached the highest branches. After some careful climbing, he shimmied up the trunk and looked out across the landscape. A steady wind at this level caused the top of the tree the sway, but it didn't bother him. The view and the pleasure of the climb completely obliterated any concern or fear. *I feel like I could just jump and fly.*

"So why don't you?"

"Ok, I think I will." He spread his arms and jumped from the tree, flapping as hard as he could. What started as a graceful swan dive, continued into graceful soaring as he banked around the treetops. Euphoric at moving effortlessly through the limbs without touching them, he grinned uncontrollably. He couldn't remember a time when he didn't like to fly.

"How long are you going to stay up there?"

Gunnar looked back down at the tree.

"I would never come down if I thought I could get away with it." He banked sharply around several trees in different directions and swooped beneath the limbs of a couple more before he landed on his feet next to the big tree. "I can think of nothing better." He sprang straight up, rocketing above the treetops, then extending his arms, came to a halt in mid-flight.

"Do you think it wise to be zipping around like that after what you've been through?"

Gunnar held himself still for a moment, feeling the breeze moving around him and enjoying the warmth of the sun on his face. Twisting his hands in a vertical position, he slowly sank back to the ground, keeping his eyes closed and his face turned to the sun. Touching back onto the grass, he opened his eyes.

"What do you mean, what I've been through? What have I been through?"

"You've been shot up, fallen from a ship and nearly broken in half. Then drenched in a downpour and to top it off, you crash land a ship and about break your neck. Don't you think that's plenty?"

"Shot? Broken neck? What are you talking about? My head is
moving just fine." Gunnar turned it side to side and rolled it in every
direction, checking for any restrictions; nothing. "And I would think if
I had gotten shot, I'd certainly know all about it." He checked his
body parts. There were some odd feeling spots on him, but…
    "Are you sure?"
    "Sure, I'm sure… Ouch!" Gunnar suddenly didn't feel so good. His
body started to ache painfully. He looked down at the areas that hurt
the worst. There was blood spots appearing in several places.
"What's happening to me?" Alarmed, he couldn't understand where all
this was coming from. For a moment, he saw himself trying to push
Tonnie through a boarding hatch and feeling the painful pinch of
ordnance slugs striking his leg and side, then the scene was gone and
he was left with pain and blood. "What should I do?" he asked.
    "Sit down on this pile of leaves and rest against the tree. You
really shouldn't be flying all over the place in this condition. You need
your rest."
    Gunnar gingerly sat down and tried to relax.
    "Who are you anyway?"
    "Well, I like that. You don't even recognize me?"
    Gunnar looked up at a grey faceless figure looking down at him
from behind the tree.
    "I should know you."
    "Yes, you should."
    "I'm sorry, I've had a pretty rough couple of days. My head is a
little mixed up."
    "It's Audra…"

The Funnel

Jayda awoke with a start when the assault craft jostled gently while entering Skadil's atmosphere. The bright reflection of its sun glared through the windows of the tiny ship as it settled through the upper cloud layers, then started for the surface. She noticed Dãsha had perched herself in the upper turret while Greg had taken one of the forward positions. Rick sat in the other turret watching as Dacey piloted the ship toward the sandy orange colored ground far below. She made her way up front next to Dacey and watched as they steered toward a set of coordinates depicted on a screen to the right of the pilot.

"Ok, here goes. We'll see if I remember how to do this," Dacey said activating his com system. "Oslerian Approach, this is SK Assault four requesting vectors for landing dock ten, acknowledge."

"SK Assault four, Oslerian Approach. Be advised of the weather front moving in. Follow ILS marker five and proceed to dock ten. State your assignment here."

"We're assigned to find a list of prisoners for further questioning and transport if available."

Jayda was impressed with how cool Dacey sounded.

"Affirmative, Assault four. Send us the list and we'll see if we can have them brought up. Get you back on your way before that front blows in." Dacey looked over at Rick, a little surprised they were to land without more interrogation.

"Sending encoded file now," Dacey said, touching several buttons on the panel next to him. While waiting for the controller, they made a wide turn over the mining base and headed for the docking bay.

"This is a tough list, Assault four. Most of these names aren't on our data base. Afraid two of them were disposed of months ago. Sending their files up to you now. The Watch Station reports one of the other ones left alive is slated for disposal later today. We'll have her and the last one brought up immediately. You'll meet with Watchman Gentoo when you land."

"Thanks for your help, Approach." Dacey checked the names on the file, then turned the display to the General. Rick frowned, reading the names of the deceased and the two remaining. "Weren't there supposed to be eight total?"

"Constance Fowler and Manx Quayle," Jayda said, reading the names.

"Why did they not send all the females directly into the slave trade?" Dãsha asked, watching the approach of another ship.

"Maybe they weren't suitable for the slave trade," Dacey offered. As they made their final approach to the dock, Rick looked over at Jayda, then up at Dãsha.

"It's a sure bet they'll think something is up if they catch sight of you two onboard."

"Why, we can be prisoners just like anyone else," Jayda objected.

"I think they would take particular exception to you, Dãsha," Rick said looking up at the dark-haired woman. Dãsha was quick to vacate the upper turret, the men in the craft having to look the other way as she climbed down.

"And what is wrong with me?" she asked, indignant.

"Nothing's wrong with you," Rick said looking back at her. "It's your dress."

"What's wrong with my dress?"

"It's very revealing."

"What?"

"It's too short," Jayda blurted. "Way too short and so is the one I'm using as a shirt now."

Dãsha angrily turned and rummaged around behind one of the seats, pulling out another pair of pants and slipping into them. Once she had pulled them up under her mini dress, she stomped back up front.

"There, just like your Jayda."

Rick grinned broadly, while the other two men snickered quietly.

"What?" Dãsha demanded. She looked down at the pants she had put on and realized she was having to hold them up by the belt loops. "Fine," she sighed humbly. "We'll stay out of sight in the back of the ship. But if you get into trouble and I have to come out to save you again, these pants are coming off."

"Fair enough," Rick snickered. He motioned the two women to the back as Dacey set the Assault ship gently on the landing pad. He left the environmental systems running to keep the internal compartment cool.

"There is no need for courtesies here," Dacey informed the other two. "You are the Drake military and everyone here respects that. Just keep the attitude to a minimum and we should be fine." Greg passed out the rifles while Dacey passed out a couple of soft strap hoods and dark googles.

"What's this all about?"

"Put them on. You'll thank me when we step out."

After getting themselves set, Dacey opened the hatch. As the three disembarked, the oppressive heat instantly started to bake their exposed skin.

"Hopefully this doesn't take too long."

"You got that right," Greg said, pulling his googles down into place.

"This way," Dacey motioned. "The Watchman will meet us inside."

"You'd think they'd provide docking bays under cover," Rick said. The three immediately made for the shadows of the outer receiving areas and the closed door.

"Will all the water this planet is pulling from Acuity going to do any good?" Greg asked as Dacey touched a control next to the door. "It's so hot here, won't it turn to steam before it ever gets close to the ground?"

"You heard the controller give me the advisory about the weather front?" Dacey asked. "As the upper atmosphere saturates with moisture, it super cools all at once and comes down pretty hard. Nearly impossible to fly through something like that. The water and ice-way between here and Acuity is even tougher. That stuff isn't just water and ice."

"Whatever Acuity's ocean has in it, is pulled up and sent over here." Rick said.

"Imagine a chunk of old ship or rocks dropping on you; even a chunk of ice."

"That would be some surprise."

Presently, the door slid open and the three stepped through and toward a desk. Dacey kept his weapon on his shoulder, but Rick and Greg kept theirs raised in a defensive stance. As soon as Dacey touched the desk, another door opened and a short skinny man appeared, his eyes glued to a device.

"The female isn't in very good condition," the little man said in a squeaky voice. "Not sure why you're bothering with her." Another door next to the first opened and a table levitated in with a woman strapped to it, followed closely by a bent man in shackles. Both looked in deplorable condition. "These the ones you looking for?"

Rick pulled a tiny device from his belt and held it up to the woman and the man. As the binders were removed from both prisoners, he gave the device a quick look and nodded.

"These are them," Dacey said, grabbing a couple of loose rags from the desk and motioned to the outer receiving area. "Thanks for your help." After getting them to the outer door, Dacey draped the rags over their heads, and lead them back out to the ship. The woman moaned pitifully when the sunlight and heat hit her, the man whimpering softly. Once onboard and situated, Rick and Greg manned the forward turrets while Dacey got the craft airborne. As they lifted from the docking bay, they were met with a blinding flash of lightening followed closely by a horrific clap of thunder that sounded like it might have hit them. A shadow passed across the ship as it turned and headed away from the landing area. An enormous wall of black clouds rolled over them as the ship throttled away. Jayda and Dãsha were out of their hiding places and immediately began attending to the two emaciated officers.

"That would have been tricky if we had gotten caught in it."

"Assault Four, this is Oslerian departure. Did you make it out ok?"

"Oslerian departure, this is Assault Four, affirmative. We got up and out just in time. That lightening would have scrambled our circuits for sure."

"Be advised this storm reaches up into the moisture ring. It's going to be a wet one down here for a while."

"Thanks for the heads-up, departure. We'll steer for a pole exit and run wide of the funnel."

"Departure acknowledged, have a good trip."

"The funnel?" Greg asked.

"The gravity conduit of water being pulled from Acuity to here, look," Dacey pointed out the side window.

They were now high enough in orbit to see the natural phenomenon in real time. As Skadil and Acuity passed each other in their normal solar orbits, they're proximity to each other was close enough that Skadil's gravity pulled on Acuity's mass. Huge shafts of water vapor, ice particles and debris were lifted into an immense conduit stretching between the two planetary bodies. The sun's rays refracted through the outer layers of this conduit creating several misty rows of rainbows. As the conduit reached Skadil's rotation, it curved in a wide arc around the planet forming a great ring above its equator. From the rear turrets, they could see much of the ring's mass extending directly to the surface in an enormous storm.

"How are our passengers?" Rick asked, getting out of the forward turret.

"I almost can't recognize either of them," Jayda said examining Captain Fowler.

"These two require immediate medical attention," Dãsha concluded, on her knees in front of Captain Quayle.

"There should be a couple of med kits in the back somewhere," Dacey suggested.

Rick promptly retrieved the kits and helped tend to the two officers. For the most part, Captain Fowler remained unconscious, but Captain Quayle seemed at least partially coherent; enough to look at Rick and Dãsha.

"Why are you taking me?" he muttered, disoriented.

"Captain Quayle," Rick spoke, trying to get his attention. "Manx, it's General Niker; it's Rick. Do you recognize me?"

"No, General Niker isn't here. He's gone after Croft Heckla. He commands a Starbird now."

Rick patted the disoriented man's shoulder to relax him and looked over at Jayda.

"Constance," Jayda spoke softly in the woman's ear. "Can you hear me? It's Jayda Niker. Can you hear me? We've got you. You're going to be ok. We're going to get you some help." Jayda looked up at Rick and shook her head. Captain Fowler was unconscious and if they didn't get her help soon, she would be beyond anyone's help.

"General," Dacey said from the pilot's seat. "You better come have a look at this."

Rick gave Captain Quayle another look, then turned forward.

"This doesn't look like normal military maneuvers to me," he said pointing at his scanners. "There's a squadron here, but there's one over here too."

"Not likely we can outrun them I suppose?" Rick asked, studying the readouts.

"Not from this positioning."

"Assault four, this is Oslerian departure, acknowledge."

Dacey glanced at Rick, who nodded.

"Oslerian Departure, this is Assault Four, go ahead."

"Assault four, you are ordered to return to docking port ten immediately for inspection."

"Is there a problem, Departure?"

"Your pickup appears to be unauthorized. You are to return at once for search and seizure."

"I guess there's little point in continuing this conversation," Rick advised. "What are our options here?

Dacey looked back at Rick trying to think of any. What he came up with wasn't much of an option.

"Run like you stole it?"

"Best plan I've heard so far."

Dacey pushed his throttles forward and steered along the gravity funnel toward Acuity in the distance as Rick stepped to the upper turret ladder.

"I like the top turret," Dãsha objected.

"I have little doubt," Rick replied, climbing up into the seat. "But I need all eyes forward if we're going to make it back to Acuity."

"Men," Dãsha muttered, stepping to one of the back turrets. Greg climbed in the other rear facing turret and strapped in. After making sure their two incapacitated passengers were secure, Jayda climbed into the bottom turret and charged the guns. Dacey glanced repeatedly at his scanner, hoping the two Drake squadrons wouldn't detect them and they could pass unseen. But he knew it was wishful thinking. If he could see them, they could see him.

"I think we've been made," Dacey called back to everyone. "These are P-90s though, so if you can shoot at all, you'll have no problem hitting them."

"It's how many there are," Rick said looking at his targeting screen.

"Not sure why they're so pissed at us. All we did was steal three slaves."

"Don't forget we blew up a royal transport," Dãsha reminded everyone.

"Oh, yeah, that too."

"Mister Dacey, stick close to the funnel. We may have to duck inside if things get too intense," Rick said.

"Better to get blown up out here, than trying to run through that mess," Dacey responded.

"Just do the best you can." Rick studied the screen in front of him and made a couple of adjustments. "We'll get two waves. If we're going to survive this, we'll need to take out the first wave before the second can engage."

"Here they come," Jayda announced, turning her guns to bear on the incoming fighters. There came a vibration to the assault craft before Jayda touched her triggers. She gave the ship's hull a quick glance seeing sparks bouncing off the thick armor plating around her turret. They were already in range.

"Are these the veteran pilots?" Rick asked, firing his guns.

"If they're hitting us, they are," Dacey said.

The entire ship's hull was aglow with ordnance striking its armor plating and streams of tracers flashing past. Inside was a chaos of noise from the strikes the ship was enduring and the turret guns clanking loudly with every recoil. Top and bottom turrets spun almost continually, while the rear turrets swung back and forth with every pass of a fighter through their gun sights.

"Seems like a waste to send all these fighters out here after one assault ship when they can't do much damage," Greg commented looking for his next target. There were only a couple left and they seemed to be fading back.

"They've done enough damage," Dacey replied.

"Report," Rick spoke up into his com mic.

"They've gotten to the thrust induction sensors and they've shot the crap out of the yaw stabilizers."

"Your opinion; can we survive a second wave?"

"Not sure we have any other alternatives, Sir."

"Well, we do. They just aren't good ones. How effective are the turret's targeting computers in the funnel?"

"Not much. Maybe you'll get a couple of seconds notice before something hits you. Pilot scanners are only marginally better."

"You said this ship has light pulse tech?"

"Every gun has one. It's the secondary trigger behind the primary. You charge them with the controls to your left; two switches."

"Any overload issues?"

"No, Sir. This ship is a tough rock and built with a tough power plant. If it's still running, and the power conduits aren't damaged, it'll keep firing."

"Second wave coming up behind," Dãsha announced.

Everyone immediately turned their turrets and targeted the approaching second squadron. The few remaining from the first wave, now joined forces with the second. But there was something a little different this time. Dacey checked his scanner closely, making adjustments as he maneuvered the speeding assault craft to just above the funnel's surface. There were a couple of target returns that looked different from the regular fighter returns. A closer inspection would have to wait.

"How are you supposed to know if you're hitting anything?" Greg asked.

"Things should start blowing apart out there," Dãsha replied.

"Every time you fire your pulse gun, it also fires a tracer round," Rick said. "But yeah, what Dãsha said."

The ship shook with a barrage of concentrated fire. Dacey began to weave while the others returned fire. For several minutes, they weaved all over, just above the surface of the funnel as they raced toward the safety of Acuity's ocean. Dãsha glanced at a section of armor plating that seemed to shred right next to her gun position and fall away as a shower of tracers slammed across the back of the ship. She pulled back on her handles and swung the big guns to the side, spraying out a stream of tracers and light pulse at several fighters that had just riddled the rear plating of the ship. Two broke apart in an instant while the third made a half roll and swung right back at the side of the ship, its guns blazing. Dãsha called the maneuver out just as Jayda swung her turret around with the triggers down. The fighter crumbled and broke apart, just missing the back of the ship as it passed.

Dacey did his best to continue to maneuver in such a way as to keep any fighters from getting a good lock on them. He glanced at the scanner every chance he had. He recognized the target returns of two more Assault craft gradually gaining on the running fire fight. Passing the display another glance, he observed two more targets, some distance ahead of them.

As the fighters were whittled down to only two or three, he took a moment to examine the readouts closer. The ships ahead were still too far out to know what they were, or their intensions, but the other craft coming up behind them became quite distinguishable.

"Two Assault ships gaining on us," he announced.

"Say it isn't so," Greg called back. "We're torn to shreds back here!"

"This ship is incapable of enduring any more attacks," Dãsha yelled.

Rick turned his turret in a complete circle, looking at the ship's exterior. Its armor was pocked with ordnance strikes and broken plate seams. The two upper thruster ports weren't working.

"How long before we reach Acuity?"

"Too long and we've got another bogie coming at us."

The ship lurched violently, taking a direct hit from the pursuing Assault ships.

"I just saw a huge chunk of armor fall off," Greg called forward. All guns were set to the rear to try and stunt the progress of the two attacking assault ships as they closed in on them, but the pounding continued mercilessly. The remaining fighters and assault craft pressed their attack hard, determined to stop, or destroy the fleeing assault craft. A direct hit next to Rick's turret blasted armor plating everywhere, sending out a shower of sparks that nearly blinded him. A sudden blast from the rear of the ship and several warning alarms blared throughout the ship's compartment, bringing Rick out of the turret and next to Dacey.

"She's taken a hit to the right main thrust regulator. We're losing power."

"Take us into the funnel," Rick ordered. "Where's the regulator assembly?"

"Opposite the back hatchway. Far side of the main engine bulkhead."

Rick started for the rear of the ship.

"Be careful of any regulator over-pressure," Dacey called back. "That fuel can flash without warning if it ionizes." Dacey gently pushed the nose of the ship over and sliced into the thick ice particles suspended in the funnel shaft. The interior instantly darkened and the noise of ice shards pelting the hull of the assault craft became deafening. The ride turned rough as Dacey kept the ailing craft diving deeper into the mirk. Looking over at his scanner, there were only shadows of the remaining pursuit ships tracking their path just above the funnel. It soon became apparent that the ship couldn't take the punishment. The turbulent funnel was handing them multiple strikes of ice chunks and other debris, causing more damage. Controlling the craft was becoming increasingly difficult with every passing second.

"I've got to pull us out of this or we're going to be dealing with a hull breach and a cabin full of ice," he called while pulling back up on the controls. Thinking of something he had learned a long time ago, he throttled way back and circled a moment, then turned the ship back up to the surface. "As soon as you see anything, you need to shoot," Dacey called to everyone. "Aim for the soft spots under the turrets and the engine nacelles." Dacey heard a shuffling from behind, but was too busy to take notice until Greg clamored into one of the forward turrets.

"I would have taken the top turret, but the lady in the mini dress beat me to it," he said scanning the space ahead of him.

"Probably better that way anyhow," Dacey said, seeing the mirk brighten a little. "Here it comes." Moments later, the assault ship breached the funnel and leveled out. No sooner did the horizon stabilize than both enemy assault ships appeared directly ahead of them at close range. There was an explosion of gun fire from Jayda and Dãsha in the top and bottom turrets accompanied by Greg in the right front turret. Their aim was on the rear end of the closest assault ship. The back of the ship flashed with ordnance strikes and pulse energy, large pieces of plating flinging away. Splitting in opposite directions, both ships carved a steep arc to turn back on their quarry. Dacey's craft started taking hits from the three fighters that had been buzzing around a little farther off, but the turret gun to Dacey's left suddenly came alive, cutting two of the fighters in half. The third closed to point blank range. Manx Quayle began screaming obscenities as he held both triggers down on the turret guns, firing right into the nose of the closing vessel. The fighter appeared to wobble, parts flying off as it nearly collided with them. Manx kept the triggers held down even after the fighter disappeared into the funnel.

"At the assaults!" Dacey yelled to Manx. He hadn't noticed the Captain climb in the turret. He looked like death warmed over. "Point it at the assaults!"

Manx turned the turret to fire at the two assault ships coming at them. There was a sudden explosion in front of them as one assault ship disintegrated, but at the same time there came an unexpected shudder rumble through the ship. Jayda looked back toward the rear to see a terrifying flash and bellow of smoke roll from the engine compartment.

"Rick!" she screamed, pulling herself from the lower turret and dashing to the back of the craft.

Everything abruptly went dead, even the gun turrets, then the lights flickered out. The pounding from the pursuing assault ship continued until there came another blinding flash outside, then everything fell silent. Looking around bewildered, Dãsha and Dacey saw no sign of the second assault ship, nor any other ship. Except for the movement of the funnel below them, all was still.

"No! No! No!" Jayda screamed in the darkness from the rear of the ship. "Help me, please!" she called again in a panic.

Dãsha was out of the top turret and to the back of the ship followed by Dacey and Greg. After finding the emergency lights, they peered into the engine room to find Jayda sitting on the floor holding Rick's limp body. He looked a mess. His clothing burned and still smoldering, his face and arms were blackened and badly burned. Both hands were bloody wads of flesh and his eyes were only half open, looking around bewildered. He opened his mouth to speak, but only a high pitch hissing sound exited. Dãsha rushed in and carefully pulled him from Jayda's arms, then carried him back into the main compartment and set him down next to Captain Fowler.

"Get the lights up here, above," Dãsha ordered, examining Rick. "The medical box, now!" She worked with him for a moment, all the while Jayda cradled his head in her arms. His eyes grew glassy and still while Greg and Manx looked on. Dacey tried to get a better view as to what Dãsha was doing, but detected a gentle vibration envelope the hull of the assault ship, then perceived a presence outside. He cautiously climbed up into the top turret and looked out. The jaws of an opening hangar bay door gapped wide at them, swallowing them into the belly of a larger ship.

*   *   *   *

Unfocused light gently found its way between the eyelids. He tried to pull them tight again to keep the light out, but as his mind cleared, he wanted, he needed to see the light. He became aware of voices around him, in the same room, but could not understand anything being spoken. There was an odd smell in the air; a light chemical odor. He relaxed his eyelids again, allowing the light to creep in. This time, he recognized a ceiling above him; a white ceiling. As the gap widened and grew more pronounced, the other eye lid split open. He focused on the ceiling above him, then became aware of the rest of his body. He was warm and comfortable; so much so, he didn't want to move. He finally blinked and shifted his eyes around the room. Directly above his head, a medical monitor flashed information about his condition. Rick blinked again and turned his head slightly. Captain Fowler was lying on the bed next to him. He turned and looked the other way, now recognizing the voices. He tried to speak, but found his tongue nearly glued to the roof of his mouth. Turning his head back, he stared at the ceiling again, trying to recollect how he had gotten here. He recalled the fire fight over Acuity's funnel and working on the engines to get power back up. He was working on the regulators when he smelled something overpowering, then a flash of light and searing pain to his face and hands. He remembered Jayda finding him and being carried out of the engine room. After that; nothing. He turned again to the voices on the other side of the room. Caidin Mantose noticed his movements this time and moved to Rick's side.

"You should be dead my friend," Caidin spoke quietly without looking back from the medical monitor.

Rick tried to speak again, but his tongue remained inhibited. He pointed a finger at his mouth and tried to speak; still nothing but hissy noises. Caidin finally understood the problem, grabbing a small hand implement with a clear flask attached to it and spraying the inside of his mouth.

"Sorry," Caidin apologized. "See if that does you any good."

Rick savored the moisture and motioned for more.

"Do you feel like sitting up?" Caidin asked.

"No," Rick rasped, choking on thick phlegm. "Need about three gallons of that."

"Got as much as you want," Caidin said handing him the flask. "There are a few people waiting outside that would love to know you're all right."

Rick put the nozzle to his lips and pulled the trigger. Taking several gulps, he stopped to cough and choke down the remaining gunk clearing from the back of his throat.

"What happened? Where am I?"

"I'll let your Jayda fill you in on what happened. You're in your medical bay aboard the *Athena*."

Rick looked around, now recognizing the bay and noticing several stasis pods neatly stacked in the corner. He looked back beyond Caidin, but the only two patients were himself and Captain Fowler. He gestured to the Captain on the bed next to him.

"Captain Fowler? She'll be just fine. She was in pretty rough shape when your team got here, but she is one tough woman and let's face it, you and I both know I've got some wicked good medical skills. She's sedated for now. I suspect she'll have some psychological difficulties and I want to make sure the rest of her is fully healed before she has to deal with what's inside."

"What about the others?" Rick rasped, pointing at the empty stasis pods.

"Oh, yes. You're crew. They've been up and about for several days now. There's a lot of work to be done here."

"How long have I been out?" Rick took another drag from the flask. "Did I actually die?"

"Kinda, sorta. You were almost dead by the time Dãsha got you on the table. I worked on you for about three days, but you've been out for almost a week. I wanted to give your body time to heal itself. I'm sure you'll be quite sore for a while."

"A week?" Rick was astonished. "A week," he repeated. "Why didn't you just heal me, like you did Dãsha?"

"I did," Caidin answered. "Having the knowledge to heal is one thing. Having the wisdom to know the right way to heal is something completely different." Caidin picked up Rick's hand and held it up. "Remember Dãsha has Nano-Mech swimming around inside her, you don't. Your hands were nearly blown off. I've restored them for the most part, but I'm allowing your body to do some of the healing work. It needs to know it can perform without my assistance. I've found that the body will heal stronger in this way."

"Ok, if you say so," Rick said clearing his throat and taking another drink. His voice was almost back to normal.

"And now, like it or not, I think you'd better see at least two visitors or I'll be in trouble." Caidin activated the door. Rick turned his head to see a beaming Jayda gliding towards him and the tall form of Dãsha right behind her. He stiffly rose up on one elbow, but Jayda wouldn't have it.

"Lay back, mister. That's an order." Jayda's voice abruptly shifted back to *wife* mode. "I'm just glad you're ok. Scared me to death. Pull something like that again and I might have to kill ya."

"Imagine how I felt," Rick mumbled. "Nice to see you back in uniform."

"It's far better than the long shirt I was wearing." Jayda looked down at her uniform.

"I have been worried for your welfare as well, Richard Alexander," Dãsha said stepping to the other side of the bed with her hands clasped behind her. She was wearing another mini dress and knee high boots, this time a bright, colorful pattern.

"I'm supposed to ask you how I got here," Rick stated, laying back on the pillow.

"CORA 500," Jayda snickered. "She talked Caidin into taking *Calypso* out with the *Athena* to make sure we got back ok." Jayda looked across at Dãsha. "But just so you know, the twins brought the assault craft back onboard the *Stark*. Dãsha insisted on pulling you out and carrying you here to sick bay."

"I suppose I'll never hear the end of that," Rick said looking up at Dãsha's emotionless expression.

"It is what you have done for me."

"So, what's happened while I've been out?" Rick asked, turning back to Jayda.

"We've gotten all the ships out of the ice and have left Acuity. We're under way back toward the Nulark system."

"You got all these buckets moving?"

"Well, not at full power," Jayda answered. "We could only get about half sub-light out of the freighters, so we're holding at their speed."

"And the Drake haven't objected?"

"No sign of them. We're on a different route back to the Nulark system. The hope is that they couldn't follow it even if they wanted to. Mister Dacey says the Drake have no navigational buoys in this direction."

"What about the cargo?"

"Work is proceeding on all four ships as you ordered. The *Athena* is being refitted with a new FTL engine as we speak."

Rick tried to sit up. He understood that while the Massey FTL engine was modular and designed to be readily removed and replaced, it was still a technical and precise operation. There was no one onboard that had ever done it.

"Yeah, no," Jayda said having none of it. "You just stay put, mister," she said with a firm hand to his shoulder.

Rick remained defiant until another hand, more forceful, pressed him back down. He looked up at Dãsha and seeing the determined look, relaxed.

"Do I need to leave Dãsha here?" Jayda threatened.

"I can read to you if you'd like," Dãsha grinned.

Rick gave the tall woman a double take and turned back to Jayda.

"Who's overseeing the operation? No one here has ever changed a Massey out before?"

"Relax," Jayda said folding her arms. "I attended the same engineering courses in this procedure as you did. I'm overseeing the project and the Korack twins are doing most of the work with the help of our other crew members."

"Do you have an estimated time to completion?" Rick asked.

"Why did I know you were going to ask that?" Jayda responded. "It'll be done when it gets done. There's no rush, until you invent one."

Dãsha looked at Jayda curiously, then down at Rick.

"Caidin and I do not speak to one another in such a manner. Do you fight often?"

Jayda snickered, looking down at Rick who was now smiling.

"Trust me, this isn't fighting. This is officer in command making sure a general stays put long enough to heal properly."

"Besides," Rick popped. "You're a little different than the rest of us. I suspect Caidin wouldn't stand a chance."

"Truly he would not, but there are rarely disagreements between us."

Jayda and Rick looked back at Dãsha and smiled. Jayda finally turned to leave, but came back and bent down to give Rick a kiss.

"Please tell me you'll stay put."

"I promise."

She kissed him and headed out after Dãsha.

My new assignment

Gunnar opened his eyes. It was dark outside and quiet in his room. He was used to always having some kind of noise in his ears, but here, there was nothing, which made the silence deafening. He sat up stiffly and swung his feet out of bed. Noticing a dull glow from under the door, he stood up on tentative legs and shuffled to the door, listening. He could hear muffled voices coming from somewhere in the house, but was unable to make out what was being said. Seemed odd that Eldon and Rayna would be up in the middle of the night. He looked at his wrist band for a moment, then turned to the dresser where he had left the other band and memory chip. They were both missing. *Did I leave them on the patio?* He didn't even remember taking them out when he had eaten dinner. Making his way quietly down the hall, he slid up next to an open door.

"This is some of the most sophisticated code I've ever seen," Eldon mumbled.

"Can you tell what it is?" Rayna asked.

"Not even a clue, babe. Our transcoders can barely display it."

"Were you able to get into the band?"

"No, same problem. I can see the translator, but how it works is way beyond me. I guess I've been retired too long."

"There's not some kind of identifier, anything?"

"Nothing, not even a symbol. It's nothing like anything I've ever seen before. I guess that's a good thing. He's not a Colonian operative or one of those Ratronian rat-ba..."

"Don't say it!"

"What?" Eldon stuttered. "I was just going to say, 'bad guys'."

"Sure you were..."

"I just don't see how we're going to be able to help this guy," Eldon continued. "I haven't even been able to find anything on any of the military channels that would indicate any active search or rescue missions."

"There was that incident on Dither early yesterday."

"Yes, but they've accounted for all the dead."

"Did they publish names?"

"It's the military, sweetheart," Eldon reminded her. "What do you think?"

"Well, regardless of how he's feeling in the morning, I think we need to get him somewhere he can get better medical care."

"Agreed. Question is, do we just take him as far as Pincock station at the dam or drive him all the way to Kemper headquarters?"

"I guess we can figure that one out when we get to Pincock…" Eldon twisted his head toward the door of the office. Both of them had heard something and cautiously rose to their feet, then stepped to the door. Looking up and down the hall, they saw only the walkway night lights illuminating the darkness. "Here," Eldon said handing Rayna the band and the memory chip. "You're lighter on your feet than me."

Rayna took the devices and headed quietly down the hall and into Gunnar's room. She paused at the door long enough to see their guest still snuggled in his bed, then glided silently to the dresser and replaced the band and chip. Turning back for the door, she paused again, looking at Gunnar. He looked comfortable enough in a deep sleep. Moving to the door, she stopped again and looked back at the slumbering stranger.

"Was he still asleep?"

"Soundly," Rayna admitted. "Not sure what we heard."

"We live out here in the mountains. No telling what it was."

"No, sentry alarms."

"How about the wind?"

"Take me back to bed, babe."

*　　*　　*　　*

Eldon woke up late. He was cussing being up in the middle of the night for no good reason. The snooping they had participated in had left him awake for some time. Standing out on the deck, he sipped his hot drink and scanned the horizon of the lakebed. In the distance, he caught sight of several ships flying low from one end of the dry expanse to the other.

Maneuvers. He hated seeing the military using the lakebed as a training ground. Though it didn't happen often, they had even used heavily armored ground vehicles on this side. In his mind, if they really wanted to do any good, they'd destroy the Wali dam on the other side and let the waters flow back into their natural course. The lake would refill and whoever or whatever would still have the same amount of water flowing down river. What really ticked him off was while they originally built the dam for a specific purpose, technology had changed to the point they didn't need the dam anymore. *Why not remove it?* A shuffling noise brought his attention back and he turned to see Rayna sitting down at the kitchen bar inside.

"What are you doing up already?"

"I could ask you the same thing," Rayna countered, still looking droopy.

"It's mid-morning. Do you think we should wake Mister Bridger?"

"If we're to take him anywhere we probably should get going pretty quick."

"I'll wake him," Eldon volunteered, setting his cup down and disappearing down the hall. Moments later, he returned, scratching his head.

"How's he feeling this morning?"

"Apparently pretty good," Eldon said. "He's not in there."

"Not in there? What do you mean he's not in there? Where is he?"

"Do you think I was gone long enough to know where he went?"

"Well, we need to find him," Rayna said moving to the hallway. "He's in no condition to be out and about." A few moments later, Rayna emerged from the hallway with a white look on her face. "Your hiking boots are gone. You don't think he left on foot, do you?"

Eldon shrugged as he went to the rail of the deck and pushing a pair of electro binoculars to his eyes, scanned the area around the settlement.

"He couldn't have gotten far in his condition," Rayna worried.

"I think there's more to that guy than he's letting on. I don't see anything out there."

"I can't even imagine him getting very far."

"Not sure how we can attempt to go after him either. I suppose we could ask one of the..." Eldon was cut off by the sound of turbines winding up somewhere beneath them. He looked over the rail trying to see if something was against the foundation of the dwelling. *Maybe one of the neighbors had pulled up to say good morning.*

"I know that sound," Eldon exclaimed, turning to Rayna. She looked back at her husband and realized what he was talking about.

"The Talladega," they said collectively, turning for a gate leading off the deck to the ground. Carefully working their way around to the back side of the cabin, the two finally stood before the transport doors. Now the winding had turned to a high-pitched whistling accompanied by a low throbbing. Eldon grinned, recognizing the sound of the engines that had come to life behind the doors. He touched several tiny buttons on his wrist band and the doors pulled back into the walls, revealing the glassy nose of Eldon's Talladega Five Hundred. The driver's side door was up and a figure was moving inside. Gunnar looked out at the older couple and smiled. Throttling the vehicle back to an idle, he climbed out patting the engine cowling of one of the side motors as it sat quietly humming.

Eldon was elated to see the ground based transport running again. Rayna grinned with glee seeing her husband so happy.

"These are some sweet power plants," Gunnar said walking around the front to the other engine and looking into the intakes. "I bet if you put some wingtips on this thing, it would fly, easy."

"Well, it is based on an air racer design," Eldon said, running his hands along the nose and the side windows. "It's the fastest hover design ever to come out of Vandmire manufacturing. But they haven't made any of these for a long time. Hard to get parts for it. How did you ever get it to go?"

"Vandmire industries," Gunnar smiled.

"You know them?"

"Sounds familiar." He shrugged and continued to examine the intakes. "I've been around enough engines to know Isom turbines and critter's nests don't mix very well. Plus, your control valves were all mucked up." Gunnar closed several of the access doors, walked around to the driver's side again and checked the intakes on the first engine.

"Shoot," Eldon grumbled, following him. "I must have forgotten to purge the injector pumps after I shut her down."

"I'm not much of a mechanic," Gunnar said closing the other panels. "But I can figure out the basics. Question is, will it move?"

"Well, the Trilix coils are guaranteed to never fail." Eldon looked back at Rayna and motioned for her to climb in the open door. She held her hands up and shook her head.

"Nope, not until we've all had something to eat and we've accessed Mister Bridger's information. Then we'll all go for a ride."

Eldon frowned, but finally nodded and climbed into the driver's seat, working to shut down the quietly purring vehicle.

"How do you access something you have no credentials for?" Gunnar asked.

"Eldon is pretty handy with that kind of thing. Part of his military service was in the encryption branch."

"Why didn't you just get it when you first brought me here?"

"We were more concerned about saving your life."

"I can appreciate that."

Eldon finally climbed out of the Talladega with a huge grin pasted across his lips.

"Looking forward to blowing the cobwebs out of this thing. Let's eat!"

Following a quick mid-morning meal, the three sat down in front of Eldon's terminal and brought several screens to life. After only a couple of moments, Eldon had active windows of information open, interfacing with each simultaneously.

"Ok, let's have your band," Eldon motioned.

"Which one?" Gunnar asked.

"The one that works."

"They both work." Gunnar smiled holding up his wrist, then pulling the other band from his pocket. He exchanged the bands and set it on the pad next to Eldon's terminal. General default information instantly appeared on the screens in front of them.

"Here's where it gets interesting," Rayna whispered, resting her chin on Eldon's shoulder as he started accessing the encrypted files.

"It's not like this stuff is necessarily top secret, but there are stop gaps in place to keep people from just scanning your data and assuming your identity." Eldon maneuvered his fingers quickly through the myriad of information displayed in front of him and presently gained the access they were looking for. "Here we go." Eldon widened the screen so everyone could clearly see.

"Captain Mace Bridger…"

"Yeah, yeah, yeah," Rayna pressed, shaking is shoulders. "We know all that. Get to the part, get to the part."

"Will you calm down." Eldon glanced at Gunnar as a picture came up with a page or two of statistical information surrounding it. "Uhm, this doesn't look anything like you; unless this was your enlistment picture."

Gunnar waited quietly.

"Pilot, special forces… blah, blah, blah, we already know all that. Hometown is Straunsen, Albia. That's on the other side of the planet. Birthdate… Married to Malina Cass. Her age is stamped as the same as yours. Says here, you're dead. Killed in action on Dither in a skirmish with Colonian terrorists. Yeah, this definitely isn't you." Eldon and Rayna looked back at Gunnar, his eyes remaining glued to the information on the screen.

"No, it's not me," Gunnar said, standing up straight.

"You're not going to kill us, are you?" Rayna asked pressing a little closer to Eldon.

"No, why would I do that?"

"You killed this Captain Bridger, didn't you?"

"I don't know any names, but yes, I probably did. I was protecting my friends." Gunnar took note of the frightened looks and decided this had gone on long enough. "My real name is Gunnar Conrad. I came to retrieve some artifacts from the Dither repositories that will change the political climate of your galaxy and put an end to this war."

"Are you Colonian?"

"No. I come from outside your galaxy."

"Then why are you trying to stir up trouble?" Eldon asked.

"I've got nothing better to do." Gunnar's response did nothing to relieve Rayna and Eldon's anxiety levels. "Look, what's the cause of the disputes between the Colonians and the Albions?"

"It's not just us and the Colonians," Rayna passed a glance at her husband. "The whole galaxy is at odds right now."

"It's the blood heir dispute," Eldon offered. "The Colonians have no blood heir, but have chosen to rule with an illegitimate royal."

"Exactly," Gunnar agreed. "I was protecting the actual blood heir."

Rayna and Eldon looked at each other, then back at Gunnar with skeptical expressions.

"There's a blood heir here, on Albia?" Eldon finally asked.

"Well, not Albia specifically, but yes. We came to one of the Dither Repos stations to retrieve royal documents and artifacts, but we had a difficult time getting away. Several troopers, including this Captain Bridger were killed in a fire fight."

"Did your friends get away?"

"I think so. They're in a pretty fast ship."

"I hope for their sakes, you're right," Rayna said sitting down. "So, what are you doing here?"

"During the firefight, I was hit several times and fell as my ship was leaving. I hitched a ride aboard that transport ship, but apparently it had some problems on reentry and the next thing I know, I'm waking up here."

"How do you know we won't just turn you over to the Albion military?"

"I don't. But I'm getting the impression you're not all fired up about doing that."

"So, what would you like from us?" Eldon asked.

"I need to get to the *Tarzana*."

The room fell silent for several moments.

"You're serious..." Eldon blurted, not believing what he had just heard. "I think I'd be trying to go in the opposite direction. Why in the world would you want to run straight for trouble?"

"During our little skirmish on Dither, the Princess dropped one of the artifacts; a ring. Without it, it'll be impossible for her to prove her legitimacy."

"She's one of the Oxlind Princesses?" Rayna asked. "But they were all killed."

"No, the youngest was held with her royal Au Pair here on Albia for a time and then exiled to a planet on the outer rim. It was dumb luck that a friend and I stumbled across her."

"I can tell you why she wasn't killed," Eldon puffed, indignantly. "KC Dismon needs her to legitimatize his attempted takeover of Hadrian."

Rayna gave her husband a shocked look.

"Honey, you shouldn't talk like that."

"Come on, Ray," Eldon snorted. "We've talked about this before. He's in cahoots with Benetar."

"We have no proof of that."

"It's only obvious."

"Maybe it is, but you can't go off what you have no proof of."

"Actually, that makes sense," Gunnar said, thinking. "The Royal Au Pair explained a lot of it to me. After Queen Oxlind passed away, the Duchess Benetar married into the royal family. She then arranged to kill off the royal Oxlind line and took control of Colonia, using her marital status as her claim to the throne. Of course, the rest of Hadrian is going to contest it and civil war breaks out. In the

meantime, the youngest ends up here along with her Au Pair. In the hands of the Albions, she couldn't be discovered by the Colonians, but to keep her from being discovered by the Albions or anybody else, she is marooned on the outer rim. It appears their plan was to use the Princess as a pawn to somehow gain control of the throne. With the Duchess already holding onto the Colonian throne and your King Commander secretly backing her, they could manipulate the Princess into making changes to Hadrian law that would place them into power. When they figured out that together they could make a duel claim to the throne at the Pintar rite of Hadrian, they decided to just dispose of the child. So, your KC Dismon sent an encrypted transmission to the Au Pair to flood the biosphere and drown the Princess. No one would ever know of her existence. But, the order to terminate the Princess went against the Au Pair's prime directives; protect the Princess. She sacrificed herself to keep the biosphere from flooding and drowning the Princess. This gave the Princess a chance to escape if anyone were to find her."

"So, what about this ring?" Eldon asked. "You think it's on the *Tarzana*?"

"Isn't it?" Gunnar asked. "Didn't you say Captain Bridger was stationed onboard? His unit would have returned to the *Tarzana* and delivered the ring to their commanding officers. I need to get to it before that happens."

"Well, that's probably already happened," Eldon said. "They don't just put things like that in their pockets and hold onto them. They'll deliver it during a debrief and it'll work itself up the chain, especially if they know what they have."

"I doubt anyone, even the King Commander or the Duchess remember anything about any ring."

"Bridger's unit was probably just trying to capture a couple of Colonian terrorists," Rayna said.

Eldon thought a moment, looking over at Rayna.

"It'll show up in a report on the unit commander's desk and maybe sent up as far as the ship's commander. But how in the heck do you think you're going to be able to get on that ship? They don't just let anyone onboard. Only certain branches of the military are allowed on and we don't even know if it's still in orbit."

"Well, I guess you could look and see," Rayna suggested.

"Even if it is still up there, that doesn't explain how he's gonna get onboard," Eldon said turning back to his terminal.

"Just look." Rayna positioned his hands on the terminal control. Eldon rolled his eyes and went to work.

"The *Tarzana* is still here. Looks like its scheduled for a late departure though, sometime this evening. But that doesn't mean a whole lot. Unless they're in for service, military ships come and go as needed. They're rarely tied down by schedules. What have you got in mind?"

Gunnar tapped his finger against his lip as he paced the room, thinking.

"What about smuggling you aboard during resupply?" Rayna offered. "It's a sure thing anytime they're in port."

"That's what the support ships are for, Ray," Eldon said.

"Yeah, but wouldn't it be easier to load directly whenever it's possible?"

Eldon nodded, and kept scanning through the information. He stopped several times, looking closer.

"Maybe we can get you into a fighter resupply…" Eldon started to turn, but then went back to his information. "No, that won't work. We don't have that kind of time."

"I'd love to fly some of the stuff they have," Gunnar said. "The Black Tiger looks like fun."

"Those things are a bit of a handful. Takes a good pilot to run one," Eldon said.

"I can fly anything they have," Gunnar stated.

"You think you're that good?" Rayna smiled. "You can't even understand our language without a band."

"If you can do it, it ain't boasting." Gunnar smiled, nodding at Rayna. "No, even if I could get to a fighter, that would likely draw too much attention. I need to be able to get onboard and move about the ship as freely as any officer. If only…" Gunnar abruptly stopped and looked over Eldon's shoulder at the information. "Wait a second. Pull up Captain Bridger's profile again."

"What good will that do, he's dead?" Rayna pointed out, moving closer. Eldon brought Captain Bridger's information back up and started scrolling through it, while Gunnar scanned the information.

"That's it," Gunnar said.

"What's it?" Rayna asked.

"Can you manipulate any of this information?" Gunnar asked straightening up.

Eldon looked up at Gunnar.

"Manipulate it? Manipulate it how?"

"Make a few adjustments and change the picture?"

"You want to assume Captain Bridger's identity…" Rayna said deliberately.

"I can, but it won't stick," Eldon informed him.

"What do you mean, it won't stick?" Gunnar asked.

"I mean, I can change all this information, but once you're cleared into the system, the data will start to conflict with their database. It'll start throwing out errors and alerts until the problem is resolved in the system."

"How long does that take?"

"I don't know," Eldon said. "I've been retired a long time. I have no idea how much their systems have been upgraded. It may take days, hours or it might flag you immediately."

Gunnar looked at Rayna, then turned and paced the room a couple of times.

"I'll have to chance it. All I need is to get onboard."

"Gunnar," Eldon shook his head skeptically. "I think you'd be better off smuggling yourself in, rather than altering this profile. Even if it doesn't throw any errors, how are you going to find your way around that ship? That thing is a city with guns mounted to it."

"I just have to convince the deck officer I am who my ID says I am, get to the command offices and retrieve the ring, then borrow a ship and slip out with a patrol."

Eldon and Rayna kept the skeptical looks coming.

"I've been on the *Tarzana* before," Gunnar mentioned casually. "I've flown barrel rolls in formation over her bow to stern and did a couple of conning tower flybys."

"No need to exaggerate to try to make us feel better about this," Rayna chided, giving Gunnar, *the look.* Eldon shook his head, turned back to his information, and started working.

"I'm going to need a picture of him, babe. Give him one of my old uniforms. Just make sure you take off all my identifiers. Those will really cause a problem, and not just with the database."

Everyone went to work and after considerable effort, Eldon emerged from the office holding the Albion band. After double checking his work, he handed it to Gunnar. Rayna was just pulling the last of the identifiers from the uniform as Gunnar took the band and stretched it around his wrist opposite his own band.

"Is helping me going to create a problem for you guys? I have a little information on how your military works and it would seem aiding and abetting could get you in a lot of trouble."

"If we had been worried about that," Eldon responded, "do you think we would have scraped you up and nursed you back to health when you crashed? Besides, if you go and get yourself killed, which is likely, there'll be no reason to try to trace anything back. Just don't get yourself killed."

"As Albions, it's our experience that most of us do not believe or act as our military does," Rayna smiled. "We both know neither the Albion nor the Colonian government have been upfront with its people. We just want what's right for Hadrian and to live in peace, the way it once was when the Oxlinds occupied the royal House of Pintar."

"I hope I can help make that happen again," Gunnar said quietly.

After a moment of silence, Eldon gulped down a drink he had picked up and picked his activator keys.

"Ok then, let's get you back to your ship, Captain Bridger. I'd let you drive, but I doubt you have any idea where we're going…"

"And Eldon always gets to drive," Rayna said snatching the activators from her husband. "So, I'll be your pilot today." Without another word, she breezed down the stairs at the end of the hall.

"Besides, apparently Ray never gets to drive." Eldon leaned a little closer to Gunnar. "Hate it when she drives," he mumbled shaking his head.

"Does she show you how it's done?" Gunnar asked moving for the stairs.

"She's defiantly going to show you how it's done," Eldon said following him. "Just make sure your harnesses are on good and tight."

*   *   *   *

Gunnar counted himself fortunate the road to Pantos cut across the dry lakebed. The garage doors had barely cleared the Talladega's rear spoilers when Rayna had engaged the Trilix coils and shifted the craft into drive. She slapped Eldon's hands when he tried to pull back on the throttles after she nearly hit several outbuildings on the corner of their neighbor's property.

"I think you're enjoying this far too much," Gunnar said from the back seat. He generally felt more comfortable up front. If not in the pilot's seat, then the copilot's seat, but in this instance, he surmised there was no copilot. Rayna was in total command of the controls and everything that went with it. Her squiggly smile was one of absolute glee.

"It's been a while since we've been able to take this ole' girl out," Rayna snickered.

"Clearly," Gunnar grimaced as they careened around several large boulders. Eldon glanced back at him, his eyes looking more at his harness.

"How ya doin' back there?" Eldon looked forward and tensed up. "Watch out for the log, Ray!"

"Yeah, it's a big one," she said, twisting the controls to maneuver around the obstacle. Gunnar felt the Talladega shudder a bit as it connected with the log, but their increasing speed didn't seem to diminish. Once past the ground obstacle, the flat lakebed opened up into a seemingly endless expanse with only the horizon laying in the rocketing craft's path. Rayna steadily pushed the throttle farther forward, the acceleration pressing everyone back in their seats. Gunnar was a little taken aback by her intoxicated appearance as she pushed the craft faster, until Eldon put a firm hand on hers and carefully pulled the lever back to the low cruise settings.

"Ray, I think you've blown all the cobwebs out of it."

Rayna looked over at her husband, then back at Gunnar. A look of embarrassment streaked across her face as she released her hold on the throttle handle. Eldon kept his eyes on her as she turned on the proximity scanners and set the auto-drive, then plotted a course to Pantos. Gunnar couldn't help but chuckle a little. Everyone who loved to fly or feel the thrill of an accelerating craft at their control seemed to act in a similar manner. Didn't seem to matter how old you were, a man or woman, the love of a machine never got old.

"Guess I got a little carried away," Rayna said sheepishly.

"That's her definition of a little," Eldon chided her as he pushed his headset down into place. Rayna gave Eldon a good-natured slap to the shoulder and turned back to Gunnar.

"I never got a chance to ask about your wife."

Gunnar looked back at Rayna and smiled. She had made mention of it before, but the conversation somehow got skipped over. He pulled his side window open halfway, letting the morning air fill the interior of the Talladega.

"I assume you wear the ring because you're married."

"Yes, I'm married." Gunnar leaned back, feeling a deep hole develop in his chest. Instinctively, he brought his fingers to Audra's chip.

"So... what's her name?" Rayna asked settling in for a fun conversation.

Finding the chip, Gunnar held it firmly in his fingers.

"Audra Atlanta."

"No middle name?"

"Yes, there's a middle name, but she never used it. I couldn't even get her to put it on her ID documents."

"Does she hate it?"

"She never said." Gunnar stared out the window as the dry lakebed rushed by.

"Where did you meet her?"

"At a music concert." Gunnar snapped out of his glum face. "Funny thing was, I had been talking to her for almost a year before I met her."

"I don't follow."

"She was a long-range traffic controller, calling my traffic in and out of controlled space. I finally met her on a blind date with a good buddy of mine. We hit it off instantly."

"Was it love at first sight?" There was a glint in Rayna's eye as she smiled, picturing that first meeting.

"I wouldn't go that far, but looking back, I'm pretty sure I knew she was the girl within about five minutes."

"Five minutes?" Eldon repeated. "I'm still not sure I got the right one." As expected, Rayna's hand contacted the back of his head. "Ouch, hey, what was that for?"

"Do you need another one to jog your memory?"

"Do you see what I have to put up with?" Eldon asked.

"I feel your pain," Gunnar laughed, clinching the chip.

"You're the luckiest man alive," Rayna said planting a slobbery kiss on the side of Eldon's face.

"Ack," Eldon said wiping the slobber off. "Hate that!"

Gunnar let out another healthy laugh thinking how similar he and Audra had interacted. This was like looking in a mirror. He felt perfectly at ease with these two.

"Do you feel like you need some hazard pay?" Gunnar asked through his chuckle.

"If you know what's good for you, you won't answer that." Rayna held her hand up to the back of Eldon's head. He tried to lean forward and put a hand up to keep from getting hit. "Don't say it," Rayna warned.

"Say what?" Eldon laughed.

"What you think is gonna be funny."

"What, the fact that they don't pay me enough hazard pay?"

Rayna's hand contacted Eldon's head again, her lips drawn up into a tight grin.

"Hey, I'm driving..." Eldon laughed hysterically.

"It's on autopilot."

"See? Hazardous to love this woman!"

"I'll give you some hazard pay." She motioned like she was going to strike him again, but turned back to Gunnar. "You were saying..."

Gunnar smiled, feeling both angry and happy at the same time. He had been doing fairly good since the crash, but now he wondered if his body wasn't going to start ramping up again.

"We got married a short time later and were together until two years ago."

"You're fortunate," Eldon said causally. "Most marriages can't survive military life, especially if you're in the flying service."

"Didn't you say you flew?" Gunnar asked.

"Yes, I did, early on, but then shifted over to Intelligence. I met this little bunch of honey-melon right after I was transferred. She's like a little kid that has wrapped themselves around your leg; I can't shake her loose."

Eldon felt Rayna's hand slip around the back of his neck, her fingers slithering up behind his ear and softly caressing his earlobe. He let out a yelp when she suddenly applied pressure and twisted the soft fleshy part between her fingers.

"Admit it, I'm the best thing that could have ever happened to you." Rayna planted a big kiss on his face while still holding onto his ear.

"Hey, I'm driving!"

"You've used that one already, remember? It's on autopilot; now say it!"

"You're the best thing that's ever happened to me." Eldon's tone sounded more like he was just trying to pacify her rather than admit anything, but it was clear they were deeply taken with each other. Rayna melted back into her seat, smiling. The silence lasted long enough for Gunnar to drift in his thoughts. It was actually quite nice to be at peace with his emotions and his physiology. There was still a bit of a headache in the background, but it was hardly noticeable right now. He fingered the chip around his neck while gazing at the ground sweeping by at a blur. His thoughts turned to Audra and the times she would act in similar fashion to Rayna. He tried to play the tough guy and she would cut right through his tough exterior with her sweet talk. He was nearly defenseless when Audra turned on the charm.

"Wait," Rayna said quietly, turning back to Gunnar. "So, what happened two years ago?"

"Ray? What are you asking?" Eldon asked, not following.

"Gunnar, you said you and Audra were married until a couple of years ago. What happened?"

"Ray…" Eldon cautioned. "I think if Gunnar had wanted us to know, he would have told us."

Rayna remained silent, looking at Gunnar, who was still staring out the window at the passing lakebed. After several moments, she shifted to turn forward, but stopped when Gunnar spoke.

"Audra died two years ago."

Rayna continued watching Gunnar reverently. He pulled the chip from around his neck and held it up to the light coming through the open window.

"I-, I'm very sorry," Rayna apologized quietly. "How did it happen?"

"Ray!" Eldon scolded.

"It's ok," Gunnar said turning from the window. "I don't talk about it enough. Audra and I were in command of a vessel that got caught in the gravitational field of a black hole. My buddy came to our rescue but got caught as well. We ended up using worm hole theory to escape, but we lost structural integrity during the attempt and sustained heavy damage. Audra was crushed when a section she was in collapsed on her." Rayna groaned, watching Gunnar's emotionless face recount the scene. "I was able to pull her free, but she died of her injuries. We buried her in space right after we arrived in Hadrian."

"Gunnar…" Rayna said putting her hand on his. "I am so sorry. Your heart must be broken. The chip, it has her memories on it, doesn't it?"

"Yes, you could say that," Gunnar smiled holding it up again.

"No wonder we couldn't read it or your wrist band," Eldon said remaining focused forward.

"Yeah, you guys are a little behind where I come from."

"Probably kind of hard to get her out of your mind," Rayna pressed back.

Gunnar thought a moment, putting the chip back to his lips.

"There isn't a day that goes by…"

"No offence," Eldon said carefully. "But if it's been that long, shouldn't you be over it by now?"

"Eldon!" Rayna, scolded back. "The man has a right to grieve."

"For two years?"

"For however long it takes!"

"I don't think it should take that long."

"You better be grieving for me a lot longer."

"To be fair," Gunnar interjected. "I'm at a bit of a disadvantage here,"

"How do you mean?" Rayna asked.

"I'm not human."

"Not human?" Rayna gave Eldon a glance.

"You look human to me," Eldon said still watching where they were driving.

"Thank you," Gunnar chuckled. "Sometimes even I forget I'm different."

"How are you different?" Rayna asked. "I'm with Eldon on this. You look normal to me."

"Normal is a relative term," Gunnar said, still smiling. "For the most part, my kind look like anyone else, but there are some visible differences in some cases. For me, they aren't noticeable on the outside, but give me a physical and you'll wonder what you're looking at."

"Please don't tell us you're an android," Rayna hedged.

Gunnar's thoughts shifted to Janox's nanny, Tonnie. He wondered if Alex had been able to get them to Cross safely.

"No," he smiled. "No metal parts. My body structure is a little more robust than a normal human. Tough bones, tough skin, and…"

"But you can still be hurt," Eldon pointed out.

"Yes," Gunnar hesitated, deciding not to finish the description of his insides.

"As evident from when Eldon pulled you out of that wrecked transport, and all the bullet holes we patched up," Rayna said. "By the way, how are those doing?"

"I'm fine," Gunnar said. "Anyway, my insides are prone to heightened stimulus, such as emotional stress. Mostly they're manifested through fits of anger. It has always been something I've had to contend with, but over time, I've pretty much conquered those demons. But I'm afraid Audra's death has changed something inside me. Since she's been gone it's been almost impossible to control those demons. Lately, it seems to be getting worse."

"We haven't noticed you getting upset about anything," Rayna said.

"No," Gunnar said after a moment of silence. "Maybe that crash did me some good after all." The cockpit went quiet again with only the soft, muffled sound of the Talladega's motors permeating the cockpit. He stared at Audra's chip, thinking about what Eldon had said earlier. *Why was he still holding on? Doctor Yamoto had asked a similar question. Was this how Audra would have wanted him to be? Always weighed down by her memory to the point he could hardly function? Would she be happy with how he interacted with people, especially his crew?* He glanced over at Rayna. She was looking at a readout in front of her and Eldon was watching the autopilot displays. He looked back at Audra's chip.

Let me go... he heard Audra's whispered voice. A clear vision of Audra came to his mind and in a split second, the chip was gone. He didn't even remember letting it go, only the wind whipping at his fingertips as it flew away in the Talladega's slipstream. He thought a moment, wondering if maybe he had made a mistake, but after waiting for feelings of dread to come and finding nothing, he felt good about his actions. Smiling slightly, he pulled the window closed and tried to get comfortable.

"We'll be an hour or so at this speed before we leave the lakebed and have to slow down," Eldon announced.

"Big lake," Gunnar said, noticing their speed.

"Maybe you ought to try and get some sleep," Rayna suggested. "I have a feeling you're going to need it."

"If she's driving, you'll need a lot more than sleep," Eldon piped up. Rayna gave him a look that brought a tentative grin to Eldon's face.

Smiling, but feeling a bit tired again, Gunnar nodded and let his gaze return to the outside. The next thing he remembered was thumping his head on the glass of the Talladega's interior. He sat up with a start.

"The suspension was meant for parking, not actual contact with the road," Eldon belted out. Gunnar grabbed hold of seat handle as he was pitched against the window.

"Just slow down," Eldon yelled.

"Not as much fun," Rayna chirped.

"This is why I've left this thing in the garage for so long," Eldon complained.

"Why did we leave the lakebed?" Gunnar asked, leaning forward.

"We ran out of lakebed," Rayna said, steering the craft around a long bend in the dirt roadway.

"Ray," Eldon said firmly. "Slow down. We're in a controlled zone now. You're gonna get us into trouble. One can only hope if we do get stopped, they'll take away your rights to drive anything mechanized."

Gunnar watched Rayna's lips draw up tight.

"Please slow down. Let the city's drive automation do all the work, for my sake," Eldon requested, putting his hand on hers. Rayna looked at her husband's expression and relented, gently pulling back on the throttles and setting the auto-drive controls. As the Talladega slowed, its sound softened considerably. No sooner did the craft slow down to something akin to normal speed, than Gunnar notice buildings lining the paved roadway and other ground transport craft joining them on the road.

"I'll take control now," Eldon said pulling the throttles back even further.

"Why?" Rayna objected. "You made me put it in auto-drive."

"Do you know where we're going?"

"No," Rayna finally mumbled, sitting back.

"Thanks." Eldon gave her a glance and took note of the pouting face. "You know I can't love anyone as much as I love you?"

Rayna tried to remain in pouting mode, but after a few moments of Eldon waiting for a response, she formed a smile and leaned over to exchange a kiss.

"Now," Eldon said glancing behind him while maneuvering the Talladega through the thickening traffic. "We need to get you to a sub-transport station."

"Why not just take him to the main hub?" Rayna asked.

"Because there's too much traffic downtown where it's located. Besides, if his ID doesn't work for some reason, we can stay close and get him out."

"It will work," Rayna looked at Gunnar and then Eldon.

"It'll work," Eldon reassured them.

"Is there anything special I need to say in order to get headed in the right direction?" Gunnar asked. Eldon shook his head.

"Shouldn't be. Once they scan your ID, they'll see who you are, where you belong and where you need to go. Just act like you know what you want and there shouldn't be any questions. This is a civilian transport station. It's likely they'll route you to a military pickup depot and then make sure you're delivered to the *Tarzana*. Once you get there, you're on your own." Eldon turned another corner. "Ah, here we are." He pulled into a darkened entryway and under several structures before emerging a vast open area full of transport craft loading and unloading people and materials. "We'll stick around long enough to make sure you get off ok."

"I can't thank you guys enough." Gunnar opened the side door and clamored out. "My Albion friend told me there are lots of Albions who are great people. You two have been wonderful."

"There are lots of us who are wonderful," Rayna said leaning next to Eldon. "You just happened across the two best." Everyone chuckled softly.

"I owe you guys big time."

"We'll hold you to it," Eldon said. "Someday, you'll do us a favor."

"I look forward to it. Do I look ok?" Gunnar asked standing up and straightening his uniform.

"Good enough to shoot," Eldon said. Rayna nudged him good.

"You look perfect," she reassured him.

"Do I need anything to get on one of these," Gunnar asked, looking around at the different ships clustered around the space port.

"You're military," Eldon looked out at him. "And a Captain in the Special Forces at that. You have the right to bump anyone if necessary. There is no charge for you."

Gunnar took a deep breath and turned for the entry port.

"Ok, here we go," he said waving goodbye to Eldon and Rayna. As they watched him go, a sinking feeling developed in the pit of Rayna's stomach. So much so she took control of the Talladega and parked it next to the entry portal.

"What are you doing?" Eldon asked.

Rayna kept her eyes glued to Gunnar as he approached the counter where the entry agent stood waiting.

"Get your hand glass out."

"My what? What for?"

"I feel it. Something's wrong."

"Ray, he hasn't even reached the desk yet."

"Get it out."

*   *   *   *

Gunnar looked around as he approached the entry agent, wondering if he was supposed to do anything specific.

"Be with you in a moment," the agent said without looking up. Gunnar observed several other people having their ids scanned and placed his wrist over the scanning glass on the counter.

"Just a moment," the agent stopped him.

Gunnar's hearts began to pound a little and his anxiety levels started to spike.

"I'm having some difficulties with my scanning program. Be just a moment." The agent still hadn't looked up from her terminal. After several anxious moments, she looked up. "There, I think I have it working now. Oh," she hesitated a moment. "I am so sorry, Sir. I didn't mean to keep you waiting. It's just my terminal has been glitchy all morning. Had I known, I would have had you step to another port and got you right through."

"It's ok," Gunnar settled. "You just tell me what I need to do and we'll both get through this in one piece." Gunnar smiled, casually dipping his sunglasses to look at the woman over his lenses. The agent smiled and motioned to the sensor glass. Gunnar looked at it and carefully waved his communicator band across it. The agent looked at her terminal and hardened her expression. After fumbling with her controls for a moment, she looked up.

"It didn't read right. Try it again."

Gunnar looked down and realized he had scanned the wrong wrist band. He promptly brought the other wrist up and waved it above the glass.

"There we go," she said looking at the information coming up. "Captain Bridger."

Her gaze hardened again. Gunnar could hear her fingers moving at lightning speed to input different commands into her terminal.

"What in the name of?" she grumbled frustrated.

"Something wrong?" Gunnar asked.

"I'm sure it's this stupid terminal. I am so sorry about the delay."

"Well, what's it doing?"

"It came up with the information, then there was an update and it had all sorts of weird information on it. Wasn't even your picture. Really odd."

"Is it working now?"

"Yes, Captain. You're good to go. I assume your destination is the *Tarzana*?"

"Got to get back to work so the war can continue."

The agent smiled and activated the gate.

"Take shuttle nineteen to the interior military terminal. You'll have a short ride to the Dullen depot. From there, they'll see that you're delivered to your ship."

"Thank you so much," Gunnar said with a cheery grin and passed through the portal. Taking a deep breath, he headed for his assigned transport and boarded without further incident. After finding a seat at a long empty row, he closed his eyes and settled in for the short flight to Dullen. As the shuttle doors closed, he detected a bustling approaching as two individuals sat down next to him.

"That was a close one," Rayna said in an excited whisper. "I knew this would happen."

"Yeah, yeah, yeah," Eldon complained. "You knew it was gonna happen. Now get over yourself." Eldon held his hand glass up and started working with it. "I don't understand. In the civilian networks, that should have worked, at least for a little while. If that's going to happen in that network, the military one is going to be a real challenge."

"Well, if this isn't going to work, then maybe I need to rethink my direction," Gunnar suggested. Eldon shook his head, keeping his eyes on the display.

"No, the more I think about it, the more I'm convinced this is the only way to get you where you need to be. We'll just come along for the ride and try to stay ahead of the security protocols."

"You're not thinking you're going to follow me onto the *Tarzana*?" Gunnar asked.

"That would be so cool," Rayna whispered, leaning into Eldon.

"It would be, but out of the question," Eldon snickered. "Just take plenty of pictures and send them to us when you get the Princess where she needs to be."

"I promise," Gunnar agreed. As the shuttle became airborne, Rayna looked excitedly over Gunnar at the sprawling outskirts of Zepplin. It was a beautiful city with wonderful spiracle architecture for as far as the eye could see.

"Do you not get out much?" Gunnar asked, grunting a bit as Rayna was nearly crawling over him to see out the window.

"Like we told you back at home," Eldon said. "We're kind of naturalists and rarely venture from the lake area. It was a little harder for Ray to leave the city life behind."

"I love this place," Rayna admitted gladly. "The lights, the hustle and bustle, the shopping…"

"The bills, the noise, the crowds," Eldon reminded her.

"Yeah, there's that too," she mumbled, her attention remaining out the window.

"If the civilian transport depot was able to scan my ID, why can't they just deliver me directly to the *Tarzana*?" Gunnar asked.

"Inefficient security procedures," Eldon responded. "Imagine how many crew it takes to man that ship and its flotilla. Population of a small city. Try and get that many people on and off a ship every time it docks and keep everything secure. Easier to just load everyone on one shuttle and take them to a central location; in this case, Dullen."

"Makes sense," Gunnar agreed. "They'd have shuttles all over the place."

"Exactly."

Gunnar finally pushed Rayna back into her seat and got up.

"Eldon's gonna start wondering who you like more," Gunnar said motioning to the now empty seat closer to the window. Rayna giggled softly and jumped to the window.

"We'll be docking in about five minutes," Eldon informed Gunnar as he activated his small glass display. "I watched you with the port agent when you tried to enter and while I would love to have passengers act the way you did, it's not indicative of a special forces officer."

"You mean your military are people with a stick up their rears?"

"Most of them. Remember, most of the Albion people are required to serve in the military and as it is somewhat of a thug style organization, service men and women aren't exactly excited about service. I suspect your character, Captain Bridger, had to do some things he wasn't necessarily proud of to achieve his rank."

"So, I need to be a little tougher?"

"Well, you don't want to draw attention to yourself as a bully or something, but lose the smile and cheery disposition. You said you have anger issues; use them. Let people know you mean business."

"Trust me, my current anger issues aren't something people want to see, let alone deal with," Gunnar said as the transport began to descend toward a large port hub with much bigger ships coming and going.

"Just be more assertive."

As the transport touched down in one of the docking spots, the doors popped opened. Rayna was the first one out, becoming completely engrossed in the sights and sounds around her.

"Hard to believe she's only a little younger than me," Eldon smiled, watching her. She was like a child seeing her first snowfall.

"The Military portal is right over there." Eldon pointed to an entryway with a short line of officers waiting to be scanned. "We'll be sitting right there in those seats making sure you get through."

Gunnar took Eldon's hand and gripping it firmly, shook it gratefully.

"Thank you so much for your help. I value true friendship and count you as a couple on a short list. If there is ever anything I can do to repay your kindness, I'll be disappointed if you don't somehow get a hold of me."

"Just get the Princess back where she rightfully belongs, and we'll call it good." Eldon pulled Gunnar close and they embraced. "Actually, if you ever get in a position to influence someone, you might see about getting our lake back."

"Done," Gunnar chuckled and turned to Rayna. "You're the hardest to leave," he said opening his arms. Rayna grinned and threw herself at him.

"I have that effect on everyone." Rayna gave him a good squeeze. "You be careful. You still have a lot to live for and I have a feeling something wonderful is on the horizon for you."

"Thanks for your help," Gunnar said pulling from her and turning for the portal. After several minutes of waiting in line, he stepped up to the attendant and put his wrist over the scanner. The attendant watched the information flash in front of them as Gunnar looked back at Eldon and Rayna. Eldon was madly working with his glass display.

"Is there a problem?' Gunnar inquired sternly.

"One moment, Captain," the attendant paused. "The scan is being slow for some reason. I'm getting a lot of glitches in your telemetry."

"Do you need to rescan?"

"No, I think I can get it clear. What's your destination?"

"Where does it say I'm stationed?"

"*Tarzana*, but..."

"Then it seems logical that's where I'm heading, doesn't it?"

"Yes, Sir."

"Good, now, is there a problem or not?"

"No, Sir. I can clear you here, but you'll need to have your wrist ID reimaged the first chance you get." The attendant deactivated the entry barrier and gestured to the opening. Gunnar gave Eldon and

Rayna a glance and a wink, then disappeared through the crowded portal.

"I'm gonna miss that guy," Eldon said, turning to help Rayna to her feet.

"Me too," she echoed. "Now, you need to feed me before you take me home."

Sanctuary

Diord stared at the moving portrayals on the opposite wall from where his desk sat. Several of the larger ones were landscapes of various destinations on Cross. There were a few starscapes depicting various quasars in motion and while they were all mesmerizing, he wasn't really looking at them, but thinking of something far off. Sitting for several minutes, he realized he was so focused on his thoughts, he was barely breathing. He finally shifted his eyes to a window. Outside, both of Cross's moons were still visible, one just above the horizon and the other slipping past his view at the top of the window. He let his eyes drop to the smooth glass of his desktop. A variety of images were tiled across its surface. These weren't security cameras by any means, but they did give him a general overview of what was happening with his interests planet wide.

Leaning forward, he gently tapped the surface and a keypad appeared in the glass. He touched several points in sequence, but then stopped, hesitating to finish what he had started. Twiddling his thumbs with indecision, he looked around the room and finally tapped the glass. The monitors in his desk winked and a myriad of photos popped up. He leaned down on both elbows and gazed at images of him and CJ Barker. Though the number of pictures seemed endless, he examined each one, thinking of those earlier times when they were together. Looking at them now, they felt so distant, such a long time ago. Indeed, they were definitely younger people back then. CJ's hair was about as red as it could be with no white locks as she had now. Many of the snapshots were of them arm in arm in exotic locations around Hadrian. There were even a few of them kissing. As he continued to look through them, he stopped on her portrait. Touching the keypad again, the other pictures disappeared as the portrait took up nearly the entire desktop. Gazing at her made something inside him stir. Not that it hadn't before. Normally he kept these pictures concealed for just that reason. This time, he didn't care if it stirred or how much; he just let it go. For several minutes he admired her, looking away for only a second, then quickly coming back to her lovely green eyes.

A summons came to his door and he touched another control on the keypad, causing all the images to disappear. Standing up, he moved to his window, wiping his eyes.

"Come in."

"Sorry for the interruption, Administrator."

"You're not interrupting anything," Diord assured the younger gentleman.

"You wanted to see these production reports as soon as they were available." The man handed him a small viewing device. "I would have just sent them directly to your desk, but you left instructions not to…"

"Yes, this is fine."

Diord walked across the room and took the reader. After looking at it for several minutes, he looked up at the man standing uncomfortably patient in front of his desk.

"Tyrel, has your group been able to account for the drop in production output in the command and defensive sectors?"

"Yes, Administrator Vandmire. If you'll look under the fourth heading, it gives all the numbers and the conclusions drawn based on the available data."

"Do you agree with these conclusions?" Diord kept his eyes glued to the viewer.

Tyrel fidgeted slightly, giving Diord cause to look up.

"Well come on then, out with it."

"It's your personal projects you've been sending off world, Administrator. There are no payments coming from these. We haven't even gotten a name to bill to. We can recover from these burdensome expenses, but the shareholders are asking questions that are becoming harder to explain away."

"Yes, this would seem to be a problem." Diord sat back down and dropped the viewer on the desk. "Have you been able to track where the materials are coming from?"

Tyrel developed an odd look. Diord grinned broadly.

"If you'll go further back up the manufacturing chain, you'll find that all those projects sent out were returned change orders or project overruns with nowhere to go. The original clients had already paid for them, but couldn't use them, so they returned them to us for resale. But these were the custom orders that couldn't be used anywhere else. Wouldn't you think we would be money ahead if we could get them out of our hair?"

"We generally dump them somewhere or melt them down."

"Exactly," Diord said smiling. "Was there anything else?"

Tyrel picked up the viewer and started for the door, but stopped before he reached it.

"Administrator, why isn't all this declared in the general ledgers? I assume the transport fees for these projects are accounted for."

"If you dig deep enough, you'll find everything is accounted for. I wouldn't be in this position very long if I were embezzling. It's buried under layers to keep Cross and my position, protected from political vipers constantly creeping about looking for a way to usurp our way of life. You'll find the transport fees under my personal account."

"You paid for all this, yourself, out of your own funds?"

"They are my projects…"

A look of relief sprang to Tyrel's face as he realized his employer was indeed, an honorable man and concerned for the welfare of Cross. As he turned back to the door, Diord stopped him.

"Anything from Albia on the military channels?"

"We've monitored some action in the Nulark system, but nothing directly from Albia. There was a curious landing request from a Kalamarion vessel, but they couldn't provide us with any…"

"Kalamarion vessel?" Diord was out from behind the desk and to the door before Tyrel could react. "How long ago?" Diord was rushing down the hall towards his personal turbo lift.

"We rejected their approach request about twenty minutes ago," Tyrel called after the administrator. "They couldn't provide the correct approach clearances."

"What station?" Diord asked activating the lift.

"Clearance station nine on level three, Controller Tillerssen."

The door couldn't close fast enough, neither could the lift descend fast enough. Bursting from the door when it finally opened on level three, he nearly ran into a crowd of pedestrians passing by. Spinning and dodging the crowd, he finally rushed into the clearance station and came to a sliding halt at position nine. The controller cautiously turned around, thinking they were either under attack or in trouble for something and didn't want to further aggravate the situation.

"Controller Tillerssen?" Diord was trying to control his breathing.

The controller glanced around, waiting for the guards to show up.

"Yes…?"

"You denied approach to a Kalamarion vessel about twenty minutes ago?"

"Yes, Sir…" The controller was still quite wary. "Was I not supposed to?"

"You did just fine," Diord answered. "Do you still have them on your scopes?"

"Not directly. Zulu patrol is escorting them away from our space."

"Do they still have them?"

"One moment, Sir." The controller turned and adjusted a control, then started speaking while Diord scanned the room. "Yes, Sir. They were just about to release them and come back."

"Have that patrol bring them back. Give that ship top clearance and assign it four corvette escorts."

"Four escorts?"

"You're right, that's not enough; make it six, and tell Zulu to stay with them. If there are any other patrols nearby, they are to join the escort immediately. That ship must be protected at all costs. See to it they're brought down into my personal landing bay. Have security team Echo and Helix meet me down there immediately."

Diord turned on one heel and dashed out. This time, he made his way to a transport portal and caught a ride down into the underground decks of the Alvadore complex. Once past the security check points, he slowed his pace a little and headed to the VIP quarters. Checking the time as he entered, he looked up at several security men coming to their feet in the lounge.

"Thank you for coming so quickly gentlemen," he said stopping in front of several of the lead security guards.

"What's the target, Sir?" one of them asked.

Diord stepped toward one of the windows on the far side of the room. Looking out, he had a full view of an adjoining landing bay.

"In a about ten to fifteen minutes, a ship is going to be landing in this bay. I want every entrance and window secured. If you have to pull in more people, do it."

"What are we to expect?" another asked.

"You'll know when I know. Move out." Diord glanced at his watch again, then looked around the room. He wasn't sure what to expect. It was either going to be Colonel Gunnar Conrad or his General friend, Rick Niker, and if they were manning their Assault Corsairs, they would have their crews with them. CJ hadn't said anything about finding General Niker's ship, so it would have to be the Colonel's ship. In either case, Diord understood the need for security and secrecy. The Albions and Colonians were hot to find these ships and would likely start a war with Cross if they knew they were here. Sitting down to relax, his communicator went off.

"Administrator, this is Approach control, level three. You wanted to know when we got a visit from the *Executioner*."

"I really don't want to hear this," Diord groaned.

"Sorry, Administrator. Aura isn't in orbit, but he is waiting on the outer border asking to come in."

"What a change. Of course he wants something. Leave him where he is and we'll deal with him when I'm through down here in the VIP bay."

"Excuse me, Administrator, but he said to give you a message."

"What?"

"The Colonians have found Aster."

Diord shuddered. A myriad of scenarios began running through his head. *How could they have found it? A better question was how did Lou Aura know about any of this?*

"Administrator?"

"I heard you," Diord responded.

"What response would you like me to send?"

Diord thought a moment; things were starting to get more complicated than he was comfortable with.

"Send no response, but bring him in under escort."

"With the amount of heightened security we're dealing with already, we're running a little low on available escort ships, Administrator."

"I'm sure we are. Do the best you can and we'll release these six corvettes as soon as they've finished down here."

"Yes, Administrator."

Diord dug into his shirt pocket, pulling out the antidote vile CJ had given him and thought a while. Gunnar would probably be glad to see this. Diord was well educated in the toxins and germ warfare prevalent in war. The countermeasures generally made the use of chemicals a moot point and so warring factions didn't bother. As he sat, the sound system in the VIP lounge came alive.

"Kalamarion craft on approach to VIP landing bay, standby bay doors."

Diord came to his feet and looked out the bay overview window just as the doors began to slide back, revealing the bright Cross sky. Folding his arms, he waited anxiously for the familiar shape of the Starbird to dip into the bay opening, instead a Kalamarion Interceptor glided to a smooth landing as the doors began to close behind it. The curious V-winged craft was hurriedly surrounded by a small platoon of security troops, their weapons drawn. Diord stood motionless, fixated on the fighter. The fact that it was here and not the entire Corsair was a red flag. He finally headed down to the bay floor to join the security forces.

After only a moment of waiting, the lower hatch dropped open and a small white droid was lowered to the floor by a pair of arms. Moments later, a young woman climbed down and turned to help another person out. Diord recognized Alex 7001 rolling directly toward him and held a hand to the barrel of the guard's drawn weapons as the little droid came to a stop in front of him.

"Administrator Vandmire, we need your help."

Diord dropped to one knee, but looked up at the two women making their way towards him.

"I thought you could fly, uhm, Alex is it?"

"My antigrav systems have been damaged, but I am still mobile."

Diord rose to greet the two women.

"Janox, it's good to see you, though I'm a little surprised. I assume there's a reason you're here."

Janox stopped short of being within reach, and held onto Tonnie's arm and a book. Sensing her discomfort, Diord gestured toward the door to the VIP lounge.

"I have a place close by where we can talk privately." Diord, motioned for the guards to secure the area as he followed Alex and the two women into the VIP lounge. Watching Alex struggle with some of the stairs, Diord finally picked the little droid up and carried him the rest of the way. Once inside and convinced they were alone and safe, Janox sat down next to Tonnie, holding her book on her lap. A somber mood fell on the room as Diord waited for someone to speak.

"Who's your friend?" Diord inquired, trying to break the awkward silence. He held out a hand to Tonnie.

"My name is Tonnie," the Au Pair spoke, carefully taking his hand and letting Diord pull it up to his lips.

"You guys look like you've had a busy day. Want to tell me about it?"

Diord sat down across from Janox and waited for someone to speak. He glanced down at Alex, who sat facing the two women.

"Has something happened with Gunnar and his ship?"

Still nothing.

"Alex, can you break the silence?"

The droid turned its head around to the Administrator, but remained silent.

"He's gone," Janox rasped through tear filled eyes.

"What do you mean, he's gone? Did his ship come under attack?"

"No... I don't know," she sniffled.

"Shall I explain everything, your Highness?" Alex inquired.

Tonnie shook her head, then encouraged Janox to continue.

"I, I kidnapped Alex and Gunnar and made them take me to Reako while Gunnar's ship was on a mission to Carolon."

"You kidnapped them?" Diord looked away, trying not to smile. "Why in the world would you ever want to go back to Reako?"

"I knew Tonnie was still alive. She just needed help. Alex and Gunnar helped her."

"Wait, you mean to tell me your friend here, was still down inside Reako? By herself?"

"Gunnar brought her out, Alex helped to fix her."

"Fix her?" Diord repeated looking at Tonnie.

"She was hurt, they helped to rescue her and bring her out of Reako."

"Ok, I'm certain I'm only getting the nibble version here, go on."

"Tonnie is my Au Pair. She tells truth about me. Said we need to get evidence of my real self and bring to you. We had to go to Albia to get it."

"Albia?" Diord cried. "Are you serious? I told Gunnar to keep you as far away from those people as possible and here he takes you right into the thick of it! What the heck was he thinking?"

"It was the only way to retrieve the evidence of the Princess's royal lineage," Tonnie interjected. "It was hidden in a records vault on Dither."

Janox pulled her fingers across the binding of her book, tears dripping from her cheeks.

"This is my book. My father wrote in this book and left me message before he died; telling me who I am and what I must do."

"And who are you?" Diord asked, knowing full well her identity. He smiled, realizing she was just coming to a knowledge of her royal

heritage. He could see she was working up the courage to make her first royal proclamation.

Janox looked down at her locket, then at her mother's ring. She looked at Tonnie, who nodded slightly, then turned back to Diord.

"I am Jana Tilee Oxlind, Colonian Princess of Hadrian. Fifth daughter and seventh child of their royal majesties, King Tiev and Queen Mila Oxlind of Colonia and the House of Pintar." By the time she had finished, she sat up erect and confident.

Diord smiled proudly and kneeling in front of the Princess, kissed her hand, then bowed his head.

"Your Majesty." The Cross administrator looked up into Jana's tear filled eyes. "How may I serve the House of Pintar?"

"The Princess Oxlind requests you provide her sanctuary," Tonnie announced, rising to her feet.

Diord rose and bowed again to the Princess while nodding his head.

"Yes, of course. Can you tell me what has happened to Colonel Conrad and his ship?"

Jana tried to speak, but was again overcome, her grief spilling out in the form of more tears, so Tonnie spoke.

"On Dither, we were tracked and ambushed before we could reach Gunnar's fighter. The Princess and I were nearly taken. It was only through Gunnar's bravery that we were able to get aboard his fighter and get away from the troopers tracking us. But we lost one of the royal rings during the fight to get away."

"That's going to be a problem," Diord mumbled.

"Tonnie and Gunnar were hit many times in order to see to my safety," Jana sniffled, barely under control. "I was able to help Tonnie inside, even as she and Gunnar took hits from ground fire. Gunnar did not make it," Jana finally let go, spilling her grief unchecked.

"He took several more hits and fell into the forest as we were taking off," Tonnie finished. "We didn't see him hit the ground, but at our height, it's not possible for him to have survived." Tonnie took the grief stricken Princess in her consoling arms."

"He ordered me to bring the Princess here, to Cross," Alex announced.

"He said you would know what to do," Tonnie said.

Diord nodded grimly as he fingered the antidote vile still in his shirt pocket.

"You'll be safe here," Diord finally said, looking curiously at Tonnie. "I have everything you will need here in these living quarters and my security forces will see to your safety. If you'd like to freshen up and rest for a bit, I'll see if I can arrange to have all three of you examined and something to eat."

"We do not require examinations," Tonnie insisted.

Diord gave all three a good looking over.

"You've been in a fire fight on Dither and who knows what else down in Reako. Alex here can't even fly any more. The Princess is no doubt suffering from flak poisoning and you're still bleeding whatever that is you call blood," Diord indicated pointing at Tonnie's arms and legs.

Tonnie looked at herself, then at Jana.

"Perhaps a bath would do us all some good."

"No water for me," Alex insisted. "But if you have any Tentorium, I might be able to synthesize it to refill my antigrav anodes so I can fly again."

"I'm pretty sure we've got something to offer everyone," Diord reassured them. "Once you've had a chance to clean up, rest and something to eat, we can study your father's lineage and figure everything out." Diord looked after Tonnie as she headed to one of the rooms adjoining the main room. As Jana picked up her things, Diord stopped her. "Your Highness, may I ask another question?"

"Please, Administrator," Jana said quietly, but with elevated dignity. "I'm still new at being a royal. It will take me some time to fully realize my position and the responsibilities that will come with it. Can you try to call me Jana?"

"I will try when conversing at a personal level," Diord said. He smiled watching her wipe her nose and eyes.

"What is your question?" Jana asked.

"Your Au Pair, Tonnie." Diord looked to the door the royal nanny had disappeared behind.

"What of her?"

"What race is she. Clearly she isn't human?"

"Gunnar called her an android."

"How did he come to that conclusion?"

"Tonnie told him."

"She's a machine?"

"She's an android. I do not pretend to understand exactly what that is, other than if you believe the teachings of the Thane, she is a life form just like you and me, only different."

"Will she require maintenance, like Alex?"

"I believe she will, but she will have to be the one to indicate what that is."

Diord's communicator went off as Jana turned for her room. He waited until she had closed her door before he activated the com.

"Yes?"

"Lou Aura is ready to meet with you. Where shall I put him?"

"I'll meet him down in the Letoh Blue Lounge."

"Administrator?"

"He'll be more comfortable where drinks are available."

"Yes, Administrator."

Diord turned to leave, but nearly tripped over Alex.

"I am so sorry, Alex," Diord said, clamoring to hold his balance and not step on the little white droid. "Would you prefer I have the materials you need brought here or would you like the use of one of my workshops?"

"As long as you wouldn't mind me creating a navigational map of your complex so I can move about freely, I would prefer the workshop. But, Administrator, I would hope that you would honor our culture's policies on giving away our technological secrets to inferior cultures."

"Not sure how I'm supposed to take that," Diord reacted with a chuckle.

"I meant no offense."

"I'll take you to the shop on my way out. Would you like to follow along or should I carry you?"

"As long as there are no stairs, I'll be fine as I am." Diord turned and started back toward the main Alvadore complex, stopping at a small workshop on the way.

*   *   *   *

Diord sat lazily in a booth in the Blue Lounge on the main floor of the Alvadore Letoh complex. On the small drink table sat a dish of hors d'oeuvres and a couple of glasses of a red fluid. He looked around. This time of day, there weren't a lot of visitors to the bar. Most were out having fun, doing what they did on a destination planet such as Cross. As he glanced around, he took note of several individuals scattered throughout the bar, each looking for a little solitude. If they were hoping for quiet, they would get none at this particular time. Just as he was about to touch his wrist com, he noticed Lou Aura enter the bar main doors, flanked by two others; a man and a woman. It took Lou only a moment to zero in on the Cross Administrator and make his way toward Diord's table.

"My friend!" Lou called boisterously.

Diord's expression didn't change much, but he did hold a glass up as Lou shuffled into the booth and motioned for his companions to find somewhere else to sit.

"Hey, Lou." Diord took a drink. "How much is this going to cost me?"

"Cost you? What are you talking about?"

"Remember the last time you were here?"

"If anything, that cost me and if you hadn't let me go, I might have lost my Command seat to Yarnell."

"Yeah, well it would have served you right. I still haven't been able to get everyone's belongings back to them."

"What about the room?"

"They've been able to get the doors and walls back on, but it's still a mess up there."

"After all this time? Can't you just throw some filler on it, do a little laser sanding and call it good?"

"Let me put it this way. My guys are having to go through the entire floor with metal detectors looking for ordnance. They've found rounds on the opposite side of the building."

"Those Vivitars are nasty machines." Lou picked up something to eat and started chewing. "I'm assuming your friends got away ok, since it would appear you've stationed them out on Aster."

"Or so I thought," Diord said taking another swallow. "What's it going to cost me for the information you've got?"

"What are you willing to pay?"

"I'm pretty sure we can come to an arrangement, provided the information is credible."

"Oh, it's credible," Lou said stuffing his face. "Hey, these are really good. Where did you get these?"

Diord watched the Tomplie eat for a moment, then reached over to the plate and tried one of the hors d'oeuvres. Surprised, he tried another one.

"Num, these really are pretty good."

"You had these made special, didn't you?" Lou asked, grabbing the last one.

"Actually, I've never eaten anything from this place," Diord said looking around.

"Well, if you'll include a crate of whatever these things are in our little deal, I'll be fat and happy for a long time." Lou took a drink then became serious, leaning down on his elbows. "A week and a half ago, a couple of my boys were buzzing through the Spartus quadrant in Skillman territory."

"Brave boys," Diord commented flatly.

"Well, they sort of got off track a little."

"A little?" Diord leaned in closer. "Your guys were so far out into the Spartus they encountered the Skillman? You're lucky they aren't part of the Drake military now. So, what happened, you have to barter them out?"

"No, they made it back out ok, but there was a Colonian Cutter group waiting for them. I went in with half my battle group and all of a sudden, they were all over us."

"They were that good?"

"No, the usual, but they were joined by four other groups, and within about two minutes, they had us surrounded. I lost half my group and a bunch of great officers and men."

"Seems to me like that would make you want to look for a different way of life, and while I feel bad for your loss, what does any of this have to do with the Colonians finding Aster?"

"Because they captured one of my disabled scout ships intact. It had Aster's exact location in its navigational data banks."

Diord stopped in mid chew, thinking of the ramifications, especially considering the current events.

"Yeah, but Aster is moving…"

"You really going to try and pacify yourself with that crap?" Lou retorted.

"Yeah, I know. Just trying to think of some kind of hope. They've got a pretty good defensive array around the place, but if the Colonians decided to really put the pressure on, they could liquify that base pretty quick."

"I suggest you get them out of there as soon as possible."

"This couldn't come at a worse time," Diord complained.

"More production problems, my friend?"

"You know, the Pintar rite of Hadrian? The Colonians have to come up with a legitimate Royal heir to the throne or legal rule turns over to the strongest faction in Hadrian. That'll mean all-out war."

"It's just about an even split between the Colonians and the Albions. The Albions wouldn't stand a chance without the Ratronians."

"If the Rats knew what was good for them, they would disavow themselves from the Albions and just sit back. I'm not one who gives a flying fig about what goes on with governments, but this latest instance with my fleet has me on edge. I can deal with our little engagements, in fact, I live for them, but having a full-scale fleet chasing after you makes it impossible to get any pirating done with any efficiency."

"Wouldn't want to disrupt your efficiency."

"Come on, I'm serious! You and I have a great thing going on here. You manufacture for every knot headed military in these two quadrants. I keep the space around the area clean and honest."

"Honest? You're calling what you do, honest?"

"If Albia becomes the ruling faction in Hadrian, they'll stop paying for their hardware and demand you work for them for free. Then they'll come after me."

"You're suggesting we band together then?"

"Unless you have a better idea. I just can't see things getting any better."

"Why not just dash out into the Spartus and make new friends out there?"

"Tried that already. It didn't work out so well. The Skillman weren't very nice."

"Well, there are larger issues at stake than just what business can produce."

"You're not suggesting a noble cause, are you? Where would you find such a thing?"

Diord thought carefully, considering the options.

"Are you in a hurry to be anywhere?"

"Well, I usually like to patrol the outer traffic patterns of Teal, just outside Jurass…"

"Anywhere important?"

"No, not really. What are you thinking?"

Diord scratched his head, trying to decide what was to be done. He understood the need for quick action, but it had to be the right action with the right people. Was it possible that forming an alliance with pirates was the right course?

"Can you come with me? I want to introduce you to someone."

"Only if my guys can come along," Lou said, motioning to his companions.

"You don't trust me?" Diord asked motioning to his men as well. All around the booth, every occupant rose to their feet and began moving toward them. Each seemed a bit tense, some of them holding a hand inside their jackets or behind them. Lou and Diord grinned broadly as they looked around.

"Ok, we'll do it your way," Lou said, knowing he was outnumbered.

"We'll bring them all with us until we reach the secured area. I've got a place they can all take a load off, so long as they'll behave themselves."

"Fair enough," Lou said gesturing for Diord to lead the way. As they left, the bar emptied out, Diord's and Lou's men following the two leaders through Alvadore.

*   *   *   *

"I've never seen so many clothes," Jana exclaimed. "How can one person possibly need this much?"

"The better question, your Highness," Tonnie said watching the young Princess. "Why does a man like Administrator Vandmire have so many female clothes?"

"He must entertain a lot," Jana replied.

"I don't know much about him, so I'll have to take your word for it."

"I don't know much about him either other than he helped Gunnar, CJ and I when we first came out of Reako. I think the administrator and CJ used to have feelings for each other."

"How could you tell?"

"I can see it in them, the way they talk to each other and the way they look at the other."

Tonnie thought a moment processing the information available to her, then hearing movement in the outer chambers, motioned to Jana to get dressed. As the nanny closed the door behind her, she turned around in time to see Diord and Lou walk in.

"You're looking better," Diord commented, giving the Au Pair a good looking over.

"Yes, we are feeling much better, thank you for your hospitality." The nanny smiled graciously.

"Tonnie, this is an acquaintance of mine, Lou Aura. We'd like to request a formal audience with her Highness. Is she available?"

"Yes, I believe she is," the nanny smiled. "One moment please."

"Her Highness?" Lou asked leaning a little closer to the administrator. "Have you got Benetar in the next room?"

"Or what," Diord whispered. A moment later, the door reopened and Tonnie emerged.

"Her Royal Highness, Princess Jana Tilee Oxlind, Fifth daughter to their royal majesties, the late, King Tiev and Queen Mila Oxlind of Colonia and the House of Pintar."

Jana stepped into the room and stood in front of the two gentlemen.

"Is this some sort of a joke?" Lou asked, watching Diord bow respectfully.

"Not a joke," Diord whispered sideways. "Now bow."

Lou bowed awkwardly, then went to sit down, but straightened back up when he realized the Cross Administrator wasn't moving. A pleasant expression formed on the Princess's face as she looked behind her and finding a seat, sat down. Once she was situated, Diord and Lou sat.

"The Princess has requested asylum here on Cross and I have agreed to provide her with whatever protection she needs."

"You'll forgive me for being suspicious, it's in my nature," Lou started.

"He's a professional pirate," Diord added with a wink.

"There is such a thing as a profession of piracy?" Jana asked, looking at Diord, then at Lou. "Should I be worried?" she asked looking back at Diord.

"No don't worry, he's harmless."

"Wait a minute," Lou said leaning forward. He gave Diord a double take, looked over at Tonnie, then back at Jana. "You think you're the rightful heir to the Hadrian throne..."

Jana nodded slightly. Lou looked back and forth at everyone in the room.

"You guys are messing with me," he grinned. "You don't actually think..."

"Was there are reason you brought this man with you?" Jana asked looking to Diord.

"It's a bit of a stretch for my friend," Diord hedged.

"Tonnie, will you bring my book, please?" Jana requested quietly.

"Book? What book?" Lou asked in a whisper as Tonnie went into the other room.

"The Pintar genealogy from the original Royal Pintar line down through the Oxlind Royals."

"There's no such book," Lou retorted still in a whisper.

"Clearly there is."

Tonnie reappeared and handed Jana her book. With the book on her lap, Jana pulled her locket out and held it up for Diord and Lou to see.

"This is encoded directly to my DNA and biosignature. You're welcome to try this before me if you'd like."

"I'd like," Lou said, searching for more evidence of authenticity.

Tonnie took the book from Jana's lap and handed it to Lou, then gave him the locket. After twisting and turning it, he sat looking at it, trying to decide if he was making it too complicated.

"Here, let me give it a whirl," Diord said taking the locket and placing it in the indentation. Fumbling with it for a moment, he finally gave up. "I believe you," he said.

Tonnie returned the book and locket to Jana, who held it close, smiling.

"It has taken me longer than it should to understand and accept who I am and my rightful place. I've spent many hours during our travels here, learning my history and coming to know my parents. I am seeking assistance in repatriating my parent's bloodline to the throne of Hadrian." Jana set the book back in her lap and gently inserted the locket orb into the indentation. Everyone watched as the device began to glow, the tiny words appearing around its surface. After turning the ball several directions, she pushed on it and everyone watched amazed as the mechanism released the book. Once the pages were open, Jana placed the book on the table in front of Diord and Lou, bidding them to examine its contents.

For some time, they poured over the pages of the book, tracing back the bloodline of the Oxlind genealogy and learning a little bit about their own lineage along the way. They watched parts of the message Jana's father had left her and examined her mother's ring. As they wound down their examination, Lou took the book in his lap to read some items a little closer while Diord chatted with Jana and Tonnie.

"I have zero doubt you were being used by someone or some faction of Hadrian to try and make it look like there was a legal precedent to assume the throne. As Tonnie has relayed to us, it sounds like the Duchess Benetar and Lord Dismon could be at the center of this. Confront them and you could expose the entire plot."

"The problem is, how can you confront them?" Tonnie pointed out. "You can't just march up to the palace doorstep on Tintee and demand to be heard, plus you wouldn't be able to prove it to more than a couple of people. It would have to be in a manner all the factions of Hadrian could witness."

"Hey," Lou exploded. "Look! I have royal blood! I'm a descendant of the Duke of Quinn!" The leader of the Tomplie clan gleamed

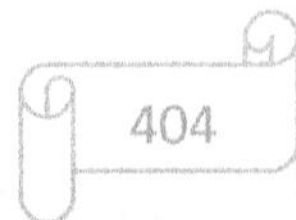

broadly pointing at a name on the page in front of him. Diord looked closely at it, joined a moment later by Tonnie.

"If you can show your lineage documentation," Tonnie said. "This man, Darington Spegal Waldron of the House of Waldron would be your great, great, great grandfather."

"So, what is the Quinn?" Diord asked, methodically following the genealogical spreadsheet.

"It doesn't say, exactly. Only that it is a clan that was located in the Spartus quadrant," Tonnie answered. "Quite possibly a smaller realm subservient to another kingdom. Logic would suggest your ancestors immigrated to this quadrant. You said you're Tomplie? It's likely your ancestors fell out of favor with the Quinn and they chose to ride with the house of Tomplie. From there, it doesn't take much to figure out how the pirate part got added."

"Not sure if you've just insulted me or not," Lou said.

"Quinn, Cross or Tomplie, we all stand to lose our basic freedoms should we do nothing," Jana asserted. "Will you help me?"

Diord and Lou looked at each other, then back at Princess Jana.

"Well, I am royalty, after all," Lou boasted. "So, count The House of Waldron in on whatever you have in mind."

"All you needed was a noble cause," Diord smiled, shaking his head. "Your Highness, we pledge our support in a coordinated effort to bring the House of Oxlind's rightful blood heir back to the throne of Hadrian."

"Thank you, Administrator Vandmire and, General Aura. Will you present me with a plan?"

"As soon as we can think of one," Diord said. "First we have a lot of prep work to do." Diord motioned for Lou to follow him out after they bowed. As they left the room, Lou gave Diord a good-natured push.

"Who would have ever thought you and me would be on the same team?"

"Well, I wouldn't exactly call this a team, but it is rather strange to think we're going to be working together for a short time."

"Yeah, and what about that Tonnie?" Lou asked in a low voice, looking behind them as they started down the hall. "She's a nice package. Do you suppose there would be some time for...?"

"Lou..." Diord blurted as they continued. "Is that all you think about?"

"Not the only thing I think about."

"First off, you have how many wives?"

"Four."

"Just four?"

"I don't count the two on Junkers. They wouldn't allow me to consummate."

"I wonder why? And let's count how many concubines you have."

"Concubines aren't wives, they're… concubines."

"The point is, you have more female companionship than any one man ought to have. In your case, any man has a right to have. Why in the world would you think you need to ruin another woman's life?"

"Ruin? I don't ruin, I *enhance*."

"Shall we set up some interviews? Besides, she's not your type."

"I like all types."

"I guarantee she's not you're type."

"Come on," Lou persisted. "I'm irresistible."

Diord stopped and turned to Lou.

"She's an android, Lou. She's not your type and you certainly aren't hers. I'm not sure whose type she is, other than another android and the closest thing to that would be that little Kalamarion droid, Alex 7001."

"An android," Lou repeated. "But she looks so real."

"I think that's what the original design of an android is all about. Come on, we have a lot of work to do."

"An android," Lou muttered, still standing in the hall. He finally broke from his stunned silence and caught up with Diord. "So, what have you got in mind to get the Princess in front of everyone in Hadrian? That'll be one big feat and that doesn't include all the resistance we're bound to meet trying to make it happen."

"The Pintar rite of Hadrian happens in three days at Calliope. We need to get her into that ceremony."

"How? That place will be crawling with Albion and Colonian forces under the command of whoever is behind this plot."

"Well, first off I'm going to recall Colonel Barker's command on Aster. Bring all her forces back here to join ours. That will bring my fleet strength up sizably. Then we join our two fleets together, exceeding either fleet's total strength."

"But who's going to command them?"

"You are, of course."

"Me? What makes you think your boys and Aster Command are going to listen to a bunch of pirates?"

Diord and Lou turned a corner and headed toward the VIP lounge where their men were waiting.

"I'll make sure they do," Diord answered.

"I'd much rather you command, and I'll play backup to the entire operation."

"Now is not the time to show the wrong colors, Aura."

"What wrong colors? I'm a pirate, we have the same black ones all the time. Besides, my men will never get along with yours. There's just too much bad blood."

"They'll be fine, you'll see."

Diord and Lou stopped short as a body came hurtling out the lounge door and landed against the opposite wall. The woman slumped over unconscious as Diord and Lou leaned forward to look inside the room at the ruckus exhibited.

"Is she one mine or yours?" Lou asked.

"I don't think I had any females in my group," Diord said slowly, glancing back at the unconscious woman. Another body came free from the brawl inside and was sent hurtling through the open door. "This one's mine."

The man got up, gave his commander a quick glance and barreled back into the thick of the fight.

"Looks like it. Two against; how many did you bring?"

"I don't know," Diord replied in disgust. "At least they've all got the fighting spirit. We better break this up before they destroy everything." Diord carefully made his way into the room, followed by Lou who had to slam himself against the wall in order to keep from getting struck and pulled into the fray.

"Glad I didn't bring any more with me?" Lou said over the noise.

Underdog

The darkness of space is endless. Thinking about occupying a given point in space, turns the mind to thoughts of what actually remains unseen around that point in space. In the grand scheme of all things visible, an object occupying a given point in space is never really isolated, just so far from another object as to seem distant. Whether aboard ship or free floating in isolation, thoughts of how far objects are from any given point naturally come to mind.

Billy Moon was no different. Although he had spent a good share of his career in space and had logged countless hours in different types of space suits, he couldn't help but think of how far away from anything he was.

For first-timers, a spacewalk is a bit of a challenge. The body isn't accustomed to the rigors of such harsh environments. Despite what the suit can provide the physical, there is also the psychological effects on the mind. As Fuji Yamoto had freely admitted, she's a whimp when it came to anything approaching open space. She never could adjust to it and to hear her talk about her adventures helping Audra Atlanta rescue Tiana Mantose, she sounded proud of that fact. But Billy had to admit, even with all his years in space, his first time out created a bit of a quandary while the body made the adjustment. The feeling of constantly falling usually sends the mind into a tailspin.

Billy looked down at his boots. He could barely see the tips for the respirator control panel mounted to his chest. The suit itself was a marvel of modern technology. Being the most streamline of any design, it was still more cumbersome that just wearing pants, a long sleeved shirt and a jacket on an outing to the forest. He sort of wished the suit was an older design. The kind you could almost turn around inside of because of the bulk. At least then he'd have a chance at getting at some of the electronics mounted to the upper back of the suit.

Gazing at his feet, he looked past them into the starfield beyond. It was the same whether he looked up, down or side to side; endless stars and nebulas. He touched the booster control on his glove and slowly turned around. Now, the bright sphere of Carolon came into view in the distance. Most people felt more comfortable seeing a large object relatively close by; it did nothing for Billy's frame of mind. If it were a ship, that would be different, but a planet was only a place to be drawn toward, eventually burning up on entry in the atmosphere. The best way to come back to the surface of a planet was aboard a craft designed for such operations; not in a spacesuit. He turned back to the last known position of the *Constellation*. If his HUD unit were working properly, he'd know exactly where the *Constellation* and the Albion ship were. He held on to the hope his actions had bought his crewmates time to make good an escape.

Allowing himself to gradually rotate, Billy let his mind wander through the possibilities that could evolve in his near future. If nothing else were to happen, his air supply would eventually run out in a couple of days and he'd suffocate. Then things would get hot in his suit's atmosphere and he'd start to suffer from carbon dioxide poisoning and hypoxia. If still undamaged, his suit would take care of his body fluids and waste materials. He had been floating long enough he was sure his heaters were still functioning correctly; he wasn't cold. The suit's batteries were designed to last for days as well. The problem here didn't seem to be whether he could remain alive for an extended period of time, but what was he supposed to do during his isolation? *You can't just pull up a chair and wait for something to happen,* he thought. Weightlessness did provide for simplicity as it pertained to sleeping. *No need to worry about a kinked neck or the blood running to your head.*

Continuing to rotate, Billy detected a myriad of flashes appear off to his right. His first instinct was to hit his booster button to get closer for a better look, but he understood his size relative to the space around him. As he was sure he was traveling outbound from Carolon's influence, trying to reverse his trajectory seemed pointless. Still, it would be interesting to understand what he was observing.

Asteroids? No, there wouldn't be any flashes from the collisions, and what are a bunch of asteroids colliding with out here in one place? Those are just flashes. Perhaps explosions from ship structures coming in contact with each other? That makes perfect sense! There are several dozen Albion ships out here we disabled or destroyed. Idiot Albions should have known better than tangle with a Starbird!

Bumping his booster to decrease his spin, he could make out a vast field of wrecked ship sections. As Carolon began to rotate out of his view, he caught sight of several larger pieces moving slowly in his direction. Another set of flashes appeared off to his left. Whatever the cause, they would converge close to his position. He touched his booster again checking his spin to focus on what was coming at him. As most of the ship debris was moving in the same direction as he was, their speed didn't worry him. Perhaps if he had an idea of how fast he was traveling, he might have been more alarmed.

His eyes widened, realizing he was in the path of several of the larger pieces of wreckage. Processing, he felt something strike his suit as two of the smaller sections collided right in front of him. Billy touched his booster, watching more fragments splinter in front of him, brilliant sparks showering away where they made contact. In a split second, there came a loud *clank* to his helmet, then the tell-tale sound of carbon fiber cracking. He searched his glass for the cause and

located a crack growing in the lower left quadrant. He looked up in time to hear another strike to his suit and helmet. This time he flinched, expecting whatever the objects were to breach the glass or the suit. When he opened his eyes, he noticed a crush spot right in the center of his view with hairline cracks developing from its center.

There came a sudden flurry of strikes to his torso and leg. He looked down and brought up his left knee. There was a small hole and something dark coming from it. Then came the pain. Bringing his hand up, he found his glove covered with blood. He bumped his booster control again to control the tumble created by the encounter. As he turned, something enormous shadowed over him. In an instant, a pair of dark giants had come to put an end to his impending misery. He instantly recognized the structures of two more torn bulkheads moving much faster than the others, coming at him.

Jamming his fingers on both booster controls, he felt the acceleration from the tiny thruster nozzles jetting inert Thorine gas. Recognition hadn't come soon enough. *This is the end! So stupid!* Bracing for impact, he realized at the speed these parts were tumbling at him, the end would most certainly be instantaneous. He felt a spray of bulkhead grit peppering his suit. The noise clanging through his helmet was deafening. *Come on, come on! Let's get this over with!* As the noise faded, he realized he was still in one piece. He hesitated opening his eyes for fear of seeing the impact actually happen. Moments passed and he finally opened his eyes to several brilliant flashes and his HUD system winking on for a moment, then off again.

Breathing a sigh of relief, he touched his thruster controls again to stabilize his movement and gathering his wits, held himself perfectly still, just breathing. *Not my time just yet.* There came a slight crackling sound in his ears and his HUD unit suddenly came back on. His hopes for information were dashed when he realized there was no telemetry in any of the display fields. *Wished my coms would come back on too.* He touched his arm monitor and checked his systems. The immediate problem had been avoided, now his suit breach would have to be dealt with or he'd be out of air in short order. His leg was starting to get cold; an indication the heaters in that part of the suit had been damaged. He not only needed to find a way to stop the suit breach, but get his heater working again. Both problems seemed insurmountable considering his environment.

Billy checked his helmet glass again. There were fractures everywhere, but he couldn't hear anymore tell-tale sounds of the clear composite cracking any further. Looking back down at his boots, he brought his injured knee up. Blood continued to dripple slowly out of the damaged suit like tiny little balloons. Trying to study the affected area, his broken safety strap floated next to his helmet. The end was frayed where it had separated from its safety hook. Checking the suit monitor on his wrist cuff, he acknowledged several flashing alarms. It was information he already knew about; a breach alarm and a couple of environmental fault indicators. His suit was decompressing due to the damage in the leg area. Working as swiftly as conditions permitted, he used the broken safety strap to cinch around his leg, above his injury. This seemed to address two of the biggest problems; the suit breach and his injured leg. Indeed, that silenced the breach alarm and looking back down at the injury, there seemed to be no blood escaping. He understood this was only temporary, but for now, it simplified the current equation.

The helmet glass seemed to be holding, but now the suit monitor was not only indicating low oxygen reserves, but the entire environmental system was offline. He was already feeling the entire suit starting to cool. What used to be days of survival time had been instantly reduced to hours or minutes. Now he was faced with freezing to death or suffocating sooner than later. He preferred freezing to suffocating. At least with freezing, the body gives the mind the perception of warming up, becoming calm and comfortable before death.

Frustrated with his circumstance, Billy bumped his thruster again to restart his spin.

Ok, important safety note; situational awareness at all times. Looking up and down relative to Carolon, he made sure he wouldn't be struck by more ship debris that might be coming at him. *I need to change my circumstance.* His best hope lay in the amount of ships around Carolon that had been disabled or destroyed. *If I could find a disabled one and reach it before my suit gives out, I might have a chance. Another option would be distress signals. With this many ships operating in the area, surely they've got search and rescue operating close by.*

Keeping with his visual scanning, he took note of several ship parts moving passed him on all axes. *I guess if the Constellation hadn't been so good at its job, I wouldn't have to be doing this,* he thought trying to humor himself. He touch his thrusters again, to speed up his spin. *Wished I was closer to Carolon. I'd be able to see this stuff better.* Watching the bright glow of the planet slide from his vision, he witnessed several more pieces colliding and then something else drew his attention. He caught the apparition out of the corner of his eye as he rotated away. Making sure everything was clear in all the other quadrants, he focused his gaze as Carolon came back around into view. Searching carefully along its distant curves, he caught a glint of something, a metallic flash. Another flash followed by a stream of flashes and a thread of dotted light swung in a tight arch.

"What the..." Billy muttered. Several more bright flashes, more beads of light spreading out in different directions, then an explosion. He nearly lost himself, watching the spectacle as the horizon of Carolon rotated out of sight. He made a hasty scan of his

surroundings as he continued to spin back around. Making sure he
was clear, he focused in on the light show again. This time, it was
bigger; much bigger. Several specs made mad circles around another
larger spec, making its own path around the others. As he rotated
around again, he started counting players in this complex atomic
structure. As he did so, he noted two of the specs get brighter and
appeared to multiply. Trying to make an identification, he bumped his
boosters in the opposite direction, stopping his safety spin. More
flashes and another explosion flared. Instinctively, Billy thrusted
forward for a better look. Several minutes slipped by as he watched
the light show. While he was far enough away from Carolon not to be
under its influence, it still commanded a sizable portion of his vision.

The specs were now large enough to see they weren't just specs of
light, but reflections of light off actual objects. Two of them broke off
from the rest of the group and made a wide arc against the backdrop
of Carolon.

"Wait a second, those look like…" He strained to confirm what he
thought he was looking at. As he watched and waited for another
opportunity to make an identification, he perceived something behind
him. Touching his booster controls, he spun around, coming face to
face with a sea of steel. The burnt out bulkhead was close enough, he
could almost reach out and touch it. He looked around for any other
pieces that might be cruising by, causing a deadly collision. The hulk
was large enough he couldn't see anything else. He touched his
boosters, ascending to the top and peered over the side. He couldn't
see anything but stars, so he turned back around to watch the cluster
of objects working their way closer.

Perching himself on the jagged edge of the hulk, he looked up in
time to see two more objects streak away from the rest. As they
presented their profiles against the orb of Carolon, his suspicions were
confirmed; *Fighters! What are fighters doing out here and what were
they shooting at?* Following the myriad of beaded light trails, he was
still having a hard time making sense of it all. There were times he
could make out a couple of different shapes against the glow of the
planet in the distance. Several more explosions flared momentarily,
then the beaded light show resumed. Like threads of pulsing flares,
they swung around in differing directions. Most of them displayed the
same patterns, but occasionally they were more concentrated, several
pairs pulsing together.

As he sat watching, he realized his perch was shifting, slowly
leaning forward. Stepping off, he maneuvered himself up to the other
end and sat back down. This time, he got a better look at the two
fighters swinging close by his burnt out hulk. The Albion symbols on
the wings of the Black Tigers were unmistakable. As they swept by
him, they were close enough he could see the occupants. He thought
about hiding, but it was too late for that. They were moving much too

fast for him to have even responded. Once past him, the fighters split and came back around, slowing considerably to get a closer look at the lone astronaut. As they circled, Billy developed a sinking feeling in his gut. Perhaps it was his suit's failing systems affecting him. As the fighters crept past him, he closed his eyes and let his arms float out as if he were dead. The Albions circled several times, then accelerated away. Once gone, Billy relaxed and resumed watching the dogfight draw closer.

His perch was once again shifting, only this time, instead of it simply rolling over, it started to dip on one side. Billy touched the boosters again and skimmed along the surface until he reached the upper end and settled inside a crushed hall cavity. Watching the fight draw closer, he could make out several different types of fighters. He glanced down at his arm monitor, scanning the flatlining environmental indicators. *This'll be the last excitement I'll ever see. Things should start to get stuffy in this suit pretty quick. Let's see, who's the underdog here? I like underdogs.* He looked up in time to see several weapon tracers string out past his position, followed closely by several more fighters spreading out through the debris field. It was then he realized they all seemed to be concentrating on a lone craft. Watching the fight closely, he was finally able to pinpoint the focus of their attack as a single fighter maneuvered through the swarm as if it were an invisible observer. Its six wing guns blasting deadly bellows of blue flares at the other ships. *That's the guy! That's my hero! Come on dude, give 'em what for!* Several Albion fighters broke apart while several more burst into momentary flames and disintegrated. As Billy studied the tactics being used, he came to the conclusion the pilot was not on the defensive, but using a laid back offense tactic.

As the big fighter banked away from Billy's position, it was struck repeatedly as it rolled then let out a quick burst at several Albion craft which instantly crumbled before it. The Albion numbers were quickly being whittled down at an astonishing rate. *A good squadron leader should realize a single enemy has them outgunned. They need to turn tail and run. Single enemy? They're all against one guy! Why are they firing on one guy? Who would they be firing at? Wait, I should know this... Let's see, I'm out here to... I'm going to... Why can't remember what I'm doing?* He looked at his helmet glass again. *There are a lot of cracks in my helmet; that can't be good. Shouldn't I be on the Constellation? Tiana is going to skin me alive when she finds out where I am. Where is the ship anyway?* He flinched as several more fighters silently crumbled in front of him. Now the fight was all around him. He ducked as his perch was pummeled with broken fighter parts and ordnance. He held on tight to a makeshift handhold as the burnt out hulk was sent spinning, crashing into other pieces. There came a flurry of explosions, some he was certain were hitting the hulk he was holding on to. As the spinning increased, there came a sudden blast near his position, then spinning stars. *What's happening?* Static blasted through his helmet's com unit. He could hear someone calling his name. *Who's speaking? That voice sounds familiar. What are they saying? It's so hot in this suit! I'm not feeling very good...*

"Billy, stabilize! Hit your auto stabilizers!"

Who... out here... knows my name? I should know who that is... shouldn't I? Auto stabilizers? What are those? I'm so sleepy... My head hurts...

"Billy, can you hear me? You've got to turn on your stabilizers!"

Billy blinked several times, seeing only a swirling mass of stars and nebula.

Wished everything wasn't spinning around so much. Those lights out there are really pretty. He looked at his hands. *This button does something... Those stars are making me sick...* He squeezed his thumb down as his eyes drooped. *I'm out of oxygen, aren't I?* He tried to focus on the empty information fields on his HUD display, but his eyes didn't seem to want to cooperate. *Oh, the stars have stopped spinning; so much better. They're so pretty... Who's calling my name? This must be the end... I'm so tired...*

There came a brilliant flash off to his right, followed shortly by another one to his left and directly behind him. He couldn't keep his eyelids open. He felt himself bump into something. *Another burnt out hulk? Stupid Albions should have known better than to tangle with...* He forced his eyes open again, seeing a stable starfield and a slab of grey metal. He looked down at some writing on the slab he was pinned against. *Oh, look at that! It says something stupid.. What does...* His vision faded at the same moment he felt something grab his leg.

"I've got you, Billy..."

He felt his suit strike something several times from different angles, then everything went dark. He dreamed of being in his easy chair on the porch of his parent's home on Randle. There was nothing like the atmosphere of a planet. The sun shining on your face and the wind blowing across you on a warm day. His nephews would shake him to try to get him to come play with them out in the yard. He hated being shaken awake during his nap time on the porch.

"I hate it when you guys do that," he scolded. "I'll come play with you when I'm done with my nap."

"You need to breath deep, Billy. Take a deep breathe."

"I'm napping! Leave me alone!"

"Breath, Billy! Breath!"

"I'm breathing already! Now, if you don't leave me alone, I'm gonna turn you over my knee and give you what for..."

"At least you'll be breathing. Just relax and I'll be back with you in a minute."

"Yeah, that's a great idea. You do that and then come back in an hour or two and tell me all about it." There came a rumble to the porch and a droning sound all around him. "Now what's grandpa up to?"

Billy's mind faded in and out of several dream scenes, the last one found him leaning back on his porch, looking at the opposite support pillar, wondering why it had different colored flashing lights on it. Opening his eyes, he realized he wasn't on the porch. His helmet was gone. Now he was wearing an oxygen mask. His head was pounding, and he felt like he was going to throw up. He shivered, feeling perspiration evaporating from the back of his neck. He blinked repeatedly, trying to clear his vision. A display and several indicator lights on a panel across from where he was sitting, jittered and doubled in his vision. Looking around, he recognized familiar surroundings and tried to get up, but had no strength.

"Look who decided to join the living," Captain Logan Dalley said from the pilot's seat of Interceptor Two. "Or is this what being dead looks like?"

"I think I'm gonna puke. Did you finish them off?" Billy asked, pulling the mask away from his mouth.

"Well, not all of them, but enough to stop and pick up your sorry behind."

"Yeah, thanks for that. I thought I was a goner."

"If I hadn't gotten to you when I did, you would have been."

"How'd you find me?" Billy asked, realizing it would take a while for his head to clear.

Logan pointed at one of his scanning displays.

"Personnel transponder scanner; never leave home without it."

"I knew that. Hypoxia will really do it to you..." Billy burped stomach gas and started to dry heave, but somehow repressed it.

"Lucky for you the scanner is still working. This bird has taken a pretty good beating."

"Do you know where the ship is?" Billy asked, trying to look outside.

"Afraid some of my equipment isn't working anymore. I've lost long range sensors; my com antennas are gone and the ship's ident transponder system is shot; no one but you knows I'm here. I've used up almost all my ordnance load; two of the main guns are burned out. Remind me to tell the engineers about it."

"Duly noted," Billy smirked. "What about the Colonel?"

"Haven't gotten anything from him," Logan said shaking his head. "I've keep my scanner tuned to his signal this whole time, but I've not seen him." He looked down at his readouts and made some adjustments. "Hard to tell from this distance and the fact that my scanning equipment has seen better days, but if I had to make a guess, I'd say what's left of the Albion flotilla has the *Constellation* surrounded," Logan said looking at his scanning displays.

"So what do we do?"

"You tell me. I'm pretty sure the *Realistic* could see the entire thing. Captain Reader had orders to bug out if anything happened, so I'm sure he's halfway back to Aster by now. Is it going to do anybody any good to dive in there with guns blazing?"

"That Mark V blast did a lot more damage to the ship than we thought."

"Yeah, that was quite the light show," Logan agreed. "Still can't believe Dakota lit that thing off."

"Then, the Albions kept hitting us with some kind of energy sucking death ray."

"I assume there's a logical reason why I found you out here in the middle of the damage path... almost dead."

"Tell you all about it as soon as I don't feel like puking my guts up," Billy replied.

"You'll recover a lot faster if you'll keep that oxygen mask up where it'll do you the most good." Logan reached back and nudge the mask back over Billy's chin. "I don't know how you feel about it, but I'm inclined to hang back here in the junk yard until we know what they're doing."

"I've got nothing better to do," Billy agreed, breathing deeply into the mask.

No Entry

In the dark confines of the *Constellation's* ball turret, Captain Abrams looked long and hard at the broad side of the Albion destroyer floating directly beside them.

"The *Dominator*," BachTL said, standing next to him. "Class four destroyer. It's an older model with a lot of mods." The Albion ship took up the entire view of the turret portal, so was difficult to see all of its armament.

"It's pretty big when you get up close and personal," Dakota said trying to study the details.

BachTL pointed at several large openings in the side of the hull. "The tugs will move us into the bottom one."

"Why use tugs? Why not just grab us with a tractor hawser?" Dakota asked. Looking at the turret window, he noticed condensation had started to form around its edges; a sign of poor air circulation and a continuing drop in temperature.

"Only our larger ships have tractor technology," BachTL replied. "Even those a little less than reliable though."

"And you don't consider this one large?"

"Didn't you said you have capitol ships where you're from?"

"Well, yes we have capitol ships," Dakota confirmed. "Certainly bigger than this. But we've discovered that size isn't necessarily what matters."

Dakota studied the armament on the visible side of the destroyer as the tugs maneuvered the *Constellation* closer to one of the gapping openings on the side of the Albion ship.

"Will this thing move at all?" BachTL asked looking back at the turret controls.

"There might be a little power left in the batteries," Dakota said touching several controls on the panel and moving the pan control. "I think as long as we move slowly, they won't notice." The turret inched around until they were looking away from the destroyer. Besides the tugs clamped to their four quarters, several corvettes held perimeter positions, while several others patroled a wide circle in all quadrants.

"The Torag," BachTL said pointing at a badly damaged ship being towed toward the same landing bay. One of its thruster pods was completely gone, while the second dangled uselessly by several crumpled conduits and twisted cables. Nearly a third of its outer Starbird facade had been torn away to reveal its undercarriage. An ungainly ship to begin with, now it was a torn wreck, rendered useless by an exploding cannon breach. Keeping the turret moving, Dakota followed the Torag until they were again looking at the launch bay opening looming ahead of them.

"Captain," Lynette Starman called from below.

Dakota turned and leaned over the rail.

"It looks like we're ready to try this."

Dakota glanced back at BachTL and grabbing the handrails of the ladder, slid down. Touching the floor, he didn't even wait for BachTL, but burst from the elevator access coming to a stop next to Hayden Hunter. Everyone was gathered around the engineering console watching Tiana Mantose run her fingers across the immense glass console as if she were playing a magnificent musical instrument. Pushing through the crew, Dakota stood himself next to the independent contractor, observing her work with hopeful patience. After watching her fingers move at a near blur, he drew in a breath to ask a question.

"We'll know in just a moment, Captain," Tiana said quietly, looking up at the display on the back end of the torpedo tube. She widened her stretch across the glass, looking up at several overhead displays. Dakota looked back at all the cables dangling to the floor from the Mark V torpedo tube and the energy shield drive panels nestled in the wall of the engine room.

Dakota and Fuji glanced out one of the port windows as the interior of the destroyer's landing bay filled the view. As the *Constellation* came to a halt inside the landing bay, all eyes turned back to Tiana as she continued to configure the systems. Dakota felt the ship make contact with the bay floor and turned anxiously back to the glass console. Tiana had stopped moving her hands and just stared at the immense display. Trying to hold his anxiousness at bay, Dakota glanced back at the window, then at Tiana, who had turned her eyes to him.

"Well?" he breathed.

"I wish Billy were here," she whispered, letting her fingers contact the glass. All sections of the console went dark, except for one in the lower corner. They both shifted their gaze at the illuminated area and moments later everyone turned to the torpedo as it began to whistle quietly. Tiana turned to the shield generator as it came alive. A blue hue developed around the entire unit as its indicators began to glow with a flurry of information.

"Is it working?" Scott asked, looking down at the console, then up at the displays.

"Look!" Fuji called, pointing to the window. There was a blue glow filtering through.

"You did it," Dakota breathed, looking at the blue glow. "It's working!" He grabbed Tiana by the shoulders and planted a big kiss on her lips. Realizing what he had done, he released her and straightened up, taking a step back. "Uhm..." he croaked, clearing his throat. "Well done, Miss Mantose."

"Don't worry, I won't tell Willis. Just see that you pay my bill," she said. After a moment of jubilation, Captain Abrams turned back to the console, watching other sections come back on.

"So, what does this get us?"

"Not much, shields and some power to environmental," she responded studying the readouts. "Maybe a few other systems."

"Enough to keep them out and us from freezing?"

"Probably, but not indefinitely."

"How long?"

"You've got four torpedoes back here. Maybe six or seven hours a piece. Do the math."

"I'll take it," Dakota snapped. "Now, what can we do to help get the power back on?"

Tiana drew in a deep breath and folded her arms, looking at the overhead displays.

"Do a lot of praying." Tiana hoped that would be enough of a hint for the Captain to give her some time to think; *nope*.

"Tiana, after all this, I know I don't need to remind you..."

"Yeah, yeah, yeah," Tiana cut him off. "Geez, no wonder Billy was so grumpy all the time. We'll start with the power couplings and ion regulators, then work our way backwards." She turned to the engineer's mate. "Scott, take Nigel with you and start on the couplings. Lieutenant Hunter, you and Pip start getting those other three torpedoes prepped for milking. The Captain and I will dive into the buffering matrix."

"Have room for me down there?" Lana asked, stepping quickly forward as Tiana started for one of the pit openings.

"Sure."

"What about the rest of us, Sir?" Doran asked. Dakota turned and looked at the rest of the crew huddled together trying to warm their hands.

"The rest of you are runners," Dakota said peeling off his uniform jacket. "Pick an area and park yourself there. If someone needs something, you get it for them. Just stay clear of the windows until we can get them dimmed out."

Everyone quickly dispersed, filtering to the different areas of focus, leaving BachTL standing alone. As the crew went to work, he was amazed watching them. In all the environments he had worked in or observed, he had never seen this much cohesiveness. Stepping carefully over the floor clutter, he made his way back to the engineering console. Parts of the console remained devoid of information, but others were flashing numbers and symbols at an astonishing rate; too fast to read even if he understood the alphabet. He tried to access several different areas on the glass console, only to be rejected with a warning he could only assume meant it was restricted.

"Here," Dakota said stepping up next to him. He tapped several areas of the panel and widened a display window. Taking BachTL's finger, he pressed it to the glass. "Now, when I tell you, I want you to touch a couple of these controls."

"Does this mean you're giving me access to your systems?" BachTL asked, watching Dakota step back toward the largest access pit.

"It means you're in the same boat as the rest of us. Now pay attention when we call out." Dakota turned and stepping onto a Lev-lift, floated down into the pit, disappearing beneath the rim. BachTL looked back at the console in front of him. He studied the characters in the windows panes Dakota had opened up and waited.

*　　　*　　　*　　　*

The outside hatch to the *Warbird* was so badly damaged it had to be forcibly removed. Dalton SoKnack finally stepped out, a bit shaken and battered, but with a grateful expression. As he stepped away from the Torag, he turned to survey the damage to the Starbird decoy. Much of its facade had been torn away in the energy pulse explosion. Several outer parts lay scattered around the craft; having fallen off as the ship was dragged into the belly of the *Dominator*. He stepped toward the rear of the ship, studying the damage to the enormous gun. The thruster bell that hadn't been blown off was hanging precariously against the rear of the ship. He slowly shook his head while walking around the back side of the *Warbird*.

"Commander SoKnack," a voice called from behind. "You made it back."

Dalton turned to an officer in a straight pressed uniform, saluting sharply. Dalton loosely saluted back, and continued looking at the damage to the Torag.

"May I be the first to congratulate you on your victory. It's a job well done, Commander. The Queen Captain and the King Commander will be pleased."

"Congratulate me?" Dalton asked, sounding irritated. "Major Tiffin, even you should know better than that."

"But you've brought in the alien ship. Wasn't that the objective?"

"Yes, but at what cost? How much of the flotilla is left out there?" Dalton turned expecting an answer but got none. "I want to see a full report on the flotilla's status as soon as possible. I also want to know how this happened," he demanded, pointing at the twisted broken metal of the energy cannon breach.

"We assumed this was battle damage incurred while you were engaging the alien ship."

"The Alien ship was unable to fire during most of our engagement," Dalton fired back, visibly shaken. Perhaps the Torag had become closer to catastrophic failure than any of the Albion commanders had thought. "Where's the alien ship?"

"The other side." The Major motioned over the wrecked Torag.

"Have your men taken the crew yet?" Dalton asked, giving the Torag a wide birth. He stopped short when the Starbird came into view.

"Their energy shield came on just as we got it onboard," Major Tiffin said stepping in stride with Dalton. "I thought the energy pulse weapon was supposed to drain all their power and render everything inoperative?"

"Clearly that wasn't the case," Dalton snapped. "Have there been any signals or movement from the ship while you were bringing it in?"

"Nothing, Commander. Either they can't communicate or they won't communicate. We performed a basic scan while we were pulling it in. We know there's a crew onboard. From the information we've been able to gather, their life support isn't working.

"Are your men still trying to hail them?"

"Yes, Commander, but it's like they're ignoring us."

"Wouldn't you?" Dalton asked, coming to a halt several steps from the softly humming hull. "It blew two destroyers to pieces with just one torpedo and how many other ships?" Dalton turned to the Major, who looked away as if not wanting to answer.

"How many, Major?"

"Five."

"Battle damage is expected to be that high, but how many were destroyed?"

"Five."

"Five destroyed? How many damaged?" Dalton's unibrow rippled.

"With or without the destroyed number?"

"I can add..."

"Three others out of commission and six more damaged."

"All from one ship..."

"No, Commander. This ship took out all the destroyers and several of the corvettes. One of its heavy fighters took out the other corvettes and their accompanying fighters."

"You're telling me, one fighter took out most of the fighters we launched?"

"Not most... all."

Dalton drew in a deep breath, rubbed his eyes, then starred at the Starbird.

"It certainly is a beautiful ship," Major Tiffin commented.

"Beautiful, but apparently quite deadly. Have you started a comprehensive scan?"

"We have a couple of Hessons on it right now," the Major said pointing at two men standing near the nose of the Kalamarion ship. "But with their shields back on, I don't know what we're going to get."

"Make sure no one, and I mean no one, gets too close to it." Dalton walked slowly around the entire ship, stopping only for a moment to look at something closer and to watch the Hessons work. "Let me know what they find."

"Yes, Commander."

Dalton turned to leave, but something caught his eye in one of the aft windows of the Starbird. He turned back and took a step closer. Through the blue hue of the buzzing energy shield, Dalton detected movement. Stunned, he recognized BachTL, Drax's personal aide, moving past the window. BachTL glanced at the window, then disappeared from view.

"Commander, is everything all right?"

"Not sure," Dalton responded hypnotically, still staring at the alien ship. Moments later, the window dimmed to black.

"I'll be up in the communications room making my report to the Queen Captain." With that, Dalton turned and headed for an exit, looking back several times as he went. He wasn't looking forward to making his report. While he had succeeded in securing the Kalamarion ship, the operation had not gone at all as planned. The loss rate they had suffered at the hands of the Starbird was unacceptable and he was certain there would be repercussions. He recalled serving with Colonel Barker and how she delivered a dismal report to the Queen Captain. While there were usually sharp words, Colonel Barker always seemed to know how to handle Drax Blair.

An invitation to dinner

Gunnar felt strangely comfortable sitting with the other officers in the shuttle as it cleared the atmosphere of Albia. Unfortunately, since leaving the entry portal, his head was starting to ache again, and his anxiety levels were rising. Still able to feel the shuttle roll gently, he took notice of Albia's binary suns, their light rays shifting through the shuttle windows as it reoriented for docking. As they made their approach, he looked around the passenger compartment. He took notice of several younger women at the far end, dressed in civilian clothes. That didn't make too much sense to him. Yes, Kalamar Command used civilian contractors all the time, CJ had even indicated the Colonian military used civilian contractors to a small degree. But he had gotten the distinct impression that independents in the Albion or the Ratronian militaries, just weren't done onboard the *Tarzana*.

He suddenly became aware of a great presence enveloping the shuttle and twisting to the window, watched a great steel envelope loom over the tiny shuttle as it was swallowed into one of the great ship's lower landing bays. Gunnar scanned the cavernous bay, taking note of endless rows of Black Tiger fighters. Suspended above the Black Tigers were gantries full of several other types of fighters he didn't recognize. He marveled at the endless numbers, wishing he could just move from one type to another examining them and contemplating what they were designed for.

As the shuttle came to a halt and he prepared to disembark, he did a double take at several transports sitting next to them. Following the line of officers to the exit hatchway, he held back so he was the last one out. Stepping down the ramp, he slowly moved up next to one of the Metro-Stars. There were four of them sitting neatly in a row. Walking around the first, he recognized the Albion alphabet on the side. He looked over at the next one, smiled slightly and shook his head slightly.

"Nice to see these things up close, instead of chasing you through a cave."

He turned and stepped quickly to catch up with the rest of the officers moving toward an exit. As he went, he let his gaze turn all around him. The landing bay was truly cavernous, and this was just one of them. The upper decks were so high up, it would require binoculars to see any detail on the edges of the decks. There were several decks lined with observation windows and control spaces. As he caught up with the rest of the officers, he observed another group of officers moving toward them. Leading them was a woman in a familiar green cloak. It wasn't until the groups were nearly parallel with each other, that he recognized Drax Blair conversing with the officers surrounding her. He dropped his eyes to his boots, tilting his head away as the groups passed in opposite directions. After being sure he hadn't been recognized, Gunnar looked back as they continued across the docking bay, then disappeared through the exit doorway.

After getting hopelessly lost for hours in a labyrinth of hallways and corridors, Gunnar finally stopped a younger looking Ensign to ask for directions. Making up an explanation for his disorientation that the Ensign neither cared about nor fully understood, he received a set of directions to the personnel quarters. Once he found them, his frustration grew as there seemed to be no identifying marks on any of the doors. Turning up another corridor to try to find some type of signage, he was confronted by a security detail bearing weapons.

"You seem to be a little lost," one of the security officers said as the other stepped behind him with his weapon up.

"Well, truth be told, I'm a little disoriented. I can't seem to find my quarters."

"How hard can it be? What's your Idents?"

"Captain Mace Bridger, Chief pilot, Special Forces."

"I thought Captain Bridger was reported dead?" the officer behind him spoke up.

"Well, clearly I'm not," Gunnar firmed up the inflection in his voice.

"I knew of a Captain Bridger," the lead officer said. "Seems like he was a much younger guy."

"Is that a crack about my age?" Gunnar noticed someone moving quickly up the corridor towards them.

"It's just I overheard that the Captain was killed by a terrorist on Dither two days ago," the officer maintained.

"Do you have any group mates that can vouch for you?"

"Special Forces pilots are lone wolves," the other officer said. "They operate independently. Called on only when needed."

A figure suddenly blew passed the lead officer and landed a hard-right across Gunnar's jaw, spinning him into the wall and nearly knocking him to the floor.

"You, worthless piece of...!" The woman was seething and in agony from the punch.

"Hold on a moment, ma'am," the officer said, stepping between Gunnar and the short woman with long brown hair. "You know this guy?"

The woman turned and tried to land another punch, but the two officers held her back.

"Yea, I know this unfeeling pile of garbage." She backed off, seeing there was no way for her to get at Gunnar.

"So, you can vouch for him?"

"Yes, he's my husband, although I was hoping he was dead this time."

The security officers looked at Gunnar, then back at the younger woman, then back at Gunnar again, giving him a slight grin.

"Guess you've got some explaining to do, buddy boy. Follow the little woman to your quarters and get what's coming to you instead of wandering the halls and getting us all riled up." The officer turned to the woman. "If you're going to beat him to death, do it inside and not out here for everyone to see." They turned to leave, but stopped as Gunnar and the woman just stared at each other. "And try not to make too much noise."

"Are you done hitting me?" Gunnar asked holding his hands up. He was doing his best to hold himself together.

"Depends... maybe." The woman was puffing slightly, and still very animated.

"Well, like the man suggested, can we take this inside?" Gunnar kept his hands up in case she decided to attack again. He noticed a ring on her finger as she pointed at one of the doors at the end of the hall. She sneered at him as they moved carefully down the hall together. He had to wave his wrist over the sensor pad a couple of times before the door finally popped open and they stepped inside. Once the lights came on and the door closed behind them, Gunnar felt a little relieved and found a comfortable spot in a soft chair next to a window. The surface of Albia took up most of the view; the *Tarzana's* flotilla took up the rest. He looked back at the woman who stood with her arms folded looking at him.

"Ok, so what's your story?" she asked stoic.

"No, high honey, I'm home?" Gunnar mused. He got no reaction. "You must be Malina Cass, Captain Bridger's wife."

"And you're not him," she retorted quickly. "Not that I'm surprised." She finally moved to the kitchen area of the small apartment and pulled a drink from a cabinet.

"I don't understand," Gunnar responded.

"He's dead this time, isn't he?"

"This has happened before?"

"Well, yes, he's been reported dead several times and every time he waits a couple of days and then magically shows up to a long-lost hero's welcome. So is he actually dead or am I to expect him back as soon as you're done with whatever cockamamie scheme he's roped you into?"

Gunnar watched her as she downed most of the drink without even taking a breath.

"No, no cockamamie schemes... He's dead."

"Are you sure? How'd it happen?"

"Firefight with terrorists on Dither."

"So what's your play in all this? What did he get you into?"

"I never knew the man."

"You have his ID band," she said motioning to Gunnar's wrist.

"Yeah, I'm still not sure how that happened."

"So what's your play? Why go to all the trouble to alter his band and then come back up here? Were it me, I would have high tailed it the other way?"

"Let's just say I need to retrieve something valuable that belongs to me."

"What's it worth to you?"

"I don't follow."

"Nobody risks espionage and treason unless it's worth a lot of credits. Come on, I've got no love for the Empire here, it's just a tool and so was Mace."

Gunnar thought for a long moment while Malina swallowed down the last of her drink, then stepped into the adjoining bedroom, leaving the door open. Gunnar could see her shadow as she changed into something a little more casual.

"I'm not sure how much it's worth, but it's certainly valuable."

Malina reappeared wearing long-legged shorts and a sleeveless shirt. She plopped down on the couch, looking at Gunnar as if trying to figure something out.

"Let me guess, Mace stole it from you?"

"You certainly don't have much faith in your late husband's integrity."

Malina leaned over onto the armrest.

"Mace was a good officer, a decent pilot and had great ambitions in this military. There were a lot of times when he would have been willing to jump in front of a launching transport if he thought it would get him ahead in the military game. But he also had a greedy streak in him." Malina leaned back. "Same as me. He was sure someday soon, he'd score the big one and then he'd take me away from this man's military and this silly war that goes along with it. We'd go find a nice rock to live on, together." She looked up at the ceiling, then closed her eyes. "The longer it took, the more out of reach that seemed to be."

There came a summons at the door, bringing Gunnar and Malina to attention. They looked at the door, then at each other for some kind of direction.

"Who is it?" Malina asked touching a control on the end table.

"Personnel Security. We're here to check your IDs."

"Come back later, we're in the middle of something."

"Sorry, ma'am. We have orders to search these premises and validate personnel IDs."

"Come back later!"

There was silence for several moments, then the door was activated from the outside and several officers stepped in. Only a split second elapsed before they found the occupants on the couch in a heavy embrace. Malina popped her head up, rolling her eyes and scowling. The officers looked down at Gunnar beneath her. Fumbling as they backed up, they stumbled against the door.

"Sorry, we didn't realize you were..."

"Didn't realize that I haven't seen my husband for over half a deployment and when I finally do get to see him, a couple of perverts want to come in and watch!"

"This is your husband? Mace Bridger... Captain?"

"Yes, now get out!" She threw one of her boots at them as they cowered and sprang back through the door, shutting it just in time for the second boot to strike it. Once she could see the door activators change color, Malina looked back down at Gunnar, giving him an odd look.

"Kissing you is weird."

"Really?" Gunnar flapped irritated. He pushed her off and sat up. "Let me guess; it's because I'm older. Getting a little tired of all the cracks about my age."

"You are a little older than most men you'll find on this ship," Malina said smiling. She shifted to the other side of the couch and looked back at Gunnar.

"Yes, I've heard all about how most guys my age are retired and living the highlife somewhere."

"So, you gonna tell me about this item you've risked life and limb to retrieve?"

"Promise not to tell?" Gunnar asked, still considering.

"I threw my boots at those security officers for you," she said springing to her feet. "Which by the way, I hope I didn't lose that first one." She moved to the door, finding one of them. "Oh good, here it is." She tossed them both through the open bedroom door, then grabbed another drink. Taking a big swallow she handed the container to Gunnar. He looked at her for a moment then at the drink, finally taking it.

"A ring," he said after taking a long drink.

"You're serious?"

"You asked, I told; a ring."

"That's what this is all about, a ring? What, does it have some super high value stone in it, cause I gotta tell ya, that doesn't sound like it's worth enough to get killed over?"

Gunnar stared at Malina for a moment, then finally decided he had taken a chance on Eldon and Rayna, this woman seemed somewhat levelheaded. *Somewhat...*

"No, not just any ring. The Royal Oxlind ring."

"What makes it so special?"

Gunnar popped a surprised look. It hadn't even occurred to him that not everyone knew the history of the Hadrian war.

"Do you really not know what this war is all about?"

"Who does?" she responded sarcastic.

"You should at least know why you're putting your life on the line every time you board this ship," Gunnar complained.

"Look, I'm just trying to survive and get out of here as soon as my time allotment is complete. Unlike Mace, I have zero aspirations for this military."

"Ok," Gunnar muttered with wide eyes. "Alien guy knows more about the galaxy than the indigenous life forms."

"Who are you, really?"

"At this point, is it important?"

"Hey, I bought the rights to know about you when I saved you from the security boys… twice."

"Fair enough. Gunnar Lee Conrad. I come from a galaxy a very long way from this one."

"What are you doing here?"

"It's a very long complicated story. Suffice it to say, I got here by accident and I'm just trying to find my way home."

"Well, I hate to break it to you, but this ship is not the place to be trying to make that happen. Besides, if you're just trying to get home, what does this royal ring have to do with that?"

"Well, until I'm able to figure out how to get home, I might as well keep myself busy. The ring belonged to the King of Hadrian."

"There is no King of Hadrian."

"Well, not anymore, he's dead."

"What happened to him?"

"He was poisoned by his wife."

"That's rough. Who was this woman?"

"Stephanie Benetar, Duchess of Teleknee."

"The Colonian Queen? She's the witch that's caused this whole war." Malina sounded indignant now.

"I thought you didn't know anything about it?"

"I don't."

Gunnar shook his head.

"I guess, she did kind of start this in a roundabout way."

"What other way was there?"

"She's been operating with someone at the highest levels of the Albion government from the start."

"Not likely," Malina forced a laugh. "Colonians and Albions hate each other with a passion."

"And why do you think that?"

"Because the Colonians stole power from the Albions."

"So the Albions have a royalty that used to rule the galaxy?"

Malina thought a moment, then realized she had stepped into pure conjecture on her part.

"I have no idea. Why are we talking about this? I don't even care."

"You asked and so I'm telling." Gunnar smiled, watching the confused look on her face. "Look, it's not complicated; a little confusing maybe…"

"Can you just give me the uncomplicated version and I'll do my best to follow?"

"It appears that the Duchess Benetar devised a plan to take overpower from the Oxlind family. The Oxlinds, of the House of Pintar are the legitimate ruling line in Hadrian since whenever."

"Ok, if you say so, we'll go with that."

"Benetar killed off the royal family except for one, the youngest, a daughter. The child was exiled to a planet on the outer rim until she was old enough to be used to legitimize Benetar as the royal heir. Until then, the good people of Hadrian have demanded a ruler. Hadrian law requires it."

"I'm still with you," Malina said.

"So here's where your war started. Benetar proclaimed herself Queen, but she has no royal blood line. She's only a Duchess. The smaller factions of Hadrian joined forces or were assimilated by the Albions. They've been waging war against the Colonians, demanding they produce a blood heir or give up rule to the Albions, as dictated by Hadrian law."

"That's the whole war thing?"

"Correct, let's buy this girl a drink."

Malina smiled, and Gunnar continued.

"So here's where it gets interesting. The exiled princess escaped her planet prison and made her way here to Dither to retrieve the proof that she's the only blood heir to the Oxlind throne. But someone high up, discovered what she was up to and sent troops down to arrest her and in the firefight, she lost her father's ring."

"And she has to have the ring in order to prove she is who she says she is?"

"Yes and no," Gunnar hemmed a little. "No, there were enough materials included with what she found to prove her blood line, but, yes, she has to have the ring because Hadrian law requires that her proof include her parent's rings; together. I believe her father's ring was found by the troops sent to arrest her and brought up here somewhere."

"I'd hate to hear the long-complicated version of this story." Malina took a deep breathe. "It's a big ship, where do you think it ended up?"

"Not sure exactly how the Albion military works in a situation like this, but I would think if the ring had been picked up as evidence, it would have been brought to the Special Forces Commander. My guess is, it's sitting on a desk or a shelf in an office somewhere."

"Or somebody saw something shiny on the ground and picked it up and kept it. For all you know, it's halfway across the galaxy by now.

Or, better yet, it's lying on the ground under a tree or chair or something stupid like that." Malina ran her fingers through her hair and pulled it back into a pony, quickly wrapping a band around the tail.

"I don't think so," Gunnar said watching her work her hair. "I saw it drop, but didn't see where it landed. I know it wasn't under a chair or outside. I think it ended up here. The troopers that came to arrest the Princess were Special Forces from this ship. They should have taken anything pertaining to the operation to their Incident Commander. The IC might not know what any of this is all about and figures a ring is just a lost trinket, some random evidence with nowhere to go, so it's just sitting on his desk."

"Well, Pops…"

"Please don't call me that," Gunnar fumed.

"Gunnar," Malina corrected herself. "You're in luck as the Special Forces branch works a little differently. Yes, there's an Incident Commander, but that's as far as it goes. The actual personnel aren't attached to any one group. There are no squads or platoons, only individuals from which a group or squad commander can draw on. When a mission comes up, the commanding officer picks someone in his command chain to make the assignments and they in turn drop the orders down to an operations commander. That commander picks from a pool of individuals to be on the mission, based on their qualifications and service records. You can get called anytime to go anywhere with anyone."

"Do you know where the IC's offices are?"

"Knew you were going to ask that. Four decks up, starboard side. I suppose you'd like to go right now?"

"Probably not a good idea just yet. I'm a little tired from the day's activities."

"You look like hell," Malina replied.

"Besides, the programing on this ID band is a little glitchy. Maybe if we give it a little more time, it'll resolve itself."

"What about the other one you've got there?" Malina leaned a little closer. "Wait, that's not even Albion. Is that a Colonian band?"

"No, this is Kalamarion. This is my actual band."

"They do things the same way in your galaxy, huh?"

"Not exactly, but similar."

"Well, if you've altered the information on Mace's band, it's going to continue to be glitchy unless you fix it in the ship's database. Maybe on the way over to the IC's office we can stop in at Digital Services and get it fixed."

"You can do that?"

"Sure, piece of cake. I had to do it every time Mace came back from the dead. You're sure he's dead?"

"Quite sure."

"Did you actually see him die?"

"Yes, I saw it."

"How'd it happen?"

Gunnar hesitated a moment, looking back at Malina.

"I think I broke his neck."

Malina stared at him for a long time, then got up and walked toward the bedroom. She stopped at the door and turned to say something, but ultimately disappeared, closing the door behind her.

*　　　*　　　*　　　*

Gunnar had no idea how long he'd been asleep. He was just grateful he hadn't had any more weird dreams. Sitting up, he looked around, finding Malina sitting in the dark next to the window.

"How come you don't snore?" Malina asked.

"Genetics," he stretched. "How long have I been asleep?"

"A half cycle."

"What's that? Six, eight hours?"

"Ten."

"Have you been watching me this whole time?"

"Some of it. I have to sleep too, ya know."

"Kinda weird, you watching me sleep, don't you think?"

"Not considering the circumstances."

"So now what? Are we ready to head out?"

"Not quite. The Command office personnel will thin out in a couple of hours after all the days orders are processed and assignment rosters are published. That'll give you and I time to chat some more and come to an understanding."

"An understanding about what?"

"About this," she said holding Mace's wrist band up. "We've got to get some things straight or I take this to security and rat you out,"

Gunnar remained silent, considering. Seeing he had few alternatives, he nodded.

"First off, I don't want you to feel guilty for killing my husband."

"Well that's going to work," Gunnar cut sarcastically.

"It was an act of war as far as I see it and I'm over it. You need to get over it too."

"Dealing with death doesn't come easily for me."

"That's your problem, not mine. I'm sure you've already figured out there wasn't much love there to begin with and I knew this was going to happen sooner or later anyway, so I'm good."

"Ok," Gunnar hedged. "What else?"

"You're wearing a ring; does your wife know what you're up to?"

"She's dead."

Malina toned down considerably, changing her mindset.

"Are you over her?"

"Yes."

"Are you sure?"

"You asked, I answered."

"What happened?"

"It's complicated."

"Spell it out."

"I thought you didn't like complicated?"

"I need to know what I'm dealing with."

Gunnar drew in a deep breath and held it.

"Ok," he said, letting the air go. "Audra and I got married a long time ago when I was still a flight Lieutenant with the Kalamarion Flight Ministry. We've spent most of our lives serving in the Ministry. A short time before we got here, we were given command of a small assault vessel; she was my first officer. The ship lost structural integrity while traveling here and she was killed. We buried her in space right after we got here."

"And why aren't you over it yet?"

"I told you earlier, I'm over it."

"I don't believe you."

"I guess that's your problem then."

"It's in your eyes and the way you sound when you talk about her."

Gunnar thought a moment, searching. He finally nodded slightly and looked over at Malina.

"I guess everyone is different. I've come to the realization that anyone who has ever truly loved and lost someone never *really*, gets over it. It's a little more difficult for my kind than for humans."

"You look human to me." Malina raised an eyebrow. "You're not?"

"I have a couple of extra parts. My skin and bone density is a little tougher than a normal human."

"That explains why I nearly broke my hand when I punched you," she said flexing her fingers.

"I also process things a little differently, including emotional and psychological responses. Add to that, your big boss, Drax Blair had me pumped full of something that's sent my system into a tailspin. It's all I can do to keep from exploding."

"So you've had run-ins with the mighty Albion military before?"

"Oh yes," Gunnar chuckled. "Drax and Blinda Koss are my biggest fans."

"So you're the one that escaped from the Queen Captain's Guardian." Malina smiled, impressed.

"I was assured Blinda didn't have any say in the matter."

"You realize they're both onboard?"

"I'm sort of counting on it," Gunnar said thinking of passing Drax when he landed. "They won't be looking for me right under their noses."

"You seem to love courting things from the wild side." Malina smiled. "I think I'm liking you more and more all the time." She held his wrist up and looked at his band a little closer. "This band is either going to get you killed or you'll get away with this little caper for no good reason. Either way, the only thing that's going to seal the deal is if you and I can sell this whole married thing."

"But kissing me is 'weird'," Gunnar joked.

"Now that I have a better understanding of what I'm dealing with, it's not so weird," she snapped. She gave him a quick look over. "You're not *that* much older than me. ...and you're a pretty good kisser."

"Is there anything to eat around here?" Gunnar asked looking toward the kitchen area.

"Mace and I never kept much here, but I've got some credits saved up. We can make a stop at the officer's club on our way to the DS offices."

"You better get dressed."

"Be just a minute." Malina sprang from the couch and a moment later, returned from the bedroom, buttoning her uniform. After giving each other a quick look over, they left and started down the hall toward an elevator.

"I haven't spent a whole lot of time on big ships," Gunnar said. "How do you know when anything is happening?'

"I never know, unless I'm told, or I have an assignment that makes it obvious. It's kind of weird. I'll board from Albia and next thing you know, I'm shuttling down to a planet in another system, then back to the ship and maybe later on, I'll shuttle down to another planet in a completely different system."

"Exactly what is your job?" Gunnar asked, as they stepped into the elevator and started going up.

"Ordnance resupply."

"Any ordnance?"

"Large or small, if it hits something or explodes, I deliver. Anytime, anywhere, doesn't matter what the conditions."

"Seen any action?"

"I've seen a few hot zones. Carolon was the hottest. I don't think I've ever seen action that intense though. The Colonians really put up a fight. I made about six runs total. Our ship even took some damage. Hard to explain; you kind of had to have been there."

"I'm sure it was," Gunnar agreed, grinning broadly.

The elevator door opened up and they stepped out, turning to the officer's club. After a casual meal, they made their way toward the office suite levels. Entering the DS offices, a technician looked up as they walked in.

"Report the problem," the attendant said, not really caring if there was one or not.

"What makes you think there's a problem?" Malina asked, sarcastic. "Maybe we just stopped in to see how you guys are doing in here and tell you you're doing a great job."

The attendant gave Malina an indifferent expression and sat looking at them. Finally, Gunnar leaned in and held out his wrist.

"Having a little trouble with my ID band. It's really glitchy."

"Take it off and have a seat," the attendant said, pointing to a bench against the wall.

"You see, my dear," Gunnar said, removing the band and leaving it with the attendant. "You just have to be upfront and let them do their job."

"Sorry Darling, I just thought they could use a little positive reinforcement."

The attendant kept his head down, but turned his eyes up at them. Catching the look from his peripheral, Gunnar put his arm around Malina and pulled her close. As if it were natural, Malina responded in kind, turning and kissing him, then snuggling into his shoulder. Gunnar cracked a grin, noticing an eye roll from the attendant as he handed the ID band to a tech. Several minutes passed as Gunnar and Malina remained closely snuggled together while they waited. Constantly trading whispered comments and hushed snickerings, they barely noticed several security personnel appear at the door and take up positions around the couple. Gunnar looked up at an officer in front of them.

"Is everything ok? What's this all about?"

The guard put a finger to his ear-piece, then held his rifle up; his companions following suit.

"We need you two to remain seated for a moment."

"We're just having a little difficulty with your band," the attendant spoke up from behind the counter. "It's just procedure."

"This is some procedure," Gunnar complained loudly.

"What's happening?" Malina asked. A frightened look streaked across her face when she saw the guns surrounding them. "What's this all about? It was only a glitch."

"Calm down," Gunnar said. "I'm sure this is all some kind of big misunderstanding." Gunnar scanned the group in the room. He was developing a sense that things were starting to unravel; Gunnar could hear the guard's earpiece buzzing.

"I'm gonna have to ask you two to put your hands on your head."

"Mace…" Malina whined. "What's wrong? Why are they arresting us?"

"I don't know, honey. Just do what the scary man with the gun says." Gunnar and Malina slowly rose to their feet, put their hands in position and waited. Gunnar felt a set of electronic binders snap into position and one arm was brought down behind his back.

"Wait a minute," the lead officer said. There was a pause; long enough for Gunnar to pass Malina a quick look. She still had her hands on her head. "Turn 'em lose," the officer ordered. "His ID's have checked out." The binders were quickly removed, and the officers backed away. "Sorry for the bother." The lead officer saluted and turned as the rest exited the room without another word.

Bewildered, Malina looked at Gunnar who stepped to the desk.

"Just what the heck was that all about?" Gunnar gripped the countertop and did his best to hold control of his voice inflections. The attendant remained aloft, studying the information on the screen in front of him.

"Your band was really messed up. It was throwing all kinds of errors and conflicting information with our master database."

"Like, what kind of errors?" Gunnar growled, still fuming.

"Breach errors, stolen and fake identity."

"How can that even happen?" Malina jumped in, still half panicked.

"We're fighting a war, ma'am. Any and everything is possible."

"Unbelievable," Gunnar complained. "Biggest, badass ship in the fleet and I'm getting scammed. Is there no place sacred?"

"I'm sorry, Captain Bridger. We try to keep ahead of it, but there is always something or some group trying to breach our security. It was a good thing you brought your ID band in when you did. It could have been a lot worse."

"Only if your goon squad had been trigger happy."

"It's happened before," the attendant said, handing the band back.

"Come on, honey," Malina urged, taking his arm.

"That isn't very reassuring," Gunnar snorted. Yielding to Malina's promptings, he let go of the counter and they left. After getting a short distance away, Malina looked up and down the corridor.

"Ok, I think I peed my pants a little on that one. I thought the jig was up for sure."

"Yeah," Gunnar grumbled taking a deep breath. "If you hadn't been so deep in character, I might have lost it."

"What can I say," she said flipping her hair back. "I was born for the *theater*. You weren't so bad yourself."

"I should be, I wasn't acting. Which way to the IC's level?" Gunnar was still revved up and trying to calm himself didn't seem to be working. After several twists and turns, they took several flights of stairs, finally coming out on a wide deck filled with busy workstations."

"You've got to be joking," Gunnar said. "Command and Control?"

"This is 'the chain'." Malina pointed to a long row of office windows and doors. "Special Ops is over there with Main Ops at the far end."

"Based on our previous conversation, any idea which one of these 'holes' my orders would come from?"

"No idea, but there's a good way to figure it out. You go that way, and I'll go this way. We'll cross paths in the middle on the far side. If an office is open, step in, take a look around and then move on to the next one. We'll meet back here."

"What if one of us gets stopped?"

"Remember, we come from the *theater*." Malina turned and started off with Gunnar looking after her.

"No fear with this one," he mumbled, turning the other way. Several times, he cast a look across the room as Malina made her way towards the command walls in the other corner of the enormous room. She didn't seem phased by anything or anyone who might have taken notice of her.

After looking in on several of the Incident Command offices, he ducked into another one just as the officer exited. Scanning the room, he was about to leave when something caught his eye. Pushed back a bit beside a com panel, was the reflection of something blue and red. Passing a quick clearing glance through the outer window, he reached back and pulled out the Oxlind ring. His hearts pounding excitedly, it was all he could do to keep from bolting from the room. Instead, he took a deep breath and pushed the ring onto one of his fingers, turning it inward. Malina was just passing by the door when he nearly plowed into her.

"Here," he said taking her arm. "Shall I be your escort?"

"What? Why?" she asked in a hush. "Where are we going? We haven't looked in all of the IC offices. I could only get into about half of them. We'll have to make a couple more rounds."

"No time, we need to get out of here, now."

"Why? I don't get it," Malina complained.

Gunnar took her hand and squeezed it, pressing the ring into her palm. Malina's eyes widened and she jerked a look at him.

"There's no need to linger unnecessarily in places such as this," Gunnar said, winking at her. Malina tightened her grip on his hand.

"I get it. Take me home, Darling."

Once in the elevator, Malina excitedly opened Gunnar's hand and examined the ring.

"Holy heck O' mighty, that's one big, ugly ring. Why would anyone wear such a monstrosity?"

"I think it's mostly for show or when performing royal duties," Gunnar suggested.

"So now what?"

"We get back to the apartment and figure out how to get off this boat and back to Cross."

Remaining arm in arm all the way back to the apartment, Gunnar and Malina were finally behind closed doors again. Gunnar set the ring down on the counter and pulled a liquid container out and took a long drink. When he set the drink down, Malina was examining the ring. A glint of excitement sparkled in her eyes as she held the ring up to the light.

"I've been credit poor all my life," Malina said slowly. "The government offered us credits to bring us in line with the masses, but my parents refused. They thought it was better to hold your head up and support yourself."

"And you didn't hold with those ideals?"

"Ideals like that make for piss poor people and no hope of ever reaching an ideal that only happens to others. With this, I could be those other people who always have everything; or at least a good portion of it."

"Why not just take what the government offers you?"

"What do you think service in the military is? You serve your time and they provide you with a pension that isn't much better than had you taken the support to begin with. You're just another one of the masses that never make a difference."

"I've seen a lot of people with all the credit they could ever want. I don't recall a one of them that was even remotely happy about it. The ones that made a difference were those who had no idea they were doing it. But without exception, they all had one thing in common. They all had ideals and principles and they stuck with them, no matter what their circumstances were."

"Is that what you have, ideals and principles?"

"I only know what I feel is right and am compelled to act on it."

"Pish! Sounds like a sucker's creed."

Gunnar finished his drink, then looked to the bedroom.

"Got a shower?"

"Bedroom, door in the corner," Malina responded, still glued to the ring.

Gunnar watched her for a moment, then disappeared to clean up. After a long shower, he carefully examined his wounds, most of which had closed up. A few were still weeping, but seemed to be healing well. Certainly, if he ever got back to the *Constellation*, he'd have Fuji properly tend to them and work some of her magic to do away with any scarring that might eventually take place. In the closet, he found a couple of clean uniforms. The shirts fit, but the pants didn't. He tried several pairs, but was disappointed each time as he tried to fasten them around his waist.

"Are you serious? I thought Fuji said I wouldn't be gaining any weight? It really sucks to get old," he mumbled. "Hey, Malina. What do you think about a personnel shuttle? Like the way we boarded? Any idea what our next stop is?" Gunnar finished dressing and stepped back out into the kitchen and living room. It was empty. He looked all around the room, but found he was quite alone. Turning to the counter, he noticed the ring was gone. He went back into the bedroom to make sure Malina hadn't somehow ducked in while he had showered. Anger quickly swelling, he searched the entire apartment, making sure she hadn't hidden herself or the ring. Trying to think the best of her, it might be possible she had to go out somewhere and didn't want to leave the ring just sitting out on the counter. A myriad of scenarios played out in his mind as his judgment started to cloud and his anger continued to ratchet. He had come so far only to be tripped up by the greed of a credit hungry widow.

Opening the door, he looked up and down the corridor; nothing. Gripping the door frame harder, he gritted his teeth, trying to hold it together. Now was not the time to lose it, besides, there was next to nothing to break in the hall. He could always barricade himself in the room and tear everything apart behind closed doors, but he was able to reason that wouldn't quench what was happening inside him. Mustering his senses, he stepped out into the hall and gently closed the door. He wished he had a pistol with him. At least then he'd be able to defend himself without making a lot of noise. His best bet would be to try to make his way to a launch bay, find a ship and get out. If he happened upon Malina on his way, he'd break her neck, take the ring, then grab a ship and make good his escape. As he moved carefully through the corridors of the billeting complex, he couldn't help but lament how much easier it would have been if Malina hadn't double-crossed him. Her knowledge of the ship and even her military assignment could have greatly increased their chances of escape.

As he worked his way further from the apartment, he spotted a large band of guards working the corridors. No doubt they were searching for him as Malina would have put them onto him to throw them off her trail. Not seeing an opportunity to reach a launch bay, he casually worked his way back the way he came. Finally back to the safety of the apartment door, he ducked back inside and watched the corridor.

"There you are. Where did you go?"

Gunnar jumped, whirling around to find Malina leaning against the counter. Furious, he slammed the door and stormed at her, grabbing her by the shoulders.

"Where is it?"

"Where's what? Put me down, you're hurting me!"

"The ring! Where's the ring?"

"It's in my pocket! Gunnar, you're hurting me, put me down!"

Dropping her, he groped in her pockets, finally pulling the ring out. As he examined it, he noticed Malina rubbing her shoulders, a twist of pain rippling across her face. Looking back at the ring, he realized he had lost control. This could have been a lot worse, but to him, that was no excuse. Setting the ring on the counter, he reached for Malina's hands. She recoiled at first, but he caught them before she was out of reach. Holding them carefully, he gently pulled her closer.

"Malina, I'm sorry. Please forgive me. The ring was gone, and you weren't here. I thought the worst."

"I told you where I was going," Malina said relaxing with the apology.

"I was in the shower. I didn't hear you say anything," Gunnar said.

Malina pulled free of his grasp and backed away to the chair in the living room. Sitting down, she coiled herself up and closed her eyes.

"I'm sorry," Gunnar apologized again, still fuming. He sat down across from her, both of them remaining silent for what seemed like an eternity. Watching him carefully, Malina finally got up and knelt in front of him. She slowly raised her hands to his mirrored glasses and pulled them carefully from his face. Gunnar winced a little, but the light in the apartment wasn't so bright he couldn't keep his eyes open. A little stunned, Malina sat back watching his eyes modulate through the color spectrum.

"What did they do to you?"

"My kind has anger issues already and my eyes will change color, but not like this. I feel like it's unsafe to be around me. I've never struck anyone in anger under these conditions, but I worry for anyone's safety if I ever lose control."

"Is that what happened to Mace? He got too close and you lost control?"

"He was right next to me."

Malina slowly nodded and gave his glasses back to him.

"We're due in the Darkin Cluster in a couple of hours," Malina said getting up and heading for the bedroom. "Might be helpful if we try to get some more sleep."

Gunnar looked after her. She was right, but for different reasons. She needed to think and recover from his uncontrolled behavior. He needed to calm down and allow his body to return to some state of equilibrium.

*   *   *   *

Malina awoke to the alarm she had set and sat up. She could still feel where Gunnar had held her, but it didn't hurt. She slipped back into the front room where Gunnar lay quietly asleep on the couch. Again, she sat across from him, watching him until he slowly opened his eyes, staring at her.

"Tell me you took a nap too," Gunnar said yawning.

"Yes, but it's time to report to our duty stations."

The room remained silent for a long while until she observed a planet appear out the window. Twisting around, she scanned the area around them.

"This is looks like Darkin Two. They're stopping here for an hour or two, then they're supposed to go to Calliope. If we're going to get off this boat, this'll be the place to do it."

"Do you have anything in mind?"

"While I was out and about, I got us on a couple ordnance shuttles helping to move gear to the surface."

"A couple?"

"Yes, I figured if we traveled down separately, there would be less chance of detection. If for some reason, something goes wrong, the other person still has a chance.

"Listen to you being all tactical and everything," Gunnar said.

"There's minimal to no personnel onboard the shuttles during final unloading. We take which ever one is easiest, clear the atmosphere and make the jump to Quadra-light before anyone realizes what's happened. I've got a set of coordinates we can use to get to Cross."

"Sounds like a walk in the park," Gunnar said standing up.

"We need to grab a couple of things first," Malina said heading for the bedroom. A moment later, she returned with two personal backpacks.

"What's this?" Gunnar asked as Malina handed him one of the bags.

"His and hers," she said holding them up. "Change of clothes and a couple of odds and ends to live on. Mace and I kept them ready in case we needed to *bug out* or disappear for a couple of days, and as we're heading to Cross, wouldn't it be nice not to be dressed as Albion officers and risk getting shot before we can deliver your little package?"

"We'll be driving an Albion ship. How are you going to explain that one?"

Malina stopped and thought a moment.

"Uhm, paint over the insignias?"

"I'm sure we can talk our way through it," he said smiling at the hasty idea. He deliberately turned her around and nudged her toward the door.

"That hadn't even occurred to me," she grumbled. "Can we stop short of Cross and do a spacewalk to cover it up?"

Gunnar's smile turned to a big grin.

"It's the ship's electronic signature you can't erase and I'm not any good at hacking into that kind of thing. It's ok, I know a guy on Cross. We might have some explaining to do, but he'll help us out."

"What if we get separated?" Malina asked.

"You're trying to think this through too much," Gunnar warned, chuckling at his own impetuous nature. "You're gonna get yourself worked up into a tizzy and make people nervous. But if we do get separated, which we won't, but if we do, this ring has to get to Diord Vandmire at all costs." Gunnar dropped the ring into one of the small pockets on the side of his bag. "It's here in the side pocket."

Malina opened the door and the two headed out, holding hands. Winding through corridors and changing decks multiple times, they

finally arrived at a check-in portal. Scanning right through, they made their way to the assignment grid, found the launching identifications and the shuttle assignment.

"We'll have to take a ground launch," Malina said, pointing to a transport vehicle being loaded with various containers, including personnel. They hopped on just as the vehicle started moving towards one of many narrow tunnels.

"Geez, don't stand up or fall off," Gunnar said looking all around. There was barely room in the tunnel for the vehicle and no room to avoid hitting anything that should happen to be in the path of the ground transport. A moment later, the tunnel opened into a cavernous launching bay, filled with a myriad of different craft. Fighters were lined up on the floor and mounted to the upper walls and ceilings. Several rows of shuttles sat in a line in front of most of the fighters. There were many other larger assault style ships dotting through the mix of craft. *It would be fun to test fly them all, or at least walk around them and sit in them,* Gunnar thought as he looked around.

As their craft turned up one of the long rows, he spotted several smaller groups of troopers marching in quick-time from several directions, converging on a location down the row. *Must be ground troops for replacements or something,* he considered as they continued on. He detected yet another cluster of troops, this bunch marching much slower and surrounding several officers. The line of ground transports they were following peeled off to their various destinations and began unloading their personnel and cargos. He finally put his hand to one side of Malina's head and pulled her close.

"No matter what happens, stick to the plan."

Malina gave Gunnar a questioning look and picked up her pack as the transport came to a stop.

"We'll be fine. Like you said, this is a walk in the park," she mumbled.

Gunnar grabbed his pack and headed to his shuttle, next to the one Malina was boarding. As he did so, he observed the converging troopers taking up positions around the vehicle he was stowing his gear in. Trying not to get spooked, he turned to a mound of gear being loaded and started to help. Many of the larger containers were brought onboard with mechanized lifters. He caught a glimpse of Malina working, but there were no troopers around her craft. As he started back down the ramp for another load, he stepped aside to allow a heavy lifter to move through. When it had passed, he turned and abruptly stopped. A short woman, dressed in a skintight, blue body suit and spiked heels stood at the bottom of the ramp.

Gunnar noticed a blaster on one hip, and recognized the Balkrum on her other hip. *Blinda Koss,* he thought, stepping down the ramp in front of her. *Bet she's still pissed?* He looked around at all the troopers now surrounding his assigned shuttle. *They look quite formidable, but no one has their guns pointed at me, always a good sign.* He looked over his shoulder to make sure he wasn't just standing in the way of what they were really after, but saw nothing but loaded cargo. *I think the jig is up.*

"You don't look nearly as dashing in that Albion uniform as you do in your own," Blinda said stepping toward him. She furled her long, shimmering black hair from her face.

"My other uniform was being pressed," Gunnar replied, undaunted by her approach. "Have you done something different with your hair?"

"It's the new me. Do you like it?" Blinda ran her fingers through it, enjoying its feel.

"Black suits you."

"You're a very long way from home," Blinda said stepping right up to him. She looked around him into the cargo bay, then at their surroundings. "I'm not seeing your friends here. You made it up here all alone?"

"It wasn't too hard," Gunnar said, stoic. "I assume you have different levels of trained people."

"Well, yes, the military does, but as I'm not in the military, I don't have any firsthand knowledge of those details."

"I don't believe you."

"Ok, you got me. I do know all the details. But I wasn't lying about not being in the military."

"Then why are you here doing their dirty work?"

"Let's just say, I've got a score to settle."

"I'm hoping you're not going to hold our little tussle on Dither against me."

Blinda did a half turn and suddenly sprang back with a right hook to his jaw. The Thane instantly recoiled in pain, shaking her fist, then holding it. She looked back at Gunnar who was checking his lip.

"Apparently you are," he breathed.

"I owed you that," she grimaced.

"Was it worth it?" Gunnar asked shifting his jaw.

"I'll let you know when my hand quits hurting. I was hoping your friend would be here." She shook her hand again, then fingered the Balkrum on her hip.

"This would be a very different conversation if he were," Gunnar said.

"Yes it would. So, I guess the question at present is; will you be coming quietly or are you in the mood to show off?" Blinda gestured to everyone watching. "Keep in mind, you don't get the opportunity to knock me senseless here like you did on Dither."

"Well, I would hate to interrupt the Albion war machine at work," Gunnar said pointing a thumb over his shoulder at the open cargo bay. "But I get the distinct impression you really want me to show off."

Gunnar suddenly launched over her, landing on top of one of the craft in the next row. Guns were instantly up as everyone turned.

"Hold your fire!" Blinda turned to the ground commander. "Get these ships out of here. Make some room. You troops, back up!" Blinda turned back to Gunnar, smiling. "You called it," she admitted. "I was so hoping you'd resist."

"Glad to oblige," Gunnar said looking around for his next opportunity.

"There'll be no saving you this time."

"No, there won't," Gunnar agreed, watching the rear doors of the shuttles close up. He looked to Malina's transport as it rose from the bay floor and turned to make its exit. He caught site of her looking out at him as her craft started to move toward the launch doors. Only their eyes could speak.

"So you can jump," Blinda commented, stepping toward him. The shuttle he was standing on gently rose from the floor. "Are you going to show us you can survive in space without a suit?"

"Not that I couldn't," Gunnar said as Malina's transport disappeared through the launch doors. He noticed several troopers exiting the vessel he was to ride down in, holding his backpack. Blinda looked behind her, then turned.

"Let me have a look at that," she ordered holding her hand out. "So, let's see what you were willing to risk your neck for." Blinda went through the entire pack, including all the outer pockets, then looked up at Gunnar. Keeping her eyes on him, she spilled the contents on the bay floor. "Girl clothes? Oh, I really like you."

"Someone's going to be mighty upset when they've found you've dumped all their delicates out for everyone to see."

"Have all the ships searched," Blinda snorted angrily. She turned back to Gunnar. "Actually, I don't care why you're here. That's someone else's job." She pulled her pistol and turned it on. "Now, come on. Surely your protector gave you a fair description of my capabilities. So, come down from there before you get hurt."

"I think I'm inclined not to acquiesce with your request."

"I'm not sure you used that word properly."

"I'm alien, I can use it however I want." Gunnar turned, ran across the top of the hovering shuttle and jump again, this time landing between two ships several rows away. He could hear the clamor of boots as he took off running behind a row of Black Tigers.

Ok, Gunnar, what have you got in mind? he thought as weapons fire riddled the wall behind him.

"I said hold your fire!" Blinda yelled from somewhere on the other side of the row.

Gunnar made a quick shift and jumped up onto the rear fin of one of the transport craft close to him. Peering across its back he could see inside the open cargo bays of the other shuttles still parked in the

next row. Cargo sat around several of the craft waiting to be loaded.
As he considered his options, the sounds of clappered trooper boots
resonated in his ears, mixed with the distinctive echoed sounds of
Blinda's spikes heels, slowly clicking closer to his position. The
engines on the shuttle he was hunkered down on suddenly came to
life. Gunnar looked beside him at the intake vents opening up, letting
a concentrated burst of engine noise escape. As the ship began to
turn in a hover, he sprang from his hiding place next to the vertical fin
and sailed across the aisle next to another transport. Before he
landed, there came a volley of shots fired from a smaller weapon.
Tucking and rolling, he saw Blinda pointing her pistol at him as he slid
under the belly of the craft. Scanning his immediate surroundings, he
peered around the loads of cargo in front of him, recalling what Malina
had said they were hauling to the surface of Darkin Two. Fumbling
with one of the containers, he pulled several oblong objects out and
examined one of them.

"Come on, Colonel," Blinda taunted. "This isn't very sporting."
Blinda stepped carefully toward the pallets, her pistol pointed up.
Instinctively, she turned and pointed at several objects rolling across
the floor at her. Each made a distinctive high pitched chirping sound.
One clanked up next to her foot. She looked down at it and bumped it
with her pointed boot.

"Really? You're gonna start throwing things?" she exclaimed,
kicking the thermal detonator away and swinging her arm out, making
a half turn. The other detonators instantly spun away, most of them
becoming airborne and exploding in a wide circle. Blinda waved her
arm over her head, keeping the tiny metal fragments from showering
her. Turning back to the pallets of ordnance, she clasped her hands
together and swung both arms in one direction. The cargo instantly
slid across the floor, settling close to another pallet behind the next
shuttle. Bewildered, she expected to find Gunnar crouched on the
floor; nothing. She scanned the area, trying to sense his presence;
still nothing. She glanced back at the transport behind her as it rose
from the floor and moved toward the launching portal. Turning back
to the open cargo doors, Blinda dropped to one knee, looking under
the craft as its two pilots were unceremoniously tossed from the side
door and the hatch slammed shut. She hurried up the loading ramp
with her pistol ready as the engines came to life. Feeling the ship rise
into a hover, she made her way forward. Approaching the front, the
cockpit door suddenly cracked open and several objects came tumbling
out, scattering around the Thane. Blinda looked down and rolled her
eyes.

"Not again," she grumbled. A twitch of her fingers and the
detonators launched toward the rear of the shuttle. Her eyes widen as
she turned to find the hold doors had closed. Blinda dove for cover as
the ordnance exploded against the heavily armored doors. Hot

shrapnel sprayed the entire compartment, peppering the Thane where she lay. Rolling over, Blinda forced a smile and shook her head. "Nice one."

The hold was now full of smoke, but with a twirl of her finger, the air cleared around her and she sprang to her feet. Forcing the cockpit door open, she burst inside. *No one is at the controls!* Scanning the instruments, she realized the shuttle was moving. Looking outside, her eyes widened seeing the craft was making a wide arc that would direct it into the next row of transports waiting to depart. The vessel shifted abruptly, causing her to lose her balance. Looking back out, the transport's course had been dramatically altered, now pointed directly at the next shuttle. In its path was not only the next ship, but both loads of ordnance. Beyond the imminent collision, Blinda spotted Gunnar sprinting for the far wall of the launch bay. Smiling, she snapped her fingers and the escape hatch above her disappeared. A rush of air filled the cockpit and catapulted her straight up and out. Moments later, troopers and loading personnel scrambled to get clear as the shuttle collided with the one parked next to it, setting off a tremendous explosion. A larger secondary blast erupted in the middle of the fireball, expanding the destructive circle. Alarms blared and emergency fire suppression instantly filled the area with a foamy sea of bright red fire retardant. In the confusion, personnel scattered, trying to escape the disaster. More shuttles became airborne, moving away from the melee.

As the smoke and flames were brought down, Gunnar casually stepped away from the end transport as it rose into a hover and turned for the launch portal. He had just about made it to the bay wall, heading toward several doors when he felt the air moving around him again. Breaking into a sprint, he glanced around for the source, but was unexpectedly thrown sideways. Bouncing a couple of times against the wall, he tried to jump, but lost his footing and fell, coming to a sliding halt in one of the doorways. Shaking his head, he detected a set of boots directly in front of him and looked up at a figure wrapped in a green cloak.

"You've just demonstrated the need to have maintenance do a better job of keeping the floors clean," Drax said looking back at the smear mark Gunnar had just left. She looked beyond at the smoldering mess in the bay. Shaking her head, she smirked slightly seeing Blinda moving through the confusion, looking all around. Gunnar was quickly brought to his feet by the Queen Captain's guards. "Am I interrupting anything?" she asked, looking over his shoulder.

"You would be Drax Blair," Gunnar acknowledged, looking at the men holding him.

Drax smiled broadly, folding her arms.

"Sorry, they don't mean to insult your intelligence, but my guards know nothing about you. Please forgive them. Guards, release...

Colonel Conrad, is it?" Hesitant at first, the guards finally released Gunnar just as Blinda softly landed right behind him.

"My reputation proceeds me," Gunnar assured her.

"Yes, I've been looking forward to this meeting for a long time."

"Delivered as promised," Blinda snickered from behind. Drax gave Blinda a hard glare, giving the Thane cause to melt a bit. Drax stood silent, looking at Gunnar for a moment, then stepped to one side of the doorway.

"If you can spare a moment, I'd love to chat with you about a few things."

"I'm sure you would," Gunnar said. "So why not just shoot me up with more of your 'happy juice' and get whatever it is you want?"

"Well, I was hoping it wouldn't come to that. Yes, you could certainly take most of my troops apart and probably manage to get away from Blinda, again..." Drax said pointing at the Thane. Blinda gave the Queen Captain a sneer. "Then you'd try to hide out on the ship, and it being a very large ship, it would take my men a considerable amount of time to find you. Then they'd have to shoot you up with more 'happy juice'. I suspect you already feel like you've got enough floating around inside you. Probably causing all kinds of, shall we say, *side effects*? So, my hope is to avoid all that and just sit down for some dinner and a little conversation. Then if you want to try and make a break for it, well, we can address that topic when we come to it."

Gunnar looked all around. He was several layers deep in troops and couldn't even see the hallway beyond the door Drax was standing in for all the guards behind her. He could feel Blinda next to him, his eardrums gently throbbing.

"Well, since there's food involved, how can I refuse?"

"Excellent! We best get you out of here," Drax chuckled softly. "The commander of this ship will want answers about all this mess."

A trooper stepped forward with a pair of open wrist binders, but stopped short when Drax put a hand on them.

"Lieutenant, those won't be necessary. Besides, they wouldn't stay on anyway. Position your guards in front and behind him with stun weapons and rifles. Am I correct, Colonel?"

"Yes, I got stunned a couple of days ago; It didn't feel very good."

Drax motioned for Gunnar to follow her guards as he stepped into the adjoining hallway. Blinda gave Drax a hard look as she joined the entourage moving through the hallways.

A Gift

Hard as it was, Rick made good on his promise to stay in bed. It seemed his quarters were his prison for a week, until Caidin finally gave him the go ahead to resume limited duty status. Caidin and Dãsha agreed to let him walk the corridors of the *Athena* for a short time each day, but Jayda wouldn't permit him on the bridge or in engineering. After several more anxious days, she finally consented to letting Rick return to full duty status with a warning that she was watching him closely.

Rick took his time inspecting the four Starbirds now parked in one of *Calypso's* hangar bays. He had seen the new AI systems before while he and the 7000 series droids were designing the original Starbirds. His understanding at the time, was that this new AI tech was still under development and far from ready for deployment. The AI systems were capable of operating the ship without human assistance, even in combat. Each ship was loaded with a full complement of advanced Pin missiles, but the load of torpedoes were only the conventional short range Mark IIs. Certainly capable of inflicting substantial damage, but nothing like what the Mark V was capable of. Perhaps these new ships were being delivered to a secret testing area for evaluation before being cleared for actual deployment. He considered it peculiar that he had not been privy to such a radical concept. Even in military circles, humanity required human thinking and interaction in order to make critical judgement calls.

Of course, with his service record in fighters, Rick found the new Interceptors of particular interest. Each was equipped with advanced weaponry and energy shields. The onboard AI systems didn't require human control to function in combat either. The large fighter was basically the same as its older brother, but faster and capable of reaching FTL speeds matching its mother ship.

Taking more of an active role in seeing to the *Athena's* engine refit, Rick spent most of this waking hours in engineering or his desk, studying the star charts Caidin had provided them. As he considered the options that lay before them, there came a summons at the door.

"Come in," he said without looking up. He heard multiple footsteps behind him shuffle into the room and finally turned around, facing three officers standing at attention. Captain Lisa Dayton, Toby Mavis and Lieutenant Laura Habba stood in a neat row looking straight ahead.

"What's this all about, Captain?" Rick asked coming to his feet.

"We wanted to come see you, Sir."

"Well, now you're seeing me."

"Permission the speak freely, Sir?" the Captain edged, looking behind her.

Rick looked over her shoulder to see who she might be looking for. It was then that it dawned on him what this was about. He smiled and clasped his hands behind his back.

"What's on your mind?"

All three officers looked at each other and then relaxed, smiling.

"The Kendalons, Sir."

"Yeah, what about them?" Rick stepped closer when he got no response.

"We can't do anything without them questioning everything," Toby complained, glancing at the other two who nodded in agreement.

"Yes, yes, yes, I get it, but you have to understand they've had to operate under some pretty strict conditions in order to maintain any kind of discipline. It's how they've survived all this time out here on their own with very little command guidance. Their branch has always been a little uptight."

"More to the point, Sir, we never really had a chance to give you a proper thank you for... You know, saving our lives."

"Well technically, I didn't save your lives. Caidin Mantose is the one you have to thank for that."

"Yes, we know he revived us from the stasis pods."

"Did more than just revive you. You three were the only ones left alive on the *Athena*."

"Yes, Sir, but you were the one that found us, and secured us in the stasis pods. If you hadn't, Doctor Mantose wouldn't have had anything to revive."

"I don't think you guys are privy to Caidin's abilities."

"Sir, we thanked the Doctor. Now we're here to thank you, personally."

Rick stopped trying to explain everything and looked at each of them, feeling a great emotional attachment to them. He caught a great lump in his throat, feeling tears shooting into his eyes.

"You guys are family," he finally choked. "And I'll do whatever it takes to see to your safety."

"Thank you, Sir."

"You're welcome." Rick observed wet eyes across the row of officers in front of him and couldn't help but be overcome. He wrapped his arms around each one individually, embracing them as he would his own child. He finally stepped back, wiping the moisture from his eyes and sniffling slightly. "Now, get out of here," he said trying to cough as he turned back to his work.

Sitting back down, he heard the door close behind him and leaned back, thinking. He had covered a lot of time and distance to have all these people back together again. He had set out to find Jayda and in the process, found many friends who had become his family. Now, he felt an urgency to find Gunnar. He hoped his friend was ok, but somewhere in the back of his mind, he felt something wasn't right. He couldn't put his finger on it, but he had a feeling his friend was once again in need of his help. The com panel on his desk lit up and he tapped one of the buttons.

"Yes, Lieutenant Habba."

"Sir, I'm getting a transmission."

"I can only imagine the things you hear at your station, Lieutenant."

"Yes, Sir. It can be a noisy place out there, but this is on our battle channels."

"Our battle channels? Are you sure?"

"Sir..."

"I'm just teasing, Lieutenant. Send it in."

There was static at first, then garbled transmissions, then a clear voice.

"Mayday, Mayday... Kalamarion SAC Ten transmitting in the blind on Kalamarion Alpha channel twenty-six. Mayday, Mayday... Captain Dakota Abrams, acting Commander of the *Constellation*, transmitting on all emergency channels as well as all lower Hadrian emergency channels. We are under attack by overwhelming forces of the Albion Empire over the planet Carolon in the Nulark system. We've lost main power and defensive weapons. If anyone can assist, please help us..." There was a flurry of technical data in the form of high speed tones providing spacial coordinates. Time variations induced by natural phenomenon between where the *Athena* was located and the source of the transmission were also included. The message then repeated itself until Rick put a stop to it.

"Thank you, Lieutenant. Are we in any position to respond?"

"I can reply, but not with our own equipment. I believe the best way to do so would be aboard *Calypso*."

"Have Caidin or Dãsha come see me if they have any questions about making the reply."

"Uhm, Sir. Would it be all right if you made that request? I think it'll carry more weight if it comes from you."

"You're afraid of Dãsha, aren't you?"

"She's a bit overpowering."

"It's ok," Rick chuckled. "She can be intimidating. I'll have a talk with her." Just then the door behind him opened. "Oh, and Lieutenant? I'm afraid of her too."

"Thank you, Sir."

"Afraid of who?" Jayda asked, settling into the chair next to his desk. Rick turned to see Dãsha parking herself on the couch across from them. He couldn't help but wonder if the tall slender woman had overheard the end of his conversation.

"We just got a Mayday transmission from the *Constellation* on the emergency battle frequencies."

Focused, Jayda sat forward.

"What's their status?"

"At least you know your friend is still alive," Dãsha commented, casually looking at her fingernails.

"It sounds like they came under attack by the Albions over Carolon in the Nulark system."

"What in the world are they doing there?"

"The transmission sounded automated to me, but if I had to guess, Gunnar went after the Asium deposits he found there." Rick paused a moment, thinking. "Dang it," he burst quietly. "I told him it wasn't a good idea to try it without backup."

"I'm sure he thought he could handle it."

"I'm not so sure Gunnar was even there."

"What do you mean?"

"The transmission was made by, Captain Abrams. That's not too unusual, but in Gunnar's case, I'm guessing he's off somewhere chasing after something or being chased by someone... again."

"Your friend sounds like he has a propensity for finding trouble or trouble finding him," Dãsha commented amused.

"You don't know the half of it," Jayda replied.

"He's the best fighter pilot I have ever known," Rick defended calmly. "He's also proved to be a top notch Starbird commander. Those two traits alone are key to being good at what he does."

"It would seem to me that being a good fighter pilot requires a certain amount of careless abandon that doesn't mix well with the required calm and calculation of being a good ship commander." Dãsha's black eyes stared straight through Rick, remaining emotionless in both tone and expression.

"You don't even know Gunnar," Rick retorted coolly.

"I know enough from what you've told me to draw a conclusion. Have I not?"

"You have no clue about what kind of a commander Gunnar is," Rick bristled, becoming hard.

Dãsha came to her feet and stood towering over Rick and Jayda. She put her hands on her hips and looked directly at Rick.

"I have upset you and for that, I am truly sorry. You are correct, I don't know your friend as intimately as you or your Jayda. I am sure he is a great commander. I can only compare him to what I am. I do have the ingredients to be a good fighter pilot, but I also understand that I would make a poor ship commander. The requirements for both do not mix well. But if your Gunnar has figured out how to make those qualities coexist, then he is indeed the man you proport him to be." Dãsha turned to leave but stopped at the door as it opened. "Tell your Lieutenant Habba I would be happy to escort her to *Calypso* to send your transmission. And I promise not to be scary."

The door closed, leaving Rick and Jayda looking at each other.

"I think you may have hurt her feelings," Jayda suggested.

"Not likely," Rick came back.

"You don't think she has feelings?"

"Oh, she most certainly does," Rick said, smiling. "I guarantee she has feelings. The difference between us and her, is where she keeps them and who she let's see them."

"I get the feeling she wants you to see them."

"Can't even begin to understand why."

Jayda watched her husband for a moment, then looked at the display on his desk.

"Ok, let's hear this Mayday transmission."

After listening to the transmission several times, Rick looked to Jayda for her observations.

"Well, the location seems to check out," she said pointing at a glowing spot on the star chart in front of them. "Just can't imagine where Gunnar could have gone."

"The answer lies with Captain Abrams and the *Constellation*. We need to get to it before the Albions do."

"What does the time telemetry indicate? How old is this transmission?"

"A day or so."

"Even at full sub-light, it would take us weeks to reach the Nulark system from here."

"Then we need to get in touch with Aster Command or Administrator Vandmire on Cross to find out where they're likely to take them if captured."

"The only way to send a transmission like that is from *Calypso*."

"Yes," Rick said getting to his feet. "I'd like to have a little chat with Caidin anyway. I haven't seen much of him lately."

"Me either and it seems like Dãsha has spent far more time here than on *Calypso*."

"She hasn't been a problem, has she?" They walked out and turned toward the bridge.

"Oh no. I've enjoyed her company," Jayda admitted. "There has been lots of opportunity for girl talk."

"Oh, brother, that's all I need. It was bad enough when Audra was alive."

"I wouldn't worry too much about it. We have vastly different ideas about dress styles."

As the door to the bridge popped open, they were confronted by Dãsha and Lieutenant Habba. The young com officer sported a tentative look.

"Ah, General Niker. I was just taking your young Lieutenant Habba here with me to *Calypso* to make her transmission."

"Yes, I appreciate your willingness to do so, but there's been a change of plans. We need to send more than one transmission, so I will be going in the Lieutenant's place."

Dãsha looked at Rick for a moment, then at Jayda.

"And will your Jayda be accompanying us?"

"No, she'll remain aboard the *Athena* as Officer in Command."

Dãsha remained silent for a moment, then looked back at Lieutenant Habba, then turned back to Rick and Jayda.

"Very well, I assume you will need to leave immediately?"

"If that's ok...?"

"As we were just leaving anyway, it seems logical. Thank you, Lieutenant Habba. Commander Jayda, I hope to see you soon afterwards. I enjoy our interactions."

Laura Habba silently mouthed a thank you from behind and backed up to her station while Jayda gave her husband a smile with raised eyebrows as she passed into the bridge. Dãsha started down the hallway with Rick hurrying to keep up.

"Do you really have to walk so fast?" Rick puffed, nearly trotting as they headed down the boarding ramp.

"I am sorry," Dãsha said. "I can't help that I have such long legs. It lends to a long stride and a different cadence. I will attempt to adjust to your speed."

"Those high heels can't be helping either," Rick observed, glancing at her knee-high boots.

"For most women they would be a challenge, but for me, they are comfortable."

"You mean you really like wearing them?"

"I do like the way they look on me, but it is more than that." They weaved through the other Starbirds toward the bay exit. "My high-heel boots are designed to support my frame better."

"I can't imagine standing on your toes all the time as being comfortable."

"While your initial assessment would be accurate for the normal human female, as you are aware, I am far from normal. With these boots, I am able to apply equal pressure to the ball of my feet as I do to the heel. It feels natural to me."

Exiting the hangar bay, they turned and boarded a pneumatic transport. Beginning their journey to the conning tower, Dãsha turned to Rick.

"Richard, do you find me attractive?"

"Do I find you attractive? Why would you ask me that?" Rick's voice cracked getting the words out. "What does it matter?"

"I value your opinion. I have found you to be an honorable man. You have never given me erroneous information."

"Ok, I'm flattered you think I'm honorable, but that doesn't answer my question. Why would you ask me that? Better put, why would you ask anyone that question?"

"I am finding my interaction with your crew to be somewhat awkward and my attempts to adjust my behavior have proven unsuccessful. If I am unable to integrate with your crew, what hope do I have of ever integrating with a planet society? As you can imagine, I have not had much interaction with other humans in any kind of social environment. It's hard for me to know what is proper or acceptable."

Rick couldn't help but smile, thinking of Lieutenant Habba's reaction when he let her off the hook.

"I can see how you'd feel like you don't fit in," Rick said. "But, wasn't your former life as Danis full of social interaction?"

"I would not categorize that life as being normal social interaction. It is my sincerest hope that no one ever know what life as Danis Knox was like."

"Danis still resides in you."

"Deep down," Dãsha replied quietly. "Danis keeps the memories of her life before locked away. It is necessary for me to lead some semblance of normalcy."

"You're unique in just about every aspect of human female physiology. I suspect most of your social difficulties are a by-product of the Nano-Mech Caidin infused you with."

"He has tried to tell me as much. I just feel so mechanical."

"It does make sense," Rick nodded, watching Dãsha's expression. "But why are you worried about if I think you're beautiful? Doesn't Caidin tell you how beautiful you are?"

"Constantly," Dãsha answered, looking forward. "I know he loves me, and I him."

"Then why ask the question?" Rick asked.

Dãsha remained silent until the pneumatic transport came to a halt. As Rick stepped out of the car, he turned and offered his hand to Dãsha. Cocking her head, she looked at it, then back at Rick.

"Yes, Dãsha, I find you very attractive."

The expression on Dãsha's face instantly shifted and smiling softly, she gently took his hand. As they exited the vehicle, she turned to Rick.

"I ask the question because I have wondered if I will ever be anything more than an object."

"I don't understand," Rick said. "Who views you as an object?"

"The way the men of your crew look at me. I've seen these looks before, a long time ago. The women of your crew look at me with distain and longing. You and Caidin are the only men I have met so far who see me differently."

"As a woman, you are a gift and Caidin is lucky to have you."

"Thank you. Those are wonderful words for any woman to hear. You are a true gentleman."

Rick smiled as Dãsha leaned in and gently kissed him on the cheek, then turned and started walking towards the elevator complex. As he looked after her, he considered for a moment, her statement about how the women on his crew looked at her with distain and longing. He understood full well what she was referring to. Her voluptuous figure, tight top and miniskirts, even the knee-high, high-heel boots stood directly in the face of cultural modesty. But not just that, every woman longed to have and keep a figure such as what Dãsha had.

"Maybe you could take a lesson from Jayda," Rick suggested, catching up to the tall woman. Dãsha stopped and turned to Rick.

"A lesson? What is meant by a lesson?"

"You want to fit in; to not be an object of distain or desire, but a woman admired for her beauty, both inside and out, right?"

Dãsha cocked her head again, looking at Rick as if trying to figure out if he had other motives in mind.

"If you have information that could help, please enlighten me."

They continued walking and entered the elevator. Rick turned Dãsha to one of the full length reflective panels and stood next to her.

"Tell me what you see."

"I see me, Dãsha."

"Exactly; and you are truly beautiful. What is it that you find different about yourself?"

"My eyes are black, but they are genetic to my race."

"Yes, you have black eyes," Rick agreed, looking at her stark black eyes. Gazing at them in the reflection for a moment, he realized after all the time they had spent together, he had become accustomed to them. "What else do you see?"

"I have big hair. It too, is black."

"Yes, but I don't think anyone has a problem with your hair."

"No one else has to deal with it," Dãsha snickered lightly.

"Anything else?"

"I have large breasts and a thin waist."

"Yes," Rick gulped, trying not to look.

"Is this not a desirable trait in a woman?" Dãsha turned sideways to admire her shape.

"Well, I guess… For every man it's different." Rick scratched his head, unsure how to proceed.

"You said I am attractive," Dãsha pressed her hands down her sides past the curves of her hips. "You like the shape of my breasts and waist? Is this not correct?"

Rick coughed a couple of times, half on purpose.

"I don't think either of those things are a problem," he finally said, turning her back to the reflection.

Dãsha looked back at Rick, sensing distress in his voice.

"I am sorry. I've given you cause for discomfort. What have I said or done to make you uncomfortable?"

"I'll get over it," Rick said, hoping to change the subject. "What else do you see?"

Dãsha stared at him in the reflection for a moment. She looked over at him observing that his face was flushing full of color.

"Are you feeling all right?"

"Yes," Rick replied. "What else?"

Dãsha slowly looked back at the reflection and cocked her head. After several moments, she seemed to give up on trying to guess.

"I feel like I have covered everything that is obvious," she said. She turned her profile again. "Unless, you think it is my clothes?"

"Have you met anyone else since you've known me, that wears the same types of clothes as you?"

"Only Jayda and she didn't seem to like them. In fact, she couldn't wait to get out of them." Dãsha turned to Rick. "I have changed the colors, the patterns, even from dress to a skirt. Is this the lesson you speak of?"

"In my culture," Rick began. "A woman is valued more by what she doesn't show than by what she does show. Modesty in dress is a revered quality that is highly sought after."

"But I thought this is what male humans preferred," Dãsha said, starting to sound distressed as she turned, looking at her reflection. "The memories of Danis indicate human males prefer short dresses or skirts, bare legs and tight fitting clothes. These are more desirable than loose fitting clothes that hide the skin. Your crewmen seem to prefer my current attire. I am confused by your lesson."

It was impossible for Rick to completely understand what was going through Dãsha's mind. He wished Jayda was the one having this conversation, not him. Dãsha was correct about his crew; even he had witnessed the looks as the tall slender woman would pass in the halls. The elevator came to a stop and the doors rolled to one side. As they walked out, Dãsha was back to her long stride, leaving Rick trying to keep up as they neared the control room of *Calypso*.

"Dãsha, I'm sorry. Now I've hurt your feelings."

"Are you sure you can tell I have any?"

"Dãsha, don't be like that."

"Like what? Like a machine? Like an emotionless drone present only for the pleasure of others?"

"Dãsha…" Rick couldn't keep up with her unless he broke out into a trot and he refused to talk to the back of her head.

Dãsha remain steadfast, moving directly to the vast communications station and began setting controls. When Rick finally caught up to her, his breathing was elevated. He leaned down and tried to look into her face, but she only turned in another direction to set more controls.

"As I was able to understand from your Lieutenant Habba, these controls should now be set to your battle frequencies. This display here, shows your emergency frequencies. The controls for changing these are right here. You indicated you wanted to send additional transmissions? Just dial and press."

"Dãsha," Rick said taking her by the arm and turning her to him. He was unable to get any words out before she firmly took his hand and removed it from her arm. Grasping it firmly, she held it as far out as she could, moving Rick away from her.

"I need to think. When you have completed your transmissions, please come and find me and I will take you back to your ship. Or if you would rather, you can find your own way back."

Dãsha released his wrist and turned in a mechanical fashion, stepping to the vaulted bay windows at helm control. Rubbing his wrist, Rick watched her take up a position next to the two pilot stations and fold her arms. She appeared to freeze in position, facing the windows.

He hesitated, thinking he ought to continue his attempts at talking with her. Jayda had indicated that she got the impression that Dãsha wanted Rick to know about how she felt more than anyone else. Probably because of how much interaction they had had since their meeting. But if Rick had learned anything about being married to Jayda, it was that even the best of women become angry or wrestle with hurt feelings. Sometimes it's best to just leave them alone and let them deal with those feelings internally. In this case, he chose to let Dãsha alone. Right now, the important thing was to get these transmissions made.

He turned back to the communications equipment and went to work, making sure he used all the appropriately coded encryption. Looking at the vast array of controls and readouts in front of him, he thought for a while if there was anyone else he could contact, but he was drawing a blank. He could spend a lifetime trying to figure out how to work all this gear. He had to wonder how the Drake, who seemed so low tech, had built such an amazing ship. Indeed, he had his suspicions as to whether the Drake had anything to do with her construction at all. *Calypso* was so large, even bigger than any of the Colonian or Albion ships he had encountered. If this ship and its technology had not been built by the Drake, then who had she been built by and what happened to her crew?

The immense station next to him caught his eye and he pushed his chair over to the nearest display. Looking at the information, he realized he was looking at a plotted course back to the Jurass system. This route looked significantly shorter than the one he had intended through the Nulark system, then through the Helix system and finally Jurass where they could then make their way to Aster. Studying the charts carefully, he located Tintee and Albia. As he sat considering, a wild idea came to mind. Something so far out there, he wasn't sure it shouldn't have come from Gunnar. Hesitating a moment, he suddenly pushed his chair back over in front of the communications panels and went to work resetting the frequency controls. After making sure he had configured everything the way he wanted it, he entered a series of messages and then with a single tap of a button, the additional messages were sent out. He sat back and thought a moment, wondering if he had done the right thing.

"Did you find what you were looking for?" Caidin asked approaching Rick.

"Just sending some reply transmissions to my friends in the Nulark system."

"Is your friend in trouble?"

"It sounds like it."

"Then am I to understand you will be wanting to go to his aide."

"He'll be expecting it, but even if he weren't, I would still go."

"Certainly," Caidin said nodding. "How can I help?"

Rick looked around at the bridge of the great ship. He recalled his Interceptor's computer giving him an analysis of *Calypso* when he first boarded her. Her light speed engines were intact, but they had been so preoccupied with getting the sub-light engines up and running, he hadn't even considered if the old ship was still capable of light speed operations.

"Can we have a look at your light speed controls?"

"Certainly," Caidin said motioning toward the far end of the navigation station. "Let me have Dãsha help you. She knows far more about these controls than I do." Caidin turned to Dãsha standing motionless on the pilot's deck. "Dãsha, will you join us?"

Caidin and Rick stopped in front of the light speed console and looked it over. It certainly looked like it was functional. Every indicator, display and readout was flowing with information. As Caidin started the basic introduction, he glanced over his shoulder expecting to see Dãsha, but she wasn't there.

"Dãsha, please, you know these instruments better than I." Caidin turned all the way around and faced the woman standing at the helm. "Dãsha?" Caidin looked back at Rick.

"I'm afraid I've upset her," Rick admitted sheepishly.

"Upset her, how?" Caidin asked.

"By suggesting she dress differently."

"I hardly think that's a reason for getting upset," Caidin shuffled back to the young woman. Rick watched him struggle to the platform and take Dãsha's hand. She remained firm where she was, so he stood next to her and began to speak low enough Rick couldn't hear what was being said. It appeared Caidin was doing all the talking. After several minutes, Caidin finally stepped back down.

"I'm sorry, Caidin. She was asking me how she could get along better with my crew and I'm afraid she took offense to what I had to say."

They looked back at Dãsha's slender form standing unmoved on the helm platform.

"Let me guess. You suggested she lose the mini-skirts and the tight tops?"

Rick popped a surprised look at Caidin. The older gentleman looked back at him smiling and put a hand to his shoulder.

"It's not the first time it's been suggested."

"Then why is she so upset?"

"Dãsha is a byproduct of Danis, who was required to wear those types of clothes all her life. Naturally, Dãsha retains bits and pieces of Danis; they give her comfort until she can resolve within herself what the environment around her would have her be. As Dãsha comes to grips with her own humanity, modesty will become more of an issue."

"So, what's the silent treatment all about?"

"She's processing. She has always done it when confronted with change she perceives as difficult. It's the Nano-Mech inside her. It doesn't understand emotional things, only facts and logic. It sometimes takes a while for that part of her to catch up." Caidin turned back to the light speed consoles. "As I understand it, this section here," Caidin said pointing at the panels directly adjoining the navigation consoles, "this would be where you would set your navigational information for the light speed computers to use when plotting the course axes. Current location in orientation to your proposed destination, and the route traveled in between; you don't want to run into anything."

"Well, everything here is problematic for any of the Kalamarion data bases," Rick said, looking closer at the readouts. "We're still picking up bits and pieces of navigational information from any Hadrian ship we can access, but to try and plot a light speed course right now, at least in this part of Hadrian, wouldn't be a good idea."

"You are correct, General," Dãsha cut in quietly. Both men turned as the tall beauty appeared between them. "As you are no doubt well aware, there are many obstacles in space. Most of them are just tiny particles of rocks, some no larger than a grain of sand, but that grain striking the hull of a ship at even the slowest of sub-light speeds can pierce the thickest armor plating. Image what a rock or tiny asteroid could do." Dãsha moved to the center station. "These other sections are for speed calculations, control and finally, light speed monitoring. *Calypso's* light speed engines are a combination of several stepping engines."

"Get one going and the ship up to speed and then add another to go faster," Rick suggested looking at the console closely.

"You are correct again," Dãsha replied. "As far as I have been able to discern, *Calypso's* light speed engines are all operational and everything you see here, appears to be functioning as it should. Up until you came along, our trouble has been with the sub-light engines. You can't start the light speed engines without already being up to the fastest speed in the sub-light range. There are fail safes designed in the system to keep that from happening."

"Understandable," Rick said. "Without those fail-safes, you could end up shredding the low end of the lightspeed drivers. Kalamarion technology struggled with that one when we used Ultra-light drives. The speed mismatching was just too high and when they finally came up with the Massey light drive engine, it included all the speed ranges. We still need to be moving on the low end of the sub-light range to jump to light speed, but we don't have to worry about blowing something up."

"What do you need this information for?" Dãsha asked, her tone controlled.

"With your permission," Rick said turning to Caidin and Dãsha. "I would like to use *Calypso* to mount a rescue."

Dãsha folded her arms, staring at Rick while Caidin ran his fingers through his whiskers.

"We've received a distress signal from the *Constellation*, in the Nulark system, just off the planet Carolon. Right now, *Calypso*, is the only ship that's light speed capable."

"What about your ships?" Caidin asked. "Are you just going to leave them behind? And what good will *Calypso* do you once you reach the Nulark system and find your friend; she has no weapons?"

"*Calypso's* hangar bays are more than large enough to hold all the freighters and Assault Corsairs. Once we arrive at Carolon, we assess the situation and launch our Starbirds to mount the rescue."

"We have never tried *Calypso's* light speed engines," Dãsha informed Rick. "We have been marooned here until you repaired our sub-light engines."

"What did the last diagnostics on your light speed systems indicate?" Rick asked.

"It has been some time since we did one. The last one indicated all systems were operational," Dãsha admitted. "But, we have no way of knowing for sure if they're going to work unless we try them. I would certainly not recommend any long-distance operations without thorough testing."

Rick turned and took a couple of steps away from Caidin and Dãsha, thinking. While Dãsha was correct, they didn't have time to spend on a thorough testing. They needed to go now. Caidin walked over to Rick, who was still deep in thought.

"Of course, *Calypso* is yours. If she'll still jump to light speed, I think she'd be glad to have you all onboard." Caidin looked around at the interior of the mammoth ship. "I think she'll be glad to have a use again."

"Are you sure?" Rick asked, looking around as well.

"Certainly. And, Dãsha and I need to get used to a new way of life. A life that moves and has other people in it." Caidin took Dãsha's hand as she stood next to him. "Please, tell us what we can do."

Rick smiled and nodded.

"Make sure your landing bays can seal and I'll start the preparations." Rick grinned broadly shaking Caidin's hand then strode from the bridge. There were so many things running through his mind now. One big one was crew staffing. He and Gunnar had planned to have a new crew for the *Athena* when he returned to Aster, but right now, that didn't seem to be the natural order of things. Now he was going to have to staff four Starbirds with the number of crew it took to staff just one; and that was crew only. Each Starbird required a command officer that knew the ship and what it was capable of. Even as he reached the elevator, he was contemplating who would need to sit in those center seats. He would resume command of the *Athena*, while Jayda would take command of one of the other Starbirds. Thinking about who would best fill the other seats, Rick reached for the elevator control.

"Richard," a quiet voice said from behind. Dãsha stopped in front of him, somewhat closer than normal. "It is my hope…" Dãsha looked down, fumbling with her fingernails. "I wanted to apologize for my behavior earlier. I am sorry. I understand that you are only trying to help."

"It's ok," Rick smiled, trying to get her to look at him.

"No, it is not ok," Dãsha said, still quiet. "Stomping off like an android to have a robotic tantrum is not the type of behavior I wish to cultivate."

"You needed your time to think."

"Normal people do not act as I have."

Rick finally put a finger to her chin, bringing her head up so he could look into her jet-black eyes. As he gazed into them, he had the strangest feeling he was looking at Dãsha and Danis, standing together, deep within.

"Dãsha, if *normal* people can't see you for who and what you really are, then they're having issues with what's considered *normal*.

"I wish I felt the same way you and Caidin see me."

"You said it yourself, Dãsha. We have never lied to you. Why would we start now? Especially about something like this?"

"Change is hard for me, especially when it comes to my appearance," she said looking down at her outfit. "I really do love what I'm wearing."

"And you look incredible in it, but remember, is shows only the outside and not what's within."

"I want people to see who I am."

"Just because you do, doesn't mean you have to become someone you're not. But it doesn't hurt to make a shift or two here and there."

"What is meant by... shift?"

"Ask Jayda the next time you see her," Rick said, backing into the open elevator, leaving Dãsha watching him until the doors had closed.

She stood thinking for a moment or two, then turned back for the bridge. As she reentered, she was met by Caidin.

"How long will it take you to run your light speed diagnostics?" Caidin asked.

"Much less time than last we tried. With the sub-light engines functioning again, there is far more power available."

"You are a true marvel, my dear."

"As are you." Dãsha leaned down and kissed her husband. "Do you think I'd look good in a long dress or pants?"

Caidin grinned broadly and looked her over.

"Dãsha, you'd look good in a paper bag. Why do you ask?"

Dãsha turned for the light-speed consoles.

"Hoping to be more than just what you see."

Caidin looked after her for a moment, then smiling broadly, turned and shuffled back to his lab.

*　　　*　　　*　　　*

Following a compressive study of the options before him, Rick assembled all the command officers, including Captain Constance Fowler and Captain Manx Quayle in the conference room. Conspicuously absent, were Caidin and Dãsha Mantose. They had not been heard from since Rick had left *Calypso* earlier in the day. With Caidin's knowledge of the quadrant, Rick was insistent the older gentleman be present, so much so, he ordered Jayda to retrieve him from *Calypso*. As Jayda departed, Rick took the opportunity to explain what he and Gunnar had gone through prior to his departure to find Jayda and the *Athena.* He finally turned to Captain Fowler for their story.

"We've already kind of got an idea of how you got here, Captain. I've read yours and Captain Quayle's reports, but everyone else here would be interested in hearing the nail biter version."

"We got stuck in the Oneida," the Captain started. "In much the same way you and Colonel Conrad did, except we went in on purpose."

"On purpose?" Captain Zak asked leaning back in his chair.

"We were given orders from Starbird Flight Command to keep our cargo safe until we rendezvoused with a Benton capital cruiser called the *Zebra Phar* in orbit over Genis Two."

"Genis Two?" Captain Zek questioned. "That's nothing but a glob of moss. No human life there at all. Why take Starbirds and parts there?"

"We were only given orders, Captain. We didn't even know what our cargo was until you guys opened up our holds."

"The Kendalon freighters were each carrying a Starbird with advanced AI and weapons systems," Rick said. "This includes several extra Interceptor advanced fighters, Starbird engines and a complete array of spare parts."

"It doesn't make any sense," Mister Mavis spoke up.

"We were to establish an orbit around Genis Two until we were contacted," Constance reiterated."

"A drop off point maybe?" Captain Zek postulated, looking over at Rick. "Were there any special instructions?"

"Just rendezvous with the *Zebra* at this specific time and place. We would be contacted using a special code to transfer the cargo," Captain Fowler offered.

"The *Zebra Phar* is a Benton light cruiser," Rick pointed out. "They're friendly to everyone, including the Valkyrie. The code you were given is one only Starbird fleet command has access to. I didn't even have those transfer codes. I have security access to the holds, but not the transfer codes." A hushed mumbling rolled around the room as everyone seemed to shift in their seats.

"In route, we were intercepted by a couple of Valkyrie T-class destroyers. We were able to break away and jump to light speed, but it was a fast jump with hasty coordinates. We had to drop out near the Oneida and try to drive around it at sub-light. But the Valkyrie managed to follow us. The only thing we could do was drive into the accretion ring and hide out until they were gone. By the time we realized we'd be hop-scotching in time by being that close to the event horizon, it was too late. Manx had heard of a scout vessel that had managed to jump out of an accretion ring, directly to another point in the quadrant, but we didn't have any hard numbers, so we took our best guess."

"Pretty good guess I'd say," Toby Mavis said, thinking of the astronomical odds.

"It wasn't without problems," Captain Quayle said leaning forward. "The spacial wormhole we drove through burnt out our guidance systems and scrambled our Navi-computers."

"Any structural damage?" Toby asked, thinking of their own tangle with the wormhole.

"None," Manx replied. "Really not much to break in a Q-class freighter. They're just a great big tube with rounded ends. It took about ten minutes to drop back out of the wormhole. It was certainly an exciting ten minutes though."

"You had some wild yaw characteristics, I bet," Captain Dayton suggested.

"Uncontrollable for us," Constance said. "Our anti-grav was unable to compensate for the gravity bubble we were bouncing through. Somewhere in that ten minutes, we lost our light drive stabilizers and the light engines burned out shortly afterwards. After we got our sub-light engines back up, we headed for the closest system we could find. Turns out, everyone wanted to be helpful, but everything in this part of the galaxy, universe, wherever you want to call it, was so behind our technology, it would have been against Command directives to show superior tech to inferior cultures. We wandered around for several months, testing the waters of different planets before we encountered the Drake and the Skillman." Constance paused, thinking. For a moment, she flashed back to her incarceration at the hands of the Drake. The horror of the assaults she had endured and the torture as a slave deep in the mines of Skadil, still tore at her mind. Manx finished the explanation.

"The Skillman didn't seem to be all that interested in us, but the Drake certainly were. They had us surrounded in Acuity's orbit," Manx said still watching Constance. "So, we dove into the ocean, but they caught up to us and cornered us in the ice flows. All four Captains and their first officers were taken prisoner and forced into the Drake military. When they found out we were just freighter Captains and had next to no military experience, they sent most of the female officers to Conti Nine and the rest of us to Skadil. We've never heard from those that were sent to the station."

"And those that went to Skadil with you?"

"All dead. You don't live long in the mines of Skadil."

"How did you two survive?" Captain Zek asked.

"If you can make alliances quickly, as a group you can survive longer than you can on your own." Manx looked back at Constance, who was still deep within herself. The room fell silent as everyone contemplated what the freighter crews had endured. Manx finally turned back to Rick. "General, on behalf of myself, Constance and our crews, those who are still with us and those who lost their lives, I want to thank you for your efforts in our behalf. I know if there had been any hope for the others we've lost, you would have made every effort to bring them back as well."

Rick looked around at everyone watching for his reaction. He wasn't much for the spotlight, but in this instance, understood the need for everyone in the room to hear from him now.

"In my travels through these two galaxies, I have come to understand the need we all have for each other and the important roles we play. We've all lost people who are near and dear to us. You have to know there could be more losses ahead of us, but if there is any way it can be avoided or if someone gets into trouble, I'll be the first one there." Rick looked over at a smiling Captain Dayton, Lieutenant Habba and Mister Mavis. "Now, we have a lot of work to do yet, namely getting the *Athena* and these four new Starbirds operational."

"Why not just leave them where they are?" Terry Gillespie asked.

"Where we're heading, these freighters wouldn't last very long. The Albion and Colonian militaries will have you before you could route around those systems to try to get to the Nulark system. Not to mention you have no light speed capability and no way to make those kinds of repairs."

"What about *Calypso*? Doesn't it have light speed engines?"

"Yes and no. Yes, she does have light-speed capability, but those capabilities haven't been tested for who knows how long. Caidin and Dãsha Mantose are currently running a functional system diagnostic to see if *Calypso* can actually achieve light-speed. I should know within the hour. Another concern with her is her lack of armament; as in she doesn't have any. She doesn't even have energy shields. She was designed with just armor plating for hull defense."

"But she's a warship, isn't she?" Captain Zak asked.

"Yes, a long time ago and while it would take quite the punch to pierce her armor, there would be little point to putting her in harm's way. She was designed to be manned by a crew the size of a small city and without guns, well, you see the problem. Our biggest dilemma right now is manpower."

"We have enough to crew five Starbirds, don't we?" Terry asked.

"It takes at least ten bodies to run a Starbird in combat," Captain Zak informed the Lieutenant. "We have only half that many between five Starbirds."

"I'm more concerned that we don't have enough command personnel. No offence to any of you. You've all performed your duties admirably, but with the exception of Captain Fowler and Quayle, you don't have any command experience. I need four ship commanders, but I'm one short and one questionable." Rick looked over at Constance. "This is nothing against you Captain Fowler. You've been through a lot and it's going to take you some time to recover. Do you think you're up to commanding a Starbird?"

"I'll give you my best, General," Constance nodded.

"Why not assign me and Zak a command?" Zek asked, throwing the idea out there.

"You both are certainly very capable, but you're also the only ones who have even an inkling of what has to be done in engineering to make these birds go. Sorry guys, but you'll be teaching these Kendalon Chief Petty officers a crash course on Starbird engineering. Captain Dayton, you're the only Starbird pilot here and you've got to not only teach these freighter pilots how to drive, but run our weapons and navigation equipment at the same time. Toby, you've got to run a bridge that's only half staffed and teach other crewman how to make it work while still being the long eyes for all five ships. I'm just not sure how we're going to make all this work. The center seat is the most important position for any combat operation." Rick perceived movement at the door and turned to see Caidin walk slowly in, stopping just inside.

"Ah, good, you're here." Rick maneuvered over to a large viewing screen. "We need to get a report on your light-speed diagnostics and have a good look at the star charts you mapped earlier. What's going to be our best route back to Aster? We're going to need to avoid as much traffic as possible."

Caidin remained silent as he side-stepped away from the door. Rick turned back to the older gentleman as Dãsha passed through the doorway. Rick grinned a bit, seeing her wearing a nice pair of dress pants with a top neatly draped below her waist. A solemn expression dominated Dãsha and Caidin's faces.

"What's wrong?" Rick asked, a bewildered expression developing.

"We understand you are short on command officers," Dãsha said, standing to one side of the door.

Rick smirked slightly trying to picture Dãsha in command of a Starbird. While she exhibited a great deal of fortitude and definitely had a commanding presence, she was still somewhat unpredictable. Considering her background and makeup, it would be an interesting experience to say the least.

Jayda appeared in the door, a profound expression deeply etched across her face. Her eyes were a little red, as if she had been crying. She stepped to her husband, her eyes shifting to the map.

"Are you all right?" he whispered trying to look into her eyes. Jayda nodded reassuring him, then turned up a smile, taking him by both hands. Rick looked back at Caidin and Dãsha.

"You're not suggesting I put you or Caidin in command, are you?" Rick asked, detecting another figure moving into the doorway.

"Certainly not," Dãsha replied abruptly. "Someone with far more experience."

Jayda tighten her grasp on Rick as he looked past her at the figure standing in the entrance. He felt himself physically jolt. Staring in utter disbelief, he forced himself to blink. He glanced at a smiling Caidin, then back at the uniformed officer.

"Your fifth command officer," Jayda half whispered, half choked. "And no... she's not a hologram."

"Lieutenant Commander Audra Atlanta reporting, Sir." Audra smiled broadly and stepped forward.

Rick was completely paralyzed, disbelieving his senses. Jayda shuffled back a little, her eyes tearing up again.

"Do I get a hug or something?" Audra asked holding her arms out.

Rick slowly opened his arms, still wondering what was happening. She couldn't be real! It wasn't possible, or was it? She felt warm and alive and as he embraced her he found himself weeping uncontrollably, so glad to see her, to touch her, to know she was here with them again. Another set of arms wrapped around them as Jayda couldn't contain her joy either. All three wept for several moments, feeling the time of their separation rapidly melt away. Rick became aware of others standing around them and pulled back, wiping his eyes.

"I don't understand," Rick sniffled, turning to Caidin and Dãsha. "What have you done?"

Caidin and Dãsha looked at each other and grinned back at him.

"What we had to do. What we knew you needed us to do, but didn't dare ask."

Rick turned and looked back at Audra who was enjoying more welcome hugs from the other crew members who knew her.

"I don't know what to say," he fumbled.

"You could say, thank you," Dãsha blurted.

"Thank you, of course, thank you. I just don't understand how."

"Certainly you do," Caidin responded. "The fact Dãsha is standing here as is your Audra, is a testament to that."

"But she is... she was... she's been..."

"No, she was never dead. Remember the conversation we had about Dãsha? Your doctor put her in the stasis pod before her life energy had left her body. I just repaired her damaged molecular structures using the methods we discussed earlier."

Rick looked back at Audra and Jayda, hugging again and wiping tears from their eyes. His thoughts turned to Gunnar. Now, he couldn't get these ships operational fast enough. In fact, light speed wasn't going to be fast enough to get Audra back to his friend. Audra and Jayda finally approached Rick, Dãsha and Caidin.

"Where's Gunnar?" Audra asked, cheery and full of energy. She looked around the room, expecting to find him sitting casually in a corner, waiting to be noticed.

Rick passed Jayda a quick look.

"Probably in a lot of trouble."

Robert James Schultz

Robert is a graduate of Ricks College, now called BYU-Idaho. He currently works for BYU-Idaho AV Productions as the Head of Engineering. Robert holds a private pilot's certificate and works on general and experimental aircraft avionics at the Rexburg Airport in his spare time. Water sports, RV camping and riding motorcycles are some of his favorite hobbies. He is a 2013 and 2015 Ironman Coeur d'Alene Triathlon finisher. Robert has loved writing since his early teens, most dealing with the science fiction genre. Married to Lola Hazel VanLeishout in 1983, they are the parents of five children and the Grandparents of three. Robert and Lola reside in Sugar City, Idaho.

If you liked this story, please take a moment and write a short review and post it on Amazon and Barnes and Noble. Just input the title into the website search bar.

www.ingramcontent.com/pod-product-compliance
Lightning Source LLC
Chambersburg PA
CBHW071959110726
47910CB00005B/1587